Secrets

Volumes 5 and 6

The Best in Women's Sensual Fiction

Secrets

Volumes 5 and 6

The Best in Women's Sensual Fiction

Red Sage Publishing, Inc.

SECRETS Volumes 5 and 6
The Best in Women's Sensual Fiction
These are original publications of Red Sage Publishing and each individual story herein has never before appeared in print. These stories are a collection of fiction and any similarity to actual persons or events is purely coincidental.

Red Sage Publishing
P.O. Box 4844
Seminole, FL 33775

SECRETS Volume 5
All Rights Reserved/December 1999
Copyright © 1999 by Red Sage Publishing

Published by arrangement with the authors and copyright holders of the individual works as follow:
ALIAS SMITH AND JONES
Copyright © 1999 by B.J. McCall
STRICTLY BUSINESS
Copyright © 1999 by Shannon Hollis
INSATIABLE
Copyright © 1999 by Chevon Gael
BENEATH TWO MOONS
Copyright © 1999 by Sandy Fraser

SECRETS Volume 6
All Rights Reserved/December 2000
Copyright © 2000 by Red Sage Publishing

Published by arrangement with the authors and copyright holders of the individual works as follow:
FLINT'S FUSE
Copyright © 2000 by Sandy Fraser
LOVE'S PRISONER
Copyright © 2000 by Mary Janice Davidson
THE EDUCATION OF MISS FELICITY WELLS
Copyright © 2000 by Alice Gaines
A CANDIDATE FOR THE KISS
Copyright © 2000 by Angela Knight

ISBN 0-7394-1430-5

Printed in the U.S.A.

Contents

Volume 5

Volume 6

Secrets

Volume 5

Alias Smith and Jones

by B. J. McCall

To my reader:
A chance meeting. A handsome executive. Anything is possible.

Chapter 1

Smith Wilding scanned the crowded airport bar. Thanks to a sudden snowstorm, his morning flight to New Orleans had been delayed. Odds were he'd be stuck for the rest of the afternoon, perhaps the night. His gaze caught and held on a shapely pair of nylon-clad legs. Ever-so-slowly he assessed the woman sitting alone at one of several tables lining the floor-to-ceiling windows. The runways were barely discernible, and the woman's attention remained on the swirling snow. Her conservative grey suit and simple hairstyle told him she, like the hordes of business-class travelers mingling around the gates and concourse, had been caught off-guard by the fierce storm.

Thankfully all the barstools and tables were occupied. Every single seat, except one. Focusing his gaze on the woman's long legs, he headed for the empty chair which just happened to be the molded plastic seat at her table.

"Excuse me," he began. "I could use a drink. Do you mind?"

She gave him a brief nod, then turned her attention back to the storm. Although her face wasn't knock-down gorgeous, something about her intrigued him. Perhaps her eyes. Large, slightly tilted, dark brown and seductive. Bedroom eyes.

"It looks like we have a bit of a wait," she said, without looking at him.

He'd barely taken his seat when a barmaid hustled over. He noted the empty glasses on the table, ordered a martini for himself and another white wine.

"How'd you do that?" she asked, swiveling around in her chair. Her knee bumped into his. "I had to wait so long, I ordered two. That waitress hasn't been within ten feet in the last hour."

"Should I call her back?"

After a long assessing stare, she grinned. "No, I have a feeling she'll be around. Come here often?"

"Only when there's a blizzard."

She pushed aside the two wineglasses. "Lucky me."

"I'm Smith —"

The grin disappeared. "Sure you are. I guess that makes me Jones." Abruptly she turned her attention back to the falling snow.

Surprised by her rudeness, Smith considered returning to the first-class lounge and the complaining gaggle of elderly couples who'd driven him to the public bar. "Would you rather I left?"

Those big brown eyes locked with his just as the waitress delivered their drinks. While the girl took her time removing the empty glasses and crumpled cocktail napkins, Smith enjoyed the amused expression on his new companion's face. The fine lines about her eyes told him she had recently slipped into her thirties. She wore little make-up, giving her a fresh, no-nonsense look he liked. Her mouth bordered on seductive, but her stubborn chin guaranteed she wasn't easily impressed or con-quered.

Swinging her long legs around, her skirt slid several delightful inches up her thighs before she stood. "You stay put … Smith. I need to brave the line at the ladies room."

Sexy and bossy.

As she turned and marched through the crowd, Smith decided legs like hers made up for bad manners and assertiveness training. Briefcases and garment bags were pulled out of her path by admiring men in three-piece suits. Executive management written all over her, she acknowledged their efforts with a slight nod rather than a smile.

Retrieving his cell phone from his briefcase, Smith called his friend at the airport management office. Verifying the worsening storm would close down the airport for hours, he disconnected and called a nearby hotel. Since his grandfather's corporation had recently acquired the hotel chain, obtaining the best suite took less than a minute. Looking around the bar, he felt sorry for the mass of travelers, the majority of whom would spend the night on the uncomfortable chairs and floors of O'Hare International.

But not him, and hopefully not the bossy number in the grey suit.

A few minutes later, overcoats, briefcases and carry-on luggage parted like the Red Sea as she returned. Tall, with legs that never ended.

Smith wanted to see every fabulous inch of her.

His grandfather would be perturbed by his delay, but Smith had about as much control over the weather as he had of his imagination. Just the thought of those long legs wrapped around his waist made him welcome the tempest slamming the Chicago area.

Meredith Collier knew that look. She'd seen it before. On *Smith* it wasn't blatantly horny, just casually sexy. Sexy as hell if the truth be told. That waitress was nobody's fool. She'd spotted the knock-out build be-neath his expensive tailored suit, and the Rolex complementing his manicured, but masculine, hands. Never mind his mesmerizing, green-flecked, hazel eyes and classy looks that literally shouted good breeding. While everyone else looked tired and rumpled, each mahogany-colored hair on his head lay perfectly in place.

Smith was no chump decked out in a good suit.

She'd been interested, a little, until he tried that old trick. When he'd introduced himself as Smith she'd looked for the telltale imprint of a wedding ring. Seeing none, she classified him as engaged. Only a fool would let a guy as attractive as Smith run around without a ring.

When women ruled the world, and that day would come, marital status would be planted in a chip. She smiled at the thought of simply scanning a prospective lover. She'd like to scan Smith.

At least he was good for fast waitress service and holding her chair for a much needed visit to the ladies room.

Thanking him as she slid into the molded plastic seat, she turned her attention once more to the snow.

"You must not be from Chicago."

"Why's that?" she asked without looking at him.

"When you grow up around here, you lose that look of wonder by the time you're eight."

"It doesn't snow in San Francisco."

"Lucky you. What's your business in Chicago?"

She liked his voice. "Training conference."

"What do you train?"

Hearing the smile in his question, she swallowed the quip on her tongue and glanced at him. "Bank employees. Everything from how to answer the phone to regulatory requirements."

"Sounds interesting."

"No it doesn't." She turned and leveled a *don't fuck with me* look across the table. "What do you want, Smith?"

"Your undivided attention would be a good start."

Meredith picked up her wine. She knew she should keep her attention on the swirling snow and ignore this handsome stranger, but she couldn't resist his challenge. As his interested gaze slid over her face, the thousand facets of color in his eyes changed. Colors ranging from green to grey to light brown. All of a sudden she felt warm. She leaned forward. Her lips parted. His hand moved. Heart suddenly pounding, she anticipated his fingertips caressing her cheek and skating across her lower lip. That old tingle began.

"A good start? Is there more?" She missed being touched, missed the feel of a man's arms. How long had it been? A while. Months since her fiancé had confessed his infidelity then crushed her with the revelation that he'd wanted to marry someone else.

Smith's eyes gleamed in anticipation, as if it were a given she'd soon be in his arms, his bed.

To hell with men. She leaned back in her chair and stared at the snow.

An odd silence stretched between them. She thought about apologizing then dismissed the idea. She owed Smith nothing.

"Would you like a cup of coffee?"

She nodded. He barely lifted his hand and the waitress was at their table asking in her breathy voice what she could do for him.

Turning from the snow, Meredith met his gaze. It was damn hard to ignore him. "I'm sorry. It's been a long day."

"And a longer night. All incoming flights have been diverted to other airports until morning."

"And every hotel is booked by now."

"Not necessarily."

"What's up your sleeve, Smith?"

"I can get you a room —"

"Your room, right?"

"Your own room, but I'd like you to have dinner with me."

"What else?"

"That's up to you, Jones."

"You're good."

He said nothing, but his silence told her he hadn't missed the double meaning of her words. He probably was very good.

When the waitress reappeared with two cups of coffee, Meredith considered Smith's offer. As soon as the waitress walked away, she asked, "You don't own the hotel do you?"

"Not exactly."

She picked up her cup. The coffee smelled fresh. She wondered if the waitress had made a new pot just for this man. "How exactly?"

"My grandparents are the major stockholders."

"My own room? My own key?"

Smith nodded, but the delicious grin on his face made her suspicious. She sipped her coffee. "Just dinner? In the dining room?"

He lifted his cup and eyed her through the rising steam. "If you insist, but my suite has a dining room. You can watch the snow."

"Why me? I'd think our waitress would jump at the chance."

"Perhaps, but I like a challenge."

As he sipped his coffee, she wondered if he kissed as good as he looked. "Tired of sweet young things falling at your feet?"

He looked straight into her eyes. "You excite me, Jones. I'd like to spend the evening with you."

"The *evening*?"

"What happens after dinner is entirely up to you."

Meredith knew exactly what she wanted for dessert, but it wasn't her style to gush. "I'm supposed to be flattered?"

"Just offering an alternative to sleeping in a chair."

"What … what makes you think I'm interested?"

"If you weren't, you would have told me to get lost by now. And your voice wouldn't have softened and your eyes —"

"My voice did not change," Meredith said despite the fact she knew it had. This entire episode shrieked *fantasy*. Trapped in a blinding snowstorm with a sexy stranger. No commitments. No heartache. Just pleasure.

"What do I have to do to convince you? Shall we exchange ID's?"

"No," she blurted out.

His eyes narrowed. "You don't have a husband do you?"

She shook her head.

"Shall we start again. I'm —"

"No names." Meredith leaned forward and crooked her finger. A half-smile curled his lips as he matched her stance, his face mere inches from hers. Deliberately, she dropped her voice into a husky whisper. "I like the mystery."

He did the same. "Don't tell me I just walked into some wild female fantasy?"

"It's a possibility."

"Shall we go?"

"You'll never get a cab."

He glanced at his Rolex. "A car is picking us up in fifteen minutes."

As soon as he stood, the waitress hustled over. He handed the girl a fifty and told her to keep the change. Beneath the warmth of his gaze, Meredith rose. When she picked up her coat, he plucked it out of her hand and held it for her.

He shouldered her garment bag, then picked up his briefcase and coat. Facing her, he smiled. A smile so genuine, she matched his easy stride out of the bar and down the length of the concourse.

Once inside the car and sitting beside *Smith*, Meredith reconsidered her decision. It was foolish to go to a hotel with a stranger. He could be a sexual deviant or worse.

Despite her usually cautious nature, Meredith trusted Smith. Maybe it was just his direct approach or the way he looked at her with snowflakes dusting his eyelashes, but for once she wanted to act out one of her fantasies.

Then she'd fly home and forget all about him.

At least he's first class, she thought as the bellhop opened the door to a spectacular suite far larger than most homes. Her modest two-bedroom, one-bath house would almost fit into the living room. She glanced at the dining area. Her home would fit with several feet to spare. Crackling flames drew her to the fireplace. She crossed the marble foyer and the carpeted area between two plush sofas, down two steps into a conversation pit complete with thick carpet and soft pillows, to the circular fireplace. She turned and faced her host. The logs were fake, but she welcomed the heat licking her cold legs.

Smith directed the bellhop to deposit her items in a room to her left while he opened a pair of double doors to her right. Good to his word, she had her own room.

Did he suspect she had absolutely no intention of sleeping in it?

After tipping the bellhop at the door, Smith removed his suit jacket, laid it across the back of one sofa and strolled toward her. "May I?"

Meredith turned toward the fire. Another kind of delicious heat struck her body as he slipped her coat off her shoulders. The image of him undressing her flooded her mind. Heat coiled low in her belly.

"Jones?"

He stepped close behind her. So close she could feel the warmth of his body. His hand settled on her upper arm. His breath feathered the ribbon of skin between her hair and her collar. "You must be chilled to the bone. If you'd like a hot bath …"

As she turned to face him, her arm brushed his chest. The brief contact made her want to touch the rest of him. Instead, she nodded.

He began to step away, then paused. Her coat slid to the carpet as he grasped her waist and tugged her close. His mouth closed over hers and she welcomed the sweet warmth of his lips, relished the pressure of his body against hers. Her senses sparked. Needing, seeking the contact, she clung to him.

He broke the kiss and buried his face in her hair. "I've been wanting to do that since I first laid eyes on you."

When he pulled away, Meredith stifled a moan.

"Your bath?" Placing his hand on the small of her back he led her into the bedroom. Her pulse leaped at the muted watercolor hanging on the wall above the king-size bed. Two figures, locked in embrace, their legs entwined. Forcing her gaze from the painting, she skirted the bed and joined Smith at the bathroom door. A large round tub, big enough for two, was built into one corner and a glass shower stall stood beside it. Double sinks beneath a row of lights above the mirror. Several white rugs covered the marble floors.

"Satisfied?"

Not yet. "The room is beautiful. A definite improvement over the airport waiting area."

"Take your time."

As he closed the double doors, Meredith wished he'd kissed her again, acted on the consuming rush of desire flowing between them. Although she and *Smith* didn't know a thing about each other, she felt he wanted something special, something more than a few impassioned minutes.

Meredith definitely wanted more. She wanted to be touched, caressed, pampered.

Eager to be with Smith, she stripped off her clothes, and stepped in the shower. Welcoming the hot fingers of the spray on her breasts, belly and thighs, she thought of his hands, his lips, caressing, touching, easing the ache inside her. She cupped her breasts, kneading them in anticipation, relishing the surge of raw desire.

She definitely needed Smith.

Smith opened a bottle of champagne, his thoughts lingering on Jones's response to his kiss. Even now he could feel the sweet pressure of her firm breasts, her inviting mouth. She'd been an exquisite temptation, but Smith had learned long ago that quick, heated exchanges were only a momentary relief. He preferred the sated feeling after a long night of lovemaking, savored the complete exploration of a sensual partner. These days only a fool would jump into bed with every willing female. Unlike the waitress, Jones was cautious. She'd choose her lovers carefully. And after she'd taken what she wanted, she'd kiss them goodbye and never look back.

But she'd leave you satisfied.

How the hell he knew that, he wasn't sure. But he had good instincts and he'd learned long ago to follow them. He wasn't going to regret a night in Jones's arms.

He wondered what she liked. Would she cry out when she came? Would she want him to go down on her? Smith intended to explore, in detail, every pink fold until she was wet, until he tasted her heat. The thought alone made him hard.

When he heard her bedroom door open several minutes later, Smith turned. A soft, dove grey sweater and short black skirt hugged her curves. As she approached, his gaze lingered on the smile teasing the corners of her full mouth, then slid to the gentle sway of her breasts. His breath caught at the sexy motion of her thighs brushing one another as she slowly placed one long leg before the other. His gaze slid lower, hugging the tempting curves of her knees, her calves, lingering at the sight of her bare feet. The image of her naked slammed into him. He looked into her exotic eyes and hoped she'd walk right into his arms and demand he please her now, on the rug, before the fire.

Instead she took the glass of champagne from his hand and sipped. She glanced at his obvious erection, licked her red lips. "I'd like to watch the snow."

Smith strolled over to a hidden panel, opened the small door and punched a series of buttons. The lights dimmed, and to the left of the fireplace, automatic drapes silently slid apart. Outside snow swirled before the floor-to-ceiling, double-paned glass.

She stood, a delicate silhouette before the immense window, waiting, making his blood thunder.

Meredith sighed when his arm wrapped about her middle. Without speaking he stood behind her. She offered him a sip of champagne. Together they finished the glass.

His breath caressed her cheek, his lips brushed her neck. At the touch of his tongue to her skin, the crystal flute slipped from her fingers. In a heartbeat she was in his arms, her breasts crushed to his chest, his lips pressed to hers.

Rocking, one against the other, they strained against the cloth barriers separating them. He clutched at her short skirt, bunching the soft material between his fingers until her buttocks were exposed. Like fire-brands, his fingers slid beneath the narrow ribbon of her thong panties. She gasped, breaking their ardent kiss, as his warm fingers slid forward tantalizing the skin along the strip of black lace, down the crease of her thigh, between her legs.

Smith was amazed how tightly she held his fingers. How wet she was. Stretched to the limit, his erection throbbed painfully. He needed her wetness.

Slowly he eased his fingers from her tight sheath and touched her partially open mouth. He nearly came when she suckled gently on his fingers. Blood pounding in his veins, he unzipped her skirt and slipped it over her hips, then slowly removed her sweater. Except for the scraps of black lace barely covering her breasts and thatch of curls, her skin gleamed, soft and delicate.

Her breath labored as much as his own. She unclasped her bra, and her reflection caught his eye. An image, provocative and bordering on the perverse, popped into his head. Long-legged with high, firm breasts, flat belly and slim hips, Jones had the build to make it work.

Taking her about the waist, he turned Jones toward the glass. As he tore off his clothes, he focused on the lacy thong between her buttocks and grinned. Grasping her breasts from behind, he watched her face as he fondled her breasts. As her nipples peaked beneath his fingertips, her lips parted. Their gazes locked and held as she leaned against him. Her expression, daring and wanton, shot pure lust to the tip of his penis. When she shifted her legs in readiness, he released her breasts, then retrieved a foil packet from his pants.

Condom in place, he slid his hard cock beneath her slim buttocks. Splaying his hand over her belly, he lifted her slightly and guided the tip of his penis under the thong and between her slick folds. Then he leaned forward pushing her flush against the glass.

Trapped between his hard body and the smooth window, between fire and ice, Meredith's breath caught as he eased his length deeper inside her. Their position demanded his control. His exquisite progress heightening her awareness of his size, his length, her tightness. Each movement gentle, yet intense. Each slow thrust pressed her sex, her nipples firmly to the glass, forming a triangle of sensation. He rotated his hips, each measured penetration searing her clit to the glass, bringing forth a unique friction, a cool burn.

Driving her wild.

Hot skin. Cold glass. Testing the boundaries of sensation.

His feverish skin sealed to hers, making her aware of his straining muscles, his strength. His breath came in hot gasps, grazing her neck, inciting a thousand fiery ripples to race along her skin. He stroked the sides of her breasts; she moaned and strained against the slick glass. Aching for release, she cried out. Her drenched sex burned, the sweet pressure increasing as his slow, intense thrusts edged her closer to climax. He nipped her shoulder, then laved his own sweat from her skin, the slow, sensual strokes sending her over the edge.

Chapter 2

"That was …"

"Amazing?" Smith asked through labored breaths.

"That too," Meredith admitted, breathing rather heavily herself.

He took a tentative step back. Free of the glass, she splayed her hands against the window and leaned her torso forward. Beyond the window, the heavy curtain of snow created a surreal mirror. It was as if the world had gone white and nothing existed but this room. This moment. This man.

She looked at Smith's shadowed reflection, savored the strained ecstasy on his face as he pushed his solid erection deeper within her. Secured about the waist by his strong fingers and thumbs, Meredith slid her hands lower, balancing her weight against the glass, inviting his penetration. His strokes, slow and shallow at first, soon turned to deep, pleasing thrusts.

She needed him. At this moment, she needed him more than anything else.

The need, mutual, almost desperate, dampened their skin with moist heat. Her knees trembled from the sheer force of their mating. Together they peaked, his eager thrusts and her taking of them stilling into one amazing moment of shared bliss.

He held her until they both regained their senses, then stepped back, forcing their flushed bodies to separate. Needing the warmth of his arms, Meredith turned.

He pulled her tight and held her.

He was all muscle. Hard and masculine. Her breasts, her belly, even her thighs felt pliant and warm. She hugged him, crushing her breasts flat against his chest and burying her face in the hollow of his neck.

Afterglow. She hadn't believed it existed until now.

A bell chimed softly, breaking the spell. Smith grasped her hand and headed toward his bedroom. The front door opened as he pulled her inside and shut the door. Once again she was crushed to his sweat-dampened chest. "I ordered dinner," he said, sliding his hand through her hair. "How about a quick shower, a meal, then something delicious for dessert?"

Once inside his bathroom, Smith opened the shower door. Meredith slipped out of her thong and stepped inside the generously proportioned stall. Adjusting the temperature, she stood beneath the spray. The hot water pummeled her belly and thighs. Her heart, her womb still thrummed from Smith's lovemaking.

She turned. He stepped into the stall. His gaze studied her every curve and hollow, reminding her of a boy before a candy store. But Smith was no boy. His wide shoulders, flat stomach and muscled legs, every masculine inch of him, perfection.

Without speaking he pulled her to him and kissed her. For several minutes they stood beneath the spray, content in one another's embrace, exploring each other with their lips and tongues as if this was their first kiss, so gentle and sweet they could be fully dressed standing in a public place.

When the kiss ended, Smith continued to hold her. "I like you, Jones."

"I like you, Smith. I like you a lot."

His hands slid from her back, then he reached around her to turn off the water. His gaze fastened on her breasts, and her nipples contracted beneath his sensual stare.

He reached out and grazed each taut peak with his forefinger. "I like your nipples," he said in a slightly husky voice. "They're big and inviting."

Although his words pleased her, Meredith sensed Smith didn't expect a thank you or an exchange of compliments. He guided her out of the stall, then grabbed two towels and handed her one.

She dried off quickly, then slipped into a white terry cloth robe provided by the hotel. As she tied the sash, she glanced at Smith. He stood before the mirror, a towel draped about his trim waist, fingercombing his short hair.

When he walked up behind her, their gazes met in the mirror. His smile was sexy. Like her, she knew he was thinking of how they'd watched each other's reflections in the window as they'd made love. He leaned to his right and flipped a switch. A bank of heat lamps bathed the bathroom in a golden glow.

Smith turned Jones around, took her by the waist and set her bottom down on the marble counter. She wrapped her legs around his waist and her arms about his neck. He kissed her. Her lips moved beneath his, hungry and demanding. She was making him hard again. Her demands dissolved into soft touches of tongue and lips. "What's for dinner?"

"I'll check." Reluctantly he pulled away from her embrace. When her sultry gaze slid to his erection, obvious beneath the damp towel, his cock jerked.

As he walked out of the bathroom, Smith thought about the hours until morning. Despite the fact he'd just had the best orgasm he could remember, he wanted her. If any woman could keep him going all night, Jones could.

Smith opened the bedroom door, glanced about to make sure the hotel staff had set the table and left, then strolled into the dining area. He lifted a silver plate cover. A small billow of steam assured him their dinners were still hot. Smiling he replaced the cover. Did Jones realize she was dessert? Still grinning, he headed back to the bedroom, dropped the damp towel and retrieved a robe from the closet.

He pulled the sash tight as he entered the bathroom. Before him Jones lay across the marble counter, robe open, with knees bent and feet wide apart. She glowed, golden and alluring, marvelous and naked, beneath the lamps.

Mesmerized he stared at the enticing slit between her legs. Shades of rose and pink, soft and inviting, lay nestled in a dark thatch of curls. Sensual and sexy, she was obviously comfortable with her nudity.

Who was she, really?

Come morning, Smith intended to end the mystery. After all, San Francisco was only a plane ride away.

Meredith propped herself on her elbows and looked through her legs at Smith. She knew he'd been staring at her crotch. She'd sensed his slow perusal while she bathed beneath the hot lamps. Unfortunately he'd wrapped a thick robe about himself making it impossible for her to judge his physical reaction. He certainly looked sexy. The casual interest he'd displayed at the airport was long gone … .

Pushing herself up to a sitting position, she swung her legs around and slid off the marble counter. Wrapped snugly in her robe, she walked up to Smith, kissed him briefly, then headed for the dining room.

Meredith licked her lips. The food was delicious, the thin-sliced beef cooked to perfection, but her interest focused on the man sitting across from her. His hands moved with grace and deliberation. Masculine hands with deft, pleasing fingers. She shifted in her chair and crossed her legs. When Smith lifted his gaze, she laid down her fork and reached for her wineglass.

His hand closed over hers. Exquisite sensations ran along her arm as his thumb caressed her palm. Meredith's heart pounded. Smith had a way of touching her, looking at her. She recalled how he'd held her after his provocative style of lovemaking. His kisses, ranging from lusty plundering to sweet exploration, were soul satisfying. He made her feel wanted, appreciated, utterly desirable. Candlelight and romance danced in his eyes.

This is how love is suppose to feel. Tender and aching. Quiet and raging.

But Smith didn't love her. He'd only been blessed with the ability to make her want to pretend for a few, short, potent hours.

Later, as they lay naked in each other's arms before the fireplace, Smith asked, "You're not … is there anyone?"

Although he'd spoken softly, the quiet enchantment had been broken. Thinking briefly of her ex-fiancé, Meredith pulled away.

"Don't." Smith reached out and took her hand. "I'd like to know your heart isn't elsewhere."

The firelight played on Smith's handsome face, obscuring his eyes. Part of her wanted to embrace his words, but logic told her, come morning, she'd just be a memory. A one-night stand with a stranger. A diversion from the storm. In six months, would he even remember her at all?

"There's no one waiting for me," she answered truthfully.

He rose to his knees and leaned forward, pushing her down on the padded bench surrounding the fireplace. "That's going to change."

She bit back words of protest as his mouth covered her breast and suckled her tender nipple. She grasped his torso with her thighs, urging him on. They'd made love after dinner and despite two glorious orgasms, she wanted him again. Wanted him so much. Too much.

His lips grazed her belly, sending tremors of delight along her skin. She arched her hips, and moaned when his mouth rested against her already pulsing center.

Honeyed and hot, Smith tasted her desire. She bucked wildly, thrusting her sex against his mouth. He flicked his tongue over her clit until it budded and Jones raised her hips high, demanding release. Closing his lips over her, he suckled, drawing on her needy clit. She tensed beneath his lips, her legs trembled as she came.

Smith eased his tongue between her quivering folds to taste the hot nectar of her climax.

Her thighs relaxed and Smith lapped one last time at her sweetness before she lowered her hips. She'd made him hard again. So hard all he could think about was being inside her, bringing her to climax again. But this time he wanted to watch her. He needed to see her face as she came.

Smith groaned as Jones straddled his thighs and accepted his sheathed length. Her gaze locked with his as she moved her hips in a wanton display of grace and desire. Riding astride, she took him, drawing him inside her, over and over, making him forget she'd brought him to a heart-stopping climax followed by near exhaustion a short hour or two earlier.

But this time the fire built slowly, fueled by her supple undulations. The provocative sway of her breasts, tipped with large, dusky nipples held him spellbound, kept him hard.

"Is there someone waiting for you?"

Her whispered question came from left field, hitting his sexually saturated brain like a hard blow to the temple. He hesitated. Let her words penetrate.

"No," he gasped as he regained his rhythm. "No one is waiting."

Already caught in his special fire, Meredith accepted, reveled in his passionate thrusts. When his lips closed over her breast and drew lustily at her nipple, she denied the sharp pain his hesitant answer had driven into her heart, acknowledged only her physical need of him.

Increasing the tempo of her hips, she rode him, challenged him to match her hunger. Thrusting her fingers into his hair, she pulled back his head, then kissed him.

A forceful kiss, devoid of love, savage and lust-filled.

She dug her fingers into his shoulders, driving her nails into his skin as she forced the hard length of him, deeper, pounding her sex against his.

He slapped her buttocks. The light stinging impact of his hands drove her wild.

From somewhere inside her womb, her climax wrenched itself free. Unlike anything she'd experienced before, Meredith welcomed its intensity, wresting every morsel of gratification from her flesh.

Finally she stilled.

Smith's chest heaved beneath her hands. Her own breath puffed in harsh gasps.

"Christ, I thought you were going to pull it off."

"You didn't like it?"

"I loved it. For a moment there, I thought I was having a damn heart attack. My chest still hurts."

"Next time I'll be gentle," she teased.

"Next time you're liable to kill me," he said, then quirked an eyebrow. "But I'll die happy."

Hours later, Meredith quietly left the hotel. Smith slept soundly in his bed, unaware the quickly moving storm had passed over Chicago and now pummeled the southeast. As her plane broke through the cloud cover over O'Hare, Meredith closed her eyes and wished she'd had the courage to leave her phone number. But as she'd looked at her sleeping lover, common sense had prevailed. The hesitancy in his answer had spoken volumes. She didn't need to deal with an unfaithful man. Once was enough.

No way in hell would she be the other woman.

Meredith steeled her heart. Smith had been a fantasy. A night of pleasure. No one fell in love with a one-night-stand.

Smith raced along the concourse, dodging travel-weary passengers and various pieces of luggage. He still couldn't believe she'd gone. Not after a night like that! He'd called the terminal for her flight gate number, dressed and headed straight for the airport. As he reached the gate, the digital lights behind the airline counter scrambled and a new flight number and destination appeared. Frustrated, Smith walked to the window. Jones's flight was already on the tarmac.

Didn't the damned woman realize he was more than a convenient layover? Hadn't his lovemaking convinced her he wanted her in his life?

Despite the crowd of people filling up the gate area, Smith leaned his forehead against the glass and wondered if he could obtain the passenger list from his buddy in airport management. But what if Jones didn't wish to be found? What if she was married? Or engaged?

Pulling away from the glass, Smith shook his head at the empty airplane bay. Deep inside he believed Jones had been truthful. She had no husband, no lover. She just didn't want him.

That was the hell of it. He wanted her and she was gone without so much as a goodbye.

Even if he had the passenger list, how many names would he have to chase down? The hell with the passenger list, he knew what she did for a living. How many banks could there be in San Francisco? Not enough to deter him. And when he found her … what then?

One thing was certain, he would accept the directorship on the board of West Coast Bank his grandmother had offered. As the bank's major stockholder, she was ready to step down and enjoy retirement. At seventy-five it was about time. And Smith needed a respite from his grandfather's escalating attempts at matchmaking.

Besides, West Coast's headquarters were in San Francisco and so was Jones.

Chapter 3

Meredith stared out her office window. Far below heavy rain pounded the narrow streets of San Francisco's Financial District. She touched the cold glass, with an odd sense of longing, of something missing. A feeling she couldn't ignore or deny. Strange after so many weeks to still hunger for Smith, still ache for his special touch. She'd expected to file him away, a wonderful memory, nothing more. Instead, she felt an intense sense of loss, as if she'd left part of herself abandoned, lost in that Chicago storm.

Her heart?

She slapped her open hand against the glass in sheer frustration. Smith wasn't going to appear like a knight in shining armor and tell her he loved her. Undoubtedly, her one-night-stand had returned to his wife or girlfriend. What had she expected when she'd asked him if anyone waited for him?

No one is waiting for me. She'd wanted to hear the words, but she'd known the moment he'd hesitated before he said them, he would lie. And he had. It was the nature of men. Smith was no different.

Better they'd separated as strangers.

At the familiar sound of Jim Murphy's voice, Meredith turned from the window and greeted the President and CEO of West Coast Bank. Jim stood at her open door, his pleasant bespectacled face beaming at her.

"There's someone I'd like you to meet," Jim said, as he stepped inside her modest office.

Meredith, used to Jim bringing around anyone from bank executives to neighbors, was about to speak, but when she saw Smith standing just outside her office the words caught in her throat. In a heartbeat she took in his polished good looks, the way his broad shoulders filled her doorway. Every hair in place, his grey suit, crisp white shirt and burgundy-patterned tie gave him a conservative look from head to toe. Except Meredith knew beneath those executive's clothes, Smith wasn't the least bit conservative. A vision of him, muscles straining, skin damp with sweat, caught in the throes of lovemaking, filled her heart.

His eyes narrowed. Meredith could swear he looked more angry than surprised, while she felt … . She couldn't move. Her lips were frozen. Her fingers twitched, and her heart thudded against her ribs. What on earth was he doing here? How had he found her? Had he been looking or was this some awful twist of fate?

"Meredith's in charge of training. Considering our recent merger with Great Pacific, we've kept her pretty busy," Jim began. He glanced at her. "Is something wrong?"

Meredith's brain refused to connect with her lips and tongue. She shook her head.

"Good to see you again, Miss Jones," Smith said, taking a step toward her and holding out his hand as if they'd never shared that passionate night. "Smith Wilding. We met in Chicago about two months ago. We shared … a table. It is Miss Jones?"

Smith? His name is Smith? Oh God, he wasn't lying. "Meredith Collier," she finally managed.

"Collier." He said the word slowly as if memorizing it. "My mistake. I could have sworn the name was Jones. Sorry, I'm usually very good with names."

"Smith's our new director," Jim offered. "For the next few months he'll be familiarizing himself with our operation."

I screwed a director. As if he'd read her mind, Smith gave her a price-less grin. She couldn't have heard Jim correctly. "Director?"

"Mrs. Wilding has decided to retire. Smith will be taking her place on the board. I have to tell you," Jim said, turning to Smith. "I'll miss your grandmother."

Wilding? Wilding! The bank's major stockholder Wilding? Oh my God.

Wondering why the corporate gods hated her, Meredith forced a smile and a grip on her tangled emotions.

"My grandmother loves this city and West Coast is her pride and joy," Smith said. Meredith resented his poise and ease. As if the two of them had shared nothing more than a table. "Once I've settled in the family apartment, I'm sure she'll visit."

Apartment? "You're moving to San Francisco?"

Before Smith could answer, Jim Murphy's secretary interrupted the conversation. When Jim excused himself to take a phone call, Smith's gaze focused on her, pinning her to the spot. "If Miss Collier doesn't mind, I'll wait for you here."

After Jim had hurried out of the room, followed by his secretary, Smith asked, "Does my moving to San Francisco bother you, Jones?"

Unsure of the play of emotions on her face, Smith waited. Murphy had introduced him to over a dozen employees. His foolish heart banging against his ribcage, he'd followed Jim from office to office. Meredith Collier, he'd repeated the name dozens of times thinking of Jones, the woman he knew so intimately. The woman he loved. After dozens of calls pretending to be an attendee of the Chicago conference looking for a fellow trainer whose name he'd forgotten, Smith had found her right in his own backyard. He'd thought about calling, but he wanted to see her face, needed to see her reaction.

She'd plagued his thoughts, his dreams. The moment he'd stepped into her office, he'd wanted to sweep her into his arms just to assure himself she was real. Then he'd wanted to shake her and ask why the hell she'd walked out on him. Instead, he'd managed to keep his emotions in check and explain the dumbfounded look on her face. Obviously she hadn't expected to see him again.

Cold steel right to the heart.

He'd been fooling himself. In his dreams he'd seen Jones rushing into his arms. But Meredith Collier hadn't moved a muscle. Not so much as a polite smile.

"Smith. You didn't just want a one night stand?"

"It's not my habit to disappear at dawn."

"It seemed less complicated that way."

"For whom?" Smith waited, but she didn't answer. Except for the hairstyle, and the business suit, Meredith Collier looked nothing like the assured woman he'd met in Chicago. His sudden intrusion into her real life obviously made her uncomfortable. Even her breath came in ragged little puffs. Was Jones just some fantasy, a personality she assumed while having assignations with strangers? The thought he was merely one of many slammed into his ego with the force of a good left hook.

Could he have read her so wrong? So damn wrong he'd changed his whole life on an illusion?

"No one here knows … I haven't told anyone about … about you. I don't intend to."

There, she'd let him off the hook. They could pretend they'd had a momentary chance meeting in an airport bar. Maybe for him that was exactly what it was.

His lips twitched, a half smile teased the corners of his mouth, but his eyes held no laughter. He stepped forward, his stride eating the short distance between them. Then he touched her. His thumb traced the line of her jaw, his fingers slid along the contour of her neck as his warm palm came to rest against the telltale pulse drumming in her throat. "Just our dirty little secret, right, Jones?"

"If I'd known who you were —"

"You didn't want to know." His voice had dropped to a husky whisper bringing forth all sorts of memories. Wild, wanton memories. "When I was inside you, loving you, you still didn't want to know."

Her pulse leaped. Blood pounded in her veins, throbbing eagerly against his palm as their gazes locked, then heated. How many times in

Chicago had he looked at her like this; wanting, demanding, challenging her to climax once again? Her lips parted as his fingers slid into her hair. All she could think of was being in his arms, feeling him inside her again.

Jim Murphy's hearty laughter, booming from the hallway, dropped an invisible curtain between them. A rush of cool air touched her skin as his hand dropped away. She barely heard his polite goodbye as he walked out of her office.

Until recently, Meredith had loved coming to work. Over the years she'd adopted a routine of purchasing a morning coffee before joining her co-workers for the slow elevator ride to the fifth floor offices. Now, she nodded politely as Smith joined the group crowding the elevator. His hazel eyes barely made contact with hers as he divided his attention equally among the bank's employees, especially the females. He treated her as if they were passing acquaintances, easily dismissing the events in Chicago. How long had it been? How many weeks since …

Only nine weeks. Nine torturous weeks.

If only it had been a table they shared that night, and not a hotel room, she wouldn't be having such annoying dreams. Images of Smith came in the night, reminding, teasing her. Even now her breasts tingled.

She sipped her latte. No more decaf since Smith had shown his handsome face at West Coast. Last night she'd tossed and turned until the sheets and blankets were twisted and tangled. If only he'd kissed her that day in her office. Surely, her memory of the night in his arms was all out of proportion to reality. Over the weeks she'd built it up, made the fantasy more special than the reality. If he'd kissed her, the spell would have been broken and she'd be free of this night fever, free of the erotic images and thoughts. She couldn't concentrate on the job. She couldn't sleep.

Somehow she had to rid herself of Smith. Dismiss this fascinating male. Forget his touch, his voice. Deny her own physical reactions.

As she stepped into the elevator Meredith knew the corporate gods had chosen to punish her. Smith's spicy cologne filled her nostrils. When she turned to face the doors, he stood in front of her. Unsmiling, but polite. She hated the way he said Miss Collier he might as well have said *Miss Liar.* The effect was the same.

A flippant remark came to her lips, but the presence of co-workers restrained her tongue until he turned and blocked her view. When several employees crammed into the already crowded elevator, Meredith moved into the corner. Smith followed.

When he deliberately wedged her into a small triangle of space, Meredith reached up and cupped one firm buttock. What possessed her, she didn't know. But once she touched him, she couldn't stop. Beneath her exploring fingers, the muscles of his buns and thighs tensed. Her actions were foolish and risky. If anyone noticed … . But everyone's attention was focused on the senior accountant and the joke he was telling.

As the elevator stopped on the third floor, she pinched Smith, hard. When several employees exited, Smith shifted along with the remaining riders, but didn't so much as glance in her direction. At the fifth floor, everyone stepped out, except for Smith. Before Meredith could follow her co-workers, Smith placed his finger on the open door button.

"I requested a tour of several of our branch offices. Jim suggested you as my guide. I'll pick you up at ten."

After what she'd just done, how could she spend the day with him? She'd pinched a director on the ass! What had gotten into her? Meredith backed out of the elevator. "I have several reports —"

"The reports can wait. I can't."

As the doors slid together, Smith winked. For several heartbeats, Meredith stared at the closed doors, then hurried to her office. What couldn't he wait for?

She pushed aside the thought that he wanted her. What had happened in Chicago couldn't happen here. That night they'd been just a man and a woman caught in a storm. No identities, no job titles, no connection other than a short-term physical bond. Now, everything had changed.

Smith practically owned the bank. While she held a position and title she'd worked damn hard for, there were several rungs left on West Coast's corporate ladder. With a remark from him, her career could climb or plummet. Meredith swore as the buttons on her telephone lit up. No man, not even a rich, powerful and too-handsome-for-his-own-good one would derail her from her long-term objectives by a short detour in his bed.

Even if he was extraordinary between the sheets.

"It's going to rain."

Undeterred by her sharp demeanor, Smith gave her a calm, but determined look. She wasn't going to avoid or ignore him. Not today. "I have a coat and umbrella in the car."

When she stalked past him without a word, he held back a smile. Bossy Miss Jones was back. Didn't she realize how much he loved a challenge, how hard it had been to wait for her to react after that first day?

He'd come so close to kissing her that day in her office. And she'd wanted him to kiss her. In that short moment he knew she'd yearned for him as much as he ached for her. When he'd touched her, he'd felt her pulse leap. And her eyes. He'd seen that look before. He needed to see it again.

He should have asked her to dinner, while her blood still smoldered.

Instead, he'd relished his foolish revenge, and let her cool off. Then she'd avoided him. He'd waited, hoped for a sign of desire, a welcoming signal. Something to tell him she needed him. Instead, she ignored him. Days turned into two weeks.

When his nightsweats had become unbearable, and his revenge unrewarded, he'd arranged to get her away from the bank where she couldn't dismiss him. Then she'd touched him, fondled him, deliberately drove him wild in a situation where he was unable to respond. But he'd gotten the message loud and clear.

She still wanted him.

He'd even welcomed her taunting pinch.

What a charmer. Meredith leaned against the headrest. She was tired. Tired of tellers, service representatives, and branch managers oohing and ahhing over Smith. Not for one second would she admit that jealousy had anything to do with her discomfort. How could she be jealous?

"How far to the Golden Gate?"

"About five miles," she answered without looking at him. She glanced at her wristwatch. "Once we cross the bridge, it will only take us about half-an-hour to return to the office."

"We're not going back. I want to see the ocean and feel something besides cement beneath my feet."

What did he have in mind? An image of Smith, his shirt, wet, clinging to his chest and arms, pulling her down to join him on a rainsoaked beach, filled her thoughts. Meredith blinked, banishing the image. The intimacy of sitting beside him within the vehicle, so close she could inhale his scent, must be getting to her. "We'll be late."

"No one expects us."

"People will talk."

"About what?"

"It's still raining." Knowing her excuses were exactly that, excuses, Meredith peeked at Smith. He was smiling. An all-knowing smile that told her he knew she wanted to avoid being alone with him.

"What's the matter, Jones? I thought you liked my company. Or is your attention limited to a few lusty hours?"

"Things have changed."

"I've noticed."

"I don't sleep with my bosses."

"I'm not your boss."

"I don't sleep with bank executives, co-workers, women, animals or married or entangled men!"

"You got me there."

But how? Did he mean executives or married? It was on the tip of her tongue to ask, but what difference did it make? He was still a director.

Once you screwed around with the men at the top, you were tagged forever. No one lived down the reputation, no matter how good they were at the job.

When Smith took the last freeway exit before the Golden Gate, a perplexed Meredith sat silent as the vehicle climbed the winding road toward the Marin headlands. On a good-weather day, winds blustered and whipped one's clothes, but no one sane would brave the grass-covered cliffs towering over the confluence of the Pacific Ocean and the San Francisco Bay during a stormy day.

Only a man crazy enough to take her, up against a plate glass window during a snowstorm.

Staring at the windshield, Meredith recalled the sensations she'd felt, pressed between Smith's muscled body and the glass. Again she experienced the heat, the sweet burn of ecstasy. Suddenly, deep inside she felt molten, liquid, game for any excursion Smith had in mind.

She glanced at him. A delicious light flickered in his eyes. "I hope you like the rain … as much as you like the snow."

His words, the timbre of his voice told her he intended to have her, to take her in the wind and rain and make her his once more. He braked the car at the termination of a dead-end road, shut off the engine and opened his door.

The wind whipped his hair as he stepped out of the vehicle and removed his raincoat, tie and suit jacket. The light rain spattered his face and shirt as he tossed his tie and jacket into the back seat. Leaning inside the car, he retrieved his raincoat, and brushed his lips to hers. Warm and inviting.

The fleeting touch held her breathless, expectant as he draped his coat over his shoulders and circled the car. He opened her door. When he held out his hand, she had her moment to refuse, to deny. But the moment passed and her hand slipped into his.

Pulling her into his arms, he backed her against the car, and pressed his chest, groin and thighs to hers. He drew his coat around them in a protective cocoon. Seduced by his heat, his strength, and commanding lips, Meredith forgot the wind and rain in the storm of Smith's kiss.

Wild and eager, their lips and tongues warred, each seeking consummation of simmering desire held in check far too long. Need beyond anything Meredith had thought possible consumed her. She held Smith about the waist, hugging him, demanding his heat, wanting his love.

And he wanted her. His rock hard erection pressed against her belly. His hips flexed, urging her legs apart. He wanted her to feel him.

Meredith welcomed his hands beneath her wool skirt, his eager exploration of her thighs and hips. Needing to reacquaint herself with the feel of his skin and the sculpted definition of his torso, Meredith grasped the tails of his shirt and pulled. Just as she touched the bare skin of his back, skimmed her fingers over his powerful lats, his fingers slid beneath the confines of her panty hose. Her flesh trembled as he cupped her buttocks and began an impatient massage.

He tore his lips from hers. Rainsoaked hair plastered to skull and forehead, he looked as he had when they'd stood in the shower that night in Chicago. But now his gaze held a questioning intensity, an edge. The air between them electrified. His hazel eyes burned with desire beneath spiked lashes. "I've missed you. There hasn't been a day I haven't thought of you. A night I haven't dreamed of you."

His words shot pleasure through her middle. He hadn't forgotten her. He'd thought about her, wanted her, missed her. As much as she missed him? His fingers pressed into the curve of her buttocks. She licked a raindrop from her upper lip. "You couldn't have told me inside the car?"

He pulled at her panty hose, baring her backside. "There's something about you and storms that get to me."

"We'll catch cold."

He slid his hand between her legs, bringing every nerve ending alive with the touch of his fingers. "You won't be cold, Jones."

She gasped as he touched her, teased her humming flesh, then slipped one finger inside. He was right, she wasn't the least bit cold. In fact, she felt hot. So hot and tight and wet, she might explode. His touch excited her needy flesh, making her welcome the cold rivulets running down her forehead, trickling along her neck.

Thrusting her hips against his hand, Meredith sought release. She moaned as he kissed the rain from her face, her neck. His heated breath chased away the cold as whispered murmurs of longing, burning need, touched her soul, set the impassioned pace of his hand, his fingers. Her moan rose into a cry as the tempo of his penetration increased. For countless nights, she'd wanted this man, needed his touch. Despite the rain and cold, she wanted to strip off her clothes and make love in the thick, wet grass alongside the deserted road.

Her climax came in sharp, urgent waves, leaving her breathless and wanting more.

"Come home with me. Let me love you. Tonight, all night." Smith felt the desperation in his voice. He couldn't recall ever begging a woman for sex. But this request wasn't about sex, it was about wanting and needing for the first time in his life. If she refused …

"I need you, Meredith," he admitted.

Her eyes were closed. Her lips slightly parted. He was a fool to break the moment, to give her the chance to cool off. She was here, hot and ready for him. He wanted her, but he wanted more than an eager climax and a friendly parting.

When her fingers brushed his erection, his breath caught.

She fumbled with his zipper, then reached inside his pants and freed his throbbing penis. "Can't wait. Now."

He dug in his pants pocket for the foil packet he'd brought in expectant preparation. Thank God.

Pushing her eager hand aside, he sheathed his throbbing erection, then lifted her against the car. When he encountered the nylon barrier, he nearly lost it. He yanked her panty hose down to her ankles, knocked off her shoe and tore the restricting fabric from her foot.

He grasped her naked buttocks, positioning her to receive him. Sliding easily into her hot, moist passage, he penetrated swift and wonderfully deep. And nearly came.

Her legs snaked around his hips, holding him firmly, demanding his vitality. Barely aware of the now pouring rain, Smith thrust his hips, driving his length over and over, willing her pleasure, needing her love, wanting her climax.

The fingernails digging into his back, the intense clamping around his cock, and the satisfied moan coming deep from her throat told him she'd peaked. Weeks of unfulfilled desires rushed upon them like a tidal wave.

He couldn't get enough of her.

Even as he broke a sweat, his shoulders and back unbelievably drenched, he remained deep inside her. He'd waited so long. An eternity.

With eyes still closed, he sought out her lips, kissing her gently, savoring their joining.

How he loved the feel of her.

The sound of an approaching vehicle snapped him back to reality. Had he completely lost his mind? They were screwing their brains out in broad daylight. He pulled out and pushed Jones's bare legs from around his waist. When he stepped back, he discovered his raincoat lying on the asphalt beneath his feet. As he scrambled to retrieve the drenched coat, he swore. Jones laughed as she hopped around trying to place a wet leg into her sodden panty hose. Finally, wisely, given the ever-increasing sound of the closing vehicle, she gave up and discarded the mangled nylons, stepped into her lost shoe and pulled her raincoat tight about her waist.

Shuddering in the cold wind, he pulled his raincoat over his wet shirt. Again he caught a muffled laugh as Jones opted for the car. As the passenger door slammed shut, he secured the belt of his coat. When he turned to face the vehicle, Smith's heart leaped. A four-wheeler bearing a national park insignia pulled close and braked.

Smith, knowing he looked thoroughly disheveled, stepped forward as the driver's window lowered silently. A young, clean-shaven park officer eyed him suspiciously. "Is everything okay, Sir?"

Smith reached up and pushed his wet hair off his forehead. "We got caught in a cloudburst. Should have taken the umbrella. But the view is worth a little wind and rain."

"Getting a little late," the officer remarked as he leaned forward.

Smith glanced over his shoulder. Sexy Miss Jones had once again disappeared. Prim Miss Collier, her wet hair miraculously styled back from her face, her lips an inviting pink from freshly applied lipstick, had stuck her head out the open window to smile warmly at the officer.

After a quick thank you to the park official, Smith groaned aloud with relief as the vehicle turned around and retreated down the road. Thank God he wasn't required to present his identification. He hadn't zipped his pants, much less removed the now uncomfortable condom. No wonder Jones had been laughing.

He spotted a trash can several yards away and began walking. When he heard his name, he turned. Jones was pointing to the ground where her panty hose lay in a tangled pile. How had the park officer missed those?

After retrieving the wet nylons, Smith again headed toward the battered bin chained to a post. Muffled laughter followed his steps.

"It wasn't monogrammed?" Meredith asked, barely suppressing a giggle. She couldn't resist teasing him. He'd looked so damned embarrassed when she'd pointed out the panty hose.

He tossed his wet coat in the backseat. "What?"

"The handkerchief you tossed."

"You're enjoying this." He turned to face her. "How would it have looked if we had gotten arrested for lewd and lascivious acts in public?"

"Is that a misdemeanor or a felony?"

"Must I remind you that it was *your* underwear I just tossed."

Meredith shifted in the seat letting him know she was more than aware she was bare beneath her skirt. His gaze dropped to her knees and his hand followed. Cold fingers dipped between her thighs sending powerful messages along her already sensitive flesh.

Although she knew they should rush back to the city and part ways forever, her flesh was indeed weak. And he knew it. His eyes danced as he leaned toward her. She gasped as his fingertips skimmed her damp curls, then teased her pulsing center. Unsated, their lips met, joined in a lusty mating.

"Come home with me," he whispered against her mouth. Her hips lifted, begging silently for more. "Let me do this right."

His invitation brought forth heated images. An evening in his arms. Another night of magic and passion.

"I want you. Naked. I want to touch your breasts, feel you against me."

Angled awkwardly, Smith pressed her back into the soft leather seat.

His hips were moving, his body arching with each probe of hand, fingers and tongue. Meredith strained against his hand.

Wrenching back, Smith abruptly stopped. She opened her eyes and looked into his. His jaw was clenched. His breathing rapid.

"My house. Your house. A hotel. Anywhere, but in this damn car."

"What are we doing?"

"What we've both wanted to do since that first day in your office. It's been a lifetime since Chicago. At least for me it has."

"I can't have an affair with you, with a director."

"You already have." His hand caressed her center as if to remind her of the situation. She clamped her knees together in protest of the liberties she'd allowed, then scowled at him. His hand remained.

"I want a decision, Miss Collier."

"This is crazy. If we're discovered ..."

He pushed his fingers deeper. "Where?"

"I think I should go home." Despite her reasonable words she wanted his hand right where it was. She wanted him. If they were at her house right now, she'd be tearing off her clothes, and his. Could she regain her senses during the short drive home?

"Your house." Slowly, he removed his hand causing her thighs to tremble as his fingers slid along her bare skin. "You don't have girlie stuff all over your bed do you?"

"Girlie stuff?"

"Stuffed animals, pillows, lace and bows."

Meredith thought about her flower-pattern comforter and buckled her seatbelt. "A ruffle here and there."

He brushed her lips briefly then started the car. "Any dogs or cats?"

"One cat. Fat and docile."

Smith turned the car around, then drove toward the freeway. "Does it sleep on the bed?"

"*It* is a male. Oliver sleeps on the bed."

"Not tonight."

"Great, another one that hates cats." Meredith realized her mistake as soon as he hit the brakes.

"Another one?"

Smith's hazel eyes narrowed. His knuckles stood out, stretched tight and white, around the wheel.

"Most men don't like cats."

"I like cats. I just don't like competition. Feline or otherwise."

He let the statement hang. She was tempted to let him think she had another lover, but there had been enough deception in their short, but intense relationship.

"I was engaged until last summer. He hated Oliver."

His hands relaxed. "No lovers since?"

"No."

"Have you seen him since the breakup?"

"No."

A smile teased the corners of Smith's face as he lifted his foot from the brake. The car eased forward, and he pressed on the gas. He felt as if a heavy burden had been lifted off his shoulders.

"No one until that night in Chicago?"

"No! No one else has —"

He wanted her to go on. He needed her to admit she cared about him. He had to know he wasn't just another guy, that he hadn't been wrong about her. "Has what?"

"Has fucked me senseless? Is that what you want to hear?"

His heart rate jumped. "Do I fuck you senseless, Jones?" he asked as he joined the flow of traffic heading south over the Golden Gate.

She was silent until they'd crossed the bridge. "You know you do," she whispered.

"Want me to do it again?"

She turned toward him and curled her legs up, forcing her short skirt high. "What do you think?"

He asked for directions to her home and switched lanes to follow the 19th Avenue signs. He drove for a while wondering what kind of fool would let her get away. Smith couldn't imagine a better sex partner. Jones hadn't lost any of her fire. He'd been ready to come in his pants again within minutes of a great climax. Lord, she made his blood run hot. He still had a hint of a hard-on as he accelerated onto the south-bound freeway. At least he'd relaxed from the utterly painful stage to pleasant anticipation.

He couldn't wait to see her naked. Just thinking about her breasts, feeling her taut nipple in his mouth caused his cock to stretch. It was damn hard to concentrate on the traffic when she gave him new directions through the narrow streets of Pacifica. After he shut off the engine, he glanced at the small, but attractive house, one of many crowded on the high cliffs overlooking the ocean.

His steps were eager as they rushed to the front door.

She turned the lock. "I'm sure there's some rule against this."

A thick heavy mist had replaced the rain. Smith shivered. He wanted to strip off his wet clothes and get naked. "Against what?"

She stepped inside, and turned to face him. "Fucking me senseless. I'm sure there's a paragraph in the employee handbook."

"I'm very good at breaking the rules," he said, daring her to send him away, praying that she wouldn't. When she stepped back to let him enter, he released a breath he hadn't realized he'd been holding.

Chapter 4

Meredith waited, near breathless as Smith's gaze was drawn to the focal point of the living room, a large window offering a panoramic ocean view. Would the expanse of glass remind him of Chicago? What would he think of the glass solarium and spa right off the master bedroom? How many fog-shrouded nights had she relaxed in the hot tub and thought of him, wanted him with her?

Thick clouds and heavy mist obscured the familiar, but still awesome view of the white-capped Pacific and rugged coastline. The last greyish light of dusk outlined the bookcase, tables, lamps and chairs, leaving one ghostly pool upon the white loveseat facing the window. Meredith reached for the lamp, but changed her mind as Smith brushed past her. The dimness reminded her of another room, another stormy night.

Familiar anticipation flared. Although they'd come together, her passion still simmered. How could it cool when his very presence held her spellbound, made her blood run hot?

At work, she could push aside her thoughts for short periods, force herself to briefly forget he was now a part of her day-to-day existence, if not part of her life. But today, after hours in close proximity, she'd been unable to reason, unable to resist.

He hadn't seduced her. She'd wanted him, needed him. Knowing she had nothing to gain and everything to lose, including her heart, she'd offered herself, willingly and passionately.

Even now she should send him packing. That might have been possible had he not walked into her home, and stood before the window. Had he not just spoken her nickname. Had not the yearning in his husky whisper been as urgent as her own.

Meredith glanced up. Silhouetted against the window, Smith waited for her. Once again the flames of passion licked her breasts and heated her center. Flames hot and wanting. As fiery, as exciting as the first time she'd been in his arms. Meredith moved toward him, dropping her damp coat heedlessly on the pale carpet. The rain had stopped, leaving a heavy mist, reminiscent of swirling snow, dancing beyond the glass.

Smith's eyes glowed. His deep breath, audible. Another reminder of another window, another night. A heat, wrought from countless dreams, from memory, coiled between her legs.

"This glass isn't as sturdy."

He shucked off his wet coat. "I'll be gentle."

She reached for buttons of his shirt. "I don't want you to be gentle. Not yet. I want it like it was."

His sodden, dress shirt dropped to the berber carpet, followed quickly by her wool skirt, her shoes. Her need flamed as he stripped off his wet clothes. Naked and splendid he reached for her. She welcomed his hands beneath her sweater, eagerly anticipating his touch as he worked the front clasp of her bra.

When he gathered her close, Meredith gasped. His nipples were hard beads beneath her palms, his skin icy. "You're freezing."

"I'm fine."

She took his hand and led him through her darkened bedroom. As she opened the siding door, Meredith flipped on a series of light switches.

Concealed lights outlined the hot tub, peaked through lush palms and ferns, reflected off the tile floor. Muted golds, lush greens, the air as soft and warm as a humid, summer night. A touch of paradise surrounded by misted glass. Her place to relax, to dream.

Circling the tub, she bent to remove the cover. He rushed to assist her. Across the intimate expanse Smith stood, his gaze, naked and passionate, caught in the pool's dancing light.

One night. It was all she would allow herself.

In two strides his arm snaked about her middle. He twisted his hand in her hair.

One night.

She moaned, already mourning his loss, knowing the emptiness that awaited her nights. His thumbs raked her nipples, bringing an ache, familiar, yet new.

He climbed into the tub and held out his hands. "You have no idea how many nights …"

Meredith's heated breath stilled in her chest. Had he too tossed and turned, ached in the darkness? She stepped into his waiting arms. Together they sank into the water's inviting warmth.

His lips brushed hers, once, then once again. Gentle touches, brief and intoxicating, a portent of things to come. His wet skin slid against hers, the water a silky lubricant as her breasts brushed his chest, their legs touched, entwined.

He cupped her face with his hands. His arms tensed beneath her palms. He held her, his gaze locked with hers. Slowly his thumb traced a path along her cheek, across her lower lip.

"You're as beautiful as I remember. More beautiful." She could hear the desire in his voice, and trembled. She wanted to believe him. And she would, at least for tonight.

Her eyes drifted closed and their lips met, wanton and seeking. The water lapped about them as their bodies tangled and sank deeper into the warmth. His hands clutched her neck, her shoulders, the length of her back, then grasped her buttocks. Lifting her against him, Smith slid onto the smooth fiberglass bench. Settling her on his lap, he licked the moisture from her breast. His mouth, hot and wet, covered her nipple, anchored her to his desire.

Although they'd touched, loved before, the impact of Smith's loving made Meredith gasp, struggle to breathe. Her mound skimmed his arousal. Her thighs clutched his hips. Heat fused as he held her in his arms, the mere contact of their flesh binding them, making them one.

Gently he built an unbearable heat, too wonderful to believe, so exquisite she couldn't speak. She could only feel, absorb, need.

Arching her back, Meredith thrust her sex to his and offered herself completely, letting him know that this night was his.

Smith felt her surrender. He knew the exact moment she'd given herself physically, lowered every sexual and sensual barrier to him. But would she ever surrender her heart?

He felt the pounding of her blood, the heavy thrum of her heart beneath her breast. She shuddered when he released her swollen nipple. Grasping her slippery thighs, he urged her to her knees. Trailing kisses along the pliant flesh of her belly, Smith paused to tease the indentation of her navel.

Wrapping his arms about her middle, he pressed his face to her belly. His heart pounded in his chest. He shuddered. Did she have any idea what she did to him? How she turned him inside out?

Lifting her out of water, he twisted, seating her on the wide rim of the tub, then knelt before her. His fingers skimmed the inside of her thighs, back and forth, until she opened, trembled from his needy caress.

Slowly, lovingly, he brushed her sex with his breath, understanding the fingernails digging into his shoulders were as much an expression of her intense pleasure as were the muted demands catching in her throat.

The touch of his tongue came softly, a reverent survey of each fold, crevice, exposing the hidden bud of her pleasure. Touching, caressing, she urged and guided him until the storm of sensation she wrought grew so intense Smith thought his heart would give out.

He relished the feel of her trembling flesh, the wild thrust of her sex against his mouth, and the sweet agony of her climax. He wanted to love her, satisfy her. He wanted to be the one she longed for, the only one she wanted.

She'd made his own pleasure secondary. That had never happened before.

An exultant cry tore from her throat, her eager thrusts shuddered to stillness. He laved her trembling flesh until her gasps eased, then mingled with soft, contented sighs.

He rose and his breath caught at the satisfied look on her face. Deliciously sated.

Nothing was more important than pleasing her. He wanted to bring her to climax, over and over, feel her quiver beneath his tongue, his lips, his urgent thrusts.

Smith's fingers trailed along her damp thigh, the curve of her hip, to the roundness of her breast. He filled his hand with her softness. Her nipple peaked in answer to his caress.

When her eyes fluttered open, an ache, new and overpowering, swelled his chest with a fierce urgency, his voice with a husky timbre. "I love your breasts."

Aching with love, his need to express his love pressed hard against her soft mound.

His lips captured hers, their tongues touched, mated, and in that moment they became one. His grasp on her breast tightened.

If only he could hold her heart so easily.

The ache intensified. His heart threatened to burst. Needing to speak, to express all the strange, intense feelings Jones evoked, he tore his lips from hers. "I love everything about you."

But did she love him?

Her lips grazed his neck, the soft, moist touch of her tongue teasing him beyond belief. He waited for her response. Waited for the words he desperately needed to hear. She didn't speak. She held him tight, her knees clasped about his middle, her sex open and exposed. He welcomed the exquisite strain she wrought, accepted what she was willing to give. For now.

He gasped, each breath a pleasure, as she rained a volley of tender kisses and tantalizing nips over his chest, across his belly. He groaned. He wanted, needed her. Intended to love her till she moaned in utter contentment.

She slid off the rim, and backed him across the pool. Willing to please her in any way conceivable, Smith complied with her gentle prodding. A provocative gleam came into her eyes as he sat on the rim of the tub and she knelt between his thighs. When she licked her lips, his erection jumped in lusty anticipation.

As she took him in her mouth, he groaned. Low and guttural, almost an animal growl. She was teaching him all over again how good it felt to be a man. How it felt to be loved.

Closing his eyes, he savored the sweep of her wet hair against his belly, the brush of her soft breasts to his thighs, and the lusty pressure of her tongue, lips and teeth, enticing his strained flesh.

He'd never felt so good. He never wanted it to end.

And if Smith had his way, it never would.

"Did you love him?"

Smith's question forced Meredith's tired brain to function. She didn't want to think of the past. Cradled in Smith's arms, she wanted to enjoy the spa's soothing jets pummeling her fatigued muscles and not think at all. Thinking would only remind her of what she was about to lose. She wanted to ignore her heart. "What difference does it make?"

"Did you love him?" His voice was soft, but insistent.

Love? She wasn't sure how to define the word. "A year ago I would have said yes. Now, I'm not sure."

"Why?"

Meredith wished he'd stop asking questions. "I don't know why."

"What's changed?"

I met you. She lifted her head from his shoulder. The solarium was filled with steam, giving the room a misty, dreamlike quality. Soft forms, no defined edges, except for Smith's eyes, Smith's questions. "Maybe I got a little smarter, a little less trusting."

"He screwed around?"

She hoped Smith didn't want details. He wasn't getting them. Moving away, she managed an answer. "Yeah."

He caught her about the waist and pulled her against his chest. He snaked a leg over her thigh, trapping her against him. "I don't screw around."

"Remind me again what happened in Chicago. Tell me again no one was waiting for you."

She waited for him to rush to his own defense. Reassure her. He remained silent. This was a conversation for the breakfast table making it convenient to separate, not one for soft lights, warm water, and entwined bodies. "She's willing to share? Or, perhaps she forgives a periodic lapse when you're gone?"

"There is no she."

"It doesn't matter since there is no us."

She felt his muscles tense, his arms tighten about her. "What we have is special."

"What we have is great sex."

"That's your definition of what we have?" His voice touched her. A husky whisper of disbelief.

"Tell me I'm the only woman you've ever picked up at an airport."

"I won't lie to you. Ever."

Did she want to know? His eyes told her he would be truthful, brutally truthful.

"Am I the only one?"

"The only one that mattered."

Was she the one? An odd pain sliced through her heart. She'd heard his husky declaration. But men could say anything when their dicks were hard.

"We're lovers. We're not in love." She'd tossed down the gauntlet. He didn't look away.

"Speak for yourself, Jones. I'm crazy about you. You know I am."

Then why don't you say I love you? Say it now. Why only lusty whispers in the heat of the moment?

"You don't believe me, do you?"

Then tell me you love me. Tell me over and over again. Tell me you want this forever.

"We have something —"

"There has to be more!" Avoiding Smith's intense gaze, Meredith looked away. She could still hear the heartbreaking news of last summer. She knew good sex wasn't enough to sustain a relationship, yet she'd hoped for more. Great sex should be an expression of the love two people shared. But she'd been wrong.

She couldn't be wrong again. She'd been loved for the sex, for being a sensual partner, but that wasn't enough then and it wasn't enough now. She wanted more than a couple of passionate nights a week. She wanted every day, every night. She wanted what Smith wasn't offering, his love, his devotion, forever. "Great sex doesn't last," she said, looking him right in the eye. "Most of our conversations have been when we're naked."

His hand slid along her spine, dipping at the small of her back, then up over her hip. "I like you naked."

"Take sex out of the equation and what do we have?"

"This isn't just about sex."

"Isn't it?"

"I love you, Meredith. I just don't know how the hell to convince you."

Meredith's heart skipped a beat. She wanted to tell Smith she loved him, but those words came so easily to men. Mistaking passion for love, she'd worn a diamond on her finger for months. Was she making the same mistake with Smith? "Love is long-term, we've only got tonight."

His eyes narrowed. "Tonight?"

This time when she pulled away, he let her go. She climbed out of the spa, grabbed a towel from a narrow, wooden table, and secured it over her breasts. "I can't afford a long-term affair with you. I'm up for a promotion, and I won't have it said that I screwed my way into it."

"I don't have control over those decisions and you know it."

"You have influence. If I get the job everyone will attribute it to you and the Wilder name."

"Office romances happen every day."

"If a man screws around, he's lucky. If he gets a promotion out of it, he's smart. But reverse the situation and what do you have? An office slut who's willing to spread her legs to get ahead."

"It's the nineties. Things have changed."

"Tell that to Alice Lester!"

His lips thinned. He didn't understand. Why should he? In his position he didn't have to compete for promotions, hope for raises. He'd been at the top of the game for years.

"Who is Alice Lester?"

She hadn't meant to expose her friend, but maybe Smith needed a lesson in reality.

"She had an affair with —" Meredith caught herself. "With an executive. Her promotion to marketing coordinator was attributed to the hard work she'd done in his bed rather than her contributions to several successful ad campaigns. Even after the affair was long over, the whispers continued. Whenever she received a raise, recognition, or won a promotion, people speculated. *Who had she fucked for this one?*"

"You can't live your life in fear of a few petty minds."

"You're a man. The same rules don't apply. You can't possibly understand."

He stood. As he stepped out of the tub, steam rose from his shoulders and chest. For a split second, she wondered if she was making a mistake by letting him go.

"No one knows about us."

She shook her head dismissing her foolish thoughts. "No one's going to know."

A bead of water slid down his chest toward his belly. Meredith's gaze followed the droplet's slow progress. Resisting the urge to stop it with the tip of her tongue, she turned away. "There is no *us.*"

He grasped her shoulders, briefly, then removed the towel. Hugging her from behind, he cupped her breasts. "Tell me that when I'm inside you. Tell me that when you shudder beneath me."

He caressed her breasts, her belly, her sex. The pressure of his erection to her buttocks, emphasized his words. "You shouldn't listen to your small brain," she quipped.

"What do you want from me?"

Everything. "Nothing."

He pushed his finger inside her. His lips skimmed her shoulder, along her neck, his tongue slid inside her ear. "Nothing at all?"

When his thumb flicked over her clit, her protest died in her throat.

"You're wet, Jones. You're wet for me."

He picked her up and sat her down on the edge of the wooden table. Pushing her knees apart, he stepped forward and thrust his hands into her hair. Molding his fingers about her scalp he tilted her head back, forcing her to look at him.

"Was it ever like this before?"

Strained with passion, his voice touched her heart. She should lie, let him think he was just another sexual encounter, but the intensity of his feelings revealed by the heat of his breath, the rapid rise of his chest, the anticipation in his eyes, and the tremor in his hands drew the truth. "Never."

His shoulders sagged with relief. The pressure of his fingers relaxed. "I had to know."

"Why?"

He smoothed back her hair. His stroke, tender, affectionate. "You walked out on me in Chicago."

"Isn't that the way it was supposed to work? No goodbyes. No awkward parting."

"If it had been someone else … but something happened. Something I never expected."

"No one's ever walked out on you before?"

"No one I wanted."

"If I had stayed?"

"We would have had this conversation weeks ago." He touched his lips to hers. "You have no idea how much I want you."

"You've had me."

He leaned forward, pressing her back until she lay upon the table. "Not as much as I need."

She welcomed his mouth on her breast, the eager tugging on her nipple. Clutching his arms, Meredith arched against him, thrusting her mound to his belly. His biceps flexed beneath her hands as one hand grasped her buttocks, holding her to him. Slowly, she moved beneath him, guided by a primal rhythm, a burning need to join, to mate, to become one.

When he slipped her legs over his shoulders, she whispered his name, almost said she loved him. The urge to speak her heart tempered by his words. He'd spoken of love, but he hadn't promised forever. He leaned over her, pressing the tip of his penis to her heat. Despite her doubts, she wanted him, and positioned her hips to receive him.

Swearing under his breath, Smith pulled back. "My pants are —"

"You want your pants?"

Smith groaned. "I'm a little too naked."

"You may be naked … ." She let the rest of the sentence hang and licked her upper lip. "In my bedroom. Top drawer, next to the bed."

He straightened and touched his fingertip to her lips. "But the *moment* has passed."

Her legs slid from his shoulders. She poked at his erection with her toe. "I'll still want you."

"But you won't tell me you love me, will you?"

"I wasn't going to tell you."

He smiled, an easy, confident, very sexy smile. "Yes, you were. Next time, I'm taping a condom to my ass."

As he walked toward her bedroom, she sat upright to gain a better view of his backside. He had great buns. "That I've got to see."

When he didn't return right away, Meredith, thinking she'd been mistaken about where she'd placed the condoms, entered the bedroom. Smith sat on the bed, running his hand along the top rail of her brass headboard. When he glanced over his shoulder at her, his eyes held a lusty sparkle that revealed he'd already thought of more than a couple of uses for the railing.

"I want to make love in your bed."

"Tired?"

Reaching out he snagged her about the waist and pulled her onto the bed. "Of you? Never."

He wanted to love her, here in her bed, fill himself with her scent, immerse himself in the place where she dreamed. Would she dream of him tomorrow? Had she ever?

He needed the memory of loving her here. He loved the silky feel of her, her scent, everything about her. Especially the appetite she had for him.

Lifting her, he slid beneath her supple thighs, tasted the heady sweetness of her lust. She moaned and grasped the brass railing. He thrust his tongue inside her, teasing, tasting, letting her set the tempo, wanting nothing more than the privilege to please her. Her sex moved, fluid and graceful, performing an erotic dance above him. When she shuddered, he almost shared her climax. Her satisfaction rippled through him, making him painfully aware of how much he needed her.

She sat back, resting her weight momentarily on his belly. Grabbing the rail, Smith pulled himself up. He reached out, searching frantically for the foil packet he'd left on the bedside table. The moment her mouth covered him, he was on the verge, caught in the magic of her lips, the enchantment of her tongue.

Clinging to the rail, like a man hanging onto a lifeline, Smith fought the storm of his own climax. He loved this fine edge, hovering between bliss and fulfillment. The latter always heightened by the intensity of riding the edge. And no one pushed him harder than Jones.

When she grasped his balls, his breath caught hard in his throat, cutting off his air supply. Her pull on his sac was measured, intense, but gentle. His heart threatened to jump out of his chest. She'd taken him to the brink, almost tasting the little death, then pulled him back to earth. Tugging lightly, she offered a tiny ration of relief, a respite from the wildness she'd wrought. Her breath, soft and hot, skimmed his pulsing flesh.

Smith was thankful when she snatched the crumpled foil packet from his fist. Understanding he was ready to burst, barely in control, she sat across his thighs and sheathed him quickly. Still the movement of her hands had him wanting to come. He groaned when she lowered herself slowly, taking each inch of him, flexing, squeezing, enveloping him with her tight, wet sex.

He cupped her breasts, filling his hands with her softness, making her cry out when he rolled her beaded nipples between his fingertips. Her sex flexed, pulled him over the edge and into a place he'd never been before. Into heaven.

He wanted to love her, fuck her, then love her again.

Exhausted, Meredith lay on Smith's chest. Her legs felt like noodles, warm, limp and utterly delicious. Threading his fingers through her hair, his thumb caught her under the chin, then tilted her face toward his. She pushed herself forward, scraping her tender nipples across his chest, to touch her lips to his.

His lips were gentle, tasting, feeling, taking nothing, making no demands. His touch delicate and warm, his arms solid. This was what she loved about Smith, his ability to need a simple kiss, his wanting to hold her once the passion storm had passed. She liked to lie in his arms, cuddling and kissing, knowing just moments before he'd been thrusting like a bull, seeking climax, tapping every primal urge in both of them.

He touched his lips to her cheek, her temple, her forehead, the tip of her nose. His eyes, warm and glowing, gazed into hers.

Could this be it? The real thing? Sex with Smith was a whole new experience. The quiet moments, the sweet kisses a refreshing change.

"I love you. You make me feel complete, fulfilled. You're in my dreams. I can't stop thinking about you." Smith's voice was soft, his poignant words touched her heart. She closed her eyes to experience the unfamiliar surge swelling her chest, making her heart suddenly too large for her ribcage.

"You're fantastic in bed!"

The pain came fast, piercing the euphoric bubble, crashing her back to reality. Her head dropped to his chest, pressing her forehead to his warm skin. She could feel his heart drumming.

"What's wrong?"

"Nothing," she managed, despite the sudden clogging of her throat. "Nothing at all."

He caught her chin with his hand, forcing her head up. "I meant that as a compliment."

She forced back her tears and faced him. "Thank you."

He scrambled to a sitting position and took hold of her arms. His eyes darted over her face, searching her eyes. "I love you. What will it take to convince you?"

Meredith swallowed the lump in her throat. "I don't want love." *Not the kind which only requires a few hours in bed.*

"What the hell *do* you want?"

Hiding the pain clawing at her foolish heart, Meredith steeled herself. "Like you said, it's been awhile since Chicago. I needed —"

"You think this is just about — that I'm —" His chest heaved. Anger raged in his eyes. "Damn you, Jones."

She pulled away, wanting to shower and wash his heady scent from her skin. He yanked her back, crushing her to him. "If this is about fucking, then I want to fuck."

She glanced down at his limp cock, thinking he couldn't possibly rouse himself again. Smiling, she looked up at him.

Smith hated to be challenged, and Jones was telling him he didn't have it in him. True, she'd wrung him dry and made him want to wallow in satisfaction till morning, but he'd be damned if she'd reject his sincerity and throw his love back in his face.

"Come morning is it over between us?"

When Meredith nodded, Smith hated her. But only for a split second and only because he finally understood what head-over-heels-in-love meant. His plan had backfired. He'd thought a night in his arms would have her declaring her love, demanding his, but all Jones wanted was a temporary lover.

Despite her callous words, Smith wasn't convinced she felt nothing for him. Couldn't believe her sighs, her cries, the catches in her throat weren't from the heart. When they came together, they loved with a passion too hot to burn out. Smith wasn't about to give up.

"Sleep with me. Tomorrow you can say goodbye."

Chapter 5

Terrible day for an interview. Meredith fastened the top button of her red jacket. Usually her power suit gave her confidence, but no matter how hard she tried, her well-applied makeup and forced smile couldn't make her look or feel upbeat.

Why hadn't Smith stopped her? So what if she'd decided to end their relationship, if two passion-filled nights could even be called as much, the least he could have done was protest. But he hadn't. Not when she'd slipped from his arms a short hour ago. Not when she'd showered, waiting hopefully for him to join her beneath the stinging spray. No, he'd waited, silently, in her bed while she'd done her makeup and hair, then watched as she dressed.

She caught his movement in the mirror as he rose from her bed. Unable to resist the allure of his strong body, she turned. Slowly her gaze slid over the strength of his legs, the thrust of his genitals, his taut belly and up to the width of his shoulders. She noticed the dark shadow of his beard, the set of his mouth, then dared to confront the challenge in his eyes. He stared at her, waiting. She couldn't say it. *I want you, but I want all of you. Not just that glorious body. I want the rest of your life.*

"Shower's all yours." Even to her own ears, she sounded lame. "I'll make coffee."

He turned and walked into the bathroom. Just before he closed the door she imagined him with a condom taped to one of his buns and smiled. But her smile died quickly. If Smith ever taped his cheek, he wouldn't be doing it for her.

A short twenty minutes later as she reached for the door handle to leave for work, Smith finally spoke. "The table in the solarium, what's it for?"

He stood close, so near she could touch his chest, his freshly shaved jaw or fondle him if she took the notion. She folded her hand into a tight fist. "It's a bathing table."

"Sun bathing?"

"That too." His eyes danced with devilish curiosity. Meredith couldn't resist tempting him. "It was designed for bathing … someone else."

She certainly had his attention. His nostrils flared and his chest expanded from a slow intake of air. "Tell me."

She shouldn't do this. She should hold her tongue, ignore the husky plea in his voice, suppress the resulting heat flooding her middle, and reject the sudden thumping of her heart.

"You lay naked on the table," she said, her voice barely above a whisper. "I fill a wooden bucket with warm water, then dip a special sponge in the water, lather it slowly with scented soap. Perhaps I'll choose sandalwood. Perhaps spice. Then I wash you. I begin with your feet. I'm very thorough. I stroke your calves. I dip the sponge again and rub your thighs. I have hours to accomplish my task."

"Are you naked?"

Deliberately she kept her voice sensually soft, her words slow. "Yes. I bend and dip the sponge again. I continue my quest. I wash your buttocks, soaping the curve of your hips, the crease at your thighs, taking my time. I slip the wet sponge between your cheeks, working the soap, back and forth. My sponge skims your balls, then I touch them, hold them, caress them. Finally, I move to your back, washing, massaging your tight muscles. Relaxing you. Soothing you." Meredith moved closer, her words, the image of Smith naked, his skin and muscles rippling beneath the sponge making her hot.

Smith raised his hand. His fingertip touched her neck at the throb of her heartbeat. "What happens next?" he asked, his voice raspy.

"I take the sponge and soap my breasts and belly. The soap runs down between my legs."

Smith spread his fingers and wrapped them about her neck, forcing her face up, her lips inches from his. "And?"

"I massage your back with my breasts, slowly, back-and-forth I rub against you using the soap and water as a slick lubricant. My nipples are hard. So hard, they scrape along your skin while my belly strokes your buttocks and thighs."

His thumb raked her jaw. "You're lying on me. You press your mound tight against me. My thigh is between your legs."

"You've heard this story before."

"Don't say goodbye."

"Why couldn't you have been a salesman, anything but —"

"And if I were a salesman, would you be bringing me home tonight? Would I be stretched out on that table?"

"I want that promotion. I worked my ass off for it. I won't have it said I didn't earn it — an affair isn't a good idea right now."

"Is that what we have?"

"We're lovers. Strangers who have connected for momentary satisfaction."

"We're hardly strangers. I know every inch —"

"You know what turns me on. You know the sensual me, nothing more."

"Some couples are married for years and don't understand each other the way we do."

"It's not enough. One of these mornings you'll wake up and the novelty will have worn off."

"You're wrong." Smith grabbed the door handle and strode outside to the car. There was no eye contact when he yanked the passenger door wide.

After a silent drive into the city, Smith pulled over to an unloading zone near the bank. Her hand shaking with doubt, Meredith reached for the handle. Smith leaned over and opened the door. "Good luck on your interview."

She was surprised he knew. "You're not coming in?"

He shook his head, pulled back and wrapped his hands about the wheel. As she placed her feet upon the sidewalk, Meredith tensed, wanting and not wanting him to stop her. When he did nothing, she whispered, "Goodbye."

"How's the new digs, Assistant Vice President?"

Meredith glanced up from the file drawer she'd been reorganizing and smiled at the man responsible for her promotion. Her new office was almost double the size of her old one down the hall. She hadn't made it to the executive floor, but that was the next goal on her career agenda. "I like it. Thanks, Jim."

"Thank Norm. He selected you as his assistant. He wants to retire in two years. All the man can talk about is that sailboat."

"Don't worry. I'll be ready," Meredith assured him. Vice President, head of Retail Banking would soon be within her grasp, so why didn't it feel wonderful? She'd worked hard for this position, knowing it would lead to the executive level. She'd earned her new title, deserved this promotion, but the victory seemed hollow.

Hollow and empty because the one person she wanted to celebrate with had jumped on a plane to New Orleans over three weeks ago. She'd gotten what she wanted, her new job, her corporate title, and Smith out of her life.

Meredith's phone rang. The caller was Jim's secretary. "Mrs. Wilding's arrived for the board meeting," Meredith said, conveying the secretary's message as she replaced the receiver. How strange Smith had disappeared without a word and his grandmother was in town for the monthly meeting. "What happened to Mr. Wilder? I thought he'd taken her position on the board."

"Smith changed his mind. He tendered his resignation and Lydia is here to resume her seat. Seems Smith's changed his mind about a lot of things lately. Has the whole family upset." Jim glanced at his watch as he headed for the door.

A dozen questions popped into Meredith's mind, but Jim waved and left her office. Why had Smith resigned? Would she ever see him again? Questions she reminded herself she had no right to ask. Smith was gone and his personal life was none of her concern.

The duties of her new position combined with the transition of her old ones to a new employee overwhelmed her Friday. When the receptionist buzzed her about a delivery, Meredith's confusion increased when a dozen red roses in a lead crystal vase were placed on the edge of her desk. With a quick "have a good day", the delivery girl scurried out of the office. Meredith glanced at the new plant sitting atop her file cabinet, and discounted her mother as the sender. Her heart pounded as she plucked the card nestled among the roses.

"Congratulations, Jones."

Meredith leaned over and inhaled the fragrance of the nearest rosebud. Anyone, even the nosy receptionist, reading the note would assume the sender was someone called Jones. For the rest of the day, Meredith caught herself staring at the roses and thinking about Smith.

Later that evening she found a card in her mail. Her heart pounded wildly when she opened the envelope to see a picture of a red rose, dewdrops beaded on the soft petals. Inside, the writing was bold, the message simple.

"Meet me for lunch, Saturday noon, at Captain's Table. I'll wait for you. Smith."

The letter bore a local postmark. He must be back in San Francisco. She wondered why he hadn't chosen to visit her at the bank or show up on her doorstep.

Most of all she wondered why he wanted to see her. Why he'd chosen a local place near her home for their rendezvous rather than a restaurant in the city?

When she walked into the Captain's Table the following day, Smith was waiting. Despite his snug-fitting jeans and navy sweater he looked out of place, too classy for the seaside cafe with its faded curtains, scarred tables and vinyl-covered booths. His loafers too polished for the scratched linoleum floor. As usual his hair lay perfectly in place.

"The roses were beautiful, thanks." She extended her hand instead of throwing herself into his arms the way she ached to do. Three weeks had been a lifetime. Her erotic dreams had returned. Now that he'd shared her bed and her spa, the memories were far too potent. Any place she looked in her home brought forth a tide of sensual images. Smith naked. His muscles bunched and straining. His face etched with passion as they came together.

He grinned at her as if reading her thoughts, then leaned down and pressed his lips briefly to her cheek. "Not as beautiful as you."

"Why are you here?" she asked taking a seat in the nearest booth. "I thought you decided to quit banking?"

He sat opposite. "I don't want to talk about work."

"What do you want to talk about?"

"You. How good you look. How much we missed each other."

"Did we?"

"Don't even try. I see it in your eyes. You're as horny as I am."

"If you believed that, why didn't you knock on my door?"

He leaned forward, his gaze intent. "I love you, Meredith," he said, his husky voice sending shivers running down her spine. "I want to make love to you until I'm exhausted, but today isn't about that."

His voice, his words triggered a heat in her middle. A simmering heat she'd tried to deny since laying eyes on him. "So what is today about?"

"We're having a date."

"Aren't we beyond the date stage?"

"We're starting over again. We're going to do all the things dating couples usually do."

"Usually do?"

"Hang out. Get to know each other. I hope you like fish and chips?"

He smiled, quite pleased with himself. She nodded, wondering how he'd chosen one of her favorite spots. Despite the rundown interior of the restaurant, the fish and chips were the best in the Bay Area. He reached out, his fingers barely touching her hand. Another set of shivers danced along her spine. Part of her loved the idea of a date, the romance of the seaside, but if Meredith had her way, she'd take him home, strip him naked and make love until the sun came up. In foggy Pacifica that might not happen until noon. "And after lunch?"

"We walk on the beach. We hold hands, we talk."

Maybe he'd lost his mind in the last three weeks. "Hold hands?"

He leaned back in the booth and picked up a menu. "Yeah, hold hands. Shall we order?"

Smith kept his word. They walked along the beach, talking and holding hands. No matter how many simmering looks she gave him, he managed to steel himself and ask another question, broach a new subject, but he did allow himself to wrap his arm around her shoulders or waist. Several hours later, they stood by her car.

"We could go home and watch the sunset." She wasn't ready to let him go. She didn't want to go home alone. The memories of Smith were far too potent, too intense to dismiss. Images forever seared into her memory.

He leaned against her car and pulled her close. "You'd end up on my lap again, and tomorrow morning you'd hate me again."

"I don't hate you."

"You're not a morning person?" he quipped. "Is that why you push me away?"

"I have my promotion. You're not a director. Problem solved."

He shook his head. "I don't want an affair. I don't want to make love all night and sneak out in the morning."

"I don't want that either."

"Don't you? Are you going to tell anyone about us? Your friends? Your co-workers? Or do I remain your secret lover?"

He'd read her right. She had no intention of telling anyone about him. The last thing she wanted was to be the subject of office gossip. "I don't talk about my personal life."

"Fine. We date until you're ready."

"Ready?"

"Ready to commit to me." His voice was firm, filled with challenge.

Was he ready to be part of her life? "Commit to you? Your life, your goals, the very air you breathe? Been there. Done that. No way."

His eyes searched hers, probing her defenses. "How about our life, our goals?"

My God, could he be serious? "I didn't mean that —"

"You don't have to defend yourself. I won't hurt you."

"I'm not —"

"Since day one, you've shielded part of yourself from me. Give *us* a chance."

"We've only spent a couple of nights together," she said, feeling the need to remind him.

"Don't push me away. We've shared a lot more than a couple of nights."

A flippant remark hovered on the tip of her tongue. He cocked his head and wagged a finger at her. "Don't you dare tell me it was just sex. If this was just about sex, I'd have knocked on your door last night."

"You thought about it?"

"I thought about it, and so did you. Tell me, Jones, how've you been sleeping lately? Do you like being alone? I don't."

"I've been busy." She couldn't tell him how much she missed him. How badly she wanted him.

"What do you dream about?"

Should she tell him about her dreams? Taunt him with the erotic images plaguing her nights. "I don't recall."

"I dream about you. I dream about unbuttoning that red suit. About stretching out on that table and being bathed. Most of all I dream about being inside you."

"Then come home with me."

He pulled her close. Even through the thick material of her jeans, Meredith felt his erection.

"Not yet," he whispered, loving the feel of her tight against him. *Not until you tell me you love me.*

Her lips curled into a sexy pout. Just looking at her made him hard. When he'd decided to court her, to earn her love and trust, he knew it would be difficult to resist her and keep his libido under control. This was just the beginning, and already he was in pain.

"How about Monterey or Carmel? The weather should be great tomorrow."

She pushed away from him, breaking the sensual contact. "You're serious about this dating thing?"

"You can bet your bank account on it." He reached over and opened the driver's door. "Time to say goodnight, Miss Collier."

Once she was settled behind the wheel, he caressed her cheek. "See you tomorrow."

The following Friday as Meredith ambled into her office, she wondered what surprise would arrive today. After a glorious Sunday afternoon, Smith had taken her home, given her a chaste kiss at her doorstep and said goodnight. Monday the gifts had begun to arrive. She'd received a selection of truffles, on Tuesday a music box, Wednesday brought balloons, and yesterday a bottle of champagne. What would Smith dream up for Friday?

She wished he'd give himself. That's what she really wanted, the intimacy, the closeness of lying naked in his arms, but Smith was determined to romance her. Despite her growing frustration, she was enjoying herself and they *were* getting to know each other. They both had been raised in the same faith and had attended parochial schools. Their stories of school had them both in stitches. Their outlook on life and politics was almost identical. They were bonding. Bonding in a whole new way that had nothing to do with sex.

But in the background, beneath the laughter, the easy conversation, desire simmered. The touch of Smith's hand, an unguarded look. Meredith felt his heat, his passion. All the more delicious because he'd forbidden the sensual. Smith's chaste kisses and gentle wooing showed a resolve, a stubborn streak Meredith admired. One she was determined to break.

When she returned from lunch, a stuffed cat, resembling her Oliver, sat upon her desk. A card tied round its neck. *Dinner at Ernie's. Cocktails at six? Meet me in the bar.*

Meredith patted the cat's head. *And bedtime at nine.*

Smith took her hand and escorted her to the car. Around them the city lights glowed like a million stars, even the street lamps sparkled. All evening he'd been a perfect date. The food and wine were delicious. Only one thing was missing. Dessert. Champagne and chocolate-dipped strawberries were in her fridge. A couple nights ago she'd dreamed of feeding him strawberries in bed, letting him lick champagne off her breasts.

"Come to lunch tomorrow, and meet my grandmother," he said, breaking into her passion-laded thoughts.

"I've met her," Meredith responded automatically.

"Not as a bank employee, but as my —"

"Does she know about us? About Chicago?"

"She knows how I feel, that I love you."

Meredith's breath caught. Her throat felt frozen. "You told her you loved me?"

"When I changed my mind about the directorship, I had to explain." He'd wanted to wait until he had a ring on Meredith's finger, but he'd done so many things his grandmother had termed "out-of-character" recently, he'd confessed. It had felt good to share his feelings. He couldn't recall ever opening himself up so completely, except when he was with Meredith or speaking of Meredith. She'd broken him open, his mind, his heart, his soul and taken him to the extreme, to ecstasy. When he'd come back to earth, he'd realized he belonged to her. Exclusively.

Exclusive hadn't been part of his vocabulary, as far as women were concerned, ever. His grandmother had looked shocked.

As shocked as Meredith looked now.

"What are you saying?"

Smith wanted to tell her everything; how he'd upset his family when he decided to live in San Francisco, how he'd been willing to spend days, weeks, whatever it took to find her. Why his work, his family had become secondary to her. Instead he waited, hoping she'd put into words the questions he knew were spinning in her head.

"Giving up the directorship couldn't have anything to do with me?"

"Why not? You made the rules."

She shook her head. Her dark hair swirled about her cheek. "What rules?"

"You couldn't have an affair with a director, and you didn't want me, us, to interfere with your promotion in any way. I gave you what you wanted."

"But what about what you want?"

"I want you. I love you." He leaned down and brushed her lips with his. "One of these days you'll believe me."

He was pleased, but not surprised when she thrust herself against him and wrapped her arms about his neck. Her innate sensuality had kept him spellbound from the beginning. He loved sex, and he needed a woman in his life who not only appreciated his drive, but enhanced it. Meredith not only met his needs, she challenged them. But she was far more than just a bedpartner. He now had a friend, a companion, and hopefully a wife. Unable to resist, he wrapped his arms around her and kissed her.

Her lips were soft, and tempting. Her hands slipped beneath his jacket, around to his back. She caressed, teased and cupped his buns, pressing herself tight against him. He understood she was trying to seduce him, and he loved every minute of her effort. He was hard and she was very pleased with herself. Several minutes later they were both breathless, hungry for each other. When she fondled him, Smith knew he had hit his limit of control. "Time to say goodnight."

Dropping his hands to his side, he pushed his weight from the door, forcing her to step back. He had to let her go, allow her time to think, to consider his words. If she told him she loved him, he didn't want it to be in bed. When she agreed to be his wife, she couldn't be naked.

She had to be dressed, her mind unclouded by sex. She must never regret her decision. He opened her car door and pressed a piece of paper in her hand. "The address, and my private phone number. Call me anytime."

"While you're in bed?"

"Consider it your personal nine hundred number."

As she drove out of the parking lot, Smith wondered what time she'd call. If he wasn't careful, he'd be proposing with his dick in his hand.

Chapter 6

Meredith picked up the phone a couple of times, then set it aside. She had every intention of calling Smith and having phone sex, she'd even thought of several steamy scenarios, but his invitation to lunch with his grandmother had taken her by surprise. All the way home she'd thought about his declaration of love. The dating, the gifts, his determination to forego sex convinced her Smith was serious. But meeting his grandmother added a whole new dimension to their relationship. An official dimension. Was she ready to declare herself, to commit?

She and Smith had begun as passing lovers, but that had changed the moment he'd walked into her office. She'd been his prey from the beginning, but hadn't seen it until now.

Meredith rolled onto her side and picked up the phone. She liked being chased, and Smith was sure to make getting caught a sexy adventure. Did she want to remain caught?

Yes! The word turned over and over. Her answer would be yes. Yes, she loved him. Yes, she wanted him forever. If he didn't ask her to marry him, she'd kill him.

Meredith giggled as she punched in his number. The phone barely rang. He'd been waiting.

"Are you naked?"

"What took you so long? I'm hard already."

His words formed a delicious image. She wiggled her bare bottom against the sheet. "I've been thinking about you, about us."

"You belong to me, Jones. You have since Chicago. I claimed you that night."

"Do you belong to me?"

"When I breathe, it's your scent. When I ache, it's for you. When I dream, it's of you."

"With a line like that, how did you ever remain single?"

"I hadn't met you."

"You're good," Meredith teased. "But I told you that in Chicago, at the airport."

Smith chuckled. "I remember. We're good, Jones. We're good together."

Meredith waited for the question, telling her just how good he thought they were together.

"Make love to me, Jones. With your feelings. With your words. Tell me how you feel, how much you want me. Make me come."

Swallowing her momentary disappointment, Meredith closed her eyes and let the images emerge. "You're naked, standing before me, your desire blatant, pulsing. A feast for my eyes. I lick my lips in anticipation, but I'd rather lick you. Just the thought of my tongue, my mouth, my lips on you, makes me hot." Sighing, Meredith ran her hand over her heated flesh, over her breasts, her belly, pausing between her legs. "I'm forced to rub my thighs together, to ease the pressure."

"Are you touching yourself?"

"Yes, but I need more."

"What do you want?"

"You. I want to feel you in my mouth."

"Take me," Smith coaxed, his voice thick with desire. "Make me come."

"I kneel before you. My hands clutch your thighs. Your muscles tense beneath my fingers. My nails dig into your flesh."

"I've never been so hard. It hurts. It's wonderful."

"I take your straining flesh in my mouth, back and forth, moistening your skin, easing your pain. Over and over. My tongue presses you and I can feel your blood pounding, vessels pumping against my mouth, filling you, making you hard as steel."

"Your mouth is wet and hot. You feel incredible."

"I am hot. You make me wet," Meredith admitted, her own fingers easing the intense pressure between her legs. "I take you deeper, I want all of you. My lips caress you, squeeze you, my mouth tugs and pulls. I'm too excited to be gentle. Too hot to be a lady. I fondle you, you're tight and full. The pleasure builds, you ache for release. I wrap my hand around you, my eager fingers kneading your needy flesh, increasing the tempo. I touch you, I lick you. My mouth throbs with pleasure. I'm so wet. Faster, hotter, until you're swollen, ready."

The only sound Meredith heard was Smith's ragged breathing, her own gasps of pleasure.

"My God, I haven't done that in years."

A smile wrought from satisfaction curled her lips. "Did you come?"

"By my own hand, alone in my bed."

"You weren't alone."

"I'm glad. I was feeling selfish."

Meredith wadded the sheet between her legs. Despite her climax, she still throbbed. "The next call is yours."

"I can't wait."

"You could come to me," she coaxed, knowing the relief was momentary. "Sleep with me."

"I still don't know how you feel, what I mean to you."

"You're everything. My pleasure. My —"

"Lover? I want to be your heart, your husband. Think about it. I'll see you tomorrow."

The phone line went dead. Meredith stared at the receiver in disbelief. Had Smith proposed?

Meredith smoothed back her hair, then rang the doorbell at the tenth floor apartment. She'd chosen her grey wool suit and pink silk shell. A strand of pearls and matching earrings complemented her outfit. If Smith decided to get down on his knee, she'd be ready.

Smith's grandmother, dressed in white wool and pearls, gave her a quick, but thorough appraisal, then welcomed her. Lydia Wilding looked sweet and endearing, maybe a tad little-old-ladyish, but Meredith remembered Jim had told her that behind that white hair and genteel, Louisiana demeanor was a shrewd businesswoman. Even Lydia's eyes, penetrating, hazel, accented with flecks of green, reminded her of Smith.

Despite the expanse of glass providing a breathtaking view of the city, the dining room was intimate and inviting. The gleaming table, an elegant blend of fine china, sparkling crystal, polished silver, and linen napkins complemented the arrangement of pink roses in the center.

And Smith, dressed in a dove-grey suit, completely at ease in the midst of this refined opulence as he'd been at the Captain's Table with paper plates and plastic forks.

Over poached salmon, the conversation was sprinkled with the proper amount of the getting-to-know-you small talk and inquiries about Meredith's duties at the bank. After lunch, tea was served in the living room. When Smith left the room to answer a phone call, Lydia smiled at Meredith. "How nice, we have a few moments alone."

Wondering if Lydia had arranged the call, Meredith returned the smile. For the moment the small talk was through. Mrs. Wilding had something to say.

"I had to meet you," Lydia began, then paused. Instead of responding to the stretch of silence, Meredith waited. "Since you've come into my grandson's life, he's been doing the most unpredictable things."

"Things?"

"We've raised him like a son. His father was our oldest. Our only son. We're concerned."

"What things?"

"He reneged on an agreement with his grandfather, and practically within the same breath announced his decision to move to San Francisco."

"I thought he moved here to assume your chair on the board."

"He did. I made that request two years ago. Four months ago he decided to accept then changed his mind again. Because of you."

"Are you sure?"

"You've had quite an impact on Smith. You've even put the *M* word into his vocabulary."

Marriage? Was Smith thinking of marriage? He had used the word commitment. Needing clarification, Meredith asked, "The *M* word?"

Lydia smiled. "Monogamy, dear."

Her cheeks suddenly hot, and her heart thumping hard against her chest, Meredith hoped her shock hadn't been written all over her face. Since marriage and monogamy were synonymous in her mind, she'd been unprepared for Lydia's choice of *M* words. Should she be complimented, or was Lydia merely warning her?

Meredith picked up her cup of tea. The china cup clattered loudly against the saucer. "You were so astounded, you had to meet me?"

Lydia's eyes narrowed. Meredith had wanted this woman to like her, wanted her approval, but Lydia Wilding seemed more curious than seriously considering a possible new family member. In a heartbeat Meredith knew monogamy alone was unacceptable. She wanted it all, and she wasn't about to settle for an affair, even a long-term one. Feminist ideals be damned. She wanted his name, his commitment legally. She wanted more than a promise of fidelity. Smith had said she belonged to him. Well, if he belonged to her, she wanted it on paper. But what did Lydia want?

"Smith is all we have. We, his grandfather and I, want him to be happy."

Meredith set her tea aside. She'd heard the unspoken *but* at the end of Lydia's sentence. Her soft southern accent belied the importance of the conversation.

"You don't really like tea, do you, dear?"

"No, right now I'd like a —"

"Sherry?"

"Sounds perfect." It didn't, a dry martini would have been perfect.

Smith strolled back into the room. "Fix us all a drink," Lydia ordered with sweet, but absolute authority. "Meredith would like a martini, and so would I."

Waiting until Smith was across the room with his back turned, Meredith challenged Lydia. "Why do I bother you, Mrs. Wilding? Maybe it would be good for him to be monogamous for awhile."

"What are you two whispering about?"

"Nothing," they both answered, simultaneously reaching for the glasses in his hands.

Meredith noted the quirk of Smith's left eyebrow as he sat next to her on the sofa. "What have you been doing, Grandmama? Meredith is full of questions, I can see it in her eyes."

"I told her I wanted to meet her."

"And?" Smith asked, without glancing at his grandmother.

"I told her you've been peculiar lately."

"I'm in love," he said, in a matter-of-fact tone. "Isn't that explanation enough?"

"What was the agreement with your grandfather?"

Lydia reached out and placed her hand on Smith's arm. "Let me explain. Otherwise I fear she won't believe you."

Smith focused his attention on his grandmother. "What makes you think she'll believe you? The idea is so outdated, I don't believe it myself."

"I'll decide what I believe. Go on, Mrs. Wilding."

Smith relaxed back into the sofa. Meredith sipped at her drink as Lydia began.

"My husband wanted Smith to settle down, raise children. Since he's shown no inclination to do so, my husband told him if he wasn't married by age forty, an old Wilding tradition of bride selection would be revived."

"The night I agreed, Grandpapa and I had had a few drinks."

Lydia glanced at Smith. "Not a few, dear. Lucius had opened a second bottle of Southern Comfort. If Smith didn't find a suitable female by his fortieth birthday, he had to marry the bride of my husband's choice."

"You'd let your grandfather select your wife?"

"The practice was quite common in the last century," Lydia interjected.

"I'd forgotten until he reminded me last Christmas," Smith explained. "It had become a point of honor, a gentlemen's agreement if you will. I was on my way home to meet *my grandfather's choice* when the snowstorm closed O'Hare. I couldn't go through with it, I reneged."

The expression on Smith's face told her his decision had plagued him. "What did you tell him?"

"Lucius had planned an engagement party," Lydia explained. "The whole family had been invited. He'd chosen a distant Wilding cousin. He was positive once Smith met her —"

Met her?

Smith ignored his grandmother along with her question. His gaze locked with hers. "I told him I had met the woman I wanted to marry."

"But how could you tell him that? You didn't even know my name.

No one falls in love in one night," Meredith blurted out. "Or was I a convenient excuse to get out of a difficult situation?"

Smith's eyes narrowed. His mouth thinned into a straight line. Meredith glanced at Lydia whose mouth had dropped open in a most unladylike fashion.

Lydia picked up her drink and stood. "I think I should leave. I'm sure I have a phone call to make."

"You weren't an excuse," Smith said as Lydia disappeared down a hallway. "I told them the truth, I just didn't offer any details."

"It was a fluke we ran into each other. You couldn't have planned on finding me."

"It was no fluke. You told me you worked for a bank and you'd been in Chicago for a training conference. It was a matter of time."

"I didn't tell you what bank."

"If you had I wouldn't have had to wait two months."

"So you flew out here and started calling banks? I don't believe it. Do you know how many banks there are in San Francisco?"

"Actually I do. I called most of them before I had the sense to call my own."

"You expect me to believe within one night, you fell in love, decided to cancel *your* wedding, and move to San Francisco to find me?"

"Actual wedding plans hadn't been made."

"And if you hadn't met me?"

"I'd given my word."

"You were going through with it?"

"I had just turned forty. My grandfather was relentless. A wife, children to carry on the Wilding name sounded reasonable."

Disgusted, Meredith jumped to her feet and stalked over to a large plate glass window overlooking the bay. The sun had just broken through the low clouds and sailboats skimmed across the glimmering water. She touched the thick glass with her fingertip.

"So I was your excuse? Surely by now your grandfather has given up on this silly notion of picking out your bride."

"I didn't need you as an excuse." He stood directly behind her. His voice low and sexy. "As for coming to San Francisco, that was because of you. Otherwise, if I wanted to remain single, the family holdings are nationwide. I had my choice — Chicago, New York, Atlanta … I may have disappointed my grandfather, but he wasn't about to relieve me of my corporate responsibilities."

Meredith glanced at his reflection in the window. "I don't know what to believe."

Smith placed his hand over hers, pinning her palm against the glass. "If you believe anything, believe I love you. Only you. Maybe it's not supposed to happen in one night, but it did."

He stood behind her, watching her reflection in the glass as he'd done that night in Chicago. She'd fallen in love that night, and it had scared her. Her feelings for him had been far too intense to deal with rationally the next morning.

"All my life I've avoided a commitment," Smith said. "Not this time. We are different. We connected. Even after weeks apart — I thought you felt it, too."

"Last night, on the phone, was that a proposal?"

Smith touched his lips to her hair. "I'd planned it differently, but I meant it."

The memory of what they'd been doing came to mind. "It was different all right."

"I could do it again."

"It wouldn't be the same."

Smith grasped her about the waist and turned her to face him. "What are you saying, Jones?"

"I love you."

"And?"

"I'll marry you, anytime, anywhere, under any circumstances."

"How about here as soon as we get a license?"

Meredith glanced at the well-appointed living room. "You'll want to live here?"

Smith shook his head slowly. The green flecks in his eyes sparkled and his lips curled in a sexy grin. "The bathing facilities are inadequate, but some night when the fog is thick as snow, we can borrow the place."

"You'll want me to sign a pre-nuptial?" Meredith asked outright. She'd rather know now, than have some Wilding lawyer slap an inch-thick agreement on her desk tomorrow with the expectation she'd willingly sign on the dotted line.

"Pre-nups are advance divorce agreements. Divorce isn't an option I'll consider. You have my word."

"A gentlemen's agreement, then," Meredith teased, relieved that Smith had placed no conditions on their marriage, but love. "Shall we drink on it? Perhaps a glass of Southern Comfort?"

"For my bride, Dom Perignon."

Strictly Business

by Shannon Hollis

To my reader:
In this high-speed, high-tech world, sometimes you just have to stop and let love catch up to you…

Chapter 1

Elizabeth Forrester closed her office door and fell into a chair before her knees gave out.

Settled.

One hundred thousand dollars, but it was still less than they would have had to pay in court. She leaned her forehead on a stack of evidence, the laser-printed type blurring in front of her eyes. She had every e-mail message in the stack practically memorized. The chronicle of a seduction, from the first innocent messages to the latest three-page document that detailed a middle-aged man's sexual fantasies with a twenty-four-year-old woman.

Online sex on the company network. Elizabeth groaned. Every keystroke sitting right there on the system backup tapes for the lawyers to extract. How could a man so smart be that dumb? The woman had used him as skillfully as any craftsman used a tool. It was enough to make her grind her teeth. Giving one hundred thousand dollars to Malinda Burke offended every principle Elizabeth possessed. But the thought of sitting in court beside the shaking husk of what had once been a senior Director offended her even more.

What she wouldn't give for a cool glass of wine.

But it was only three in the afternoon. She had to make an employee retention pitch in half an hour, and then interview two people for the compensation manager's position. She pushed the thought of the wine away. As Director of Human Resources, one of her responsibilities was to make sure a lawsuit like this wouldn't happen again. She called up her freshly written policy on her computer screen — the fruit of the last four months of hell.

"Stratton Hill management realizes that healthy relationships among its employees are key to their quality of life. However, personal relationships must remain within the best interests of the business. In order to encourage focus and productivity, management requests that employees adhere to the following principles: (1) Relationships between persons in the same management chain are discouraged. In particular, a romantic relationship between a manager and his/her employee is prohibited due to the risk of favoritism and conflict of interest. (2) If the behavior of two employees disrupts or causes discomfort to their co-workers, disciplinary action may follow. Should the employees require three warnings, transfer or termination may result. Thank you for your understanding and compliance."

She tapped the "send" key and the policy went out over the system to every Stratton Hill employee in the country. God help them if they didn't comply. She wasn't going through this ever again.

Her administrator, Jenny, poked her head in the door. "Are you OK, Elizabeth?"

Elizabeth pulled *Burke v. Stratton Hill* together and locked the files in one of the cabinets against the wall. "I am now. I just sent you-know-what out over the wire. Be prepared for the deluge."

Jenny braced her shoulders and shook her curly hair back — the soldier before the final charge. "I've been taking self-defense classes."

Elizabeth laughed. "That's what I like about you — you're so proactive. Can you give me some pointers?"

"Nope, just a reminder." She relaxed back into informality. "You've got a meeting with Garrett Hill in ten minutes. About the technician theft problem in the Canadian office."

"Right." One problem down. Another to go. They'd just got the retention situation in Portland under control, and now the brightest minds in the Vancouver office were being lured *en masse* over to AlphaTech Computers, their biggest competitor. Elizabeth wished AlphaTech would quit opening offices in cities where Stratton Hill had already hired the best development techs the industry had to offer.

She took a deep mental breath and looked on the bright side: she was going to spend a whole hour in a strategy meeting with Garrett Hill, the most beautiful man in Silicon Valley. Taking her presentation folder and laptop from Jenny, Elizabeth headed down the hallway to the executive offices. You'd never catch her complaining about the time she spent listening to that voice, or watching Garrett's sexy backside as he pointed out profit margins on the wall screen. Sitting next to him, she had to resist the temptation to reach out and touch his thick, dark hair as it curled on the back of his neck.

She put the images out of her mind as she slipped into the conference room. Thinking about Garrett Hill was crazy, after the afternoon she'd just spent. Her heart and her body might crave him, but her head had to keep her own strict policy in mind. He was the Chief Technical Officer of the company, and one level above her in the management chain. No matter how strong the urge, hell would freeze over before she'd let her deepest, most secret fantasies see the light of day. Not only would she lose all credibility in the insular world of human resources for breaking her own policy, she'd lose her job.

But there was no harm in looking. No harm in enjoying his company.

She was fourth on the agenda, and presented her key employee retention proposal with as much presence of mind as if Garrett weren't sitting two chairs away, watching her intently out of darkly lashed blue eyes. She tried not to play to him, but every time she turned to explain a concept, his gaze would flick up and meet hers. The presentation material had his interest, anyway. It certainly couldn't be her sober, dark blue suit with the skirt only her grandmother could call short. Little did he know, she thought as she finished the proposal and sat down, that under the suit jacket and jewel-necked silk blouse, her nipples had tightened in an involuntary response. If she couldn't have his hands on her, at least she could capture his gaze.

He waited for her as she gathered her materials at the conclusion of the meeting.

"What was the verdict?" he asked. She glanced toward the open door. The entire workforce probably had their ears to the walls of the conference room. But Garrett was a senior executive, and the former boss of the departed victim. It was her responsibility to tell him first before submitting a formal report.

"Settled," she said quietly. He stood close, his attention absolute. She could smell a faint whiff of his cologne, and resolutely blocked it out.

"How much?"

"One hundred K."

"My God." He turned away, one hand on his hip, the other rubbing his face. "She could make a living at this."

"I hope not. Her attorney does, of course." She couldn't keep the bitterness out of her tone.

"It hurts."

"I know. But dragging us all through court would hurt even more."

He nodded, and turned back to her again, his eyes somber. "Nice job. Thanks for sticking with it. I know this has been your whole life for the past couple of months."

"Not quite my whole life." She smiled, and was rewarded with an answering smile. She pushed her response to the warmth of his praise back down to a professional level. "I try to keep my perspective on this job. If I let it take over at the risk of my personal life, it will consume me."

"That's right. You're at the helm of the Quality of Life program." He changed the subject. "So let's talk some more about the problems in Vancouver."

She nodded. "Looks like we have some work to do if we want to stay ahead of AlphaTech. The salary structures in Canada are very different, but I'm not sure it's salary alone. I know a motivation consultant out of Seattle who might help."

"Whoa," he said, sitting sideways on the conference table. "Hold on a minute. I was thinking about another approach to the problem. Sit down and let's think about this."

It was no wonder Garrett Hill had been written up in *Fortune* as one of the most influential executives in the Valley. He made her feel as if her input was the single most important thing he would hear all day. When you talked with Garrett, even something as trivial as a good morning in the hallway, you knew you had his attention.

This was one of the sexiest things about him.

Elizabeth didn't want to sit in one of the low conference chairs. His masculinity was potent enough without the domination of physical space. She edged the chair out of the way, dropped her laptop and folder on the seat, and leaned against the table a cautious few feet away.

"What did you have in mind?" she asked.

"A personal visit." His gaze held hers, and she lifted a dark eyebrow, prompting him to continue. "There's a feeling of disconnection out there, of being cut off from what's going on at Corporate headquarters. A little bit of visibility, some one-on-one conversations, and some plain humanity would go a long way to bring them back to the fold."

She nodded. "I think so, too." With a smile, she added, "And it's a little more friendly than a motivation consultant, I suppose."

He smiled in return, and her concentration narrowed on his mouth. What wouldn't she give for just one kiss from that mouth, with its Duchovnyan lower lip and sculpted outline …

"So I'd like you to go with me," he said, jerking her out of her five-second fantasy.

Travel with you? Spend hours on an airplane beside you? Hotel rooms?

She clamped down hard on the first rush of instinctive self-doubt. She'd never survive the trip without making an utter fool of herself.

But he was looking at her expectantly, waiting for an answer to what was, for him, probably just another unwelcome business trip to solve a problem that shouldn't have occurred in the first place. She pulled her professionalism around her, a guise as sober as her navy blue suit.

"Sure," she said. "When do we leave?"

❦

Garrett folded himself into the first class aisle seat next to Elizabeth and tried to find a comfortable position. Alaska Airlines only thought these seats were bigger. Men who were six foot two knew better.

His daughter Jessie's good-bye still sounded in his memory. "Be good to yourself, daddy," she had said. "Don't worry about me. I'll have that bug fixed before you get back."

He smiled. If she could write that software fix for her science project before he returned Wednesday morning, he'd hire her himself. His thirteen-year-old genius. They were quite a team.

"I brought along some ideas," Elizabeth said, bending to slide her laptop under the seat. "My market analyst says that —"

"Elizabeth," he said solemnly, the smile still curving his lips, "for the duration of this flight I don't want to hear a word about retention or market analyses or even lawsuits. I want to have a drink and relax and talk about something completely trivial and unrelated to work." He touched her arm. "Okay?"

She froze, gazing at him with those wide grey eyes that reminded him of winter rain, and looked down at his fingers.

He removed them. "Got it?"

"Got it." Her voice sounded muted. He hoped he hadn't offended her. She took her job so seriously.

As the plane headed north for Vancouver, he accepted a Scotch from the flight attendant and risked a glance to his right. Elizabeth was looking out the window at the Sierras below. Her dark hair waved away from her face, swept into a roll at the back of her head. He'd never seen it any other way. Well, once. At the summer picnic she'd pulled it back into a French braid, but that hardly counted. At that same picnic she'd worn denim shorts that had knocked his socks off. Her legs were sensational, long and slender, with firm thighs and delicate ankles. He'd never seen that much of them since, and he wanted to.

In the six months since she'd joined Stratton Hill he'd found himself wanting more of Elizabeth Forrester in every way. He knew about her professional background, but nothing about her personal life except that she did a lot of volunteer work. He knew her marital status, but nothing about the people or things or places she cared about. He'd seen glimpses of her body, but other than that brief contact moments ago, had never touched her. What he did know was that when she walked into a room, people smiled. Her joy in life was catching, her caring involvement with people, sincere. He wanted her to share some of that joy and care. With him.

It was frustrating and challenging at the same time. And now with this Malinda Burke harassment thing, the possibility of satisfying his desire and his primitive craving for Elizabeth's warmth was more remote than ever.

At least they'd accomplished something together. She'd proven him right in his strategy to humanize the firm. Too many of the software engineers spent long hours cooped up in their offices, sweating over microcode in order to make Stratton Hill number one in its market. He admitted he had once been the worst offender. From their first interview, he'd known Elizabeth Forrester could take on the job — human resources and public affairs — and make the company's work atmosphere so appealing that people would compete to hire on with them. And she had. The fact that she was single and gorgeous and made his adrenaline pump every time he passed her in the hall had nothing to do with her success.

For the flight she had put on black slacks and a black angora turtleneck. Not much of an improvement on her business suits, unless you noticed the details. And he was a detail man. The slacks outlined a smooth pair of hips and a waist curved to fit a man's resting hand. She had a hell of a walk, too, a sort of graceful sway that drew his attention to her backside and kept it there all the way down the jetway to the plane.

She sighed, her breasts lifting and falling, and settled into her seat. He swallowed and glanced away, afraid she would notice the direction of his gaze. That thin angora sweater had been designed for only one thing. He imagined how the angora would feel under his palms. Thank God she hid under wool or linen jackets in the office. He'd never get any work done otherwise.

Garrett spent an entirely enjoyable few minutes speculating on the kind of bra she might be wearing. Not the wired, push-up kind. Those curves were anything but artificial. And no padding. Her nipples poked at the soft angora just enough to be utterly distracting every time he glanced over. Big nipples. He loved big nipples. They were so sensitive and erotic. Suckable. He shifted in his seat as the blood rushed to his groin, filling him, making him stiff.

Jesus. Think about something else.

Women's nipples were supposed to subside. Then why didn't Elizabeth's? Why were they still hard, poking through her bra, through her sweater, making him crazy?

She was turned on. That was it.

So what was she thinking about, there with her head tipped back against the seat, eyes closed? What was making her nipples tight and delicious and too damn visible for a public place? The guy across the aisle thought Garrett hadn't noticed him sneaking peeks at Elizabeth's breasts. She was with *him*, dammit.

"Penny for your thoughts?" he blurted abruptly, and then wished he could just get blown out the nearest window. What a stupid thing to say. He didn't want to know, anyway. She was probably thinking about the latest man in her life and the fact that because of him, Garrett Hill, she wasn't going to see him for three days.

Good.

Elizabeth smiled. "I was just thinking about Vancouver. I used to spend my summer vacations there. My aunt and uncle had a couple of acres out in White Rock and my brother and I would come for a month every year."

The first personal information she'd ever given him, and it had to be a fib. Summer vacations did not make a woman's nipples hard. He was right. She was thinking about her boyfriend, and that annoyed him no end.

"You know the area? Great. You can drive the rental car." He tipped his head back and stared at the door into the cockpit. He would not look at her breasts any more. Let that horny jerk across the aisle have the pleasure.

For all the good it was going to do either of them.

Elizabeth dropped her suitcase on the floor in the hotel room and sank down on the bed.

She'd done it.

She'd actually managed to spend two hours on a plane beside Garrett Hill without climbing into his lap and begging him to make love to her. She was going to have to buy a padded bra — or tape herself down. This was ridiculous. She was glad he was a cranky traveler. If he'd been charming and attentive, the way he was in the office, she would never have been able to sustain what little control she had.

Oh, Lord, she had to keep control. Her career depended on it.

Elizabeth began to unpack. One black skirt, with three silk blouses and coordinated jackets. One black dress for Tuesday night's management dinner. And one pair of grey leggings and a comfortable grey sweater to watch *The X-Files* in. Her favorite show would start in half an hour, giving her enough time to change, press tomorrow's blouse with her travel iron, and take the pins out of her hair.

At five minutes to nine, she settled in the middle of the bed and zapped the television on with the remote control.

Someone knocked at the door.

She crossed the room and looked out into the hallway. There was no one there. Frowning, she locked the door. When the knock came again, she realized there was a discreet door on the far side of the room, next to the bureau.

Adjoining rooms.

Great. As if this weren't difficult enough. Why hadn't she paid attention when the clerk had handed them their room keys?

"Elizabeth?" Garrett called softly, his voice muffled.

"Be right there."

A combination of anticipation and dismay spritzed into her bloodstream as she opened the door. What did he want? In her dreams he would flatten her against the wall and kiss her into a frenzy. In reality he probably wanted to go over the retention strategy one more time with a captive listener.

She opened the door, and her breath caught in her throat.

He leaned easily on the jamb, his arms crossed. The top three buttons on his shirt were open, enough to show the dusting of black hair on his chest, and his tie hung down either side of the open placket.

Don't do this to me, she thought, dazed. *It isn't fair that you look this good.*

He looked her over slowly. "Your hair's down," he said in a soft tone of surprise, as though he thought she might wear business attire to bed.

"I'm watching TV," she said.

His boyish grin made her bones melt. *"The X-Files?"*

She nodded, smiling sheepishly as though he'd caught her with her hand in the cookie jar.

"I saw the previews last week. You know what they say. You don't want to watch it alone."

"Is that an offer to protect me from paranormal activity?"

He opened his mouth as if to say something, then changed his mind. "I'm a fan too. Can I join you?"

Not dressed like that, you can't. "Sure." She stepped back and he closed her side of the twin doors behind him, leaving his side open.

As the show's teaser scene came on, he settled against the bed's headboard with a couple of pillows behind his back, while she sat, cross-legged, on the end. When the opening theme began, she looked over her shoulder.

"I'm glad you're here. This has to be a ten on the Chris Carter Creep-Out Scale."

"Does that bother you?"

"I like the UFO and psychic ones. No blood."

"I'll protect you."

"Ha. I'll remind you of that at three in the morning, when I can't sleep." The minute she said the words, she heard the double entendre and wished she could bite them back.

His eyes crinkled with a slow smile, his lashes dropping over a glance that acknowledged her slip as clearly as if he'd said so. And that he liked it.

Mortified, she turned back to the television, hugging her knees protectively against her breasts. She was going to have to watch her mouth. It was bad enough that she was sitting on a hotel bed with the Chief Technology Officer. Clumsily veiled come-ons only made it worse. He was going to think she was so desperate that she'd break her own policy to get a chance at him. He could sue for harassment, whether he had invited himself into her room or not.

She got through the rest of the hour by concentrating on the show.

The episode made her blood run cold, but it kept her from falling into forbidden fantasy about the man on the bed behind her.

She shut the television off at ten o'clock and got up. "I'm glad I didn't set my VCR to tape that one."

"I told you. It's a mistake to watch that show alone." He swung his legs off the bed and pulled his tie off. "So. Are we ready for tomorrow?"

"Yes, sir. Presentation, budget, encouraging words. All here."

"Elizabeth." His voice was low, a bass caress. Oh God, that voice. It was enough to crumble her resolutions and make her throw her ethics out the window.

"What?" she whispered, her throat dry. He stood two feet away, rolling his tie up in a neat engineer's coil.

"Don't call me 'sir'."

She tried to turn it into a joke. "But you're the veep. We all have to call you 'sir'."

"No, you don't. We're co-workers. We're here to get the job done." He moved over to the door. "Join me for a drink? I've got some wine in the minibar."

She wrestled temptation to the ground. "No, thanks," she whispered. "I need to go over my notes one more time, and then I need some sleep."

"Call me, won't you?"

She looked up at him, confused. He stood so close, she could almost smell the warm, rumpled cotton of his shirt mixed with his utterly distracting cologne. "Call you?"

"When you wake up at three in the morning."

"I …" She floundered, trying to come up with a snappy retort that would break this intimate spell, but the images were too much for her.

With a smile, he slipped through the adjoining doors. Thank God. She shut hers behind him, locking it more to keep herself out of his room than to keep him out of hers.

She leaned on the door, her heart thudding in her chest. Her knees wobbled. With a featherlike brush of her fingers, she touched her nipples through the grey tunic sweater. A fiery trail of desire arrowed from the two sensitive points down to the soft, damp place between her legs, triggering the scent of her own desire.

He couldn't possibly know the effect his unconscious flirtation had on her. That was just his way. He used that softly persuasive tone on practically all the female staff, and it never failed to work. He wasn't responsible for her body's reactions. She was. And she had to keep them under control.

But that didn't stop her from taking the pillows he had been leaning on and sleeping on them, her face pressed into the warm, scented hollow where his head had been.

Chapter 2

Monday morning, when Garrett came to collect her, Elizabeth opened the door in stocking feet as she shrugged into her suit jacket.

"Hi, I'm almost ready."

"Take your time." He stood just inside the door, wearing a navy suit that made his eyes a deeper shade of blue, and brought out the smooth planes of cheekbone and jaw.

She dragged her gaze off him and retreated to the end of the bed. Shoes. She needed shoes. As she slid one foot into a high-heeled pump, his gaze traveled down her legs to her stocking-clad foot and rested there as she slipped it into the second pump.

She was acutely aware of his attention as she picked up purse and briefcase. Slowly, his gaze moved up her legs, past her conservative skirt, paused for a moment on her blouse, and stopped on her face.

"Shall we go?" he said, and held the door for her.

She felt breathless, as if he'd physically run his hands the length of her body.

Off limits. Don't even think about him that way, she told herself fiercely as the elevator dropped six floors and deposited them in the lobby. *He appreciates women. He's nice enough to pretend he appreciates you. But you work for him, and even if you didn't, he's not the kind of man who will make you happy.* His heart belonged to Stratton Hill, and he had a reputation for working longer hours than anyone she knew. Any woman who loved him would always have to take second place to his driving desire for success. She straightened her back. Her mother had taken second place to IBM for thirty years. It wasn't going to happen to Elizabeth. She wanted success, too, but not at the cost of a life outside the workplace. She had attained many of her goals — the respect of her peers, a directorship at a Fortune 500 firm, a reputation as a role model for young women. She was working on the last goal — a rewarding relationship with a loving man. Fantasies about Garrett Hill were fine in their place. But he was not the man who could give her what she needed in the long term.

The Vancouver office had arranged to have them picked up at eight-thirty, and from then on it was one appointment after another. While Garrett met with the management team, Elizabeth met individually with the engineers, gathering data and formulating her own opinions about what direction they should take to retain the talent in the area. Her path crossed Garrett's several times during the course of the day. Each time he managed to exchange a smiling look or crack a whispered joke in passing that, despite her determination not to let him affect her, lifted her spirits and made her warm inside. He had the gift of making her feel as though they were partners, up here to accomplish something that mattered.

After lunch she heard his name in a hushed conversation outside the conference room door, where she was beginning her trip report on the laptop.

"Have you ever seen Garrett Hill before?" a woman's voice asked.

"No," a second woman replied. "But I recognized his voice. He looks even more gorgeous than he sounds."

"I'll say. Who's that he's with?"

"The HR director from head office."

"Do you think they're … ?"

"For Pete's sake, Elise. You're going to get yourself in trouble one of these days. Didn't you read that policy in your e-mail? She's the one who wrote it."

Elizabeth froze in her chair, her notes forgotten. She felt cold, guilty — as if she'd been caught in the wrong. But no one could possibly know her internal struggles about Garrett Hill. Her behavior towards him was always professional and cordial. Particularly today. Those women were just speculating. It sounded as if it were a hobby.

But it made her realize how very thin was the line between fantasy and reality. The thought of the employees speculating about her ethics when she was trying so hard to live up to them chilled her. She had to be more careful than ever about hiding her feelings.

Accordingly, she opted for room service that evening, forcing herself to ignore the puzzled hurt in Garrett's eyes when she declined his dinner invitation. A little distance would be good for her. Keep her out of the danger zone.

But that didn't help to control the leap in her senses when she heard the quiet knock on the adjoining door at nine-thirty. She was dressed in nothing but a flowered silk slip that the Victoria's Secret catalog had assured her was a nightgown, with a matching short robe over it.

As she went reluctantly to the door, she wished she'd put on her sweater and leggings. This was no outfit to keep resolutions in.

Cautiously, she opened the door. Garrett stood in the opening, one hand kneading his shoulder, his face creased with lines of pain. "Garrett, what's the matter?" she asked, her voice filled with concern.

Frowning, he took in her silk dressing gown and the smooth length of bare leg it revealed, then looked away. "Do you have any aspirin?" he asked.

"No, I don't. Sorry. Did you pull a muscle or something?"

"I probably slept the wrong way last night. It's been hurting all day."

"You looked like you were in pain this afternoon, during the last meeting. Can I do something to help?" She hated to see that drawn look on his face. The thought of anything hurting him hurt her, too.

"Do you know how to give a back rub?" he asked, cocking one eye at her hopefully.

"The best. Come in and lie down." She led him over to the neatly made bed. He sank onto his back, grimacing as the movement tweaked his shoulder. "You need to lie on your stomach," she instructed gently.

Holding her gaze, he reached out with one hand to hook her gently behind the knee. Her entire leg suddenly became extra sensitive, as though his hand had passed over it from thigh to ankle. Thank God she'd shaved, she thought, and was instantly ashamed of herself. She had no business enjoying his caress. It was practically illegal.

His expression grew still and absorbed, as though his whole being was focused on experiencing the touch of her skin. He tugged again. "Come here."

She resisted. "No. On your stomach."

"Shirt on or off?"

She swallowed. "On. This is strictly business, Mr. Hill."

"But it hurts."

"I can get to where it hurts through your shirt."

"None of the professionals do it that way." He lay on the bed, holding her gaze. One at a time, he unfastened his shirt buttons, then slowly pulled the tails out of his waistband. The muscles of his chest flexed as he rolled briefly to one side, then the other, pulling the shirt out from under him.

Elizabeth knew her jaw had come unhinged, but she was powerless to control her face as her employer bared his body for her. Rumpled white cotton contrasted briefly against the dark mat of curly hair on his chest as he rolled to the center of the bed. He wadded up the shirt and shoved it under his chin to align his neck and shoulder muscles.

And oh, were they nicely aligned. There was something about the male back that had always excited Elizabeth. She took a moment to drink in the sight of all that sculpted muscle covered in smooth, tanned skin, and then at last, she knelt on the mattress beside him and gently laid both hands on his shoulders.

His muscles were warm and hard beneath her palms. She kneaded firmly, working her way down to the knot between his spine and his right shoulder blade. "Here's your problem," she murmured. "Relax and I'll work it out." She went after the knots in his muscles mercilessly until he was soft and pliant under her probing fingers. The pleasure of touching him, the smooth texture of his skin against her palms, enveloped her in a sensuous haze. With each passing moment her firm resolutions paled until her ethics seemed only a smoke screen between her and what she really wanted. He made small sounds as she worked over him, sounds she could imagine him making as he loved a woman. Her breasts, confined only by two thin layers of silk, began to ache as her nipples responded to her thoughts.

Stop it, she implored her body. She felt the secret place between her legs moistening and swelling. *Stop, before you lose it!*

She finished with a brisk karate chopping motion up and down his back with the blades of her hands, and sat back.

"That felt so good," he said as he rolled over slowly, his voice husky and slurred. "Why don't we run away together?"

His eyes were half shut with relaxation and pleasure as he regarded her. Reaching up, he crossed both hands behind his head. She saw his gaze drop and intensify, and realized two things at once.

The first was that the wrapped front of her dressing gown had loosened with her efforts, and her cleavage was exposed in its fragile covering of flowered silk. The second was that, under his pleated charcoal trousers, Garrett Hill was as aroused as she.

With a muffled indrawn breath, Elizabeth slid off the bed and turned away, pulling her dressing gown together and tightening the sash.

"If you're all right now, Garrett, you'd better go," she said in as calm a voice as she could muster. "We have another back-to-back day tomorrow, and the dinner will probably run late, too."

"What are you wearing, Elizabeth?" His voice was low, husky.

"I brought a black dress."

"No, I meant under that little silk robe."

Desire slammed through her and heat washed into her cheeks. *A snappy response, quick! Turn this into a joke and divert him!* The trouble was, she couldn't think of a single thing to say except the truth. And the truth would only make things worse.

As she struggled with her own silence, Garrett added, "I bet I know. I just saw a little silk nightie with nothing underneath. Am I right?"

"Garrett," she managed in a whisper, still with her back to him, "this is a highly inappropriate conversation. Please go back to your own room."

He didn't move. She could see him in the mirror, stretched out on her bed with his hands behind his head, all that chest exposed, that rampant male sexuality mocking her. Available yet not available. *He's your senior exec,* she told herself firmly. *Remember that. And while you're at it, remember dad and what he did to you and mom. Remember second place!*

"Elizabeth, we're not in the boardroom any more," he said. Her back burned where he watched her.

She closed her eyes briefly, trying to muster moral strength from somewhere within. "Garrett —"

Closing her eyes was her second mistake. Not making him leave was her first.

He came up off the bed behind her. She dragged in a breath as he reached around her and gently pulled loose the tie of her dressing gown. Her chest felt as if it would burst as he brushed the dressing gown off her shoulders and she stood in front of him clad only in the nightie, with its spaghetti straps holding up the silk. Should she run for the bathroom with its sturdy lock, or stay here and tough it out? Poised for flight, the indecision made her quiver.

"I've thought about this in the boardroom often enough," he whispered, his breath fanning her ear. The only part of his body that touched her was his erection, brushing her backside gently, teasing.

Fire burst inside her at the husky hunger that made its own music in his voice. The moment of anticipation hung breathlessly between them. Resistance. She had to resist. "You are off limits," she whispered as firmly as she could manage.

"And why is that?"

She took a deep breath, and her breasts swelled against the silk that covered them. He stood so close she could feel the heat of his body suddenly increase.

"You're my employer," she whispered.

"I'm not. You report to Alan Stratton. Your policy …" He placed his fingertips on her waist, bracketing it, and she jumped. "… applies to people …" Lightly, he touched her ribs. "… in the same management chain." His fingers slid over the silk, inching upward. "Not to us. You're so beautiful," he whispered against her ear. His breath made her shiver. Slowly, he tongued her earlobe, tracing a wet, erotic trail on the thin, sensitive skin. "I've wanted you since I first saw you. Watched your skirt ride up in Alan's staff meeting when you crossed your legs. Wished you'd take your suit jacket off and let your hair down. Wished you'd look at me just once with that smile in your eyes, as if I were a man, not a title." His fingertips rested just below her breasts. "And here you are, in a silky little nothing that shows and hides everything all at once. But I haven't seen your smile yet, and I want to."

"Please don't," she said in a ragged whisper, her eyes half shut in response to the seduction of his voice and his hands. "It isn't fair."

He made a gravelly sound in his throat, and she shuddered. "You aren't fair, either. You drive me crazy. You've got gorgeous breasts, Elizabeth. I want to sit behind you and touch them during presentations. Suck your nipples. Make you respond to me the way I respond to you."

She was going to die of desire. "Garrett, we —" she began, but with a touch as light as the silk that covered her, he brushed her nipples. "We can't … oh …"

Fire danced from his fingertips, lanced through her breasts and down into the wet, soft place between her legs that wept for him. He snugged his erection into the cleft of her buttocks, pulling her against him. She arched away, driving her breasts into his waiting hands. He groaned and cupped them, squeezing them, dragging his hands over the thin silk so her nipples abraded his palms.

She couldn't allow herself such pleasure. "Garrett, don't!" she protested in agony, whirling and pushing against his chest.

For answer, one arm slid around her waist, pulling her against him, and he bent his head and kissed her. *I've wanted his mouth for so long,* she thought as she gave up the feeble struggle and drowned in the delight of it, parting her lips, taking his tongue as it teased hers. His other hand cupped her breast, fingers sliding over the silk, feathering the nipple with his thumb. She wrapped both arms around his neck, pressing her mound against his rigid erection, as he stroked his tongue with hers, silently telling her what he wanted.

He pulled her backwards onto the bed and she fell on top of him.

"God," he gasped. "You're practically falling out of this. I want to look at you. Let me, Elizabeth. Please."

He was begging her. Garrett Hill, co-founder of Stratton Hill, was begging for pleasure only she could give him. The voice that turned her on in conference calls was husky with need, just as she'd imagined it. The mouth she adored lay against her throat, saying the words she craved.

"I can't," she cried. "This isn't right." She tried to roll away but he caught her and with both hands on her wrists, pinned her down. He threw one trouser-clad leg over both her bare ones and buried his face between her breasts.

"Yes, it is," he said, the words muffled against her skin. "Nothing's ever been so right." He transferred both wrists to one hand and grasped the hem of her nightie, pulling the slippery fabric up and over her head.

Then he was still.

He gazed at her body, his breath rough in his throat. She knew she should struggle, pull her wrists out of his grasp, even roll over and conceal her body in the rumpled bedspread. But she couldn't. That spellbound gaze was what she had secretly desired for months.

"Why do you hide under those dark suits?" he asked in a wondering tone. "You're beautiful. So beautiful." His voice faded to a whisper and he lowered his head.

Elizabeth cried out as his warm, sleek tongue dove into her cleavage, licking, tracing her curves reverently. He laved her breasts in wet, concentric circles, working toward her nipples, until Elizabeth was writhing and moaning with anticipation.

"Gorgeous nipples," he murmured against her skin. "On the plane … I could see them right through your sweater. What were you thinking about?"

"You," she said on a sigh, arching her back, pressing her left nipple toward his mouth with insistent, desperate movements.

"Me!" He lifted his chin, eyes wide, and she nearly cried out in frustration.

"Please, Garrett," she begged.

"For that you get what you want, darling girl," he said, and lowered his head to suckle her. She moaned and lost herself in the pleasure as her sensitive nipples responded to the short, feathery strokes of his tongue, then teasing nibbles and bites.

He released her wrists and cupped her with both hands, lifting her breasts until her cleavage was high and convex. "I want you to wear a strapless black velvet dress tomorrow night," he whispered. "One that pushes you up and out, like this."

"You do?" she asked weakly. The dress she'd brought was modest at neck and hem. Long-sleeved. Professional. The thought of displaying that much of her body to the world was frightening.

He sat up, his hands never leaving her skin, and pulled her into his lap. She straddled him, gasping, her hands on his shoulders.

"Then in the elevator I can pull the cups down and lick you, like this." He demonstrated, his mouth closing around her nipple, the areola dimpling under his circling tongue. "When the doors open again, there we'll be, prim and proper as can be. No one but you and I will know that your skin is wet underneath."

Oh God, that voice and the pictures he made with it could seduce her as easily as his body. Her thighs clutched his narrow waist, the fabric of his trousers abrading her soft skin. She wanted to feel his skin against her legs. She wanted to peel his zipper down and reveal his erection. He lifted his face, his eyelids half closed, his lips swollen from loving her, and the last breath of her resistance faded. She bracketed that beloved face with both hands and took his mouth with hers, rubbing her breasts against his chest in slow, sinuous movements as she imprisoned his tongue between her lips and stroked it.

He moaned and reached for his fly. She lifted up long enough for him to divest himself of his trousers, and took control herself, peeling his shorts off, drawing them down the length of legs honed by hours of running and working out. His penis sprang out of its imprisonment, swollen and beaded with impatient liquid at the tip.

"Look what you do to me," he murmured, reaching for her again. "Sit in my lap. Imagine we're in the office. What are you wearing?"

She settled her swollen, slick mons against the length of his shaft, her thighs tight against his waist. "Mmmmm," she murmured as he squeezed her breasts gently together and sucked both nipples at once. "A very conservative, high-necked blouse." He made a sound of protest. "And a pleated skirt with thigh-high stockings and no panties."

"No conservative blouses allowed," he said firmly, cupping her with both hands and kissing her throat. He moved his hips, stroking his length through her wetness. "I want you to wear the kind with the pleats that crosses over the front. Like your green one." He buried his face in her cleavage, lifting his hips and grinding his penis between their bodies. She arched and stroked him in response. "Sometimes in meetings your blouse gapes open and lets me see your black lace bra. You should wear it more often. It's cut so low it barely hides your nipples." His words, breathed against her skin, made her feel swollen. Heavy. Her body was close to bursting with desire. "Some days you move suddenly and your areolas peek out … on those days I never get a single damn thing accomplished. I just sit in my office and dream about doing this."

"Garrett …" she moaned as he sucked hard on her aching nipples, drawing her flesh in as if he wanted to make her part of himself.

"What, sweet girl?"

"Please."

"Please what? Tell me what you want."

"I want you inside me."

He lay back and pulled her with him. "Are you ready for me?"

She groaned. "I've been ready since we left the Valley." And for months before that, she added silently.

"Ride me, Elizabeth," he whispered, smiling up into her eyes. A smile of such warmth and passion she could hardly believe it was for her. "I want to see your face when you come. And I want to look at your beautiful breasts when I do."

Her gaze holding his, she stroked his tumescence slowly with her body, not allowing him to enter her but moistening it with her juices, leaning forward now and again to taste his mouth. He took himself in one hand and stroked her clitoris with the head. She moaned.

"Lean forward, baby," he whispered. "Let me suck you at the same time."

He suckled, pulling at her nipples hungrily, stroking her clitoris with the swollen tip of his penis. It was like being licked in both places at once. She gasped and shuddered, the pleasure coalescing in an explosion deep within. She cried out his name as he arched and pulled her onto his thick, rigid cock, sliding up into her as the last of her orgasm rippled around his urgent flesh. He filled her, stroking hard, his hips lifting and bucking, causing her breasts to quiver. He gripped her hips and stabbed upward, making her cry out as her body clasped him again and again.

With a rough cry of fulfillment, he exploded inside her, his strokes turning into shudders at the answering quivers in her body. Still sheathed inside her as tightly as a sword in a wet, slippery scabbard, he wrapped both arms around her and drew her down to lie on his chest, where their hearts beat frantically together until she couldn't tell where hers left off and his began.

Chapter 3

Garrett heard Elizabeth's alarm clock go off through the open adjoining door as he knotted his tie. She made a soft, heartbroken sound when she realized she was alone in the bed, and he moved quickly to the door to reassure her he hadn't left her.

Leaning on her elbows, her hands gripping the edge of the mattress, she looked up with parted lips. They were too swollen, too delectable for him to resist. He knelt beside the bed and took her chin in his palm.

"Time to get up," he whispered, and tasted her lips, stroking her lower lip with his tongue. She groaned, reaching for him. "No, no, sweetheart. Time to go to work." He cupped her breasts in both hands. He was ready for her again. She was so soft and pliant and desirable, all tousled from his lovemaking.

What a night. What a woman.

"Don't want to work," she murmured against his mouth. "I want to make love with you."

"You will. All day. Come on, into the shower with you."

She swung those sensational legs over the side of the bed and stood up slowly, rubbing her body sinuously against his trousers and crisp white shirt. "Come with me?" she suggested, her eyelids heavy with desire. The sweet scent of sex on her skin rose hot between them. She pouted, her lower lip glistening, waiting for a kiss.

Lord above. This was the buttoned-down Elizabeth Forrester, this sensuous woman with the body of a goddess and a mouth made for sin? He had wanted to claim some of the warm attention she showered on people for himself, but he'd never dreamed of anything like this.

"No," he said, taking her by the shoulders and aiming her into the bathroom. "I'm dressed. Go shower. And then I want to watch you dress."

She was showered and dried in fifteen minutes. "So," she said, standing by the closet door, "what should I wear?" Her challenging glance over one naked shoulder nearly undid him, but he stayed where he was, savoring the pleasure of looking at her round backside and the luscious profile of her left breast from his seat on the edge of her bed.

"Tell me you wear stockings, not panty hose," he said, his voice husky.

"Yes, I do."

"Put them on."

Her back to him, she pulled a pair of black bikini underpants from her suitcase and shimmied into them. Then she sat on the bed and pulled on a pair of thigh-high black stockings with lacy tops. Slipping her feet into black high-heeled pumps, she slowly strolled around the corner of the bed and stood in front of him.

He suddenly felt as if his shirt were a size too small.

"All right so far, boss?" she asked, reaching out to touch his cheek with one fingertip.

"Oh, yeah," he gritted.

She smiled. "Good." She reached into her suitcase and pulled out her bra, and he stopped her.

"No. No bra."

"No bra? Are you serious? I have to wear a bra."

"No." The pleasure of the day to come was almost more than he could stand, and it showed in his voice. "I want to look at your nipples through your blouse all day. I want the branch manager to suspect you've got nothing on underneath, but not really know. I want to fondle you when no one's looking, maybe even taste you. Go on. Put your blouse on now."

Her gaze clung to his and her lips had parted. She was breathing faster, and when she slipped the emerald green silk blouse on, crossing the surplice front and buttoning it at the waist, her breasts lifted and fell in a way that confirmed his fantasies had been accurate.

"Ah, Elizabeth," he breathed. The silk clung lovingly, the pleats stretching apart over her curves. The lamplight glistened in the silky-smooth valley of her cleavage. "Yes." He got up and touched her nipples with his fingertips, stroking them in tiny circles. "Nothing between me and you, between you and everyone's eyes, but this thin little bit of silk. We can make love all day simply by looking at each other. Don't you think that's erotic?"

"I think it's crazy," she whispered. "I can't possibly …"

He slipped a hand inside the V created by the two pleated halves, lifting one breast as though his hand were the cup of a bra, and her voice faded on an indrawn breath. The silk glimmered as it slipped over his knuckles.

"Yes, you can. Now, your skirt."

Frustration fought with uncertainty as she tossed her hair back and pulled away. Her black skirt hugged her hips and fell just to the point at the top of her calves which emphasized the sculpted curve. Then she moved into the bathroom to put up her hair.

Garrett leaned on the door frame, watching as she lifted her arms, twisting her chocolate-dark mane into the neat French roll. Her back arched.

"Mmmmm." His appreciation rasped deep in his throat. He waited until her hair was in place, then moved behind her and filled his hands with her flesh wrapped in warm emerald silk.

"No," she said impertinently, twisting out from under his touch and walking over to the closet for her jacket. "If delayed gratification is what you want, Garrett, that's exactly what you're going to get." She shot him a challenging look from under thick lashes. "Look only. No touch."

"We'll see about that."

She kept her jacket on through breakfast and the first two meetings of the day. But as she walked down the hall beside him on their way to the conference room, where they were scheduled to watch a multimedia presentation developed by the sales group, he was amply rewarded. The lights of the hallway glinted off the glossy jacquard surface of her blouse, highlighting her delicious double bounce as she walked.

He nodded to the people seated around the conference table, shaking hands with the sales team. The lights went down, and Elizabeth shrugged out of her jacket. As the presentation opened, he glanced to his right. He had chosen seats in the back of the room on purpose. He disliked sitting in the front of a theater, and besides, he wanted the attention of all the other men in the room firmly focused away from him and Elizabeth.

He could just make out her profile next to him, dimly lit by the colors playing on the screen. She was building barriers between them again this morning, despite the way they had made love last night, despite the way she had joined him in playing out his fantasy today. There had to be a way to break through that resistance and make her see that he was hers … and had been from the first. He craved her. Not just physically — although making love with Elizabeth was the best he had ever known — but in his heart, in that deepest part of him that had been empty and crying out for solace since Juliet had left him years before.

He was hers. And she would be his or he'd die trying.

Slowly, he slid one hand under her arm and touched her nipple. She drew in a startled breath, and her nipple hardened instantly under the silk. He traced its shape with feathery strokes. He had never met a woman whose nipples were so sensitive and at the same time so lush and erotic. And the shape of her breasts seemed to satisfy some aesthetic need within him — they were big, yet so firm and erect and round, ripe for a man's hands and mouth. It was obvious they were a source of enormous sexual pleasure for her when he touched them … a pleasure he loved to give her.

Slowly, he reached into the V of her neckline and cupped her left breast, marveling that his hand could hardly contain it. But he couldn't enjoy it long; someone at the front of the room shifted and turned his head, and Garrett sat back.

Under the table, where it was utterly dark, he ran a hand up Elizabeth's thigh, past the smooth nylon of her stocking to the skin exposed above it. She sat back in her chair and drew one foot up under her, opening her legs. He took the invitation immediately, absorbing the secret softness of her inner thigh against his fingers. Her skirt whispered against the back of his hand as he touched the damp crotch of her panties.

She shivered, echoing his own excitement. Desire pooled in his groin, heavy and pulsing. His sex thickened, stretching the fabric of his briefs.

He slipped a finger inside the band of her bikini panties, sliding down into her curly thatch. Above the table, his other hand cupped his chin thoughtfully, one elbow on the arm of the chair, as he stared at the screen. The presentation had ten minutes to go and he hadn't absorbed a kilobyte.

He found her clitoris and stroked. Her lips parted as she tried to control her breathing. As his finger slid over the creamy-slick nubbin, she bit her lower lip. Garrett drew the pleasure out, stroking on both sides, then underneath the wet little pearl of her pleasure. With every uneven breath, her breasts thrust against the confining blouse but he couldn't touch them as she came, no matter how much he wanted to. He felt a rush of wet heat and her back went rigid as her lips clamped shut on a cry. He stroked her twice more, luxuriously, making her shudder, before he slid his hand slowly from her body.

She pulled her skirt down and crossed her legs. Profile turned toward the screen, she remained still and collected until the lights came up.

The juices of her orgasm dried on his fingers as the general manager got up and began to speak. Garrett leaned his chin on his hand, his fingers resting on his upper lip, breathing deeply. The scent of Elizabeth. Rich with her own special tang.

As the meeting concluded, he dragged his mind off the woman next to him, and stood up to make a recommendation to the group. The plan he'd formulated with Elizabeth and the general manager, Brady Grant, a young man of about thirty-four whose affability and keen business sense made him one of the rising stars at Stratton Hill, was unanimously agreed to, and the meeting broke up with handshakes and smiles all around.

Garrett saw Brady shake hands with Elizabeth, his grip so enthusiastic that her breasts jiggled before she was finally able to extract her hand. Brady placed himself between her and the small crowd near the projection screen as he asked her something in low, earnest tones.

Garrett moved in beside them, his briefcase in one hand. "Ms. Forrester, may I have a moment with you?"

"Certainly." With a sinuous movement of escape, she walked to the far side of the conference table, put on her jacket, and began to slide several file folders into her own briefcase.

Garrett smiled at Brady. The man was a huge asset to Stratton Hill, even if his timing was lousy. He'd been one of the first to take Elizabeth's Quality of Life strategies and implement them in the Vancouver office. "Thanks for the great presentation, Brady," he said. "I appreciate all the work your people put into it. I'll see you this evening at dinner, all right?"

"Yes. You're welcome, Garrett. I was asking Ms. Forrester if she — er — if the two of you would like to join me for lunch? There's a little place around the corner that serves great hot and sour soup, and I promised Ms. Forrester I'd take her there if she ever got up to see us."

So he was asking her out to lunch, was he? No doubt so he could ogle her over steamed rice and get a little steamed up himself.

"You two know each other?" Garrett asked, still smiling.

"She was my first call when this tech theft thing first came up. We've been talking off and on for several months over the new programs, too."

Elizabeth smiled at Brady, and his eyes seemed to glaze over. "If we hadn't come soon, I'd have had to put a separate line on my phone just for your calls."

"Right. Elizabeth." His tongue lingered on the syllables of her name, and Garrett lost his patience.

"I appreciate the offer, but we have a lunch meeting scheduled with an outside consultant. I was hoping to take a few minutes now to brief Ms. Forrester on what I want them to accomplish during the next quarter. If you'll excuse us?"

Brady nodded and gave a halfhearted smile, clearly disappointed. He backed out of the room and Garrett closed the door softly.

Pushing the thumb lock in firmly, he turned to Elizabeth. "Months of phone calls? E*liz*abeth?" He drawled her name, exaggerating Brady's pronunciation.

"An outside con*sul*tant?" she riposted in the same tone, sitting on the edge of the conference table. "First I've heard."

"Me too," Garrett said unrepentantly. "But I saved you from becoming the object of Brady's fantasies over lunch." His slow, hot gaze perused her, and he stripped her jacket off, tossing it on a chair. She leaned back on her hands, and his lips parted as the pleats in the front of her blouse spread. "The man is smitten. He didn't take his eyes off you once." He stepped closer, and touched the fragile fabric over one nipple. "Neither did anyone else. Including me."

"That's what you wanted, wasn't it?" She stood and wrapped her arms around his neck, crushing her breasts against his chest. Their firm heaviness inflamed him, and he stiffened again, pressing against her pelvic bones. "The only one I want looking at me is you," she whispered, her breath soft against his mouth. He dipped his head and licked her lower lip, sucking it into a kiss.

"You owe me for saving you," he murmured gruffly. He slipped a hand into her blouse and fondled her breast, pushing it up and shaping deep, curved cleavage. He kissed her throat and moved down, pushing her blouse aside and licking the exposed areola with wet, swirling motions. "I bet Brady wants to do this. He thought he was hiding it, but I could tell." He suckled her nipple fiercely, and she moaned. He felt her hands close on his cock, and he shuddered. "Yeah. You owe me." She stroked him through the fabric of his trousers, her fingers tight on him, as urgent as he.

She unbuckled his narrow leather dress belt and the button at the top of his fly. His cock leaped and bucked against the backs of her fingers as she eased his zipper down.

"Mmmm," she murmured, plunging both hands into his briefs. Her arms squeezed her breasts together, and the sight combined with her hands on him nearly made him lose control.

She sank slowly to her knees and he reached behind him for the back of a chair. "Elizabeth —" he said, his voice a rough whisper in his throat. "God —"

She pulled his briefs down and devoured him whole. His body convulsed as her luscious lips surrounded his cock, her tongue swirling around the base of the head, where he was most sensitive. She sucked on him the way he sucked her nipples, pulling him in and making his knees go weak.

He pushed her blouse off her shoulders but the storm of pleasure blotted out the ability to do more. It was an effort to drag air into his lungs. Her lashes spread on her cheekbones like dark fans, closed in pleasure and concentration. Her pulsing tongue and the suction was going to pull the soul out of him, was going to make him burst, was going to —

He made a sound that could have been a shout but was strangled by the need for secrecy into a hoarse whisper, and he exploded into her loving mouth.

Chapter 4

Never in her life had Elizabeth lived through a day like this one. Nothing in her past relationships had prepared her for the sheer sensual pleasure and raw enjoyment of sex shared with Garrett Hill. In the ladies' room, Elizabeth took a wet paper towel into the stall with her. The scent of her own juices, she was sure, acted like a magnet to horny men — general managers and salesmen in particular.

She had never exposed her body like this before, never known the secret sense of power that a woman could exercise over men. Garrett was teaching her the potential of her own sensuality — and the fact that he was enjoying it to the full made it no less valuable a lesson.

She washed her hands and ran a comb through her hair, catching the few stray strands that had come unmoored when she had gone down on her knees to him. The memory of his swollen flesh in her mouth, of the sounds of surrender and passion she could tease from him, made desire ripple through her body.

It was time to stop fooling herself. This powerful emotion, this desire — face it, this impossible love she'd been denying for months — was more intense because deep in her heart, she knew it couldn't last past the end of this trip. She bit her lip and pushed away the thought. She wanted to think about the sweetness of the moment, about these few days of loving Garrett, not the price she would eventually pay.

After he'd collapsed into one of the conference room chairs, he'd drawn her into his lap and rested his forehead on her collarbone. His uneven breathing had slowed against the upper slope of her breast. The few intense moments of silence and closeness they shared were like nothing she had ever experienced before. His hair was soft under her fingers as she'd stroked him with a feathery touch. His body, so hard and warm and strong, had curled around hers in an embrace so sweet she was still flushed with warmth.

Maybe that was what drew her to him so strongly. Not his charisma and authority, although no one in the Valley could deny that. Several women had pursued him on the basis of that alone, if office gossip could be believed. No, she'd sensed a vulnerability within him — a yearning in his eyes she'd seen when he thought no one was observing him. That yearning called to the deepest part of her nature, the part that wanted to share and console and heal.

She loved him. There was no escaping it — and no sharing it, either. Not as long as either of them worked at Stratton Hill. She loved him. But she loved her self-respect and the fulfillment her career brought as well.

Elizabeth straightened her jacket and smoothed both hands down the front of her skirt. There. At least she was presentable again, her gaze level, the flush in her cheeks receding. Only two more meetings, and she and Garrett could return to the hotel. She wasn't ready yet to let the fantasy end.

Fortunately for her ability to concentrate, both meetings were with the human resources generalists stationed in the Vancouver office. Garrett would be in a different wing of the building with a focus group of technicians. She had no doubt that his enthusiasm and sheer love of the business would be catching. If AlphaTech called tomorrow, no matter how attractive their offers, they'd be fresh out of luck.

At five o'clock she commandeered the conference room to steal a few moments of quiet to enter more notes into her trip report. As she pulled the pad out of her briefcase, a folded piece of paper fluttered to the floor. Frowning, she picked it up. It was the white grid paper the engineers used, not the yellow legal pads she wrote on.

She opened the paper. The words were written in block capitals in dark blue ink.

"Harken, Jezebel, flaunting the charms of thy flesh to tempt the souls of men. Harken lest thou be damned to hellfire forever, to tongues of flame which will lick your body and consume it. Woman was made to submit to man, not to tempt him past bearing to thoughts of sin. Vengeance is mine, saith the Lord! Your soul can still be saved if you submit to His power. You must strip yourself naked of all worldly lusts and go down upon your knees before him. You must take the rod of his punishment between your lips and accept his power as it fills you. You must submit. Only in doing this can you be saved."

Somebody saw us, was Elizabeth's first panicked thought. Her stomach clenched as she did a quick scan of the conference room. Though it had exterior windows, they were fifteen floors up. There was only one door to the hallway, and no interior windows at all.

Common sense returned. She crumpled the note and tossed it in her briefcase. Stratton Hill was harboring a nut, that was all. A religious nut who couldn't handle the guilt of his own sexual fantasies and had to level the blame at the woman starring in them. In this case, herself. Well, Garrett had told her that the imaginations of Brady and the salesmen were probably running wild. She hadn't expected it to get this wild, though. Writing the note had probably been as close as the nut would come to an orgasm.

She had to remember her professionalism and call a halt to Garrett's erotic suggestions from now on. She glanced at the crumpled ball of paper. Should she show it to him? No. It was an unwelcome reminder of her own guilt, and she didn't want anything to spoil the fantasy bubble they were living in. Reality would bite soon enough. Garrett would probably initiate a manhunt and then all hell would break loose. The nut case could be any one of fifty or sixty people on the floor, and was probably harmless. She dismissed him from her mind.

Back at the hotel, Elizabeth knocked on Garrett's door. After a moment he opened it, a marbled paper shopping bag in one hand. Slipping his free arm around her waist, he kissed her with a sensuous thoroughness that left her mindless and gasping. Lord above, his mouth was going to be her undoing.

"What's in the bag?" she asked, when she could think clearly enough to string words together.

He lifted a dark eyebrow and walked over to the bed. "I meant it, you know," he said. Reaching into the bag, he pulled out a length of black velvet.

"Meant wh — oh, my God, Garrett. You didn't."

He looked pleased and feral at the same time, laugh lines crinkling at the corners of his eyes. "Oh, but I did. This hotel has a great shop downstairs. *Veni, vidi,* Visa."

He held out a strapless dress.

"Where the hell is the rest of it?" she demanded breathlessly. "Garrett, I couldn't possibly wear that to a business dinner."

"We'll talk about that later. Come on. Try it on for me."

So much for calling a halt to his erotic suggestions. With a resigned sigh that only half disguised her dismay, she reached back and unzipped her skirt. Stepping out of it, she unbuttoned her blouse, every cell aware that Garrett's eyes were locked on her. She pulled the blouse open slowly, feeling the whisper of silk as each pleat resisted and then surrendered. The blouse slid liquidly down her arms and she dropped it on top of the skirt.

"Looking at you is almost as much pleasure as touching you," Garrett whispered. "Let me touch you."

"No," she whispered back. "We're getting dressed for dinner."

He held out the velvet dress and she stepped into it carefully. She shimmied the soft fabric over her hips and leaned forward to fit her breasts into the boned cups of the bodice. She reached behind, her back arching, and sang the zipper up its track.

"Dear God," Garrett breathed.

The dress nipped in her waist and snugged over her bottom, leaving a smooth length of leg below. The rich texture of the velvet made her skin look as delicate and translucent as fine porcelain, and made her eyes and lips look even more sultry. The boned cups supported her breasts, pushing them up and out in classic round curves, a magnet for the eye.

Garrett ran his skillful, long-fingered hands over her hips, up her ribs, and cupped her velvet-covered breasts as he watched her in the mirror. "You don't need any jewelry. A pair of earrings at most." Slowly, he stroked her bare curves with his fingertips. "Does it turn you on when men look at you?"

She tried to concentrate on answering him while the pleasure rippled along her skin. "I don't know. I've never dressed this way in my life," she sighed. Other men's responses didn't matter. Only Garrett's. "It turns me on when *you* look at me. And touch me like this."

"Why do you hide this beauty under those dark suits?"

"Beauty isn't professional."

"I wouldn't say that." He kissed her shoulder. "But I must admit, it was your brains and your success that got my attention at first." He turned her to face him. They shared a look that contained the memory of their first interview, and the mutual respect in their interactions since.

"Nobody at Stratton Hill even knows I *have* a body," Elizabeth said firmly.

"Except me," Garrett whispered. "I know how luscious your nipples are, how erotic you smell after making love. I know the sensitive spot behind your knees that you like me to lick. I find it incredibly sexy that your breasts are so sensitive, and that looking at them across the dinner table will be like touching them in public. I like being the only one who knows." He kissed her, his tongue sliding against hers, hot and languid. "You're a fantasy come true."

The heat of desire in his voice and eyes kindled her responses into a blaze. He nuzzled her bare shoulder, tasting her skin, his kisses slow, as though it mattered to him that she experience the pleasure each movement brought. But his words struck a wistful chord in the part of her mind that still resisted him even when they were locked together in mind-bending love.

"I'm not a fantasy," she whispered, brushing one cheek against his hair as he bent to his pleasurable task. "I'm real. Our relationship — everything you just said — is the fantasy, Garrett."

His movements stilled and he lifted his head to look into her eyes. "What do you mean? Of course you're real. You're the most real, intense part of my life right now."

Right now. That's all it was. The hotter the flame, the briefer its life. The hurt splashed through her body and chilled her passion as effectively as a bucket of cold water. He could fit her in on a trip, where his working hours were limited, but what about later, when they returned home? Even if she could get around that damned policy, a relationship was next to impossible.

She stepped out of his arms and he straightened, puzzled.

"What's the matter? What is it?" With brisk, businesslike movements she unzipped the velvet dress and took it off, pulling her silk robe off its hanger and wrapping it around her. "Elizabeth, for God's sake, talk to me."

"I need to face the truth," Elizabeth said, trying to get the honest words out before she lost her courage. "Our ... my feelings for you may be very strong, but they don't change reality. And the reality is that not only do we now have a policy against what we're doing, we have an extremely harassment-sensitive workforce, thanks to Ms. Burke. You're the most visible person at Stratton Hill. I have a professional reputation. Add one to the other and it precludes any relationship between you and me, Garrett." She paused. She didn't dare look up into his eyes. "Also, I have strong feelings about what it takes to preserve my quality of life. Or I did," she finished miserably. "Until now."

"I told you before, that policy is for people in the same reporting structure. It doesn't apply to us since you work for Alan. It's nobody's damn business what I do with my private life, anyway. And what's this about the quality of your life? Look at me, sweetheart." He frowned as he struggled to make sense of her words. "You make it sound as if I'm having a negative effect on it."

Elizabeth laid both hands on his chest and spoke quietly. "Please don't misunderstand me. We've had an incredible two days, and I'll treasure them always. But I can't do this." He took a breath to speak, and she covered his mouth with a finger. "Let me finish. I care about you and I think you care about me. But everything else aside, our goals in life are too different. You live for Stratton Hill. I can't. I just don't see a future for us. Not the kind I'm looking for, anyway." Elizabeth's voice failed on the last words, and the tears choked off anything more she wanted to say.

Garrett tried to take her in his arms. "Elizabeth. Darling. I never thought I'd hear you say you care. I can't believe it. It's —"

"Garrett, didn't you hear any of what I just said?"

"Of course I did, but I'm focusing on the important part. We care about each other. That's what matters most."

For an engineer and a strategist, he could be surprisingly unrealistic. "But I'm looking for a future, Garrett. A meaningful future. And I don't think you can offer me that."

"What do you call a meaningful future?" His voice was too quiet.

She needed to explain this clearly, without sounding like a needy female. Her mother's behavior with her father flashed into her memory, and stiffened her resolve. "It's not as if I want white picket fences; I'm just not that kind of person. But I do want a home I can share with a man I love and respect. I want a partnership where the first priority is our life together. And some day I want children, which will make it even more important that our priorities are in the right order. Which would mean business in second place."

"Do you expect me to propose?" He was trying hard to understand. Elizabeth's heart squeezed with love and her own pain at having to deny them both what they desperately wanted.

"No, of course not. It's too soon to expect anything from each other."

He dropped her hands as if they burned him, and walked over to the window. "That's the most unkind thing anyone has ever said to me." His shoulders were rigid with hurt.

"Oh, God." For an expert in human resources, she was really making a mess of this. Where were all her communication skills when she needed them? "What I'm trying to say is that Stratton Hill isn't my entire life now, and won't be in the future." She crossed the room, and touched his shoulder blade with a gentle hand. "Garrett, my dad gave thirty years to IBM. I grew up without him. For God's sake, my mother took me to the father-daughter dance because he was tied up on a project and couldn't give me the time. I've learned the hard way how important it is to put relationships first."

He turned to her slowly. "And you think I wouldn't?"

"I know you wouldn't," she said, her voice husky with tears. "I've seen how you —"

Someone banged on his door in the adjoining room and they jumped, startled. Elizabeth twisted away from him and pushed him into his own room. If anyone from Stratton Hill caught him in her room in her present state of emotional and physical nakedness, they would both be hopelessly compromised.

"We're not done yet," Garrett promised as she tried to push the door shut against his shoulder. "Count on it."

She bumped the door shut with the weight of her body and flattened her back against it. "How can you defend what everyone sees every day?" she whispered into the empty silence.

Male voices murmured for a few moments on the other side of the door. When her telephone rang, she was concentrating so hard on distinguishing the voice of Garrett's visitor that she jumped again. *My nerves are shot*, she thought as she drew in a deep breath, trying to make her heart slow down. *This has got to stop.* She picked up the receiver. "Elizabeth Forrester."

"Hi, Elizabeth. It's Brady. I'm next door, using Mr. Hill's phone. I came to pick you both up and take you to the restaurant."

The restaurant. Right. She was supposed to face Garrett across a dinner table in front of an audience and pretend nothing had happened.

"How kind of you, Brady," she said, hoping her voice didn't sound as strained as she felt. "I'm just changing. I'll be ready in ten minutes if that's okay."

"That's fine. I'll be down in the lobby. I'm looking forward to seeing you … in a more relaxed atmosphere. It's probably been a stressful couple of days. You sound as if you could use a drink."

His voice was warm with concern and a kind of teasing friendliness. She could use some friendliness. Nice, uncomplicated, platonic friendliness.

"Thanks, Brady," she said, her voice sounding a little closer to normal. "I'll take you up on it. See you all in a few."

She hung up and turned to the bed, where the velvet dress lay twisted inside out. Innocuous. Only fabric. It had been constructed to bewitch and seduce, but it needed a woman inside it to make its designer's dream come true.

In a brief moment of weakness, she allowed herself to ask *what if*? What if Garrett shared her views? What if he and she were alone, without Stratton Hill, and with hope for the future? She could wear his gift to dinner, seduce him from across the table … could allow herself to be seduced by the hunger and appreciation in his eyes. Could look forward to the night — and the days — to come.

Elizabeth sighed. *What if* was a useless exercise. He would be a different man, and then she probably wouldn't be so attracted to him. His confidence, his success, his drive, the way he drew people to him — all these things made him what he was. She treasured that in him, even though she knew it meant her own unhappiness. Maybe she'd just imagined the vulnerability in his eyes in those unguarded moments. There was no room in this situation for happiness.

In the business world she had schooled herself to deal with reality, no matter how hard it was. And a woman faced reality in a high-necked, medium length, black georgette dress.

Chapter 5

The hurt in Garrett's eyes as she met him in the hallway was so painful she had to turn away. She had rejected his gift, had returned to her old look instead of the unbound, sexy one to which he had introduced her. It was like rejecting him a second time. She led the way out of the elevator into the lobby, her shoulders prickling with awareness of his gaze — and his disappointment. As Brady waved from the doorway, Garrett leaned over and whispered, "Stockings?"

"Pantyhose," she replied grimly. "Don't push me."

Even their banter was gone. She felt his emotional withdrawal from three feet away. He pulled his executive formality around him like a magician's cloak and they climbed into Brady's car, some kind of long, gas-guzzling classic she couldn't identify, which was running at the curb under the *porte cochère*. She slid into the wide front seat while Garrett fulminated in the back, and responded automatically to Brady's running commentary on the landmarks they passed. Anything to keep from turning around and feeding her weakness by gawking at Garrett. In his double-breasted charcoal suit and silk tie, freshly shaved and combed, he looked good enough to eat.

Bad choice of words, Liz, she chided herself as a bolt of desire zipped along her veins and made her shift restlessly in her seat.

"Your Caddy's in great shape, Brady," Garrett said in an effort to be sociable. "What year is it?"

"Fifty-nine," Brady said proudly. "My brothers and I have been restoring it for most of our lives. Do you drive a classic?"

"No. A Lexus. This kind of thing is fun, but it isn't my style."

Brady subsided, evidently believing he had been snubbed, then turned to Elizabeth a few moments later. "You told me not long ago that you're an *X-Files* fan," Brady said with a grin, unaware of the tension between his passengers. "You know it was filmed here, right?"

"I'd heard that, yes."

"Sometime when you're up here I'd be happy to take you on an *X-Files* tour of Vancouver. What a marketing pitch, eh? I'm surprised the Ministry of Tourism hasn't hit on it yet. We could go to Lighthouse Park, where they filmed 'Darkness Falls.' And Stanley Park, of course. Did you know they made Siberia out of a parking lot for 'Tunguska'?"

"No, I didn't. That's fascinating." Any other time it would be. What if she and Garrett could get away and do something like that together?

What if. Stop it, Liz. It's pointless.

"I doubt Elizabeth will be able to get to Vancouver very often," Garrett pointed out in a voice devoid of expression. "I trust we won't be having employee retention crises on a regular basis."

"No, of course not," Brady assured him in the rear view mirror, then negotiated his way around a bus. "But the techs are pumped up now that they've met you. I'd recommend twice yearly visits. At least."

"I'll be happy to come," Garrett said. Elizabeth looked out the window at the Vancouver skyline and the mountains beyond.

"Oh. Great!" Brady recovered fast. "I think the connection with Corporate can only improve morale. But you know, Vancouver is also a great place for a vacation."

"I know," Elizabeth said absently.

"Elizabeth used to come here as a child," Garrett explained to Brady, staking out unspoken rights to her personal history.

"No kidding!" Brady said, a flush mounting his cheeks as he ran a hand through his reddish-brown hair. "So I'm just telling you what you already know."

"I know the area, that's all. I had no idea about all the *X-Files* stuff," Elizabeth said. She really had to be more approachable. Garrett was going to crush poor Brady if she didn't step in and lighten things up. "That tour you mentioned sounds like a lot of fun. No moonlighting as a guide for the tourists, though. We need you full time."

"Another career path bites the dust," Brady said, shaking his head with mock regret. "But at least you'll get a preview tonight. We're meeting my staff in the restaurant in Queen Elizabeth Park. That's where they filmed the graveyard scene in the pilot episode."

"I'm not eating dinner in a graveyard!" Garrett exclaimed.

"Relax, sir. This place is one of the classiest in town."

Under any other circumstances, Elizabeth would have been enchanted by the view from the restaurant. It sat on a hill, surrounded by parkland. The lights and towers of Vancouver glimmered in the late summer twilight as the sunset faded. The maitre d' led them to their table, where the three members of Brady's immediate staff were already seated. Over the past two days she had become acquainted with Marie D'Aoust, who ran the technical writing arm of the development organization, as well as the two men who were responsible for software development and the quality and test functions.

The note she'd found in her briefcase flickered briefly in her mind's eye. Were any of these people the author? She closed her eyes briefly. *Nice going, Liz. Of course not. You've been working with them in close quarters for two days. You have bigger problems right now than obscure religious nuts.*

Brady pulled out her chair for her, and then sat down next to her. Garrett shook hands with Marie and seated himself opposite Elizabeth. His gaze rested on her — somber, watchful and very, very sexy.

It was going to be a long dinner.

Elizabeth sipped her wine as Garrett asked Brady about the employment situation in Vancouver, and how it might affect their ability to attract talent in the area. The conversation stayed businesslike until after the entrées had been cleared and the dessert menu presented.

"I couldn't," Elizabeth protested to the waiter. "The prime rib was the best I ever tasted. Anything more would be too much."

"We could split the blackberry cheesecake," Marie suggested.

"I can't even do that. I'm full."

"I'll split some with you. My daughter and I do it all the time," Garrett said, turning the charm of his smile on Marie. To the waiter, he said, "The blackberry cheesecake, please. And two forks."

Helplessly, Elizabeth watched Marie, whom she knew from their coffee room conversations to be happily married and four months pregnant, melt and dissolve under that smile. *Jealousy is idiotic and immature,* she scolded herself, finishing off the last of her wine. *He turns that smile on everyone. You have no special rights to it.*

The waiter discreetly brought a second plate as well as two forks. *You do this with your daughter?* she thought. *When do you ever see her?*

The lights dimmed, and behind her she heard the sounds of a band tuning up. As they swung into "In The Mood," Elizabeth found herself dangerously close to tears. She wanted to dance. With Garrett. She wanted to wear her strapless velvet dress and spend the rest of the evening in his arms, his body brushing hers, held close to his white shirt, the heat of his skin penetrating the fabric under her hands.

Stop hurting yourself, Liz.

For the Director of Human Resources, her choice in relationships sure was lousy. If she had any sense at all, she'd go for Brady Grant. She had to admit he was adorable. She'd never been partial to redheads, but he had nice eyes and an engaging grin. They had Vancouver and *The X-Files* in common, to start with. And Brady had one thing going for him that Garrett didn't.

He practiced what he preached. The programs they'd set up for the Vancouver office were successful because he backed them. This technician theft thing was a temporary aberration. For the most part, the employees here seemed to be happier and more fulfilled in their families and communities than those in many companies in their market. And all because Brady believed in what she was trying to do. If he had had kids, *he'd* have time for them.

The music pulled at her, making her shoulders sway and her foot tap. "Do you like this one?" Brady asked. "These guys are pretty good. They play the clubs in town a lot. My brother knows the bass player."

"Love it. 'In The Mood' is one of my favorites."

"Would you like to dance?"

A sideways glance at Garrett's face was enough to decide her. The Rolling Stones were right. *You can't always get what you want.* "Sure."

Brady grabbed her hand and led her out onto the dance floor, where half a dozen couples twisted and swung energetically to the music. He was a good dancer, smooth and easy to follow. She hadn't danced in years, but felt the steps coming back, knew instinctively when to swing out to arms' length and when to whirl back in.

The song ended, and the band segued into Bob Seger's "Old Time Rock and Roll." Brady and Elizabeth jived like teenagers. Elizabeth let the music and the beat lift her away from her misery and the hopeless waste of her love on an unattainable man. She concentrated on the steps and on the male admiration in Brady's eyes, and maneuvered so that they were dancing on the side of the room closest to the band, with a crowd between her and Garrett.

Halfway through the third song Jim Wilson, the QA manager, tapped Brady on the shoulder. "Mind if I cut in, boss?"

Elizabeth smiled, and over Jim's shoulder saw that Eric Bouvier was dancing with Marie. Though she clasped Jim's hands and responded to his conversation as they swung together, she had no control over her feminine antennae, which were continuously scoping the room for Garrett. She and Marie traded partners and she was hardly aware of it. Where was he? Who was he dancing with? Why should she care, anyway?

"I'm going to pull rank on you, Eric."

Eric faded into the crowd as his Chief Technology Officer slid an arm around Elizabeth's waist and took her hand. The band picked that moment to slide into a slow, bluesy number that kicked her heart into panic mode.

She said the first thing that came into her head. "Pulling rank is bad for morale."

"It's an option I exercise once in a while. Why are you avoiding me?"

"I'm not. I'm fraternizing with the troops."

"Are you sure that's all you're doing? Brady Grant was practically glassy-eyed when he staggered back to the table."

"Stop it, Garrett."

"I didn't see much body contact during those fast numbers, but for a determined man — or woman — I suppose it's possible."

"There was no body contact. Not that it's any of your business. You and I have no claims on each other."

She should have known better than to challenge him like that. He pulled her an inch closer, not enough for any indiscretion to be observed by their co-workers, but enough for the tips of her breasts to brush his shirt front. "Only this," he murmured under the music. "And this." He changed direction, and his leg slid between hers, his thigh hard and uncompromising. His lashes dropped low over his eyes, and the glinting heat in them made her shiver. His gaze dropped to her mouth, and she realized with horror that her lips were parted for a kiss.

"Damn you," she whispered. He watched her lips move. Garrett could make simple speech into a sexual act just by the intensity of his focus. If she licked her lips now it would be as overt an invitation as removing her clothes.

"What for?" he responded. "For making you want me?"

"Yes."

"For making it plain that I want you? Even covered to the neck in this prim little outfit?"

"Yes. I look professional, and don't you deny it."

"You look unapproachable." He pulled her another inch closer, and she tried to resist until his breath brushed her ear. "You have such beautiful breasts it makes me hard just knowing they're under there, barely confined in that black bra," he whispered. "And when you're turned on, like you are now, the scent from between your legs mixes with your perfume."

A bolt of pure desire sizzled through her. His voice was so sexy, his body warm against hers as they moved to the slow beat of the music. She was drowning in him. Drowning in his seduction in front of the whole room.

"So why are you denying the magic between us?" he demanded softly. "We're lovers for two days and it's the best I've ever known — and suddenly I'm not good enough for you any more." His hand played on her back, a delicate sensation that traveled from lumbar curve to waist to shoulder. The pleasure of his touch made her want to weep at giving him up. "Help me understand, Elizabeth."

The tears rushed to clog her throat. Another few seconds and she was going to break down and make an even greater fool of herself. "It isn't what you've done, it's what you are, Garrett, don't you see? You're a good man, a successful leader. That's great in the work place. But at what cost to your home life? I lived it once. I'm not going to live it over again."

"You don't think my personal life is a success?"

The sense of loss seemed to harden into a ball in her chest, and her body chilled. "How can it be, Garrett?" she asked sadly. "You don't spend any time on it."

She pulled out of his arms and wove through the swaying crowd back to the table. Brady looked up, startled, as she appeared without her partner. Marie, who was sitting the dance out and sipping soda water, took in her white face and trembling lips, and got up. "Come on, Elizabeth. Time for a trip to the powder room."

"Thanks, Marie. I'm not feeling too well." Elizabeth was surprised at how normal her voice sounded. "I'm going to ask the maitre d' to call me a cab."

"I can take you back," Brady put in, jumping to his feet.

"You can't leave Garrett in the lurch, Brady. In Human Resources we call that a career-limiting move. But thanks for the offer."

She gathered up her purse and, head high, left the lights and the music behind.

Chapter 6

Elizabeth tossed her handbag in the direction of the bureau and fell face down on the bed, her body racked with the ache of loss. She wept all her pent-up tears into the bedspread, then stumbled into the bathroom to wash her face and blow her nose. Bracing her hands on both sides of the sink, she stared at the flushed, disheveled reflection in the mirror.

Get a grip, Forrester. You've had your cry, now hold your head up and get on with your life.

Turning away, she stripped off the georgette dress that had once seemed so stylish. She hung it in her garment bag and picked up the strapless velvet from the bed where she'd dropped it earlier.

Of course she had to return it.

She caressed the velvet, ran a finger inside the boned cups. Damn dress. It symbolized these two days somehow; sexy and forbidden and completely unrelated to real life. Where would she ever wear a dress like this, anyway? She didn't go to supper clubs or operas. When she wasn't working she was with friends, or her brother and the kids, or volunteering, or teaching other people her practical methods in organizational management. She had a *life*, for Pete's sake.

A life that didn't include fantasy men who bought dresses like this.

Oh, go on. Just once more.

She popped the clasp of her bra and tossed it on the bureau. She stepped into the dress and zipped it up, then stepped into her black high heels.

There.

A full-length mirror hung on the back of the bathroom door. She modeled in front of it, smoothing the dress down her hips with both hands, taking pleasure in eroticizing her own body. Garrett had taught her that much, at least. She'd spent so many years covering it up for the sake of professionalism that she'd forgotten anyone might want to look. Not that there had been many takers, but as long as there were men like Brady Grant out there, she had hope for the future. Getting ahead in business had taken a lot of her energy, though she'd learned to find a balance. She'd chosen HR on purpose as women seemed to rise faster there. *The caregiving arm of the business,* she thought. *That doesn't change.* But she was good at it.

She wished she were as good at intimate relationships.

With a sigh, she reached behind her for the zipper. If Garrett had left his adjoining door open, she could slip in and return his gift. She'd leave it on the bed, where he would see it when he came in. It would hurt him to find it there as much as it hurt her to give it back, but it was the only thing to do. The sooner they ended this, the better.

A discreet knock sounded at the door and she froze. "Who is it?"

Garrett? If he found her wearing the dress again, she'd be right back at square one and all of tonight's pain would have gone for nothing.

"It's Brady, Elizabeth. I need to talk to you."

Brady! What on earth could he want at this time of night? Had he left the dinner party early? What had happened to Garrett?

"I — I'm not feeling well, Brady." Reaching backward, she fumbled at the zipper.

"It will only take a minute. Please, Elizabeth. It's important."

She couldn't answer the door in this dress. Awkwardly, she pulled at the zipper, but it was stuck in its track.

"Elizabeth?" He knocked again.

Oh, for heaven's sake. She jerked the zipper back up, straightened the dress and yanked the door open.

Brady's jaw dropped an inch as he took her in from top to bottom. His mouth opened and closed for a second before words came out. "God almighty!"

"Come in, Brady," she said in a resigned tone, stepping aside to let him pass and closing the door behind him.

"Are — are you going out?" he asked, feeling for a chair and dropping into it. He rubbed his face and raised bemused eyes to hers.

At least he had the decency to look her in the face. "No."

"I thought you were sick. You looked pretty bad when you left and I was worried. But now you look — you look —" He paused and swallowed. "Great!"

"Thanks." This was the most ridiculous situation she'd ever been in. No explanation would make sense. And who said she owed him one, anyway? "What was it you wanted to see me about?" She tried to keep her tone professional, as if this were a formal visit to her office.

He dragged his gaze off her décolletage and made an obvious effort to remember why he was there. "I know it's none of my business, but you were so upset when you left that I felt I had to do something." He held up both hands as she opened her mouth to reply. "Now, I know you're going to say that I could have called, but I wanted to see you. To make sure you were all right."

"I'm fine."

"Can I ask what it was that upset you?"

"Nothing upset me, Brady. I was tired. Stressed out. I just needed some quiet time."

"We all need that. You know, I enjoy our talks on the phone. I feel a real connection with you. I had this image of you built up in my mind; someone young but motherly, somehow. Someone with lots of integrity who would always do the right thing. Someone incapable of cruelty or deceit."

Elizabeth resigned herself to listening to him empty his soul of whatever was bothering him. She sat down in the chair on the other side of the round writing table. "That's a lot to discern from phone conversations, isn't it? What is it that —"

"It is, but I think it's accurate. Except for one thing. You don't look … motherly."

To heck with emptying his soul. There was definitely something weird going on here. Something even stranger than her own behavior tonight. She had to find out what he wanted and get him out of here. "Brady, what —"

"You look sensational. Does anybody know you dress like this in private?" His voice took on a tone she knew all too well. A tone she hated. One that meant all her careful constructions of professionalism were about to be blotted out by sex.

"No, of course not. I mean, I don't usually dress like this."

"I like the way you dress. Discreet. Professional. I had no idea you looked like this undern …"

"Brady, this conversation is inappropriate. I think you should go before I have to register a complaint."

"A complaint? Just because a man gives you a compliment?"

"It's inappropriate between two managers of this company, even if we're in different branches of the organization."

"I'm not here as a manager, Elizabeth. I'm here as a man. I think the world of you; I have right from the beginning. I know you like me, too, and trust me, otherwise you wouldn't have let me in just now."

"I thought you had some kind of HR difficulty you wanted to discuss. If that's the case, then please tell me. If not, I'd like to get some rest." How much more diplomatic could she be?

"I have an HR difficulty, all right. I'm very, very attracted to the HR director."

"Brady …" she sighed in exasperation.

"Give me a chance, Elizabeth. Spend some time here with me. I think you're the most beautiful and — and ethical woman I've ever seen. And the sexiest, if you don't mind my saying so. The way you're dressed tonight … well, it's almost as if you walked out of a dream."

She was tired of being a dream and a fantasy. She was tired of providing an object for every man in creation to look at. It was going to stop right here.

"I appreciate your feelings, Brady, but I'm afraid I can't return them. I'd like to keep our relationship on a friendly business level, if you don't mind."

His appreciative male smile slowly faded to dismay. "I sure as hell do mind. What do you call friendly?"

"Something that's more appropriate. I believe —"

"How can you talk about appropriate when you're dressed like that? Who are you waiting for, anyway? Garrett Hill?"

She stood up abruptly, turning to show him the door before her face gave her away. "That was uncalled for. What does Garrett Hill have to do with this?"

Brady leaped from his chair and followed her, confronting her in the narrow space between the end of the bed and the bureau. "You have one dance with him and you come back to the table looking like you just lost your best friend. Then I come up here and find you parading around in a dress only a lover should see, in a room right next door to his. It looks pretty obvious to me."

"Then your vision isn't very good," she snapped. "Your logic is as warped as your ideas. Now, please leave my room and hope to God I don't decide to report you in the morning."

"Report me for what? Telling you my honest feelings?"

"Harassing me and casting aspersions on my character!"

"Your character isn't what I thought it was at all. You're a deceiver and a tease!"

"Out! Now!" She whirled for the door, but he caught her halfway there. The first cold surge of fear rolled in her stomach. One arm gripped her waist, the other was wrapped around her neck, her chin in the crook of his elbow. The fine wool of his suit jacket rubbed roughly against her skin.

Oh, God, tell me this isn't happening. Tell me this isn't Brady Grant, a man I trusted and liked! Why does nobody know how flawed and unpredictable he is?

"I'm not going anywhere," Brady whispered, breathing the words. "And you're not going to report me. I'll just tell them what a Jezebel you are, meeting me at the door dressed like a hooker, trying to seduce me." The arm locked around her waist loosened and one hand slid up to cup her left breast.

Jezebel? In a moment of horrified clarity, she knew who had written the note.

"You've brought me to this," he whispered, pressing his hips against her backside. "This is all your fault."

"What are you going to do?" Elizabeth whispered.

"Make you repent. Make you sorry you ever deceived me and led me on."

He gripped the tab of her zipper and yanked it past the spot where it had stuck. The bodice of her dress loosened and fell away. In a savage movement, he grabbed a handful of velvet and pulled it down. The dress fell in a puddle at their feet. He lifted her off the floor and kicked it away.

"Lord God," he prayed over her shoulder, and bit her neck in a paroxysm of ecstasy. He cupped one breast roughly, squeezing it as though he was testing it for ripeness, grinding his erection into her bikini panties in an unconscious parody of Garrett's passion only hours before. He clamped the other hand over her mouth, so that her scream was muffled into a high whine. Cold terror tore along her veins. *Garrett,* she prayed. *I'm so sorry. Please come. Please.* It was hopeless. His pride wouldn't let him try her door, even if he came back in time.

Brady stepped around in front of her, undoing his fly with one hand, grabbing her arm with the other and backing her into a corner of the room. "Don't scream," he snarled, flexing his fingers and making her gasp with pain. "My hands are strong. Your neck is small. It won't take much to shut you up."

His eyes devoured her, hot and filled with lust mixed with hatred, and she nodded, head moving jerkily, like a marionette's. She stood in front of him in black bikini panties, thigh-high stockings and black high heels. Undoubtedly every sexual fantasy he'd ever had. How could she make that work to her advantage? Every second she could distract him was a second where help might arrive.

Pretending modesty, she tried to cover her breasts with her hands.

"No!" he said, swatting her hands away. "I can look on sin unafraid."

"You sent me that note, didn't you?" she murmured, trying to look as if his male power overwhelmed her.

"Of course. Slut. You came to that meeting with no bra on just to tempt us all, didn't you?" He covered her breasts with both hands and squeezed. She whimpered with the pain. "You like that, do you? You wanted to tempt me. You wanted me to come to your room. That's why you put on that dress, isn't it?"

"Brady!" she gasped. "You don't need to hurt me."

"How else am I going to punish you, Jezebel?"

"You don't have to do that. We're friends, remember?"

He splayed a hand on her chest and pushed her down on the bed. "Friends!" he spat. "Don't tell me what to do! You don't deserve me or my friendship. You're just a cheap tease and you're going to get what you deserve."

Chapter 7

The evening he had planned so lovingly had backfired with a bang and gone downhill from there. What was the matter with him? Garrett groaned, running a hand through already disheveled hair and making absent circles on the tabletop with the base of his snifter of cognac. He was supposed to be one of the most brilliant and articulate businessmen in the Valley. Why, then, was he such a miserable failure at communicating with Elizabeth? What was it going to take to convince her how important to him she had become?

It was bad enough that she had walked out on him during the two minutes he had managed to claim her as a dance partner. He was unable to communicate his love with his body. His verbal skills were a dead loss. How was he going to succeed?

The answer came easily. The way he'd seen Elizabeth act when she had to get to the bottom of a problem. She tackled the thorniest issues with sensitivity, gentleness, and dogged persistence until she found a way to solve them. He could learn a lot from her. In more ways than one.

He pushed the snifter away and got up. A lesser man would have ordered another, but Garrett preferred to be clear-eyed and in control, even if his only task was to walk out of the hotel bar and get on the elevator.

You're in control, all right, his memory mocked. *Except when you're with Elizabeth. A helluva lot of control you show there.*

It was true. The only reason he was skulking in the bar after a concerned and strangely quiet Brady Grant had dropped him off was that he hadn't been ready to go to his room yet. He hadn't wanted to hear the subtle sounds of Elizabeth getting ready for bed, so close, yet so out of reach.

Maybe not so far out of reach, after all. She didn't know all there was to know about him, and he intended to rectify that ... if she'd let him.

He sighed and glanced out the window as he wove past the empty tables in the bar. The bar looked out on the rear parking lot, which was brightly lit. He frowned and stepped over to the window. How many '59

Caddies could there be in this neighborhood on the same night? And why was it parked in the back, by the restaurant dumpsters?

Garrett recalled all the friendly little hints Brady had dropped all evening. Maybe Elizabeth had taken him up on them. Maybe he should just get out of her life. She'd run it very capably before he'd come along; he was sure she'd do the same afterward.

Sure. I will definitely do whatever she wants. After I find out whether Brady's in her room or not.

The elevator was too slow. He took the stairs two at a time, and let himself into his room. Dropping his key and jacket on the bed, he opened his adjoining door and stood still, his ear against her door, trying to calm his breathing.

Brady was definitely in there, all right. Garrett heard the murmur of their voices, and pain sluiced through him. The pain of total rejection, of being supplanted by someone less worthy of her even than himself. Garrett bowed his head and was reaching blindly behind him to close the door when he heard Brady's voice suddenly intensify in volume.

"… and you're going to get what you deserve!"

Garrett's blood seemed to congeal in his veins as he heard Elizabeth scream. "No! Help! Someone h …" The word was cut off by the sound of an open palm hitting flesh.

"Quiet, Jezebel! I warned you!"

Fear for Elizabeth and a killing rage blazed up in Garrett. There was no door handle on his side, no way to get into her room save one. He backed up and with all the speed and strength he could muster, slammed his body into the door. Unbolted, it gave, and he burst into Elizabeth's room like a runaway freight. His momentum carried him over to the bed, where he tackled Brady with such force that the other man slid off the other side, Garrett on top of him.

Weeping with terror, Elizabeth leaped off the bed and ran into Garrett's room to call hotel security, her voice shaking so much she could hardly get the words out.

Once he saw that Elizabeth was unhurt, Garrett turned his full attention to making sure Brady would never assault a woman again. Brady might be younger, but he was no match for a man of Garrett's size and strength — a man who was protecting his woman. With a final blow, Garrett laid him out on the carpet and jumped up, panting.

There was no sound from his room. He crossed the carpet, and as he did so Elizabeth peered out around the jamb as if it had taken an act of courage to see which of them was still standing.

Their eyes met in one unforgettable moment of perfect clarity and understanding.

Elizabeth burst into tears and ran into his arms.

Garrett retained the presence of mind to bundle Elizabeth into his bathrobe moments before hotel security showed up at the door. The police arrived shortly afterward and took Brady away, shouting recriminations and threats of lawsuits as he was manhandled down the hall to the elevator. When Elizabeth and Garrett had given their statements and were left alone at last, Garrett led her gently into his room.

"I don't know about you, but I'll feel safer if you're in the same room with me tonight. I can call Housekeeping and they'll bring me a rollaway so that —"

"Garrett." Elizabeth laid a finger on his lips. "You don't have to. I can sleep in my own room. It's over. I'll be perfectly safe."

He tried to keep the flicker of pain from showing in his face, but from the way Elizabeth bit her lip, he could tell she had seen it. "Safe from me?" he asked bitterly. "Or just from any crazy who walks into your room?"

"Please don't," she whispered, turning away and hugging herself around the middle. "Not after what we've just been through." She began to shiver, and his heart broke.

"I'm sorry," he said. His throat closed on the words. He put his arms around her and simply held her, rubbing her back, until the tremors subsided. "You've had a horrible shock and I'm a cretin to make it worse for you."

"Stop bad-mouthing the man I love," she said, muffled, into his blood-speckled shirt front.

"What was that?" Hope leaped in his chest.

"Nothing."

"Tell me."

She shook her head and tried to pull away. "I'm sorry. It was a mistake. I say stupid things when I fall apart."

"Do you love me, Elizabeth?"

She drew in a breath and paused. His whole life passed before his eyes.

"Of course," she said, and the blood surged into her cheeks. She bit her lip. "Pointless as it is."

"Stop that. You give meaning to my whole life, do you know that?"

He'd thought to bring a smile to the lips he adored. It didn't happen. "I can't do that," she said against his chest. "Only you make your life meaningful, and you choose to do it by devoting yourself to Stratton Hill. There won't be anything left over for me or anyone else. That's why giving my heart to you is pointless."

The cold started at his fingertips and crept up his arms. "Don't tell me this, Elizabeth."

"Don't tell you the truth? You're consumed by the industry, Garrett, and in a business sense that's a good thing. But I've seen the hours you work. I've driven by at night, and the lights are on in your office. Your car is the only one in the lot. I know you have a daughter and it frightens me. If you can't spare any time for her, what would you be able to give me?"

The cold had reached his heart now as he realized the depth of her conviction. Gentleness and persistence, he reminded himself. There was a solution. He could not lose hope or control now.

He kept his voice pitched low. "My daughter's name is Jessie. She's thirteen. She's also in a special program for gifted teenagers at San Jose State. Have you noticed a pattern in the nights I stay late in the office?"

She shook her head. "I only drive by once in a while. But you're there every time. And I've heard people talk about the hours you work."

"The hours I used to work. Some stories never die. Let me tell you what I'm doing. Jessie and I are in the lab, Elizabeth. We've been there three nights a week since the beginning of July, working on her science project. She's writing software for little kids. Computer games. We're doing it together. We have a perfectly normal relationship, except that she's brilliant and I have a hard time keeping up with her. Despite my divorce — which I admit was partly due to the hours I worked back then — Jessie has been the top priority in my life since she was born. Until now."

Elizabeth felt dazed. "You mean —"

"You thought I was at the office night and day? That my quality of life was so bad I had nothing in it but work?"

Put that way, she realized the injustice she had been doing him all these months. "Yes," she admitted.

"So when you knew I wanted you to share that life, it frightened you." She nodded, her forehead against his shirt front. "And now that you know the truth? Does it change the way you feel?"

"I … I hardly know what to think. My feelings are doing somersaults."

He went down on one knee, gripping the folds of the dressing gown wrapped around her thighs. "Elizabeth Forrester, will you marry me?"

"You can't be serious."

"I've never been more serious in my life. This is scarier than a stock market crash."

She didn't smile. "Will you forgive me?"

"What for?" he asked, gazing up at her as though she were the sun rising.

"For not realizing the kind of man you really are," she whispered as a fat tear overflowed and rolled over the bruise on her cheek, leaving a shining trail in the lamplight.

"Oh, God, Elizabeth," he groaned, and clutched her around the waist, pressing his face against her stomach. "I love you so much. Tell me yes before I —"

"Yes. Now and for the rest of my life." Her sweet scent rose to his nostrils, arousal mixed with Chanel No. 5. He tried to control his body's reaction. She couldn't want this, after the violence she'd just survived. "Garrett," she whispered, a breathy little sound, a sound she made when the anticipation was too much.

His sex quivered, stiffened, filled. He nuzzled the terrycloth of the robe that wrapped over her belly, and pulled the tie away. Her fingers moved convulsively in his hair as his lips found her skin. "My love. I love the way you smell." His tongue circled her navel, then traced a path down one bare hip. She gasped as his cheek brushed her curly thatch, and she shifted, spreading her feet to invite further exploration as he kissed the delicate, inner skin of her thigh. "So sweet," he murmured, licking the inside of the other thigh. Her breath hitched, and she whimpered. He tongued the hollow at the apex of her thigh. "I want to eat you."

"Please, Garrett," she begged in an unsteady whisper. "Please. Erase what happened tonight. Love me."

His cock ached with urgent pleasure, throbbed with every beat of his heart. "Take the robe off."

She arched her back, and the robe slid to the floor behind her. He slid his tongue into her wetness, tasting her lovingly, spreading her folds until he found what he wanted. Clasping her slender hips with both hands, he licked the slick, hooded pearl, first with the hard tip of his tongue, then with the flat, kissing and sucking until her legs trembled, and she unconsciously pulled his hair.

"Garrett, oh, oh —"

She shuddered and bucked against his face, but he pulled her relentlessly onto his tongue, holding her in a kiss from which she couldn't escape.

She bit back a scream and came, the wet rush of her orgasm filling him with triumph and joy. Her legs buckled and she slid down onto the carpet in front of him, quivering and gasping.

"I need you," she managed. "Now."

All he could think of was fulfilling her need, as fast as possible. Stripping his trousers, underwear and shoes off in seconds, he pulled her onto him and impaled her, swollen and wet, on his rigid cock. Her hair swung forward and the diamond earrings she still wore bounced madly as she threw back her head and forced him deeper.

He gave her control, loving the way the tight grip of her body clasped and slid the length of his aching sex, loving the full curves of her breasts, the way her luscious nipples teased him. He cupped her breasts as she stroked him, and felt the wild pleasure surging up out of his body, tearing his doubts away in an explosive rush, giving every cell of his being to the woman he loved.

⁂

Garrett Hill laid his resignation letter on Alan Stratton's desk with a flourish. "There you are, Al. The official two weeks' notice."

Alan gave him a glare that was so patently fake they both laughed. "You bastard. After all I've done for you."

Garrett grinned. "Don't give me that. You know startups are in my blood. I've rounded up some venture capital and I'm going to diversify a bit. At Elizabeth's suggestion."

Alan's face softened. "Congratulations. You're a lucky man."

"Thanks."

"I'm not going to lose Elizabeth, too, am I?"

"Hell, no. For some reason she likes this place. Both of us can't stay here, so I'm going to be the one to leave. To tell you the truth, I'm excited about the challenge."

"How does Jessie feel about it?"

"The three of us are spending weekends together. Jessie was a little reserved at first, but they seemed to take to each other. There aren't many people who can resist Elizabeth."

"Including you." Alan waved a hand. "Can't understand what she sees in you. Now, get out of here and earn your severance package, dammit. Don't go giving me short-timers' syndrome."

Garrett laughed and strolled back to his corner office, where Elizabeth waited. She laid an urgent hand on his coat sleeve. "Well, what did he say? Did he bite your head off?"

Garrett shook his head and gathered her into his arms, waltzing her in a circle and pulling her down with him onto the leather couch. "I've known Alan a long time. He wants us to be happy. The only guy biting anything around here is …" His voice faded into a muffled murmur of satisfaction as he traced the silk-covered curve of her breast with his cheek.

"Don't you dare! I have a meeting at nine!"

He chuckled and lifted his face for her kiss. "The down side of office romances," he grumped.

"I guess you'll have to make up for it tonight," she whispered, touching his cheek.

They smiled into each other's eyes. "Tonight and for the rest of my life," he said, echoing her own promise, and he kissed her.

About the author:

The shape and texture of words — their sensuality — have fascinated Shannon Hollis since she learned to read. She got her first positive review at the age of eight on a school composition, and completed her first novel at seventeen. Shannon has an Honors BA in Creative Writing from the University of California, and works in a high-tech company in Silicon Valley. The beauty of romance, she believes, is that its focus is on the things that are important to a woman: laughter, learning, friends, family ... and a committed relationship with the man of her choice. In romance, no matter what the obstacles she must face, the woman always wins. Like her heroine in "Strictly Business," Shannon fell in love with and married her boss, and they live in the house he built for her after the 1989 earthquake.

Insatiable

by Chevon Gael

To my reader:
I have always been fascinated by the games people play
when they fall in love. They go to great lengths to avoid,
deny, ignore and even refuse what they feel. Alas, love
latches onto you like a bad virus — with a lot of the same
symptoms — and never lets go. Love doesn't play fair and
lust throws all the rules out the window — as my hero and
heroine find out. Enjoy the game!

To the girls of the Golden Horseshoe Chapter, thanks for
not censoring me. I love you Mom and Dad for believing in
my dream. And for CM in Chicago who woke me from a
long, long, sleep!

Chapter 1

Marcus Remmington finished reading the directions on his frozen microwave dinner in time to be startled by several successive rings of the doorbell. He tossed the package into the kitchen sink and shouted, "Hold your horses, I'm coming."

Before he had a chance to wonder who was playing his doorbell like a piano, his gaze fell on the entry his assistant had made in his diary. Daagmar's spidery scrawl was spread across the page as a cue to block out the entire evening. He barely noticed the words, "Ashly-Tate"; then beneath it, *"Bedroom Eyes."*

"Shit," he muttered. The appointment had gone right out of his head after the ugly scene this morning with Yolande Johannsen, his latest runway diva. She'd shown up while he was in the shower, ready to scratch out his eyes. Of course, she'd quit on the spot. Marcus had expected as much so he wasn't terribly disappointed. He also wasn't disappointed at the shots he took yesterday, so Yolande's bailing out wouldn't cost him a job, but she'd never work with him again. Losing her as a bedmate didn't bother him. Losing a model to sit for the gallery opening did. Professional models of his acquaintance weren't interested in working for nothing. Besides, if Marcus was completely honest with himself, he was tired of the single name supermodels with their super-egos and over-inflated breasts or the underfed, wasted-waifs with their heroin-haunted eyes and six figure contracts. They wanted the runways at the end of the rainbow; not the hungry, artistic, pay-me-nothing-but-experience jobs that meant working in rain, snow or triple digit humidity. Just working period.

He no longer had the patience to scour amateur portfolios of thirteen-year-old virgins who offered to let him change their status in exchange for their first job. Nor did he have the cash flow to indulge in big money contracts for temperamental spoiled brats like Yolande. If it wasn't for the extra money coming from his *Bedroom Eyes* work, he couldn't afford his share in the gallery at all. So if his evening appointment was late and he missed out on supper, he didn't mind. He was grateful for every job.

He flipped on the outside porch light and prepared his professional side to flatter some bored housewife. He opened the front door and braced himself. The sight of the petite, dark-haired woman in the red cocktail dress stunned him into silence.

Her slightly glazed, green-gold eyes stared back at him in surprise. The halo of the yellow porch light reflecting in her glasses made her seem like some smoldering angel from wet-dream Heaven. She swayed slightly and shivered. Instantly, Marcus stood aside to allow her to enter. When she hesitated, Marcus was afraid she might be someone who just had the wrong address. Luck was with him, however, when she finally spoke.

"Is this *Bedroom Eyes?*"

Her voice was soft and uncertain. Marcus felt his groin stir as he breathed in the heady scent of an unfamiliar brand of perfume, mixed with the candy-sweetness of licorice. "Miss Tate?"

His assumption was answered with high, bubbly laughter.

"No, I'm not Lola." She stared down and critically assessed the bodice of her strapless dress. "Definitely not," she confirmed.

Marcus stood there in the open doorway, still not quite certain who had shown up for the appointment. But he didn't object when the woman walked past him into the hallway. Suddenly the heel of her shoe caught the end of the carpet and she toppled off balance. He lunged forward and caught her, his hands grasping her bare shoulders to steady her. Instantly, every nerve in his body was alive with sexual energy. He marvelled at the satiny texture of her skin, smooth and flawless in the dim light. The overwhelming urge to caress the rest of her surprised him. This woman was a stranger, a client.

Instead of turning around to face him, she leaned back against his chest until her head rested beneath his chin. She sighed loudly and tilted her head up to look at him. The corners of her frames poked the side of his jaw, knocking her glasses askew.

"You're tall," she said, one arm slowly reaching up, almost touching him. He held his breath for a heartbeat, hoping she would touch him and was disappointed when she only re-adjusted her glasses and slid them back up her nose.

Marcus gently pushed her away, his body strangely protesting the loss of her warmth against him. "And you're tipsy. Listen, we can do this some other time."

She answered him by removing her strappy sandals and pointing at her polished toes. "We match." She smiled and lifted the hem of her cocktail dress to reveal part of a dimpled knee beneath a slender thigh.

Marcus found himself unable to tear his gaze away from her legs. He jiggled his suddenly tight shirt collar. When had it turned so warm?

"We?" He cleared his throat and leaned against the wall in the shade of a potted hibiscus tree, happy to observe this strange elfin creature.

"I forgot," she giggled. "You don't know. I went and had a paint job this afternoon. I wanted everything to match." She held up her hands and splayed her fingers out toward him. "Fingers, toes and dress."

"I know I'll hate myself for asking, but why do you have to match?"

She planted her hands on her slender hips. Again, he found himself following her every move. Was she trying to hypnotize him?

"Because I'm not a blonde," she frowned, her ruby-red lips forming a plump, luscious pout.

Marcus' keen eye feasted on her lips. As a man he found them inviting. As a photographer he was aware that their fullness was refreshingly natural. Yolande would kill to have a mouth like that. Her overzealous surgeon injected too much fatty tissue into her lips. They looked ridiculously large compared to her tiny sculpted nose and the scooped-out hollows of her cheeks. While he was aware of Yolande's flaws, the memory of her face had suddenly vanished. The woman in front of him had overloaded his senses. He forced himself to continue the conversation.

"Since when has not being blonde been a crime?" Marcus wondered what she would do if he took her in his arms and showed her that it wasn't.

She looked at him then, and answered in a tone which made an explanation totally unnecessary. "Greg."

Marcus held his tongue. He wasn't even going to ask. Instead he steered her toward the purpose of her appointment. "Is Greg the one you're doing this for?"

A petulant frown touched her lips. "I'm doing this for me. Greg can go to hell," she snapped.

So, Greg was history. He was strangely relieved to hear that. "Miss … ah," he searched his memory for the notation in his date book. "Ashly, is it? Follow me to the studio."

"Have a seat and I'll be back in five minutes. Here," the man who greeted her at the door handed her a glass of wine. "Relax and think about the kind of look you want." Then he vanished up the stairs and into another part of the house.

Ashlyn sat in a black leather easy chair and surveyed her surroundings. The entire evening since leaving the restaurant was a blur. Only one detail remained perfectly clear, her now ex-boyfriend, Greg, leering at the enlarged chest of his date.

Ashlyn took her mind off the memory by concentrating on the walls of the studio. They were covered in black and white photos of what she guessed to be past clients. Women of various ages and tastes stared back at her. In her present state, their toothy smiles and eyes signalling invitation seemed to be making fun of her. She could almost hear them snickering. *They* probably had boyfriends or husbands who would look at their pictures and appreciate them in the ways that only intimate couples could. She sighed and sipped her wine. Might as well make the best of it now that she was here. Come to think of it, her host — who had introduced himself as Marc somewhere along the way — was making her visit as comfortable as possible.

The man himself was extremely comfortable on the eyes. He reminded her of Brad Pitt. Tall — but then, everyone was tall compared to her, and compactly built. No wasted space anywhere. His dark, wavy hair was lightly peppered with grey. It was a little longer than what she was used to, but she liked the way he pulled it back in a rakish queue. It made him look classical yet exotic at the same time. Not every man could pull off that look.

She watched him take the stairs when he left and was conscious of the way his slacks tightened against his butt each time he took a step. Some men had such flat rear ends. She couldn't decide what shook up her erogenous zones more, his butt or his blue eyes, so blue they were almost silver.

She leaned back completely and sank into the leather chair. She closed her eyes and thought about Marc. No doubt about it, the man was a hunk. Hell, when it came right down to it, the way she was feeling she just might take off her clothes if he asked her to. It was, after all, her birthday present.

"Wake up, beautiful." Marc's voice made a pleasant intrusion on her thoughts. He'd changed into a track suit with some kind of sports logo on the front of the sweatshirt. He flashed her a faintly amused smile.

"Is it time to work?" Ashlyn stretched her arms over her head, unaware that the bodice of the cocktail dress sank down enough to reveal the shadow of a cleavage.

And an impressive cleavage it was, thought Marcus. Her breasts were not overwhelming and most definitely natural. He caught himself wondering how they would photograph. Natural breasts were an erotic road map full of wonderful flaws. One was usually larger than the other; the nipple shapes uneven, areola's differed in shade. Their individual fullness was sensitive to the camera's eye. In his ten years of photographing women, Marcus found that breasts were like snowflakes; no two were exactly the same. In that respect, Miss Ashly would be no different.

"Here," he handed her a red satin bathrobe. "You can change in the corner bathroom over by the hot tub."

When she didn't immediately take the robe, he laid it across her lap. "Whenever you're ready. Want a refill?" She didn't object when he refilled her glass with white wine. Marcus sensed her uncertainty. He thought about offering her the option to back out. Immediately, he discovered there was a war heating up between the fantasies his mind was spinning and the lectures his conscience dragged out.

He damned himself, then half-heartedly offered, "We can do this some other time. It doesn't have to be tonight. The coupon is good any time."

She took a swallow of wine and seemed to be considering his offer. Then she shook her head. "I wouldn't want to disappoint Lola. She's my best friend. She's the one who bought me my makeover this afternoon and these pictures tonight."

Marcus sat down on the ottoman. "Okay, beautiful. You're calling the shots."

She picked at the bathrobe. "Do you have anything else? I mean, what if I don't look good in this?"

Marcus stole a glance at her legs, exposed now by the way the skirt of her dress fell to one side. "You'll look good in anything, Ashly."

She sat forward then until her face was inches from his and he could see his reflection in her glasses. "I like that name," she whispered as if bearing a secret. "It belongs to someone else. Tonight, I want to be someone else. Will you make me someone else, Marc?"

She was dead serious. Marcus read the plea in those luminous eyes, hidden as they were behind the briefcase-and-boardroom style frames. He helped her out of the chair and she slung the robe over one bare shoulder. "That way," he pointed toward the far corner of the studio. "You change and I'll set up the background."

By the time she opened the bathroom door and stepped out, Marcus had finished arranging a neutral beige background behind a sky-blue, satin covered divan. As a force of habit he looked up at the noise. As a force of nature, he looked again.

The robe was short, just barely covering her buttocks. Her shapely, bare legs spoke a language he was all too familiar with. They weren't the longest pair of legs he'd ever seen. God knew, he'd seen his share! And certainly, they weren't perfect. Perhaps it was their imperfection that attracted him to them. Whatever it was, he certainly intended to get his share of those legs, even if it was only on film.

Then, as an afterthought, he loaded the black and white film in another camera and positioned it on a spare tripod. His *Bedroom Eyes* photos were always in colour, but something, an instinct maybe, told him to get some b&w's. Marcus relied on that little "something" that stirred in his gut when he was feeling out a shoot. It told him which shoots were going well and which ones, like Yolande's, were disastrous. His "something" was busy again. It was a signal he couldn't ignore. And, when it came right down to it, this girl — this woman — was sending out signals he couldn't ignore.

An hour later, Marcus wanted to kick his "something" right in the ass. Ashly wasn't working for him. At first she sat rigid on the edge of the divan with her arms folded across her chest. She tugged at the short hem of the robe, trying in vain to cover up those delicious legs of hers. Marcus knew she was no professional but, at least in the past, most of his **Bedroom Eyes** clientele would try and pose. Marcus would joke with them and say racy things like, "Smile and think of your man when he sees this." That usually got rid of some of the tension.

But when he tried it with Ashly, her smile died and a sadness crept into her eyes. She reminded Marcus of his apprenticeship days in the department store baby portrait studio. He almost wished he'd kept that old, stuffed, Sesame Street character. All he had to do was wave it in front of any child and he couldn't get a bad shot if he begged for one. Once again he looked through the camera lens to check the angle.

She cleared her throat. "Could I have another drink of something? I guess I'm just nervous." She shivered and crossed her legs. "And a little cold, too."

The camera lens caught that simple action and channelled it straight into his expert eye. He adjusted the focus in time to pick up her body's reaction to the cold. Her nipples sprouted against the smooth, red satin. Suddenly he needed a drink too. But not before his "something" had crawled out of retirement to kick him in the stomach again.

Marcus could hardly contain himself. The ghost of something exciting revealed itself in that innocent shiver. If only he could get Ashly to loosen up some more. He could chip away at that glint of diamond he saw buried beneath the coal.

He walked over to check her height against the camera angle. She bent forward to retrieve her empty glass. "Okay, I take the hint. Let's take a break. I'll get you something from the bar. In the meantime, why don't you freshen up your lipstick and clean what's left of the old off your teeth. Here," he tossed her a blanket. "Wrap up in this for a few minutes." He picked up her glass and strolled over to the bar. He heard Ashly get up then close the bathroom door behind her. Suddenly, it occurred to him how she could get warm. A second later he was at the hot tub, setting the whirlpool timer and checking the temperature.

He set both their drinks on the ledge, being careful to first transfer them into tall, opaque plastic tumblers. He shed his track suit and slid into the tub before Ashly opened the bathroom door. He motioned for her to join him.

"Ta-da. Instant heat."

Ashly clutched the blanket around her shoulders. "I can't get in there."

"Why not? It's not like you have to know how to swim." He raised his drink and saluted her. "Cheers, beautiful. Now, come and warm up.

Then we can get back to work." He followed his argument with more coaxing. "My time is yours tonight, remember. This is your birthday and I haven't had the chance to buy you a drink."

He was charming and irresistible, as were the bubbles that churned around him. She watched their hypnotic patterns swirl against his chest. His words swirled around her ears. *My time is yours tonight … it's your birthday.*

Lola's words at the restaurant crowded her thoughts. *A night to remember …*

The implications of what was happening finally dawned on Ashlyn. What had Lola really bought for her? Glamour photos for her bruised ego, or a fantasy night of passion for her battered heart? Either way, she had to get things straight now while she still had the strength to walk out of here. Her vision was a little out of focus; her brain, fuzzy. Abstract visions of Greg rose to haunt her. His distorted voice taunted.

Daddy's little yes-girl … but you won't say "yes" to me. You're a tease, Ashlyn. You needed Duncan to get you a date.

"Ashly?" Marc's voice burst Greg's ugly bubble. Marc. If it weren't for Lola, she wouldn't have him either. The truth was always ugly. Her ego fought back. She didn't need anyone to get her a man and she wasn't a tease. She was just … careful. And good.

"But I don't want to be good tonight," she whispered, forgetting for a moment that she wasn't alone.

"Huh?" Marc slid over to the edge of the hot tub and examined her, uncertainty crowding his handsome features. And he was handsome. She didn't need all those glasses of champagne to convince her of that.

"I'm sorry, I meant I want to look good, for the camera and the pictures." For you. For me. She knelt down to sit on the side of the hot tub and dared to dip one toe into the churning water. Steam rose up to cloud her glasses and dampen the beautiful satin robe she wore. She should shed it before it became ruined. She found herself slightly embarrassed about revealing her all in front of a strange man. Her mind searched for a way to discreetly suggest that he turn his back.

Marcus found himself staring up at Ashly, a little confused but willing to go along. It hit him then why she was hesitating. And he suddenly realized what being around all those willing young models had done to him. *Marcus, you're an insensitive ass.* He silently tore a strip out of himself. At the same time, he was amazed that her modesty had rescued a scrap or two of moral behaviour. He discreetly turned his back. When he heard her settle into the hot tub, he retrieved her drink from a small utility shelf above him where he noticed she had placed her glasses for safekeeping. He turned to hand Ashly her drink and discovered she was neck deep in bubbles. She lay back, eyes closed. Her feet floated to the surface, just inches from his chest. Marc had the ridiculous urge to reach out and tickle her toes.

"This is wonderful," she purred.

"Don't get too dehydrated," he warned. "Here. There's plenty of juice in this."

Ashly straightened up until her shoulders peeked out of the water. Marc had to fight to keep his gaze from slipping beneath the water line. She took her drink and pressed the icy tumbler against her cheek. He watched intently as cool droplets of condensation slid down the side of the tumbler and splashed into the hot water. Through the churning water he imagined the tell-tale dark shadow between her legs. He knew she sat against two water jets; one massaged her middle back while the other, more strategically placed jet, pulsed between her buttocks no doubt sending hot tongues of water between her legs to lick at her clitoris.

His mouth went dry at the thought of his own tongue taking on the task of her arousal. His graphic musings sent his cock shooting straight up. *Down, boy!* He slid deeper into the water, unsure of what her reaction would be if she knew his thoughts, but not imagining the best case scenario. Marcus knew he had to get his mind back on track — fast!

She moved the edge of the tumbler to her lips and Marc stopped her. "Happy Birthday." He touched his tumbler against hers in salute.

"Thank you." She took a big gulp — which she instantly regretted. "Wow!" she gasped. "What's in this, rocket fuel?"

"Just a little imported rum," he assured her.

"Imported from where, NASA?"

He chuckled; a low, comfortable rumble that must have started deep in his chest. Ashlyn wasn't immune to that sound. It certainly was much more pleasant than the short bursts of loud guffaws that came from Greg when he watched All Star Wrestling.

Marc didn't seem like the wrestling type. Well, maybe some intimate wrestling perhaps. She stole a covert glance at him over the rim of her tumbler. Could they be any more intimate here in the hot tub, nearly-naked and not even an arm's length between them? She shifted her bottom to relieve the pressure of the water jets. The rushing water created an interesting stimulation; slipping between her outer lips, drumming against the tiny bud of her clitoris, causing it to swell. Not even Greg's faint attempts at manual foreplay had aroused her like this. A few more minutes of this and …

"That's the rum mixing with the sugar in the passion fruit."

"Huh?" Her mind tumbled from her near climax and she felt herself blush. "Passion fruit? I've never had that before." She sidled away from the perilous jet and took another sip, slower this time. "It's good. Well," she presented her drink to him once again. "Here's to passion … fruit."

Marc swallowed the tight knot in his throat. Passion. Right. The temperature of the water was rising. And that wasn't all. His raging hard-on forced him to stay on his own side of the hot tub — at least for a while. His drink and his libido needed some ice.

"Am I being rude if I ask you how old you are today?"

"Not at all. My twenties are officially behind me."

"Ah, I remember when I hit the big three-oh — barely. But that's another story. What I want to know is, why a beautiful, mature —"

"Careful —"

"— woman such as yourself is spending her birthday alone."

"It's not a crime," she defended, her shoulders inching a little higher out of the water. Bubbles danced around the shadow of her cleavage but she seemed not to notice either the rushing cascades or his look of longing as he watched the pattern of those bubbles.

"Like not being a blonde?" he reminded.

"That's different." Her free hand toyed with a cluster of bubbles circling close to her right breast.

Marcus watched her casual water-play and decided he had either died and gone to heaven and was about to be reincarnated into a bubble; or the devil had finally taken him after all and the nagging pressure in his groin was there to stay. He felt droplets of sweat bead across his upper lip. He licked the dampness from his mouth before trying to swallow past the burning hunger building in his chest which he knew had nothing to do with his missing supper.

"He must be crazy."

"Who?" She upended the tumbler and drained the last of her drink.

"The guy who dumped you."

"Oh, him." She reached into her glass and fished out an ice cube. It melted quickly between her fingers and her tongue darted out to catch the falling drops of cold water. She pressed the melting cube against her cheek then casually trailed it down her neck and across the vee of her exposed breasts. Marcus had never wanted to be an ice cube so much in his life.

"Greg's not crazy. He's not too bright, that's all."

Marcus agreed. And it was a good start. Apparently, she was getting over Greg fast. And that was good, at least for her. On the other hand, Marcus knew the warranty on his self-control was about to expire. Time to get on with it, whatever "it" was going to be.

"Do you want to carry on with the shoot?" Nice, safe territory.

"Not yet," she replied, completely oblivious to his predicament.

Okay, kid. Go ahead and torture me. I deserve it for what I'm thinking.

She obliged him. "Just a few more minutes. I feel much better now."

Marcus couldn't decide how he felt. He wanted her in here. He wanted her clothes off. He wanted her relaxed. So far, he'd gotten everything he wanted. So what was the problem? There was an old proverb about getting what you wanted. Whether it was good or bad, Marcus couldn't remember. He didn't care.

"Five more minutes, please Marc."

Marcus, old boy, you're the one who likes it when they beg for more.

"Ashly." His voice was ragged and her name rolled off his tongue like a plea. "Ashly, I'm warning you, I want to —"

"If I tell you what I wished for tonight, will you promise not to laugh?" She was serious.

"Okay, beautiful Ashly. I promise."

"I might not get it because I missed the candle the first time."

"Sure you will." Whatever her wish, Marcus wanted to make it come true.

"I want to have a wildly mad affair. I want to do something crazy and impulsive. I want to lose control completely and not care. That's what I want."

Marcus was stunned into silence, again. *Say something, stupid. Something polite, benign.*

"I … I want to … that is … I hope you get your wish, Ashly." The thought was genuine but the words sounded phoney. Apparently, she didn't notice. Before Marcus could stop her, she slid over to his side of the tub with her back facing him. "Rub my neck, please Marc."

Damn! There it was again. *Please, Marc.* He didn't have any more time to think as she pressed her naked back against him, trapping his erect flesh between them. He felt her stiffen then. A strangled "oh" escaped her lips and floated across the churning water.

At that moment, Marcus realized two things. First, regardless of how many candles she missed, Ashly was going to get her birthday wish. And second, no matter how bad she wanted that wish, she was still wearing her panties.

Chapter 2

Marcus sat in the hot tub, trapped between the hard wall of the spa and the silken back of the woman reclining into his crotch. He knew Ashly was too far gone from the drinks, even if she didn't. To take her now was asking for trouble. Even if she was aware of what she was doing, which he doubted, she would certainly regret it later. She'd feel used, he felt sure of it. And, if he were honest, so would he. Yolande's boot heels were still fresh in his mind. It wasn't fair to Ashly to go to bed with her simply because she was available and he was in need. He had a list of willing fingers ready to scratch such an itch. Besides, no matter how much she might want it now or how sweet or hurt she was, his lack of protection in the water was reason enough not to proceed.

Instead, he slid out from behind her, smoothly climbed over the side and quickly wrapped a towel around himself. "That timer goes off in about 30 seconds," he warned. "I'll duck into the bathroom and change."

As he disappeared through the bathroom door, Ashlyn heard him say, "We better think about getting back to work, if that's what you want."

"Okay," she replied dreamily. But what did she want? The offer was certainly there. He was obviously ready, no doubt sufficiently able and definitely willing. Yet, he hadn't come right out and made a direct pass at her. He seemed to be waiting for her to initiate the action.

Her confusion was lost in Marc's warning about the timer. Instantly the bubbles dispersed and the water became clear and calm. She should get out and dry off while she still had her privacy. She could hear Marc moving around in the bathroom. The muffled sound of the tap water running; the whirring of a hair dryer. She towelled off and slipped the bathrobe back on. Dry satin contacted with wet nylon reminding her that she still wore her panties. She slid them off and wadded them up in the towel.

Now, where to hang them? She would wait for Marc to finish, then lay them over the shower curtain rod to dry. Maybe she could use the hair dryer to get rid of the excess moisture. Whatever she did, she suddenly realized that the short robe left her in a very revealing position. She wrapped the wet towel, sarong style, around her waist in time to hear the bathroom door open. There stood Marc looking very refreshed and very covered in his track suit.

"Hey, beautiful. Ready to continue?" He shook his slightly damp hair which he now wore loose. It fell to just below his neck. Ashlyn wondered what it would be like to touch it; to feel it wild and flowing across her fingertips. His whole nature was so totally removed from the men she usually had to deal with in her life. Duncan, her ultra-conservative father who was so set in his ways or the too-chic and delicate look of Greg who wouldn't be caught dead with a short, mousse-sculpted hair out of place.

Next to the in-bred pedigrees of her acquaintances, Marc was the lovable mutt who begged to have his ears scratched and his belly rubbed. And Ashlyn was a soft touch when it came to strays.

Tonight, when she confessed her wish to Marc, he hadn't laughed or criticized or any of the things she might have expected from Greg. Marc seemed so laid-back and comfortable with his life. He loved his work, as demonstrated by the photos on his wall. To a degree, Ashlyn was envious. Success at Fraser and Associates was measured in quarterly reports; never an encouraging word or gesture from her father.

Good was unacceptable; best was passed over for perfect. Seduce, persuade, brainwash, even lie to the public if it meant increased sales. Just keep the client happy. Keep Duncan happy. Marc didn't seem to care about success yet he came across as being completely satisfied with his lot. Could he teach her his secret, she wondered?

"You can toss the towel in the hamper," he said, motioning to the wicker laundry basket beside the hot tub.

The moment of truth had arrived. And, by God, tonight she was going to play by her rules. *I'm going to be happy.* A self-indulgent smile tugged at the corners of her mouth. She suddenly felt as if she had climbed out of her body and was watching someone else. Slowly, she loosened the towel from around her waist and allowed it to slide to the floor in a heap. The lace of her discarded panties peeped through the folds, offering her one last chance to change her mind. She knelt down, picked up the towel and strode carelessly over to the basket and dropped it on top of Marc's already discarded one. The last of her armor gone, she squared herself and walked over to the divan.

"I'm ready, now." For the first time in months, she really meant it.

Marcus adjusted his lighting, changed the background again and set the tripod to the correct height. He deliberately kept busy until Ashly was sitting comfortably on the divan.

"Slide down to the end," he instructed. "Good. Now, tilt your head up. To the right. Okay. Shift your left shoulder towards me." He issued one instruction after another, all while making corrections through the camera lens. He looked up several times and critically surveyed her from different angles as if trying to convince himself of something. Finally he said, "can you lose the hair?"

"My hair?" Instantly her hands were behind her head to protect her precious French roll. "This hair cost a fortune and you want me to ruin it?"

"Yeah. You know, take those pins out and let it down?" Marcus recognized the feminine defense mechanism. Professional or not, no man crossed into the sacred territory of changing a woman's looks without meeting some form of resistance. But Marcus *was* a professional, and ready for a counter-attack.

"It looks great, but the effect would be far more sensational if you let it down. If only you could see yourself through the camera the way I do, I think you'd agree." Marcus was a master at dealing with difficult subjects.

"Well, if you really think —"

Before she could finish, he was standing in front of her, his fingers gently working on the pins. He tilted her head forward until her forehead rested on his waistband. Too late, he realized the shock of touching her was about to undo all his concentration. He practically wrenched the last pin from her hair, making her wince. "Sorry," he muttered and stepped back.

He studied her for a moment then pointed at the bridge of his nose.

"Off," he ordered.

"Off?" She repeated, confused.

"I know my studio is acoustically perfect. I built it myself. There is no echo." He levelled a stern "me Svengali" look at her.

"Chill," she mouthed and removed her glasses.

"Much better," he assured. "Now, shake your head. That's it. I — Wow." The effect *was* stunning. A hue of reds and browns swirled around her shoulders, picking up the gold in her eyes. The color cast shadows in the hollows of her cheeks. Marcus hadn't seen natural beauty like hers since the Scavullo exhibition at MOMA. She had the air of a classic celluloid diva, a cross between a young Katharine Hepburn and Lauren Bacall.

With barely contained excitement, he realized he'd found what he was looking for. The savior of his exhibition was sitting right in front of him. He tried to imagine what she'd look like silhouetted naked on a nine-foot-high matte of black and white splendor. His expression became dreamy. *Oh, yeah!*

"What are you grinning at?"

Her question brought him back to the studio as she grinned back at him, letting her head fall to one side and sending a cascade of hair across one shoulder. Instinctively, he snapped the photo.

"Hey, no fair. That one doesn't count. I wasn't ready."

"Candid, beautiful. I want you natural. No fake 'say cheese' photos for you. Just let yourself go. Pretend I'm not here. Get up close and personal with the camera lens."

"You mean 'intimate' don't you?"

Marcus tried to ignore the teasing tone in her voice. "Exactly. I'll dim the lights a little for you. There, now I'll bet you can hardly see me. Right?" He stepped behind the tripod.

"Actually, I can't see anything without my glasses on. You're just a blur, Marc." She squinted in the direction of where she thought his voice was coming from.

"Well, that's one I've never been called before," he quipped.

"What?"

"Nothing, just lay back. That's it," — click — "Now, lean forward, cross your legs and prop yourself up on one elbow." Another click. "Perfect."

Ashly was aware of low, soft music and she recognized Kenny G playing in the background. Safe sax — her favorite. The generation-aged disco Greg loved grated on her nerves. She'd gone through the 70's and once was enough, thank you. She closed her eyes and allowed the fluid rhythm to guide her movements. Gradually a sense of freedom took over and she began a wonderful journey of erotic self-discovery. A storm of trapped images, whispered sounds and repressed feelings flowed up to vent themselves.

She straddled the divan and purred like a kitten for Marc who urged and coaxed and begged her into impossible positions and instigated her transformation. The role-playing was unfamiliar yet exciting. She was a slave to Marc's masterful commands. She dared the camera with every click, teased out every flash. Marc's encouraging words became a litany.

"You're beautiful. Be sexy. Fantasy time, give me more. Great. Now, tease me. That's right. Pout, close your eyes, big sigh. Terrific."

The music was a turn on. The camera was a turn on. Having Marc tell her what to do and how to do it was a turn on. She felt like a teenager again, exploring the danger zone of the back seat. Daring. Pleasurable. Taboo.

She'd reached into the candy jar, copped the biggest piece and lingered on the decision of whether or not to bite quickly or suck slowly. She decided to bite.

Marcus' resolve, already pushed to the breaking point, foundered completely as Ashly slipped her arms out of the robe and clasped her hands in her lap. She sat cross-legged on the divan, facing him. Her creamy white breasts shone like two luscious pearls under the lights.

Their pink tips stood poised before the camera lens. Marcus lifted his head from behind the camera to make sure he was seeing the proper image. The image he saw was anything but proper.

Gone were the inhibitions of the shy, mousy working girl. This woman was a feast for the eyes, *his* eyes. His fingertips stood poised on the flash button. At that moment, she was totally and utterly his. If he depressed the button, she would be his forever, captured in his fantasy to look at whenever he wanted for as long as he wanted. But she also might belong to someone else some day; someone she might be intimate enough with to show the pictures. The thought of sharing his Ashly created an uneasy and unfamiliar feeling that lodged in his gut. He couldn't imagine another man looking at her the way he was and wanting her the way he did. A sudden possessive urge distracted him from his purpose and he flinched to clear it. In one hair-trigger reflex, Ashly became frozen in time forever as he heard the click and saw the flash. A satisfactory blush rose up from her waist and ended at her hairline.

But to his horror, she wasn't through. She bent slightly forward, pressing her arms into her rib-cage and forcing her breasts together to meet in a deep 'v'. It was the act of a woman in the throes of a seduction. A deep, throaty whisper confirmed his suspicion.

"Marc."

It was all the invitation he needed. In seconds he was kneeling beside the divan with Ashly wrapped in his arms. To his surprise, he found himself trembling inside, the thrill of anticipation doubling his pulse. He wasn't sure who started the deep passionate kisses that fed the fire burning inside him, he only knew that she aroused him like no other woman ever had before.

He pressed her warm body against him and cursed the clothes he still wore. Yet, he hesitated to break the kiss. She tasted of sweet wine and citrus. Marcus could feel her lack of experience in the way she kept her mouth closed at first. Then gradually, she became bolder, more secure with the feel of him as he pressed her down on the divan. He broke their passionate embrace long enough to whisper, "Baby, let's come up for air."

But Ashly would have none of it. "Want to drown," she murmured and drew his face back to her own.

"Then at least open your mouth, sweetheart, so I can drown, too."

Ashlyn willingly obeyed and was rewarded with a long, slow, deep kiss, the likes of which would have knocked her socks off, if she'd been wearing any. Never had a man kissed her the way Marc did. He was gentle yet sure of what she wanted. He didn't mash his teeth against her own while carelessly fumbling at her breasts. He took his time. He took *her* time.

The feel of his warm, hard body against her own naked skin excited her. There was something pleasantly erotic about almost wearing someone else's clothes, especially when someone else was still in them. If this was foreplay, she'd take all she could get. This new pleasure prompted her to try a little foreplay of her own.

Ashlyn slid her hands underneath his sweatshirt and trailed her hands up his back. His sudden intake of breath nearly stole her own. He broke away and in one swift motion, peeled off the sweatshirt. He was back on top of her before she missed the heat of his body. For the first time, Ashlyn had the luxury of his skin against her breasts.

His springy chest hair tickled and teased her sensitive nipples. He fed off their arousal. His husky moan encouraged her to continue her exploration. Her fingertips followed the muscle-play of his arms and shoulders as he expertly kneaded and nibbled her breasts. Her breath caught and she heard herself gasp from the sheer pleasure he gave her.

Ashlyn indulged in one of her earlier curiosities and tangled her fingers in his long, dark hair. The silky strands slid across her hand. She toyed and played with it, winding it around her fingers. One by one, she freed each finger being careful not to tug too hard. Gradually she caressed a path down his back before settling in the downy-soft patch of hair at the base of his spine. She ached to go further but waited for a sign of acquiescence. Instead of giving her a sign, he opened the door for her by reaching down and placing her hand on his half-exposed buttocks.

She heard her own soft, surprised sigh at the intimacy of her new discovery. She gave in to the urge to gently knead the hard, muscular cheeks of his ass. She always considered herself an "ass-woman." Most of her girlfriends giggled and speculated about the bulge in a guy's crotch. Ashlyn's fascination had always turned her head to watching men walk by her. It afforded her the pleasure of a long, lingering gaze, instead of having to avert her eyes suddenly or hide an embarrassing flush.

Marc had a great ass! Tight, not too much hair covering his skin, hot to the touch and sensitive! He expelled a sudden growl when she firmly grasped one cheek then the other. His hot breath between her breasts created a tingling inferno of pleasure. She arched up to give his mouth better access to her breasts. She wasn't disappointed.

"Beautiful," he murmured as he took one swollen nipple into his mouth, then the other. "You feel like silk … so natural … all pink and white … warm perfection …" He suckled each breast in turn until the rosy tips became hard and puckered. Then he captured the nub between his teeth and flicked his tongue over the very end in a torturous frenzy.

Yet there was no urgency in his lovemaking. He gloried in scraping at every raw nerve in her body. He began a tortuous rhythm of insinuation as he nestled his crotch against her thighs. Her hips copied the motion and she opened her legs to cradle him. The length of his hard cock prodded her naked mons before sliding between her tender outer lips. She felt her own dewy moisture dampen the cotton fabric of his pants. Marc began to rock back and forth against her swollen clit.

The unfamiliar feel of rough cloth against her sensitive flesh only heightened her pleasure. It was a keen reminder that very little stood between her and the point of no return. She couldn't stop now if she wanted to. And she wouldn't stop Marc from removing the final barrier.

And he was going to. He told her, in searing detail, exactly what would happen.

"I'm going to fill you up, baby doll. Take you, inch by hot, lovely inch. I want to feel those dimpled, little knees strapped tight against my ears while I give you full penetration. Then, I'll turn you over, come in from behind so I can play with your clit at the same time. Would you like that?"

Ashlyn was at a loss for words; mesmerized by the images he described. She could do little but dumbly nod her head.

"I didn't hear you."

"Yes," she managed to whisper.

"Yes, what?" he demanded and reached down between them to explore her thatch of pubic hair.

The feel of his fingers gently probing her outer lips caused her to cry out in frustration and beg for more. He teased her instead.

"Not until you tell me what you want," he gently chastised, then allowed one finger to brush over her swollen bud.

Ashlyn nearly screamed. "Now! I want you inside me now."

"Patience, my love. The first time's going to be hard and fast. Not time enough for both of us to enjoy it. But then we'll do it again … and again … and again."

Ashlyn accepted every word as easy as drawing breath. And her next breath mingled with his as he shared a deep, lingering kiss. Ashlyn was sure he was stealing her soul, but it didn't matter. Nothing mattered now but the man in her arms.

The air filled with his soft growls and her own urgent groans. The louder she groaned, the faster and more forcefully he ground himself against her until she felt her last groan being drawn into a sudden gasp. A rush of sensations erupted into a powerful climax. She wrapped her legs tighter around his waist in an effort to try to force him inside. She wanted him deep, penetrating. She wanted to hear the sharp slap of his balls against her ass. She wanted to come again only this time with him fully imbedded inside her. She wanted to feel the splash of warm come against the sensitive walls of her canal. Was it a dream or did she hear herself emptying her soul of all these secrets to the man who held her?

Marc tore his mouth from hers and kissed a path to her ear. She thought she heard him whisper something coherent and sensible like, "protection." Instead of responding to his question, she gently bit the hollow of his neck.

"Don't go. I want you inside me." He was making magic and she'd be damned if she'd let him break the spell. But break it he did. He struggled to sit up, taking her with him. He held her close and kissed her head. And her eyes. And her nose. Finally, he landed a series of short kisses on her mouth as he spoke.

"I'll … be … right … back," he whispered and climbed off her. He turned and strode across the studio to the door that led into his private living area. In the dim light of the studio, Ashlyn had a perfect view of just how aroused Marc was. His erection created a tent inside the once-loose sweat pants, giving startling evidence that he was generously endowed. Ashlyn couldn't keep her eyes off the site. A thrilling shiver rushed through her thighs and she pressed them together. They tingled with anticipation while the delicate, still sensitive bud of her clitoris quivered, ready to jump back to life. No wonder she'd come off like a rocket! And that had been with his clothes on. She tried to imagine what it would be like once he was inside her buried to the hilt.

As she watched him disappear behind the door, a thought struck her. She was not being invited into his bedroom. A more horrifying thought gripped her. *Oh my God, what if he's married?*

The champagne, combined with the liqueurs, wine and cocktails made her brain fuzzy. She couldn't remember if he was wearing a ring, not that it was an accurate sign of any permanent attachment. She tried to recall seeing any womanly signs as they walked through the house to the studio. She remembered seeing a picture of someone in a red dress flirting with Marc. The scene drifted by her in slow-motion and became part of a distorted jumble of images. The room spun at a dizzy angle. If she could just lay down for a few minutes, she might feel better.

She closed her eyes against the lights of the studio. They had suddenly become harsh and glaring. Why had he turned up the lights? A thumping noise poked through the haze. She tried to lift her arms to cover her ears but they seemed weighed down. Someone called her name but she couldn't respond. She felt something rough and heavy settle over her body. She relaxed into it's warmth and was eternally grateful when the room became dark. She managed a slurred "thank you" before falling asleep.

She didn't hear the disappointment in the voice that answered.

"You're welcome, beautiful."

Chapter 3

Marcus pushed his way through the crowded streets of Hazelton Lanes toward the gallery. Briefcase gripped tightly in his hand, he was only vaguely aware of knocking it against a woman pedestrian as she walked past him. He disregarded her cheerful smile and only muttered a curt, "excuse me" after the hard, square leather connected with her thigh.

His foul mood, a leftover from the past three weeks, was instigated by his waking up that Sunday morning and finding Ashly gone. Nor could he find any trace of her in the days following her disappearance. He cursed Daagmar a thousand times over for not getting Ashly's telephone number. He badgered her for days about any detail she could remember until finally, Daagmar told him where to go.

"Ashly whats-her-name didn't make the appointment. Somebody-else-Tate did," Daagmar snapped and promptly told him to piss-off.

He wasted no time in developing the film he'd shot. The results fortified him. Ashly was magnificent; the most perfectly proportioned collection of black and white dots he'd seen in a long time. He spent hours examining film negatives through the magnified light box. He enlarged print after print and then faxed her picture to every modelling agency in the city, and a few in L.A. and New York. Each time he got the same answer. No one had her under contract or had even seen her before but, could she be persuaded to sign?

Marcus was less than amused. He was aware of the less than professional remarks being circulated as a result of his queries. She had slipped through the experienced fingers of Marcus Remmington and was now known as "the one that got away." It was purely by accident that Marcus discovered some of the agents he'd sent Ashly's picture to were working behind his back to find her.

He answered a frantic summons from Alexis Tremayne, his partner in *Nirvana*, the up-scale art gallery located in an exclusive shopping section of downtown Toronto. He arrived in time to speak briefly with the construction foreman working on the renovations. Most of the crew had already packed up and were gone. News that the project was on schedule should have pleased him. He suspected that wasn't the only reason Alexis wanted to see him. He wasn't surprised when she raked him over the coals about his behaviour and the entire Ashly incident.

"Marcus, dear boy." Alexis embraced him through the cloud of cigarette smoke that always surrounded her. Marcus constantly harangued her about the habit. She, in turn, bitched incessantly about his long hair, his scruffy but very expensive designer jeans and his fondness for bourbon. It was her right, she argued, and a privilege of her age to decide to commit ritual nicotine-induced suicide, and he could go to hell. Marcus defended his right to breathe and warned her that she would not live to see her next and fifty-third birthday.

Alexis used to own a modelling agency and had learned about Marcus' problem through a mutual contact. She was concerned enough about Marcus to leave several strong warnings on his machine. Alexis represented a lot of money. As his partner, he knew he couldn't afford to rile her. The wisest thing to do was to hear her out and get his "sorry ass" down to the gallery!

"So show me this little piece of tail who's tied a knot in your, ah," she paused and pointed her cigarette holder at his groin, and gave him a teasing smile, "reputation."

"My psyche," he snapped. "She's screwed me up, Alexis." Except for the two of them, the half-renovated gallery was empty. Marcus listened to his words as they echoed off the high ceiling. Admitting them out loud didn't make them any easier to bear. The naked truth was painfully sad and honesty plain out sucked, big time.

Because there were no other chairs besides the one Alexis sat in, Marcus pushed back a corner of the protective tarp and sidled onto her desk. Alexis made a disapproving face and leaned forward, planted one elbow on his pant leg and propped her chin in her free hand. Marcus could feel himself being scrutinized through the wraparound sunglasses she always wore, day or night. He had the urge, but never the courage, to ask if she wore them while entertaining one of her many lovers. In her other hand she clutched her cigarette holder, another permanent fixture. Alexis was eccentric enough to be the kind of person who might conceal a weapon in the tip. Marcus swore that if he met her without her two props, he wouldn't recognize her. She tapped the end of her holder on the oak desk top, drawing his attention back to her.

"I'll lay it on the line for you Marcus, since it seems to be the only way I'll get through to you. *Nirvana* opens in two months — that's 60 days, if you're keeping track. I want to know if, in two weeks, you'll have your exhibition ready. If not, then … well, dammit Marcus, I'm a business woman. Don't sit there and pout like some little boy mooning over his first crush. The only way to get over this is to take out your black book and …"

She stopped when Marcus silently handed her one of Ashly's photographs. Marcus nearly fell off the corner of the desk when Alexis slowly raised her sunglasses while angling the photo into the dim light. The woman had eyes — bloodshot — but they were there and they were scrutinizing his Ashly. And it suddenly occurred to him that he wanted Alexis' approval — badly.

He counted the heartbeats until Alexis slid her sunglasses back into place. He waited for her to toss the photo back at him, as she had with countless other infatuations. When she didn't, he held out his hand and raised his eyebrows to question her hesitation.

"I'll hang on to this, if you don't mind."

He did mind, but she closed any objection by exhaling a large cloud of smoke in his direction. In retaliation, he coughed loudly and fanned the air, using several exaggerated arm gestures, and one not so subtle hand gesture. She answered with a peevish grin and slid the photo into a faded, leather portfolio under her desk. Case closed, as it were.

"If I were you, Marcus, I wouldn't spend too much time on this obsession," she warned.

Marcus rolled his eyes in defence. "I'm not obsessed."

"Some men hang fuzzy dice from their rear view mirrors; others carry a rabbit's foot." She took a long drag off her cigarette and continued. "But not our Marcus. No sir. He carries around women's underwear." She pointed the cigarette end of her holder towards Marcus' open briefcase where a swath of pink silk and ivory lace peeped accusingly from one of the worn leather pockets.

Marcus glared at her while he stuffed the treasure back into the zippered compartment and snapped the lid shut. He cleared his throat against the image that had haunted him ever since that night; the image of Ashly, the fledgling seductress, teasing off her robe to reveal herself naked as the temptation of Eve. He'd discovered the silky swatch while sorting through the laundry hamper. Impulsively, he decided to hang on to it. Just in case.

"Interesting concept you have, Marcus. You know, Prince Charming carried a glass slipper from door to door. What *are* you hoping will fit into those?"

Her laughter, meant to embarrass him, only served to fuel his resolve. "I'll find her."

"Where?" she demanded.

"I don't know. Yet," he managed through gritted teeth.

"You have two new competitors following in your footsteps. I'm surprised you haven't noticed them scratching at your heels," Alexis said casually and butted out her spent cigarette.

Marcus scoffed, he knew where this was leading. "If you mean that rich kid, shutterbug wannabe and his latest mattress decoration, I've noticed them. So he got a few shots of daddy's yacht into the Toronto Island Yacht Club Directory. It doesn't mean shit, Alexis."

"Brian and Ellen are very talented. They're eager. They're *hungry*. You remember what that's like, don't you Marcus?"

Marcus was ready for the remember-who's-putting-up-half-the-cash-for-this-venture speech. "You don't scare me, Alexis."

"Wipe that smug look off your face. Yolande's been spreading a lot of crap about you. Word on the street is she wants your blood. And she'll get it if she isn't up on these walls as the star of this exhibition." She waved her empty cigarette holder at the newly finished drywall partitions.

Marcus followed the gesture and stared at the bare walls, the freshly sanded hardwood floors and the gaps in the ceiling where the imported light fixtures would soon hang. He only hoped they had enough money between them to finish the renovations on time. Alexis didn't need to know that his line of credit was almost non-existent or that the money from the Bedsong shoot wouldn't arrive until after Christmas — after the opening. His next job was almost a given. If he could arrange an advance against the job, then he could breathe easier. His next appointment would tell the tale. In the meantime, he would live like he always did, by his wits. He nodded toward Alexis's portfolio. "Yolande can be replaced. She already has."

"If you can find her," Alexis reminded.

"I'll find her."

"Why?" Alexis let out a frustrated growl and slumped back in her chair. "You don't need her. You've worked hard and helped launch the careers of dozens of young girls. Clients want you. Agents want you. So what if this Ashly doesn't want you? You're practically a legend in the industry and after this exhibition you'll be a household name. Your work will be in demand. Art snobs and celebrities will buy up your prints and drive up the price. You'll make money," she paused for emphasis. "*I'll* make money." She grinned wide, displaying two sets of extraordinarily white teeth in contrast to the amount she smoked. "And that will make your bankers very happy." With that, she got up, stretched lazily and yawned. "And you, my darling Marcus, will be a star."

Marcus squirmed when she came around and tried to pinch his cheek. "And all without the help of Ashly whoever." She finished by tugging none-too-gently on his freshly secured pony-tail, causing errant strands to fall out of place.

"Stop that," he admonished and slapped her hand away. "I have a meeting this afternoon with the DiAngelo brothers."

"I heard the pride of Milan was in town pushing their new perfume.

I'm surprised you have time for them, what with combing the city for Cinderella," she quipped.

"I'll find her," he promised.

The words haunted him as he made his way to Fraser and Associates later that afternoon. He walked from the gallery in Hazelton Lanes to Fraser's University Avenue address. It gave him time to mull over the problem.

I'll find her. But how? It was one hell of a big city. He was almost ready to admit that Alexis was right. He was obsessed.

I'll find her. If he ever found her again he wasn't sure what he'd do first, lose his temper, or himself.

❧✣❧

"You wanted to see me, Dad?" Ashlyn took a seat across from her father and hoped the trepidation in her voice wasn't too obvious. Duncan never called anyone into *the red room,* as Brian once dubbed it, unless there was a lecture involved. Duncan's office was a sea of burgundy leather and antique brass studs. Over the years Ashlyn occupied herself during numerous lectures by counting the brass studs that outlined the huge leather-topped oak desk and two matching wing chairs. She knew exactly how many studs were on each piece of furniture. She hoped Duncan wasn't offering her another chance to refresh her memory.

She watched him briefly flip through, then discard, the portfolio containing the mock-up ads she and Sharon painstakingly put together during the last week. Lines of disapproval crowded his forehead. Any hopes of reprieve were lost in those furrowed brows.

"Did you enjoy your trip to Europe?" she asked, hoping to lighten his mood.

Duncan answered without looking at her. "I met with the DiAngelos in Milan."

"Did you go alone?" The recent wedding was so quick and quiet that Ashlyn didn't want to admit the name of her father's fourth wife had slipped her mind.

"Your stepmother went with me."

"I hardly think that someone who isn't old enough to drink in some states qualifies as my stepmother."

"That's enough, Ashlyn. You don't have to like her."

"Like her? I don't even know her. You'll have to introduce us one of these days."

"Don't be sarcastic. You *were* invited to the wedding.

"Was Brian?"

He ignored her probe and continued. "I left a message on your desk."

"A pink telephone slip does not a wedding invitation make. Come clean, Dad. Why all the secrecy?"

Duncan heaved an impatient sigh. "Her name is Kirsten, or Mrs. Fraser, if you prefer and yes, she went with me to Europe. Are you finished prying?"

Ashlyn rolled her eyes. "My father marries a teenager he's never introduced to his *grown* children and he thinks I'm prying. I have a right to pry."

"You're covered if I die tomorrow. That is what you're worried about, isn't it?"

"If it is, then I have a long wait behind the three ex-Mrs. Frasers. No thanks, Dad. I have no desire to watch them all shop together after you're gone."

"I settled with your mother years ago and the other two remarried," he snapped.

"Yes, Stephanie and Jennifer got smart. Why mother still carries a torch for you is beyond me. What I can't figure out is where Miss Teen Idol fits in. Unless … Oh, my God! She is, isn't she! That's why everything was so hush-hush. I'm going to be a … a sister."

"I would appreciate it if you wouldn't talk about this around here. It's no one's business but mine."

"Oh, I'd say it'll be everyone's business in about six months. Tell me, Dad, are you sure its yours?"

"That's enough. I'm old enough to choose what I want in life."

No, it wasn't enough. Her father was acting like an idiot. His temper be damned. "Did she even give you a choice, or did her parents threaten statutory rape? It must have been some choice, marry me or it's off to court we go, not to mention the newspapers. Did you ever hear of safe sex? By the way, have you been tested for any contagious diseases?"

"Ashlyn! That's enough!" He bellowed loud enough for anyone on the same floor to hear him. Ashlyn shut her eyes against the picture her life would present for the rest of the week; the circumspect glances from her fellow employees, silent pity ringing out from their faces. If he flogged her publicly in the town square, the humiliation couldn't be worse.

Determined to recover what little self-esteem she possessed, she changed the subject. "Can we please get back to discussing some strategy?"

Ashlyn listened to her father's input. With each passing minute, her hopes sank lower and lower. 'My-way-or-the-highway' was what Duncan meant by strategy. The so-called strategy was nothing more than a platform for Duncan to solicit her opinion, discard it, and go with his own. Ashlyn knew the ads were rough by her standards, but they were something to show the client. And she was proud of them, even if Duncan wasn't.

Ashlyn had learned to deal with Duncan's constant criticism by handing him benign, satisfactory answers. Schooled in the art of deception, she no longer blushed or lowered her head when battered with Duncan's public corrections. She would rather die than admit that her own father embarrassed her. Instead she reinforced her resolve by squaring her shoulders and lifting her chin. Duncan often commented on what excellent posture she had, never realizing he was the cause. The only outward sign of her discomfort was her nervous habit of adjusting her glasses. Just as she found herself doing now as she listened to him lecture her.

"This account is very important to the company. It could make up for the business we lost during the recession. I can't afford to have you screw this up."

Ashlyn's answer was designed to cause him no less stress. "I'll be fine." Of that she was sure. She knew better than to commit herself or her ideas. Duncan's lips pressed into a grim, flat line. Ashlyn knew he wanted her to say something else. Something to reassure him that he had produced at least one clone of perfection. *Sorry, dad. The world isn't ready for another Duncan Hardwick Fraser, and the world isn't going to get one, either.*

Ashlyn was relieved when she heard Duncan's name over the paging system. He answered the page from an interoffice phone on the wall. He barked into the receiver. "Yes. I see. Show them in and offer them coffee. We're on our way." He replaced the receiver and snapped his fingers toward the door. "Let's go," he ordered, as if she were one of the half-dozen thoroughbred hunting dogs he owned.

Ashlyn dutifully followed behind. For the first time in her life, she found herself hating her job. She hated herself for not standing up to Duncan. And she hated what's-her-name, the current Mrs. Fraser, for involving her father in such a cheap scandal. Surprisingly, she didn't hate Duncan. She pitied him and the idea that the company he loved more than his family was now running him. She didn't envy the financial responsibility he had to bear. Perhaps it was that pressure that drove him to the bed of a pretty, gold-digging Lolita. Ashlyn thought about her own recent indiscretion and knew she shouldn't be casting stones at her father. She might have ended up in the same situation. That Marc guy must have used some protection, since her period came as regular as clockwork the following week.

The night in question was still a muddle, but it gave her a secret source of pleasure to know that for one moment, a man wanted her because he thought her attractive and not because she was a savvy business opportunity. That knowledge brought a smile to her lips and raised her spirits. It was a revived and confident Ashlyn who entered the boardroom, ready to gamble the future of her father's company on a slender bottle of scented water.

Chapter 4

If Duncan hadn't realized Ashlyn wasn't perfect before now, then he knew it ten minutes into the *Insatiable* presentation. He sat at the back of the room, scowling in the dark as she narrated the merits of each advertising program. As she talked, she kept one eye on the two representatives who chattered in Italian between themselves. Clearly, they were not overwhelmed by what they saw.

"I'd appreciate your comments, gentlemen," she said. Finally they stopped talking.

"The woman," one of them, a man named Giuseppe — Joe, her father had introduced him — made an hourglass shape in the air. "Where is the woman?" he asked in exaggerated English.

"As I mentioned previously, Mr. DiAngelo, every perfume on the market uses a Hollywood personality or a supermodel to endorse their product. Our research department has found that the celebrity's name is remembered first, and then the product. We want your product to be noticed for its unique qualities, not for some actress who has to be replaced every time her contract runs out. That's a lot of money to spend on a short term advertising campaign. You'll find the cost figures on page 14 of the report."

Which lay unopened in front of them, she noted disheartedly. Ashlyn knew she was losing this round. What was worse, she knew Duncan knew it too. And, since he usually sided with the client, he made his displeasure no secret.

"I understand what Mr. DiAngelo is getting at. He's thinking along the lines of what I had in mind all the time."

Thank you, Dad, for the translation and the vote of confidence.

Instantly the reps turned toward Duncan. Ashlyn stood forgotten and had no choice but to sit down and listen to what Duncan had to say.

"If I hear you correctly, Joe, and I think I do —" he gave the men a conspiratorial smile, "in order for us to get the message to women consumers, then it should come from one. After all, these women know how to talk to each other, eh?" The men laughed among themselves and nodded agreeably.

Ashlyn fumed in silence but swallowed her anger and attempted to reason with them. "I thought we were selling perfume, not sex." She didn't miss the look of reprimand from her father, or the lack of interest from the DiAngelos. She tried one more time. "I've been wearing the sample of *Insatiable* and I —"

"Of course we're not selling sex, Ashlyn. We want to get the message across that if you wear the perfume then you feel sexy. And if you feel sexy, then you are sexy. Right?"

Ashlyn thought carefully before answering. *Right, Dad. You know everything about women. Just ask Jennifer or Stephanie or the most recent one whose name escapes me.* Then she remembered her recent conversation with Gerry Dolan, their chief accountant warning her of their unstable financial position. "Of course, gentlemen. If that's what you want we'll certainly work towards putting together a suitable campaign." She redoubled her efforts to smooth things over, not because she agreed but because the interest on the bridge financing was due.

Duncan reinforced the offer. "Yes, of course," and motioned for her to back up his assurance.

"We can get a draft to you by, say, next —"

"By tomorrow," Duncan interjected.

Ashlyn flashed him an incredulous look, which Duncan quelled by marginally narrowing his eyes and ever-so-slightly lowering his head in her direction before he continued. "As a matter of fact, the photographer should be joining us shortly."

"Photographer?" Ashlyn tried to hide her confusion and was losing the battle. She ground her frustration between her back teeth. She felt the heat of anger flame her cheeks. Disappointment stung her eyes.

Duncan stepped in. "I invited Marcus Remmington to join us. Don't you remember, Ashlyn?"

At Remmington's name, the reps responded with favorable "ah's", and made impressive remarks to Duncan. "His work is *molto bene.* How you say, very good. Yes?" Francesco nodded enthusiastically, forcing another benign but polite smile from Ashlyn.

She was aware of Remmington's reputation. He could turn a respectable ad campaign into a peep show before you could say 'market share'. There was nothing like a nude, bronzed butt cheek to catch the eye of the potential perfume consumer. It made perfect sense to her.

"I believe he's just finished shooting the Bedsong account with Yolande." Of course Duncan would keep on top of his own idea. He knew what he wanted all along. All he needed was her own bad handling to slide right in and catch the unwary client. Another demonstration of the golden rule at work. His earlier words took on a menacing double meaning. *Get this account at any cost.* Even if he had to ruin Ashlyn's career in the process. Brilliant strategy. *And you walked right into it, didn't you Ash?*

And Remmington. His ace-in-the-hole. How had he managed that? Remmington had a notoriously strict code of independence. Ashlyn conceded that it was probably another one of those male bonding efforts. A few beers, some chatter about sports, a handshake later and it was done. Who said the old boys club was dead?

Duncan stood. "Now, Francesco, about that tour of the country club I promised you …" As they turned to leave, Duncan tossed her a crumb. "Ashlyn will stay here with Giuseppe to discuss the campaign. When Remmington arrives the three of you can brainstorm some ideas. I'm sure you'll have a draft by the end of the day." The words 'or else' hung unspoken between them.

Francesco bid her, *"Ciao"* and Duncan escorted him out. Giuseppe reseated himself right next to Ashlyn. The overpowering scent of his cologne caused her to wrinkle her nose and cough discreetly. There was nothing discreet in the way Giuseppe leered at her.

"You like work with you papa, no?"

NO! The silent scream echoed in her head. Politeness intervened. "I appreciate the opportunity, but I have to work as hard as anyone else." There was a fine line between truth and contempt.

Giuseppe leaned closer, casually trailing his index finger along the sleeve of her shell pink linen jacket. "We have been to other companies with our product but we think you have much more to offer." He smiled, his gaze drifted from her face down to where her thighs met the hem of her matching linen skirt.

"Th-there are many talented people here at Fraser & Associates. Perhaps you'd like to meet some of them." She started to rise but Giuseppe's hand on her arm stayed her.

"Your papa, he say you not married." Guiseppe's stare raked over her slender figure like a wolf eyeing a plump, innocent rabbit.

An alarm sounded inside her head. Was she being used as bait for *Insatiable?* Did he think Duncan was willing to offer *anything* for a chance at the account? Duncan was devious but she was still his daughter. It was time to draw the line between business and pleasure.

"My father is correct, Mr. DiAngelo. I'm not married, but I have a boyfriend," she added quickly and continued the lie. "It's quite serious." She saw confusion in Giuseppe's face followed by the discreet withdrawal of his hand.

For a moment, she could think of nothing to say to him. She filled the gap with small talk about his home in Milan and his trip to Toronto. At last, the intercom buzzed. Thankful for the distraction, she picked up the receiver. "Thank you, Marie. Show him in." She turned to Giuseppe. "Mr. Remmington is here."

At last, the Fraser receptionist escorted Marcus to the boardroom. He tried to clear his mind and prepared himself to flatter the DiAngelos. It was a common ploy and he used it whenever he expected any resistance from a client. And he always got his own way. He prided himself on it. The Fraser executive would be no trouble. Perhaps the day wouldn't be a total loss.

He acknowledged the familiar form of Giuseppe DiAngelo with a handshake. Giuseppe's thick, broken English was worthy of a *Godfather capo*. He immediately turned toward the account executive and held out his hand.

Then he froze — but only for a second. Suddenly he couldn't breathe. The air was gone. No it wasn't. He'd just forgotten to inhale. And it was hot. So hot he could feel the blood pounding against his temples. He was breathing again but it was hard. It was always hard when your heart was slamming against your chest, trying to break free.

He smiled at her. He shook her hand. He took in the suit, the sensible shoes and the prim topknot of hair. He looked past the plainness, right through the glasses and into Ashly's panic stricken face. His Ashly. At last, he'd found her.

He fought for control and smiled politely. "Pleased to meet you, Miss, ah …"

"F-Fraser. A-Ashly, er, Ashlyn. Ashlyn Fraser."

Her voice was barely a whisper. A slight tremor rocked the hand that took his. He stared down at their clasped hands and felt her tugging from his grasp. He leaned toward her, out of Giuseppe's earshot and whispered, "You left the ball a little early, Cinderella. I have something that fits you." Then, louder, "but *you* Miss Fraser, can call me *Marc*."

The next hour was sheer hell on Earth for Ashlyn. She sat across the boardroom table from Marc, her knees clenched tightly together, her toes curled and sweating inside her flat shoes. The realization of what she had done refused to settle in. Had she really gone to bed with the infamous Marcus Remmington? Could there be two Marcs with the same silvery eyes and seductive smile? Could Marcus Remmington, the arrogant, smirking womanizer, be the same Marc that seduced her into her own wanton split personality?

She concentrated on the wall just above the men's heads, never looking directly at them when she spoke. Her gaze shifted from one side of the room to the other. She talked down at the layout on the table, to the presentation easel, but never once did she raise her eyes to meet Marc's.

Marc, on the other hand, delighted in distracting her. He whistled through his teeth, drummed his fingers on the table, coughed and cleared his throat until Ashlyn was sure he was having some kind of an attack. Through all of the distractions, his eyes never left her.

She summoned all her will to remain professional. Perhaps her indifference would convince him that he wasn't seeing Ashly, that he'd made a mistake. Later she could take him aside and explain that she was often mistaken for other people. She even thought of dropping a slutty twin sister into the picture. Anything, so long as she didn't have to admit to being the wanton creature Marc so hastily seduced in his studio.

Giuseppe was saying something to her. "Excuse me? I'm sorry, would you mind repeating that, *Señor* DiAngelo? Yolande? No, I don't think she's the proper spokesperson for *Insatiable*. Besides, I believe she's contracted to Bedsong." Ashlyn silently applauded her recovery. But it was short lived.Marc snapped open his briefcase and drew out several photos; black and white head shots of assorted models he probably worked with from time to time.

"I believe *Insatiable* deserves a new, fresh face, not some over-exposed glamour girl whose face is in every current magazine, ad nauseam." He paused and stared pointedly at her, his silvery eyes twinkling. "I have another model in mind for the shoot. A new girl, very beautiful, very talented."

"Really?" Ashlyn answered, but heard the word as if it was spoken through a dream.

"Oh, yes," Marc gave an exaggerated nod of approval to Giuseppe. "Trust me, *Señor* DiAngelo, she's perfect."

Ashlyn felt her mouth go dry and swore the pounding of her heart could be heard by everyone around the table. She held her breath while Marc sorted through his pile of photographs. He took the very last photo and pushed it toward Giuseppe. A flash of fire-engine red silk and the spill of mink and gold curls proclaimed her nightmare officially underway.

"There's your girl," Marc announced.

Ashlyn didn't have to look at the photo to know who Giuseppe was ogling. She kept her head lowered and toyed with the frames of her glasses. From the corner of her eye she caught a glimpse of her reflection in the chrome-plated water jug in front of her. Her cheeks were flushed scarlet, her lips drained of color. Through a haze she heard Giuseppe murmuring, *"bella, mille bella"*.

"Now, she's *Insatiable*. Don't you think so, Miss Fraser?" His voice was light and deliberately mocking.

Ashlyn looked up to find Marc's gaze leveled at her. She fought the urge to bolt. Quickly, she recovered herself. "Personally, I find the exploitation of women to be demeaning and bordering on sexual harassment." There, she'd said it. Duncan be damned. And as soon as she'd said it she knew it was the wrong thing to say in front of Giuseppe

DiAngelo. She met his disapproving scowl and tried to explain. "Wh ... what I mean is, your advertising budget will go a lot further if we don't have to pay an inflated agency fee for a model. I've heard rumors for months that heroin is ravaging the modeling industry. Do you really want to take that chance? Couldn't we just use the floral garden sequence? We don't have to pay flowers to pose or spend endless hours retouching make-up."

Marc clasped his hands behind his head and leaned back in the swivel chair. He idly swayed back and forth drawing out an ear-itching squeak. He stared thoughtfully up at the ceiling. "If memory serves, Miss Fraser, didn't this agency have the True-Taste Banana account a couple of years ago?"

Damn his memory! Ashlyn knew what he was leading up to. Since it was useless to deny it, she nodded.

"And didn't someone here write that obscene banana-eating commercial?"

"For which we won a *Bessie* —" she defended.

"— and which was censored?" Marc lowered his gaze to Ashlyn's face. He raised his eyebrows in declaration of winning their game of one-upmanship.

"I want-a her." Giuseppe tapped his index finger sharply at what Ashlyn could see was her own partially exposed left breast. She fought the urge to cross her arms over her chest to protect herself. She could almost feel the pressure from Giuseppe's poking fingers.

Anger and tears welled up inside her and she fought them down. How dare Marcus Remmington display her body as if it were some table centerpiece. The man had no morals, no ethics. He'd betrayed their professional relationship and violated a personal trust. She would never forgive him.

"You give me this girl and I give you the account." Giuseppe's ultimatum left no room for argument.

She longed to snatch the picture from Giuseppe's hands, tear it up and order them both out. The responsibility of meeting next month's payroll stopped her. She could feel Marc's eyes on her as she weighed her decision. Finally, she relented. "I'll see what I can do, *Señor* DiAngelo. If this is the girl you really want ..." her voice trailed off. She knew she was beaten.

"Then I guess it's a done deal," Marc announced and shook hands with Giuseppe. He smiled sweetly at Ashlyn. "Miss Fraser."

Ashlyn glared at him but said nothing. Instead, she shook hands with Giuseppe and walked him to the door.

"*Ciao*, Miss Fraser and congratulations. *Insatiable* is yours."

Chapter 5

Once Giuseppe departed, a pregnant silence was all that remained. Marcus stared at Ashly's rigid back. The language of her stance was unmistakable. The defiant tilt of her head, the aggressive poise of her delicately curved shoulders as she thrust them back in a challenge to anyone who dare cross her, right down to the muscle play of her shapely calves as they flexed in readiness to either charge or retreat. Lady Ashly was ready to do battle — with him. Marcus steeled himself for the onslaught.

"You scum!" Her voice cracked through the air like a whip. "How dare you!"

She turned sharply and advanced on him, ever so slowly. Marcus swivelled the chair from side to side in a lazy rhythm and studied her as she continued to stalk him. The once golden hues of her eyes now burned a glittering shade of topaz. His cavalier attitude threatened to slip when he thought of what all that beautiful anger might become if positively channeled into the right kind of emotion, namely, passion.

For the moment, however, he knew he was caged with what might turn out to be a very dangerous animal. He should watch his step. She was ready to draw out his punishment and he eagerly awaited the confrontation. Yet, he wouldn't let her off the hook just yet. His ego was still smarting from her abandonment.

"Relax, babe. He didn't recognize you. I thought he might have for a moment when he first looked at the photo. He was simply a man being struck by a woman." Marcus shrugged his shoulders. "Happens every day."

"I don't know how you have the gall to sit there so casually and just throw my picture out for the entire world to see."

"It looks like the entire world will see it, if Giuseppe has anything to say about it. Would you like to see the rest?" he asked innocently.

"Give me my pictures and get out." Shaking, she pointed to the closed door.

"Not before I give you a business proposition."

"Screw your proposition. I could sue you, Marcus Remmington, and then where will your precious reputation be?"

"And I could pull out of the shoot and then where would your precious account be?" he mimicked.

The point settled on her, briefly. But she was far too angry to consider the consequences. And she thought Duncan had humiliated her. It was a love tap next to the blow Marcus Remmington dealt her. But before she threw him out on his butt, she'd make sure he knew exactly how she felt. "You think you're the only bloody photographer in this city?"

"I'm the only one who photographed you in the buff." There was a meaningful twinkle in his eye. Not a threat, not exactly. It sounded more like he wanted her to know the kind of ammunition he had at his disposal.

"You think this is some terrific joke, don't you. You could have ruined my career."

"Hey, don't look at me like that." He unclasped his hands from behind his head and leaned forward to unlock his briefcase. "Besides, I have something else that belongs to you." He bit his tongue to keep from grinning as he flipped up the top and removed Ashlyn's panties. "Here," he tossed them onto the table. "Your glass slipper, m'lady."

Ashlyn gasped, blushed, then lunged for her underwear. Before she could snatch back her panties, he grabbed them and held them up out of her reach. His large fingers kept a tight grip on the delicate lace trim as he teased her. "Not so fast."

"You — you ... b-bastard!" She sputtered, balancing on her toes and wildly grabbing at the prize he carelessly dangled just inches from her grasp.

"Uh, uh. Temper, temper, *Ashly*. Or should I call you, *Miss Fraser.* Miss Ashlyn Fraser, all straight and starchy like everyone else does around here."

"Stop it!"

"*Miss Fraser.* With her hair pinned up and her geeky glasses, looking like a refugee from some convent. Where's the mystery woman who walked into my studio? Where — Oh!"

He doubled over from the unexpected force of her punch to his unguarded middle. But even while clutching his stomach, he maintained his grip on her panties.

"Hell of a ... a right hook you ... you've got there," he managed between breaths.

"Just a man being struck by a woman," she replied smoothly.

Marcus seethed, not because of her retaliation but because she was right. He was lost the moment he walked in and saw her. He winced again. "Geez, I think you broke something."

"I hope so."

He regarded the smug satisfaction on her face and clutched his treasure even tighter.

"Give me my panties," she demanded, "or I'll hit you where I can do some real harm."

"Why?" He baited her but instinctively lowered his hands in front of his groin.

"Because they belong to me." The stubborn press of her lips told him she wasn't ready to give in.

"Why else," he demanded, eager to challenge her; determined to break through the wall she'd hastily erected since he first walked through the door. He saw a glimpse of the real Ashly. The woman who bewitched him in his studio was inside her somewhere. In her determination to recover her lingerie, her hair had slid out of its topknot. The top button of her blouse had come loose and dangled by a single thread. She was red from embarrassment and shaking from spent rage. She'd never looked more beautiful. At that moment Marcus would have sold his soul for a camera, even a cheap disposable. But somehow, he doubted if he would ever forget her like this.

He wanted her, all of her. Right here, right now. To hell with anyone else. But he also knew she'd never give in. So he decided to take the only piece he could get. He shoved his silk and lace trophy back into his briefcase. In one swift movement, he closed and locked it.

Ashly opened her mouth and started to swear at him again but stopped. She looked longingly at the closed briefcase and then back to Marcus. It was then he noticed the glistening betrayal behind her glasses.

"Please," she whispered. "Haven't you shamed me enough?" A solitary tear escaped from behind her dark, square frames and slid down her brightly colored cheek.

Oh God, Ashly. Please don't cry. Marcus reached out and wiped the tear away. He noticed more gathered at the rims of her eyelids like watery little soldiers, ready to assault his conscience. This was all his fault. A lump suddenly lodged in his throat and he tried to deny how it got there. He had a feeling he might be developing a sudden case of the guilts. His stomach churned, and not from the impact of her fist.

He found himself holding her hand. The touch of her petal-soft skin soothed his aching mid-section. The site of her lovely eyes, shimmering with tears, created a new and different kind of pain. He hadn't meant to hurt her; only tease her a little to get back at her for leaving him without a way to find her.

"Truce?"

A tiny nod of her head and he raised her hand and pressed a gentle kiss across her fingers. "I'm sorry, Ash — I ... Hey, what do you want me to call you anyway?"

She tilted her head to look at him, regarding him as if considering the question at great length. Finally she answered. "I'd like it if you'd call me Ashly."

Marcus answered her smile with his own. "Okay. Ashly it is. But only between the two of us, okay?" Confident he was back in her good graces, at least temporarily, he folded her into his embrace. He held her gently and she lay her head against his chest. After a few seconds, he tucked the loose strands of her hair back into its lopsided topknot. "There's something I've wanted to do since the moment I walked in here," he murmured.

"Me too," came her muffled reply.

"I mean besides take you here on the boardroom table," he teased.

She tried to struggle away from him but he held her fast. "I'm only kidding," he soothed and she settled back into his arms. He wasn't really kidding, but now that he'd found her, he decided to stick to a conservative strategy. No use scaring her off again. Still, that nice, flat boardroom table was awfully tempting. All they'd have to do was lock the door and privacy would be ensured. Then he'd lift her pretty little bottom onto the table and start kissing each of her stockings — or whatever she was wearing underneath — down her gorgeous legs. *Yeah!* Marcus smiled dreamily at the thought. He'd start at the top of her silky-smooth thighs, all white and pink. Stop and breathe in the tempting scent of her, maybe even plant a tantalizing kiss on her —

"Marc?"

... bite the little creases on the backs of her knees —

"Marc."

... raise her skirt, lay her down and —

"Marcus!"

He winced at the sharp poke to his mid-section. The subject of his fantasy was creating an annoying distraction. He became aware of her body, trapped between his own and the edge of the table. There was an alertness in her eyes and he obligingly nudged himself against her. Her soft gasp confirmed his discomfort. His body was definitely ready to indulge in the fantasy.

"You want me to let you go?" He barely recognized the edge in his voice; the kind of edge that comes with losing something valuable, finding it, only to risk losing it again. He chased the thought away by squeezing her possessively. A strained moan escaped her lips and he loosened his grip on her. But his mind branded her. *Mine, dammit.* He stopped the thought before it reached her ears but the feel of her body against him created an unmistakable sign. For the second time, he found he could not control his reactions. He couldn't summon the objectivity that came so easily with his job. He was used to being around women, stunningly beautiful women wearing less than nothing and sometimes nothing at all. They were business, nothing more. He had catalogues full of assorted feminine body parts. Yet none of them had the effect a fully clothed Ashly brought on. He'd felt himself go stiff as a flagpole the moment he laid eyes on her. It was unnerving and embarrassing, to say the least.

Tension and frustration fueled his erection. He stroked her with a hard, mock thrust. Instead of moving away from him, as he expected her to do, she parted her legs and invited him to settle between them. It was almost too much to bear. Marcus had a vision of coffee cups, pencils and file folders flying off the table.

"Ashly?"

She shook her head mutely and surprised him by hopping up on the table and wrapping her legs around his hips. Spurred on by weeks of unspent desire, he was unable to resist her invitation. He kissed her hard and deep, savoring the taste and feel of her. A groan of satisfaction rumbled from somewhere deep in his throat. The moment his lips touched hers, he knew it hadn't been a fluke. Lightning had struck — again.

The scent and soft heat of her flooded his senses. Her pictures just weren't enough, would never be enough. He had to have her, all of her. His lips became more urgent, more demanding. He explored her body, his lips and hands claiming new yet familiar territory. Her soft moans drove him on. He ground his pelvis into hers, creating a torrid, raging fire in his crotch.

"Ashly, my love. My sweet, sweet, love." He lifted his lips from hers and was pleasantly surprised when she combed her fingers through his hair, directing his face back to her. Her instincts had kicked in. She wanted more. "We have to stop this now," he warned, "or I might not be able to."

"I don't want to," she confessed between kisses.

And she didn't, she realized. Somewhere between losing her temper and losing her dignity she had also lost control. Marc! Marc! her heart sang. He hadn't forgotten her. He carried her in his memory. He carried her pictures with him. Hell, he carried her underwear.

She couldn't recall exactly when her glasses found their way off her face but she knew Marc meant business when he carefully placed them out of harm's way. The last thing they needed was one of them rolling on top of her glasses and breaking the lenses.

"Just a moment, darling," he whispered and his blurred figure darted across the room for a moment. She was about to question him when she heard the sharp click of the deadbolt lock. He was back before the heat of his body left her fevered skin. His thoughtfulness on all accounts amazed her.

There was no champagne-induced dullness for her senses to hide behind this time. And her senses were raging, along with her hormones.

The feel of Marc's warm hands fondling her buttocks was to die for. She ached for him to touch her everywhere, just as she was touching him. Suddenly, their clothing became an annoying barrier.

Ashlyn was determined not to let that stop her. She nipped at his lower lip, buried her mouth in the sensitive skin along his neck. His face was rough and stubbly from the day's growth but she welcomed the feel of it scraping her cheek, ached for the same chafing sensation between her thighs. Her mind raced ahead of the game and she imagined his face buried in her mound and kissing her where no man ever had. In a sexual frenzy, she covered his lips, teased open his mouth and treated them both to a deep, soulful kiss. Their tongues danced and lapped at each other. Suddenly she knew where she wanted his mouth. He had crept into her dreams these last weeks. She reveled in the visions of his dark head buried between her thighs, his magic tongue easing the tension, only to awake, finding herself alone and frustrated. This was one time she wouldn't leave frustrated.

She broke the kiss, eager to share her desire with him. "I want you to kiss me," she whispered. "Everywhere … I want you to touch me," she breathed and snuggled into the heat of his embrace. "Touch me in all the secret places I've dreamed of sharing with you."

Marc answered her demand with a throaty growl. "Anything else m'lady wishes?" he asked, giving her a hard nip beneath her earlobe.

"Oh, yes," she sighed, shivering from the electric chills shooting down her neck and pooling deep in the pit of her abdomen. Dare she expose her fantasies to him along with everything else? Her body made the decision for her as Marc's fingers contacted with the front of her blouse and fondled her silk-covered breasts. She gasped sharply, suddenly, and pressed herself into the waiting palms of his hands. She felt the momentary tug of buttons releasing, the rush of cool air against her heated skin, then new waves of acute sensations as Marc slid a hand inside her bra. He gave each breast an intimate caress, pausing to fondle the ridges of each taut peak, before expertly releasing the front clasp of her bra.

"Do you approve?" he murmured before kissing her again.

Approve of his possessive touch as his fingers roamed freely over her naked skin, or the hard press of his groin against her tender inner thighs? Ashlyn couldn't think to answer him. Somehow, she knew she didn't have to. Her body was doing all the talking.

He shifted his weight and leaned into her. The hard surface of the boardroom table groaned beneath her bottom. She rubbed her stockinged feet up and down the back of his thighs. From her position on the table, she couldn't do much more. Certainly, she couldn't do what she wanted which was to dig the balls of her heels into his hard, muscled buttocks. A moment later, she got her wish.

She found herself lying flat on her back on the table, blouse open to the waist, bra loosened and pushed to one side. Marc all but climbed on top of her then and buried his lips into the hollow of her neck before making his way to the valley between her breasts. He captured each swollen tip between his lips, nuzzling and sucking each in turn. Waves of pleasure cascaded over her and she wrapped her legs around his hips, firmly planting her feet across his backside.

Ashlyn coiled her fingers tightly in the long, soft hair shielding his face from her. Sometime during the seductive frenzy, his pony-tail slipped out of the leather thong which had so sleekly secured it. Now it hung in wild tangles across her skin, brushing and teasing her as much as his hands and mouth were. He reminded her of a lusty barbarian; saying little but demanding all. All is what she would give. She knew he would take no less. She lifted her hips slightly off the table and pressed herself against him.

Marc looked at her. In spite of his fever-laden eyes, he asked her, "Are you sure, Ashly? Once you say 'yes' there's no going back. I won't stop, even if you beg me." There was something hypnotic in that dark, hooded gaze, something that didn't allow her to hesitate. No wonder he had gotten his way with her so easily that first night. Marc wove a tapestry of sex magic around women. She was no different.

Even before she had a chance to reconsider, he stripped her panty hose off her legs. And she helped him. What's more, her hands were fumbling with his belt buckle, deliberately passing over the bulge which protruded at an angle from his zipper. Ashlyn hated things that were out of place. She followed her compulsive behavior by tugging down the metal zipper of his pants and reaching inside to grasp his sex through his briefs and lay it flat against his belly. She heard Marc gasp, saw his eyes widen and felt the pulse of his rod quicken at her touch.

"Oh, God! Baby, touch me. Reach inside and put your hands around me. I want to feel you. I've waited so long for you. Don't torture me."

Ashlyn found herself grinning wickedly at his demands. For all that he'd put her through today, she now had him eating out of her hand, begging for the slightest favor. She kneaded the hot length of him, feeling the girth increase slightly with each firm squeeze. How much larger would he get? The tip was already peeping over the top of his briefs. She released him then in favor of grabbing another handful of his hair and urged him to kiss her again. Naked skin met naked skin as Ashlyn felt the round, velvety tip of his rod sear her stomach. A tiny drop of fluid dripped onto her belly, then Marc thrust against her. All the while he breathed love words, sex words, into her ear.

"I'm going to bury it deep in you. Flood you when I come. Brand you forever, like you've branded me. You've cast a spell on me, little witch. I'll never let you go. The way you smell. The way you taste. The way you feel, especially the way you feel."

Through his heavy breaths that mingled with her own, she was vaguely aware of his hands gripping her bare buttocks. She didn't remember taking off her panties, couldn't recall how her skirt had bunched up around her waist. It didn't matter. Nothing mattered but the feel of his fingers slide between her thighs and dip into the well of her sex. Wetness oozed around his fingertips and he rimmed her outer lips with her own moisture.

Marc carefully positioned his cock at her entrance, kissed her once, roughly, and quickly thrust into her. The jolt hit them both. Marc arched his back and gasped suddenly like a swimmer breaking the water's surface after staying under too long. Ashlyn raised her legs higher until her knees bumped his elbows. Full penetration caught her off guard. He was hard and hot and the engorged tip rubbed deep inside her. The friction brought her pleasure unlike anything she had ever experienced, including the night in Marc's studio.

Now she was completely sober, her body alive and absorbing every ounce of passion, every nuance, every raw and primitive urge that Marc awakened inside her. She couldn't lay still. Her inner muscles milked him. She ground her pelvis into his. She raked furrows across his ass with her fingernails. She raised herself off the table to bury her face in his chest, bite the corded muscles in his shoulders and suckle his flat nipples. She felt a demon being unleashed inside of her. The dark side was free at last and she recognized something of the woman she'd discovered in Marc's studio. Wild, untamed, a sexual predator.

Marc thrust against her womb, forcing himself deep inside her. With a sudden toss of his head, he reared up, gritted his teeth and let out a strangled gasp. He shuddered in a series of sudden convulsions. Hot semen flooded against the walls of her womb. Hard and fast, it was over for him. A moment later, he collapsed on top of her.

An eternity passed before she heard him whisper an apology. "I'm sorry," he mumbled against her neck. "You were just too much. Too tight, too hot, too wonderful to bear. Next time I'll wait for you." He moved to one side to adjust his weight on top of her. Ashlyn started to sit up.

"Damn! My purse is in my office. I think there's a hand towel in the coffee cart." She climbed down off the table, trying not to notice how wobbly her legs felt and avoiding the large gilt mirror at the far end of the room. She picked up her panties and hosiery on her way to the wheeled cart. She opened the lower doors and breathed a sigh of relief. Thank goodness, Marie had filled the cart up before the meeting. She pressed the small terry-cloth towel between her legs and began to repair the damage.

Behind her came the sound of Marc smoothing his own rumpled clothing, the muffle of cotton settling over his body, the metal rush of a refastened zipper. She pulled the remaining pins from her hair, shook out her tangled mane and reshaped the mass into the prim knot she'd started out wearing. What other signs would give her away? She cast a sidelong glance into the mirror and was horrified. Her clothes were a mass of wrinkles, her cheeks flushed and her skin red in spots, bearing the imprint of Marc's teeth.

She wiped a trace of lipstick from her chin and stopped. She raised the palms of her hands to her nose and sniffed. Fragrance of a man clung to her; a lingering whiff of male cologne, the tangy odor of expensive shampoo, the musky scent of enraged sex hormones. The potent mix had permeated her clothes and mingled with her own warmth. A sinful smile stole across her lips as she realized she would carry the scent of him around with her the rest of the day. What would her co-workers think when she left the boardroom, clothing rumpled, hair disheveled, and smelling like Marc's aftershave? On second thought, they'd probably applaud.

Marc put his arms around her. She shivered at the sound of his voice next to her ear.

"I woke up and you were gone. That's never happened to me before," he confessed as he kissed a trail between her earlobe and the nape of her neck. "I was a little put out. I wanted to find you, to find out what I did to scare you off. I thought everything was fine. I," he paused and tilted her head up so he could look at her. "I felt good with you. Things felt … right," he explained.

Ashlyn knew exactly how he felt. They had bonded. The magical force that had found so many of her happily attached friends was suddenly revealed to her in all its splendor. She was a member of the club, part of an ancient society of women who had been both hunter and hunted — often by choice. A primitive longing unleashed itself inside of her. She knew what it was like to be in lust with a man. The awkward experiences of her teen years were clinical, at best. Certainly Greg's sloppy, tongue-twisted attempts never unleashed a raging torrent of desire. When Marc kissed her, the jolt was enough to blow the toes out of her sensible shoes. Was she actually falling in love with him?

The idea frightened and excited her, although neither one had yet to speak the word. Maybe that came later. Right now, she didn't care. Marc brought so many new ideas to tempt her away from her safe, comfortable life. And oh, how he tempted!

"It felt right for me too … after a while. Things just happened so fast. I've never done anything like that before," she murmured lazily, still savoring the thrill of his kisses.

"What," he chuckled. "Fallen asleep on a man's couch?"

Ashlyn opened her eyes and looked up at him. "No, I. — I …" She lowered her eyes and grinned sheepishly. "I mean going to bed with a man on the first date."

Marcus stopped stroking her hair. He looked down into Ashlyn's face. There was no sign of the usual coy tricks or mock innocence. She was dead serious. Her flushed cheeks were all the proof he needed. The realization of what she insinuated hit him like a sledgehammer. No wonder she came at him spitting like a wildcat. She thought he'd taken advantage of her after she passed out. If it had been any other woman in his past, he might have laughed at the situation. Did she really think he was low enough to resort to something like that? He must have made some first impression. Not only his pride was damaged but his integrity as well. He let her go and stood back.

"I know it must have seemed like it was the kind of thing I do all the time," she continued, "but with the wine and everything, I guess I got carried away."

Marcus digested her words. *It. Thing.* Like what they almost shared wasn't worth labeling properly. She considered their aborted lovemaking a trivial experience; an experiment perhaps. He had given those kinds of lessons countless times and to pupils more willing and with far more experience. What kind of euphemism would she use to describe what just happened between them? How would she excuse it this time?

"Happy to be of service," he snapped.

Ashly's smile died. Her expression clouded and her eyes mirrored the hurt in his own soul. But at the moment, he didn't care. After all, why should she be upset? Wasn't she the one who left him?

"You *do* think I do this all the time," she accused. She pushed him away and stalked across the room. She bent down, retrieved a shoe from under the table and jammed it on her foot. Marc fervently hoped she would calm down before leaving the room. She probably didn't realize her panty hose were strung around her neck, or that her skirt was twisted around backwards. He stepped closer to help her but she froze him with an icy glare.

"What did you think to accomplish by seducing me, Marc? A docile executive who won't cramp your style on the set? Or is it …" she paused then, the anger on her face dissipating into hard realization. Marcus felt a knot growing in his stomach. He knew what was coming, knew what she supposed to be the awful truth. The problem was, she was half right.

"You want *her. Ashly.* You need *her* for this job."

"No! You're wrong. That's not what happened here. Ash —"

"You can't have her. She doesn't exist!" Ashly spat her denial at him, almost challenging him to prove her wrong. His own anger took up the cause.

"Oh Ashly does exist. Maybe not all the time. But she's here. She's hiding behind some spoiled little rich girl who lets her father walk all over her. The real Ashly would have the guts to defend herself and take control like she did in my studio and even now." He stopped and slammed his fist on the table, on the very spot which still bore the damp evidence of their lovemaking. "Unless she only comes out after drunken birthday parties and behind locked doors."

Marcus braced himself for the slap that never came. The silence in the room was louder than any of Yolande's projectile tantrums. He watched Ashly raise herself to her full height. With as much dignity as she could muster, she straightened her glasses, buttoned her blouse and swept back a loose tendril of hair. The purring kitten he held in his arms a moment ago became a spitting tiger. Dammit all anyway, he'd done it again.

Ashlyn glared at him and pressed her love-swollen lips into a thin line. She took a long, slow deep breath and exhaled sharply, expelling the remains of her earlier mood. Her mind worked quickly, searching for some way to show him that she wasn't ready to be used and then tossed aside. She'd had enough male browbeating for one day.

Whether he knew it or not, Marc had just become the cause of an impulsive decision, the second one in her life since she'd met him. He was becoming a bad habit, one she intended to break immediately. She thought of the flurry of consequences she would have to endure because of that decision. *Well screw the consequences!*

She could land the *Insatiable* account without the help of Marcus Remmington. She could find another photographer for the shoot, one who wouldn't try to blackmail her out of her clothes. *I'll get Brian,* she thought quickly. Her own brother was struggling to make a name for himself, why not give him the opportunity? She wouldn't tell Duncan. Let Dad see for himself that Brian had talent. It might even help mend the rift between them. And all without having to endure Marc or the emotional head games that went with him. She could direct the shoot herself and use her own ideas. Of course Duncan would blow a gasket, but he'd get over it. After all, the man had been married four times. It wouldn't be the first time a woman had disappointed him.

Satisfied she had made the right decision, she turned her attention back to Marc who stood beside the chair he had occupied during their meeting. He was a mask of closed emotion as he rifled through his briefcase. His scowling features had eradicated any trace of the passion that filled his eyes only moments before. So much the better. It would make her next task easier to accomplish. She leveled her gaze at him. She thought her voice sounded oddly flat and unemotionally cool as she heard herself say the words.

"You're fired."

Chapter 6

"I can't do this." Ashlyn repeated the phrase over and over again. Even as she sat in Vlad's make-up chair in the portable on-site dressing room, her mind reeled at the idea.

Her world was in turmoil, her plans crushed. How was she to know that Brian was out of town and couldn't be reached? And Marcus hadn't been feeding her a line. She turned the city upside down looking for a reputable commercial photographer, but she couldn't get anyone to fill in on such short notice. Duncan hounded her as the deadline for a draft ad loomed like a threatening, black cloud. At the eleventh hour, when the storm threatened to burst over her head, she had no model, no photographer and no hope of finding a replacement for either one. In the end, she was forced to admit that Marcus was right and that *Ashly* remained her only hope. But even when she'd fired Marcus, she'd known she couldn't model for anyone else.

Daagmar sat across from her, nodding her head each time Vlad asked for approval, although she never took her eyes off the raspberry-colored negligee she was hurriedly altering.

"What's taking so frigging long?" Marcus bellowed from outside the trailer. "If you don't hurry up, I'll miss the sunrise. The day will be shot!"

"I wish someone would shoot him," mumbled Daagmar as she held the cloth up to her mouth and severed a loose thread with her teeth.

"Get in line," Ashlyn murmured as Vlad applied another coat of fresh lipstick. She checked her watch and tried not to yawn. She had been up since three thirty this morning. "The sun won't be up for another hour, what's he worried about?"

"He worries about everything," Vlad snapped. "Now hold still, I have to proportion this blush properly, or Marcus will have a bug up his ass about that, too."

"There." Daagmar stood up and shook out the garment. "I'll just give this a quick press and we'll be ready to go."

A moment later, Daagmar and Vlad eased the gown over Ashlyn's carefully arranged hair. Ashlyn felt shy and embarrassed with

Daagmar's intimate fondling as the woman arranged the gown around Ashlyn's body. But Daagmar was all business when she reached between Ashlyn's cleavage and adjusted her breasts. "Perfect," she announced.

Ashlyn turned toward the full-length mirror and gasped in horror. Her breasts spilled over the top and sides of the slender garment like water over Niagara Falls. The front of the gown was cut clear to her navel and the skirt was slit so high up the centre, Ashlyn could see the dark shadow of her own pubic hair. To make matters worse, the bodice of the gown was fitted with a sheer lace fabric while the rest was nothing more than a hint of translucent chiffon which left nothing to the imagination. Ashlyn would have felt more covered in a band-aid.

She saw her cheeks flame bright red with shame as she tried to cover herself by crossing her arms over her chest. "I can't go outside like this, I'll freeze. Besides, people will see me. Oh, he can't be serious."

Vlad and Daagmar circled around her like a pair of vultures, poking at this, re-arranging that. "Come now, darling. Try and relax. I'll fix you a double cappuccino supreme if you promise to sip it through a straw. Marcus has photographed hundreds of girls wearing a lot less in front of a lot more people. Ingenues," Vlad clucked and reached for a small lip brush. "I swear they'll be the death of me."

At least Daagmar was sympathetic to her plight. "Here," she tossed Ashlyn a full length chenille bathrobe. "Put this on. At least you can keep warm until the absolute last second Marcus needs the shot."

Ashlyn gratefully accepted the robe and wrapped it around her, securing it with the matching belt. Her skin warmed instantly and she relaxed a little. At least now she could go outside. She left the trailer, careful not to trip over the bathrobe as she descended the narrow metal stairs. A faint glow started to appear on the horizon, adding a soft blue tint to the black sky. The stars were beginning to fade and the quarter moon looked pale and soft in the October sky.

"Okay. Positions, people." Marc shouted instructions and orders to the set assistants. Ashlyn took in all the paraphernalia. Between the spot lights, flash umbrellas and tinted screens, she wondered why Marc didn't simply wait for more daylight.

Then he appeared behind her. "What the hell is this?" he barked and tugged at the belt holding her bathrobe.

Ashlyn turned and faced his disapproving frown. A shock of black hair spilled idly across his forehead. He looked more like a petulant schoolboy than a professional photographer. "Daagmar said I should stay warm until you were ready."

Marc planted his hands on his hips. "Well, I'm ready. Off with it. Now."

Ashlyn's anxiety returned at the thought of losing her shield. "I won't.

I can't," she cried and then lowered her voice. "At least let me put a pair of panties on."

"Nope. No underwear. It will spoil the silhouette. I don't want a lot of nasty lines I'll have to brush out later. Now get up on that rock and look longingly into the sunrise."

But Ashlyn was determined to argue the point. "I don't get it. I thought the layouts called for upper torso only. The DiAngelos' approved the mock-ups. Nothing was said about a full body layout."

As she spoke, she could see Marc was losing his patience. His frown deepened to a scowl and his brows knitted together in obvious irritation. It was on the tip of her tongue to tell him to go straight to hell and cancel everything.

As if he read her thoughts, he leaned and whispered harshly in her ear. "Behave yourself, darling. We have a bargain, remember?"

She remembered.

"Oh, all right," she grumbled and gave the belt an angry tug. Marc took a half-step forward to help her but she skirted around him and yanked off the bathrobe. She let it lay where it fell to the ground in a fluffy puddle. She turned and stalked over to the outcropping of rock.

Instantly, Marcus felt his mood change from irritation to admiration. He couldn't imagine getting through this without the old Ashly coming to life and sparring with him.

The location he'd chosen was in a northern provincial park, now closed for the season until the following spring. Featuring several rocky outcroppings and sand dunes, it simulated a desert.

The park was fairly remote and deserted this time of year. It was miles to the nearest comfortable accommodation and Marcus had chosen it just for that reason. He planned to stay out here for a few days and try to mix a little pleasure with business, no matter what Ashly said.

And she had said a lot the night she phoned him, humbled and desperate. Perhaps that's why he'd given in so easily. That, and the fact that he knew she didn't have any other choice, no matter how hard she tried to disguise her motives.

"I have some good news for you, Mr. Remmington," her voice on the phone that night sounded cool and condescending. "I've decided to re-hire you to shoot the *Insatiable* campaign."

Marcus bit his tongue to keep from laughing and played along. "That's very generous of you, *Miss Fraser*."

"Generosity has nothing to do with it. I'm only interested in what's best for my client."

"Then your client is going to be disappointed." Marcus counted the seconds before she answered.

"I — I'm afraid I don't understand. The DiAngelos said they … I mean, Giuseppe is expecting you ..." Her voice faded and Marcus picked up the erratic change in her tone. It was time to bait his hook.

"Look, Ashly. I know you're in a spot. It's a busy time of year for commercial shoots. Anyone worth their weight in film is already booked up. So why don't you just come out and admit that you need me."

Just as much as I need you. But Marcus bided his time. Her rejection in the Fraser boardroom still stung and he was sure that she knew nothing of the follow-up phone calls he'd received from Duncan himself. That rankled Marcus more than anything. He'd stood in the reception area while he waited for the elevator and tried to reconcile what had just happened between them. His feelings were raw, his emotions high. He was elated and excited beyond belief one minute, angry and vengeful the next. Only a special kind of woman could do that to him. And she was special. But why didn't she believe in herself? Why didn't anyone else?

The answer, of course, was right in front of him.

Although Ashly's tempestuous decision to fire him stung his ego, he couldn't help remembering the way her father all but humiliated her in the boardroom. Duncan didn't treat her like an employee, much less a daughter. It bothered Marcus that Duncan didn't recognize Ashly's talent and intelligence. Ashly had a vision of where she thought the company should go, and it was a good one. Why then did Duncan snub the very woman who could be the key to the company's success? The answer had come in the form of an annoying giggle.

Marcus had turned around to the site of white-haired Duncan Fraser fondling that little piece of tender tail he married. Marcus frowned and shook his head. He quickly stepped into the open elevator door, eager to be out of Duncan's domain. The scene still left a bad taste in his mouth. He'd hoped to God he wouldn't be like that in twenty years.

Why Ashly allowed Duncan to treat her that way was beyond his thinking. He would have given the old man the kiss off long ago and wondered why Ashly hadn't. His thoughts were still with Ashly when the elevator doors slid open and he stepped forward without looking to see if the way was clear. It was then that he ran smack into Miss Tate, to whom he apologized and offered to buy her a coffee. When he realized she was *that* Miss Tate, the best friend who made the original appointment for Ashly, the opportunity to gain some insight into Ashly was too powerful to ignore, so he joined her.

What he learned about Ashlyn Fraser not only surprised him but made him realize that she'd been telling the truth when she believed she had slept with him. He also learned that Fraser & Associates was in dire straights and the fate of the company hung on Ashly's next move with *Insatiable*. When Marcus got home later that day, he had already made up his mind to call her.

But she had beaten him to it. He could barely control the fluttering in his gut when he'd picked up the phone and heard her panicked voice. She came right to the point.

"If you want me to stroke your ego, then fine. Whatever. You artist types are eccentric, so you better tell me in advance what buttons you want me to push."

Marcus laughed softly into the receiver. "In the first place, Ash," he emphasized her name to gain her full attention. "It's not my ego that needs stroking. Secondly, you don't have to push my buttons. It's enough that you've swallowed your pride and called me. I know you're the kind that doesn't swallow." He let the innuendo hang in the air. He expected some kind of terse dressing down, but it never came. She must be doing one hell of a job of holding on to her temper, he thought admirably.

"Then tell me what I have to do to get you back." Her voice sounded sincere and contrite, almost desperate. It was the closest he could expect to an apology, he supposed. But he couldn't afford to lose his chance to bargain with her. He tumbled carelessly onto his bed, rolling onto his back and letting the cordless phone rest lazily against his ear. He sighed loudly into the receiver, knowing he held all the cards.

"This is really going to put a crimp in my schedule. Let's see," he paused and grabbed a newspaper and rattled it noisily. His gaze momentarily fell on one of his favorite color photos of Ashly smiling back at him from behind the glass of a pewter frame. "I could fit you in here … no, no wait. I have something tentatively planned. Hmm. Here? Nope. I'd have to change an appointment —"

"Marcus!"

He ignored her impatient retort and the soft curse that came after it. "I think I can squeeze you in …"

"Next week, Marcus. I'm on a deadline and you know it."

"Next week sounds fine. Does that suit your schedule, Miss Fraser? Think you can squeeze a big guy like me into your tight, little deadline?" Marcus grinned and was sure the phone line was burning in her ear. He'd almost bet if he looked out his front window, he could see the sky reddening in her part of town.

"Fine," she snapped.

"One condition, honey."

"I suppose you want me to sleep with you again."

Marcus grinned from ear to ear, nodded furiously and patted a pillow beside him. His better judgement held him in check. "Aw, gee. Thanks. But if we're going to make the deadline then we won't have time for that sort of thing. I was thinking of something more along the lines of some extra photos. You see, Ash, making room for you will mess up my plans for a very important exhibition near Christmas. In order to accommodate you, I'll have to cancel the sessions I had planned with my models. I'm afraid you'll just have to fill in for them."

This time there was serious silence over the phone. Marcus assumed she was thinking over the proposition. He was willing to let her off the hook if she said no and he would have bet his contract that she would. But once again, she surprised him.

"Fine."

Marcus jumped on her answer. "You mean it, Ashly? No backing out. It's a deal?"

"Deal."

It was the last word he spoke to her until this morning. Their offices traded faxes and contracts and the result was that both of them were here in Sandy Beach Park, with the late Autumn frost covering more than the grass. They hadn't said a civil word to each other. Having Daagmar alter Ashly's gown to his specifications was just the beginning of what Marcus hoped would be an interesting day.

The sun was high in the sky before Marc ordered a break. It was only ten o'clock and already Ashlyn was trembling with fatigue. The temperature was a balmy 45 degrees and she was sure her butt was frozen as hard as the uncomfortable rock he ordered her to lay on. So much for her preconceived notions about the glamour and excitement of modeling. Back in the dressing room trailer, she huddled inside the bathrobe trying to warm her freezing fingers around the cup of cappuccino Vlad had promised her hours ago. Daagmar sat across from her, readying another skimpy costume. Her face mirrored Ashlyn's thoughts.

"This is ridiculous," Daagmar muttered. "You really will catch cold and die if he keeps this up. What's going on anyway? You both act like this is some kind of penance instead of a job. I thought you two had it big time for each other."

Ashlyn blew the steam off her drink before answering. "What we have is a love-hate relationship. We love to hate each other."

"Sounds more like you hate to love each other."

Ashlyn almost choked on her coffee. "I don't think so. Maybe in the beginning it was lust at first sight, but then I found out he was just a macho pig like my ex-fiance."

Daagmar eyed her, apparently unconvinced. "Uh-huh. That's why he's got your photograph on his night stand with your flashy greens staring him in the face twice a day. I think your brain froze out there. Why do you think you're here and not Yolande? When she found out Marcus was shooting *Insatiable* for the DiAngelos, she showed up at the studio crying, begging and pleading to work with him. Marcus threw her out on her surgically altered rear."

Ashlyn listened half-heartedly. "So, how do I know that he won't do the same thing to me someday? What'll happen when the next pretty face comes along?"

Daagmar finished sewing the last sequin on a pair of slippers. "I guess you'll have to stick around and find out, won't you?"

"No, thanks. I only have one heart to break and it's bruised enough already."

"Suit yourself. Just remember, while he's putting you and everybody else through pure hell, he's also going through hell himself. I know. I've watched him the last few weeks and this is more than just infatuation. I don't agree with the shabby way he's treated you today, but I do care that he's putting his own battered heart on the line. If he didn't care about you, Ashly, he would have thrown you to the dogs. Having you around is hard work for a man like Marcus, a man who is used to having his own way, used to being boss, not bossed. Here," she stopped and tossed a slipper in Ashlyn's direction. "Try this on and see how it fits."

Ashlyn shed the robe and stood in front of the mirror while Daagmar helped her change gowns. When they had finished, Daagmar yelled out the door that it was safe for Vlad to come in and touch up Ashlyn's hair and make-up.

"Before you go back out there, Ash, just remember one more thing. Marcus loves to push the envelope with people. You have to stick up for yourself. If you feel he's getting on your nerves, and God knows he's getting on everyone's today, then give him a taste of his own medicine." She stood back and tugged at the gown's seams so that they fell in whispy layers over the curves of Ashlyn's hips.

"You've got power, girl. Use it." She winked slyly at Ashlyn, gathered up her sewing box and left the trailer.

Ashlyn stared at her reflection in the mirror and contemplated Daagmar's words. *You've got power.* She began to pace the trailer. What had she done that first night at the *Bedroom Eyes* studio to make him so anxious to take her photograph? Was it the wine? The music? The hot tub? Memories of that evening crowded into her mind in no particular order yet none of them spurred her consciousness. What she remembered most about that night was the way he talked to her, looked at her in that all too convincing way that made her want to please him. That was the magical ingredient and it was missing.

She heard the trailer door open and saw Vlad peek in to see if it was okay to enter. That was something else. They didn't have an audience that night. Maybe that's what bothered her the most. If she was going to conjure up "Ashly," it would have to be with far less prying eyes. She waved Vlad into the trailer. She caught sight of herself in the mirror once again, her brows firmly etched with the labour of her thoughts. Perhaps there was a way, after all.

She whirled around. "Vlad, when you finish with me, I want you to take Daagmar and those two harassed set people and disappear. Tell Daagmar I said it was okay. She'll understand."

A moment later she watched the foursome climb into Daagmar's station wagon. The doors were barely closed before the car disappeared in a cloud of sandy dust, leaving her alone with Marc.

Chapter 7

A sudden sound startled Marcus and he looked up from his camera in time to see his entire on-site crew speeding away.

"What the hell —"

He tossed the camera aside and ran after the car, yelling and waving his arms. When he reached the spot where the car had been, he found himself looking into a cloud of dust.

"Son of a bitch!" He yelled and kicked at the sand. It was then he spied Ashly, looking innocent, too innocent.

She shrugged. "Maybe they thought it was time for lunch."

Fists clenched in anger, he stalked over to where she stood.

"You put them up to this," he accused. "You … you …" He couldn't get the words out. He stood shaking his finger at her in impotent rage and mute frustration. His bottled emotions had been at the breaking point for hours. His excitement and energy at starting a new project; the sheer joy of seeing her again and above all, his burning desire for her, barely controllable but gnawing inside him. He couldn't wait for the day to be over. He hoped it would never end.

"Tsk, tsk. How unprofessional. I thought we were here to work, not to argue."

Marcus exploded. "How dare you talk about work. So far you've had all the enthusiasm of a snail. I could get more life out of a statue. You're supposed to be selling perfume. You couldn't sell lifeboats to the Titanic."

Through it all Ashly stood there, idly tracing a design in the sand with the toe of her slipper. "You know, you're handsome when you're angry."

He stared, open-mouthed, while she continued. "In the boardroom, remember? You said I was beautiful when I was angry. Well, so are you. Handsome, I mean."

He became aware of shock yielding to understanding. So, that's what this was all about. How could he have been so blind? Turnabout was truly fair play. Ashamed and unsure how to react, he stared down at the ground. His bottom lip twitched when he noticed that she had traced the shape of a heart in the sand, only this heart had a jagged line through it's middle. He scrubbed his hands through his hair and muttered, "They're still in my briefcase. I'll get them for you."

"Get what?" she questioned.

"Your panties. You're still mad because I embarrassed you in front of the DiAngelos and wouldn't give you back your panties. All this is my fault," he sighed. "If I hadn't been so eager to avenge your abandonment of me, we wouldn't even be here. How could I have been so … so …"

"Stupid?" she offered. "Pig-headed. Selfish. Shall I continue?"

Humbled, he stood there staring at her. Yes, he was all those things and more. What had started as a practical joke could cost Ashly her father's company. He'd only meant to tease her with the pictures but the strategy blew up in his face. He was as surprised as she was when Giuseppe DiAngelo decided she was the right girl to represent *Insatiable*. He'd never intended any of this to happen. Of course, he resented her firing him from the project and, for a while, it looked like he might even be out of a job. But then Duncan had gone behind Ashly's back and Marcus had been tactful enough not to mention the altercation.

Between that and witnessing the scene in the reception area with Duncan and his wife, he'd seen enough of Ashly's family to realize they were using her as a doormat. That was the last straw. She didn't deserve the way they treated her. She was smart and beautiful and dedicated. Then, when he learned how desperately she was working to hold her father's nearly bankrupt company together, he decided to help her any way he could. If only his wounded pride hadn't got in the way. Listening to her beg back his services broke his heart rather than soothed his ego. He knew she would die rather than admit she needed his help.

He wanted her to know just how much she had hurt him and decided that making her wear those ridiculous costumes would be just the ticket. Instead of humiliating her, he found it nearly impossible to control his desire for her. The part of him that always demanded control, the part he could always count on to be professional and impartial, had deserted him. *She* was in control, whether he liked it or not and that irked him.

Now he was alone with her. It was a situation he longed for and now feared. He wouldn't blame her now if she wanted to bury him alive in the sand. Hell, his head was as thick as the rock he had forced her to sit on for hours. How could he ever make it up to her?

Tell her how you feel. Tell her what's in your heart. Tell her you love her.

He took a breath, ready to reveal himself to her when her tiny voice quelled his courage.

"I would have said 'yes', you know."

Marcus stared in astonishment, unsure of what he heard. "You mean sleep with me?"

"That, too," she blushed and lowered her gaze.

Understanding phased him. "Oh, you mean the pictures."

"Duh! Yes, the pictures. I really resented being forced into them, but now that we're here we might as well do them. I suppose I really wanted a little more time for the idea to settle in. I'm not exactly a professional."

Marcus grinned at her choice of words and almost laughed at the face she made when she realized her mistake.

"Don't we have some work to do?" she snapped.

She turned her back to him and slithered out of the bathrobe. She left it lying in a heap in the sand, on top of the jagged heart. She practically strutted over to where he had changed the set, leaving him no choice but to follow. It was as if she had slipped an invisible leash around him. The thought of having her in control sent a thrill of excitement through him and he felt himself grow hard. His crew was gone at least for the remainder of the day. The trailer held all the comforts of home, including a bed. But first, they had work to do.

"Maybe the DiAngelos will like the pictures you took this morning. It may buy us a little time to get the gallery photos done," she said as she started to climb back up on the rock. Then she stopped. "Wait a minute." She jumped off the ladder, picked up the hem of the red satin negligee and ran through the sand over to where the unused equipment was sitting. She retrieved a portable CD stereo along with a handful of CD's and ran back to the rock. He watched her set the stereo down and ponder over which selection to play. Then she popped in a disc and turned the volume up loud.

The deserted set suddenly came alive with the sound of *Legs* by ZZ Top. Marcus watched her climb up the ladder, each foot taking a step in cadence, her bottom swaying to the rhythm of the music. Now she stood on the rock, towering some six feet above him. Her entire body started to move with the beat. She raised her arms up to the sky and threw back her head, totally destroying her carefully arranged hair. Then she whipped herself forward, bending at the waist and hung there limp. A second later, she reared up and kicked off her slippers.

Marcus watched, fascinated, as she undulated from side to side, teasing him, using the center slit to expose each of her slender legs in turn. He stood there, awstruck. Ashly, *his* Ashly had returned. He knew he should be taking pictures but his arms refused to move. Only one part of his body was seeing any action. It too, pulsed to its own beat.

"Well, don't just stand there. Take some pictures." When he didn't move, she danced to the edge of the rock and dropped down on all fours so her breasts could take the full force of gravity. The effect teased all of Marcus' senses and he staggered forward for a better look. It was then that Ashly changed the game completely. She shook her shoulders slightly and let the micro-thin satin straps slide down her arms. What little protection the lace cups offered slithered downward as she shed the straps, leaving her magnificently naked from the waist up. Her rosy nipples reacted to the cool air immediately and the areolas blushed a deep pink.

Marcus felt his mouth go dry. There was plenty of bottled water on the set but he knew only one thing could quench his thirst and that was to bury his face between her breasts and start licking.

She sat back on her heels and crossed her arms. "Well, I'm waiting. Better get to work before it gets too cold. Ashly might get bored and run away again."

Her threat spurred him into action. "No, you don't. Don't you ever go away again. Understand?" Instead of using the small step-ladder, he took a run, lunged at the side of the rock and scrambled up onto the flat surface where Ashly sat waiting.

"You forgot the camera." She sounded mildly annoyed.

He sat down and wrapped his arms around her. "Screw the camera," he growled softly before he kissed her. She responded immediately, opening her carefully painted lips so Marcus could deepen the kiss. She was an intoxicating mix of honey and silk. She affected him like one of the high-priced drugs he knew were abundant in Alexis' crowd, although he had never been tempted to alter his own reality. Nothing could compare to the high of holding Ashly's warm, soft body in his arms. This was the only reality that mattered to him.

He felt her slip a hand up the back of his neck and tug at the cord that held his neat pony-tail. With a sudden jerk, the black leather thong became part of the scenery. His hair fell forward in an unruly fashion but he hardly noticed. In fact, he barely felt Ashly grab a handful as she started to pull them down on the rock's flat surface. The stone felt warm from the sun and it occurred to Marcus that he had told one of the set assistants to spread a tan-colored blanket across the surface to shield out the glare from bright specks in the granite. He located the still folded blanket and quickly shook it out. Then he eased her down onto the blanket as if she was a precious, fragile treasure.

He kissed her again, letting his tongue slide through her generous, wet lips. He felt the contact of her smooth teeth and wondered if she would allow herself the luxury of experimenting in a bit of oral sex. He groaned into her mouth at the thought of the hard tips of her teeth grating up and down the length of his fully erect cock. He would, of course, return the favor.

As if his own fantasy had wandered into her thoughts, he felt her teeth gently close around his tongue. He allowed her to suck and stroke him before breaking off the kiss. When she protested, he reassured her.

"You know, there are ways of asking for something if you don't feel comfortable using the words. Am I correct in assuming you just asked?"

She looked away from him and nodded. Marc smiled and caressed her cheek, coaxing her back to him. "Look at me, Ash. I won't make jokes about this. Have you ever done this before?"

She shook her head, answering him in silence again.

"It's okay. If you don't want to, you don't have to. But if you do, I'll guide you through it. You can stop anytime you want. And," he trailed a finger across her forehead and down to the end of her nose. "I promise to reciprocate."

Her wicked smile returned and he kissed her again. "That's my girl. Care to help me off with these?" He started to unzip his jeans when she stopped him.

"I think I can manage this without any help."

And Marcus lay back, allowing her to finish undressing him. He only helped her by lifting his hips off the ground so she could slide his jeans down his legs. A cool breeze brushed his nearly naked body. It was cold! And to think he had put her through this and she'd performed with few complaints. Marcus was surprised he hadn't ended up with one of her slippers up his arse by now.

But then he felt her hands slip under the top of his white briefs and the chill he suffered dissolved into a slow-burning fire. He closed his eyes and gave himself up to the pleasure she created. And when her hands closed around his erect shaft, every muscle in his body sounded out a three-alarm blaze. Maybe he wouldn't make it through her first lesson.

"Now what?"

He opened his eyes to meet her questioning gaze. He licked his lips and swallowed before answering. "Sweetheart, this is oral sex. Just do what comes naturally."

Easy for him to say, thought Ashlyn. His organ throbbed between her palms and the full, round head made a wet stain against the white cotton. These, she decided, would have to go. As she did with the jeans, she slid the garment over his hips and down his legs.

Now he lay naked before her. His rigid organ sprang straight and proud from his groin. The tip was wet and shiny in the sun. Tiny blue and purple veins pulsed beneath the skin. Ashlyn began to wonder what that great pulsing member would feel like against her skin. She didn't run from the urge to taste him, to find out how he would react to her kiss.

She knelt down until she was face to face with his massive erection. Her mouth quivered with anticipation.

"Go ahead," he urged in a shaky voice. "Take me in your mouth."

She licked her lips and placed them gently over the smooth tip. She delighted in hearing Marcus gasp loudly. She placed her hands under his buttocks, fearful that he might pull away. She loved the muscular feel of his round butt and she dug her fingers into his flesh. They contracted under her touch and his penis pulsed double-quick in her mouth. She moved her tongue experimentally along the length of him, licking him slowly, exploring every rigid contour. The taste of him was slightly salty but not unpleasant.

She noticed how he especially liked it when she ran her tongue around the head. His breathing quickened, becoming almost ragged. His body trembled and his head thrashed from side to side. For a moment, Ashlyn thought he was in agony, that she had inadvertently nipped something that caused him pain. When she paused to question him, he pleaded with her.

"Don't stop. Oh, God. You don't know how good you feel."

Ashlyn giggled wickedly. "Not yet, but I will." She continued her ministrations, alternately licking the head and kissing his shaft. During this process it seemed to her that he actually grew larger. Soon she would have him deep inside her. A tremor passed through her and she responded by applying more pressure on him with her teeth. After a moment, he placed his hands on her cheeks and urged her off of him.

She looked up at him in question. "Just a precaution," he chuckled softly. "Don't want things to end too soon." She kissed the glistening tip one more time and impulsively buried her nose into the velvety soft sac where his balls hung. He smelled clean and musky and she took an intimate, womanly delight when the small globes swelled slightly when she nuzzled them.

"Do all men grin then when they get touched like that?"

"Just the ones in heaven, honey. Just the ones in heaven." A moment later he joined her on the blanket. He wrapped his arms around her, kissing her while easing her down to the blanket.

"My turn," he whispered.

Ashlyn was quick to understand when he kissed a trail down her neck, between her breasts and across her belly to the nest of soft, dark curls and the swollen outer lips just beneath. A cool breeze brushed the hood of her aroused clitoris where it peeked anxiously through the moist lips and she shivered. As if sensing her discomfort, Marcus bent his head into her lush thatch and nuzzled her mons. Low, growling sounds came from him and she soon joined in the music, free to cry out her pleasure in the security of their isolation.

And Marcus gave her a lot to cry about. What began as a hesitant, kittenish sigh soon gave way to an exotic howl of supreme delight. Her blood rushed faster, her heart pounded a fierce echo. It seemed that the harder she cried, the more effort he put into torturing her sex, as if he were taking vicarious pleasure in her heightened state. Ashly realized then that he was enjoying this as much as she was.

He nudged and teased her clit with his tongue. The sensation caused her belly to tighten and her toes to curl. He nipped and nuzzled the little bud until it swelled larger with anticipation. It was as if every sense, every nerve had flowed to that one tender little spot beneath her bush. At that moment, the man whose head was buried between her thighs owned her soul.

Yet he proved himself a considerate lover, plying her supple breasts as if it were possible to entice more pleasure from her already over-wrought body. He reached up with one arm and stroked each one in turn and tweaked the nipples as they hardened under his palm.

Ashlyn groaned out loud as his tongue dipped into her inner flesh while his other hand teased the entrance to her body. She gasped as one strong finger slipped into her. Her pelvis automatically tilted toward him as if it had a life of its own. Marcus was playing her like a fine instrument, strumming, stroking until he got the right pitch from her. Right now, her pitch was near a frenzy. She moaned softly and bit her lip.

"More," she begged.

Suddenly he stopped and eyed her thoughtfully. "More?" he questioned. "Are you sure?"

"Oh, yes. Yes!"

"Say, 'please', my hot little witch."

The delicate grasp she had on her control slipped dangerously. She was going over the edge. Fast. And she wanted to. She deserved to. For the first time, she let go.

"P-please. Please don't stop."

"That's what I want to hear," he soothed and kept his promise by slipping another finger deep inside her. He forced open her outer lips once again and nibbled in earnest. His tongue flicked over the sensitive bud again and again. Each pass drew a ragged groan from her. Pressure built.

Her whole body writhed uncontrollably. Arching her back, she tilted her pelvis up and offered him a sexual feast. He noisily devoured her, making low slurping and sucking sounds deep in his throat. He was a many-tongued fire licking flames of need throughout her body. She heard her own voice, shrill and demanding as she begged for more. Seconds later, the pressure broke and a blissful release flooded her. She cried out his name over and over again.

Minutes later she became aware of his dark head resting across her belly. With shaky fingers, she reached down to play with the silky strands of his hair. He turned his face toward her and nuzzled her hand with his chin, then proceeded to gently suck each one of her fingers.

"Ouch!" she cried when he bit a little too hard on her thumb. She gave him a playful swat.

"I think you should change your name from Miss Fraser to Miss Roman Candle," he teased.

Ashlyn laughed nervously. "More like Miss Nuclear Explosion. What the hell was that, anyway?"

Marc rolled over on his stomach, inched up beside her and kissed her. "I believe *that* was an orgasm." He stroked her hair lovingly. "What's the matter, Ash, no man ever take the time with you before?"

Ashly closed her eyes, giving in to the magical shivers his fingers through her hair created. She sighed. "Let's just say my last lover couldn't spell foreplay, let alone acquire any finesse. Greg should have been named, 'old two-stroke'. He barely got the condom on in time before his world came to an end."

"Ah, so that's the Greg whose neglect drove you to my arms." Marcus chuckled softly and shook his head. "I must thank him if I ever see him, although I don't feel the least bit sorry for him about what he threw away. Some men wouldn't recognize the ideal woman if she were surgically attached to him."

Ashlyn moved to lay on her side to face him. "And you would?"

Marc looked taken aback. "Look at the trouble I went to just to get you here." He swept his hand around the site. "Not to mention the fact that I hounded you, coerced you, bargained and finally blackmailed you. What else am I supposed to do? For God's sake tell me because I've run out of ideas. Please, I'm begging you. What moves Ashlyn Fraser?"

What indeed, thought Ashlyn, as she stared up at the cloudless sky then back to the scenery past Marc's shoulder. What part of herself did she give up to be here, naked in the middle of nowhere with the most perfect specimen of masculinity she had ever known? Sure, Marc was a sexy looking guy, a savvy business man, an artist in his craft. But how did one get to know the man inside? She was certain that under the silk shirts and camera equipment lurked an ordinary person who wore dirty socks and never put the toilet seat down.

Being honest with one's own self was painful but necessary, if she were to grow beyond the sacred walls of her father's company. She had already taken the first step, she had found a man who believed in her. Now it was time to believe in him.

She took a deep cleansing breath before answering him. She turned her head so that their eyes met and locked. She saw honesty in his rugged face and expectation in his gaze. And there was something else, something she had seen in herself. One half of a raw emotion reaching out to find its mate, to become whole. And she accepted the fact that she was in love with this man, realized that it was possible he felt the same way. But now was not the time or the place for either of them to confess their love.

So, what moved her? She knew he was waiting for her answer. She reached up and gently brushed a stray lock of hair from his face. She smiled then, knowing she held the secret in her arms.

"Just be yourself, Marc."

Chapter 8

Without any further discussion, he did just that. He helped her up off the blanket and enfolded her into a deep embrace. He surprised her by kissing her tenderly at first. Then he became anxious and impatient. His lips parted to allow his tongue to intrude forcefully into her mouth. He growled softly and crushed her against his body. Soon she discovered the reason for the change in his mood.

He wanted her. Now. She knew this time would be for him. He made bold thrusts against her inner thighs, silently expecting to be admitted. Ashlyn gave a mute response by parting her legs. Her permission spurred him into action and he broke the kiss. "C'mon. Let's get back to the trailer. It's cold out here."

He snatched up the tan blanket, shook it out and placed it around her shoulders. He stopped to don his briefs before helping her down the ladder. They strode hand-in-hand across the sand back to the trailer.

"The benches in the kitchenette fold down into a bed," he explained while they walked. He paused to pick up a couple of cameras, some lenses and to shut down the lights. Ashlyn had a feeling they wouldn't be working any more today, at least outside.

She started up the metal stairs when Marc stopped her. "Uh, uh." He shook his head. "We're doing this properly." With that, he swung her up off her feet and into his arms. He ascended the three steps, paused to fumble with the door handle and then they were across the threshold. Inside, as well as outside on the set, Marc issued instructions.

"Lock the door while I make up the bed. There's some champagne in the bar fridge and glasses in the cupboard."

Ashlyn searched the cupboard, barely aware of the sounds of Marc readying their love nest; the creak of the middle table being stowed and benches being lowered, the muffled flap of sheets being spread across the foam mattress, the fluttering of her heart and quickening of her pulse. When Marc finished, he stripped off his briefs and climbed in. He leaned back against the pillows and held out his hand, silently beckoning her to join him.

Ashlyn padded toward the bed, weighed down with the cold bottle and two fluted goblets. Her legs still felt a bit wobbly, as if she were walking the deck of an unsteady ship. Outside on the rock Marc had played her body like an instrument of Eros using only his hands and mouth and her insides still hummed to his intimate tune. She almost hesitated to think what he would do with her now that he intended to use the rest of his body. And his intent was obvious by the way his stiff rod poked against the white satin sheet like a sleeping volcano ready to erupt under a mountain of snow. The large mass quivered slightly under the sheet. A tiny dark stain emerged where the tip pressed against the cover, proof that he was more than ready for her.

Ashlyn was aware that she was staring at his arousal. For the first time, she didn't feel the least bit embarrassed by her bold curiosity. She was relieved that he wasn't making fun of her. In fact, he seemed to be enjoying her silent perusal. She looked away, slowly, her gaze travelling up and across his bare, muscular chest with its springy dark curls. Finally she had the courage to look at him directly. What she saw more than pleased her.

His eyes seemed to darken under her intense gaze. His lips parted slightly and he swallowed. There was only the sound of their breathing broken by the occasional loud hum of the refrigerator. The calm before the storm.

Ashlyn broke the spell by setting the glasses down on the ledge above the bed. When she came near, Marc greedily nibbled at one of her breasts through the bodice of her gown. With her breast trapped between Marc's teeth, she had no choice but to sit beside him. He nuzzled the teat with his mouth and tongue, dampening the thin material. Her tiny, round nipples hardened under the assault. Satisfied by the response, Marc rubbed his nose across the silk-covered bud, teasing her even more.

Enjoyable as they were, his playful actions made an impossible task of unwrapping the gold-colored foil from around the neck of the champagne bottle. Frustrated, Ashlyn finally ripped it off. Then she worked on the wire holding the cork in place. Her efforts were hampered by his hands which had suddenly found their way to her shoulders and were deftly sliding the thin silk straps down her arms. Ashlyn tried to ignore him as she untwisted the wire cradle and pressed her thumbs against the stubborn cork. All at once, the bottle released its plug with a fierce "pop". The force sent her toppling back against Marc. At the same time, her breasts slipped out of their restraints and into his waiting hands.

Ashlyn tried to right herself, ever mindful of the open bottle in her tenuous grasp. But Marc's fingers were busy massaging her bare breasts while his lips played with the sensitive area below her ear. A thrilling shiver shot through her and she sighed, full of soft, warm pleasure. "If you don't stop, I'll spill something."

"So will I," he muttered, burying his face into the hollow of her neck.

Ashlyn gave a shaky laugh and forced herself to move away from him. Marc pouted but relented while she filled each of the glasses in turn. She handed him his drink and snuggled in beside him.

"What shall we drink to?" she asked once she was settled.

A twitch of his lips played into a wide wolfish smile.

"What, Marc?"

"I was just thinking about the last time you and I shared a drink together. It was your birthday and you were wearing far less than you are now. Honey, you have no idea how close I came to taking you right there."

"You mean all that steam didn't come just from the water?"

"Hah! Your innocence is wasted on me. My love, you are a sadist. You tortured me mercilessly and all I did was find you irresistible. Just like now. Let's toast to you taking off the rest of that dress," he grinned over the rim of his glass.

Ashlyn trailed a finger across his chest. "I thought I'd let you do that. A reward for your, um, torture."

"Ah! I get to be in control, is that it? About time." The smirk on his face told her he was only kidding.

"I thought you liked being in control," she teased.

The eyes behind his smile were serious. "Honey, I haven't been in control of Jack Shit since you walked into my life. Not my assignments, my staff, and especially my libido." He gave his protruding member a hardy pat in emphasis.

Ashlyn was taken aback by his confession. It was the closest he had come to admitting that they shared an attachment on an emotional level. And she thought *she* was the only one whose life was in turmoil. Marc was revealing himself in more ways than one. Still it wouldn't hurt to remind him of his part in the *Insatiable* conspiracy.

"Oh, yeah?" She raised her glass menacingly over his dark head. "And just how did I come to be out here in the first place? Talk about a control freak. Who picked the middle of nowhere, not to mention my skimpy wardrobe? My buns are just starting to thaw out. I'll probably die of pneumonia."

Marc slid down under the sheet, trying to evade a possible champagne bath. "Okay," he cried, his voice laced with mock defeat. "I surrender. I give. Guilty. Now stop that or you'll drown us both. Besides, your buns look cute in that shade of blue."

They laughed together as Marc righted himself again and picked up his glass from the ledge. "I have a better idea," he said, tipping his glass towards hers. "Here's to the successful mix of business and pleasure, emphasis on pleasure."

Marc's heated stare locked with her own as their glasses touched. A clear "ping" sealed the bargain. To Ashlyn, it was like the sound of a boxer's bell intoning the end of a round. Right now it looked as if they had both won. But the day was young.

The afternoon sun had positioned itself right above their window and Marc reached up to draw the curtain. "No need to corrupt any wildlife," he said with a sly wink. "There now. All nice and cozy. Lots of privacy. I don't want any prying eyes or big ears listening in."

Ashlyn slowly sipped her champagne. "And what would anyone hear if they were listening?" It was a leading question but she was becoming quite fond of Marc's verbal foreplay.

Marc drained his glass. After topping up hers and refilling his own, he set the half empty bottle on the floor. Then he wrapped his arms around her and placed his warm mouth next to her ear. His breathing tickled a stray lock of hair around her earlobe and she allowed him to tuck her hair back out of the way. The feel of his hands made so common an action feel like the most intimate caress in the world and she shivered with delight.

"First we're going to finish this glass. That will make you relax a little. Then, I'm going to play with your nipples, like this," he paused to illustrate his meaning. His warm fingers closed around her bare breasts. Then he moved his callused palms across the soft, sensitive tips in a circling motion. He sighed deeply against her ear when he received the anticipated response. He captured the taut peaks between his thumb and forefinger, gently, but firmly kneading them. Ashlyn could see the deliberate rise and fall of her chest, stronger and a little faster than it had been just a few moments ago.

"Then what," she managed to breathe.

"Well, now that the twins are hot and bothered, I'll move on to nuzzling your neck. But I won't do that yet. Slowly. I want to move slowly with you. Shall I continue?"

Ashlyn could do no more than nod her head weakly.

"Good. Now, just a reminder. Who's in control?"

Ashlyn sighed. His hands wove a magic spell around her that started in her nipples and travelled directly to her anxious pelvis. She could feel herself getting wet. She should do something about getting undressed soon or the garment would be ruined. She was less worried that her reputation would suffer the same fate. She tried to wiggle out of Marc's grasp but he tightened his hold on her until she winced from the pleasure-pain of her pinched nipples. His silky voice threatened her. "Did I tell you to go anywhere, slave? I asked you who is in control and you didn't answer me. Do I have to ask again?"

She vigorously shook her head. She could get into this game. Maybe he had a little bondage in mind. Who knew what lurked in Marc's lascivious imagination? She wanted to find out so she decided to play along. "Y-you are," she stammered, trying to sound sufficiently meek and subdued.

"I am what, little pussywitch?" he hissed into her ear and bit down softly on the fleshy part of her earlobe. Ashlyn vaguely recognized the sound of an earring hitting the floor before she answered.

"You are …" quickly she searched her ragged senses for something that would please them both. "You are … master. My hot, dominating master. Teach me to please you. Show me what I need to know."

"You learn fast." He sounded pleased. But no more than she was. She was unbelievably wet. Her inner flesh tensed and twitched, impatient to be pleasured. The game was incredibly exciting. How did he know she would like it?

She felt the tension on her nipples ease. "Now, when I let you go, what are you going to do?" Ashlyn hesitated before answering, unsure of which phrase to use.

"Nothing until you tell me to."

"I would have also accepted, 'anything you want' but I'll take your first choice. And if I tell you to suck my cock, will you do it?"

She nodded.

"And if I say, 'peel off that rag, I want to lick your pussy' would you do it?"

Again she nodded.

"Then do it. Get rid of that dress." He released her and she got out of bed to stand in front of him. So, he wanted the dress off. The possibilities presented themselves to Ashlyn. What would he like? Another sexy dance? A striptease? With her mind engaged, she didn't notice the bottle until she almost kicked it over. She bent down and righted it before the game had to be called on account of broken glass.

"Ahem." The master called, his empty glass balanced between two fingers. He tipped it up and over and back again, eager to demonstrate what it was he wanted. Ashlyn was instantly on her knees, kow-towing like a harem slave. Then she picked up the bottle and refilled his glass. He smiled a thank you before leaning back against the pillows. He gestured impatiently for her to get on with his wishes. Ashlyn stuck her tongue out at him and decided to give him what he asked for. If he wanted a show, then he was going to get it.

She stood up. With her legs planted shoulder width apart, she grasped the skirt of the dress where it hugged her hips. Slowly she inched the material up her legs; first sliding the hem across her ankles, then brushing up her calves, skimming the dimples and curves of her knees. When the bottom of the dress finally met the shadowy 'v' between her thighs, she stopped, leaving only a teasing glimpse of glistening curls. Then she turned her back to him so that he could see her bottom was still covered. She ran her hands over her buttocks, flipping up the hem once in a while to give him a flash of round, naked flesh. Her butt cheeks might no longer be blue but her own cheeks felt flushed. She widened her stance and began to bend at the knees, plié style while she swished her bottom from side to side in what she thought was a hypnotic motion.

Just for variety, she bent over every once in a while, a quick, thrusting movement that exposed her pubic curls to his view. She longed to see his face and what kind of reaction she was getting. Her gaze slid to the full-length dressing mirror. Bingo! He might have a front row seat but so did she. She kept her head moving from side to side so he wouldn't notice her own voyeurism. Somehow, she doubted if anything could pry his attention from her.

He lay spellbound, his untouched glass gripped by fingers that were nearly white at the knuckles. His head was tilted slightly so he could see her when she bent down. His hips under the sheet partnered her every move and she knew his cock must be pulsing madly. She smiled and increased her momentum. Now for the finish.

The dress stayed bunched up around her waist as she slid both hands between her legs and bent over straight-kneed. She looked like an upside-down V in the mirror. She saw Marc inch closer to the edge of the bed for a better look. He licked his lips several times before he seemed to remember the drink in his hand. He downed the entire contents of his glass in one swallow. Ashlyn grinned wickedly and let her fingers do the walking around the back entrance of her swollen outer lips. She carefully parted them as if to reveal a sacred treasure. She rimmed the entrance to her vagina, forcing her sex juices out where she could best display what she had to offer. She stroked her clitoris until it felt wet and creamy. The little bud swelled with her effort and it was all she could do to avoid lingering there until she climaxed.

Suddenly, as if reading her mind, Marc left the bed and was behind her on his knees. His warm, wet tongue licked and probed, driving her to an unbearable frenzy. His lips nibbled her clit to her first orgasm and she yelled as her wobbly legs nearly collapsed underneath her. But he didn't stop there, his tongue invaded her slick opening and he suckled noisily. Then there was a moment when his tongue left her and she felt herself being pulled toward the bed. Then something bigger, harder, forced its way between her lips and into her body. With one quick thrust he slid inside her. Marc had sat on the edge of the bed and taken her with him. Now she was sitting on top of him, but with her back to him. At last she had the feel of his hot flesh inside her. It took only a moment for her to become accustomed to the stinging stretch his presence caused. The intense pressure of him prodding the neck of her womb was unlike anything she had ever known.

He tugged at her hair until her head was tilted up. She realized he was watching them both in the mirror. *He knew! Damn him, he'd known all along.* His voice became an echo somewhere in her mind.

"So, the little pussywitch likes to watch. Don't hide from it, babe.

Watch me. Watch your lover take you. Can you feel me deep inside you, stroking you? Can you see me buried to the hilt?"

She could. He lifted her off him slightly so she could see his cock, all shiny and slick with her juices. He played with her clitoris and once again, the sweet, tense pain boiled in her belly. She gave herself up to Marc's ministrations and once again she slipped over the edge, along with Marc who yelled sharply behind her and buried his face in her wildly tangled hair.

After a few moments they crawled back into the bed. Ashlyn lay locked in Marc's embrace. Both their bodies were slightly damp from their efforts but neither minded. They could shower later, together, even. Ashlyn closed her eyes and gave herself up to the languid after-glow. Soon she began to drift off. She heard Marc stir and she heard the sound of him quenching his thirst with the last of the champagne. She felt she should say something but her mind was empty. Finally she murmured, "nice game."

Marc set his empty glass on the floor and hugged her to him. "Yeah, especially when *some* people play by the rules. And speaking of rules, don't forget about the gallery. We still have a lot of film to shoot. I've got less than a month to prepare." His voice was lazy and heavy with fatigue.

She yawned and buried her face in the pillow. "Sleep first."

He snuggled against her. "While you can."

Ashlyn smiled, drowsy against his warmth. "This is lovely," she breathed.

Marc wrapped his arms around her and settled in beside her. "No, Ashly. This is love."

She cautiously opened one eye. "You mean love making."

"No," he whispered. "I mean, I love you." Then he kissed her, as if to seal the bond.

Ashly kissed him back, ecstatic at the revelation yet too exhausted to do more than wiggle her bottom against his groin. She managed one final thought before allowing fatigue to claim her. "With all the arguing and trying to outmaneuver each other, how did we ever manage to find time to fall in love?"

He sighed and his hard, warm breath tickled her ear. "I think falling in love *was* the game."

"Then who won that round?"

"You did," he murmured against her hair.

"Cheater," she whispered. "You'll want revenge."

"Later," he mumbled and minutes later, Ashlyn discovered she was a lone audience to his light snore. Later, indeed. Tonight, tomorrow. It didn't matter. She'd always be ready for him. She closed her eyes to wait for sleep, satisfied that this time, they had both won.

About the author:

Chevon lives in a small town east of Toronto along with two dogs, a cat and ten thousand books. Her animals are the perfect audience for her work — they don't blush when she reads out loud! When not writing, Chevon passes the long Canadian winters on the ski slopes.

Beneath Two Moons

by Sandy Fraser

To my reader:
Change time and place, past to future, city to desert, Earth to the stars. One constant endures: the fiery passion of a man and a woman. Lose yourself in the fantasy.

Chapter 1

The shuttle from the Tarquin set down in a cloud of fine red grit, and Dr. Eva Kelsey peered through the shield for signs of life. Nothing moved except a lone dust devil.

"See anything, Leon?"

"Looks like the Texas Badlands," the pilot said. He hunched over the console. "No welcoming committee. But I got the right coordinates and time. How long do we wait?"

A hideous roar split the low hum of the shuttlecraft, and Eva started. An immense splay-footed beast, a brown lizardy nightmare masquerading as a horse, shuffled from a sand canyon. The animal was saddled and bridled. And in the saddle sat a huge man.

He urged the creature close to the shield. The lizard rolled its eyes and stamped its feet, but it obeyed.

Confident, relaxed, the rider leaned forward and his penetrating stare burned Eva, as if he'd crisped her neosuit to explore the possibilities beneath. She fought an urge to cover her breasts with both hands, to protect herself from the attack of his eyes.

"Conor." Eva caught her breath, her mouth tightened. Low in her belly a hot memory woke.

He held his seat on the nightmare nonchalantly, reins loose in his lap. Always in control, Conor, even when he looked sleepy-eyed and careless. That's when he was most dangerous. His steel-grey eyes never shifted from Eva's face, and unsettled, she smoothed her hair in its confining Baradian twist, and tucked in a stray curl.

Damn! She knew better than to signal that he'd unnerved her, but it was too late. A smile flickered across Conor's lips, a smile that implied she'd come off-world to re-ignite an old fire.

He was more man than most women could handle. Except Eva. Conor's aura of intense maleness presented no danger to her. She'd had the experience, like some exotic disease, and she was immune. Her self-control had intensified in the last two years, and he wielded no power over her.

"Is that *the* Conor? The legend in the flesh?" Leon adjusted a stabilizer and chuckled. "Hey, Doc. I'm impressed."

"Then you're a chump for personality cults." Eva patted his back and rose abruptly. As Conor backed his creature into the shadows of a dune, Eva touched the pilot's shoulder. "Thanks for the ride, Leon. You can take off after I unload. I've only got the two cases."

Minutes later, ankle-deep in the planet's sand, she was assaulted by the thirsty air, and heat shimmered over the arid earth. Every breath scorched her lungs, and tiny beads of sweat collected on her upper lip and evaporated in an instant.

Leon shot her one last wave and the shuttle slipped away, shrinking in an instant to a silver dot of light and then vanishing, separating her from the Tarquin, leaving her on Feldon-9 for months. For the first time, she couldn't suppress fears that accepting the assignment had been a bad idea, a risk. But assignment refusals alerted the Psych Board, and files were pulled, notes were made.

And she'd had enough notes to last her a lifetime, all the same complaints. Diminished objectivity, personal involvement. There would be no more notes to call the Board's attention to her loss of self-control.

Delaying the inevitable, Eva fiddled with the neck of her white neosuit, and raised one hand to her eyes. Red dunes and flats and the total absence of green, the stark landscape imposed itself on her, brutal and unforgiving. This was a man's planet.

Conor's planet.

Suddenly, she was in shadow, a giant, broad-shouldered shadow. As always, Conor invaded her space, radiating his own special brand of heat. His presence coiled around her, weakening her knees and emptying her mind of cool reason.

"Dr. Kelsey. Welcome to Laredo." Resonating, deep, like a primitive drum, his voice rumbled, vibrating a string between her navel and her core. In her very depths, in her soul, the voice, criminally compelling, like a sexual command, echoed and rippled, and her breath came shallow.

"Dr. Kelsey?"

Eva closed her eyes, straightened her shoulders, and masked her nervous trembling. The trick, she knew, lay in avoiding locked stares. She forced a friendly smile, a textbook picture of the objective colonial investigator, and turned to Conor.

He reached out one hand, almost daring her to take it. As if staring at his hand would buffer her from the necessity of meeting his eyes, she focused on the hand. Like his body, enormous, tanned and rough, these callused fingers had tugged her nipples into stiff peaks, had cupped her wet flesh, had elicited her helpless moans. Caught in the memory, her nipples hardened. But her skin-tight neosuit hid no secrets, and, blushing, she sneaked a quick upward glance to check Conor's reaction.

Conor was looking down at her breasts. He licked his lips, and met her eyes. Stark hunger rode across his face.

"Eva." His voice roused need in her belly as his hands once had roused her body.

Eva swallowed her memories to study his hand again. It was just a hand. And Conor, he was just a man. Simply a man like any other. Not a legend, not a fever dream from long ago. And while she was here on official business, she'd prove it to herself. And him. But her guts twisted and she clung to the lie even as it disintegrated.

Conor was not a man. Conor was a hunter, a demon whose mere presence excited the prey, hypnotized them into his arms.

Eva flicked her gaze everywhere but his eyes. He'd pulled back his long sable hair and tied it with a leather thong. And curiously, he wore buckskins, shades of the old trackers and explorers she'd seen in compuvids.

His face was hard planes and angles, even the nose, as if chiseled from granite, strong-jawed, the lips cruelly masculine. Except when, hot and electric and devilishly practiced, they had ravaged her breasts, captured her mouth. Softened in the flame of contact, they'd curved and swelled as he'd slanted them over her protesting lips.

"How very nice of you to meet me." Summoning her reserves of professional self control, Eva took his hand, and tilting her head, met his gaze. Her fingers quivered, lost in his grip.

"My pleasure, ma'am." Conor checked his smile and his hunger. Eva Kelsey could pretend till the end, the final surrender, the final scalding fusion, no matter how coolly she stared him down now, lying to her body that she didn't want him. But if it took the rest of her stay, he'd have her, wet and begging and frantic.

He ran a hunter's swift inventory. Had she changed? No. Still creamy-skinned, hair like gold silk, almond-shaped blue eyes whose ice he'd melted into hot liquid compliance, the full rosy mouth he wanted to bite. Tight-assed as usual, she'd followed the rules and poured herself into the crisp white uniform that proclaimed her scientific status even while it hugged every soft curve.

Gorgeous high breasts and legs that ended in heaven, a heaven he'd never forget. He pried his attention off the hint of that sweet cleft he'd caressed until she'd spread her legs and whimpered.

"Let's get to town. Mayor's nervous as a long-tailed cat in a roomful of rockin' chairs." He hoisted her cases and led her to the beast. "Cayuses, we call them here on Laredo." He whistled and from around a sandhill slithered another of the critters, apparently an elephant-sized baby version of the colossal cayuse.

"He's darling. Is this my mount?" Eva took a tentative step toward the monster.

Mount. Beneath the snug buckskin, Conor's erection strained the tanned hide of his breeches, heavy and hot. By God, one suggestive word out of her mouth was all it took to make him hard. After two years, one look, one touch, and he wanted to drop her in the red sand, peel off her neosuit, expose her like a ripe fruit. Tease her, suck her breasts and drive into her till she came and came, screaming his name.

"What's this little guy's name?" She stroked the cayuse. It gurgled, closing its eyes, sappy at her touch.

Like Conor himself.

"Hondo," Conor grated, the craving for her now a throbbing ache in his groin. "But he's too young to ride. Just a pack animal for now." He positioned the cases in the rope slings, and patted Hondo's leathery hide.

"But where do I ride?"

"On Sweetheart." He gave her a wicked grin. "With me."

"With you? Up there?" Eva blinked and tipped her head back to measure the saddle on the giant cayuse.

Sweetheart flattened her floppy ears, eyed Eva, and squealed. Casually, Conor gave the beast an elbow to her tree trunk of a front leg. Sweetheart snuffled at his neck, begging until he stretched to pat the thick hairless chest.

"Just jealous. A female." He shrugged and bent, lacing his hands. "Up on board, ma'am. Sit behind me. You can hang on."

Eva anchored her foot and Conor lifted her slowly, inhaling as her feminine mound grazed his nose. His nostrils flared, and through the neosuit, he detected her wet heat.

Conor held, stroked one long leg as Eva ascended the rope ladder onto Sweetheart's back. With practiced moves Conor climbed into the saddle and took the reins, grateful for the dry, faintly acrid reek of the cayuse that overpowered Eva's wildflower scent.

Straddling the huge beast, Eva squirmed to make herself comfortable. Her thighs clasped Conor's firm rump and molded the hard muscles of his legs. Humiliated at the intimacy, she struggled to gain distance between them.

"Arms around my waist, unless you want to fall thirty feet. Crack your head on a rock, and I have me a carcass to haul into town," Conor growled.

Eva glared at Conor's thick neck, the cluster of black hair, and tried to hang on by grasping the buckskin shirt. Impossible. Obviously, the man must've worn a size too small to show off the taut carving of his frame.

"Around my waist," he roared.

Eva laid her cheek on the steel of his back, and wrapped her arms tightly. No matter how she flexed and strained, she couldn't encircle him. Her breasts mashed into his solid torso, and her areolas puckered. The softness between her legs ground into him, an electric friction.

The rise and fall of the animal's gait, the gentle rocking and swaying, produced a fine irritation, then warm pleasant pain, wetness. Her woman flesh felt swollen and yielding. Eva gritted her teeth and closed her eyes. This could not be happening. Unlike animals and wild people like Conor, she was so civilized, she had been selected to judge the civility of the colonists.

She controlled her body, fed it intelligently, exercised it, limited its desires and needs. And she neither desired nor needed the persuasive rubbing of her clit against Conor's spine, against his buttocks.

She squirmed a few inches away, holding herself at an angle to escape the contact until her back ached and Conor roared again. "Damnit, woman. I said, hang on."

At first the cayuse strolled among the barren dunes, but as the land rolled flat, Conor clucked and Sweetheart picked up a surprising speed. The sway increased, the jiggling too, and Eva held her breath. Conor's iron velvet massaged her sensitive breasts, and tingling heat raced up her legs. She was pilloried on his unyielding body. Tension built almost to the bursting point.

"Please," she gasped. She jerked at Conor's arm. "My legs are killing me. Is there some other way I can ride, Conor?"

He glanced over his shoulder. "Yeah. But I'm only going to stop once. If you choose it, you're stuck with it."

For a second Eva read a quirk of his lips, but she gave a mental shrug. Anything was better than being brought to orgasm by the mere touch of Conor's backside.

"Anything," Eva agreed.

"That's my baby. Slow down, darling, and I'll give you what you want," Conor murmured, his voice low and seductive, and Eva's cheeks flamed.

"If you think you can take advantage of this situation," she began, gearing up to set limits to this barbarian.

"I was talking to my cayuse. Jealous?" A mocking laugh lay under his words, and Eva clamped her mouth shut. A smart reply would only spur him on.

Obediently, Sweetheart slowed, stopped, and twisted her neck for a stalk of dried vegetable treat Conor offered from a brown saddlebag. "Is that good, baby?" Conor crooned.

While Sweetheart munched and worshipped with her yellow eyes, Conor extended both brawny arms over his head. He reached back.

"Grab on and stand up, Doc. I'll haul you over my right shoulder. C'mon. One leg at a time."

Eva rose gingerly, her muscles quivering with the hour of rigorous stretching. She found her footing, and clung to his hands for balance.

"I won't let you fall." Utterly the master, Conor gripped her left hand and levered her until she straddled his shoulder. She had a sudden image of Conor taking advantage of her precarious position to nuzzle the moistness between her thighs.

And she was horrified that she was so aroused she imagined jutting herself toward his face, impatient for his tongue like all his bed partners, inviting him to taste the evidence of her desire, to rub his face into her.

"Other leg now," he ordered, the perfect gentleman. He slid her down into his lap over buckskin so tight he might as well have been naked.

"Sidesaddle for ladies." Conor adjusted her in his lap. "You can sleep. Better?"

For the first few moments, she held herself stiff and aloof, but Conor pressed her head against the slabs of his massive chest and forced her to lean into him. Then he bent toward her, and his beard stubble grazed her cheek.

"Look at me, Eva." His frown, dark and compelling, was the equivalent of his elbow in the cayuse's leg. "Is this better?"

"Better," she whispered, ashamed that she thirsted for Conor to cuddle her. And as if he read her mind, he cradled her in his arms, picked up the reins, and Sweetheart galumphed into the silent sands.

Silence. Flailing herself for her weak will, Eva searched for a reason to provoke his disturbing voice, to measure her strength against him. Tentatively, she placed her hand where his buckskin shirt revealed the outline of the flat male nipple over his heart. Conor sucked in a great breath, and beneath her hand, his heart thudded.

"Is the colony scratching so hard for survival they can spare only one man to pick me up?" Unobtrusively, she studied the tension in his jaw muscles for the telltale signs of a lie. "I told the mayor I'd get you." He pierced her with a single look.

"You *told* him?"

"Surprised? Why? You saw pack leader/top dog syndrome in my psych-form when you knocked me out of the program. What clever heading did you paste on it, my pretty professor? Alpha-male behavior?"

"I classified you under *prefers to work alone*," she said defensively.

"And almost cost me the opportunity to colonize Laredo." His laughter rumbled under her hand. "But despite your damndest, I got here." He tugged the reins and Sweetheart veered left. Little Hondo gave a squeal and rushed out in front, wagging his long lizard tail. Conor grinned. "Smells the lake from miles away."

Conor shifted and faced the horizon bounded by a blue-green sky. He swayed from side to side on the leather pad, and made a low sound in his throat. His shaft swelled against the soft flesh on the underside of her thighs. Her face flamed.

She cursed herself. Why hadn't she bitten her lips and endured the painful ride on the too-broad rump of the cayuse? How could she have missed the implications of nestling in his groin?

"My cramps are gone," she said cheerily. "Look." She pointed her toes and stretched her legs. "If you don't mind, I'll take my original seat now."

"Oh, but I do mind." His hard hand clamped down about three inches below her knees, and he killed her stretch. "I told you, I'd only stop once." Slowly, he exhaled and rocked her in his lap, forcing her to feel the steadily increasing thickness of his erection. "Besides, Dr. Kelsey, I like you exactly where you are."

His lips had lost his arrogant smile, and he closed his eyes, but his dominant maleness enveloped Eva as surely as if he'd staked her out and covered her with his body.

She shuddered and remembered the first time Conor had bruised her with that voice, burned her with his heat, the first time he'd manhandled her.

Against her will, she remembered every detail of her first meeting with Conor.

Chapter 2

"Dr. Kelsey, Dr. Kelsey." Judy had scurried around her receptionist's desk. She'd pointed at Eva's seclusion room. "He's in there, your first appointment. He, I mean Mr. Conor, got here early and you're five minutes late."

"Thank you, Judy." Eva raised one eyebrow. "And you let him into seclusion unattended?"

Judy failed to control a scarlet blush. "He asked, and somehow — well, I just couldn't say no."

"Really? You've never broken the rule before. Quite persuasive, this Mr. Conor." Eva patted Judy's arm and smiled. "Now stop the hand-wringing. What's done is done."

Putting on her professional face, Eva swung her porta-bag and waited a second for the slider to recognize her, to part and welcome its owner.

Suddenly she understood Judy's fluttering. Conor's presence over-whelmed the sim-walls, the soft brown rug, and almost overwhelmed her. Physically, he was a giant, sprawled in a chair that for the first time had stretched its flexible limits to accommodate him.

Casually he rose, towering over her, deep-set, steel-grey eyes appraising her from under dark, heavy eyebrows. A mane of black hair fell to the shoulders of his black jacket. His firm lips opened to reveal perfect white teeth. Animal vitality filled the room. Eva swallowed. Hard.

A successful predator flashed across Eva's consciousness. She pictured his powerful legs pumping, running down his hapless prey, the brawny arms seizing the struggling creature, rendering her helpless and compliant, the sharp teeth biting her neck. My God. *Her?* Had she lost her mind? Eva resisted an impulse to shake her head to roust the picture. *Get a grip, Kelsey. He's just a man. An immense man, the kind of man who diminished other men, but just a man.* She'd evaluated hundreds of these guys.

"Mr. Conor." She extended her hand, and, with a hint of a smile, he covered it in his enormous grip. A galvanizing jolt of sheer sexual power coursed from his hot touch up her arm, shot through her body, and raced down to tell her knees to buckle, to tell her to fall on her back and spread her thighs.

Eva battled her desire. She had too much at stake. The instant attraction would skew her analysis of the man. If she lost control, she'd color the interview, and invite another file note from the Psych Board.

She dragged her hand out of his grip, and scuttled behind her desk. "Please," she murmured. "Please."

"Please what?" His voice resonated and sounded even when his words ended.

"Please … make yourself comfortable," she croaked. She perched in her chair, hid her hands under the desk, and pinched the tender skin between her thumb and index finger. The pain restored her common sense, and she folded her hands. "Let's get started, shall we?"

Conor was standing before her. He'd left her two choices. Either stare at the hefty bulge straining his pants, or tilt her head to meet his penetrating eyes. She closed her eyes and waved, praying he'd resume his seat.

"Oh, lady, I'd like to get started," he rumbled and folded himself into the lounge. He smiled again, a quirk of his lips that signalled some dark question she wouldn't acknowledge. He crossed his ankle over the opposite knee.

Eva clasped her hands on the desk. "I have all the records. Physical, psychological profiles, and work and personal history, Mr. Conor."

"Conor. Just Conor." It was a command.

"*Mister* Conor," Eva insisted. She had to take control. "You know all the paperwork and what it entailed. But we need to get the feel of you." The heat of a wild blush surged up her neck and into her cheeks. Conor grinned.

"I mean, the emotional nuances that compsychs and paperwork won't divulge."

"Take your best shot," he invited.

"What's your dream, Conor? Mister Conor," she corrected hastily. "Is it colonizing Feldon-9?"

"My dream," he repeated, locking his hands behind his head, and contemplating the ceiling. He straightened, uncrossed his legs, and riveted her with those piercing eyes. "To be free and open and big on a world that's like me."

"Free?"

"Of all the bowing and scraping a man has to do to be honest and open."

"Ah, you'd prefer a place without laws and manners?" She tried to restate him, incriminate him. "A lawless, loose, primitive world?"

"C'mon, Dr. Kelsey." He cupped his hands over his knees and arched one brow. "We both know what I mean. You know my past, safari guide, mercenary, bodyguard. Hauling people out of tight spots. I need adrenaline rushes. I need to ride to where the boundaries have vanished."

"Very poetic, Conor. But the need for adrenaline rushes, in your case, have included — how can I put this delicately — avidly searching for boundaries in the beds of other men's wives." She displayed a list printed on the pink sexual history sheet.

"I told you I ride to where the boundaries vanish. And I've given some of those stifled women the best rides of their lives."

His infuriating grin enraged Eva.

"This list," she flapped it at him "fairly shouts of incredible breaches of respectable behavior, besides being quite clearly against moral law." Her heart was pounding. "Explain yourself, Conor."

"Ah, may I?" Smoothly, he leaned forward and snatched the paper from her hand. He perused it for a second. "What's the point of compiling a list like this? More evidence of government prying." With contempt, he tossed it back, defiling the perfectly organised surface of her desk. "Lonely women, sad women, some desperate for a change in their lives. Some just wanted to play, to taste a little tabasco on their meat."

Eva pursed her lips. "Although I disapprove of your behavior, it is not punishable by law. But you are a time bomb, an ember waiting to inflame and torch a colony. A disruptive, macho influence and a threat to family harmony."

"That's me, Doc. One powerful, reckless bastard."

"Did you know, Mister Conor, not one of these women stayed with her husband? Not one! I can see from your expression that comes as news. And what do you think that means?"

"Hell, Doc. What do *you* think that means?"

Eva adopted her frostiest tone. "I assume a man of your type doesn't hold himself accountable."

"And what type would that be, Doc?"

"The rutting stallion type, Mister Conor, the bull, the dominant kagalon inseminator of Pastor-12." She leaned back and steepled her fingers to allow herself a satisfied smirk. "Have you any questions?"

"Yeah. How come it's *Mister* Conor again? And how come my little flings seem to annoy you?"

"They do not annoy me," Eva blurted in a huff. "I don't care how many beds you gallop through like a stallion who's caught a whiff of a ready mare. Be my guest. Have at it. What is it they used to say? Men like you are limited only by opportunity and stamina."

"I get the distinct feeling you don't like me, Dr. Kelsey."

"I do not, Mister Conor." Eva rose. "And because I play no games, I will give you my evaluation now. I cannot recommend you for colonizing Feldon-9."

"Because I've fucked too many women?" He came out of the chair like a steel spring. "Or because I haven't fucked you?"

"Get out of my office." Eva trembled. Her hand shook as she pointed to the door. "Before I —" She groped for the security button and missed.

"Before you what?" He reached and pulled her across the desk, one hand an iron band around her waist, the other tipping up her face. She thrashed her head from side to side, but Conor stilled her, gripping her chin and pressing her back against the holo-desk.

"Look at me, Dr. Kelsey. We're in seclusion, so save your breath. Unless you want to scream with pleasure when I do this." He brushed his mouth across hers. Fiercely she bit his lower lip. She tasted his salt blood. In an act of defiance, she spat in his face.

"Now you have to pay." He slanted his mouth over hers in a punishing kiss that forced her mouth open and tore a whimper from her throat. Like some strange drug, Conor's touch paralyzed her into submission, sapping her will, making her an accomplice in her own seduction.

"I hate you," she got out, but she couldn't even convince herself. Her lashes swept her cheeks, her eyes half-closing in lust, but she made one more effort. Eva struck his face, a thin, anemic blow. She had no strength against him. Conor chuckled, and her fists opened, palms flat against the wall of his chest.

"Such little fists," he whispered. "Is that the best you can do?" He held her closer, kissed her softly, hushing her like he'd calm a frightened doe.

Conor tapped the catch of her neosuit, and swallowed her weak protest in another kiss. He yanked the snow-white suit down to her waist, immobilizing her arms in her own clothes, rendering her helpless.

His eyes, grey as a winter storm, scanned her breasts. "God, you make me hard. I want to rip this suit off, throw your legs over my shoulders, and ride you like a bull." His voice was strained and rasping. "Tell me you want it."

She licked her dry lips and moaned. He was worse than an animal at stud. All those women, panting and wailing under him. Eva's cry of protest died in her throat.

"You're very beautiful. Do you know that? Feel what you do to me." He nudged her legs apart and rubbed the rigid bow of his erection on her cleft.

Then he weighed her breast, his big hand cupping the undercurve while he thumbed the taut nipple. He kissed her and rolled her sensitive peaks between his thumb and forefinger.

Slowly, he took his lips from hers and his eyes were dark as smoke. "I'm going to kiss your breasts now, Eva, suck you until you want me to do more." He bent his head, biting her neck, gliding a provocative string of kisses lower and lower.

Battling even as her will drained out of her, Eva moaned and arched into his hand, instinctively offering her breast with its pebbled areola. He closed his teeth on the hard nub while she whimpered. His tongue twirled and lapped, and Eva strained to thrust more and more of her breast into his mouth.

He flicked his tongue wickedly, paused to blow on the moist skin, then plucked at her nipple while he licked and nibbled her other breast.

She squirmed beneath him, and Conor slid his fingers into the curly nest between her thighs. "You're beautiful here, too. So hot and wet." His fingers worked in and out and his thumb rubbed her clit, faster and deeper, and Eva tensed and moaned, wanting and afraid to want as the currents of desire pulled her far from herself into a blinding place where everything spiraled down to Conor's enormous hand boring into her swollen vulva, and his steely eyes boring into her soul.

On the edge, the split second before she fell over the brink into an electric oblivion, Conor stopped.

He withdrew fingers wet with her essence, and wiped them in the curls on her mound.

In an agony of lust, she swiveled her hips shamelessly. "Finish. Finish me."

But Conor raised her and slipped the suit up till it fastened around her neck. He swung her into his arms as if she weighed less than the pink sheet of his harem, and carried her into her private bathroom. He set her before the mirror, and held her braced against his massive torso.

"Look, Dr. Eva Kelsey."

Eyes glazed, Eva stared into the mirror at her fragile feminity, her pale gold melded to Conor's dark maleness. She reached back and clasped his muscular thighs to support herself. The mouth of the woman in the mirror had lips swollen with his kisses, wet and smeared with lust. Her skin glowed, dewy with the heat of passion.

Her turgid nipples marred the smooth skin of the suit, and even as she stared at the flare of her hips, Conor took possession of her mound. He cupped her, the hard heel of his big hand rocking, rubbing her distended flesh, again dragging her closer to orgasm. She shook and trembled, poised on the brink.

He stopped again, bent to suck the lobe of her ear, and flashed a cruel smile.

"Why? Why are you doing this to me?" Eva heard the begging note in her voice, the pleading, and she didn't give a damn. She was desperate, needed him to complete her anyway he could.

On tiptoe, she thrust into his retreating hand, fighting to maintain the sweet pressure.

"I dreamed about the colony, pretty Dr. Kelsey, lived for the dream, and I've passed every test. But yours." He released her and stepped away. Eva clutched at the cold sink and still his eyes held her gaze.

"I wanted you to know how much you can want something and have it taken away at the last second." He clenched his fist and a muscle twitched in his strong jaw.

"Wait, wait, Conor." Her own voice was strange, pitiful in her ears.

"It's been a treat, Dr. Kelsey." He mocked her with a bitter smile and a salute. "And thanks for all the fun."

Barely able to stand, Eva heard the sliders whoosh, and she was in seclusion again. Alone. She pulled in great gulps of air, and her pulse raced. She averted her concentration from the mirror and counted the green glass tiles. When she reached ninety, her pulse still thundered, her respiration was shallow and too fast. She gave it up as a bad job and took a long, calming breath.

"What do we tell patients? Look yourself in the eye and deal with the truth." Still shaking with the need Conor had waked in her, she lifted her head and stared into the mirror. Hair disheveled, lips branded with his kisses, Dr. Eva Kelsey had confusion written all over her face.

"But I know, I *know* who I am," she declared, "and a ten-minute lust bout with a bed-hopping hunk can't change me.

"Logic and reason. Logic and reason." She repeated her mantra until her cracked and whispery words made her desolate, made her cry. Eva touched her throat. She bit her swollen lips, and she hated herself as she watched fear replace confusion. Who was she if Conor so easily destroyed her civilized, analytical philosophy?

As tears coursed down her cheeks, Eva forced herself to ignore a heavy ache of frustration, of emptiness. And what had it meant to him? Another almost-conquest? The Conors of the world, men who oozed hormones and charisma, took great pride in reducing women like herself to mindless females, pliant, eager for sex.

Not that Eva hadn't had sexual encounters, the sophisticated trysts recommended by the professional guilds. Her partners had always been other pros anxious to fulfill their own guild requirements. Dr. Eva Kelsey knew her duty and had referenced her sexual activities in her guild file to prove she was fully experienced. The Psych Guild insisted their members be competent to minister to patients with mating dysfunctions. Conor escaped that category. Conor had his own category.

Tentatively, Eva fingered her mouth, remembering his mind-drugging kisses. She had endured the mechanical efforts of partners determined to practice the maneuvers of sexual athletes on the compuvid's Kama Sutra channel. When the man was through, she'd clock the minimum three minutes of afterplay and give a sigh of relief. She'd dress and scurry to have the institute's door robot verify her visit with the pink seal. Sex never had meant anything to her before, nothing except animalistic stimulus and response, sweaty wrestling.

Until today. Until Conor.

He had shockingly skilled hands and lips. But it was more than his natural gifts. Eva had felt truly safe, protected in his arms, free to be a different Eva. With his knowing caresses he had released the passionate woman terrified of intimacy, the woman who struggled to present a picture of a cool and collected psych doctor. A woman above reproach, above challenge from her peers and the Psych Board, a woman who slept in her lonely bed, detached, aloof from desire, untouched and invulnerable.

Logic reminded her Conor was a man with an erotically charged past, a man looking forward to a blazing future. Reason warned her that chaos lay in her wild response to him.

"Logic and reason," she said and splashed her face with cold water. "Logic and reason," she said as she completed her neat Baradian twist, every hair in place.

The simple act of smoothing her neosuit made her close her eyes and imagine Conor's hands cupping her hips and drawing her into his arousal. Her eyes flew open. No. His effect on her had been an aberration, a weak, needy momentary lapse on her part.

Again she heard his husky voice. "Save your breath, unless you want to scream with pleasure when I do this."

Eva covered her lips. She'd solve the problem of Conor by relegating him to a mental limbo where she isolated disturbing events. And as for seeing him again, she had few worries. No doubt he'd find a slot as a squad leader in Mercenary, Inc. She could see Conor in the jungle, or a desert's edge where, her official inquiries noted, he was respected and liked by his men.

Eva's belly tightened. The reports praised him as a fierce, intelligent, relentless fighting machine whose special gift was an uncanny ability to sense danger. And then to fix it with whatever it took. What an asset for Feldon-9's civilian colonists!

What an asset she'd thrown away on the basis of the pink sexual history sheet. Eva checked her suit's power tab and met her eyes in the mirror. Guilt flickered across her face.

And then the tough Dr. Eva Kelsey jerked the controls from this new, soft Eva.

Dr. Kelsey mocked her reflection. "Grow up. You followed your best professional judgment. He's a menace to peaceful settlement. In a few hours, we'll do emotional housecleaning and toss out Conor."

"Lord help me," Eva whispered. "Make it so I never see him again."

Chapter 3

Though a week had passed since Conor had shamed her, and cold logic demanded she hate him for exploiting her weakness, Eva's traitorous body still hungered for his probing hands, his plundering tongue.

During lunch with a friend or a run in the park, in the middle of a seclusion session, the memory of Conor suckling her breasts surfaced, a flush reddened her cheeks, her nipples erected into stiff, tingling buds, and a creamy dew slicked her private flesh.

Sometimes a friend, or her secretary, or an evaluatee asked, "Something wrong, Dr. Kelsey?" And glibly she lied, and poured water from a carafe.

But of course something was wrong when she opened a folder and the glassy surface of the holo-desk lay cool under her hands. And like the stab of a sharp knife, the memory rose of Conor. How he'd lifted her, spread her out, shivering on the glass, a half-naked sacrifice to his revenge.

And now, forced to sit politely, professionally in the setting where he'd played with her body like a living toy, Eva squirmed. If Conor aroused her, a woman he'd just met, to a fever pitch to punish her, what did those others feel? Those women he flirted with, seduced for his pleasure? Had he kissed them until they wept, tongued and fingered them until, crazy with lust, they begged him to bury his engorged arousal deep in their wetness?

Desperately, she tried to erase a kaleidoscope of Conor with willing women, Conor masterfully changing their positions, driving into them, bringing them repeatedly to climax, until they lay limp in his arms.

"He's an animal without conscience," Eva shouted in the dark quiet of her air sedan. And she hated him for showing her what was missing in her life, the cost of her detachment.

She heard again his mocking questions. "Do you hate me because I've fucked too many women? Or because I haven't fucked you?"

On the verge of a decision about Conor, she snapped awake. Her sleek Austin slid around the last curve, pulled to a smooth stop before the gates, and announced, "We have arrived at our destination, Miss Kelsey, the estate of Roger J. Kelsey, your loving father who would like a grandchild before he's too old to take the kid on safari."

"Thank you, Austin," she said. She sighed. Her father insisted on his staff maintaining her vehicle, and no matter how often she'd erased Austin's reminders, the mechanics carefully reprogrammed him at her father's directions.

Wearing a huge smile, Randall, the gateman, stuck his head in her window. "Go round back, Miss Eva. Your papa's invited damn near half the city."

Eva saluted, and Austin glided onto a sideroad, and into the estate's garage. While Austin exchanged greetings with the other vehicles, Eva set off on the wandering path toward the house.

"Some house. I really grew up in a giant theme park." She lingered in the Shakespeare garden and the herbarium her mother had loved. In the cool damp of the fern forest, she heard faint music escaping from the house, the perfection of a world-famous string quartet.

The music grew in volume as she entered the house by the solarium door. In the main salon, she navigated clusters of movers and shakers, nodding and smiling until she found her father, tall and distinguished and used to imposing his will. A kiss and a hug, and he resumed talking.

Eva circulated and joined a group of laughing friends. The knots of sophisticated guests swirled, formed and reformed. Eva, in an instant becoming aware she was the target of an intense stare, struggled to sustain social chatter. She glanced over the rim of her wine glass. Suddenly the crowds parted. And *he* was there, leaning with one elbow on the Carrera marble mantelpiece.

Conor, as jarringly out of place as a panther in a farmyard. From twenty feet away, she read the challenging smile on those lips she'd bitten, read the dare in eyes that knew her secrets. "Go on," he seemed to be saying. "Tell Daddy and have my ass kicked."

Despite her drink, Eva's mouth went dry, and the wine quivered in the champagne flute. Conor in her family home. Another violation, almost as personal and ruthless as his penetration of her seclusion room. *And herself.*

"Excuse me. Excuse me," she said, automatically planning her route through the guests to her father. Then she'd have her real revenge when Conor got dragged off the estate. And how would Conor maintain the slavish admiring gaze of the silly females he'd drawn like filings to an erotic magnet?

She'd managed to get halfway across the parquet floor when a massive hand captured her elbow. The scent of woods and jungles and wild places, the scent of the untamed animal. Conor. Her nostrils flared, and she stiffened. Around him the temperature rose. Conor radiated extraordinary heat, the hunter's heat.

But she was no one's prey. Not Conor's, not any man's. Though the top of her simple coiffure barely reached his heart, she inclined her head and shot him a venomous glare.

"How dare you touch me in a public place?" Her voice shook with indignation, even as her knees weakened.

"I'd like to touch you in a private place."

"My father will have you castrated when I tell him what you did."

"Ah. You haven't told him yet?" Far from hanging back, Conor ran interference through the throngs.

"I *had* no intention of upsetting him," Eva said. She put an edge on her voice even as Conor's touch unleashed desire in her belly. "Until you intruded here. My father is a hard man who doesn't take kindly to men who manhandle women. But now I see my silence has done nothing but encourage you."

"Guess I'll have to pay the price, Dr. Kelsey." He smiled, hugely satisfied, and Eva burned with the urge to slap his face.

He brought her in front of her father.

"Daddy, this man —"

"You've found Conor, I see." Her father patted her cheek. "Good show. Fences mended after the evaluation problem?" He tapped the ice cube in his scotch and raised one bushy eyebrow.

"Problem?" An ominous chill raced down Eva's spine.

Casually, Conor draped his arm over her shoulders. "I haven't told her yet, Roger."

"You call my father Roger?" She blurted, her voice brittle with astonishment.

"On safari, I called him *bwana*." Both men laughed and exchanged fake punches.

"My dear, you are as precise in the colony selection process, they tell me, as a surgeon with a scalpel. The teams you qualify reek with success." Her father considered his drink, looked up quickly, and his gaze bored into hers. "But Conor has been exempted from your approval."

"Exempted? You went over my head?"

"He's a rare man, Eva. Feldon-9 needs his rare qualities."

"I see. The propensity for bedding every female between eighteen and eighty? Is that sleazy trait among his so-called special qualities?" Her eyes flashed, and she dislodged Conor's arm violently as if repulsing a snake.

Eva stormed out, slowing only when she reached the private family terrace, and clung to a giant oak. The frivolous music mocked her. Furious tears wet her cheeks, and she fought to maintain her self-control. How dare her father interfere? How dare he use his influence to shove Conor down her throat?

Conor down her throat. The innocent words changed, the common saying developing in her imagination like a vidscreen show. Eva kneeling between his legs, weighing his heavy sac in one hand, holding his enormous cock to her lips, his fingers tangled in her loose hair. Her own flesh slick and heated by the act of pleasing him, by the promise of the intense pleasure he'd give her after her lips and teeth and tongue had brought him to the edge.

"No," she moaned. She pressed her face into the bark, hurting, welcoming the harshness. From the house a reggae band off Luna cranked up the volume, and the guests shouted and danced. She heard not a single footfall until Conor was upon her, smooth and deadly silent as a panther under the cover of darkness.

Easily he gripped her wrists in one hand and stretched her arms over her head. His muscled torso and iron thighs, as efficient as a vise, held her against the tree.

"Get your hands off me," she directed, cold and determined to show him no weakness, no willingness.

"Going to scream, Doc?" He rolled the heavy arc of his erection into the hollow of her back.

"I won't give you the satisfaction."

"Oh, but you will."

He nudged her legs farther apart, absorbing the ineffective kicks she aimed with her heels. There was more than one way to shrivel the ego of a beast in human clothing.

"You amuse me, Conor," Eva said. "I've had a chuckle or two over the years from you and your ilk, a pitiful dying breed of testosterone-maddened males. If you're expecting —"

"Expecting this?" He lessened the pressure, leaned down and jerked up her silk skirt, and tore off her lace panties. With a fever-hot hand, he explored her buttocks, caressing the firm cheeks. "If a man could be maddened by testosterone," he whispered, "the sight of you would drive him crazy."

Eva flinched as his big demanding hand worked its way between her and the tree, briefly toyed with her breasts, followed the curve of her belly and ruffled her pubic hair. She was drenched, slippery, and with one blunt finger he massaged her erect clit, delved into her swollen vulva.

He rested his tongue on her throat where her pulse fluttered like a snared bird, bit the curve of her shoulder, and whispered into her ear. "Unless you've been playing with yourself and thinking about some other guy, you're wet and creamy and ready for me."

"Is this your answer to everything, Conor? Sex? Is this how you defeat women?" Her voice grew faint, she slumped, her knees buckled. "Sex whether they want it or not?"

"You want. You've wanted me from the first time I walked into your office." Conor loosed his belt, tapped the catch and his arousal sprang out. "And God, I've never wanted a woman as much as you." He groaned and shivered as the sensitive tip slid between the cheeks of her buttocks and found her sweet heat.

He inserted just an inch and stroked her clit, her labia, pressing her against his engorged tip.

"I'll scream if you don't stop." In spite of herself, Eva jutted her hips into his erection to give his hand free access.

Conor grazed her nape with his teeth. He bit his lip and clamped his eyes shut. No woman, not any, from the very first when he was fourteen to the Australian model he'd fucked a week before seeing Eva, had inflamed him like this woman.

Cool and pale and restrained, she was everything Conor was not. So sophisticated, looking down her patrician nose at "the animal" as she called him, yet like an inferno under an ice cap, she simmered.

Now he battled the desperate urge to spin her around and bury himself between her dripping petals, but he held off. She flung her head back, panting, resisting, in the throes of the most intense sexual temptation she'd ever felt. Her golden hair escaped from its taut coils.

Inhaling the provocative scent of her mane, Conor danced his fingers in her heat and growled, "This means nothing?"

"Nothing," Eva gasped. Her thighs loosened. "*You're* nothing but a sex machine."

"Want some more?" He gave her another two inches and tormented her with his callused thumb. Eva shuddered, and he thrust half his cock in. She was shimmering on the brink. He read it in the trembling of her legs.

"I hate you," she got out between ragged breaths. "And you — you can't force me — to experience sexual satisfaction. If I don't want to."

"You can't help yourself." He tried to produce a mocking laugh, but he had started to shake, and the muscles of his legs quivered. Conor pushed the remaining four inches, at last fully lodged, and held himself motionless in her velvet sheath. A series of tiny spasms, constricting ripples, squeezed him. He gritted his teeth. He broke out in a sweat, fighting for control.

"Conor," she moaned. "Let me go."

"I can't," he said, no longer capable of remaining still.

"I've got to have you, Eva. If I roast in hell, I'm taking you."

In a heartbeat, her protests melted into soft, mewling cries. "Conor. Conor." She arched her back to give him total access.

Instantly, he withdrew, spun her around, and a low sound was ripped out of his guts as her shaking hands inserted him. He buried himself up to the hilt, lifted her till her legs encircled his waist. With a bruising kiss, he swallowed her scream of pleasure-pain. Rhythmically, his tongue plunged into the sweet wine of her mouth in tandem with his thrusts.

Her hips rocked into his, slapping into his hard pelvis, and his enormous hardness stretched her beyond thought, beyond reason, beyond all but total sensation. She sucked his tongue, then broke the kiss, and concentrated, shrinking her world to the juncture between her legs where Conor's length burned.

"Give it to me, baby," he groaned, and pumped. His strokes grew shorter, and the dense curls surrounding his shaft brushed her clit until, like a firestorm, she blazed.

"Now, Eva, now," he demanded.

And Eva froze in a paralysis of sensory overload, and climaxed, a furious, heart-stopping orgasm, with blood pounding in her ears, deaf to anything but Conor's roar of completion matching her own howl. Hot sperm jetted and met the pulsing contractions of her fevered core.

Eva shuddered and wept and forced her pelvis into his groin. Only Conor's powerful legs kept her from collapsing. He cupped her buttocks, and gently continued his strokes into her wetness, into her sweet aftershocks.

"Let's go someplace," he rumbled into her hair. He thrust again and she whimpered. "Someplace close."

"Garage." Savagely, she rained bites on his throat, his cheek, his lower lip. "No. Please, Conor. Stay inside me, don't put me down." She lowered her voice to a soft murmur. "I don't think I can walk, darling beast, my darling animal."

"What if somebody wanders out of the party, finds their way into this garden?" Conor tested her need, found her mouth. Her kiss spoke a desperate, rising hunger.

"Let them." She was limp in his arms. And in the silver moonlight, she traced the strength of his jaw, threaded her fingers through his midnight hair.

"Does it excite you, knowing we could be seen?"

"*You* excite me." Eva fastened her mouth to his, and he carried her, speared on his throbbing flesh, down the winding walk. Eva moaned and sobbed. She shrieked softly, and around his shaft, she pulsed and contracted. Her sharp nails raked his neck.

"You're coming again, without waiting for me," he teased. And imbedded in her body, he felt more masculine, more the master, more the protector than he'd ever felt in his life. This was the one. This was Conor's woman.

Wordlessly, she nodded and clung to him, her perfumed breath in his ear making him harder, more swollen than he could endure.

At the end of the path, she gave an order to the garage, and the slider opened.

"Hello, Miss Kelsey. Did you have a pleasant time?"

"Lovely, Austin." She unwrapped her arm from Conor's neck long enough to point at the chauffeur's bedroom door. "In there. Quick." She nipped Conor's ear.

He navigated the door, kicked it shut, and with a sharp intake of breath let her slide off his penis onto the bed. Wanton, her eyes shuttered, Eva slid her silk skirt up to her waist. Conor shucked off his clothes and in the dim light of a small bedside lamp, took in her beauty.

Her nipples, thick as cherries, peaked, pointing through the thin mauve silk. And Eva ran her hands down her sides, let them linger on her thighs. She spread her legs, and Conor stared greedily at the tiny wet curls of wheaten hair on her mons, at the pink fleshy folds. Her nub seemed to ripen as he feasted his eyes on her.

"God, you're beautiful," he rasped.

"Touch me. Come deep inside me. Do everything." Her words were strangled. "I've never felt like this." The tip of her tongue wet her lips, and she raised her long nails to her breasts, lightly scratching her nipples. "Do everything, Conor. Please." Eyes bright with desire, she thrust her hips higher, offering herself to his mouth.

His arousal knocked against his belly, and he stroked himself, his hand gliding over the creamy residue she'd left, the gift of her depths. He bent over the bed, and ran a finger over her. Eva whimpered and writhed beneath the slow touch.

"Open yourself," Conor said, his voice aching with need. She parted her core, and he held his breath as her mauve fingernails glistened against the wet pink petals. Conor slipped his finger in and out, and held it to her lips.

"Suck on it," he said softly, "the taste of your sex and mine." Her gaze locked on his, and she nursed his finger between her tongue and the roof of her mouth.

Impatient, Conor pushed her hands away, and tore open the silk dress. She lay completely exposed and vulnerable and wanting him desperately.

"Eva." He groaned. "I want to fuck you. But not yet."

"Do me. Do me now," Eva begged.

He cupped her mound, juicy with his come and her own heated gushing. He let his fingers wander over her ripe, distended vulva. Conor gently took one nipple between his teeth and suckled, then the other as she arched and writhed into his hand. He thrust two fingers deep inside.

Eva imagined his erection probing her again, stretching her, her core magically accommodating his impossible thickness, his incredible length.

"Conor, Conor." Her nails dug at his shoulders. "Come inside me. I need you now."

Conor glanced up from his suckling, and smiled a lazy smile.

"Not until your nipples are raw, and you show me you're ready to come. I want you to come, Eva. Can you come for me? Still holding back? Come for me." He brought her on until she screamed and bucked, and her tight sex gripped his fingers, and milked them with waves of muscular contractions.

In the throes of orgasm, Eva clutched his head. When her moans of pleasure died away, subsided into croons of after-pleasure, she smiled up at him and raised herself for a kiss.

"No one has ever made me feel this way, Conor. No one but you." Light kisses, butterfly kisses, and she sank against the bolster.

"What way? Talk to me." He massaged her mons, played with the wet curls.

"Fishing for compliments?" Eva reached for the rails of the headboard. "Ah, Conor, I'm naked and soft and melting, and totally at your mercy. And you're not even in bed with me yet." Her voice dropped, low, seductive. "Do you like playing with me? Hmmm? Or do you like this?"

With an eager sigh, she reached for his shaft and thumbed the smooth head. With her sharp fingernails, she traced the thick veins, and Conor hissed through his teeth.

"I want you in my mouth," Eva whispered, replaying her fantasy.

"And I want my mouth on you."

Conor flung himself on the bed, lifted her like a cougar might grip a rabbit, and turned her till her head rested on his thigh. "Spread your legs."

Straddling his chest, she licked the tip of his cock just as his tongue found her clit and lightning shot through her.

"You taste like wild honey," he breathed into her wetness, and she shuddered. "Take me, Eva. Take all of me."

Eva weighed his heavy sac in one hand, and thrust him into her mouth. She flicked the pulsating vein on the underside, explored the crevice where the plushy head divided, and withdrew the huge organ. She moved her hand up and down his smooth length until his massive sex jerked involuntarily and jumped with a life of its own, and Conor's hips came off the bed.

Eva engulfed it again and bobbed her head, her own body shaking under the delicious titillation of Conor's tongue, finding herself mirroring on him each stroke he laved on her vulva. And when he plunged his tongue rapidly, she whimpered and squirmed, and he gripped her buttocks, forcing her mons down onto his mouth.

Frantically, she scraped her teeth on his flesh, and he responded by nibbling her inflamed clit. Eva rotated her hips wildly over his skillful lips, sobbing for release.

"Finish me," she wept, "Oh, God, please finish me."

Conor bucked up until he gushed into her mouth, and she screamed while her own juices trickled onto his mouth and jaw.

Instantly, he pulled her under him and, still iron hard, lunged while the frenzy rocked her. In a haze of mindless pleasure she clung to him, savoring his salty tang on her tongue, the bruised tingling of her nipples as they brushed the pelt on his chest.

A second wave of electricity shot through her, and she dug fiercely into Conor's shoulders. His black hair a curtain over her face, he plunged like a stallion on a mare. Eva opened her mouth to shout a mindless prayer, but pleasure overwhelmed her, sent her flying high into a midnight place where only she and Conor existed, locked together, and finally fell to earth, mute with exhaustion.

His sex beat inside her, the throbs gradually slowing until he rolled over, maintaining the connection, banding Eva to him.

"Stay with me, Conor," she had murmured. "Sleep with me, my wonderful animal."

⁕⁓⁍⟨☾⟩⁌⁓⁕

The cayuse thundered along at high speed and jolted her out of the memory, the unforgettable memory of making love with Conor. And in the here and now, Eva lay nestling into Conor's chest, nestling into the smell of woodsmoke and the smell of a heat that had no name but Conor.

She yawned and half-raised her lashes. Tiny hairs on her skin prickled, and an ominous dry wind weighed on her.

"Conor, what's changing?"

"You should live on Laredo, lady. You've got the fine tuning to survive." He raised one arm and extended his finger. "North. See the dark cloud moving this way?"

"Aren't we at the lake yet?"

"Not close enough to beat the storm. But there's a canyon cave just ahead. I keep the outer caves stocked." Sweetheart stretched her long neck and raced toward a looming mesa.

At the mouth of the cavern, Conor swung Eva down, pulled her inside, and thumped the cayuses's leg twice. Sweetheart gave a complaining squeal, and sank to her knees. The giant creature folded herself. Her bulk barricaded the jagged opening of the cave.

They'd barely unpacked blankets and water when the storm hammered them. Amid the dizzying effects of changing air pressures, Eva paced the confines of the small cavern and twisted her hands nervously.

"The animals, Conor. Sweetheart and Hondo. How can they survive out there?"

"The wild ones live on the desert, and ride out storms like this every week." Conor grinned and started a fire. "See? Old Sweet Thing tucked herself up like a camel and closed her eyes. She'll snooze, and so will the baby."

Shaking her hair loose, Eva sighed, accepted a cup of herb tea, and settled into the downy blankets.

He caught her studying him over the rim of the cup, the ice-blue eyes reflecting the flames near her white boots.

Conor hunkered next to the fire and filled his mug. Through the hour of the ride, Eva's nearness had tortured him, and he'd had visions of the past, fragments, quick scenes of Eva under him, and under his control.

Eva, the cool professional, her shell destroyed under his busy hands, moaning for satisfaction he'd withheld to teach her a hard lesson about frustration.

Eva trapped against the tree on the estate while he caressed her sensitive breasts, her wet flesh until she welcomed his penetration.

Eva impaled on his erection while they recklessly hunted for a private place to continue. Then the dark hours of frantic pleasuring until they both lay exhausted, awash in the strange sweet sadness of completion.

All of it, every scene replayed during the cayuse ride, with Eva molded to his thighs, his torso, cherished in his lap. Yeah, he'd replayed every scene but the last, the one so painful and perplexing, Conor usually cut it from his erotic reveries. The last time he'd been with Eva.

※☆(づ♡)づ☆※

Conor, wary as an animal, had wakened with Eva in his arms hours later, listening for footfalls, for voices. Out in the garage, the cars traded gossip and endless recountings of their repairs.

He grinned. After the night's sensuous bouts, *he* needed repairs. He feasted his eyes on Eva, melded to him in the narrow cot. She cradled her head on his bicep, one hand trying and failing to encircle it. Delicate and white, her other hand lay on his chest. His heart swelled. Her tiny hand lying in the valley of his pecs made him feel ten feet tall.

Conor pressed a kiss on her disheveled blond hair and tightened his arm around her. His woman. Eva. This was his woman. A wave of protectiveness surged over him. Pink and gold Eva, so strong yet so vulnerable and yielding in his hands. He would kill to keep a stone from her path. He would never let her go.

In her sleep she murmured and snuggled closer to him, her breasts swollen, the peaks and areolas soft and relaxed, silk. Her long mauve nails hid like exotic creatures in the forest of his thick pelt. A tiny tremor, a shiver, coursed over her, and Conor grabbed the quilt from the floor and spread it over them. The night light barely illuminated her face. He smoothed her lips, lips bruised and ripe with his savage kisses. Beneath her eyes lay the evidence of hours of love-making, lavender-blue smudges whose weariness he kissed reverently.

He tucked his arm under his head and wondered at himself. In all the encounters, all the women, all the warm and sex-scented beds, Conor was notorious for escaping, for slipping away. No excuses, no apologies. A final kiss and he was gone.

But in this small bed he cuddled a woman, and the thought of letting her go, dressing and returning to the concrete canyons and crowds of the domed city, those thoughts failed to get a toe-hold in his mind. He wanted to hold her against his length all night, wake up to her in the morning. Keep her.

Eva squirmed into his warmth and opened her eyes. "Conor," she breathed. "For a second, I wondered if this was real." She laughed unsteadily and sat up, tossing the wild fall of her hair behind her shoulders. "Conor." A lilt of amazement tinged her voice. "We really happened."

"Want us to happen again?" Conor gripped her waist and trailed his hand up her ribs to her breast. Instantly, her nipple sprang erect, and her eyes went smoky.

With a little moan, Eva bent over him and kissed the tip of his nose. She smelled of sex, the rich, heady smell of sex. "I'd love to darling, but I really can't stay." She swung her long legs over the side of the narrow cot, and stretched luxuriously on the braided rug like a golden cat.

Stung, and covering his disappointment, Conor leaned against the headboard, his balls tense, his cock lengthening, a fierce ache developing in his groin. "Going out there naked?" He dangled the ruins of her silk dress before her.

"Come prepared is the Kelsey motto." Mischievously, she put her fingers to her mouth and gave a two-note whistle. Out in the garage an engine thrummed to life. When Eva opened the slider, there Austin was waiting, his trunk open.

With a small case and a duplicate of the dress she'd worn, Eva popped into the bathroom and when she emerged, she was clean and fresh, the perfect replica of what Conor'd seen hours earlier at the start of the party. Not a hair out of place.

"I'd love to kiss you good-bye, Conor," she closed the clasp of her case, "but I think you have other things in mind. And I know better now than to get within range." She laughed, a soft tinkling laugh like a sweet weapon. "See you later."

Conor had lain stunned, staring at the closed door, the perfumed musk of sex billowing around him, his body sticky with dried sweat and smeared with both their juices.

No woman walked away from him. Then why should the one he desperately wanted to stay saunter off, as if she'd discarded him like a used toy?

⁂⟨✿⟩⁂

In the garage, Eva leaned against the slider and let the tears come. Conor left the women he pleasured. Was she the first to walk away? The first to avoid the agony of losing him by running?

Eva set Austin to travel backroads. She trusted the air car to navigate the traffic, but she couldn't trust herself to drive, not with eyes blurred with tears, and an ache in her throat. Worst of all, logic and reason reminded her she was suffering the pain of loss for a passionate melding that would never happen again.

Despite her shower, Conor's scent had imbedded itself in her skin. Conor's touch still tingled on her nipples, Conor's lips still pressed her mouth. Eva drew a shuddering breath. The intense pleasure of their joining — how could she ever forget wildly indulging herself to the limits? How could she forget the magic of being covered by Conor's hard body, hearing his dark promises?

"Conor," she said. His name sounded stony and final. If only he'd go away. If only he'd spend the month till boarding for Feldon-9 doing what his files showed that he did best. He'd escorted refugees through battle zones, slipped behind enemy lines to sneak POWs out of prison and nuns out of jail.

He was an enigma, a savior, a rescuer, and at the same time a charismatic seducer. What lay in his heart? Surely, not commitment to a true relationship. She was just another mark on his score sheet. She closed her eyes, utterly miserable, and a fresh flood of tears rolled down her cheeks.

Was Conor really through with her? Had he relished her capitulation, her eager surrender, melting her resistance? Had he paid her back enough for cutting him from the colony list? If he decided to extract another payment to salve his ego, could she escape with her resolve never to see him again intact?

And what would she do if he came to her, coaxed her with his rough, knowing hands, his lips whose touch drained her of the power to fight?

"Please, Conor," she whispered aloud. "Let me go. Help me. I can't see you again. Ever."

"Why?" Austin inquired.

"Be quiet. I'm not talking to you."

"This Conor, was he the specimen lying on the chauffeur's bed?" Austin deliberately reduced speed and dawdled. "I heard the two of you, you know, the shrieks, the loud moans." Austin's voice carried a tinge of curiosity. "We *all* heard."

"Stop it, or I'll override." Eva paused with her finger on the control panel. "Who heard?"

"Well, Mrs. Pinchot's Silver Cloud Rolls Royce almost boiled over. The old girl has led a sheltered life. Then Rodney Lee's Instigator said — but its response was predictably coarse. So, why don't you want to see this Conor again? Has he hurt you in some way?"

"No. Yes." Telling Austin was like telling a mechanical friend, a robot ear who'd make sympathetic noises until she had shed her burden. Eva dabbed her eyes with a tissue. "How can I stay objective when this man, with a single look, can make me forget my status, my dedication to my job? Conor made me love sex for the first time in my life."

"Is this not a good thing?" Austin sounded perplexed.

"Yes. No." She clasped her hands and sighed. "Good sex should enhance an individual's life. But some people, Austin, maybe some people find it too disturbing, too invasive. Hormones instead of logic."

"Like a mechanic tampering with my turbo-carbs with a cold tension probe?" Austin was trying.

"More like a car-doc fooling with your original program."

"Changing the real me?" Austin's voice rang with shock.

"Exactly. Action, that's Conor's appeal. Oh, Austin, he's got a month to come after me. I can't face him."

"In that case, you need a long vacation, Dr. Kelsey. How about the polar resort, The Ice Queen? Would he track you there?"

"Ah, brilliant, Austin." Eva felt a ray of hope. "The guest list confidential, no unauthorized landings. By the time Conor tracks me down, he'd be AWOL from the project. He won't sacrifice his berth on the ship anymore than I would my psych rating."

Austin chuckled and slid into the slow lane of the skyway to Metro from where Eva would escape to the icy north. She'd never again see Conor, never again hear the deep compelling voice.

Chapter 4

"So quiet, Conor." In the cave, Eva made a simple statement that he knew was really a test.

He used both hands on the cup, and stared into the ashy film dulling the randoo branches. Spurts of flame escaped from the nexus where sticks crossed. Idly, Conor sipped his tea and poked at the fire.

He'd planned to sandbag her, wait her out, spoil the revelation she'd extract from him through an innocent remark. But sly Dr. Kelsey was good at waiting too, and that damned perfume, like musk camouflaged with roses, coiled a sinuous finger around his neck, turning him to face her. Conor stalled for another minute.

"Can't hear the storm through tons of cayuse flesh, Doc."

"I meant *you*, Conor. *You're* so quiet." In the echo of the cave her voice seemed stifled, unnatural. Tense?

Conor stretched out, propped on his elbows and ran a slow inspection of her from toes to teeth. He was gratified when she fussed with the tap closure at the collar of her suit, and he hid a grin.

"Dr. Eva Kelsey." He paused and studied her from shuttered lids. "Seems to me if I'd answered your question with a remark about how I was daydreaming or thinking, you'd have laughed and said you meant the storm. Isn't that the way of it, ma'am?" He sucked the cinnamon crust off a randoo twig. "Keep a man off-balance? Geld him with the sharp comment like you'd castrate a steer?"

Eva's voice dropped thirty degrees. Into the ice zone.

"When you finish parading around as Old Texas Billy Bob, I'd like a straightforward answer."

"You mean, you want to get something straight between us? Doc, we did that a couple of times." Conor lightly fingered his crotch. "Damn, lady, my straight thing memorized you chapter and verse. As we'd say here on Laredo, almost wore hisself to a frazzle, pore feller."

Eva's eyes glittered, her lips tightened, and her calmness seemed to take great effort. "Of course. How had I forgotten? Everything must be on the very lowest level or you're unable to deal with it. Deal with it? You're not able to give it a second's room in your head."

With a swing of his cup, Conor dowsed the fire. One small branch gave light, and flickering shadows decorated the rough walls.

Conor heard her gasp of surprise, the rattle of her gourd cup as it bounced off a rock. In the dancing light she was struggling to maintain her equilibrium, but she was in shock. And that was enough, all it took to open her up. One abrupt act, one act close to the edge, and despite her starched control, her professional demeanor, Eva lost her ability to sit perfectly at ease with folded hands and prim lips.

He'd needed another signal, a sign that their night together had imprinted itself as deeply on her heart and mind as it had branded itself on his consciousness. Every cell was marshalling his body to move, to follow the surprise with a kiss, an embrace, a melding of bodies to induce her open-mouthed, open-thighed surrender.

"Now," he began, trying for a reasonable tone, "you ask me why I'm so quiet. You know. But you want to hear me make a fool of myself, hang myself up as your target."

Eva struggled to her feet and flung back the riot of hair that had escaped from the Baradian twist. "I don't know what you're talking about, Mr. Conor."

"Damn, you're good! That *Mr. Conor*, now, that sure put me in my place." He chuckled. "But we're not tip-toeing around Metro City. We're not pretending. We're not civilized anymore, Doc. See, I rode out to get you. Alone. I have you locked in a cave in a storm miles from the settlement in an uninhabitable desert."

Fighting to rein in her tone, Eva said, "What I see is that once again, my assessment of you was uncannily accurate. Conor. An anachronism, a throwback to primitive ancestors who had their way with club and force. You are as unsuitable, as dysfunctional here as you were on Earth, except for the occasional bizarre job niches you occupied to satisfy the unspeakable needs of similarly deranged employers."

Conor threw back his head and loosed a roar of laughter. "Ah, you give yourself away, lady. The more hifalutin' you get, the more you've lost a handle on the situation. Eva, Eva, you can't even admit I was the reason you opted for this assignment."

"Of all the egomaniacal —"

He was across the cave in two strides, bent slightly, and swung her into his arms. She weighed nothing, and felt like everything he'd hunted for his whole life.

"I want you under me, close to the fire. I want to see your eyes open wide, and then close when you take me inside." His throat constricted with need, and in that moment in the light of the savage, primitive scene, her fire-burnished hair cascading over his arm, Conor craved her like the caveman of ancient times lusted for a mate. "Kiss me, Eva. Kiss me like you mean it."

She felt his uneven breathing warm her cheek, the ragged rise and drop of the great pectorals as he lost the regular rhythm to wild panting. He crushed her to his brawny torso, and her sensitive flesh, tormented by his hard nearness during the long ride, shrieked for her to find his lips and plunge her tongue into the alien cinnamon scent of his mouth. Shrieked for her to strip herself, let her breasts revel in the harsh brush of his beard stubble, wrap her arms around his neck and force her nipples into that devilishly knowing mouth.

With a soft moan she met his lips and began to slip away into his hunter's heat and the lure of the kisses she had spent two years aching for. She gave herself up to the drugging kisses, turned in his arms to press her swollen breasts into him, to meet more of his flesh and bone.

Like a panther, he growled into her mouth. "You're what I've waited for, burned for. You burned for me, too, my pretty lady." He took her lips in another bruising kiss. And when she had to break the kiss to gasp for air, he tightened his hold. "Tell me how bad you've wanted me, Eva."

His words penetrated, and shocked awake, Dr. Eva Kelsey, champion of cold logic and utter objectivity, swam to the surface Conor had clouded. Mentally, she listed his heroic acts, his bravery, his larger-than-life exploits.

The diagnostician woke and evaluated his request to admit she needed him. His overwhelming, granite arrogance was revealed in that simple command. How badly *she* had wanted *him*? Dr. Eva Kelsey should've laughed in sheer, stunned astonishment.

For in the end, Conor was Conor was Conor. His heat had reduced her to a whimpering female offering her genitals to sate his animal needs, tearing away her rational surface and exposing an emotionally unstrung bitch animal with a pink cleft made wet and hungry by his masculinity and his strength.

And did Conor have a kind of scoreboard here, too? A coterie of slavish females and a peanut gallery of admiring males to cheer him on? "The legendary Conor," Leon the pilot had said.

Gathering her willpower, Eva attempted to free herself from the bonds of Conor's raw sexuality. She thrashed, eluding his bids to still her mouth with his kisses, trying to find the cave's floor.

"Conor. No. Not now." She shuddered, her reactions too swift, too violent to convince him to wait. "Put me down, Conor, please … please."

"Let me, Eva. Just a little." Conor possessed her mouth, his tongue following the seam of her lips, coaxing her to yield despite her determination to withstand him.

He went to his knees in the soft sand, still anchoring her to the wild thudding of his heart, and her pulse skittered, an erratic crazy dance that sent hot blood to pool in her loins. Deep inside, her resistance shattered like flawed glass. And she sent Eva Kelsey, Ph.D, mute and enraged, back to some quiet place within her mind.

Eva closed her eyes to shut out the shadows playing on the stalactites, to shut out the strangeness of the cave. Behind her lids, there was only the image of Conor. Conor, all man, who made her all woman.

Whimpering, she hoarded her energy, directed it like a tight laserino to pinpoint the fevered flesh at her center. She moved her hips restlessly, and Conor slipped his hands between her loosened thighs and thumbed the hint of her clitoris through her neosuit.

He fastened his teeth on the rise of her nipples through the suit, and the rub of the fabric like a second skin over her wildly sensitive flesh jolted her.

"Conor, Conor." She clutched his clubbed black mane and fumbled with shaking fingers to untie the leather thong.

Then he stopped, lifting his head, his gaze dark and penetrating under his thick eyebrows. From the depths of his deep-set storm-colored eyes, his stare, like a scalpel, excised the shreds of her self-control.

Lightly, he brushed her lips, and weakened his hold on her. And though she felt the stiffness of his massive shaft, he only traced the curve of her cheek and brushed her hair from her face.

"Conor?"

"From now on, Dr. Kelsey, the guy you call animal will be tame as a pussycat." His grin should've reassured her, but underneath the gleam of white teeth and loaded promise, Eva sensed a darker purpose. With a final gentle kiss, he deposited her on the warm sand beside the feeble fire.

He knelt beside her, and raised his hands above his head, the enormous tanned hands that had forced her to his sexual will, confining and restraining her until he'd elicited an outpouring of desire.

Eva's hands trailed down the powerful muscles under the taut buckskin shirt. She fondled his swollen erection and watched the muscles tighten in his jaw.

"Tame? Is this tame?" Eva teased him, her voice throaty and low.

"From now on, you show *me* how much you want me."

"What kind of game is this, Conor?"

"You spell out everything you want me to do. Teach me, poor untrained bastard that I am. After all, what can you expect of — what was it you called me — bizarre? dysfunctional critter? A throwback to the times when men dragged screaming, but secretly delighted, women back to their caves by the hair." Conor folded his arms, biceps bulging.

"I said those things." Eva licked her lips and hooded her eyes, letting her fingers slide to his iron thigh. Defiantly, then, even as the urge to en-

gulf his thick penis in her willing flesh tortured her, she added, "And I
see no evidence to change my opinion."

"Exactly. I'm Laredo mud in your hands, Doc. Won't make a move
without orders from the all-knowing Dr. Kelsey."

She reined in an outburst of temper. "You're giving me total control
of your body and mind?"

"Only way I can give you evidence I'm —" he coughed into his fist,
"civilized."

Her pouting labia lay slick against the crotch of her neosuit, and she
squirmed as unobtrusively as possible, needing the relief Conor held
just out of reach.

"You make no move, say no word unless I command it?"

Conor nodded and dropped his hands to his sides.

A collage of luscious possibilities raced through Eva's imagination.
She sat back, crossed her legs Indian-style, and tested him.

"Stand up, Conor."

He rose without so much as a quick breath and looked down on her.

"Strip. That shirt. And boots, too." Eva put her hands behind her,
bracing herself while Conor caught her stare and slowly, oh so slowly,
gripped the hem of his tunic and inch by inch raised it.

Eva's mouth went dry. He exposed the black tip of hair that pointed
to the huge treasure below his belt, and widened into a matted pyramid
as he pulled the shirt higher. The pelt swirled around his flat male nipples, and Eva remembered her tongue on the pebbled surfaces.

Conor dropped the shirt and kicked off his moccasins. He waited,
bronzed in the pale firelight, a perfectly chiseled archetype of virility.

"The pants," Eva got out after a long hesitation, determined to best
him at his own game.

As if to call attention to what she should look at, he brushed his groin
briefly, and Eva felt a tide of warmth creeping up from her collar and
glanced away, only to be drawn back.

Without a grain of self-consciousness, Conor untied the leather
strings at his waist and slid the trousers down, revealing the thick patch
of black curls at the apex of his legs.

He paused for a few seconds with gritted teeth to stretch the pants
over his jutting penis. Freed from the constraints of the skins, it sprang
free.

With one hand, Conor brushed the angry swelling erection.

"I didn't order you to touch yourself," Eva snapped.

A quick duck of his head in agreement, and Conor shucked off the
pants and threw them aside. He stood before her, heart-stoppingly
male, every taut muscle, every articulation of bone and ripple of tendon
and sinew releasing a flow of creaminess from her core.

"Fix the bed, I mean, the blankets," she stuttered and he bent to spread the feathery quilts, his strong toes digging into the soft dirt. At the sight of his testicles, furred and high and tight, Eva's fingers curled involuntarily.

When he turned to her, his great erection knocked against his belly and she shivered imagining his thickness pushing, stretching, thrusting into her dripping vagina.

She'd planned on directing Conor to undress her slowly, to kiss her breasts, to suck her clit until he was half-maddened with lust. She'd planned to make him wait before he emptied those heavy balls in her body.

His eyes, gleaming with sexual excitement, measured her fierce readiness. She met his gaze and tried to play the ice queen but it was a joke. She was shaking with need for him. Waiting be damned. Teasing be damned.

With one trembling finger she indicated the tap-catch on her collar. Huskily, she pleaded, "Open me, Conor."

He undid the lock and stepped back.

"No. Get it off me. Make me naked." She could barely hold back the urge to scream at him to hurry.

Conor stripped her of the suit as neatly and quickly as peeling a glove off her hand. And stopped.

"No," she moaned, reaching for him. "Carry me to the bed. Lie next to me." Conor swooped her up and held her high on his chest, keeping her well away from the throbbing she wanted to feel skimming her buttocks.

He laid her close to the wall and stretched out beside her. He laced his fingers as primly as a solo singer and stared at the ceiling, pretending to be oblivious to his mighty penis with its enlarged veins and head.

Eva bit her lip. Hot and aroused and furious with need, she wanted Conor to take charge. Though she'd initiated the game, Conor knew all the right moves to drive her insane. But she could still win. After all, how long could a man like Conor keep his hunger in check?

Should she play with him, the way she had in the estate's garage room? Flicking his sex with her tongue, teasing with her fingernails?

Or should she drive *him* mad with instructions to play with her body? And at the last minute, command him to stop? This wasn't, after all, really about lust and satisfaction. This was about revenge, the payback for Conor's smooth dismissal of her power and importance, his treating her like an inconsequential cog in the bureaucratic machine.

From somewhere in her mind, the eminent Dr. Eva Kelsey sneered and mocked. "Revenge? This assignment was all about pursuing a man you couldn't forget." Then she went silent.

"Lick me, Conor," Eva whispered. "All over." Half-closing her eyes, she raised her hands over her head and sifted the sand through her fingers.

She expected him to start with her face, but Conor rolled over and, bracing himself on the other side of her waist, he nuzzled into the delicate skin under her arm. His warm tongue, wide and wet, laved her repeatedly. She moved slightly, urging him without words to her swelling breasts, to suck her nipples.

But Conor by-passed her breasts and licked down her rib cage.

When he plied his tongue in the crevice between her thigh and torso, Eva moaned and fought to keep her hips still. He would soon bury that wonderful tongue deep inside, lap up the cream that had been flowing since her first sight of him, since he'd ridden out of the canyon. Dominant, devilish, all-controlling Conor.

He knew what she wanted, damn him, and was not giving it to her without a fight, without her croaking nonsensical commands. Squirming, she turned her mound into his face, feeling the accidental, heavenly grain of his beard stubble scratch her clit.

She shuddered, but Conor's knowing tongue skipped over the aching nub and slid down her leg.

"No, Conor. Eat me." She spread her legs, embarrassed to say the words, but too desperate to care. "Or fuck me. Or do anything you want. The game's over," she groaned. "I want you so bad I hurt."

"Don't you want me domesticated, tame?" he said. "Tell me, Eva. What's it going to be? The real me or the civilized, sanitized version?"

"You. Oh, you, Conor." She choked with craving for him, her breath shallow. "Please. The game's finished."

Smoky-eyed, Conor shifted, placed a heavily muscled forearm over her belly to hold her in place, and, with his rough fingers veed to keep her open, worked his mouth over her distended flesh. Finally, her jouncing against his mouth became so violent, he immobilized her with both hands on her hips in an iron grip.

Then he stopped, and whispered into her wet, heated core. He spoke soft, dark words, words she could guess, love words from the Cygnus system, from Mars, sounds from the rustling feathers of mating pteradrakes. He blew tiny gusts into her until she cried for the feel of his mouth again.

At her cry, Conor loosed her hips, and sucked on her clit while his hands massaged her breasts, and plucked her painfully erect nipples.

Just as she arched her back for relief from the impossible tension, Conor freed her, lifted her shaking legs over his shoulders and had barely penetrated when she shrieked and reached to claw at his shoulders.

"So wet and creamy, so ready for me, but so tight." He pulled out except for the tip and raised one eyebrow. "Too tight. Why? Tell me, Eva."

"No." She rocked her head back and forth on the feathery blankets. "Come in me. I won't scream."

"How far? This far?" He shoved in an inch and she tensed her vaginal muscles. "No more, my pretty lady, until you answer."

She touched his face, closed her eyes and turned her head to the wall. "Conor," she breathed raggedly. "There've been no other men since that night."

Then she realized she'd said the perfect words. Across his face she saw flickers of wonder and tenderness and delight. His immense penis swelled even larger, and he pushed its stiffness in slowly.

"I don't want to hurt you, lover," he said, his voice rough with shock and happiness and restraint.

"If that's the only way to have you, hurt me," she whispered, and suddenly she surged upward and engulfed all of him. Her whisper built into a long, painful scream that rang in the cave. But she would not let him withdraw.

After endless moments of Conor between her thighs, suckling her breasts, and kissing her deeply, he began to test her with slow, measured thrusts. Eva felt herself adjust to his massiveness, his fullness stretching her body's limits, and she lifted her hips to meet his hard pelvis in a magic, ancient rhythm.

Chapter 5

Eva's trembling gradually ceased, and she clung to Conor, imprinting tender kisses on his flesh, tasting the beads of sweat.

"I'm too heavy," Conor whispered, and loosed her arms from around his neck. He kissed the tip of her nose and grinned. "Pay attention now. When we get to town, we have to set some limits, Doc, or we'll both be dead, exhausted." He bent and lazily licked her nipples. He tried for a light tone, but he missed and hoped she'd see his gaze was serious and penetrating.

"Limits?" Eva stretched like a cat beneath him and ran her fingernails through his hair. "What limits do you mean, lover? One position fits all?" She laughed, a sleepy, teasing laugh, but her eyes clouded as if she knew what he was asking.

He braced himself on his forearms, and let his thumbs play where her breasts softly grew from her ribs. "If you ever tell anybody I said this, I'll swear on my cayuses's head that you're a liar." Conor drew a deep breath. "Eva, you're the only woman I've ever had who sucks the stamina, that animal energy out of me. You even block my sixth sense, my female-sensor, and who needs other women, darling, when I've got you?"

"Why, Conor, I do think that's a compliment." She bit his lower lip, and his guts boiled in a spasm of need. He clenched his jaw. Without withdrawing, he got hard again.

"So we need limits. Limits as in, how often we see each other like this." He moved in her, and elicited a moan. "Answer me, Doc. What's it going to be? Maybe three nights a week? And the weekends?"

Eva massaged his shoulders, and palmed his chest. Her voice was a whisper and all the lightness had vanished. "Let me sit up, Conor. I can't think about anything when you're deep in me, except —"

She slid away from under him, pulling him from the dripping velvet of her sheath, and he gritted his teeth against the pain in his groin. Eva tossed back her mane of wheaten hair, while a very small smile played on her lips. "If I did sexual calisthenics like these five days a week, Conor, I'd be as limp as a Venusian gel-eel, and twice as useless."

"That's how I like you, woman. Limp and wet," he growled, "but only afterward when we've dowsed all our fire." He lay on his back, brawny arms and torso glistening in the dimness, his hands stacked behind his head.

Eva felt for her suit, conscious of his hot inspection, conscious of the picture she made, her breasts, full and ripe, weighed by gravity, within Conor's reach, aching for his touch and his mouth.

But he was right, and she blushed with shame that she, a professional, had been forced to think of her obligations by a colonist.

She slipped into the suit and collared up, locking the tab. Swiftly and efficiently, she coiled her hair, fished a stay-pin from her suit, and was once more, on the surface at least, the respectable cold fish, Dr. Eva Kelsey, Colonial Selection Specialist, Investigator.

She cocked her head and listened to a diminishing roar. "Has the storm blown over?"

Conor rose and dressed quickly. "You've got the ears for this place." He tied his hair in its leather thong. "Like I said before, Doc, you were born for Laredo. Should've tested and settled here yourself."

At the cavern door, Sweetheart grumbled and shifted, lowered her rhubarb-eared snaky head and peered in with a squeal of delight. In the brilliant shafts of light allowed into the dark by the cayuse's movement, Eva folded blankets while Conor kicked the rantoon sticks apart.

"Quit dodging the question, Doc. How many nights?" Hands on hips, Conor stood with his legs apart, planted like a stone monument, with no intention of going anywhere until she answered.

Eva had a flash of herself with Conor constantly on her mind. The renowned Dr. Kelsey, approaching every problem, every evaluation, every test, with the silky false perceptions of the truly satisfied woman. She could almost hear the rushed interviews, larded with omissions because all she'd want was the damned things to be over, for Conor to bed her, recklessly, with total mastery, reducing her to compliant sexual slavery. Like all the women he'd seduced and abandoned, made mindless and wanting.

How long before the Psych Board found out? And they always did. She could see the five old gentlemen, Freudian-trained and Tatroset-depth sharpened, impassively reviewing her files. The quintet shaking their venerable heads, sighing as they added another note, another accusation of personal involvement.

She'd shown some spunk, that time on the estate, when she'd walked out on him to repay him for humiliating her at her office, his easy manipulating of her father to bypass Eva's judgement. But the truth was simpler than revenge. She had been terrified of wanting Conor. Loving Conor.

And now, he'd reduced her to an emotional, quivering jelly.

Was this Conor turning the tables, laughing at her under the guise of sincerity, pretending to be on the verge of declaring love? Conor getting even? Conor jeopardizing her standing?

The down blankets held protectively over her breasts, Eva said, "We hardly know each other. I really am at quite a loss to explain any of this." She nodded toward the depressions in the sand next to the wall where they'd lain, where he'd brought her to one stunning climax after another.

"Quite a loss, you say?" Conor's grin was devoid of amusement. "You're so full of doubletalk, your suit must be straining at the molecular level." His laugh chilled her. "The damn thing should explode and leave you naked."

"Ah, there it is, what I was waiting for, the old Conor, the beast so near and dear to all our hearts." She snapped out her words like the crack of a whip. "I will not be seeing you three nights per week, or the weekends, or anytime during my visit. I am not here for your pleasure, but to improve my file, do my job."

Conor grabbed the saddlepack of utensils. "Nothing surprises me about you, Doc. What surprises me is that, after all my hunting experience, I let you ambush me twice."

"What are you talking about?" Eva's stomach somersaulted, as if the planet spun and Conor had floated out of range.

"The garage. You let me know I was scum when you dressed and ran home." He strode toward the opening, and turned back. "And today you put me in my place again."

Flustered and furious, Eva stamped after him and shouted, "You're delusional with obvious tinges of paranoia. How dare you equate my professional concerns with your bizarre notions that somehow I'm wreaking revenge on you?"

"Yup, that's me. Crazy Conor. I'm a sick bastard. But don't offer me free treatments, good doctor. Your methods only make things worse." He threw down the pack, snatched the blankets from her and lifted her onto the ladder as impersonally as he'd hoist an elderly man.

"Get aboard. Sit still, and for God's sake, keep one of those blankets between you and me. I've had plenty of women —"

"Hundreds!" Eva shrieked. "Thousands!"

"— but I never had one who got off rubbing herself on my butt while calling *me* an animal."

When he climbed up and stowed the pack, Eva shrank away and obediently stuffed the blanket between them, the fence, the barricade, the wall to keep them apart. "Happy now, Conor?" she said evenly.

He didn't bother to answer, just clucked to Sweetheart, whistled for Hondo, and guided them across the flatlands to the lake.

"Laredo City. Population 400," the weathered sign proclaimed. The sun was casting angular shadows when they rode into the settlement by the lake. Shards of light, broken by a brisk breeze, danced on the water. Eva licked her lips. The sight and cool smell of the blue-green water made her even more thirsty.

Twice Conor had offered her his canteen, and she'd refused. *Stupid, she chided herself. Stupid to ride for hours craving a drink just for the satisfaction of saying no to him.* But she brushed aside her self-accusations, and studied the efforts of the colonists.

Fastform buildings imitated the raw structures of a western ghost town and lined the main street. On boardwalks, men in blue trousers and cowboy hats mingled with women wearing sunbonnets and calico dresses. Was that the right word, calico?

Where were the efficient neosuits with their bright colors and occupational designations?

Almost as if reading her mind, Conor spoke. "These clothes work best in the climate. The women patterned one of the fabricators, and pretty soon they had us all gussied up. Gussied up," he repeated, "means dressed nicely."

"Thanks. I've been reading a dictionary of western old-speak." Eva could've kicked herself. Obviously, Conor was making gestures, almost apologizing for his attitude, and she'd rebuffed him. A few miles before town, she'd let the blanket slide down, then draped it across her shoulders like a cloak in the cooling air.

Conor had seemed not to notice the press of her breasts. His posture, his breathing, his position in the saddle, nothing changed. She smiled and scanned the clumps of welcoming folk and couples at the roadside, but the ones who stood out, frantically waving, were women. And the bonneted ladies were not wasting their waves on her.

How many of them had he taken? How many had been drawn into his enveloping, musky heat? How many had eagerly spread their thighs, opened themselves to his ravages?

When Conor raised one hand over his head, the crowd cheered. These people knew the real Conor, the one who led and hunted, and protected, the one she'd penalized in Metro City with her biases. She'd made a mistake. Untamed, he mirrored the rawness of Laredo. The perfect world for him and his power and his arrogance.

Eva gave a polite wave or two, quickly returning her free hand to Conor's waist. Nodding at a cluster of older men in quaint suits, she wondered how many of them would be cheering Conor astride his cayuse if they knew Conor had also been astride their wives.

At the tug of Conor's reins, Sweetheart halted. A gang of little boys, grubby from play, shouted Conor's name and rushed to greet him. He waved, swung out of the saddle, and urged Eva to climb down the ladder.

Men unloaded Hondo, and stacked Eva's cases next to the general store. But no one came forward to help with Sweetheart who froze, rigid, her immense ears flattened against her neck.

"Dr. Kelsey, welcome to Laredo." The mayor doffed his hat, and bent to kiss her hand, the remnant of sunlight splashing on his bald head. He jammed his hat on, and took her arm. "I'm Mayor Tim Ballard, and this here is Noah Rain, our young sheriff."

"Pleasure, ma'am." Noah touched the brim of his hat, tilted rakishly on blond curls. His file raced past in her memory. Only twenty-three, killer good looks, great body. If anyone on Laredo could give Conor a run for his money, it was the young sheriff.

And, if she had appraised him, he was returning the favor. His bright blue eyes took her in from teeth to toenails. No secret, he liked what he saw.

Take that, Mr. Conor, she gloated.

But a shrill squeal ended her flirtation, and sent her into Noah's arms. When she jerked around, Conor, head high, hadn't paid the slightest bit of attention to the sheriff and herself measuring each other for a jump in the sack. Instead, he'd climbed aloft, signalled, and he and Sweetheart had begun trudging down the middle of Main Street.

"Conor and that damned critter," the mayor apologized.

"I'd think the men would have helped him with her," Eva said.

Around her the group chuckled. "Ah, she don't take kindly to anybody touching her but Conor," the sheriff informed her.

"What's more, she don't take kindly to anybody touching *Conor* but herself."

"Fair warning, hey?" The mayor offered his arm. They deposited her work cases in the office which he shared with the sheriff, and he escorted her to Mrs. Donovan's boarding house.

The plump and apple-cheeked Mrs. Donovan must've drawn herself off a compuvid landlady of 1950's horse operas. She made a wonderful fuss over Eva and got her settled in a room at the front of the house. The settlers had decorated the walls with a rose-bouquet paper, and the theme was repeated in a white hobnailed vase of newly-cut cabbage roses.

"Now, after your shower, missy, put on these. I ran the fabricator myself. Gingham." Proudly, she displayed a blue print dress and a bonnet hanging on the back of the door. "Here's your little leather slippers." She lowered her voice. "Now we don't wear underclothes here, my dear. Too hot."

"This is extraordinarily kind, Mrs. Donovan, but for professional reasons, my suit —"

"Oh." The landlady's face fell, she put her hand in her apron pocket, and suddenly smiled. "Well, landsakes! How foolish of me. 'Course you must wear your neosuit. Now, you freshen up and come down for dinner." She bustled down the stairs, leaving Eva to contemplate the dress and her silly feelings of guilt at hurting the kindly woman's feelings.

Eva sat on the thick mattress and stared at the toes of her suit. Mrs. Donovan must've known that the suit had a cleansing mode, and that Eva really didn't need a shower. Watching her eyes grow smoky in the shadowy mirror atop the dressing table, she stroked the warmth between her legs.

On the ride in with Conor, she'd tabbed in the hygiene program, with special limits. The suit, per instructions, sanitized her, but had avoided her most private place. On the chenille bedspread, Eva squirmed, and her delicate woman parts, swollen and slippery, slid wetly against each other, closing the ripe crease Conor had fingered and pierced and licked.

Eva shuddered in a small orgasm, unable to fight off the memories of Conor, his dark head moving between her legs, his mouth searing her, tasting her, thrusting his tongue deep, nibbling and sucking her clit until she'd screamed and tore at his hair in her wildness.

"Stop this. Right now. Stop this," she hissed at her image.

Eva skinned off the suit and popped into the bathroom. Under the warm spray, she scrubbed off all evidence of Conor's musky, male scent, Conor's savage love-making. She closed her eyes and her traitorous body remembered his teeth grazing her hard nipples, her buttocks, the sensitive skin on her throat.

Her eyes flew open. Her throat. Eva leaped from the shower and lifted her chin. Huge love-bites, Conor's brands, stood out like purple blooms in a kind of sex-necklace.

Eva panted with fury. Who had seen the damned things? The mayor, she'd bet, and that sharp-eyed young sheriff. Eva clapped her hands to her face, and felt the blood beating in her cheeks.

And, of course, dear Mrs. Donovan must've got a good look.

Wrapping herself in the fluffy towel, Eva dried herself. She slid into the neosuit. But the mirror showed her that the collar was too low, and the bruised skin flashed like ion-signs above the whiteness of her uniform.

Close to tears of rage, she tore it off, flung it on the rag rug, and pulled the gingham dress from its hanger. But even the high neck's sweet frilly finish wasn't enough. Eva had to leave her hair down, too soft and girlish, trailing over her ears, and down her breasts. Mrs. Donovan had left her no petticoat, no underwear, just the long dress whose tiny blue bows winked down the bodice. For all the length of the skirt, Eva felt more naked than she'd ever felt in her life.

Who could take her seriously during her investigations, decked out, "gussied up" like some pioneer adolescent advertising for a husband?

"Damn Conor to hell for this." Remembering Austin's cry of disbelief about a man who changed the original self into a new creature, Eva snarled into the mirror. "I let him change *me* because I wanted him. I let him do this. I hate myself." She dashed tears from her eyes, and tried to decend the stairs with the dignity befitting her official status.

In the foyer, she tugged at her skirt, arranged the cascade of hair over the fitted bodice, and arranged a smile on her face. As she entered the formal dining room, she parted her lips to greet the diners, but her eyes widened, her mouth stayed open, and the greetings locked in her throat.

Framed before the filmy batiste curtains at the enormous, lace-covered table sat Conor, as out of place as a cougar in a rabbit hutch.

Chapter 6

Conor rose, dwarfing the two normal-sized men and a middle-aged woman. His eyes glittered, reminding Eva of their shared sensual secrets, and the shock of seeing him was so acute, Eva felt the blood drain from her face, then return in a flood of heat and embarrassment.

Mrs. Donovan rushed in from the kitchen, cooed welcoming cries and introductions, and seated Eva directly across from Conor. Eva bit the inside of her mouth, draped the napkin on her lap, and addressed chunks of squash in a steamy broth.

At first, she was grateful to whatever fates had plunked her on the opposite side of the table from Conor. Next to a balding chemist who hardly seemed to generate enough thermal units to warm himself, she smugly congratulated herself at avoiding Conor's fire.

But as Mrs. Donovan cleared the soup plates, Eva felt something brushing her ankle, something encased in soft buckskin moccasins. She glanced up at Conor. With a corner of his napkin he was dabbing those demanding lips that had forced screams of ecstasy from her throat.

He wore a perfectly straight face, features that were a model, an example of self-control, even under torture, all except for his eyes taking in her nipples, erect, frictionized by the sturdy cotton.

By the time Mrs. Donovan arrived with the platter of roast gilk, Conor was well-satisfied that Eva could not face him without the picture of their terrific fuck fueling the flames. Leisurely he moved his foot higher, intruding under the protection of her dress.

Eva glared at him, and tried to back away, but where was there to go? What could she do? Excuse herself and run from the table? He knew it wouldn't happen. She'd do it verbally. That was her style.

"What a curious name. Gilk. Whatever does it mean?" Eva poked a thick slice swimming in the gravy on her plate.

"Why it's a meat creature from the forest, Dr. Kelsey," the chemist explained. "Gilk. That's the cry it makes as it expires. Or so we townfolk are told."

"And you don't believe that story? A wise skepticism, if you've never actually killed one yourself." Eva smiled, and took a bite. "Delicious. My kudos to the hunter and the cook. I know the cook. Do you trust the hunter?" Laughter around the table punctuated her question.

Conor used the distraction to slide his foot back and forth over her knee. He put food in his mouth. It was tasteless, and he was aware that the fever of wanting Eva had shut down anything extraneous to his goal of having her again. It was like being on the hunt, when he was numb to heat, insect stings, and he zeroed in on the prey.

His erection stirred, and he shifted. He was in pain, but not enough to abandon tormenting himself, touching her with his toes through the thin buckskin. God, he wanted to clear the table with one sweep of his arm, throw that damned dress over her breasts, and pump till she begged for mercy.

"Everybody trusts Conor. This guy hunts and stocks the caves. That was his idea, stocking the caves in case somebody got caught in a storm." The chemist buttered a scoop of potato-like starch. "He rides the perimeter every day."

"And don't forget catching the wild cayuses," Mrs. Donovan added. "And all his exploring. My, my. Did you see how even the little boys admire him?"

"Oh, yes. He's quite remarkable, a regular pillar of the community. And a real catch." Eva wore a small proud smile.

Mrs. Donovan snorted. "He says he's got no time for women."

Conor forced his foot between Eva's closed thighs, and caressed the soft skin with gentle urgency. He watched for any sign of desire on her face, but like a marble statue he'd once seen titled "Purity Assaulted," Eva ignored him and pretended to be taking part in the dull conversations.

She coughed genteely, her napkin to her mouth, her gaze burning him over the white hem. She clamped her thighs on his foot, but it was too late. Conor was on target, the tip of his moccasin wet with her juice, rubbing her nakedness, moving in slow circles on her mons, in the downy triangle, on the stiffening nub that loved his attention though Eva's manner denied it. Her body made a liar out of her.

She fidgeted, chatting up the chemist, playing with her silverware. She sipped water, inched the salt cellar away from the pepper mill, asked for the vegetables to be passed, and surreptitiously read her time band. The boarders discussed the weekend.

And Eva chimed in, as if she cared. "What a challenge, trying to recalibrate my circadian rhythm to a ten-day week."

"You have been sadly misinformed," the chemist said. "We have only five days in a week."

"But Conor, Conor said —" she tried to go on, but stuttered to a halt and fixed her eyes at a point just over his left shoulder.

Now she realized his wanting her three days plus the weekend meant wanting her *all* the time. The way he wanted her now, to come in polite company with only his hidden manipulation.

Her nipples looked immense, and, as he imagined rolling them in his mouth like sweet, hard candies, Conor's penis thickened, and he hovered on the brink of explosion just by looking at her, feeling her. Damn, that was a kid weakness he'd put behind him when he was fifteen.

Eva's breathing quickened, and she dropped her napkin on her plate. "A lovely dinner. And so nice to meet everyone." Her eyes were glazed, unfocussed, and her breathing rapid and shallow.

Come, Eva. Come. Imagine my tongue lapping all that hot pink flesh while you let go. Imagine my cock stretching you. Come for me, baby. Conor gave silent commands and smilingly agreed to a statement he hadn't heard from the maiden lady.

"Nonsense, Doctor. You shall have some perciple pie," Mrs. Donovan insisted. From the sideboard, she transferred a gigantic ceramic pastry dish, and placed a wedge of flaky crust bursting with syrupy yellow fruit on a dessert plate. "It's our favorite, peachy and crisp. Now you sit still and take as much as you want."

Conor licked his dry lips. "That's right, Dr. Kelsey. Sit still and take as much as you want."

Eva turned crimson, and despite herself, opened fully and rotated her pelvis. Conor worked with more speed, finally centering on her clit and teasing mercilessly.

Suddenly, her fork clattered on her plate, and she gasped, eyes tightly shut. She gripped the table edge, white-knuckled, and froze in a spasm. "Ooh, ooh, my God." She shuddered and slumped forward.

"Lord, she's had some sort of allergic fit," cried Mrs. Donovan. "It was the pie! I'll never forgive myself."

Before the boarders could move, Conor strode around the table, lifted Eva, and cradled her in his arms. "Finish your supper. I'll carry her to her room."

Mrs. Donovan rushed before them, and had a damp cloth waiting for Eva's brow. "Yes, put her atop the coverlet, Conor."

"Do you think I should call the medic?"

"No medic," Eva whispered. "Just a little rest. Go back to your guests. I'm so sorry to have been a bother."

"I shall not leave you here alone," Mrs. Donovan said firmly.

"I'll stay. You should be with the roomers." Conor's voice brooked no argument, and he sat beside Eva, turning the washcloth to its cooler side.

"Dear, dear. It never rains but it pours. Look here. You've spilled something on your moccasin, Conor."

"Some juice," he said. "I'll fix it later."

As soon as the sound of Mrs. Donovan's footsteps ended in the foyer, Eva opened her eyes. Conor was practically on top of her, and her response to him left her weak, out of control. Again.

The submerged Dr. Eva Kelsey rode to the rescue, protected Eva's vulnerability, barricaded her from the urge to throw herself into his arms. She jerked the cloth from his hand and struck him across the face. Dr. Kelsey put words in her mouth.

"If you knew how much I detest your vulgarity, you would wither and dry up," Eva ground out between her teeth.

Conor cupped her mons through the gingham skirt. "No fear of that happening down here," he said, his voice low and husky. "You're like an oasis, all nectar and cream, and I'm dying to drink. But tonight I'll have to settle for this. Making love in your office, in the cave, seems like a hundred years ago. Seems you're burned into me. Eva, don't you feel it, too? I'm complete for the first time in my life."

He squeezed her rhythmically. Eva jolted into a series of aftershocks, staring into his eyes, clutching his wrist. Conor stayed his hand till the last tiny crisis passed. When he rose, his fingers were as wet as her dress.

He ran his tongue over them, savoring her essence. "Second-hand. But better than nothing, my beautiful Dr. Eva."

"Enjoy the moment because after tonight, that's what you'll get. Nothing." Her eyes were bright with self-anger and shame.

"Nothing? Not even when I've saved this for you for two years?" He captured her hand and pressed it to the bulge pulsing and struggling to escape his breeches. "There's been no one. Damn it, woman, you know it. I love you, Eva."

Eva wrenched away. Her thoughts whirled in a stupid jumble, all mixed up, the attraction to his domineering maleness, her compulsion to touch him, to tremble at his hungry look, to melt in surrender. The now and needy high tides of lust inspired by Conor's nearness had colored her habits of careful deduction and analysis. Worse, the most heinous Psych Board sin, involvement.

She stifled a moan and tried to sharpen her voice. "I have professional responsibilities, Conor, that take precedence over personal feelings. Besides, I don't intend to join your list of discarded women. I can't see you again."

"But you will." He straightened her skirt, brushed his mouth on hers, and headed for the stairs.

The next morning, the Mayor waved her into his office. It smelled of dust and disuse, and she made a mental note to chart that under the column entitled "Community Energy." Dust motes floated in beams creeping through the smeared windows. The lone jail cell was empty.

Swelling with pride, Ballard pointed at his desk. "The Sheriff and me, we put your cases here. And allow me to add, ma'am, you're sure fetchin' in that sundress and bonnet. Same blue as your eyes." He drew a heart in the dust on a ledger.

"So, Dr. Kelsey, not askin' you to commit yourself to anything, whaddya think? A general impression of our little village?"

Eva perched on the edge of the chair. "On the basis of limited observation, Mayor, I've never seen happier citizens. All smiles, grins, hugs and kisses. Is it in the air?"

"So some say, so some say." Their chuckles blended.

Eva gathered scattered pencils to clear a workspace. "I'm all set, and thanks for your efforts, Mayor."

"Now don't get too involved in paperwork today, Doc. You got months, and, after all, you better know the landscape, the plants and critters. So I made arrangements for you to get the grand tour."

"The grand tour? Oh, I'll do that later," she said hastily. "I really must begin interviews." Suddenly, the windows rattled, and the floor quaked under Eva's feet.

"All the time in the world," he insisted, ignoring the earth-shattering thumps. "Yup, I asked Noah to take you round —"

"Ah, the Sheriff." Eva breathed a sigh of relief.

"— but that young scamp, he's caught up today. So I asked — by gum, speak of the devil. Here's your guide, pullin' up to the old hitchin' post this minute."

Eva leaped up. Through the dirty glass, Sweetheart's yellow eye discovered her. The cayuse opened her fearful mouth and uttered a screech. She vented her bad humor by darting a bite at a second cayuse standing quietly in the middle of the street.

And then Conor performed the empty ritual of draping the monster's reins over the log. What a joke. Nothing could hold back that creature if she wanted to stampede.

"I know it's important for your records to check the lay of the land, so to speak. I'll leave you in Conor's capable hands for now. Me and the Missus, we got some … , well, let's call 'em chores." He winked and slammed the door behind him.

Eva frowned. He couldn't have possibly meant what the wink implied, could he? Of course not. A man of his age and his position would have strong notions of propriety, the rigorous requirements of his status. And damn his stupid plans. She reseated herself and punched a few file buttons.

Tight-lipped, she bent to her bio-com, wearing an expression of professional interest. True, it was necessary to visit the outlying environs, but there was no way she'd get dragged out of this office by Conor.

"That's better, Doc. Sidesaddle good? Just the thing for ladies who don't wear britches." Conor grinned. "Now don't get testy and saw at the reins."

"What I'd like to saw is your skull from your neck," she said. She labored overtime to steel herself against his charm. "Did you or did you not hear me say we couldn't see each other anymore?" Summoning all her self-control, she waved at the Sheriff lounging across the street with his gaggle of girls.

Conor completely ignored her reminder and instead nodded at the cayuse's wiggling ears. "I notice Hercules likes you. And Sweetheart approves." The male ducked his neck, crooned, and bathed Eva in a bashful stare. He had very long eyelashes. "Poor guy, he can't help himself."

"Then he's ridiculous," Eva said, secretly pleased at her conquest. Conor wasn't the only one with a devoted beast. She scratched Herc's neck, and he rumbled a thank-you. The cayuses lumbered down a wide path where the town met the sparse woods. Eva inhaled the freshest, most fragrant air she'd ever tasted, air permeated with the faint scent of cinnamon and lavender.

Some of the trees twisted and displayed a peculiar variety of barks, and one, a brilliant green from root to branch stunned her with deep-lobed purple flowers. On its trunk a dead fox-like creature hung as if he'd been glued.

"Conor, what's that?" Eva leaned forward in the saddle and pointed.

"Gripper tree," he said. "Anything that strolls too close gets invited to stay … permanently." He exhaled. "No matter how beautiful a planet or a person, there's always a dark side. But who'd know better than you?"

Eva struggled for composure. Her trips into the wild, anywhere, were rare. Later she'd confide in Conor that this was only her second off-Earth colonization report. "Of course, of course," she said abruptly, and, despite the aura of security he exuded, she dug for a question to conceal her nervousness. "But it's so horrible. Have these trees any practical value to the colony other than snaring small animals?"

Conor raised one knee and planted his foot on the saddle as casually as if he sat in his living room. "I don't want to tell tales out of school, Doc, knowing how you're collecting data about us and all. Some couples like to take walks out here, use the gripper trees for fun and games. Shameful, hey?"

Swallowing a laugh, Eva clucked at Hercules and, over her shoulder yelled, "Is there anything, absolutely anything that doesn't remind you of sex?"

"Nothing, when I'm with you," he shouted, brimming with sheer wickedness. "And when I catch up with you ..." He roared, his bigger-than-life, bold laugh.

But Hercules poured it on, skirting the dense forest and carrying her out into a meadow of blue-green grasses where orange and yellow birds flitted. The flatlands stretched out in a forever vista, out to the horizon. A tug at the reins, and the cayuse stopped and munched on a clump of grass.

Eva strained to listen. No voices, no thrum of machinery, no mechanical attention from robots or talking cars. A twitter from a flock of the tiny birds, the sweet whisper of a soft, scented breeze enveloped her. The sound of joy.

From deep inside, Dr. Eva Kelsey imperiously delivered curt jabs of iron self-control, interview schedules, and a wealth of complicated social diagrams, a planetary caseload of reports.

But the soothing aromas, the hypnotic undulations of the grassy fields, stilled Eva.

Astride an ugly creature whose tonnage she couldn't guess, on the outskirts of a small town sprung from myths three hundred years old, all the shields and restraints began to crack, and a great peace descended on her.

Conor rode up and signalled with a jerk of his head. "We'll ride around the lake, if you like," he said, his deep-timbered voice disconcertingly muted.

This is a first. Conor asking instead of telling. But his gentleness disarmed her. She tapped her skills as a psychologist to search for causation. Maybe the combination of the liquid air and fragrances and Conor's deference to her wishes had melted the rest of her shell. And, shockingly, forbidden illogical thoughts whirled through her brain.

Who gave a damn about her proper behavior? Who cared? Did she care? No. Not any more.

"Thank you, Conor. That would be lovely." Her tone surprised her, feminine, compliant. From the depths of her soul, the crisp Dr. Eva Kelsey gave a despairing shriek and vanished. And suddenly the safe world of repressing her desires, subjecting her ideas to relentless analysis and criticism seemed very far away. The Psych Board could fill her file with condemnatory notes, if only her man could fill her emptiness.

Conor's smile was inscrutable. In the lead, Sweetheart found a wide trail at the edge of the woods, and Hercules hurried to walk beside her.

"So beautiful, so peaceful, so ... so kind." Eva almost sang the words. "I love this place. And I feel wonderful." Overflowing with exuberance, she flung her hands over her head. "Oh, Conor, all of you, free of the crowds, the noise, are incredibly lucky. And you're just being yourselves."

"You could be lucky, too. Stay here with us, Eva." Conor reined

Sweetheart closer, and his eagerness infected her. "Do your report. It should be easy now that you've got a feel for Laredo. What have you got to go back to?"

Eva felt the pull of her icy professionalism, and for a moment, all her obligations and training battled the temptation of genuine freedom. Her hand flew to cover her mouth. "I couldn't. I have —"

"Another man?"

"Oh, Conor." His face darkened when she laughed. "Since the first time I saw you, there's been no room in my life, in my bed for anyone but you. I've analyzed the situation, and decided on a course of action."

"And?"

"And there's simply nothing to do but this." Eva lifted the gingham skirt. The capricious wind played, and she gave herself to the sensation of coolness. She riveted her gaze on Conor while she slid a finger into her mouth and sucked.

Conor's breathing grew ragged, and when she dipped her other hand into her nest of curls, he swung out of the saddle, and climbed halfway down the rope ladder. Then, wild with haste, he pushed off and plummeted to the ground.

"Come to me, lover," Eva breathed.

"Come to *me*," Conor countered and stretched his arms toward her.

Without a second's hesitation, she leaped, her skirt billowing around her like a crazy parachute, and fell into his embrace.

Chapter 7

The two moons, pale and lopsided, had risen, and the townsfolk had gone to bed, but Eva sat at the mayor's desk, idly twisting her hair.

A month, twenty days, the happiest in her life, had flowed by, one into the other like the movements of a graceful ballet, seamless and rich. The bio-com had recorded all the interviews, and she'd replayed them endlessly, struck by the curious lack of edge in her questioning, amazed at laughter she'd shared with her subjects. The good-natured, friendly colonists.

Happy. That was this place's secret. They were all happy.

She was happy. Obscenely happy. She, stiffly correct Dr. Eva Kelsey, Colonial Selection Specialist and Investigator, deliciously liberated and intensely sexualized, hungry for Conor. Always ready for Conor.

Was there something wrong with this picture? She sighed, and pushed her fingers through her hair, unbound, untethered, undisciplined. Like herself. She examined her hands. Her nails had resumed their natural pinkness. Mauve seemed cruelly artificial, out of place on Laredo.

Her lips had changed, she knew, had grown fuller, poutier, riper, suffused with her blood's redness instead of gloss. Her very flesh and skin shone with vitality and, there it was again, a kind of sensual readiness.

"Ready?" Conor had whispered not two hours earlier, buried to the hilt in her, teasing, withdrawing until her legs vised his waist, and she shook with lust. "Ready to come?" he'd asked, the teasing tone fading into a low growl revealing his own violent hunger, his need.

But she had been on fire, ablaze, and her silent answer had been the sudden contraction that grasped him tightly and repeated, narrowing her passage in a chain of palpitations.

And she didn't care who heard her cries of passion as intellect and reason abandoned her, and Conor spurted his seed, and bruised her lips with his kisses and filled the emptiness of Eva's heart with love.

"Conor," she announced to the deserted office. Her voice rang with determination and decisions forged. "Do you hear me, gentlemen of the guild? Write the note and write me off." Her anxiety, her eagerness to rise in the Federation of professionals dissolved. Thousands of light years from Earth, she'd have no opportunity to practice colony selection. But she could return to her first love, counseling. And she could stay.

"It begins and ends with Conor. I want him. I want him enough to stay."

Her simple declaration melted the last shards of Dr. Kelsey's icy restraint, and Eva sprang to her feet and spun, dancing the joy that bubbled in her laugh, in her heart, and finally she was fully alive.

⁂

"I have to what?" Eva squeaked. She let Mrs. Donovan's screen door slam, and stamped out onto the front walk. The noon sun beat down, she was sweating, and her three hours of sleep had left blue circles under her eyes and the grit of Earthside temper in her craw. And the girls lingering beside the garden gate to flirt with the handsome sheriff added nothing to her thorny disposition.

"Sorry, ma'am." Noah tilted his Stetson and dangled a straw between his lips. "That's what Mayor Ballard said, to come fetch you for a fitness evaluation by the town council."

"This is an outrage," Eva sniffed. "*I* am the person who qualifies candidates for colonization teams. *I* have the training and expertise to select skilled, compatible individuals. I am professionally objective enough to verify my competence and emotional stability."

"You sure can talk, once you set your mind to it," Noah remarked admiringly. "Think you could teach me to talk like that? We'd best stroll right quick, ma'am. The Council don't like to work too long. And that Conor, he purely hates squatting indoors."

"Conor? What has Conor to do with this? Some kind of character witness?" Ah, blessed relief. They all adored Conor. Her problems were solved. Her beloved Conor would make it right.

"Oh, no, ma'am. Conor, he's the one suggested it. Says you ought to get a taste of your own whip." He whistled "Buffalo Gals," and lengthened his strides.

Eva's throat hurt from quelling a shriek. She pressed her hands to her diaphragm and breathed deeply. "Well, well. Conor. Imagine that. What a clever fellow, supposedly on a hunting and exploring trip, and still finding time to attend a hearing. Sheriff, what are we waiting for?"

Eva practically ran down Main Street, her skirt flapping behind her like a pangabark's sails. Swallowing her chagrin, she paused long enough to tuck her hair behind her ears, realized the sweet bruises of Conor's teeth on her throat would be on display, and yanked her hair forward again.

She straightened her shoulders and entered the meeting house, the perfect lady. It was hot, and a rivulet of perspiration slid down her side.

At two long tables sat the mayor and his five councilmen. She recognized them all, remembered grilling three and marking their applications questionable.

She had sweated them during their qualifying interviews, and her stomach churned with anxiety.

They removed their hats and mopped their brows. On a stand in the corner, a rotating fan treated them to occasional blasts of air.

Fancying herself a modern Joan of Arc at the Inquisition, she curtsied and asked humbly, "Gentlemen, how may I help you?"

"Good-day, Dr. Kelsey. I s'pose you wonder what the heck we're about, eh?" The mayor's chuckle dwindled under Eva's frown.

"Not at all. I understand perfectly." She turned a venomous gaze on Conor, decked out in his hunting clothes, who straddled a chair in the first row. Despite major efforts at self-control, just the sight of him, the thick biceps that flexed when he positioned her, the enormous hands that stroked her breasts and her aching wet folds, opened floodgates of desire, and dew slicked her sex.

"Seems like you're the applicant here, asking to stay on Laredo. Is that the gist of it?"

Eva nodded, torn by conflicting emotions, and not trusting herself to speak.

"Shucks, ma'am. We know a bit about you, your hifalutin titles and all, and that's right as perciple pie. But, well, the main thing is … the main thing is … damn, what is the main thing, Conor?"

Conor shifted and hung one meaty arm over the chairback as if he roasted professionals every day. He grinned, evilly. "The main thing, Dr. Kelsey, is your lack of sexual experience."

"My lack of — ?"

"The folks of Laredo have had two years to shed the old repressions, to know themselves, and enjoy their bodies. We've got our priorities straight. What've you been doing for the last two years?"

The council members leaned forward, all ears and moustaches.

"Answer the question, missy."

Her mouth went dry, and she blinked with bafflement. It was a simple question. She could answer it.

"I worked, worked hard, for the welfare of … of off-world teams," she stumbled over her thoughts. "I exercised. I read." And her mind went momentarily blank. "Oh, I was active in Federation professional societies."

One councilman scribbled on a pad. Another contemplated the ceiling.

"What about sex?" Conor demanded.

"I was really very busy," she croaked. "Time. The time."

"Are you saying here in front of the council and everybody," the mayor sputtered, "that for two years you slept alone?" They buzzed and whispered and shook their heads.

Eva looked down at the plank floor. "Yes. Yes, I slept alone. I had no sex, but it wasn't my fault."

"And whose fault was it, Dr. Kelsey?" Conor rested both arms on the toprail of the spindle-backed chair.

"Yours, Conor," she shouted. "How could I ever, ever forget you? And how could I ever let another man touch me?"

The councilmen grinned and nudged each other and talked. Dimly, through the roar of her own blood in her ears, she heard their comments.

"Well, 'course, after Conor, what would you expect?"

"She got gumption to speak out."

"Good enough for me. He can catch her up."

"Two years' worth? Hell, that's a piece o'cake for Conor."

A chair crashed, and Conor was striding down the aisle, crushing her in his embrace, savaging her mouth. He swung her up into his arms, and spun to face the cheering council. Eva hid her blush in Conor's buckskin shirt.

"How say you, gentlemen?" the mayor hollered.

The room rang with ayes, and Conor whispered, "I love you."

He didn't have to kick the door open. Noah tipped his hat and obliged.

"Where are you taking me, Conor?" Eva murmured. She kissed his bronzed skin, inhaled his man-smell. "No. Don't tell me. I don't care."

※⟨ᑕᏀᎵ⟩※

Night fell, and in complex, shifting shadows fragmented by moonlight, Eva strolled hand-in-hand with Conor under the trees.

"Eva." He took her around her waist, sheltered her under his massive arm, and massaged her breast until the nipple begged for him. But she slipped out of his hold, stepped away.

"Even in the dark, I know what your eyes are revealing."

"And is that wrong, wanting you again?"

"My darling, this —" she touched the apex of her legs through her skirt "— this is raw and hot and sensitive. And full of you." She closed her eyes and concentrated on the creamy residue of their love. The lubrication, the blend of her female moisture and his come at once soothed her and stimulated her, made her want him again. Desperately. But not until …

"If you need a rest from me, don't talk like that," Conor teased.

"Don't you know a man gets hard when a woman says she's raw and hot?" He sidled up and kissed her cheek. "Now, how was that for pure innocence?"

"Oh, Conor, look," Eva said breathily, "the ferns at night, so cool and beautiful." She brushed the fonds and stepped off the path. In the dappled moonglow, she exposed her mons and lured him. "I need to be kissed."

"Eva, baby." Conor came toward her, and she launched herself into his arms. He laughed, a great masculine bark, caught her, and, slightly off-balance, he staggered backward. Eva twisted and maneuvered him into the gripper tree. She skittered left, and stood just out of reach.

"Now, mister give-her-a taste-of-her-own-whip Conor, I've got you just where I want you." Triumphantly, she paraded around the tree.

"And where would that be?" Conor inquired.

"Helpless and at my mercy." She rubbed her hands together and tried not to gloat. "Now, if you have a hope of me setting you loose, raise your arms overhead, that's right, so all of you is stuck fast."

He made rocking motions, muscles bunching under his tunic. Finally, he leaned back, still. "So you've got me. What of it?" Conor's voice was cool and studied.

Eva detected a hint of a smile, his teeth white in the darkness. She tapped her chin and examined the captive. "Thought you were cute, did you, forcing me to admit I had no sex for two whole years because of you, how you turned me into a lust-crazed female. Oh, don't lie. I know you loved it, loved hearing me give a testimonial to your cocksmanship."

"I wish I could shrug my shoulders, Doc, but I can't, so I'll have to say it without the gesture. If you got it, flaunt it." He seemed oddly comfortable, and she couldn't tolerate it.

"Then flaunt this." Eva untied the flap over his groin, and gently lifted out his genitals.

"Don't, Eva." Conor tried for a conversational tone, but he delivered her name with a distinct note of pleasure.

"Of course, Conor. Anything you say, Conor." Busying both hands, she weighed his sac and smoothed the ridges of his fast-hardening cock. Slowly she played, ringing her thumb and index finger around it, announcing with fake surprise, "Look, Conor. I can't make them meet. Will I have to tell that at the town meeting, too?" And then she knelt and lipped the thick round head.

Eva glanced up. Conor's jaw was clenched, and she couldn't see the dappled moonlight reflected in his eyes because he'd closed them.

He sucked air between his teeth and groaned. "Pull me free. Now, Eva."

Eva, her own flesh overheating, rose. On tip-toe, she lifted her skirt and brushed her nakedness on his nodding erection.

"So big, so hard. Do you wish you could drive it up me? Push it into me to the hilt and take me here under the moons?"

Her voice cracked with need, and her composure hovered on the verge of shattering, but Eva was determined to wring this last bit of revenge out of him. Then, when he was totally aroused, she'd work him loose from the gripper tree's clutches. If she could hold out that long herself.

"I think you'd like me to drop you here on the forest floor, on your hands and knees, lodge myself good and tight." From low in his guts, a tormented groan escaped, and he said, "Admit you're praying for me to take you from behind, reach around under your belly and tickle that bud you're dancing against me." He was panting. "Keep you bent over, speared on my cock, massage your breasts, drive you crazy. Would you like that, Eva?"

Frantic, her need boiling inside her, she clawed at his hide shirt. "I can't, I can't get you loose. Oh, Conor. Please."

"It's easy. See? I just walk away." And he did, laughing at her confusion, capturing her.

"But you were stuck. I saw you struggle," she managed between kisses. She arched into him and moaned.

Against her lips, he whispered, "You were having such a good time getting even, I didn't have the heart to disappoint you. But a gripper tree hangs onto things too weak to struggle. Are you listening? I love you Eva. Marry me." Masterfully, he kissed her until she gasped in an agony of wanting him, and her knees weakened.

"Don't lecture, Conor. Do me. I want you so bad I'm hurting. I need you deep in me."

Conor stripped her and himself, and they collapsed to the leafy forest floor. Eva, trembling with desire, rolled onto her hands and knees, and jutted her buttocks.

He licked and kneaded the firm globes, and teased her swollen vulva with the tip of his cock.

"Are you too weak to struggle, Eva?" he whispered before he was engulfed. In the silence, he mounted her and, losing all control, made the first thrust hard and deep like a stallion on a mare in heat.

Whimpering, Eva lowered herself onto her elbows, and rocked with his pounding surges. In her core, heated honey flowed, and taut nerves collected their energies for a colossal outburst. She began to moan his name in rhythm to his strokes, and when his blunt fingers pinched her clitoris, and she felt his juices spurt, she spasmed, and the only sound in the world was Conor's exultant shout.

Shivering in the aftermath, they lay together on the perfumed leaves. In the safe haven of his love, snuggled in his arms, she sighed contently.

Conor slid a possessive hand over her breasts, her belly, and sleepily drew circles in her wet curls.

"I'll never get enough of you, sweet Eva," he confessed, "and like a human gripper tree, I'm damned glad you're too weak to struggle. Aren't you?"

Beneath two moons, the fragrance of alien trees washed over them, and a nightbird sang.

Eva, open and free and uninhibited, writhed under Conor's fingers. Just before she surrendered herself to his delicious attentions, before she became mindless with greedy lust, she imagined the shuttle from the Tarquin returning in a few months. The boarding door would open, and Leon would stick his head out.

And there she'd be, Eva Conor, handing over the cases, happily wearing a bonnet and a calico dress. Eva, minus breast cups and panties, the hot desert wind sneaking under her skirt, the tiny gusts fondling her, making her yearn for Conor's caress.

"About that question a while ago, Conor." She nuzzled at his throat, kissed a strand of his hair, and explored the ridges of his lean belly.

"I'm not too weak to struggle, darling. I'm too smart."

Secrets

Volume 6

Flint's Fuse

by Sandy Fraser

***To my reader*:**
Change time and place, past to future, city to desert, Earth to the stars. One constant endures: the fiery passion of a man and a woman. Lose yourself in the fantasy.

Chapter One

In the dark of the moon, a phantom shadow masked and dressed in black stalked his target. With cat-like silence he slipped down the hall to her bedroom in the rear wing of the gigantic house.

The timing and execution had been perfect. The moonless night, the disabled security system, and access to Madison's estate. He paused, listening to his breathing, preparing to make his move.

Grimly, Flint smiled. Madison had brought him off a big assignment in Australia, given him a detailed floor plan and a picture of his pretty daughter.

"A bitch on wheels," Madison had sighed. "There's not a man alive who can check her. She's a five-star general in the battle of the sexes. The good guys lose. Look, Flint, if I asked her nicely to take a vacation, she'd pry, ask too many questions. But my sources tell me International Investments is not unwilling to threaten family members to up the leverage during a merger." He leaned back in his chair and folded his hands. "Take her to a place I don't know. I'll spread the word she's on safari. Call my lawyer in Lisbon once a week. I'll leave word so you'll know when it's over."

"She'll be scared. How much do I tell her?" Flint thumbed the picture of the leggy blond.

"Anything, but for God's sake, don't tell her *I'm* involved."

The glacial captain of industry had a note of panic in his voice.

"Some simple kidnapping story should suffice. I'll pay the non-existent ransom, and you'll bring her home."

Flint rose, and Madison got to his feet.

"You've fought your way out of jungles, killed men with your bare hands, taken bullets meant for somebody else. You're not the kind of man who relies on luck." Madison shook his hand.

"But you'll need all the luck you can get now, you poor bastard."

Flint wrote off the warning as a dose of the tycoon's notorious gallows' humor. Apparently Madison thought snatching a woman was a big deal. Real operatives knew it was chump change compared to the tough jobs.

He turned the knob and eased the door open. Dana Madison was a motionless slender form under silk sheets in a room scented like Paradise. Walk in the park, he told himself.

But the instant he touched the bed, Dana sprang up and delivered a side snap-kick to his jaw. Good placement, he judged, but ineffective because the mattress gave her no base for balance, and he was too fast. Flint grabbed her ankle, toppled her, and covered her, feeling her lush breasts mash into his chest.

He gripped her thighs with his knees, and to shut off her cry slapped duct tape over her mouth, bound her flailing wrists and ankles. "Hush," he whispered. "Be still. I won't hurt you."

She growled behind the tape and tried to wrench out of his grasp. Easily he lifted her, carried her down the hall, and had to still her thrashings with a nerve block. He had an image of caressing her, burying his face in her throat.

Her sudden limpness, sweet false compliance, the softness of her nestling against him stirred his groin and announced Dana Madison was trouble. His body signalled he should sneak back to her room and return her to her four-poster.

"I blew it. So fire me," he could report to Madison the next morning, and ask for another run-of-the-mill assignment, like rescuing a double-agent from the attentions of an Israeli interrogation team. Instead, Flint cradled his captive, sneaked out through the French doors, and arranged her on a mattress in the cargo area of the van. By using surface streets, he whisked them out of Metro in twenty minutes, and ramped up the freeway.

When high noon burned the endless stretches of shimmering desert, Flint slowed the van, stopped at the edge of the highway that ran and ran until it disappeared into the horizon.

"If you behave yourself, I'll free you, let you use this." He nudged the camping toilet and opened its lid. "And then give you a drink and a sandwich." He waited, impassive. He could out-wait anything, anyone.

Dana Madison closed her eyes and nodded slightly. She was flowing gold hair, and, beneath her filmy nightgown, all tempting curves and nipples that crested under his stare.

"This will sting." Flint knelt beside her and stripped the tape from her ankles and wrists. She simultaneously ripped the tape from her mouth and found her feet. Like a demon, she gouged at his eyes and kicked his shins.

"Ooow," she screamed as her toes connected with massive bone.

Flint let her fall onto the mattress and rock back and forth, nursing her sore foot. "Want a Coke? How about a bologna sandwich, Miss Madison?"

"Bastard." He'd never heard such venom in a voice. What he recognized as the hereditary Madison gaze drilled into him. She spat, "Enjoy yourself for now at my expense, moron. It won't last long. And my father won't give you a cent. He'll hunt you down. He'll put one of his secret squads on your trail."

"Take your panties down."

Dana's lips curled in a sneer. "Can't get it for a burger and a couple of beers, eh? And too proud to pay for it?"

Flint bent, and Dana shrieked while he ripped lace and grabbed her. Despite her fighting, he put her on the porta-potty, handcuffed one wrist and clamped it to an exposed bar in the van.

In a shower of her original curses, Flint fled, slamming the door behind him. He raked both hands through his hair and leaned on the rear bumper. Heat waves rose and distorted the scrub and the dull powdered sand.

Once, in Death Valley, he'd stood unprotected, bare-headed at high noon. He'd been a kid pummelled by unrelenting heat, lost in wondering how a man could tolerate the cruel sun.

But, years later, after Wu Chin had put him on the path of inner serenity and he'd learned the control of the body-mind-heart center, he'd been thrown out of a Jeep to die in the Sahara. On the edge of consciousness, he heard the laughter of his captors when they sped away. He tasted the gritty sand sponging up his blood and last drops of moisture.

In that terrible oven, he'd gotten to his feet, dizzy, sick, and determined. Slowly, he'd centered himself, and hunted a sand shelf where he lay, measuring his breaths in the sizzling shade until night fell and he had walked out to safety.

There was no safety around this woman. His instincts spiked. Where there should have been the soft, yielding, passive coolness of *yin*, the female principle, Dana Madison seemed a wild creature of *yang*, light, heat, action.

The van rocked, she pounded on metal and yelled. Flint sighed. Well, he wasn't paid by Madison to indulge in long meditation sessions. He was being paid to baby-sit a woman whose body and face should've been declared illegal when she was eighteen. Glumly, Flint returned to the van like a man going to the gallows.

Madison's words came back to haunt him, "You'll need all the luck you can get, you poor bastard." Less than a day with this spitfire, and he'd already aged ten years. He refused to think about handling her for a month.

"Clothes," he said gruffly, pointing. "I'm uncuffing you. Get dressed."

Dana jumped up, slammed the lid, and let him apply the key to her wrist restraint. He reached for the clothes, and she caromed off him like an ace billiard shot, leaped out the open van door, and was away and running through the sand.

Flint pursued her, but not at top speed, not even working up a sweat in the heat. Approvingly, he noted she wasted no breath on futile screams. She was saving her strength. He berated himself for his carelessness, thankful that this empty stretch of road carried virtually no traffic, day or night.

He reached out, caught the nightie to jerk her to a stop, but Dana kept running, and he was left following with shredded pink streamers.

He knew all about pursuits, but the sight of her, naked and eluding him, fired an ancient, primitive instinct. His sex grew heavy as excitement pumped hot blood into his arousal. Flint was a man pursuing a woman, a mate.

As he took her around the waist, he tried to be gentle, but her violence and surprising strength demanded more muscle than he cared to use. Unexpectedly, she dropped to the sand, and Flint fell with her.

Wrestling in the harsh powder, she panted and he held her down by straddling her. Her eyes were wild, but not with fear. She exuded hate and temper and revenge and something else he couldn't name.

His cock and balls knew, though, and they tensed, ready for Flint to part her thighs and take her here at noon in the burning sand. Her nipples grew erect, and he saw they'd blushed a deep red. He raised her to her feet and twisted one arm behind her back.

"That's right. Hurt me, too, you scar-faced animal."

He kept his voice cold. "The only way you can be hurt by frog-marching is if you try to break away. Now we'll walk slowly together, back to the van."

She muttered curses, and Flint stared into the cascade of tangled golden hair deepened with dark honey. He imagined it swirling around her head, pillowed on black silk, while he sucked those huge nipples, while he wrung groans from her.

Then he looked past her to the van, ordering his tension to disperse, his breathing to regularize, and his focus to narrow on one specific. Getting the job done.

He visualized a calendar, a month, thirty days. Madison's enemies, the bright boys at International Investments, had gravely underestimated Madison's resources. The threats against Dana to force Madison into the merger would fail.

He'd shuck this wild woman as easily as he'd dispose of her torn gown smelling of the unique fragrance that was Dana Madison, a fragrance that made his nostrils flare.

At the van, Dana planted herself, and he had to lift her slick nakedness up in the cargo area. "For the second time, get dressed."

"Not until I have a Coke. *And* a sandwich." She tossed her head and jammed her hands on her hips, daring him to fasten his attention on her golden delta. He read the real message. To Dana Madison out-maneuvering him, distracting him, meant more than modesty.

"Get dressed." Flint leaned over the driver's seat. "Now."

"Is it hard for you to understand? I said no, not until I get what I want." Her eyes flashed blue fire.

"Listen carefully, Dana. Three times you've been told to dress. Now I have to do it for you." He climbed into the back, and Dana shrieked and grabbed the thin strapped blue top.

"Too late." Flint jerked it away, tossed her to the mattress, and tugged the jeans onto her legs. She clawed and fought when he boosted her hips. Despite her shouts, he trapped her arms under his knees, and completed the job by flattening the unruly curls at the juncture of her thighs and zipping her jeans closed. He sat her up like a ragdoll and stuffed her into the tank top.

Panting like a whipped animal, she regarded him with a kind of murderous respect. "*Now* can I have my food and a drink?"

He dug a soda and a sandwich bag out of a cooler, and Dana snatched them from his hands. When he bent to retrieve his water bottle, he caught a lightning move in his peripheral vision, and barely deflected the blow. Flint wrenched the red can from her, forced her to the mattress and cuffed one hand.

"I hate you," she said, and her voice was low and deadly.

"One Coke," Flint said and poured the can's contents into a paper cup. "One bologna sandwich with mustard."

Dana drank, laid the sandwich on her knee and dissected it.

"I hate this kind of mustard," she said scornfully. Then she rattled off a litany of complaints and questions while Flint drove. He opted for silence, hoping she'd run down, wear herself out.

Master Wu Chin had counseled that the temper of a woman is like a summer storm, violent but short-lived. The Master had never met Dana Madison.

Flint imagined the old man trying to reason with Dana, and he grinned in spite of himself. Dana Madison was not a woman. She was a force of nature, and Flint would have to reckon with her treachery for a hellish four weeks. His grin faded as he struggled to ignore the bulge in his pants that gave mute testimony to her bold sex appeal. Aside from the physical attraction, Flint would have to deal with her intelligence and defiance which issued a dangerous challenge to tame her.

Realizing he'd been speeding to reach the cabin, he slowed and rehearsed all the break-downs travelers suffered in the desert, all the stories of people trying to walk out of the inferno.

God help her if one of her unpredictable escape attempts worked, and she found herself in the badlands without him.

Chapter Two

"You know what your trouble is?" Dana leaned back and braced herself. She crossed her long legs at the ankle and stretched out on the bearskin rug before the fireplace.

Silent as a granite monument, Flint stared into the flames, hands relaxed on the arms of his chair. He said nothing.

"Did you hear me, Flint?" Her voice grew snide. "I'll bet that isn't even your real name. I'll bet it's some godawful wimp name like, like Lester or Cecil, isn't it?"

Slowly, Flint glanced down, his cool grey eyes examining her as dispassionately as a scientist might inspect a bug under a microscope. The inspection seemed to go on forever, until he resumed gazing into the flames.

He said nothing, the way he **always** said nothing when she sniped and needled, but once Dana started, she couldn't stop pouring out her fury and frustration. If he wouldn't give her attention, then she'd steal it, goad him until he retaliated, satisfying her ego, manipulating him into action.

"Well, I don't care about your phony tough guy name. After all, who'd be stupid enough to waste money on a hired gun named Petey or Ricky? Or are you working alone?" Her stomach twisted in embarrassment at her bitchiness. "But that wasn't the question, Mr. Strong Silent Type, now was it?" Dana got to her knees and jammed her hands on her hips.

As though speaking to an inattentive child, she repeated, "The question was, do-you-know-what-your-trouble-is?" She was acutely aware of his nearness, of the virility he radiated, aware of the flush on her cheeks. Unbidden, a shocking thought intruded.

If it were a different situation, a different place, she'd recklessly abandon common sense and throw herself at this rugged male, luxuriate in his strong arms, let him make decisions, revel in the carefree confidence he inspired. But in this time and place, Flint remained cool and considerate, the model warden, the gentleman kidnapper. And Dana chafed under his reasonableness.

"I'll be glad to reveal your weakness, O great stoneman. You can't talk." Triumphantly, she plowed ahead. "Don't deny it. Those rare one-syllable grunts you produce hardly qualify as conversation."

As usual, Flint denied nothing, agreed with nothing, and Dana trembled on the verge of slapping his immobile, chiseled face and tearing out his thick black hair. Two weeks with him had been two weeks of pure hell, two weeks of virtually talking to herself, two weeks of continual surveillance. In the end he would drive her mad. And maybe that was his scheme.

A knot formed in her throat, and tears burned behind her eyes. She wanted to go home.

Flint rose, powerful legs flexing to support his huge body, all thick thighs and massive torso, and corded neck. Behind his fly, the snaps of his Levi's contained an enormous bulge, thrust nearly into her face when he loomed over her.

"Bedtime, Miss Madison," he said, a voice cold as his eyes.

"I'm not ready for bed, thank you very much for your concern, Flint. I am an adult and quite capable of deciding when I'm tired and when I need to go to bed." With a smug smile, she clambered into the chair he'd just vacated, and pretended to relax. But how could she? Flint had left the chair imprinted with his incredible heat, and it lingered, it disturbed her.

Dana hoped that she'd disturbed him, and sneaked a look at the black T-shirt hugging the slabs of his muscled chest and straining to cover his biceps. But his respiration was regular, under rigid control, like his emotional responses to her, clock-like. The guy was a robot, inhuman.

She'd never seen Flint sweat, lose his temper, overeat, or over-react. His responses were exact, automatic, icily perfect.

He never wasted a move, never squandered an ounce of energy, as though he had a fuse box installed. No overloads, no power surges flustered the Stoneman. And he could, she knew, maintain his steady gaze and comfortable stance for hours without the least show of anger.

Damn him. Why should she make his life easy? When her ordeal was over, if he wasn't caught, he'd be a million dollars richer, and, by God she'd see to it he'd earned every last cent. Clamping her arms over her breasts, Dana dug in and tightened her mouth.

Flint stood like a rock, courteous, patient to a fault and totally infuriating. He eyed her. "Miss, for the second time, please go to bed." More than once, she'd had a taste of what he'd do after he made a third request. The quick lift, the unhurried walk with Dana Madison manhandled like a side of beef.

"You're a hateful bastard," she snapped. Out of the depths of the deep low chair, Dana struggled to her feet, brushed past him, and stamped into the bedroom. She itched to slam a door, but ten days ago in his methodical way, Flint had extracted the hinge-pins and carted the door outside, a punishment for one of her tricks.

Now he propped his bulk in the threshhold and watched her march into the bathroom whose door he'd permitted to remain after replacing the lock with a hook and eye. Probably so he could kick it in, she griped. This tiny room was the last, the only private place left to Dana, and sometimes she was astonished Flint had had the decency to free her, ever so briefly, from his spying.

She shucked off her jeans and tank-top, poured water from the chipped pitcher into the ewer, and wrung out the wet cloth. In the mirror above the wooden counter, she studied her face. Too large blue eyes, full pink lips, flyaway blond hair, and a face her nanny had called elfin. "Now listen, my little elf," she'd say as she scolded Dana, "it is truly a sin to waste God's gifts, and your gifts are beauty and cleverness."

Dana heard Flint cough to hurry her along. Well, let him barge in and get a good look. She retreated to see more of herself, everything Flint would see. She dropped the cloth, and ran her hands down the body her aerobics intructor always said was "to die for."

Dana frowned. Creamy skin, generous breasts with marble-size, dusky pink nipples. Tight abs. She smoothed her hands over the firm flare of her hips, the curve of her belly, down to the nest of dark gold curls.

Karate hadn't worked on Flint. Neither had trying to run past him, climbing out the bathroom window (after that episode, he'd boarded it over), hitting him with an andiron, or grabbing a knife. Maybe this, her body was the perfect weapon.

"A guy like Flint, a weight-lifter type, handsome if you like 'em tall, dark and dangerous," she whispered, "a babe magnet." When was the last time he'd had a woman? A couple of weeks ago? Maybe the very night he'd snatched her?

The thought of Flint sweating between the legs of a woman pleased her, Flint losing his impassive expression, going wild. Images came of Flint taking a woman like a bull, his immense cock plunging in and out, in and out, Flint sucking that faceless woman's breasts as she cried in an agony of fevered tension. Yes, sex might be Flint's weakness.

Sex. Was he hurting for sex, hurting bad? As hungry for a hot joining as Dana herself?

To her horror, Dana saw her nipples standing erect, her hand foraging in her pubic hair, rubbing her clit. She leaped to the basin and washed her fingers.

"This has nothing to do with wanting him myself," she insisted. The woman in the mirror seemed unconvinced. "Sure, I have needs, cooped up like this. But so does he, and I'll use it to my advantage. And if push comes to shove, I can fake it."

Lure him, seduce him, yes, that was the ticket, exhaust him into the heavy, dreamless state of the drained male. Then, car keys in hand, she'd speed into the night, speed to the nearest police station, and then let Flint see how he'd enjoy life in jail.

Despite the trial and error of all her failed attempts to subdue him, to hide, and sneak and run, at last she'd crafted a scheme bound to work, a plan to control the invulnerable Flint.

Never before had Dana worried about controlling a man. Her father's fortune and her willfulness anesthetized her lovers. The eager yes-men, a string of polo players, an ambassador with erotic skills, and his young assistant whose lasting power had almost fooled Dana into thinking she was in love.

In the end, all of them wilted, brought to heel by her strong personality. "I want a man, a real man," she whispered. If she'd wanted a fawning, submissive dog on a choke collar and chain, she could buy one at a kennel.

The faces and forms of her rejected lovers receded and disappeared, overpowered by Flint's commanding presence.

In the mirror she watched her smile flicker and dissolve. Through half-closed eyes, she replayed her fantasy of Flint making love, but this time instead of the unknown woman, he held Dana immobilized and plunged between her legs. Flint the master, his dark dominance protecting her, making her feel safe in his arms.

She thought of his rigid decisions, his unwavering limits that stood up to her practiced pleadings and arguments. Dana shivered. For the first time in her life she knew boundaries and consequences. And she liked it.

***

Flint heard her brushing her teeth, her white, white teeth, the brush moving between her rose lips. He closed his eyes, and imagined her naked, her top thrown aside to reveal her lush breasts, her jeans slithering over her long legs, slim ankles, dainty feet, gorgeously, completely naked, peaches and cream. And in that downy triangle, were the lips soft and pouting, was the clit a tiny button or a dark pink projection?

He fixed his stare at the paint peeling off the opposite doorjamb, and cursed himself for accepting this job. All the assignments in the past, guarding moguls, running down a crazed fan with a gun, even taking a bullet in the side for a rock star, every job had been a piece of cake compared to snatching Dana Madison.

Yeah, Flint, boxer, Navy SEAL, mercenary, he'd been around, had the expertise, the contingency plans, the quick improvs for extreme situations. But this, this grab and hold was the hardest thing he'd ever done, as hard and swollen as his cock. He took in a huge breath through his teeth, and thumbed open the first two snaps of his Levi's to relieve some of the pressure.

Pain, some new pain, would kill his desire. Flint stiffened and ground his spine into the crusty wood of the frame, forcing himself to inflict damage, a harsh rasp to cleanse himself of these distractions. But the sting of abrasion was numbed by the picture of her nakedness. He clenched his jaw. His sex grew heavier. He had to get her into bed right now.

Startled by how far he'd let his mind wander, he corrected himself. He meant he had to force Dana to go to bed now, by herself. Forget his pulsating cock, forget the damned thing, that, like an untamed, instinct-driven animal, fed on his fantasies and disrupted his coolness until he forgot his job and lasered his attention on his aching groin, on the sweetness between her thighs.

With an oath, Flint raked his hands through his hair, and looked up to see Dana in the bathroom doorway, silhouetted by the lantern behind her, the thin nightie rendered nearly invisible.

"Oh," she murmured, cupping her breasts, "I didn't know you were out here, Flint."

A lie. He'd stood in this exact spot every night for the past two weeks, supervising as she crept under the covers, turning out the Coleman. What the hell was she trying to pull?

He held his breath, willing away the throbbing. He limped into the bathroom, doused the light, and reclined on a thin futon outside her doorway. Stifling a groan, he raised one knee and stacked his hands behind his head. He hadn't had blue balls since he was sixteen.

"Flint? Flint, are you awake?"

Five feet away, Dana Madison was calling, and his cock was answering. Flint squeezed his eyes shut, as though her throaty voice could be banished by simple silence, and he remained mute.

"Flint?" She gave a little, apologetic sigh. "I'm sorry I was so bitchy. Forgive me, Flint. I — I want you to like me."

His eyes flew open. In the glow of the fireplace, the room seemed soft and feminine, the old paint and splintery furniture transformed into a romantic landscape by her voice. The cracked walls were hung with tapestries, the ratty sofa magically changed into a silk chaise where Dana clung to him, where she urged him deeper into her dripping, honeyed heat.

With a grim smile, Flint brought himself up short. He'd read the studies on the Helsinki Syndrome, the bizarre emotional state that linked the helpless hostage and the all-powerful perpetrator.

A spasm fisted his guts. The soft voice, the sweet apology seemed sincere. But was it the syndrome? Had Dana Madison, now totally dependent on him for every bite of food, every sip of water slipped into the captive's mentality?

Or was it that Dana needed his approval, and now hungry to please, craved his affection, as if any kind of relationship survived a captivity ordeal?

And he? He wanted to shake his head, to clear his libido of the contagious fantasy Dana was spinning.

Worse, he wanted to believe she had maintained her feisty independence and was engineering a ploy to lull his suspicions. Inexplicably, he preferred a fiery, trouble-making, take-no-prisoners Dana, busy plotting his ruin, to a psychologically-bent Dana who wanted him to love her.

"Flint, do you remember the night you kidnapped me?"

"Go to sleep," he growled.

"How can I sleep when I'm never tired? You never let me go out to exercise." She caught her breath and grimaced in the dimness. She had to walk a chalk line in her approach. "There I go again, complaining. I'm sorry, Flint. Talk to me a minute, like we're kids having a pajama party."

"Someone put me out of my misery," he said.

"Oh, Flint. That was a joke. I think." She giggled. "Now get serious. When you woke me that night, did you expect the karate move, the old snap-kick?" She heard him sigh.

"I surrender. If I talk for one minute, will you shut up and go to sleep?"

"It's a deal. One minute." Real excitement tinged her voice. In the dimness, she saw Flint set his watch alarm.

"All right, Miss Madison, tell me, that night, did you expect me to grab your ankle?" She saw him shift, prop himself on one elbow so he looked into her room. "Or pull you under me?"

"Nope. You were too strong, too fast, like a panther, on top of me, gripping my thighs between your legs. I thought you were going to rape me." Slip sex in at every opportunity, and try to lose my overactive imagination. "And me, taking those female empowerment classes. I beat up dummies every week, and guys wearing protective pads, you know, the fake mugger types." She gave a self-mocking laugh. "But when the chips were down … oh, Flint, I was so helpless and scared."

"Only sick jerks take a woman by force. I was on a job. Look, Dana, for your own good I had to get physical, tape your mouth, your wrists and ankles. I won't use sedative injections."

He'd called her Dana. She shivered with satisfaction. That was real female power. And she dicovered her moves were more than a game, and she needed to know his secrets, needed to break down the barricades this mystery man maintained so successfully.

"Ah, Flint, you trussed me like a Christmas package, touched my neck and the next thing I remembered was waking up on a mattress in your van next to all those boxes of supplies."

In his memory Flint had hoarded the natural perfume of her skin, the soft feel, the sweet weight and curves he'd carried as gently as he could. She'd fought furiously, wild blond mane whipping his face, her eyes wide with fear and hate, glimpses he'd caught in the flame-shaped light of a wall sconce. He'd put her out with his thumb on a pressure point on her neck.

"The way you touched me, somehow I knew you weren't going to hurt me. I trusted you. And, Flint, I still do." Her voice was a lover's voice, and Flint imagined his mouth slanting over her tempting lips that begged him for more.

Two beeps chimed. "Night, Miss Madison." Flint rolled onto his back, eyes open, listening to the sounds of Dana sighing, sliding those long, smooth legs between the sheets.

Three hours later, he checked Dana's even breathing, and, quiet as a cat stepped over the futon and slipped onto the front porch. Exasperated at himself, at the failure of all Wu Chin's emotional serenity teachings, Flint gave himself to the full moon.

He slipped into the first stage and meditated on his life, his detached, complete life that suddenly had developed a hungry yearning void in the place where he'd shielded his heart.

Chapter Three

"I won't stay here alone, you know." Dana struggled to keep her voice cool and reasonable, swirled coffee in her cup, and studied Flint's reaction.

But, of course, there *was* no reaction. As if he hadn't heard a word she'd said, he swallowed the last bite of his bread, wiped his mouth and pushed back his chair. After dusting his hands, he tossed the styrofoam bowl and napkin, and looked at her.

"Finished?"

"With lunch. But not with this discussion." Dana balanced her chair on the rear legs, and rested her hands on top of her head, an innocent gesture, and one that raised her breasts and brought her nipples to his attention. "So let's decide what to do."

She smiled to show him she was being both logical and sweetly submissive. It was her best move, the one she'd used without fail on a dozen men over the years.

"Finished?" His steel-grey eyes were inscrutable, yet almost electric in his bronzed skin. She detected the tiniest tic in his strong jaw. Dana knew when she'd got to a man, and as different as Flint thought he was, how invulnerable to her manipulations, she'd seen a chink in his armor.

With a sigh, she bounced the chair forward. Her lower lip quivered, and she covered her face with her hands. "Flint, please don't leave me here by myself. You know how scared I get."

He took her utensils and trashed them. "Time for bed, Miss Madison."

"No. I know what you're thinking, that maybe I ran away a couple of times, hit you, and, well, a couple of other things that make you believe I'm really tough. But Flint," her voice wobbled, "Oh, Flint, I'm not as tough as I look."

He held up two fingers. "Time for bed."

Dana's game plan crumbled, and she snapped. "Stop that ridiculous three-times-and-you're-out nonsense. I'm going nowhere until we talk about this." As soon as she tilted her chin defiantly, she knew she'd made a mistake.

"Time for bed."

He moved faster than any man she'd ever seen, all smooth speed and determination, and he had her in his hard embrace before she could get out of her chair.

"Then talk to me." She screamed and thrashed. But all it got her was Flint holding her higher and harder, her face in his throat, the sweat and tang of his maleness on her lips, the scent of sage and woodsmoke in her nostrils.

He carried her as if she weighed no more than a cat, and Dana fought the rising tide of her excitement, the stunning realization that Flint could do anything to her, even possess her body, and she was helpless.

But when he laid her on the quilt and released her hands, she managed a stinging slap to his face, directly on the jagged scar that sliced from his ear to the corner of his mouth. His gold-bronze skin burned with a rush of blood. And the scar stood, a bloodless vein of white, unchanged, impervious to any assault Dana mounted.

Sick at herself, she wilted. Calm, gentle, efficient, Flint clamped the metal ring on her left wrist, securing her to the bedpost.

"No one comes here. You're safe. I'll be back no later than four." Without consulting his watch, he said, "It's one o'clock. Three hours is adequate to stock up on food and water. Your water bottle is on the bedside table."

He swiveled and was at the door before Dana whimpered. "Flint, I'm sorry. Oh, God, your face." But the only answer was the screendoor banging shut, and then the engine turning over.

As the sound of the van died away in the hot afternoon, Dana wiped her eyes on a tissue and stared up at the cracked ceiling.

If only he'd talked, engaged her in conversation, she could've convinced him to take her along, then, on some pretense, slipped away, freed herself and run for help.

But no. Flint was like that scar. Impervious, unchanging, no matter what she said or did. A man hard-wired to be exactly what he seemed, the same outside and in.

Dana twisted, making herself as comfortable as she could. Flint. He was on her mind, and now that she'd been relieved of his heavy presence for the first time in weeks, she considered the mystery man.

The men in her life were nothing like Flint. Not even her father who could cause a panic with a raised eyebrow. But she, who people insisted was a chip off the old block, had always been able to twist her father around her little finger.

If girlish coaxing failed, pouting worked, or flashpoint temper, or the silent treatment, and then Dana had her own way.

Dana always had her own way. Until Flint.

She daydreamed about Flint, in a half-doze, imagining the origin of his fascinating scar. Maybe a historical setting?

She smiled at the thought of Flint duelling with sabres. Dark and bronzed like a fabled black knight, playing a waiting game with a blond Aryan **Ubermensch**, offering his cheek for the cut to gain advantage, to find the perfect opening to break the sabre loose and power his opponent to the floor.

Dana turned onto her left side and closed her eyes against the sunshine. Or maybe Flint as a Green Beret, caught in an ambush, missing having his throat slit by catching steel in his face.

Maybe something more romantic. New Orleans. Through slatted balcony windows, the music and laughter and songs of Mardi Gras filtered onto a dim bed draped with netting. Flint, controlled, on automatic pilot, pleasuring a fiery Cajun beauty with regular deep strokes, increasing his speed as her moans grew louder and faster. A violent climax, a cry splintering the reggae tunes, and then Flint rising to leave. The demanding lady, a glint of a razor, blood spurting from his cheek. Flint shoving her aside, walking out with a snowy kerchief on his wound.

Dana moaned like the Cajun woman, and slept.

When she woke, the sun had moved behind the mountains. She stretched and drank from her water bottle. Idly, she picked up her watch. "Four-thirty," she said, a little groggy from her nap. "A diller, a dollar, a ten o'clock Flint."

He was late. She giggled. Another chink in the stainless steel armor of Stoneman Flint. She took both pillows and elevated her handcuffed arm, relieving some of the strain on her wrist. Then she slept again.

When she woke, the sunlight had disappeared. The window framed a clear black velvet desert sky winking with a million stars.

"Flint?" she called, yawning the sleep from her throat. No candle, no cozy blaze in the fireplace. No sound. The utter silence of the desert prevailed.

"Flint, if you're jerking my chain, it's not funny." But she knew she was fooling herself. Where was he?

A horrible scenario flashed into her mind. Flint killed in a crash, in his dying breath trying to tell the paramedics about Dana, Dana cuffed and helpless.

Flint, purchasing food, Madison's team of private detectives waiting, Flint running, the shots, the limp body hitting the dusty street.

Flint driving toward the cabin, rubbing his cheek, fingering the thin line of his wound, the wound she'd struck. Flint meeting his own eyes in the rearview mirror, and shrugging off Dana and all the millions her father would pay in ransom. Flint slamming on the brakes and hitting the accelerator, a perfect one-eighty. Flint barreling down the road toward civilization.

Dana licked her dry lips. The water was gone. She'd read a survival guide once. She could last ten days without food, three without water. And in the end, hallucinations and a blessed euphoria.

Dana screamed and jerked at her captive wrist. The cuffs were steel, the bedpost iron. She tried to unscrew the iron finial atop the post. It was welded on. Frantically she raced through options. Trapped animals chewed off the snared foot.

She shuddered. "Wreck the bed. Break the post. Drag the whole thing out behind me onto the road." Conserving her strength, she began to jounce, to rattle the bedstead. And just behind her determination to free herself lurked the mother of all screams.

※)(ᴄ꒜)⁂

Flint lay on the brakes and the van skidded to a halt. Dana's guttural screams rang out, screams from a raw throat. Once he had screamed like that, and he couldn't get to her fast enough. He hurled himself out of the car, flung open the screen door, and rushed into Dana's room.

"I'm here, I'm here." He lit the candle and unsnapped the cuffs. In the dimness, Dana lay panting and sweating, the fan of hair tangled from thrashing. Her eyes were glazed and she looked at him without recognition.

"Baby, baby, it's all right. I'm here now." He sat propped at the headboard and gathered her into his arms. "Dana, baby, I'm here. Flint's here, darling."

"Flint," she said. Within the shelter of his embrace, she looked up as though not believing her eyes. "Flint?"

He pulled her into his lap, brushed back hair damp with the sweat of terror, and kissed her brow. Flint stroked her face, drying the tears with his thumb.

She clung to him, shivering, and raised her hand. "I couldn't get loose. I couldn't get loose and you weren't here."

Flint, even in the semi-darkness, saw the dark bruise the cuff had burned into the sensitive flesh of her wrist.

The bruising purpled her pale skin, the delicate tracery of her veins.

Guilty and torn, Flint kissed the soreness gently. "Let's soak this. And make you some soup." He moved and Dana panicked.

"No. No, you'll go away again." She held him fiercely, and her voice trembled on the edge of hysteria.

"I'll stay right here with my baby," he whispered, and pressed her head into his throat. "We'll sleep now."

Twice during the midnight hours, Flint shifted, but she cried out in her sleep, and he relaxed, cuddling her closer.

At three, she woke and fondled his bicep. "Strong man," she murmured.

He squeezed her shoulder. "Even a strong man has to use the head occasionally. How about you?"

She ducked her head, hid her face in his chest. He could feel the heat of her blush through his tee. Dana Madison, blushing? The woman who'd parade around naked rather than follow an order to put on clothes? Asked to choose between her naked beauty or the sudden, inexplicable modesty, he was stumped. Modesty sure as hell would make his life easier, yet to see Dana nude had been a saving grace of this assignment.

But Dana slid over his lap and padded to her bathroom. He got up and stretched, and headed for the kitchen. He heard water pour into the ewer, and combed his hair with both hands.

That damn fuel pump, the dumb jerks at the auto shop, no place to rent a car or even to hire a car and driver. He kept reaching for his center, remembering all the near-misses, the fringes of fatal mistakes in his adventurous life. Curiously, none of them mattered, none came close to his fear of terrifying Dana Madison with his long delay.

If anything had happened to her, if anything had happened to his sweet …

Flint cut off the renegade thought. Women were dangerous, women were mine fields in the kind of life he led. They made him feel things, want things he couldn't have and couldn't need. When he saw a guy and a woman and a kid, a lucky guy with a woman who cared where he was or if he was hurt, Flint's guts constricted with envy. Was love a forbidden luxury? Was Dana forbidden, too?

He built a fire and listened to his center. And when she came out, on tip-toe wrapping her arms around his neck, shyly burying her face in his throat, rubbing her warmth into him, he curled his fingers around her forearms and set her away.

Stoically, he met the hurt and puzzlement in her eyes and wore his mask. His voice was flat, monotone to conceal his pain.

"Time for soup, Miss Madison."

Chapter Four

For two days, Dana alternately teased Flint, nagged and sniped, and subsided into sullen silence. He had put up a wall, and in the quiet time after lunch, she suspected she knew why.

She was getting to him. The experience of being tied and abandoned had horrified her, but Flint's reaction had erased the residue of those bleak seven hours. Lovingly, Flint had held and comforted and cherished her while she nestled in his arms. He had kissed her. Not, she admitted, with passion, but with tenderness, and that was a start.

"Why don't you talk to me, Flint?" Dana sat Indian-style at his feet. "Lately you dole out about six words a day, and you know how I get bored."

Flint immersed himself in a paperback western and said nothing.

"I loved how you held me that night, made me feel safe and protected, Flint." She walked two fingers through the fur rug until they reached his boots. Compelled to make contact with him, no matter how fleeting, how trivial, she stroked the hard blackness of the boot.

Flint dog-eared a page and closed the book. "That was the point. That's what you do to a frightened person on the brink of hysteria." There was soberness in his voice, and a hint of guilt. "Even chimpanzees hug each other during a fright."

Dana hit him with a mocking laugh, and smoothed the hard leather. "Do they call each other *my baby and darling,* Flint? Do they hold each other for hours and kiss?"

"You're getting carried away," he said flatly. "In extreme situations, one does what's expedient. Here. Read an old Zane Grey." Casually, he set aside his book and strolled out onto the porch.

Dana restrained the urge to dive after him. Instead, she waited a few minutes and followed. Flint was leaning against the post that supported a rickety overhang. His powerful neck flowed into broad shoulders, the vee of his torso arrowing down to the lean curve of his butt. How many women had feasted on Flint's masculine beauty?

All women developed a low, juicy radar for men like Flint, an instinct for tracking hot, dangerous males. Oh, she'd seen women give out all the primping signals when a man like Flint swaggered past. Flirty tossing of the head, fingering hair, licking lips, dilating pupils, hordes of women must have put out the vibrations, must've thrown themselves at Flint.

With a yank to keep her tanktop taut, she sidled next to him. "I've never spent time in the desert," she offered. "It's very beautiful." Damn, she was lame. "Do you like the desert?"

"What do you want, Miss Madison?" Flint's incisive stare shut her up, and his coldness forced her to change strategies. Obviously he wasn't caving in, wasn't bowing to her seduction. Flint was as obdurate as his name, and his resistance hurt her. Dana smiled brightly as if the two had shared a joke. She wanted to cry, but as often as he'd bested her, Dana still had a few weapons in her arsenal. And now, ashamed she'd been rejected, the smart idea was to pretend they meant nothing to each other.

He'd shoved her back to square one. Then the one option was escape. But she couldn't escape her longing for his lips, her need to feel him buried in her welcoming heat, most of all, her desire to love him. Stupidly, she thought she'd seen signs that he'd cared. Her throat ached with unshed sobs.

"Can I sit in the van?" It came like a bolt out of the blue, an inspiration.

"Why?"

"A change of scenery, for heaven's sake." She reined in her testiness. "Just to do something. Please, Flint."

He shrugged. "Then go sit. I've got some firewood to chop." He sauntered off the top step, and vanished around the side of the cabin.

As soon as Dana heard the even thunks of axe on wood, she gave herself to the dry heat, meandered to the van, pausing to inspect a tiny lizard doing push-ups on a rock.

Flint left the car unlocked. After all, no one came here, no one spied. She left the door open to cool the suffocating interior, and climbed into the front seat. In case he'd bother with a quick check, Dana popped the driver's seat back, and rested her feet on the dash.

When the thunks continued, she jack-knifed, searching for the ignition wires. A few tears trickled down her cheeks before she took the final irrevocable step.

She held her breath, tore the strands loose, and twisted the ends together. Buster, her father's chauffeur, had taught her, always claiming that Dana could set up shop as a primo car thief when her father disinherited her.

Her heart pounded and her pulse raced. Escaping Flint, showing him she really was tough, that she didn't need him, that was the adrenalin rush.

A few fits and starts, and suddenly, wonderfully, the engine turned over.

"Eat this, Flint," she crowed. Dana kicked it into first gear and barrelled down the dirt road. In the side mirror, through the cloud of dust, she spotted Flint, both hands on his axe, like a dark statue.

"Oh, baby, if I'd met you on the golf course, or on a cruise, we might've set some sheets on fire," she said ruefully.

After all was said and done, Dana sported the same radar as the rest of her sex.

She sighed, peering through the windshield for the highway.

"Flint, Flint, the trouble is I'd never see you on a golf course, or on a cruise. I'd never have met you at all. And now how will I ever learn how you got that scar, how you became such a smooth criminal?" She lay on the accelerator. Somehow, the prospect of learning Flint's secrets from the police department, maybe the F.B.I. sent an uneasy shiver down her spine.

She kicked the accelerator and the speedometer zipped toward eighty. The needle had just hit its mark when the engine spluttered and coughed. "Dirt in the fuel tank," Dana said, whistling in the dark. She stamped on the pedal again, but slowly the needle swung back and the van slowed, gave a pitiful wheeze and cruised to a dead stop.

"C'mon, c'mon," Dana shouted. A red light on the dash gave her the bad news. "Empty," she moaned.

A glance in the rearview reflected an ominous sight. Her escape from Flint's clutches measured about three blocks. And worse, Flint was hiking toward her with a red gas can, a leisurely hike as though he had all the time in the world.

Dana shrieked in her fury and jumped out of the van. She looked right, left in the draining desert heat, and struck out for the highway as fast as she could. A hasty glance, the glance of the terrified prey, revealed Flint filling the tank.

She shrieked again, but Flint started the engine and poured it on, and when he jumped out and snared her, she was soaked with perspiration, coated with gritty sand.

In the van, amid a barrage of her "I hate you's," Flint locked the cuffs on her, and headed for the cabin.

"Then say something," she demanded.

"Why? You know what's coming." He seemed on the verge of laughing. "Bedtime."

Fired with frustration, she lunged and kicked at the back of his seat. "If you think you're going to tie me to that bed again —"

"You'll hurt your wrist," he interrupted in a conversational tone.

And fifteen minutes later, he stood outside the bathroom while she washed away the sand.

"Here's your costume for the day," Flint said. He stuck his arm in and dangled a clean pair of babydolls. "Put them on, and give me the road clothes."

"I won't!" Dana stamped her foot. "I am not a child, I will not be treated as a child."

"Put them on." He waved two fingers.

Panicked, she cursed at him and slipped on the outfit. At least it was clean and cool. She came strutting out. "Well, macho man, satisfied?"

For a second, his eyes clouded with hunger, and Dana knew he was anything but satisfied. Seductively, she arranged herself on her bed, lounging like an houri in a harem.

"I know you don't want to hurt my sore wrist with those metal things," she wheedled.

"I won't, so I made these." Flint tied her hands with strips of soft towels. Dana closed her eyes and wriggled her toes. Then Flint tied her left ankle, and her eyes flew open.

"What the hell do you think you're doing?" Outrage and temper sharpened her voice.

"I can't trust you. Starting now, I'll let you up every two hours. Then you can go wild." He side-stepped a vicious kick.

She sobbed and used her little voice. "I have to lie here twenty-four hours a day, alone? With nothing to do? Talk to me, Flint."

"I don't talk, remember?" He tied her right ankle.

Her howl followed him into the kitchen, out onto the porch, and behind the cabin where he chopped wood, trying to drive out the image of her oozing the promise of rich sex, bound, smelling of desire.

"Center yourself," he commanded and swung the axe higher, brought it down harder. Dana never let him or his cock forget her. She whimpered and cried between each strike of the axe.

With a mighty blow, Flint shattered the log. He only had to survive a few more days of the provocative Dana Madison. She was intelligent, but wasn't she smart enough to understand he could read her sexual overtures as clearly as the back of his hand?

She was her father's own daughter, clever, but without a sincere bone in her luscious body. She was just a job.

❧⟨ᴗ⟩❧

By the Coleman, Flint sat reading *Sports Illustrated*. A log sputtered and fell to ashes. He checked his watch and glanced at the futon rolled up beside her door. She'd been restless, talking in her sleep, and at 2:00 A.M., he'd given up and made coffee.

"Flint." A soft moan. "Flint, I need you."

He tossed the magazine, sprang up, and hovered at her bedside.

Frowning with concern, he asked, "Feeling sick, Miss Madison? Water, juice, aspirin? Something I can get you?" He felt her forehead, and it was cool. "Something I can do?"

Her answer was a velvet whisper. "Oh, yes, Flint. You can do something." In the dim candlelight, she moistened her lips, and choked back her words. "No. I can't tell you." She turned her head to the side, avoiding eye contact.

He sat beside her and cupped her shoulders. "Tell me."

She faced him suddenly, and her eyes shone with naked lust. "It's been three weeks, three weeks without sex, Flint."

As though scorched by the touch of her flesh, he drew back. "You'll be home soon. One of your men —"

"Please, Flint," she wailed. "Make love to me. It won't mean anything, I promise. Please. I'm so restless, so tense. I'm having nightmares."

The bed creaked as he rose, and Dana began to cry, sobs that shook her slight frame.

"Look, I can't do it," he said. "My rule, no fraternizing on the job."

"You tie me up, watch me all the time. I can't even take care of myself." She trembled and wept until her breasts heaved. "I need it bad, Flint. Love me. Touch me there so I can sleep."

Flint's penis stirred and thickened. His guts twisted, and guiltily he reminded himself, this wasn't about him. It was about his hostage. The weeping Dana Madison, pinioned and writhing, was a wild woman used to indulging her appetites, a reckless heiress who'd been spoiled by getting everything she wanted, except escaping this abduction.

But he had bad news for the demanding Miss Madison. She wasn't getting a fucking, or a fondling, or even a quick kiss from him, not from Flint, her baby-sitter.

Her cheeks were streaked, the tears glistening as they flowed from those incredible blue eyes, from beneath the golden lashes. Her sobs hiccoughed. Damn, she'd worked herself within a hair's-breadth of hysteria.

Madison had given instructions about his daughter, but nothing about driving her crazy or depriving her of sexual satisfaction. And this was hardly a question an intelligent operative asked a father.

Dana moaned, so sweetly desperate, his cock strained even harder against his seams.

Flint sorted through Wu Chin's advice, but despite his respect and reverence for the old master's teachings, Wu Chin had never tied a woman to a bed and walked away while she pleaded for sex. He paced to the door, pivoted, and completed a stiff half-circle, trying to work off his anger and frustration.

Hell, he'd give in and give her what she wanted, this time. But he suspected when he got through with her, she'd never again depend on relief being just a finger away.

In the half-light, she lay, the sheer cotton nightie riding up, a veil over the lush, firm breasts. "Thank you, oh, thank you, Flint. It means so much to me." She smiled then, like an angel about to sin.

With his bandana, Flint dabbed at her tears. He cursed himself for a fool and reached for the candle.

"Please, leave it lit, Flint. I want to watch you play with me." Her voice, an intoxicating blend of shame and boldness, lured him like a magnet.

In the half-light, he sat beside her, and threw the quilt to the foot of the bed. No panties. The downy triangle was exposed. Beads of sweat broke out on his brow, and a trickle slid down his spine. He fought the urge to rip off her gown and drive into her. Flint suppressed a shudder of desire and rested his hand on her mound.

She hissed through her teeth and tensed her pelvis. "Yes. Please, Flint."

Holding his breath, he began toying with the soft curls, periodically sliding his hand away to brush the satin of her inner thighs. She wriggled, spread her legs wider, beckoning him with her body to return to her vulva, to her clit.

She was shivering now, jutting her dampness into his hand. "Oh, God, don't make me wait. Please touch me."

He covered her wetness with his palm, squeezed the pouting lips, leaned over and raised the candle in its china saucer high overhead, until it cast a distorted oval of light on her flesh.

"What, what are you going to do?" she gasped, shrinking into the mattress.

"You want to watch me play with you," he got out huskily, "and I want to watch you come. But let's make it interesting." Deftly, he balanced the saucer on the curve of her belly. "Keep quiet, Dana. Hold still, no matter how good it gets." He smiled wickedly.

At first Dana concentrated on the dancing candle flame and the quivering of her belly. Then, desperately as she tried, she couldn't ignore the thrilling, insistent massaging. Flint's skilled fingers slid in her wetness, caressing the labia, finally transferring the slickness to her clit, his thumb circling the nub.

Wild sensation tore through Dana. Maintaining the candle's balance tormented her. She gnawed her lower lip and mewling sounds escaped from her throat. But the longer she held still, the longer she dammed the urge to release the fire pooling between her thighs, the longer she checked the urge to scream her pleasure, the more slowly he built the tension.

"Is this what you want? Mmm-hmm. Do you like me rubbing your cunt, Miss Madison, all open and hot and creamy?"

Dana shut her eyes, and lay silent, praying to fall over the edge, praying to drown everything in silence, to shut out questions and answers and let her whole world be the constant agony of his touch.

But Flint was having none of that. "Tell me, or I'll quit."

He stopped all movement, and Dana bit her lips and looked deep in his eyes. As always, he meant what he said. Hastily she swallowed and jerked her head.

"You know I like it. Oh, don't stop." Her words caught in her throat.

"I'd make you tell me exactly what I'm doing to you, what you like," he commented almost conversationally, "but I am not a cruel bastard."

Flint thrust a big, blunt finger into her sheath, plugging her, filling her, controlling the internal probing even as his thumb increased speed.

Hungrily, Dana called his name and arched up.

"I'm finger-fucking you. Do you want to come now, Dana?" he whispered. His eyes darkened and his nostrils flared.

Dana breathed the ripe smell of her sex, and knew Flint smelled it, too. She saw herself reflected in his eyes, two tiny Dana's spread-eagled, mercilessly teased by Flint's rough calluses, and she flexed her hips, trying to delay her spasms.

The candle tottered, the flame winked. "Let it burn me," she shouted, crazed for release at any price. But as soon as Flint felt the first powerful ripple, the milking of his finger, he lifted the candle, watching her watch him.

"Flint, Flint!" She shouted his name, wanting all of him deep inside her. Sobbing and pumping her hips, she thrashed, screaming for fulfillment. She froze then, impaled on his thick finger, feeling the pulse of her clit under his callused thumb.

Dana looked down when he placed his left hand gently on her belly and pressed as the spasmodic shudders gradually diminished.

Drenched with perspiration, she sighed. A few delayed contractions squeezed his finger, and he massaged her dewiness.

Dana groaned, exhausted and utterly boneless in happy relief.

Flint had made her burn, had built the blaze, and stoked it into a mindless, final conflagration of the senses.

"Feel better now?" He raised one eyebrow, and a very small smile quirked his lips.

"Was this a medicinal screw, an injection of Flint's finger sedative?" Dana tried to chuckle, but she was too dizzy, too mellow. Instead, she gripped the wrist ties, tensed her vaginal muscles and clung to his finger, but he slid it out, and drew her nightie over her wet curls.

Flint exhaled and rolled his shoulders. Tight-lipped, he untied the bindings. And Dana, heavy-lidded and dazed, still managed to detect the heat lightning of desire flicker across his impassive face, and the huge swelling in his groin.

Behind the bathroom door, she washed and read her total satisfaction in the mirror. By lantern light, she stretched, cat-like, gloriously loose, relaxed. Languidly as if in a dream, Dana basked in ripeness, fullness. Her nipples had softened, the aureolas smooth and content, courtesy of Flint and his educated hand.

When she drew a towel between her legs, the soft distended tissue protested, and she licked her lips. If Flint could bring her to the edge of the universe and spin her out into the void with one hand, what could he do with his mouth, his body?

She shivered and studied her expression. Oh, he was a real master of the art. She'd sleep great tonight. And it took no seer to predict that Flint would suffer from insomnia and a granite groin. For all his emotional distancing, she'd bet a million, Stoneman had a heart and a hard-on.

And for some stupid reason, she let the cynicism melt, trickling away like the mingled drops of sweat and water between her breasts. Her father had preached his motto. Take what you need, but do it with charm and style. If you have to work an opponent's weak spot, work it, but leave him smiling.

Flint wasn't smiling. She'd taken what she'd needed, an intense sexual experience her captor had given freely, believing that she was suffering. Dana draped the thin towel around her waist and leaned into the splintery wood, wishing for the first time she knew the secret of smoothing the hard lines of Flint's mouth, of bringing to his face the sloe-eyed look of satisfaction she wore tonight.

Chapter Five

From the porch, Flint counted stars, gazing at their cold perfection like his assignments, each encounter, each task clean, distinct and separate. And when the job was finished, all the ties were cut, all the feelings. The file was closed. And Flint followed Madison's next order.

In her bedroom, Dana lay sleeping, languid, perhaps drifting in a soft dream. He smelled her scent lingering on his fingers, closed his eyes, and pressed the ache behind his tight Levis.

Dana, magically golden in the candlelight, was the stuff of his dreams and fantasies. He'd looked at her as little as possible during the past three weeks, afraid of losing control, of dragging her to the floor, devouring those red lips, and taking her savagely. He'd spoken to her as infrequently as possible because her low, throaty voice spoke innocence, but his brain heard a phantom invitation, phantom moans of ecstasy while he dreamed his cock plunged and probed her wet velvet.

"Dana," he whispered. He re-ran the moments of caressing her slipperiness, fondling her quivering flesh as the candle glimmered. He'd read the wild shifts of lust and delight on her face as he varied his strokes and touches to bring her time and again to the edge, then forced her to retreat.

He passed his fingers over his lips, and inhaled deeply. Sea air and a heady bouquet. Dana. To be inside her was all he cared for, damn everything. Protect her, and love her and make love to her. Dana, in her strength and defiance, her open sexuality, an elusive mix of want and shyness, excited him more than any other woman.

Then he dredged up Wu Chin's homily on sex. "My son, what hides between a woman's thighs is the most mysterious being on the earth," he'd intoned. "For it has no voice, yet calls to a young man constantly, has no brain, but schemes and plans, has no arms yet catches and holds with the strength of a giant."

"But, Master, what is a man to do? This?" Half-smiling in the dark, Flint remembered lifting his right hand to touch the crotch of his white cotton ghi.

"The boiling overflow of the life essence must be drained, and I tell you to answer the call of the being. Yet answer to a different call each time. Or one woman will bind you and know your secrets."

One woman, the only woman for him, the ultimate woman for him, lay asleep in her bed. She would never hear his words of love. And she was the only woman he could never have.

"Snap out of it," he ordered himself. Action, action was the prescription, not replays of the Master's advice.

He washed his hands in the outdoor basin, scrubbed them with harsh disinfectant soap, and poured the intoxicating odor of Dana Madison into the thirsty sand.

Flint ran for hours over the arid landscape. In the distance grotesque forms threatened until he approached and recognized twisted cacti, deformed rocks, the meshed bulk of tumbleweed.

Returning to the cabin, he bowed, grabbed his knees, and sucked in great breaths. The moon lit beads of sweat dripping from his face. He flopped on the weathered wood planking and let the cold night wind chill his face.

Wu Chin's advice was always correct. Grim and exhausted, Flint remembered the Master's emphasis on the *yang*, action and light and heat. "Exhaust the body, and reason shall mount and rule with the whip."

Flint splashed water on his face, pulled his futon to the middle of the room, and fell into a restless sleep.

Cuffed again, Dana twined a curl around her index finger, and tried to focus on a dreary women's magazine. Seven A.M. and Flint was hacking at the wood pile. He had enough for twenty bonfires and a thousand barbecues and still he chopped away. Were they going to be holed up through winter? A tiny frisson of pure excitement and anticipation raced down to her belly, and she shook it off.

Surely, Daddy's men would track her down before long. A question nagged her. Why hadn't her father's top investigators found her, and frog-marched Flint into a black sedan?

She stiffened, and the picture of Flint subdued and arrested woke a sharp pain in her breast. No, she wouldn't let them take him, not the man who'd soothed and embraced her tenderly, the man who'd kissed her tenderly, and called her his baby, his darling.

That damnable Flint and his tenderness had muddied her motives, her purpose, her plans to escape. And he refused to sleep with her.

She sighed and glanced at the table of contents. What was this? **Getting Mr. Right into Bed, Three Steps.** Whoever wrote it had never tried to seduce Flint. Dana snorted and started reading.

During lunch and dinner, she commented about the weather and slumped into silence. Flint looked like hell. Tight-lipped, tense, deep violet shadows beneath his eyes. Dana shuttered her gaze and imagined kissing the shaded crescents, imagined the texture of his skin.

When night fell, he waved her into the bathroom. "I'll stay out here. Something I want to read." Over his shoulder, in a tone suggesting that he was having a tooth pulled, he said, "You were good today."

Dana hurried to the bathroom. "Give me a break," she whispered to herself, "my big reward, washing up without Flint on duty." Her last reward had been her father's donation of a quarter million to Dana's favorite charity. How she'd come down in the world! She chuckled, and plied the washcloth.

Moonlight drifted through the windows, painting everything falsely new. Dana, fresh from bathing, put on her nightie, picked up the hair brush, and ignored her bed. Playing close to the edge, she tip-toed into the big room to linger, to show herself in front of the fire and test Flint's mood. She bent from the waist and brushed the fall of her hair. When she sensed she'd stolen his full attention, she snapped straight to toss the mane down her back, thrusting her breasts for him to scrutinize. The abrupt intake of his breath, and the turn of a page were notes of his lovesong.

"Flint." It came out soft, wanting and compelling. And real. She wanted him, and all her scheming and conniving vanished in her need for his taut body, the heaven of his owning her, the sweet aftermath when he'd murmur —

"Forget it. Whatever it is." Gruffly, he rattled the pages of his magazine.

"I'm sorry if I've done anything to upset you. Why are you so angry?"

"Don't beat around the bush."

If Flint had ever blushed, he was doing it now. Boldly, Dana touched his knee.

"Sorry to disturb you, but it's time to tie me." She added brightly, "Of course, I could stay up late and chat."

"No. You should be in bed, all covered up." Slowly, he followed her.

Dana sashayed into her room, and lay atop the old quilt. "No quilt tonight, Flint, please. I'm so warm." If her range had fallen any lower, he'd need a hearing aid to catch it. She fanned her hair on the pillow, and stretched her hands up and over her head.

"Tie me."

The ties hung on the bedposts, but as Flint took the first one, Dana stroked his bulging crotch.

"Flint, do you want me?" Her lips were open and inviting, and she wet them with the tip of her tongue.

An image flashed in Flint's brain, Dana swirling that eager pink tongue around the head of his cock, Dana begging him to bury it deep in her mouth, then into her plush heat.

"No." He snared the trespassing hand, tied it, and leaned over the bed to trap the other hand.

"Flint, kiss me. I need you to kiss me."

"No." He delayed a fatal second, and she stayed free to massage his thickened groin. He groaned and rocked into her hand.

"Please, Flint."

He shook his head, and fell to his knees to protect his genitals from her forays. Another second and he'd be on her like a hawk on a dove. "You don't know what you're doing. You don't know what you're saying. So shut up." He fumbled for the tie and tried not to seek those lips, those eyes. He lost the struggle and knelt on the bed, memorizing sapphire and gold.

"Then kiss my breasts," she begged. Her eyes sparkled with desire. "Kiss my nipples. They're aching for you." She arched, displaying her erect, marble-sized buds. She eased his head to her, and, cursing himself as he did it, Flint instead met her mouth, probed it with savage kisses, tasted her, wanted her.

In a fog of lust, he barely felt her open his Levi's until his penis sprang free. She encircled him, squeezed and stroked his rigid length. "God, baby," he moaned, trailing a ribbon of kisses to her nipples, "do you like my mouth on you?" He glanced up, but she had no words, and he plumped the white globes and sucked until she writhed. He closed his teeth on her hard nipples.

His penis knocked against his belly, and Dana crooned and slid her hand deep to play with his balls. Then she brought his hand to her mouth, and suckled one finger. She panted, she raised her hips, she loosed a little cry of pain.

"Untie me, Flint, so we can make love."

I'm crazy. She's finally kicked what's left of my brain to the curb. Unsteady, Flint got to his feet, grabbed her left hand and bound her. Throughout, he was conscious of his cock nodding toward Dana.

"Good-night, Miss Madison."

"You pansy bastard, do you jerk off?" Dana delivered the accusation like a quick jab below the belt. Her eyes shone with contempt. She was furious, at once aroused and disappointed. "Don't you ever need a woman?"

"Yeah." He clenched his jaw and buttoned his fly. "When I need sex, I buy one. Anonymous. No one gets hurt. It's professional on both sides of the deal. And then we walk away."

Painfully, with a swollen groin bursting his seams and breath hissing through his teeth, he managed to reach the door.

"And from now on, Miss Madison, the lullabies are over."

"But I won't be able to sleep." Outrage drove her voice up an octave.

"Count cocks." He itched to slam the door, but of course, he'd carted it away weeks ago to punish her.

꿹✵(꧂)꧁✵

When he let her out for lunch the next day, she slouched in her chair, barefoot, hair a mass of gold tangles. Sullenly, she ate half an apple, drank a few sips of water. Without prompting, she rose and flung herself into her bed. She lay like a cream and pink statue, unseeing. Especially not seeing him.

A spoiled bitch, so used to getting her own way, she goes into shock every-time she hears no. When her stomach grumbles, she'll eat quick enough. Despite his dismissal of her tactics, a sick cold lump grew in Flint's gut.

As darkness fell, she'd lain silent, except for one quick bathroom trip. She'd refused a Coke, turning away her head.

At suppertime, he hauled her to the table. "I cooked for us, corned beef hash, and cactus salad." Sheepishly, he gestured at the candles he'd set out, and the styrofoam cup of dried flowers. "Kind of like a date."

And he imagined Dana on a date, a stroll along Riverwalk, an intimate dinner in a cool Mexican restaurant, a secluded booth where she kissed him, tiny, loving kisses, promises of the gift she'd give him when they wore nothing but music and bare skin.

He hung a towel over his arm, and brandished a bottle of Welch's. "A touch of the grape, Madame?"

Dana stared into her plate, her hands in her lap.

Flint poured anyway and served the hash, buttered her bread.

After chewing a few times in the silence, he tried again. "Please eat. You'll make yourself sick."

He ate his salad, and she watched her plate. "Just a little something," he coaxed. "One bite."

Nothing. Was she testing him, after all the times she'd tested and lost, egging him on to the third request? He propped his elbows on the table and steepled his fingers.

Dana picked up the white plastic fork. She ate nothing, drank nothing. But Flint, reminding himself he was a patient man, drank grape juice and pretended to ignore her.

The candles choked on melted wax. Her face was dimmed and illuminated by the dying and reviving flame. And still she sat, fork hovering over her plate, drink untouched.

A tic danced in Flint's jaw as he showed three fingers. "Last chance, Dana, before I stuff the food down your throat. Eat your dinner."

Quick as a flash, Dana was on her feet, wielding the fragile fork, jabbing at him. In the faint light, her eyes flashed with anger. "Let me go before I —"

Flint twisted her wrist until the fork fell. He kicked over his chair and, boiling with temper and fierce hunger for her, swung her around the table and lifted her.

She kicked and screamed, and threatened his eyes with sharp fingernails.

"Do it, woman," he snarled. "C'mon, give me your best shot." He threw her onto the bed. But instead of the hysterical rage he expected, Dana sprawled, legs spread, eyes bright not with fear but desire. She panted and licked her lips.

"Damn you, you hellion," Flint growled. He ripped off her tank top, tore off her shorts. In a frenzy, he skinned out of his clothes. Fully aroused, he roughly nudged her legs wider apart, slipped his hands beneath her thighs so they rested on his forearms. His big hands splayed over her belly, then her mons. His hard thumbs separated the lips, forcing her clit out and up, until it glistened and offered itself to his ravenous mouth.

"Flint, do it. Flint, please."

He ran his tongue between the lips and back down, holding her immobile against involuntary twitching and quivering. He licked faster and faster, the only sound her moans and the sound of wet flesh on wet flesh.

He stopped and blew tiny breaths onto the sopping cleft.

Dana made wanting noises, and locked her hands behind his head, futilely trying to bring his mouth into full contact.

"Are you asking me to do what you wouldn't do for me at dinner tonight? Talk to me, Dana."

She probably thought he was torturing her for holding back, but she couldn't feel the torture his need was extracting from his nerves while he prolonged the foreplay. He glanced up.

Dana was whimpering, her eyes half-closed, half-mad with lust. She could hardly get out the answer. "I don't remember, Flint. Oh, please, lick me." She tried to raise her wetness toward his mouth, but he applied pressure to her pelvis to restrain her.

"Ask me what I asked you to do." He flicked the tip of his tongue and withdrew again.

"Eat." She moaned. "You asked me to eat. Please, Flint, I've been good and answered the question." She was shaking now, pleading.

Flint buried his face in her, nibbled the sweet projection, and then released her so she jogged against his mouth, freezing as all her nerveendings fired and she sang the ancient female song of desire fulfilled, of the male pleasuring her beyond reason or sense.

Flint straddled her chest and brushed her cheeks and lips with his cock. Dana turned her head from side to side, and opened her mouth, trying to capture him. Slowly he slid down to her waist, pressed her creamy breasts together and worked himself between softness and watched as she crooned, thrust out the tip of her tongue and lapped at the drops of clear fluid on the end of his shaft.

"Come inside me, Flint," she begged. "I need this —" she kissed the engorged head "— all of you so deep inside I —" She drew in a great breath.

Flint settled between her legs, lifted them over his shoulders and drove into her. A low moan erupted from her. He arched in the ecstasy of treading the edge of self-control, of sending his whole length into her pulsing heat, of feeling his balls against her wet crevice.

He pulled out and sank into her again. "God, so tight, so ready, you were made for fucking." He rocked, abruptly withdrew, and despite her protest at the cessation, her efforts to catch him in her cleft, he let her legs fall to the sheet, caught her shoulders and supported her head.

"Kiss me, baby," he whispered. "Taste yourself on me, and then I'll ride you till you scream." Dana extended her pink tongue and licked the pearly essence of herself on his stiff flesh.

From under half-closed lids, she met his eyes. "You're so good, so good for me." She fell back and put her hands on his biceps. Her eyes were blue diamonds, her mouth a sweet prison where his tongue was welcome. Flint braced himself above her, feeling her fingers guide his massive erection deep into her.

And he grew harder than he'd ever thought possible, delving into the hot velvet, her quickening cries of rising tension joined to his ragged breaths. His powerful pistoning slid her toward the headboard, and Flint grabbed her and pulled her down toward the middle of the mattress.

"Don't — don't stop, my darling," she cried. Her hips rose faster and faster to meet his thrusts, speeding the coming of the explosion, frantic.

Her blue eyes dilated, so wide they were black, and she clutched his shoulders, slipped her hands to his slick back and kneaded the rippling muscles laddering his spine. As her control shattered, she dug in her nails.

"Oh, Flint. Oh, darling, I love you," she screamed. And the bloodrush beating like her voice in his ears, Flint pounded into her, gripping her hips, melding her to him. He threw back his head, and slammed the final thrust home, coming like a sirocco breaking over the desert, his shout boiling up from his guts.

He held her through the smaller paroxysms that pulsed around his cock. She fit him like a custom-made glove, and he wanted her to be here with him. Always. Always with "I love you" on her lips. But he knew it was a lie.

The coming separation would destroy the interlude they'd shared.

Flint brushed away a tear. He'd never believed that crap about broken hearts, yet his own drummed with physical pain. Just for tonight he'd fight to believe her lie of love would come true. Just for this one night. Possessively, fiercely, he banded her to his body, stroking the supple, woman muscles, counting her ribs, palming her breast. Learning her, engraving her on his memory.

Then Flint drifted in a cloud of exhaustion, a delicious half-dream more satisfying than he'd ever felt after the act. *Submerge yourself in feeling*, Wu Chin would advise. *And when the immersion is complete and you have taken everything you can use, erase it. Erase her cries of passion and the softness that fed your need.*

And Flint tried to slip into a river of dreams, into a perfect nirvana where sensation and thought and reason seeped away, leaving him to float mindless, empty, blank. He failed, and let the sharp questions pierce his conscience.

How many times had he brought women over the line to climax, heard them cry, "I love you, Flint"? Faceless, nameless women. And how many times had he skillfully extricated himself, ruefully slipping out of bed, dressing himself in black? How many times had he leaned over silk sheets to soothe a lady with his special *au revoir,* murmuring faintly apologetic excuses (he had to go), delivering the practiced good-bye consisting of a short tongue probe of her mouth, a lick on her breast, and a quick kiss on her mons.

All very tender, and more importantly, the ritual allowed him to slip farther and farther from her grasping hands, and let him exit without a messy final scene.

Dana didn't deserve that, wouldn't be soiled by those cheap tricks, ruses to oil his escape. He'd never told a woman he loved her, unless it was part of the job.

"Am I crushing you, Dana?" He hoisted his bulk an inch, and the suction created by their sweaty torsos gave way. "Want me to climb off?" His cock registered a no vote.

Dana ran her fingers through his hair, traced his jawline.

"Don't you dare, lover." Smiling, sleepy-eyed, she stretched, offering her breasts so he could nuzzle the softening nipples. "And don't let Flint, Jr., take a hike either." With a laugh she tightened her female muscles.

Flint flexed and came up on his toes, elevating his hips just enough to slide his hardness out almost to the head. "That critter has a mind of his own." He mouthed her breasts up to crests, teased her, poised while Dana complained deliciously and struggled to envelope his cock to the hilt.

"No, no." She wrapped her legs around his waist and urged him back inside.

Grinning, he sank deep in her again. Still connected, he rolled onto his back, and brought Dana over him. He locked his hands behind his head and worshipped her in candleglow.

First, Dana lay quietly on his chest, tickling his throat with tiny nibbles, brushing him with light kisses. Then she sat up, cradling him inside. She curled his black chest hair around one finger, trailed her nails around his nipples, lapped sweat under his arms, bit his shoulder.

"Oh, you taste so good, lover," she whispered, and ground her slipperiness into his pubic bones. "Recommended by *Dana's Guide to Five Star Restaurants.*"

"Damn cannibal woman," he growled.

"Yep," she agreed cheerfully, "that's me. And to prove it, I'm going to eat you all up." She rotated her wetness around him and bent to graze his nipples with her teeth.

"You missed dinner, so I suppose you have to eat something," he mused. He bucked up into her, ready for round two. And before her delicious kisses and more delicious squirming rendered him unable to speak, Flint whispered, "All of me. Is that a promise?"

Chapter Six

In the fading moonlight before false dawn, Dana, sated, burrowed in his arms. Flint drew her close, kissing her, tender kisses, loving kisses and gentle murmurs. They were wrapped in a cocoon of dreaminess.

"You make me feel so safe, Flint." Her toes explored the wiry hair on his leg. She slid one foot from his ankle to his knee, parted her legs and pressed herself into his thigh.

"Yeah? You make me feel like an endangered species, strong and healthy until I fell into the hands of a ruthless exploiter and was screwed to death. But what a way to go." He cradled her and nibbled her ear. "I can't move."

Dana giggled. "Then what's that thumping on my thigh?"

"Involuntary muscle twitches. No pain, no gain, they say. Are we going to sleep now, sweet thing?" He brushed his lips over her temple.

Dana touched tiny kisses to his chest. The moon lay a white path across him, and she traced scars on his chest.

"How did you get these?"

"Knife."

"No, I meant *who*?"

"Look, Dana, there's stuff we can't talk about." His voice took on an edge, the old edge he'd used on her before they'd had sex.

"And what's this puckered thing on your ribs? It's horrible. Who did this to you, my darling?" Dana bent and kissed the wound. She wept for him and his pain.

She saw Flint blink when the tears watered his chest, felt him hold his breath when she caressed his scars and swept her long hair over the violent blemishes marring the perfection of his body.

"Bullets and knives. It's the past, babe." He spread his legs, making himself loose and open. Flint carried her hand to his swollen genitals. "Do me," he pleaded, folding her fingers around his cock.

"But I want to know —"

"Know this." He played in her wetness, found her clit, and concentrated on slow, circular movements until her hand moved in the same erotic rhythm on him.

She stroked him and gushed onto his fingers until her heart pounded, and she needed all of Flint's maleness. Hastily, Dana straddled him and high on her knees rubbed the plushy head in her heat. With a little cry, she shoved him inside and slid down the iron length. Flint gasped and grabbed her hips.

In the moonlight, she braced her hands on his shoulders and rode him slowly. "Tell me," she whispered, as he'd done to her.

"You trying to pump me for information?" Flint gave a strangled laugh. It wasn't funny, and he wasn't convincing. He was burning up in another fever of desire.

"No action until you talk." She gnawed on her lower lip.

"What's to stop me from throwing you on your back and having you whether you want action or not?" He gripped her more firmly.

"Because you wouldn't do that to me." Conviction rang in her voice.

"All right." He grimaced in the blue-white light. "The knife scars, top secret. I could tell you, but then I'd have to kill you. The bullet I took when a crazy dude shot at Billie Winkler on stage during his Save the Frogs Tour. Happy now?"

Dana straightened. "I love you, Flint. Please don't get hurt anymore. I couldn't stand it."

"Fuck me," he whispered, a dark angel coaxing her to fall.

And Dana rode him to ecstasy, arching backward, one hand buried between their linked bodies, massaging the base of his root.

In the fraction of a second when Flint, too roused and bullish to let her finish on top, powered her on to the sheet and spurted into her, Dana caught the moonlit glisten of his keys on the floor.

❧⟨☉⟩❧

"Breakfast is ready, big man." Dana spooned fruit cocktail and melon chunks into his soup bowl. Half-listening, Flint fished under the cushions of the wing chair. Methodically, he'd searched his pockets, the van, and the house. Nothing. He went to the table where Dana served toast and bacon browned over a small fire on the hearth.

He ate and smiled. "Pretty good. In fact, five-star for a lady who doesn't cook, and had to make do with the fireplace." He leaned over the table and kissed the tip of her nose.

"Still can't find the keys?" Dana sipped tomato juice and wrinkled her brow. "And you only have the one set?"

In that second, Flint knew she'd stolen them. The next time she made a break for it, she'd have the advantage of a quick ignition. He gave her a curt nod.

"One. Even a careful man makes mistakes. Of course, I can always rely on your expertise to hot-wire my wheels."

"Going somewhere?"

Flint detected the lie in Dana's too-innocent question. She thought she was smooth and subtle, that her love-making had softened him, dulled his powers of observation. He munched on a hunk of watermelon and speared a cube of honeydew on his fork.

"Town."

"Ah, the weekly trip for supplies." Dana put down her glass and met his eyes. "Can I go along?"

"No." Had her voice revealed an edge of anxiety?

"Then take this." She dropped a small paper between the salt and pepper shakers. He saw a numbered list and gulped his coffee.

"Instructions? What do you want me to do, lady? Call the F.B.I.?" Flint forced a chuckle. "Or the Texas Rangers? Or Daddy? Or maybe stop by the Auto Club for a map?"

"Of course not, you suspicious critter." Dana rose, pinched the list and snuggled into his lap. "But I love you, anyway." Her body heat radiated her perfume, and the scent of roses brought back the night and scenes of the most intense joining he'd ever experienced. He froze the urge to breathe deeply, to pull in her heady aroma. Flint concentrated on the keys and her slyness.

Hell. She did exactly what I would do in her place. He flashed back to a POW camp where he'd gradually loosened fencing, sustaining burns from electric shocks until he'd wedged his body through and made a successful escape.

Flint wanted to throw away that memory and replace it with Dana's turbulent love-making that had seeped into his very bones.

A POW's first duty is to escape. The first rule of capture besides restricting info to name, rank, and serial number. Why shouldn't it be Dana's rule, even her motivation for coming on to him?

"Penny for your thoughts, lover." She bit his lips. "On second thought, can't town wait another day?" Dana moved in his lap and woke his need again despite his suspicions. What mental trick could shield him from her delicious lure?

"Kiss me, lover," she whispered. "Take me to bed." And when her tongue traced the seam of his closed lips, he fought his rebellious body, got up and stood her on the cracked linoleum.

"Have to go to town. What's on that list?" He put a few feet between them by checking the paper. "Juice, meat, canned milk, fruit. Salad greens?"

"For tonight. I've got no way to make them last without a refrigerator." She leaned against him, brushed her breast on his arm, and his groin tightened. "If I can't go along, you're stuck doing the shopping, lover."

"Dana, the terrible thing that happened when I was late can't happen again." Flint folded and pocketed the paper. "Don't worry. I wrote a couple of notes with your identity and your whereabouts. One in my jacket, one in the car, one in a safe deposit box at the local bank. I'll need an extra hour today."

"Hurry, lover. I'll be waiting." She raised her wrist for his kiss. "Cuff me." Dana walked backwards into the bedroom as if she couldn't see enough of him. "The faster you leave, the faster you'll be back."

Watching her lie before him like a willing sacrifice to his power, Flint slowly tied her hands to the bedstead. When he bent for the good-bye kiss, her blue eyes filled with tears.

Stay, his body told him, and his emotions echoed the refrain. *Stay and hold her forever and make her your own.* But he knew what Madison expected, and it was not a complicated job.

Flint took her mouth in a bittersweet kiss that spoke of heat, love, and the final, inevitable detachment.

Flint pivoted and strode to the front door. He closed his ears to Dana's I-love-you's, and hot-wired the van. On the deserted, sweltering road to Brisco, he prioritized his errands.

First, the replacement of the ignition switch and new keys. While he waited, a call to Madison's lawyer in Portugal, and a quick stop at Hopkin's Super Foods.

He remembered the bleak and empty meals before Dana. Now he'd have to resume his meals eaten standing over the kitchen counter, or the silent, lone dining with a book or a newspaper broken only by a question from a waiter.

He'd never be the same. How could he go back to that empty life without her? The life of the cold, objective professional who lived everywhere and nowhere, who had no bond to anyone. An agony built in his throat, and, on the barren road, he threw back his head and howled like a wounded animal.

Dana had left a hole in his heart.

When the van parked in front of the cabin, Dana woke from a doze. The sun was just setting, and he was early. Her stomach lurched with anticipation. "Flint," she cooed, waiting for him to bolt to her side, loosen the cuffs, and take her in a bone-melting embrace. She imagined his lips on hers, his hot tongue probing, his strong hands stripping her with an exquisite slowness to heighten her erotic excitement.

A flush of desire washed over her and her nipples stiffened, tingled, incredibly sensitive to her shirt's light cotton weave. At the apex of her thighs, creamy moisture flowed and collected. She writhed in her need.

"I'm so ready for you, lover," she called. She heard his slow footsteps. "Come make love to me before I dissolve." Her voice was steamy and inviting.

He came and leaned against the doorjamb. He looked at the bureau, at the brown braided throw rug, everywhere in the room except at her.

"Flint, what's wrong?" She strained against the cuffs. "Free me so I can love you."

"The loving is over, Miss Madison." He approached her bed.

When he freed her, Dana smiled. "I see. Anything to torment me. Come here, lover." Eagerly, she threw herself into his arms.

"It's over."

"Don't say that, Flint. Please." Fear colored her voice.

He held her and stroked her hair. "Hush, now hush. And listen. Good news. Tomorrow night you'll be going home. Happy?"

"Home?" She leaned back in the curve of his arm. Shock and bewilderment flickered across her face. "Why?"

"Hey." Flint gave her a little shake. "The deed is done. The job is finished."

"But you, me. The two of us —" She choked on the words.

"Baby, there never *was* the two of us." He gave her a quirky teasing smile. "You've been around the block. You know the story. A little stimulation, a little relief."

"No. That's not true. I love you."

"C'mon, Miss Madison. This is what you love." Flint laid her on the coverlet. Bracketing her head with both hands, he leaned down and opened her mouth with a tongue kiss, and lowered his face to her breasts. Through the thin fabric he worked on her nipples until she lifted herself for more. She sighed and moaned his name.

Flint raised his head and for a second he gazed deep into her eyes with naked hunger. Dana's heart thudded erratically. "Flint, take me. I can't wait any longer."

With a fleeting kiss he touched her cleft. He clenched his right fist and caught the punch in his left palm. "I'll make sandwiches for dinner. After a couple of meals tomorrow, we won't have any food to throw out."

"What about me? You'll have *me* to throw out, won't you, Flint?" She leaped off the bed and ran after him, jerking at his arm until he spun to confront her.

Dana screamed and beat on his chest, slapped his face in her fury and pain. Flint took it all, not catching her wrists or stepping away from the blows. A statue without feeling, a stone without pity, without remorse.

And Dana wept then, and crumpled, sliding down his strong, ungiving form, clutching him, embracing his knees. She sobbed and pressed her cheek to his thigh. "It had to mean more to you than sex. Please tell me it meant more to you than that. The way you touched me, the way you owned me, as though you could hold off all the bad things."

"Nobody can hold off the bad things, baby." Flint seized her by the elbows to lift her to her feet, but she shook her head wildly and clung to him with every ounce of her strength.

Flint disengaged himself. "You're making this rough, Dana. Use your common sense. *I'm* one of the bad things. I'm your kidnapper. Have you forgotten?"

Dana wilted and shrank into herself. She knew what he was seeing. He saw a small teary version of the defiant, brittle Dana, the overbearing princess who lived in a palace with King Madison. A woman who spoke and people snapped to, a woman whose heart had never been touched because she'd never given up control.

She hiccoughed a sob, and Flint hunkered before her. "Let me go, lady," he whispered. He cupped her cheek, and Dana tilted her head and snuggled into his palm.

"I can't," she said, miserable. "Not without being with you one last time." When Flint pulled her to her feet, she inhaled, preparing for a scream of despair.

But she was wrong, wonderfully wrong.

Flint swept her into his arms, the kiss he gave her blended tenderness and savagery and took her breath away.

"Promise me it's the last time, Dana." His gaze was fire and smoke. "Promise me this is over. Tonight."

Weak with joy, she nodded. She kissed the line of his jaw.

"Does tonight last until tomorrow morning?"

Flint laughed. "That's my girl." But his laugh died away, and under her hand, she felt the drumming of his heart.

❧✦✧❧

Hours of perfect connections played out in Dana's bed, an incredible partnering with positions changed, speeds modified, bodies squeezed and released, an instinctive dance of love in which Flint both led and followed.

"Does this feel good, this slow motion?"

"So good. Don't stop."

"Want my tongue here?"

"Yes, yes. For God's sake, you're driving me crazy."

The sound of fevered flesh meeting fingers. Licking and tasting and lapping, whimpers and groans. The bedstead creaking, faint in the still night. The slow, prolonged, deliberate working of stiff shaft in wet softness.

And finally, Dana taut and unmoving as a tightened string, her mouth open, and release that went on and on as Flint poured into her and the two joined in a duet of satisfaction and cruelly unfilled longings.

Braced on his forearms, he hovered over her, sheathed and content. He moved himself in her blood-hot cleft, eliciting tiny moans, tiny aftershocks.

"Come down on me, all of you," she whispered. "I want you against me this last time." She pressured his biceps.

Flint lowered himself, his bare chest covering her warm breasts. He kissed her throat, and rested his head beside hers. He was lost in her fragrance, wanted to submerge himself in a sweet exhausted sleep but worry kept him awake. Dana dreamed she could change the situation, change him.

For her own sake, she had to discard the notion that their meeting was somehow fated, that this had been a romantic tryst, a prelude to a heavenly forever-life together.

Reality, like a sharp knife, cut to the truth. He heard Wu Chin's sad commentary on failed love affairs. "The rift is not caused by what fools say, not the shape of the lover's eye suddenly grown displeasing, nor the laugh grown too loud. It is instead the way of life, the expectations of family and parents which intrude and crack the seamless shell."

Flint closed his eyes to blind himself to Dana's hair, silvered in the moonlight, her long lashes sweeping her cheeks, her eyes like the ocean off Tuamoto, stormy and calm and sultry by turn. He had to erase her beauty and her passion as though they had never existed.

Chapter Seven

"It's time, Miss Madison." Flint glanced at his watch as if his heart hadn't been counting the minutes whizzing by in the early dark.

Dawdling near the kitchen's dry sink, Dana scrubbed a plastic fork. "Finishing up," she said.

They'd sat at the old plank table, pretending to eat. He'd watched her moving chunks of tuna on her plate, and he knew she'd watched him covering his fish with a piece of bread.

And they'd glanced around the cabin. The fireplace, the shabby chair, the bearskin rug. He hoped a storm would destroy it, or a lightning fire. Then no token would remain of their sad little love story.

"We'd better hit the road. Don't want you hanging around the bus depot all night."

She carefully placed the fragile plastic in a drawer, as if putting things in their proper place was the magic charm to make the inevitable disappear. She wiped her hands on a paper towel.

"Guess we're finished."

He nodded, not trusting himself to speak, opened the door for her, and blew out the candle.

"Sit up front," he said. He slammed the passenger side door, and climbed into the van. He dug out his keys.

"Here." Dana dangled the missing keys before him. "It was a stupid trick to hold us in the cabin."

Flint closed her small hand around the key ring. "I bought a new ignition, different keys. Keep 'em as a souvenir." He hit the starter, a starter that ended what had only begun. Damn, if he kept up this philosophizing, he'd give old Wu Chin a run for his money. The engine roared to life. The moon shone on Dana's solemn face. Flint gripped the wheel. A wave of tenderness rolled over him and he considered driving forty to prolong his time with her.

He kicked it up to eighty and held the redline.

"Three blocks south of the intersection. You understand why I can't drive you to the door." He extended a packet. "I bought your bus and airline ticket. There's some cash for a cab if your father's not home to send a chauffeur."

"Is this how it ends, then? Tickets and a little cash? Of course, you remarked that when you needed sex, you bought it. Was I anonymous enough for you?" Dana curled her lip and lifted the papers from his fingers, avoiding his hand like a kid repelled by a snake.

Choked by furious urges to deny her accusations, to jump out and kidnap her for himself, to keep her close forever, Flint said nothing.

He'd been a fool. During the day, dreading the loss of Dana, he'd cut wood and slogged around the backyard desert. He had assumed she was making work for herself or reading or napping. But unpredictable as always, she'd been crafting an icy manner, a glacial good-bye. Under the street lamp, even her gaze was cold and dismissive.

"Hope you didn't knock yourself out entertaining me. But as you said, it meant nothing —" she unlocked the door and stepped to the curb "— a little stimulation, a little relief." She slammed the door and instantly ran toward the bus station.

Flint cursed. His acting had been too good. Did she really believe he wanted to let her go? He drove a parallel street, turned down an alley, and parked in the shadows across from the depot.

Dana appeared in the halo of the street light. Slender and compelling and desirable, she pushed the smeary glass door, and marched to the sleepy clerk behind the counter.

Flint threw the van into reverse and backed onto the parallel street. She'd seen nothing. Let her imagine he was so glad to dump her that he'd driven off and left her unguarded.

The love affair had ended with money, but it had ended the right way within the boundaries of a job. She'd scamper home to the loving arms of Madison. He'd counsel her not to publicize her mysterious disappearance, that he'd personally take care of the bold kidnapper.

Dana could return to high society, marry a well-connected man, and produce little Samantha's, Robbie's and Caroline's.

Flint might linger as a romantic memory for a while, but as the years passed, he'd be re-molded as a villain in her thrilling adventure. Finally, a white-haired Dana would reduce Flint to a big teddy bear who'd played tough guy, but had been brought to his knees courtesy of her cleverness.

By 2:00 A.M., he'd ramped onto the throughway and sped toward Louisiana. He had a couple of friends in Algiers, in old New Orleans where he'd conveniently disappear. He muttered names of parishes, saw himself driving the Causeway, drinking beer in a zydeco saloon, chugging rye whiskey shooters, getting a little wasted to dull the pain of losing Dana.

꿍ᘏᑓᒐᕒᕐ

"Time heals all wounds. Out of sight, out of mind." Dana gave a cursory glance at the framed mottoes and separated the lace curtains of the cozy sitting room overlooking the curved drive. "It is better to have loved and lost than never to have loved at all. What lies." She made a choked, desperate sound, and stared at the gardeners manicuring the lawns.

She had an herb garden she should be tending, but two long months after Flint had released her, she had slipped into a shell of solitude. Her nightgowns had become a kind of uniform.

Not that she hadn't tried to resume the old life. Hadn't she attended the Madison Foundation's board meetings where she sat distracted? Two invitations to dinner from dear friends who seemed annoying and unreal. Their mouths moved, the laughter was tinny, the teasing dull.

With crusty politeness, Dana strolled the terraces, sipping from her champagne flute. After an hour or two, she'd migrate to the exit, offer thanks. "We must do this again some time," she'd said, the statement vague enough to be forgotten.

"C'mon, c'mon," she'd coax the parking valet, slip him a twenty, and roar home in her Lexus. Fast and faster. She'd wanted to be in her quiet bed, by the weak light of a candle stub reliving Flint's heady love-making, a happy captive in his arms.

Now the walls were drenched with sun, altogether too cheerful for her mindset. Dana skipped over the embroidered heirloom mottoes her mother had adored. Two made sense. She read aloud the tiny one speckled with bluebells. "There are no reasons that explain love, but a thousand that explain marriage."

A few tears betrayed her efforts to dismiss Flint from her mind, from her life. She'd stopped trying to find reasons for loving Flint. And what did it matter? No reasons explained love. And she had a hand-worked piece to prove it.

She studied another very old motto she agreed with. Worked on frayed silk, stags and does eyed each other from the four corners. "In hunting and in love you begin when you like and end when you can."

Flint and she had begun when they liked, but her heart told her that they hadn't found the end, that despite her release and his let's-pretend attitude, he loved her.

The crunch of gravel brought her to the window again. Buster must have taken the ancient Silver Cloud Rolls Royce for its weekly exercise. Idly curious, Dana frowned. What was he doing parking? Buster's routine ended with steering the old girl to the huge garage for a shower. Instead, he braked at the porch and leaped out.

Before he could reach the passenger side, the door opened and a man stepped onto the gravel. A big man, a towering man, a man in black with sable hair.

Dana's heart skipped a beat, and then pounded furiously. He had come for her. "Oh, God, thank you. Flint. Lover."

As though he knew she hid behind the curtains, Flint looked up. No smile, no wave.

In shock, Dana watched as Leon the butler appeared and soon he and Buster were talking with Flint. A man's man, Flint was charming the family retainers. She could hear faint laughter as Flint and Leon entered the foyer.

At the sight of herself in the mirror, Dana blanched. She was no charmer. Out of control hair, blue baby dolls at three in the afternoon, eyes red from weeping.

In five minutes, she'd thrown on jeans and a tank top, twisted her hair into a pony tail, and rushed down the backstairs. She followed the voices, Flint's booming baritone that made her knees weak, her father's imperious tenor.

She crept up and peered through the crack between the double doors of the den. Was he here for more money? No, that was irrational. He could be arrested. For her? Or Lord, she prayed, make him say he came for me.

If her father had chosen the site of the confrontation, he'd chosen badly. The massive mahogany furniture covered in brown leather diminished her father. On the other hand, the den seemed designed to scale for Flint who overpowered the huge chairs and reading tables.

Shock piled on surprise piled on confusion. The meeting had no hint of confrontation. Genially, her father was chatting with Flint like an old friend.

"Heard you were hanging out in the bayous, my boy. You look like hell."

"This job's over?" Flint sprawled in the largest leather chair and stacked his hands behind his head.

"Merger complete, my little girl home safe and sound. Job well done." Madison poured sherry. "Simple and clean, that's why I like your work."

"Give me some action, Madison. Get me out of here. Africa, South America, Singapore." Flint emptied the dainty sherry glass. "Nothing civilized, like paper sabotage. Maybe a take-down in Brasilia. Or give me stuff on the high seas. What's that poem? A ship with a hard-assed crew and a star to steer her by? But no more snatch and grab, Boss. And no more women."

No *more* women? Dana's stomach churned. Jealousy and love and hate boiled over. Was making love to her an assignment, part of a job? Dizzy and sick, she leaned into the carved mahogany.

With the uncanny sixth sense of a hunter, Flint whirled and jerked open the paired doors. He arched one eyebrow and greeted her in a coolly impersonal tone. "Want something, Miss Madison? I was just telling your father —"

Dana stormed in. "If I had to choose which of you was the most despicable, I'd call it a tie." She was panting with fury. "You had me kidnapped, Father, consigned your own daughter to this animal, this throwback to prehistoric times."

"Now Dana, dear." Her father took refuge behind his desk and showed her his palms. "It was for your own good, little girl, your own safety."

"My safety? You weren't around to see this Neanderthal man-handle me. And now he walks away from his crime unpunished."

Desperate, Madison searched for support. "See, Flint, this turmoil was the very thing I wanted to avoid. If I'd explained, and asked her to leave quietly, she would've exploded. The merger —"

Flint casually moved between her and her father, as if she'd physically attack her own dad!

"You're a savage, Flint," she began when the idea came. How would Flint enjoy having the tables turned, Flint the hostage instead of the captor?

A tiny wave of anticipation rippled in her belly. Flint hand-cuffed and begging for sex. But even more, she envisioned her smile when she imposed his rule of three times and you're out. Why, she could plan a dozen tricks.

Caught in the scent and heat of Flint's presence, Dana trembled. She called up reserves of stubbornness to maintain her taste for teaching him a lesson.

But he had all the weapons, and her defenses failed in the face of his compelling gaze. He depleted her will power, and her body forgave him in spite of her anger. Her legs weakened, her dewy sheath remembered and cried for his sweet invasion. It was madness to think she could battle to get even when her every cell prepared for penetration. She licked her lips, and drummed up a crumb of resistance.

"All this for a merger?" she whispered.

"A merger," Flint said. "You do know what a merger is, don't you, Miss Madison?" Dana fixed her stare on the curve of his lips. If only he would slant them over hers in a scalding kiss, she knew she would surrender in a kind of erotic trance.

How could she concentrate when he smelled of pine and the sea and the familiar randiness of the man who had bedded her? Damn, she raged inwardly. It wasn't fair. Flint wasn't fair to make her want him so, not when she should give him a dose of his own medicine.

Sheltered from her father's gaze by Flint's broad chest, she mouthed,

"Are we over?" She slid two fingers up the sleeve of his jacket, read his thundering pulse, looked into his hungry eyes. Dana quivered with a crazy exaltation. He still wanted her.

"Dana," her father said angrily. "Go upstairs, or for a drive as far as you can get from this man. Buster will be taking him home shortly."

"Daddy?" She side-stepped, adopting a cool, civilized demeanor, restraining herself from leaping into Flint's dark embrace. "I think you're in no position to order me around when you hired this man to hold me hostage."

"Dana, please let's talk about this later. You'll make yourself ill. Little girl, excuse yourself and rest. Flint and I have business."

"Yes, Daddy," she answered so meekly her father should've heard alarm bells. To Flint she whispered, "I need to see you one last time. The Morton tomorrow night at ten."

Dana pulled the carved doors together. Then she grinned and ran upstairs to plan. The dinner, the decor, the wine, and if she could get it, a special ingredient to pacify the panther, and subdue his objections to her cage.

❧❀❧

Dana paced around the penthouse suite of the Morton, checked the bouquets of old cabbage roses with their muddled centers, red and pink white, autumn damasks dense with thick perfume. To fool Flint into thinking this meeting would be their last, she'd even scattered rose petals on the seafoam green silk sheets.

Like a nervous hostess, she inspected the table swagged in pink linen, the candles reflecting on crystal and silver. She glanced at her watch and, like Victorian ladies, felt an awful compulsion to wring her hands.

For the hundreth time, she paraded in front of the mirror.

The sapphire blue silk, carefully selected to match her eyes and show off her nipples, plunged in a daring vee between her breasts nearly to her navel. She wanted Flint to lust for her as she ached for him.

"Damn, what are Leon and Buster doing now?" She'd expected the chauffeur and butler to call her as soon as Flint came into the hotel. When her cell phone finally rang, her heart flew up into her mouth.

"Miz Madison," Leon mumbled. "He come in, set at the bar. Dint go to no elevators a'tall."

"What? Where is he? What the hell's going on?" Dana said.

"Hold on, Missy. Worked out real good."

Dana's stomach took the elevator Flint had ignored. "Oh?"

"Yeah, me and Buster bellied up to the bar, started yakking, even bought Flint a drink." He was choking on his cleverness.

Dana filled her lungs and tried to stay calm. "You've got to get up here with the stuff so I can doctor the drink. And how can I do it when you've got it in your pocket and he's on a barstool?" Her throat hurt in her effort to keep from screaming.

"Done it," Leon announced proudly. "Slipped it in his beer when he run to the men's room."

With a clenched fist, Dana silently raged at the fates in the form of her father's bizarre family retainers. Why had she trusted them to do anything complicated? "What did you give him?"

"You don't wanna know, and we don't wanna tell. Herb don't hurt none, Miss, just make him a little woozy, but he'll be able to talk and walk and do what you tell him. Lasts about eight hours. You need him down for longer, you shoulda told us."

Dana grimaced. "Listen carefully, Leon. Walk away. That's right, let him get up here *now* before he goes down in public. And follow him, but don't let him notice you."

The few minutes dragged like the hands on a bad clock, and she jumped at the knock. As she opened the door, the space between them pulsed with excitement. The air was charged with electricity.

The man she loved wore his usual black, and had clubbed his midnight hair with a leather thong. Wickedly handsome, stern and powerful, he was the man she loved.

"Flint, Flint." Dana breathed his name and threw her arms around him. "Lover."

He turned so her kiss was wasted on his jaw. Flint gripped her wrists, brought her arms down, and kicked the door shut. "Dana, we've got to talk. Madison said the estate is off-limits, or he'll turn me in. You forget me, and everything that happened. He's right. To sweeten the pot, he's assigned me to jobs that I can't discuss with you or anybody else." His tone was honed and cutting as a samurai sword.

"He told me to forget you, never to see you again. Whether he sends you to the North Pole, whether he lays down the law, I don't care. Darling, I wanted to see you one last time. Please, Flint." She waved at the little table, the intimate setting for a romantic supper, a bittersweet final meeting.

Dark and rugged as a basalt statue on pink velvet, he paused for a second. Then he exhaled a long-held breath and pulled out her chair.

Flint's lips twitched as he uncovered the salvers. "Corned beef hash, cactus salad, oysters and a steak. A trip down memory lane plus eats to give a man staying power." He reached across the table and held her hand.

Dana captured his hand and pressed her lips to his fingers, the fingers that had known her so intimately. "I love you, Flint."

He rescued his hand and picked up the wine goblet. "Don't say that."

Quickly, he scanned the room. "This was a mistake, only makes it harder for both of us, Dana."

"Ah, that's what I wanted to hear, that it's hard for you, too." Dana came around the table with her arms open, but Flint was too fast. He rose and put up one hand, as if to shield himself from her love.

"Don't touch me, don't try to kiss me. This is over. Now. It was over when I completed the transfer." His eyes were dark grey, the color of a storm.

"The transfer? You completed the transfer? Like you signed a lading bill for used cargo?" Dana heard the sorrow, the tears in her voice, gradually waking her resolve to make him pay.

"It's more than that, and you know it. This is dangerous for you, for me. Tonight in the bar —" Flint frowned and shook his head as if to clear it "— a couple of weird characters were hanging around." He rubbed his eyes, reached for the chairback and swayed. "They must've slipped something in my drink."

"Are you feeling all right?" Dana was scared, trembling as she led him to the bed. Quietly, he lay back on the pillows and rose petals. "Is there something wrong?"

"Something wrong," he said. He clung to her hand.

"Don't get up, darling. Stay here."

"Stay here," he repeated.

Dana thumbed the cell phone. "Leon. Back service elevator. Take him down like he's a drunk buddy."

It took less time than she'd planned, changing clothes, whisking Flint away, stuffing him in the van onto the mattress next to the supplies.

"Thanks. You're too smooth, guys," Dana said, thrusting the bills into their hands.

"Slick as grease on concrete," Buster said with a wink. "Now you drive safe, Missy."

Chapter Eight

When she'd driven twenty miles, compulsively eyeing the rearview mirror, she started to breathe regularly. No flashing red lights had appeared, no sirens, no state troopers or F.B.I. to haul Dana Madison off to jail for kidnapping. Or at the very least, for plotting revenge.

Revenge. An awful ache beat in her heart, and she knew she was lying, and confused. She had to have justice, and she'd find it in subjecting Flint to the iron control he'd once wielded over her. Yet she had to have *him*, his lovemaking, his hot masculine determination to pleasure her, to bring her to completion. She missed his erotic skills, missed even more his strength and his sense of humor that glimmered at the most unexpected moments.

"Just this one last time, Flint." A renegade tear crept down her cheek. "Darling, one last time." In the dark, she followed the van's frosty headlights. "Then if I can't make you love me enough to stay, to stand up to my father, I'll let you go. Did you know you're the only man I love, the only one I've *ever* loved?"

She slammed on the brakes for a stubborn armadillo, and the sharp stop took her mind off Flint. A puzzle had niggled at her for the last couple of hours. Something she'd heard or seen out of place, not right. Something about Buster and Leon and Flint.

She rolled the prickly mystery around as she zipped down the highway toward the desert cabin, then shrugged it off. Every few minutes, she glanced back where Flint sprawled, open and utterly vulnerable.

Overwhelmed with memories, Dana first tried to separate them into two categories: delicious, wild sex with Flint, and the tenderness, the softness that spoke of love. But the divisions mingled just as the days and nights of isolation had blended into a seamless union, just as hot battles of dominance blazed and left a residue of glowing coals that could burst into flame at the least puff of desert air.

Dana mulled over their short past, how the chemistry had worked between them in the rough cabin. First, the powerful physical attraction that had drawn them together, later the growing intimacy, his comforting her in his arms, her weeping over his wounds. And then a tangle of caring and sexual thrills impossible to unravel.

Dana remembered the years when she was still waiting for the right man, for a man who donated to the fund for retired polo ponies and knew how to choose the proper wine, how to impress the maitre'd.

Oh, she'd met the men who did all the right things, carried the right name, suave and sophisticated. Dana had even imagined being in love twice. But neither eligible bachelor, no matter how hard he tried, generated the heat and desire Flint ignited with a single touch, a single scorching look.

Somewhere she'd read that the act of sex allowed communion, not abstract and pie-in-the-sky, but a real melding in the flesh. And she wanted now, more than anything, to have that union again with the man who made her feel satisfied and safe and complete.

She peered at him, the sleeping giant comfortably stretched out, muscular legs parted, exposing the meaty bulge in his crotch. His rugged face was relaxed in dreams, and she smiled, hoping the dreams were of her.

⁕⁓ᑕᗝᒐ⁕

Far into the desert, she pulled to a roadside rest area and took a carton of milk from the cooler. When she knelt beside him and smoothed his hair, Flint stirred, propped himself up, and buried his face between her breasts.

"Thirsty, darling?"

"Thirsty." He fastened on her nipple and suctioned it until she gasped at the sweet pain. His teeth tugged, and shock waves of desire spread to her flowing cleft. A mere pulsebeat from urging him to take her, she pulled away from his seeking lips.

"No, no. Here." She slid the straw into his mouth. While he drank and Dana supported his head, foreboding shivered down her spine. What was romantic about Flint toying with her breasts when he didn't even know what he was doing?

She tossed the empty carton aside, and lowered him to his bed. "Sleep, lover."

"Lover," he repeated, like a warm robot.

Ashamed of herself, Dana said, "I love you."

"Love you," he muttered.

She clambered behind the wheel, and the few hours to the cabin were the longest in her life. When at last she set the brake, she hesitated before cutting the engine. Was she making a mistake, rendering Flint unconscious, giving him commands, putting him on automatic pilot? She palmed the thick leathery head of the stick shift and flashed immediately on Flint's heavy maleness. In her hands, in her mouth, down her throat.

Squirming, Dana had to whip up her resolution to force him to beg the way she'd begged for relief. In his docile state, Flint would be a pussycat, not the panther she knew and loved. Dana dragged open the sliding door, thumbed on the flashlight and led Flint to the porch through the cabin to the backroom. She propped him against the doorjamb and flapped the coverlet. A wee breeze, ripe with sagebrush, freshened the night and extended a welcome.

"Rest for a while, darling." She let him stretch out on the bed while she lit a candle.

"Darling," he murmured. In the glow of the flame, Flint smiled. Dana caressed his cheek with the back of her fingers, and had to tear herself away to bring in the supplies and food.

The newly pliable Flint was allowed up for a snack. And Dana slipped into the bedroom with a bag of surprises for the big man. She torched logs in the fireplace, not trusting Flint to do it in his drugged condition.

Meanwhile, the object of her obsession munched and drank and smiled. Beneath the heavy wings of his brows, his dark eyes studied her as if he'd forgotten her and waged a war to retrieve their secret passion.

"Darling," he said without prompting.

Uneasily, Dana brushed a stray curl off her face, checked her watch and grimaced. Buster had said the drug's life span was eight hours. Driving here had eaten up four. And now Flint was initiating comments instead of echoes.

Dana hurried, biting her lower lip. After all, it wasn't forever. Just a few hours to show Flint the cost of his playing the heavy, of forcing her to his will. Rapidly, she cleared the table while Flint stared into his glass.

"Well, now, lover." Dana leaned over the back of her chair. "Let's go to bed."

"Bed," Flint agreed. When he rose, he staggered slightly and draped one arm over her shoulder. In the dim light, she peered at his face. Was it her imagination, or had his weird complacency been replaced by the hint of a sparkle? The second before she turned him loose to fall onto the bed, she was almost sure she detected a slight squeeze on her upper arm.

The pale moon shone in the window. Two candles threw light and shadows. Beneath his lashes, Flint enjoyed the sight of Dana skinning out of her shorts. Slowly, she unpinned the gold silk of her hair, a sweet act that raised her breasts. Wearing her pink tank-top and her black bikini panties, she straddled his hips. "Flint, should I make love to you? No or yes?"

"Yes," he mimicked.

"I could be mean to you, coax you to tear everything off and put you in strange positions. But I won't," she whispered hoarsely, "because I love you."

Flint kept his gaze blank, and ineptly poked her nipples as if they were a novelty. The buds were rigid, the size of large pearls, and he bit back his desire to pinch them between thumb and finger until she moaned.

"Do you like them?" Dana pressed his hands into her swollen breasts, and moved slightly on his groin. "Oh, lover, my nipples are so hard."

Flint sneaked a quick glance at Dana arching backwards in delight. Behind tightly closed lips, he gritted his teeth, and held the pressure on her breasts steady.

"I think *you're* getting hard, lover." Dana rocked forward, put his hands over his head, and kissed him. She nibbled his earlobe, and trailed her fingernails down his black turtleneck, past his belt, to the bulge straining his slacks. "What have we here?" She massaged him and he heard the tremor in her voice. "I like this. I want to see it. But first —" she stretched and snapped handcuffs on his left wrist.

Flint raced to make a decision, fast. Let her cuff him and have her fun, or tell her he hadn't been drugged, and end the game. But why spoil a good thing? Dana had to do all the work.

He held his breath, simulated relaxation and played along, suspecting he'd hate himself for giving up control, and encouraging her need for dominance. Hell, he'd save hating himself until the morning. When he got back to Leon and Buster, he'd kick butt for buying into this crazy scenario. Dana, he noticed, had been so busy immobilizing him, she'd forgotten to take off his clothes. He suppressed a grin.

"Oh, oh. I forgot something. Your shoes." She laughed and dropped them on the floor, and cuffed his ankles. Flint expelled his breath as she found her favorite spot on his zipper and wriggled.

Dana tilted her head and touched her lips with one finger. "It's so puzzling. Why do people have sex naked?"

"Naked," Flint repeated, putting real effort into his act and inwardly admitting he'd better not give up his day job.

"Do you know the answer, darling?" She stroked his zipper and Flint did multiplication tables. "Let's have sex with our clothes on. Ready?"

"Ready," he croaked.

Through his fine cotton sweater, Dana licked his nipple, sucked it, and took the tiny nub between her teeth. He swallowed a groan as his sensitive flesh felt each thread. Dana slid lower, working his nipples with her nails, and probing his navel with her tongue.

A devil peeped out of her blue eyes. She sighed and knelt between his knees. In a sad little voice, she said "I'd love to rip this shirt and play in your black hair. But dearest, should I keep the action above your waist, or" she palmed his erection "— do it?"

"Do it," Flint echoed.

She caressed his swollen genitals, and rubbed him through his trousers. "No," she declared. "Down here, I absolutely must feel the naked man. See it all. Should I get the candle?" She chuckled wickedly.

Dana tossed back her blond mane, and eyed him as she fondled herself. Then she slid the black leather through his belt buckle and undid the button. Carefully, she pulled his zipper, opened his shorts and with gentle hands lifted him from the protection of his boxers.

Flint strained to fight off the intense urge to beg her to mount him, to give him relief. He was sweating. Dana tickled his balls, explored them with her tongue, and tasted the tiny bead of lubricant on the head of his cock. She was squirming with need, but by-passed her body's demands at the cost of keeping him powerless. She licked him from root to tip, engulfed him in her warm mouth, and bobbed her head rhythmically.

Under his mask of composure, Flint was seething, in prime shape to explode. He jerked his hips and bucked up into her mouth.

"Damn it, woman, uncuff me," he roared, glaring down the length of his torso to where she crouched, driving him mad. His come boiled, and his need to sheath himself in her was torture.

Suddenly she stopped and looked up, feigning bewilderment.

"Of course." She slapped her thigh. "Now I remember what's missing. What was it you said when you teased me? *I want to watch you come, and I want you to watch me watching you.* Where's that candle?"

Her laughter died on her lips, her seductive golden lashes slowly lifted, and Flint burned when he saw in her eyes a depth of desire matching his. Tenaciously, she returned to mouthing him, determined to humiliate him at the expense of her own sexual satisfaction.

Flint thrashed his head under the delicious titilation, and then fell still as a statue. He began with breathing exercises, the reduction of pulse rate, the gradual elimination of the stress Dana had cooked up. Thanks to the teachings of Master Wu Chin, he threw a mental shield over his genitals, numbing them to Dana's busy tongue.

"Flint? Flint? Why are you so quiet." She gasped and released his wet cock. "My God, they poisoned you! I knew it."

"Help," he said faintly. A sheen of sweat covered him.

"Oh, my darling. Wait." She fumbled for the cuff key, alarmed and almost weeping in her anxiety. Flint pondered his original decision. Was this acting or was this acting? Maybe he *should* give up his day job.

When he was free, and lying with one arm over his eyes, Dana insisted on bringing water and making him lean on her while he drank. She kissed his cheeks, held his hands, and confessed to a hundred sins against him. He frowned and couldn't remember a damned one.

"I have to get up now," he said in his usual stony way. Dana squeaked and hopped out of bed quick as a cricket, her eyes wide, her mouth open in shock. Flint grinned evilly. Then he started to strip, his jacket, the turtleneck. By the time he thrust his thumbs under the waistband of his slacks, Dana was running for the door.

"You'd better run for it, lady," he shouted. He tore off his boxers and sprinted after her. He caught her in front of the fireplace. Flint slanted his mouth over hers in a long, deep, wet kiss, and her knees weakened. Without breaking the kiss, Flint lowered them to the bearskin rug.

In the firelight, he caught her wrists and pulled her hands over her head, and sucked her nipples through the pink top until she arched. "Strip me, lover," she spoke with great effort and her eyes were glazed with want.

Flint ripped the thin top off, and caressed her breasts until she moved restlessly. "I want you, Flint." He took his time, sliding his strong, blunt fingers beneath the black lace panties. The hot dampness surrounded by a nest of curls warmed his fingers and he worked them in and out of her slipperiness.

Flint gazed at her, from her wild mane of golden hair to eyes half-closed in lust to her perfect white breasts, to the honeyed delta he needed to sip from. "Dana, I'm going to mount you. Stay inside you all night, ride you till you forget any man you've ever had."

She shuddered and eased his access to her sleek treasure. Flint, on the edge of losing control, tongued her through the lace, tasting her salt, her sweet, feeling her fleece while she uttered a low purr of readiness.

"Take me, Flint," she moaned and raised her hips so he could pull down her panties. Then she lay before him, a lithe blond cat, stretching, luxuriating in the warm light on the furry rug. "Come inside me, please. I'm so hungry for you."

Settling between her legs, he pushed, filling her with one smooth stroke through the melting liquid velvet, and he groaned at the perfect fit of his rigid cock in her cleft. She wrapped her legs around his waist, and he rocked, slick, thrusting flesh urgently building spirals of higher and higher tension, to a mutual explosion.

Flint, still hard inside her, rested his head on her breast, and listened to her heart beating while he thumbed one nipple, and then reached down to their connection and stroked her clit.

She cried out and came and came again, squeezing his cock until he began pistoning in her, and she'd climax again, a sweet circle of cause and effect.

In the breaking dawn, at the final spurt of his juices, Flint shouted, "I love you, Dana. I'll love you forever."

After their spasms had subsided, Dana laced her arms around his neck, and sighed into his ear. "I loved you from the first time I met you, lover."

"Not a contest, woman," he said with a drowsy chuckle. "Go to sleep."

"You have to answer a question first."

"Give it to me," he groaned and rolled onto his back.

Dana snuggled under his arm. "You were drugged tonight. Yes. I'm guilty. Orders from me to the family's Buster and Leon. What do you think they slipped in your drink at the Morton?"

"Nothing. They're my buddies." He closed his eyes and cuddled her.

"What?" She propped herself on one elbow.

"Mercenaries in a private army together. They were already old then and I was just a punk kid. When we fell out of work, your father hired us to do a little spying. The old guys finally retired to being houseman and chauffeur. Now will you go to sleep?"

She lay touching his muscled length with her whole body.

"Don't worry about Daddy. He's grouchy, but it's all an act. He'll probably make you head of security." She pulled a curl on his chest. "Look at me when I talk to you, Flint."

He opened one eye. "I'm looking. Now you look. Know what this means?" He raised three fingers.

About the author:

Sandy Fraser lived in Southern California, but recently passed away. Published in book-length women's fiction, she loved the opportunity to push the sensuality envelope and to tell the forbidden in **Secrets**.

Love's Prisoner

by MaryJanice Davidson

To my reader:
I've always been intrigued by good guys who have to do bad, and werewolves are prime examples of that. It's tough to be a sensitive, 21st century guy when you turn furry, howl at the moon, and crave raw meat once a month. It's even worse if you're in love with someone who not only thinks you're delusional, but at times actively despises you. Stick two people like this in an elevator, add one power outage, and watch the sparks fly ...

I hope you'll e-mail me or visit my website to tell me what you thought about *Love's Prisoner.* I love to hear from my readers, and I like getting suggestions on what you think I should write next.

Chapter One

Engrossed as she was in *Glamour*'s Do's and Don'ts, Jeannie Lawrence scarcely noticed when the elevator jolted to an abrupt halt. She *did* notice when the lights went out.

"Oh, come on!" she cried, slapping her magazine shut. Getting stuck in an elevator during a power outage was nowhere on her to-do list. Today, anyway.

"Not now," a voice muttered, and she nearly shrieked. She hadn't known anyone else was in the elevator with her. When she had her nose in a book or magazine, she wouldn't have noticed if Barney the Dinosaur was in the elevator with her.

"Well, this is a fine fix, huh?" she asked the voice. "Of all the days to drop my ad copy off early! I guess it's true — no good deed goes unpunished. What are you going to be late for? Me, I'm trying to beat the rush hour traffic to the bridge. I can't stand it when —"

"Hush."

The voice was a pleasant baritone, one she liked despite its abruptness. She hushed, not offended. Some people didn't like talking to strangers. Or maybe this guy was claustrophobic. Or — what was fear of the dark? Darkophobic? Whatever it was, he was clearly unhappy to be trapped in an elevator for who knew how long. Poor guy. She hoped he didn't get the screaming meemies. There was nothing worse than a grown man having hysterics.

"Sorry," she said, then added, "I'm sure we won't be here long."

She heard a sound and recognized it immediately: the man trapped with her had taken a couple steps back. Almost as if he was trying to put as much space between them as he could.

Exasperated, she said, "For crying out loud! I don't have cooties. Anymore," she added, hoping to lighten the mood.

"Be quiet. And step into the far corner. Now."

"The hell I will!" She turned toward the voice. "Look, just because you're feeling antisocial doesn't mean I —"

"*Don't.*" No pleasant baritone that time. That one sounded like a growl, like he'd forced the word out through gritted teeth. "Don't come near me. Keep away. When you move, you stir around the air currents and I get more of your scent."

"And that's *bad*, right?" Great, she thought with grim humor. Trapped with someone who skipped his medication this morning. Why didn't I take the stairs?

"No. It's not bad." His voice, low in the dark, was a throbbing baritone she could feel along her spine. "It's ... extraordinary."

"Gosh, thanks." Uh-huh. Clearly a nutcake, sexy voice or no. She hadn't had time to put perfume on after her shower. He couldn't smell a damn thing, except maybe a lingering whiff of Dial soap. "Do you have a special doctor you tell these things to? Someone you should call when we get out of here?"

He barked laughter. "I'm not insane. I'm not surprised that's the conclusion you've drawn, though. What is your name?"

"Jane Doe."

He chuckled softly. "What harm could it do to tell me your real name?"

"All right, but only if you promise not to freak out on me. More than you already have, I mean. It's Jeannie Lawrence." There were a million Lawrences in the greater St. Paul area, she comforted herself, so if he was a serial killer he likely couldn't track her down when this was over. "Now remember, you promised ..."

"Actually, I didn't. Not that promising would have done any good." He sighed, a lost sound in the dark. Absurdly, she felt sorry for him, this perfect crazy stranger who talked so oddly and in the sexiest voice she had ever heard. "You smell wonderful."

"Don't get started on that again," she warned.

"The moon's coming. I can feel her." She heard him swallow hard. "There isn't much time."

"Boy, have you got *that* right." She put her arms out in front of her, feeling in the dark, then stepped forward and banged on the elevator door. "Hello!" she shouted. "Anybody up there? A nice girl and a raving lunatic are trapped in here!"

"You're ovulating," he said directly in her ear, and she shrieked and flung herself away from him, so hard that she bounced off the far wall and would have fallen had he not caught her. Even in her startlement, she was conscious of the easy strength of his hand, in his scent, a crisp, clean, utterly masculine smell that she liked very much, despite her sudden fear.

"You —" Her mouth was dry; she swallowed to force moisture and finished her rant. "You scared the hell out of me! *Don't* sneak up on me like that, for the love of — and you can let go of me, too." She yanked her arm out of his grip, her heart yammering so loudly she felt certain he could hear it. And what was that absurd thing he had said? Had he really said —

"It's too late. You're ovulating," he said, his voice a low rumble in the dark. "You're … in heat, to put it a little more crudely. And I'm too close to my change."

"Then empty your pockets," she said rudely. "Let your change out."

"You don't want me to do that," he said softly. "Oh, no."

She supposed some women would be reduced to panic at this turn of events, but this weirdo with the sexy voice and strong hands had no idea who he was dealing with. She had a black belt in karate, could drill a dime at fifty yards, and had once put a would-be mugger in the hospital with cracked ribs. If this guy tried anything with her, he was going to have a very bad day.

"Look, I'm sorry you're feeling … uh … unwell, but if you just stay calm, they'll have us out of here in no ti —"

With that same shocking suddenness, his hand was behind her neck, tilting her face up, and she could feel his mouth near her temple, heard him inhale deeply. "You're in heat," he murmured in her ear, "and the moon's coming up." He inhaled again, greedily. Frozen by his actions, she waited for his next words. "I'm very sorry."

Then his mouth was on hers. Pressed against the far wall of the elevator, she could feel his long, hard length against her body, could feel his hands on her, could hear his rasping breath. She had the absurd sense he was wallowing in her scent, glorying in it. And she came absurdly close to relaxing in his embrace, to kissing him back. Instead, moving independently of her brain, her hands struggled up and pressed against his chest, hard, but it was like trying to move a tree.

"Oh, Christ," he groaned into her hair.

"Don't —"

"I'm sorry."

"— stop it —"

"I'm very sorry."

"— before I break your —"

"Do you believe in werewolves?"

"— big stupid — what?"

"I'm a werewolf. And my change is very near. Otherwise I might be able to — but the moon's too close. And so are you."

"*What* are you talking about?" she cried.

"I'm trying to explain. Why this is going to … why this must happen. Don't be afraid."

"I'm *not* afraid," she hissed, shoving at his chest again. This time, it worked. Or he stepped back.

"You're a liar." Odd, how he could make that sound like an endearment. "I can smell your fear."

"I'm not sure how to break this to you," she said through gritted teeth, "but I'm not afraid of any man. And I *don't smell.*"

"Not afraid. Anxious, then," he soothed. "I don't blame you a bit. If *I* was trapped in a box a hundred feet off the ground with a werewolf an hour from his change, I'd be out of my mind."

"About the werewolf fixation," she said, striving for a note of humor — she'd always had a perverse need to make light of any seriousness. "I confess this concerns me a bit. Perhaps there's a support group that can help. Men-who-love-werewolves-and-the-women-trapped-in-elevators-with-them."

He laughed, a throaty chuckle.

"Couldn't you have waited another hour to have your nervous break-down?" she complained, pleased that she amused him. If she could keep him distracted, off balance, maybe the power would come back on and she could —

Then she felt his hands on her arms, gently pulling her forward. "I am sorry," he said, his voice heavy with regret. Again, she caught his pleas-ant, utterly masculine scent, and again she fought her unwitting attrac-tion. Jeannie didn't plan to let him do anything he'd be sorry for. She took a deep breath and prepared to strike him, palm out, with all her strength. A crippling blow, and, if she nailed him on the bridge of the nose, a killing blow. She hoped she would get him in the forehead or cheek. She didn't want to kill the lunatic. That was her thought as she smashed her hand into his chin and felt him rock backward with the blow.

"Ouch," he said mildly.

She felt her mouth pop open in stunned surprise. She hit him, she *knew* she hit him! Her hand was numb from the force of it. He should be unconscious, or at least groaning on the floor.

"That was some punch," he continued, as if commenting on a drink and not a blow it had taken her four months to learn. "You've had train-ing."

"You're out of your mind," she whispered. Or she was. Could it be true? Was he a — ludicrous thought — werewolf? She felt for him in the dark, sure he had to be bleeding, and her fingers encountered his smooth cheek. She jerked her hand away. "You're completely crazy, you know that?"

"No." She sensed him step close to her and threw another punch, no more fooling around — and her fist smacked into his open palm.

He had blocked her punch. In itself, almost impossible unless he was also a black belt. And what were the chances of being trapped in an ele-vator in the Wyndham Tower with a crazy man who was also a black belt? More worrisome, he had *seen her strike coming*. Whereas she couldn't see her hand in front of her face.

She felt his fingers curl around her small fist, felt his thumb caress the knuckle of her first finger. Her knees wanted to buckle, either from sudden, swamping fear or the sensation his warm fingers were calling forth. "Brave Jeannie Lawrence," he murmured, his voice so low it sounded like tearing velvet. "What a pity you didn't wait for the next elevator."

Then he deftly swept her legs out from under her and she was falling — but he was coming down with her and cushioned her fall and was on top of her in an instant, his mouth on her throat, his hands busy at her blouse. She shrieked in anger and dismay, raining blows on his shoulders, his chest, his face, and he took them all without being deterred from his task. She heard a rending tear as he ripped her blouse away, tugged at her bra ... then felt the shock of it to her toes as his warm mouth closed over her nipple.

She tried to lunge away from him but he pinned her easily with one hand on her shoulders, while the other tore at her clothes. "I'm sorry," he was groaning against her breast, "don't be afraid, I won't hurt you ... ah, God, your scent is driving me *out of my mind.*" That last ended on a growl, an ominous rumble that filled the dark elevator.

She drew in a breath to scream the building down — and sobbed instead. He was too strong for her, she was punching him and clawing him and kicking at him and he was barely noticing. This ... thing he meant to do, it was really going to happen. To her. Daughter of a cop and a Special Forces veteran, a man and woman generous with their teaching, who never wanted their daughter to be a rape or murder statistic. Jeannie could pick a lock and knock out most men with one punch. But she couldn't stop this man from taking her by force. Never mind the fact that her mind kept shrieking that this wasn't happening to her, this was not, was not, was *not.* It was.

"Don't cry," he begged, and she could feel his hands shaking as he gathered her against him. "We'll be done soon. It won't hurt. I'm so sorry to scare you."

"Please don't," she whispered, hating the way she sounded — so helpless, so frightened — but unable to do anything about it. "Please don't do this."

He groaned again and squeezed her in a rough hug. "I have to. I'm not mated, I don't have any control over this, just like later I won't have any control over — but you don't believe me, so we won't talk about that." His voice was still soothing, and now his hands were beneath her, stroking her back, forcing her chest up, and his mouth was buried in her throat, kissing and licking and even — very gently — biting.

She could hear his breathing roughen in the dark, heard another rip as her skirt was torn. She remembered herself and struck out at him again, blindly, connecting hard but with no apparent effect. He shredded her linen skirt like it was paper ... Christ, he was strong! But his

hands on her bare flesh were gentle, almost languid. They were everywhere, stroking her skin, sliding across her limbs, and she felt her nipples harden so much it was almost painful. When his lips brushed across
one she almost wept with relief, even as she was pushing against his
shoulders with all her strength. He rubbed his cheek against that same
nipple, his stubble rasping across the sensitive bud, and her fingers
curled into fists so she wouldn't touch him with tenderness. She couldn't
give in to him, no matter how —

Stubble?

He had been clean shaven two minutes ago.

She shoved that thought away, hard. His rough tongue swept across
her nipples, a blessed distraction that made her want to scream, made
her want him, and she hated wanting him. She tried to remind herself
that this man was raping her, but the only thing she could really understand was that he was making her feel as no one had ever made her feel.
She was no stranger to sex, but the only man she had ever been intimate
with was her college boyfriend, and that was almost three years ago.

In the back of her mind, a constant refrain: this isn't happening. It's
not real. Ten minutes ago I was on my way home; now I'm having sex in
the dark with a stranger. Thus, this is a dream. It can't be happening,
ergo it's not happening. Tempting to believe that voice, to give in to the
pleasure he could so skillfully offer her, to …

She realized she hadn't hit him in quite a few seconds. That she no
longer wanted him to stop. That traitorous thought alone galvanized her
into raining more blows on his head, until he caught her wrists and
pinned them above her head with one hand.

"Enough," he said hoarsely, and she cringed, wondering if he was
going to hit her back. "I don't blame you one bit, but … enough,
Jeannie."

He pinned her knees apart with his own, kept her hands out of his
way by keeping them above her head, and bent to kiss her. He jerked
back and her teeth snapped together, bare centimeters from his mouth.
He could apparently see in the dark like a cat.

Or a wolf.

She put the ridiculous thought out of her mind as quickly as she
could. That way lies madness. That way lies …

His thumb was stroking the soft cotton of her panties. And moving
lower. Her breasts were pressed against his chest, her knees were flat
against the carpet, forcing her thighs wide apart, and now his damned
fingers were — were — inside her panties. His breathing was so harsh in
the dark, almost panting, and she could feel his body thrumming with
tension, could hear his teeth grinding together as he fought — what? It
was clear he was in the grip of urgent lust, that he wanted to surge inside
her and thrust until he could no longer move, but something was hold-

ing him back. And now his fingers were delicately brushing the plump lips between her thighs, stroking so sweetly and tenderly … and then his thumb slipped between her nether lips while his tongue thrust past her teeth and she nearly shrieked, so intense was her pleasure.

He groaned into her mouth and then his fingers were spreading her plump folds apart and his thumb was slipping inside her and his tongue was licking, darting, and she sobbed with frustration and strained against him. His fingers danced across her slick flesh, sweetly stroking, probing, oh so gently rubbing a circle around her throbbing clit, a circle that got smaller and smaller … and then his thumb was dipping inside her again while his fingernail flicked past her clitoris, and she shivered so hard she nearly bucked him off.

He growled. The sound did not frighten her. It kindled her blood, made her want to growl back, made her want to sink her teeth into his flesh while his flesh sank into her again … and again … and again …

She realized dimly that he wasn't growling, he was saying her name, but his voice was so thick and deep she could hardly understand him. "Jeannie — let your — hands go?"

"Yes!" she screamed, wild to touch him, to feel his flesh against hers, to rip off his clothes as he had ripped hers. He released her wrists and in a flash her arms were around him, pressing him closer, she was tearing at his shirt, frantic to get the damned cloth off him and he was helping her and now her clothes weren't the only ones in shredded ruin, after all, what was sauce for the goose was sauce for the werewolf, and —

His hands were beneath her buttocks, raising her to him, and she could feel that long, hard, hot part of him nudging for entrance. For an instant, reason reclaimed her. Was she really going to do this? This crazy thing? She had no protection and without it, in this day and age, she was taking her life in her hands. And why was she cooperating in her own rape, for the love of God?

"Wait —" she said in a thin, high voice, but he drove forward, thrust into her with power and searing heat and her good sense left her; she threw back her head and screamed until she thought her throat would burst, screamed at him to never never stop and still he came, that hot hard length parting her, filling her, and it should have hurt, it should have, he was very large and she hadn't known a lover in years, but her need for him was as great as his for her, and instead of hurting, she needed more.

When he was seated completely within her, somehow, somehow, he made himself stop; he gathered her against him and she could hear the furious hammering of his heart. His hands behind her back were hard fists and he was shaking as though he had a fever, and still he stopped. When he forced the words out she could barely understand him.

"— doesn't — hurt?"

"No," she gasped, wriggling against him, his throbbing cock within her making her frantic. "No no no please, please you can't stop now you can't you can't you —"

"You're — very small — sure — doesn't hurt?"

"— you can't you can't please I please don't make me —"

"Don't — be afraid — tell truth." He took a deep, shuddering breath; his fists were still clenching beneath her and, very distantly, she heard carpet tearing. "Can try — wait — if you —"

"— beg, don't make me beg, please please please PLEASE!"

He pulled away but before she had time to groan her disappointment he slammed forward. His mouth covered hers, his tongue mating with hers as he took her again and again, as they made love so fiercely the elevator shook. And above it all, beyond it all, she could hear someone screaming with hoarse joy and dimly realized it was she making the noise.

Her orgasm slammed into her as he was, spasms so fierce she could actually feel her uterus contracting. He stiffened at the height of her climax, threw his head back, and roared at the ceiling in pure animal triumph.

For long moments, she didn't think she would ever be able to move. She could smell the scent of their lovemaking, could hear his heavy breathing, hear her own. Her pulse thudded in her ears and she was damp with sweat and ... other things.

He pulled back and out, his hands frantically feeling her limbs, her neck. "Are you hurt?" he asked hoarsely. "Did I hurt you?"

"No," she said tiredly, ready to sleep for a week. A year. "No, it was a surprisingly painless rape."

She felt him flinch, and wondered who she thought she was fooling. It might have been rape for the first minute, but after that she had been an eager participant. Shame made her flush.

"Jeannie — I'm so very sorry. I don't expect you to understand." She felt his hand on her arm and cringed back, hating herself, hating him, and most of all, hating the fact that she wanted to do it all over again, right now. Right here. "I'm sorry," he said again, quietly. "My poor Jeannie. You were so brave."

"Don't call me that," she snapped. She tried to pull her shredded blouse together, but might as well have tried dressing with confetti. "Don't call me anything. Don't talk to me at all."

"We need to get you out of here," he said urgently, completely ignoring her order. "And quickly. The moon's almost up."

"Do *not* start that again," she ground out.

"Out," he was muttering. "Need to get you out. Not safe here."

"Brother, have you got *that* right." She started to stand and nearly pitched forward; she would have thought her eyes would have adjusted to the dark by now, but she was still effectively blind. And exhausted. And — how was this for the stupidest thing ever — she wanted him to put his arms around her and promise everything would be all right.

What if she was stuck in here with him all night? What if he decided to take her again? Could she fight him off? Did she want to?

She heard him stand, heard him bang experimentally on the elevator roof, then heard the groan of metal as he somehow forced the locked hatch. She shook her head at the sound, amazed at his strength. He could have broken my neck, she thought dumbly. Anytime he wanted.

"Why the *hell* didn't you do that twenty minutes ago?"

He gripped her waist and lifted her up, up … and through the small trapdoor. "I had other things on my mind," he replied shortly. "Like how badly I needed to touch you."

"Bastard."

"Yes," he said quietly. "But now I can think again. For a while."

"Don't flatter yourself," she mumbled, cautiously getting to her knees on top of the elevator. She heard him chuckle beneath her and then abruptly, shockingly, he was crouching beside her on the roof. Off the floor and through the trap door in one bound, apparently. It was almost enough to make her wonder …

But that was ridiculous. This was the 21st century, and there were no such things as werewolves, dammit!

"Why have we left the relative safety of the elevator, to teeter out here on top of the elevator, you nutcake?" she asked with saccharine sweetness.

"I'm definitely planning on falling in love with you," he said casually, in a tone he might have used to ask her to close the window. "Any woman in mortal danger who can tease her assailant after being terrified is definitely worth taking to mate. Just so you know."

"Save it for your parole hearing, pal," she said. Before she could elaborate on what the judicial system would do to him with her blessing, she heard their death warrant: the elevator cables groaning from stress. She belatedly realized she was in danger of more than forced sex this evening. "Oh, God," she said, abruptly terrified. Had she thought she was scared when Tall, Dark, and Horny had taken her against her will? She hadn't known what scared was. "Oh, God — what should we do?"

"Live," he said simply and, absurdly, she took comfort in that. She had to, because never was the dark more terrifying. She could hear his rapid movements, hear twangs as parts of the cable give way under the stress, hear the elevator doors two feet above her creaking as they were forced open.

"Be careful!" she said sharply.

"Always," he said, and suddenly his hands were on her again, and she felt herself effortlessly boosted and shoved. She reached out and clutched wildly, and felt the carpet in front of her. The building was as dark as the elevator had been, but she could tell he had held her up, almost over his head (no one is that strong) and boosted her through the elevator doors. In the pure dark, she could sense no one else around, which was just as well, given the shredded ruin of her clothes. Now his hands were on her heels, and he shoved, hard. She zipped across the carpet as if it was wet tile, her entire front going warm from the friction (he's not crazy, he really is a werewolf).

She turned around and crawled back toward the open doors, groping for the drop-off. "Come out!" she cried in the dark, hearing the sharp twang of more cable parting. "Jump out! Quick! You can do it, weirdo!"

"Stay back from the doors!" he said sharply. "You can't see a thing, you'll fall right back down here. Stay —"

She would obsess about that for weeks, that his last words were warnings to her. Because at that moment, the main cable parted and the elevator car plummeted five floors into the basement.

Her rapist had become her savior. And paid the price with his life. She shouldn't have cared. She should have been relieved. And she was relieved. So relieved that she put her face down on the dusty carpet and sobbed as if her heart would break.

Chapter Two

Of course, there were questions. There were always questions. And when she stopped crying, Jeannie tried to answer them. No, she didn't know the elevator passenger's name. No, she didn't know how he'd managed to break the hatch lock and lift her several feet to safety. No, she didn't know how he'd over-ridden the safety locks on the doors, forcing them open. No, she didn't need to see a doctor. No, she couldn't identify the body — when they found it — because she had never seen his face. No and no and no.

She supposed she could sympathize with the building's management. A half-naked, hysterical woman cheated death on their property and now only wanted to go home … of course they were loathe to let her go.

She had her chance to tell them what he had done to her, how he had forced her — there was even a lawyer in the room to take her statement (the building management's corporate counsel, doubtless prepared to beg her not to sue) — but she couldn't do it. As much as he had scared her, used her, she couldn't bring herself to lay charges against him. If the price for her life was forced sex and mind-numbing pleasure, she was going to count herself very lucky indeed.

She saw a doctor at their insistence, a doctor who raised his eyebrows at the shredded ruin of her clothes but said nothing, a doctor who could tell she had recently had sex but, after her rude replies to his carefully phrased questions, said nothing to the others. Probably assumed it's my nature to seek out quickies in elevators, she thought darkly, and at the thought of her "quickie" partner, crushed and dead, she nearly started crying again.

The doctor had tried to insist on an overnight hospital stay; she had been firm. Like mountains were firm. She would not stay, she would spend the night in her own bed, thank you, will someone call me a cab?

They gave her a cab voucher — her purse was at the bottom of the elevator shaft, along with her wallet, ATM card, credit cards … and her rapist/savior. The cab came. She got in. The cab dropped her at home.

She got out. Went inside. Threw her clothes away. Showered for a long time. Wept for a longer time.

Three weeks later, about the time she noticed her period was late, her martyred rapist/savior showed up on her doorstep.

Chapter Three

Michael Wyndham III stepped from the car, nervous as a bride-groom. Which, he supposed, he was. It had taken him nearly three weeks to track Jeannie down, weeks of frustration and guilt and worry. But now he was going to see her again. The thought of taking in her scent, maybe even touching her, made his pulse pound in his ears. Oh, he had it bad.

He grinned. It was marvelous, to find his mate. And in such a strange way! His father had tried to tell him, but Michael had never believed, had always figured one female was as the next. But he had found his mate through purest luck and, best of all, most wonderful of all, she was an extraordinary human! And *homo lupus*, unlike *homo sapiens*, mated for life.

Now to persuade Jeannie, who thought her future husband was nut-tier than a granola bar.

Derik and Jon got out of the car and the three of them examined the apartment building before them. Minimum security — not that that would be a problem for three werewolves in their prime — and a pleas-ing location, right on the lake, with a park across the street. Best of all, less than a four hour drive from the Wyndham estate.

"Remember," he told his men. Derik and Jonathan were his closest friends, his fiercest protectors. "She was scared to death. I forced her, and she had to assume I died. She'll be terrified when she recognizes me."

"If she recognizes you," Derik reminded him. He was as blonde and fair as Michael was dark. "Her eyes aren't as good as yours. It was prob-ably pitch dark in the elevator to her."

"If she recognizes me," Michael agreed. "I'm just reminding you, you'll need —"

"Patience," Derik and Jon echoed, then laughed at him. Michael rolled his eyes and cuffed Jon in the back of the head.

"It's true," he said, "I might be repeating myself."

"Quit fretting, Michael," Derik said. "We'll not muss your mate."

"Do you think she's pregnant?" Jon asked with hopeful curiosity. He was a curly-haired redhead with boyish features. He looked all of sixteen, and was twice that. "The pack has been after you for a long time to mate and provide an heir. It would be wonderful if she —"

"Was pregnant and happy to see our pack leader, and embraced our lifestyle with open arms, and settled into the pack as if she was born to it?" Derik shook his head at his friends. "None of this is going to be easy, for her or for us. Better that she not be pregnant. Then Michael can let her go."

"Enough," Michael said sharply. Let her go? Let that witty, beautiful, sensual woman go? In his dreams, his ears still rang with her cries of ecstasy. Let her go?

Moot, he comforted himself. She was surely pregnant. Her scent had been all sweet ripeness, like a bursting peach. And beneath him, she had felt —

"Excuse me, o mighty king of the werewolves," Derik said dryly, "but you're about to walk into that pillar."

"I am not," he said, swerving at the last moment. He grinned at his friends, who rolled their eyes. Jon had taken a mate last year, and thus knew exactly what his pack leader was going through. Derik had not, and thus thought his leader was being foolishly sentimental.

"She was scared," he said aloud, remembering, "but she never showed it."

"I still think this is nuts," Derik said gloomily. "And bad luck. Of all the times to get stuck in an elevator — with an ovulating female who couldn't fight you off, who just happens to be human and not believe in werewolves —"

"Gosh," Jon interrupted with a grin, "what are the chances?"

Derik ignored his friend. "— who's going to go right out of her mind when we try to bring her home. Man, I hope she's not pregnant."

"It will work out," Jon said, but they both heard the doubt in his tone. "Humans mate with werewolves all the time, and vise versa."

'All the time' was a gross exaggeration ('once or twice a generation' would have been more accurate), but neither Derik nor Michael pointed that out.

"Jon's right, pardon me while I choke on that phrase," Derik said, giving his pack leader a friendly clap on the shoulder that would have felled a human male. "It'll work out. C'mon, chief. Let's go get your mate."

⁂

At least, Jeannie thought grimly, I don't have to worry about chasing anyone down for child support.

She was in her bathroom, staring at the double pink line which, the instructions assured her, meant she was positively pregnant. One bout of sex after going without a partner for three years, and she was well and truly caught.

Among other things, it was problematic that her baby's father had been a little unhinged. It was also problematic that he was dead. Jeannie had no idea — none at all, not even a smidgen of an idea — what to do now. Her mind, after taking in the double pink line (such an innocuous color for such a momentous event), had shut down, and the same thought kept cycling through her brain: now what? Now what? Now what?

There was a firm rap on the door and, annoyed at the intrusion, she went to answer it. She peeped through the eyehole and saw three large men standing quietly on the other side of the door. They were dressed in dark suits; the one in the middle was the tallest, with dark hair, and he was flanked by a blonde and a redhead.

What fresh hell is this, she wondered. Normally she would have at least asked for their names before opening the door, but the shock of that double pink line was still governing her actions, and she swung the door wide.

The one in the middle was almost enough to distract her from her news — he was, simply put, one of the finest looking men she had ever seen. He was tremendously tall, with longish, wavy black hair that looked thick and touchable; her fingers itched to see if it felt as lush as it looked. His eyes were a funny, gorgeous color — the pupils were large and dark, the irises yellow-gold. His nose was a blade, and his mouth had a sinfully sensuous twist to the lower lip. His shoulders were ridiculously broad; his coat was belted at a slim waist.

"Yuh …" She coughed and tried again. "Yes?" She glanced at his companions and they wouldn't lose any beauty contests, either. One blonde, one a redhead, both fair and green-eyed, powerfully built and even broader across the shoulders than the brunette.

All three of them were staring at her. She covertly felt her face to make sure ants weren't perched on her nose or something equally disgusting. "What's up, boys?" They must be selling their hardbody calendars door to door, she thought, that's the only explanation for the abrupt arrival of three gorgeous men on her — her! — doorstep.

"Jeannie," the brunette said. With that one word, she recognized his voice — that deep, velvet voice — and went cold to her toes. Forcing her expression to remain neutral, she raised an eyebrow at him.

"Yes?" she said, with just the right amount of impatience.

His shoulders slumped a little and the blonde man shot him a look of compassion. Mouth drawn into a sorrowful bow, he said haltingly, "I — ah — this is difficult, Jeannie. You probably don't remember me … whurggggh!"

He said 'whurgggh!' because she had hoisted her sneakered foot into his testicles with all her strength. His breath whooshed out in an agonized gasp and he crashed to his knees. She shouldered past the astonished redhead and bent over him, shaking a finger in his face.

"You bet your demented ass I remember you! A) Thanks for saving my life, and B) drop dead! Again, I mean! Now get lost, before I lose my temper —"

"You haven't lost your temper yet?" the blonde asked, aghast.

"— and forget that you saved my life and remember that you *raped* me in an elevator that was about to *plummet* into a basement. If you'd taken five more minutes to get your jollies, we'd both be dead! You're lucky I don't call the cops on you!"

"I don't think he feels lucky right now," the redhead said, staring at the rapist/savior, who was clutching himself and writhing on the floor in an undignified way.

"And as for you two," she said, rounding on the redhead, who took a step back and covered his crotch with both hands, "your friend here has some serious psychological problems. He thinks —"

"— he's a werewolf," the blonde said from behind her. She whirled, part of her not liking the way the three of them, purposely or not, had boxed her in very neatly.

"You know about the delusion?" Now might be a good time, she thought uneasily, to step back into my apartment and close the door.

"We share the same delusion," the blonde said, smiling at her with very white, very sharp teeth.

"Well, *great*," she snapped, concealing her unease … which was rapidly turning to fear. At her tone, the blonde's eyebrows arched in appreciation. "Maybe you can share the same shrink, too. You — what are you doing?"

He was sniffing her, like a dog. He didn't touch her, but he got entirely too close and sniff-sniff-sniffed her neck. "Shit," he said, right before she shoved him hard enough to rock him back on his heels. He turned to her felled giant, who had been helped to his feet by the blonde. "She's pregnant."

The brunette grinned in triumph, and he stared at her with a gleaming gold gaze, a gaze too proud and possessive for her taste.

"Congratulations," the redhead said politely, "to both of you."

To her astonishment, the blonde reached out and put his hand on her flat stomach. "Here grows the next pack leader," he said respectfully. "Congratulations, ma'am."

She gritted her teeth. "Hand. Off. Now."

He complied hastily. Before she could think of what to do or say — nothing had been controllable since that double pink line — the brunette spoke up. His color was coming back, and he had recovered from a ball-stomping much faster than she expected. "Jeannie, the short version is: I'm a werewolf — as I believe you heard — the pack leader, you're pregnant with my heir and successor, I have enemies who would steal my mate and unborn child so it's not safe for you to stay here, you have to come home with us."

Without a word, she turned around and went into her apartment, firmly closing the door in their faces, twisting the deadbolt with a click. Once inside, she started shaking so hard she looked around for a place to sit down.

"Jeannie?"

It was the brunette, calling her from the hallway. Sure, like she'd open the door and say, 'Yes, dear?'

"Jeannie, get away from the door."

Having seen his strength before, she had a good idea what was coming, and went at once to the small chest on the living room endtable. There was a tremendous thud and her door shuddered in its frame. She flipped the top of the chest and grabbed her .9 mm Beretta, cursing herself for being so paranoid about gun safety that she kept the clip — fully loaded — in her bedroom. No time to go for it now —

THUD!

— her door had just been kicked off the hinges.

She turned, her palm cupping the handle of the gun to conceal the emptiness where a clip should be, and leveled it at him, sighting in on the hollow of his throat. The brunette — odd, how she still didn't know his name — stepped across the threshold into her home. His friends, she was relieved to see, were nowhere in sight.

"You're going to shoot the father of your child?" he asked with honest curiosity. He picked up the door and set it neatly aside, then strolled toward her.

"In a New York minute," she said coldly. "Stop. Turn around. Go now."

"I can't imagine your rage and hurt and frustration." His tone was serious; he never even glanced at the gun; his gaze was locked on her face. "I told you I had no choice, and I hope someday you'll be able to see me as more than a conscienceless monster."

"Kicking down my door wasn't a good start to that end," she said curtly. "Last chance, Romeo."

"Sorry."

Before she could figure out how to keep bluffing him, he had zipped forward, so quickly she couldn't immediately track the movement. He slid forward, under her gun sights, across her prized hardwood floor, and tackled her around her knees. With one hand he cushioned her back as she fell to the floor; with the other, he pulled the gun from her grasp.

Hefting it, he knew at once it had no clip, and he smiled at her. "Good bluff. I never doubted you." He tossed it over his shoulder.

"Get off me!"

"I will. Wait. Tell me now, while we have some privacy — you weren't hurt that night? After, I mean? I had to be rough when I threw you out the elevator door. There wasn't time to —"

Part of her anger — a tiny part — diminished. He was a wanna-be kidnapper and a rapist, but he was awfully concerned for her well-being. She remembered his concern that night, too, after he had taken her. Him on top of her, both of them still panting, and his hands running over her limbs, checking for injuries, making sure she wasn't hurt.

"No," she admitted through gritted teeth. "I wasn't hurt. Not even a skinned knee. They told me you died."

His gold eyes twinkled at her. "Just a couple of broken legs. But I'm a fast healer. Were you sorry? When you thought I was dead?"

"No," she said stiffly, remembering her sobs, the way it had taken her an hour to stop crying after the elevator fell down the shaft.

"If I had died," he whispered, leaning in close, nuzzling her ear — to her annoyance, her entire left side started tingling. "If I had died, I would have taken a beautiful memory with me. I would have died sated, knowing my seed had found a home, knowing the bravest woman I ever met was going to mother my child."

"Shut up," she said thinly, bringing her hand up to push his face away — he went easily, and she had the feeling he went because it pleased him, not because of anything she had done. "Shut up, I hate you, I wish you *had* died."

"I know," he said sadly. "Your opinion is not about to change." Abruptly, he shifted his full weight on her, and she felt his fingers come up and settle on the junction between her neck and shoulder ... and start to squeeze. Black roses bloomed in her vision and she felt herself fading, fading, using up precious strength to get him off her rather than trying to drag his fingers away from her neck and what the hell was that, anyway? Was that —

Chapter Four

She woke in an unidentified bedroom … and came to consciousness yelling. "What the hell was *that*? Did you actually use the Vulcan Neck Pinch on me, you freak?"

Then she realized she was alone. The bedroom was small — the bed took up nearly the entire room, and paneled with pastel-striped wallpaper. There were two large windows on each side of the bed, and …

And the bedroom was moving. She bounded off the bed, swaying for a long moment as a wave of dizziness swamped her, then lurched to the nearest window.

The bedroom was on a highway. Traveling roughly seventy miles an hour.

There was a short 'rap-rap' on the door, and then Tall, Dark, and Weird stuck his head in. "Are you all right?"

She whirled on him and he grinned as she snapped, "I am *so* sick of hearing that question from you — usually after you've done something horrible to me! *No*, I'm not all right! I'm a rape victim and a kidnap victim and a — a pregnancy victim and a Vulcan Neck Pinch Victim and now I'm in some sort of mobile bedroom —"

"It's an RV," he said helpfully, easing into the room, keeping his hands in sight. She felt like a rabbit, easily spooked, like she might bolt any second. Apparently he had the same impression, because his voice was low and very soothing. "I wanted you to be comfortable for the trip."

"How very fucking considerate of you," she said with acid sarcasm. "Why, I don't know when I've been kidnapped by a nicer man."

His smile faded. "Jeannie, I have enemies who would kidnap you and take your baby from you and then kill you, all so they could raise the next pack leader and have a voice of power. How could I let that happen to you?"

She took a deep breath and forced calm. On top of everything else — the physical power, the sexy voice — did he have to be so handsome? If she'd gotten a look at him in the elevator before the lights went out, he probably wouldn't have had to force her. Much. "Look. I'm not saying you're a liar, okay? I'm not saying that. I'm sure you believe all this stuff."

"Thanks," he said dryly.

"But the fact is, you can't force women in elevators and then show up and yank them from their homes and take them who-knows-where. You *can't*. Don't you know it's wrong? Don't you care?"

He sat on the edge of the bed and nodded soberly. "I do know it's wrong. By your laws."

She threw her hands up in disgust. "Oh, here we go."

"I do care," he continued. "As angry and humiliated as you are, I'm as embarrassed to find myself having to play the villain. But it's far worse to use you for my pleasure and then never give you another thought. Especially when I knew you were ovulating, knew there was an excellent chance I'd made you pregnant. How could I turn my back on you after using you? How could I never look in on you, make sure you were out of danger?"

"Fine!" she shouted, stomping toward the bed. "Look in on me! Tell me you're not dead! You could have apologized for forcing me and scaring me and — and other stuff, and I could have thanked you for saving my life, and then you could have gone your way and I'd have gone mine. Instead you do *this*." She gestured to the RV bedroom. "I loathe rooms on wheels," she hissed.

"There was the small matter of my enemies finding you," he reminded her calmly.

"Very small — you knew my name and it *still* took you three weeks to find me."

"Even if there was only a chance in a thousand you were in danger, do you think I'd risk you for an instant?" he asked sharply. "You're angry with me now, but what if I had never come back in your life ... but my enemies had? You would have died cursing my name. I couldn't have borne that."

"Oh, please." She turned her back on him. "You don't give two shits for me. I was a piece of ass you couldn't resist. That's — aaah!"

He had come up behind her with that liquid, silent speed she had seen before, startling her badly. His hand fell on her shoulder and he turned her toward him. His eyes, locked on hers, were gold and blazing. "Do not say that again," he said with an icy calm that terrified her, even as it fascinated her. "It's disrespectful of me, as well as yourself. I'm not in the habit of forcing unwilling females, despite what you must think."

"Sorry," she said quickly, through numb lips. Then, despising her fear, she added coldly, "Remove the hand."

His hand fell away. "And now I've frightened you," he said with real regret. "Forgive me, Jeannie."

"It's just that, since you don't even know me, I don't see how you can claim to feel anything for me," she said carefully.

His hand came up slowly, carefully, and when she didn't flinch, settled on her cheek like a dove's touch. "I do know you," he murmured. "There is much more to you than beauty."

She flushed; against her hot skin, his hand felt cool. "I'm not beautiful."

He laughed. "With all that curly blonde hair?"

"It's frizzy," she corrected him.

"And all those adorable freckles?"

"Ugh."

"And that pale skin, like the richest cream?"

"When I go to the beach I look like a fucking vampire, thanks very much, and could we get off my looks, please?"

"Then we'll just have to talk about your intelligence and courage and razor wit," he said with faux regret. "What a bore."

She laughed; she couldn't help it. And immediately bit off the sound.

"I've never heard you laugh before!" he said, delighted. "Do it again."

"I can't laugh on command. Look," she said briskly, getting back to business, wondering how long he was going to be touching her face, "let's talk facts, here. *Facts*, not delusions and you're the king of the werewolves and you've got enemies out to get me even though they don't know me — cold hard facts. Where is your home?"

"Barnstable, on Cape Cod," he said, amused.

"Ah, yes, Cape Cod," she said sarcastically, "a hotbed of shape-shifters. I always thought so. The tourists had to be going there for some reason ..."

He laughed again, and his hand slid down, toward her collarbone. She knocked it away and backed up, so fast that she hit the far wall. Startled, he went after her, politely backing off when she kicked out at him.

"*Don't* touch me there again. Ever. Ever *ever*. If you do, I swear I'll —" She couldn't think of something bad enough. "I'll do worse than rack you in the 'nads."

Understanding dawned. "I wasn't going to knock you out again," he said. To her amazement, he actually sounded hurt. "I just like touching you."

"I don't give a shit! You're contemptible, showing up uninvited, pinning me down and pinching me until I was out cold —"

"I had a feeling," he said dryly, marching to her and dragging her, kicking, out of the corner. He shoved her gently to the bed and then walked around it, standing on the far side of the room. "I had a feeling you wouldn't cooperate in your — uh — removal. Steps had to be taken. But think about this — think about the things I could do to you if I didn't cherish your well-being."

She'd been trying not to. She had realized in the elevator he could have killed her, crippled her, as easily as stomping a spider. If he wanted to hurt her, he'd had ample opportunity. Hell, she'd visited upon him the worst pain a man can know ... and there had been no retaliation.

"It's still wrong," she said firmly.

He shrugged. "You had more questions?"

"What happens when we get to Cape Cod?"

"You'll stay at my family home."

"Until?"

He hesitated. She gritted her teeth and repeated the question.

"Until you accept your destiny and freely agree to stay with me. Us."

"Forever?" she asked, aghast.

He nodded.

"You've kidnapped me forever? Unless I escape or blow the place up or whatever?"

"Yes." He paused. "I don't expect you to agree right —"

She launched herself at him. It was time to take advantage of the fact that he wouldn't hurt her, and do some major damage. Her first punch missed — he caught her wrist in time — but her simultaneous kick hit the mark, and he winced as her foot cracked into his shin.

"I hate you!" she was shouting, raining blows down on him. He held her wrists and took her kicks stoically, only blocking the ones to the groin with his thigh. "You can't do this! It's not my destiny, you weirdo, it was just *dumb luck*! I won't stay with you, I won't! I have a *life*! And it does not include hanging out on Cape Cod with a creep who thinks he's a werewolf!"

"Understood. But it doesn't matter; you're staying." At her shriek of rage, he continued. "And while we're talking, I don't like being hit, or kicked," he said calmly, wincing as she brought her foot down on his instep with all her strength, "so there will be consequences in the future."

"Fuck your consequences!" She brought her head forward in a devastating head butt; he jerked his head aside and she ended up banging her forehead into his neck.

"Starting now," he said, and pulled her to him so sharply she lost her breath. Then his mouth was on hers in a bruising kiss that stole the strength from her knees. He pinned her arms to her sides and, when her teeth clacked together in an attempt to bite him, contented himself with gently nibbling her lower lip.

"Don't," she managed, and when her mouth opened his tongue slipped past her teeth.

He pulled back before she could gather the sense to bite him again. He was breathing hard. Almost as hard as she was. His effect on her was infuriating and she practically gnashed her teeth in rage.

"So," he said coolly, but his eyes gleamed, "now that you know there are consequences, feel free to punch away. Because, afterward, I can put my hands on you without feeling a bit guilty, under those conditions."

"You should die of guilt," she choked out. "I hate you."

He was staring at her mouth, his own a line of sadness. "I know."

He left, slamming the flimsy bedroom door behind him. Jeannie sat down before her knees betrayed her.

Chapter Five

"This," Tall, Dark, and Disgusting said to the fifteen or so assembled people, "is my wife-to-be, Jeannette Lawrence."

"Ma'am," the small crowd said in respectful unison.

Jeannie opened her mouth to tell them exactly what she thought of what's-his-name, but the black-hearted bastard beat her to the punch.

"She's here entirely against her will," he went on, "and isn't happy about it. She's also pregnant by me —"

A happy gasp from the crowd.

"— and not happy about it. It happened, as some of you probably guessed, during the last full moon."

Nods. Sympathetic glances. She bit her tongue, hard, so as not to shriek with embarrassed rage.

"Thus, she will be rude, throw things, and do her best to escape," he went on casually, as if she wasn't standing at his elbow and hearing every word. "She doesn't understand her vulnerability and can't appreciate her delicate position. And she won't thank any of you for pointing it out." He paused. "Be patient with her."

Jeannie rolled her eyes. At the edge of the crowd, a petite, elfin blonde woman saw it and winked at her.

"Moira, if you'll show Jeannie to her rooms?"

The small blonde nodded and stepped forward at once. Psycho Boy turned to her and asked with ridiculous politeness, "Did you have any questions, Jeannie?"

"Just one." She paused. He waited, the crowd waited, expectantly. "What the hell is your name?"

Score! He flushed a little, and there were a few outright laughs in the crowd. Moira giggled, and quickly choked off the sound as he glanced at her with a frown. "Ah — that's right, we never got around to that, did we? It's Michael. Michael Wyndham."

"Great," she said, unsurprised. After the month she'd had, nothing could surprise her. The Wyndhams controlled a vast shipping empire and were reputed to be slightly more wealthy than God. The father of her child owned the tower she'd taken the ill-fated elevator in, probably owned the magazine she worked for. It figured. "Psychotic *and* rich."

"I'm afraid so," he said with an irritatingly sexy smile. She looked away, disgusted.

Moira led her out of the yard, into the astonishing mansion she'd glimpsed from the RV. After her last confrontation with Tall, Dark, and Wyndham, she'd cried herself to sleep. And when she woke, they had been pulling up to the most beautiful manor home she had ever seen. She was so stunned at the home's size and majesty, she hadn't said a word when Michael gently led her out of the RV and introduced her to the household staff who, the redhead (whose name was Jon; the blonde had introduced himself as Derik) had assured her, all shared Michael's "delusion."

She was so impressed with the ocean-side mansion, she could hardly fret about being kept prisoner by fifteen people who were all as nutty as Wyndham. True unease would come, she had no doubt, in time. Like as soon as her shock and surprise wore off. Then there'd be hell to pay. Then there'd —

"I hope you'll come to like it here," Moira was saying, leading her through a home that made *Gone With The Wind*'s Twelve Oaks look like a claim shanty. "We've been waiting for you for a long time."

"Waiting for *me*?"

"For our leader to take a mate," Moira explained. She was a lovely, delicate blonde with eyes the color of the sky, and skin so pale it was almost translucent. She was tiny; almost a head shorter than Jeannie, and Jeannie herself was five-ten. "He needs an heir. It's just unfortunate that …" She trailed off, seemingly embarrassed.

"You don't know *how* unfortunate," Jeannie said dryly. "Look, Moira, I don't suppose there's any chance you'd help me —"

"Don't even ask, ma'am," she said firmly. "I'd die for Michael. Any of us would."

"In other words, don't waste your breath asking anyone else to crack out of this pokey," she finished.

"Your 'pokey', ma'am," Moira said with a grin, throwing open a set of mahogany doors. Jeannie stepped into the most beautiful room she had ever seen — all gleaming blonde wood floors, lush throw rugs, a fireplace large enough to roast two pigs, and several doors. And the bed! A king-sized monstrosity, large enough to comfortably sleep a family of six.

"Bathroom, closet, closet, balcony," Moira was saying, opening all the doors.

"Whoa!" Jeannie said, staring, goggle-eyed. Moira giggled again. "Okay, so, this place ranks high on my Top Ten List Of Places To Be Held Prisoner. But it still sucks, you know."

"Hmmmm?" Moira said, turning down the bed.

"Being held here against my will," Jeannie reminded her impatiently. She waited for Moira to blush, to acknowledge guilt, to do something … something besides shrug and look unconcerned, dammitall. Then a thought struck her, and she asked sharply, "Where does Wyndham sleep?"

"His is the adjoining room," she said simply.

"Over my dead body!"

"You'll have to discuss that with him, ma'am."

"And stop calling me ma'am! I'm not ninety!"

"As you wish, my lady."

"Out!" she hissed, and to her relief and surprise, Moira obeyed at once. Jeannie threw herself on the bed, which enveloped her at once in an eiderdown embrace. She was too mad to cry again, which was a relief — she'd done entirely too much crying lately. Now was the time for action!

"Would you like to have something to eat before you try to escape?"

It was Wyndham, poking his head through the doorway that doubtless adjoined his rooms to hers. She'd like to slam that door shut, watch his eyes pop out as his neck broke.

She glared up at him from her bed. "I want to go home."

"Yes, I know."

"Now!"

"Sorry."

She reared up in the bed, tottering to stay balanced on her knees amid all the fluff of the quilts. His mouth twitched as she struggled to right herself. "Wyndham, I'm telling you this for the last time: I won't stay here with you. I won't have anything to do with you. You're a criminal *and* a jerk, a miserable combo."

"You're not afraid," he said with a satisfied sigh. "I knew you wouldn't be."

"Don't flatter yourself. I'm too pissed to be afraid. Listen, dickhead: there are going to be some horrific consequences if you try to keep me here. We're talking broken bones and FBI raids. I'm out of here the second the opportunity presents itself."

He actually looked alarmed — at the chance of losing his sex toy? Or a deeper reason? Then his expression cleared. "There will be consequences if you try to escape," he said simply, stepping into her room and softly closing the adjoining door. He had changed from his suit to khaki shorts and a white t-shirt, and if possible, looked yummier in casual clothes that showed off his finely muscled legs and upper body. He was ridiculously tan, ridiculously handsome. "Are you going to try to escape soon?" he asked, as if inquiring about the temperature in her room.

"You — you —" She sputtered wordlessly at his absurd question. "You're not supposed to *want* me to get away."

"You won't get away. We'll catch you. I don't want you to leave — it's dangerous. So, as I warned you earlier, there will be consequences if you try and escape."

"What consequences?" she asked, but had a sinking feeling she knew.

His gaze was level. "Elevator consequences."

Her mouth went dry, even as her heart sped up. "Seek help, Wyndham. As quickly as possible."

"Do you think I'm pleased with this scenario?"

"Yes! I think you're very pleased," she said bitterly.

The bum actually looked hurt. She couldn't believe his nerve. "It's the only way I can think of to keep you from trying to leave," he sighed, "since you don't believe me about the danger."

He walked to the bed and stared down at her. A blind woman could have seen the hunger in his gaze. "I won't lie — part of me wants you to try and escape," he husked. "Don't misunderstand — I'm sorry about the circumstances that brought you here. And I'm sorry you don't like my home."

"I never said I didn't like your home," she interjected sharply.

"But if you try to escape, just as if you try to hurt me again, I can take you without guilt."

"You —"

"I can hardly stand to be this close to you without touching you," he said, and for a moment she saw such pain and longing in his gaze, she had to glance away. "Having you sleeping just a few feet away is going to drive me mad. But I won't take you again by force, Jeannie — except as a deterrent. Because," he added sadly, "as much as I long for your touch, I know you can't stand to be near me, that you despise me. So lovemaking relieves my hunger while punishing you." He turned away. "I wish it could be different between us," he said without turning around. "I'd give anything for things to be different."

"You know what *I'd* give anything for?" she asked sweetly, groping behind her for something to throw at him, and finding nothing more deadly than a pillow.

He laughed shortly, and left the room. The pillow smacked into the door and fell to the floor with a fat thump.

Chapter Six

Since Wyndham, the sadistic cretin, was panting at the thought of her escape, and since he'd alerted the household she was an unwilling guest, Jeannie decided to stay put for a while, provided her situation didn't change (read: Wyndham didn't decide she was in heat again, or Moira didn't spike her milk with broken glass).

So she took lunch with Wyndham and his staff, who were obviously more friends than employees, in a dining room that had more windows than a solarium. Sunlight splashed across the table and gleamed from the blonde wood floors. She sat in the finest dining room she'd ever seen and commented on how delicious everything tasted. They had all been watching her expectantly, and seemed disappointed when she didn't throw things or leap across the table through the French doors that led to the beach.

"How long have you known you were expecting our leader's child?" Derik asked, sliding the bread basket toward her.

She helped herself to another piece of the sun-dried tomato and basil loaf and looked at her watch. "About six hours and fourteen minutes."

Wyndham looked up from his soup. "You did one of those home tests? You haven't seen a doctor?"

"I had an appointment for this afternoon. Which I missed. Guess why, King Psycho."

He remained unruffled, though she saw a few of the staff hiding smiles. "Well, then, you need a doctor. Moira, see to it." He glanced at Jeannie with a frown, then added, "A female physician, if you please."

"Yes, sir."

"Like there are *so* many werewolf doctors to choose from?" Jeannie interrupted sarcastically. "What, is there a directory or something?" As the others laughed, she had a sudden thought. "Oh, will we have to go to town for that?"

Derik, seated at Wyndham's left (she was at his right), snickered. "Nice try. The doctor will come here."

"Well, goody for him."

"Her," Michael corrected sharply.

Jeannie raised her eyebrows, said nothing, and ate her chicken. Wyndham was jealous? Of a male doctor? Ridiculous. Still, that might be a handy button to push. She filed the thought away.

"Are you mad because you think we're all crazy, or because you're here against your will?" Jon asked curiously.

"I don't think that's a fair question," Michael said reproachfully.

"Yeah, I mean, there's so many reasons for me to be furious at all of you, how can I pick just one?"

"I meant," Jon said, flushing a little, "the full moon is in three days. And you could watch some of us change, or even one of us change, and then you wouldn't think we were crazy anymore, so it might be easier to accept — um — are you okay?"

She could actually feel the color draining from her face, could feel the trembling in her hands. She dropped her spoon in her soup and fled the table, running, running, for her rooms.

Michael caught up with her on the stairs. She wrenched away from him and kept going. Never one to take a hint, he followed her into her bedroom.

"The full moon?" she asked, hating the shrill, panicky note in her voice. He shut the door to assure some privacy; she barely noticed. "The full moon again? I can't go through that again! I can't go through that *craziness* with you again! *Don't you touch me!*"

He had been reaching for her, ignored her shriek and pulled her, struggling, into a firm embrace. "It's all right," he said into her hair. "I had planned to leave the grounds when my change came. I wouldn't have forced you again. I promised you I wouldn't force you, except as punishment."

"What good is a promise from you?" she choked, resting her forehead against his shoulder. He smelled so good. It was as comforting as it was irritating.

"I've done many things to you, Jeannie, but when have I broken a promise?"

She shrugged sullenly. Then stiffened, remembering. She leaned back to look at him. "But what about the others? They all think they're werewolves, too, they all —"

"You have nothing to fear from the females, because as my mate, you're alpha female. No, listen, Jeannie — if it's a delusion, at least we all have to follow the same rules, right? And the males won't — can't — touch you without my permission." His voice hardened. "And I won't give it. Ever. So you have nothing to fear."

She choked on a laugh.

"You really don't," he said, pressing a warm kiss to her brow. "Now come back and finish your lunch. You don't want the baby to starve, do you?"

"No," she sighed. She glanced at him again; he had put an arm around her shoulder and was steering her out the door, back to the dining room. A thought struck her — late, but her thought process was continually being thwarted by shock upon shock. "What do you think? About my being pregnant, I mean? I never got a chance to ask you. Not that I care either way," she added hastily.

"I'm thrilled," he said simply, giving her a warm smile. He leaned close and she had the sense he wanted very much to kiss her. Something — belated concern for her feelings? — held him back. "I love children. The pack needs the continuity of succession. And I get to keep you now, don't I?"

His voice ended on a teasing note, but she wasn't amused. "For a minute there, I was almost liking you," she said evenly, pushing his arm away. "Thanks for turning back into a creep."

At the dining table, the other werewolves — people — were still glaring at Jon, who was miserably embarrassed. "I'm really sorry," he said at once upon seeing Jeannie. "I shouldn't have reminded you about the full moon. I forgot that —" He paused, glanced at Michael, blushed harder. "I have no excuse. I'm so sorr —"

"*Please* stop," she said, rolling her eyes and sitting back down. "I'm the one who should apologize. I can assure you it's not my usual M.O. to drop cutlery and flee for the bedroom when the word 'moon' is introduced into the conversation."

The others laughed, Michael harder than anyone. Jon smiled at her with pure gratitude. And Derik forked another chicken breast onto her plate.

❧❦❧

"How about a tour, Moira?" she asked briskly, after the lunch dishes had been cleared away. "Might as well check out my new home."

"She'll try to escape," Derik warned, finishing the last of his peach sorbet.

"I know," Moira said defensively. "You don't have to tell me everything, Mr. Right Hand Man."

"Bring her to me once you've found her again," Michael said casually, but his eyes were gleaming in a way Jeannie didn't much care for.

"Hello!" she shouted. "Prisoner still in the room, here! Can you have this conversation where I can't hear you?"

Moira giggled, and extended a hand. Surprised, Jeannie took it. "Come on," she said. "We'll start with the gardens. If you cosh me over the head to escape, try not to muss my hair."

"For God's sake," she muttered, but obediently followed Moira out the door.

She had, in fact, decided to escape in the next day or so — well before the full moon. Michael's assurances aside, she had no intention of sharing a home, however sprawlingly luxurious, with twenty people all sharing the same delusion. And she didn't plan to be in the same *state* with Wyndham when he went through that again. She wasn't afraid of being forced, so much as being forced to pleasure. Her cheeks burned with humiliation every time she remembered how he had made her scream in ecstasy. In a flash she was back in the warm, dark elevator, Michael's cock surging between her thighs, her fingers digging into his skin, wordlessly urging more, more ...

She shook herself, and concentrated on the tour. Now was no time for daydreaming. Now was the time to plot and plan and eventually escape these crazies.

In the rose garden, Moira said in a low voice, "We don't blame you. For being upset, I mean. It must have been ..." She trailed off, then asked timidly, "Was it very awful?"

"Huh? You mean being stuck in the elevator with your boss? Well, the lights went out, so we couldn't read my *Glamour* ..."

"It's kind of you to joke, but ... I can't imagine how it must have been for you — a pure human, and an unbeliever, besides. Tearing clothes and scratches and bites, and being forced on your knees and taken without so much as a 'please' ... I suppose you had to see a doctor." She looked as though she was going to burst into tears. "I suppose you — you tore and ... and — no wonder you hate him. Us."

"Uh ... yeah. Yeah, it was an unending torment. What's that building over there?"

As Moira obediently showed her the gardener's shed, Jeannie's mind whirled. What Moira imagined hadn't been at all what happened. Michael had gone out of his way to soothe her, to bring her pleasure, to make sure she was ready for him. He'd had that much control, at least. What would sympathetic Moira think if she told her it had been the most exciting, pleasurable sexual experience of her life? What did that mean, that he'd been nearly out of control, but cared for her enough to do his best not to hurt her, even to bring her pleasure?

In a flash, she was back in the warm, dark elevator —

Jeannie pushed the thought away with a firmness she didn't feel.

"You can't leave the grounds," Moira was saying casually, "until we kill Gerald. But after that, it should be all right."

"What?" She nearly fell into a rose bush. "Now you're talking about killing someone so I can leave?"

"Didn't our leader explain about Gerald?"

"Frankly, I tend to tune him out when he's babbling about all the reasons it's okay for him to break the law where I'm concerned."

"Your law," Moira pointed out calmly, "not ours."

Jeannie bent to sniff a rose so grey it was almost silver. "Okay, I'll bite. What is your law?"

"Safety of mates and children first, above and before *everything* else. Michael has to keep you safe. Because he knows it's right, and because he must set an example. How could the rest of us follow someone who can't even protect his own mate?"

"I'm not his mate," she said sharply.

"Yes," Moira said simply, "you are."

Jeannie stewed over that one for the five minutes it took them to walk from the rose garden to the beach. "How does Gerald fit into all this?" she asked at last.

"He's our enemy. He went rogue five years ago. His mate was giving him nothing but female cubs and he wanted an heir, someone he could train to challenge the pack leader. He's too cowardly to try a challenge himself; he wanted a son to do the dirty work." Cute, delicate Moira spat in the sand to express her disgust.

"Whoa, whoa, watch those loogies." Jeannie took off her shoes and wiggled her toes in the surf, scanning the horizon and judging the wisdom of swimming to England to escape. Still, this was a fascinating delusion. "His mate was giving him daughters? Did the creep never crack a biology textbook? Sperm chooses gender."

"Gerald is … old-fashioned," Moira said reluctantly. "He represents the pack before the Wyndhams took over. Savage, undisciplined. Gerald killed his mate after the birth of his fourth daughter. Michael would have killed him, but for the intercession of Gerald's other daughters, who begged their leader to spare their father's life. Michael did, but banished him. Now Gerald's rogue, and the only way he can come to power is if he gets his hands on the pack leader's child."

"Thus, I be kidnapped," Jeannie said dryly.

"If you ever crossed Gerald's path, he would kill you to revenge himself on Michael — for what is worse than the loss of a mate? Or he would keep you until you whelped, take the child from you, and then kill you. And he would be well-revenged indeed, for he would be as father to the next pack-leader, and come to power quickly. And we would be back in the days of savagery and blood." Moira turned an unblinking, wide-eyed gaze to Jeannie. "It would be the end of all of us." Pause. "You can't leave while Gerald lives."

Despite herself, Jeannie felt a thrill of fear. Determinedly, she pushed it away. It was all part of their delusion, it was a way for Michael to justify kidnapping her. She wouldn't believe it.

There had to be a way out of here.

Exhausted — either from the wild events of the last few hours, or fatigue brought on by an early pregnancy — when Moira brought her back to the mansion, Jeannie went straight to her room and stretched out on the bed to nap. The bed was ridiculously comfortable, her room astonishingly beautiful, and if she wasn't being held here against her will she'd probably be having the time of her life.

Hell, she thought drowsily, watching the light play against the rich gold wallpaper, there hadn't been anyone in her life since college. Under different circumstances, she'd gobble Wyndham with a spoon. *She'd* rape *him*. Gorgeous, rich, intelligent, and a gentleman — when he wasn't raping and kidnapping. A real catch. And those eyes … those eyes …

Yes, she could definitely wish things had been different, that they had not met in such drastic fashion. But, as her mother used to say, done can't be undone. Her mission was not to play nice with the lunatics, it was to get the hell out of here.

With that unsettling thought, she drifted into sleep. And found herself in the elevator again — for the last month, she'd stumbled into that elevator two or three times a week. Only this time, Michael didn't save her. This time, he used her and left her, turned his back on her and left the elevator in one bound, leaving her in the car, in the dark, and there was a terrifying Snap! as the cables parted and then the sickening sensation of free fall, her feet left the floor and her head banged on the ceiling and her stomach climbed into her throat and she screamed all the way down, screamed for him to save her, and —

"Jeannie … hush, Jeannie, it's all right. You're safe here."

"Ha," she said weakly, opening her eyes. To her surprise, while she dreamed she had been pulled into his embrace. He was sitting on the edge of the bed, holding her in his lap like the world's biggest doll.

As she rested her head against his chest, she was absurdly comforted by the thud-thud of his heartbeat in her ears. "Do you dream about the elevator often?" he asked, his voice against her ear a deep rumble.

"No," she lied. In a moment she would have to pretend outrage and shove him away. In a moment. For now, it was too damn nice to be held with tenderness. Even if he was crazy. Even if he'd landed her in more trouble than she'd ever been in. "No, never."

"I do, too," he said softly, as if she'd told the truth. "Only, in my dreams, I can't save you. And down you go. And I wake up with a scream in my throat."

She shuddered against him, closing her eyes. He stroked her back and murmured to her; she caught no words but was comforted by tone. "In mine," she whispered, "you leave me. You use me and leave me and the elevator falls into the basement and they scrape what's left of me into a jelly jar."

He tightened his grip. "Never. I'd die myself before letting that happen to you."

"I know," she said and, to her surprise, she knew that as a fact, as she knew her own name. "You proved it, didn't you? But I can't help dreaming about it."

"Nor I," he agreed.

She noticed his right nipple, which was about two inches from her mouth, was stiff. Probably from her; every time she opened her mouth, breath puffed across it. She had the absurd urge to kiss it. To taste it. Run her tongue across it and test the texture. Her mouth had actually gone dry from her sudden, startling need to take part of him into part of her.

He was rubbing his cheek against the top of her head and she could feel that odd tension in his body, as she had felt it the night in the elevator. He wanted her, she realized with a bolt of excitement. But he was afraid to do anything, afraid she'd fight him, scream the house down, call him names. He wanted to preserve this temporary peace between them as long as he could. What would he do, she wondered with a strange, thundery joy, if I leaned over and kissed his nipple? And slid his shorts down to his ankles and took him into my mouth?

"I came to get you," he said, and she thought his voice sounded thick, "because the doctor is here."

In a flash, she remembered herself: she was pregnant, by him, against her will, in his house, against her will. She sat up and shoved him away. Christ, she mentally groaned, standing up and walking out the door, what was I thinking? I've got to get out of here before I forget I hate this creep.

The doctor, who introduced herself as Rose Madison, was waiting for them at the foot of the stairs. Jeannie greeted her with, "Nice to meet you, I'm Jeannie Lawrence, they're all crazy and they're holding me prisoner, mind getting me out of here?"

The doctor, a small brunette with whiskey-colored eyes, was all commiseration as she explained she, too, was a werewolf, and she was very honored to be tending to the pack leader's mate as well as her future pack leader, and would my lady mind peeing in this cup?

Jeannie snatched the plastic cup out of Dr. Madison's hand, shot a sizzling glare toward Michael, ignored Derik's smirk, said loudly, "I hate every one of you," and marched into a nearby bathroom.

Within half an hour, Dr. Madison had confirmed her pregnancy and handed her what looked like — yes, it was. An ice cream bucket full of pre-natal vitamins.

"What the hell?" she asked helplessly, hefting the bucket and astonished at its weight.

"You'll need at least four a day, due to your increased metabolism," Dr. Madison informed her.

"Sure I will," she said, humoring her. Dr. Madison let that pass, cautioned her about her diet, and told her she would see her again in two weeks.

Sure you will, Jeannie thought. She glanced around at Michael, Moira, and Derik. Now or never. If any of them came with her, she was toast. "Dr. Madison, can I talk to you in private about — uh — a female thing?" she asked, feigning embarrassment.

"Of course," the doctor said quickly, even as the others did a respectful fade. "Come, walk with me to my car."

Once outside, Jeannie glanced around again, saw no one, and followed Dr. Madison to her car, a nifty little Ford Taurus. "Uh — the werewolf thing. Should it turn out to be true, will I have a litter? Will I have a puppy?"

Dr. Madison laughed kindly. "No, you won't have a litter. Two, at the most — and that is rare for our kind. And werewolves don't change until puberty. He or she will seem like a perfectly normal-looking child until, oh, about age thirteen or so." She grinned. "Then all hell is going to break loose. Don't worry about being human mother to a werewolf, though. Our leader will help you. We'll all help you."

"It takes a village to raise a werewolf," Jeannie said wryly, casually hefting the huge container of pre-natal vitamins. Who ever heard of taking four a day? The doctor had given her enough to last ten years.

"To raise the next pack leader, certainly." Dr. Madison turned to look at her with a serious gaze. "One thing, though. Your child will be highly prized. Not only because of his status in the pack, but because often the child of a human/werewolf mix is able to control their Change. To turn into a wolf at any time, not just during the full moon."

In spite of herself, Jeannie was fascinated by the complexity of the fantasy. "Is that why the others don't resent me? I'd think, if anything, a human would dilute the strain."

"Not in this case. Human mothers are prized. Smart, courageous ones even more so. Every time you snap at Michael or crack a joke, or make a determined effort to hide your fear, they like you more. *He* likes you more."

"Oh," Jeannie said, completely mystified.

"Well," Dr. Madison said reasonably, "who wants a dishrag for a consort?"

"Not me," she said, and swung the heavy container, hard sidearm, at Dr. Madison's head. The blow knocked the small woman into the car, where she bounced off and hit the gravel drive, hard. Jeannie prepared to step over Dr. Madison's unconscious body, and was astonished to see the woman was still clinging to consciousness.

"Don't," she slurred, trying to get to her feet. "It's too dangerous. Gerald will kill you."

"Sorry," Jeannie said, and she was. The doctor was almost a foot shorter, after all. But tough as hell. Jeannie jumped into the car, starting the engine with one twist of the keys conveniently left in the ignition. "Christ," she muttered, slamming the car into first gear, "hit her over the head and her only concern was for me. Damn." If she wasn't careful, she'd get attached to those loonies.

She was down the lane and out the gate before the alarm was raised.

Chapter Seven

Knowing better than to outrun them — who knew how many fleets of cars, choppers, and what-have-you Wyndham had at his disposal — she screeched to a halt in front of the Barnstable Police Station. Sprinting up the stairs, she burst into the station and yelled, "Help! I've been kidnapped by a group of nuts who think they're werewolves!"

The three people in the room — the desk sergeant, an off-duty patrolman, and a plainclothes detective — turned to stare at her. "Quiet town," Jeannie mumbled, keeping an ear cocked for the sounds of pursuit.

"I'll take this one," the detective said. He was a large man, a good four inches taller than she, with mud-colored brown hair, eyes the same color, and fists the size of bowling balls. He gestured to a door at the end of the hall. "C'mon, honey. Tell me all about the big bad wolf."

"Werewolf," she corrected him, walking down the hall. At his nod, she pushed through the door and found herself outside, in a small alley. Surprised, she turned — and ran smack into the detective's chest. To her shock, he shoved her away, hard.

"You've got Wyndham's stink on you. You must be his new bitch," he snarled, snuffling her ear. She jerked away, appalled. His tongue flicked out and ran across his thick lips; he looked about as evil a creature as she had ever seen. "And is that his little bitty babe I smell *in* you?"

"Are you Gerald?" she asked dumbly.

"I was. Now I'm going to be stepdaddy to the new pack leader." His big fist came looping through the air toward her; she ducked under it, darted forward, and snatched his sidearm out of his holster. In a flash she had the barrel jammed into the soft meat of his throat.

"Guess again, Detective Stupid," she growled. "Christ, has everyone gone crazy? Am I the only sane person in an insane world? Can it be that —?"

"If you're going to kill me, get it over with," Gerald grunted, "but don't make me listen to you whine."

"Oh, shut up," she snapped. "Who else on the force thinks they're a werewolf?"

"*Thinks* they're a werewolf?" As she dug the barrel deeper into his flesh, he added, "Three others. They're all on Wyndham's side. Too bad for you they're on patrol, eh?"

"Guess again, rogue," a cool female voice said. Jeannie snapped a gaze over her left shoulder and saw two uniformed patrolmen and another plainclothes detective — this one a woman — pointing guns at them. At Gerald, hopefully.

"Our leader told us you'd probably stop here first," one of the patrolmen said, almost apologetically. "Step away from Gerald, please, ma'am."

"You might want to mention to Michael that I had everything under control," she said, obeying.

"If I were you, ma'am," the detective said, not taking her gaze off Gerald, "I would not mention that I had even met this man, much less drew down on him."

"Good advice," Jeannie mumbled. She tucked the piece into the back waistband of her jeans, ignoring Gerald's burning glare. "I like to keep souvenirs," she told him, then let herself be escorted to a patrol car.

In the back (feeling like a POW, to tell the truth), her curiosity impelled her to ask, "Are you guys going to get in trouble? For pulling a piece on a fellow cop, a member of the brotherhood, that sort of thing?"

"Pack business is private," the lady detective said, turning around to look at her through the mesh. "And Gerald doesn't outrank *me*." Her buddy behind the wheel laughed at that one, and Jeannie shook her head, wondering what the joke was.

To her surprise, the cop-werewolves let her keep the piece. To her further surprise, upon return to the mansion she was not instantly dismembered. Instead, Dara, the chef, politely asked if she wanted to eat and, upon declining, Jeannie was escorted to her rooms and locked in. That was it. No yelling, no threats, no thunder-voiced Michael promising doom. No Michael, period.

"Well, hell," she said, looking at her watch. She'd been free for all of twenty-seven minutes. She tucked the pistol away in a bedside drawer and prepared to kill a few hours.

She amused herself watching daytime reruns (*The Brady Bunch* and *Wings* were particular favorites) until dinner time. Moira, pale and quiet, brought supper.

"What's up with you?" Jeannie asked, pouncing on the covered plates. She lifted the lids to reveal prime rib, baby red potatoes, green beans. Bliss, except for the green beans — blurgh. "And why hasn't your lord and master been in here to play 'Jeannie is a bad girl'?"

"He's so angry," Moira practically whispered. "He's staying away from you until he calms down. When he heard Gerald had his hands on you — the builders are coming tomorrow to fix the holes in the wall."

The bite of prime rib stuck in Jeannie's throat. With an effort she swallowed, coughed, and said, "So, the cops ratted me out, eh? Fascists. Did they mention when they came on the scene, Gerald was saying hello to the barrel of his gun? Held by me? Because I got the drop on the overconfident son of a bitch?"

Moira flashed a smile, which eased the tension lines around the smaller woman's eyes. "They did. They practically fell over themselves assuring our leader you were never in any danger. You made quite an impression on them."

"You should see the mark on Gerald's neck, you want to see impression," she chortled, forking down another bite of the delicious prime rib.

She was halfway through the meat before she realized it was raw. She waited for the urge to puke, or faint, but it didn't come. Moira saw the look on her face and quickly explained, "It's normal, my lady, don't fret. You're growing a werewolf, after all. You'll crave raw meat throughout your pregnancy."

"My God!" Jeannie said, putting down her fork. "I'm catching your delusion!"

❧⧉❧

Hours later, she was soaking in the tub — which was more like a miniature pool — when the bathroom door opened and Michael said, quite calmly, "You put yourself in danger. You put my unborn child in danger. On purpose."

She swallowed a mouthful of water and sat up, looking behind her to see him standing in the bathroom doorway, stone-faced. She opened her mouth, but before she could speak he said, "Finish your bath," and walked out.

An hour later, she was still in the tub. Wrinkled and shivering, but defiant. He wasn't the boss of her, dammit! She'd get out of the tub when she was damned good and ready, thank you very much —

"Jeannie. If I have to remove you from the tub, you won't like it."

— and that was right now. She climbed out of the tub, dried, and shrugged into the clothes she'd been wearing earlier. She wrapped her soaking hair in a towel and padded into the other room to take her medicine.

Wyndham was apparently a helluva boy scout, because he'd kindled a respectably-sized fire in the fireplace. He was crouched before the flames, balancing on the balls of his feet, and she had the impression he'd been in that position some time, waiting for her. He turned his head when she entered the room and came to his feet at once.

"Why aren't you wearing a nightgown? There are plenty of clothes for you to wear."

"They're not my clothes," she pointed out. "You stocked up before snatching me, didn't you? Bought a bunch of stuff in my size? I saw it earlier. Well, forget it. I'm wearing my own clothes."

By firelight, his eyes were yellow. His voice, though, was still cool and calm, which reassured her somewhat. "Everything in this room is yours."

"This *room* isn't mine. Nothing here is mine. Now, about this afternoon." She swallowed and lifted her chin. "I admit to some remorse about cold-cocking the doctor, but …"

He crossed the room and tore the shirt off her body, ignoring her outraged squawk, then leaned down and tugged at her leggings until they, too, were shreds. "Your old life is over!" he shouted as he dragged her to the bureau. He yanked open a drawer, found a nightgown, thrust it at her. "You belong to me, and you will wear my clothes and stay in my home and be safe and you will damned well like it!"

Shocked at his rage and loss of control, she couldn't grab the nightgown and it floated to the floor. "You weren't this out of it in the elevator," she said, brushing the scraps of t-shirt off her arms, hating the way her hands trembled. "What's your problem?"

"My *problem*," he said with savage sarcasm, yanking the towel from her hair and furiously towel-drying the soaked tresses, "is a willful mate who doesn't care about her own safety or, apparently, my child's."

"I'm not your mate!"

"You *are*. And all your protests won't change the fact. Werewolf law is a hell of a lot older than human law, Jeannie, and as such, you're mine, as the child is mine, forever and ever, amen." He finished drying her hair and tossed the towel at her. "So I strongly recommend you *get over it*."

"I hate you," she said hopelessly, furious at herself for not being able to come up with anything better.

"I suggest you get over that, too," he said carelessly. He pulled his t-shirt over his head, unbuttoned his shorts, let them drop, and stepped out of them.

"Wrong," she said, and oh God, her throat was so dry. "Not in a thousand years, pal. Never again."

"I'm not your pal," he said coldly, but his cheeks were flushed with color and his gaze was hot. "I'm your mate. It's time you were reminded of the fact."

"And you can't wait, can you?" she hissed. "All day you've been hoping I'd escape, so you can *rape* me. Again. Well, I did try, and now you get to play — or at least you think you do — so why are you so mad?"

"I never expected you to end up in Gerald's literal grasp," he growled, stalking toward her. She took a great, clumsy step backward and nearly tripped over an endtable. He was there to steady her, his hand on her arm surprisingly gentle. "Jesus! He could have torn your throat out and you wouldn't have known it until you woke up in the afterlife!"

"The only one in danger of throat trouble was Gerald," she retorted, and swallowed to get the lump out of her throat. "I had his gun. I —"

"There was no bullet in the chamber, you idiot!" The heat of his rage baked her face; he shook her so hard her hair flew into her face, her eyes. "The gun wouldn't have fired! Gerald knew it, he could have killed you at any time! Now he knows your status, knows where you are, knows if he gets you he gets the next pack leader. You've been reckless and you might have paid the price with your life, if my people hadn't gotten there in time, you stupid, stupid ..." Then she was crushed to him in an embrace so tight it drove the breath from her lungs. His chest heaved and he shuddered all over, trying to force calm. "How could you have risked yourself? Risked our baby? Frightened years off my life?"

"I didn't — I didn't —"

His mouth was suddenly on hers in a bruising kiss even as he moved, pulling her with him. The backs of her knees connected with the bed and she twisted away from him, gasping, only to have him casually toss her on the bed. He stripped off his undershorts and she couldn't help but stare at him, at the thing that had gotten her into this mess. Fully erect, almost curving under its weight, thrusting from a lush nest of black hair, she looked for a long moment, almost spellbound. Then her gaze was drawn upward until she was staring into his gleaming gold gaze.

"I can't," she whispered, but oh, part of her wanted to. "Not with you. Not again."

"You will. Only with me."

He climbed onto the bed, easily avoiding her kick, and then his chest was settling against hers and his hands were in her hair, tugging, forcing her head back. He dipped his head and inhaled her scent, seeming almost to savor her, but she could feel that hot, hard pressure against her lower stomach and knew he wasn't going to be satisfied with just her natural perfume.

"Don't."

"I can't help it. I've always loved your scent."

"*Don't!*" she said, almost gasped, as he licked her throat. "I don't want you. Don't do that!"

"It doesn't have to be punishment," he said, and sounded almost — could it be? — desperate. "Let me make it good. I want *you*, not your body. I don't want to take by force what you could share with both of us."

"Don't you understand?" she screamed at him, startling him, startling herself. "I *can't*! The qualities that make you like me also fix it so I can't … give … in." No matter how much I want to, she thought desperately. "Now leave me be!"

"Please," he said again, and his eyes were haunted. "I'll overlook what happened. I shouldn't have backed us both into this corner. Just let me —" He dropped a soft kiss to her throat. "You'll like it."

That's what I can't bear, she said to herself. Oh, God, anything but that — anything but me begging him again. I'd rather be taken in anger than reduced to humiliating screaming and begging, shouting myself hoarse while I come so hard I can't think straight …

And he was *wrong*. He was wrong to keep her here, Gerald or no Gerald. Her outraged pride could never escape that fact. Nobody held Jeannie against her will, God damn him.

"I'll escape again," she said through gritted teeth, as he licked the underside of her left breast. Her nipple rose, a taut pink rosebud, and he rubbed his cheek against it. She whimpered, the tiny sound escaping before she could lock it back.

He smiled at the sound. "I was so afraid," he said quietly, pressing his mouth to her cleavage for a brief, sweet kiss. "So terrified. When they told me who you'd run to. When they told me that mate-killing bastard had actually put his hands on you." His head dropped to her shoulder. "Jeannie, I was so scared for you," he said, so low she could barely hear the words.

She wanted to comfort him. She wanted to thank him for his concern. And she hated every tender feeling he was calling up in her. Forcing on her. Better to be forced, better to be victimized, than a willing prisoner. Anything but that.

"I think I could get a better deal with Gerald," she said with cruel casualness. "As soon as I escape again — and I will — I'll have to track him down. At least he'll leave me alone until the baby's born."

He froze against her and she held her breath. He raised his head and gave her a long, level look.

"I *will* leave," she said evenly, and felt shame, and felt anger at feeling shame. "I won't stay here against my will. Let me go now, tonight, or I'll find Gerald just as soon as I can." A bluff — she wasn't going near Gerald on a bet — but Michael wouldn't know that.

He said nothing. Instead, he calmly rose and padded out of the room, stark naked. She went limp with relief, unable to believe she'd gotten off so lightly.

She rose from the bed and put away the nightgown he'd thrown at her earlier. She'd meant what she had said, about not wearing clothes he'd picked out during his shop-for-my-future-prisoner spree. It wasn't to be borne, not any of this male-domination bullshit, and if he thought she was the type to …

He was back, carrying something.

He kicked the door shut behind him, his face dark with anger, then he unscrewed the top to the tube, squeezing a handful of — of something onto his hand. He rubbed the handful all over his turgid cock, until his member was shiny and slick with lubricant.

She watched this cold procedure — his expression never changed — with her mouth hanging ajar. Then understanding hit and she turned to run … somewhere. But his hand was on her elbow before she'd even taken a step. He thrust her, screaming her denial, face down on the bed. She scrambled to her knees and he let her, then he grasped her hips and plunged inside her. She shrieked again at the shock of it, the brutal intrusion, the taking of her for punishment.

He reared behind her, plunging and withdrawing, and her screams of anger — for, in truth, this didn't hurt, but it couldn't exactly be called pleasurable, either — gave way to furious weeping. He never missed a stroke, and after a minute he was shuddering behind her.

He let go of her hips and she dropped to the bed, which shook with her sobs. He let her cry for a long moment, then put a hand on her shoulder and eased her on her back. She couldn't look at him.

"That was for what you just threatened to do," he said hoarsely. "Never *think* of going near him. He'll kill you. I couldn't bear that."

He left her on the bed, going around the room and shutting off the lights. She tried to get a grip on herself, tried to stop crying, but it was all too much — the stress of the last three weeks caught up with her, not to mention the stress of the last minute and a half.

When he eased into bed beside her she cringed back, expecting to be used again, but he shushed her and pulled her, oh so carefully, into his arms, as if he thought she might shatter if handled too roughly. His large warm hands stroked her back and he pulled her face into his throat. In the dark, his voice rumbled against her cheek, sad … almost lost. "You wouldn't know this, but … that's how a werewolf punishes his mate. Using her but withholding pleasure. You had frightened me so badly, you weren't listening, I — I couldn't think of what else to do." Pause. "And I was very angry, tremendously angry." He licked the tears from one cheek and, when she didn't cringe or flinch, but just sobbed softly and steadily, he licked the tears from the other. He licked the ones that had dripped to her chest, chasing one errant tear all the way to her nipple.

He trailed soft, sweet kisses down to her naval and she could feel herself stiffen beneath him. He paused, obviously expecting a protest, but the agony of her recent humiliation was too great, and she was afraid to stop him. "It's all right," he said sadly, reading her mind, or perhaps smelling her fear. His tongue flicked out, caressed the cup of her navel, moved lower. "No matter what you do or say, I'm done with cruelty for tonight. I've found I don't have the taste for it when you're involved. Do you want me to stop? Leave?"

Wary of werewolf tricks, she said nothing, but couldn't stifle a gasp of protest when he settled himself between her legs. He started lapping the inside of her thighs, cleaning his seed from her, and a treacherous warmth began to spread through her limbs. She could feel herself relaxing by inches when long minutes went by and all he did was nuzzle and kiss and lick her inner thighs. When his tongue brushed her clitoris, there and gone again, she didn't even have time to squirm before he was back to tending to the less sensitive skin of her thighs. Then his tongue was delving inside her, darting, flicking, probing … and then back to her inner thighs.

Soon the trips to her inner thighs were shorter, and all his attention was on her cunt, which had began to throb in delighted abandon. She tried to bite back a groan, but he heard the muffled sound and murmured, "It's all right to like it."

Not with you, she thought despairingly, and nearly groaned again when he suckled her clit, swirling the impudent bead with his tongue. Then she felt his finger ease into her and her back bowed off the bed, her teeth biting her lips bloody in her efforts not to show him how his wonderfully skilled touch was affecting her.

Everything clenched within her, and suddenly her orgasm was blooming through her like a dark flower. Even as sweet aftershocks made her limbs tremble, he was pulling her toward him, and then he was on his back and she had straddled him. Murmuring encouragement, he took himself in one hand, nudged her thighs a bit further apart, and then his tip was in her, while she braced her hands on his chest to keep from falling.

He stopped. She looked at him in the near dark.

"Go ahead," he urged softly, hoarsely. "Take me inside you. Or not. This time, it's your decision."

Still she didn't move, wary, wondering what he was up to, wondering if he was going to punish her again, the black-hearted (he's never hurt you) bastard, oh, how she hated (you were no match for that crooked cop) him, wished him dead, hated him for humiliating her (if the cavalry hadn't shown up, you'd have been toast) and then bringing her pleasure. He was contemptible, and she was trapped (you don't really think they're all crazy, do you?).

She shut out the despicable voice and abruptly, hatefully, let her weight drop on him, slamming him all the way inside her, until she could feel his tip touching her womb. Then she lifted … and dropped again. And again. Beneath her, Michael gasped, a ragged sound. "Jeannie —"

Lift. Drop. Again.

"Stop, Jeannie, you're not — this is all for me, you're not getting any —"

Again.

"— *please*, stop it, stop it, let me help you come again, don't do this —"

Again.

"— don't do this, don't, don't —"

Again. She kept it up, riding him with savage intent, ignoring his pleas that she slow down, that she allow herself pleasure. She used him as he had used her, and from the look on his face, her expression was every bit as mean and ugly as she felt. After an eternity, he threw his head back, his protests ending in a ragged groan. She felt him pulse within her, felt her muscles grab at him greedily, milking him, and hated herself almost as she hated him.

Without a word, she climbed off him and curled up on her side, away from him.

I'm trapped, she thought with dull despair. They're all nutty, the whole town's infected, they're all in on it, they'll help him keep me. I can't get away, and if I try again, there's more of … of this.

I can't get away.

I can't stay.

She wept again, silently, ignoring Michael's soft entreaties that she look at him, that she forgive him, that she try to understand.

"You're pregnant with a child who will grow up to safeguard and lead some 300,000 werewolves across the globe. That's bigger than your pride, Jeannie. Your safety has to come before everything. I'm —"

"Don't say you're sorry again," she said coldly, and he shut up.

Chapter Eight

"You've broken her!"

The accusation brought Michael wide awake. After leaving Jeannie, he'd paced his room for hours, wondering what, if anything, he could have done differently. Werewolf discipline had been a mistake — or had it? If it kept her from fleeing to Gerald, it was worth the tears and hatred. He'd rather she hated him forever than love him and die tomorrow.

It all came down to their natures, to the fact that he had different rules than she was used to, but she couldn't accept this because she couldn't accept them. She thought they were all deranged. Perhaps Jon's suggestion had been correct. If she saw them Change, even one of them Change, she could look at her situation in an entirely new light.

But oh, she would be terrified, would expect to be forced again. Could he put her through that, even though he knew he was right?

Was he right?

Finally, he'd dozed off at dawn, only to be brought awake by his door slamming open and Derik shouting at him.

"What?" he asked fuzzily, blinking sleep out of his eyes. He looked out the window ... and was startled to see it was mid-afternoon. "What's the matter?"

His boyhood friend slammed the door so hard, a splinter the length of his forearm jumped off the frame and landed on the floor. "You've broken your mate, that's what's the matter. She's been curled up in the window seat all damn day, won't speak a word to anybody, won't eat a thing — *naked*, for God's sake, she won't get dressed, won't talk, won't eat —"

"You're repeating yourself," he said sharply, quelling the dart of worry that made an instant appearance at Derik's words. "Is she hurt? Has anyone seen to her?"

"She's not hurt," Derik said, aggravated, "I keep telling you, she's broken. You smashed her spirit. And we think that rots." He paused, coughed. "Sir."

"We?" he asked, sliding from the bed. "My loyal staff and pack members, you mean?"

"I can smell her all over you," his friend said quietly. "You took her again, didn't you?"

"When I heard about Gerald — that he'd actually had his hands on her —"

Derik groaned and collapsed on the bed. "Not mate-punishment, tell me, *tell* me you didn't take a human for punishment?"

Silence.

Derik sat up and glared at his pack leader. "Jesus, Michael, she's delicate! She's *human*. You shouldn't have done that, no matter how badly she scared you. You can't treat her like a werewolf, even if she is your mate."

A low growl got Derik's attention, and he dropped his eyes at once. "Okay, hell, I'm upset. I shouldn't tell you how to handle your female." He paused, then burst out angrily, still keeping his eyes respectfully downcast, "But you'd better get up there and fix it, O mighty king of all werewolves, because your mate is in a sorry state and it's all your fault. She's got to eat. And it would be nice if she got dressed, too."

"I can't go near her," he said, pacing the same stretch of carpet he'd walked so many hours last night. "I'm part of the problem. She doesn't understand our rules, doesn't understand —"

Derik looked up. "Then make her understand," he said, clearly exasperated.

"I'm *trying*!" Michael managed to restrain himself from kicking a hole in the dresser. "I'm trying, but how do you teach a blind person how to look at things? How do you tell a deaf person what a symphony sounds like? You can't make them. You can only hope they get it … even though your worst fear is that they never will. *You* know she's my mate, and I know … and we both know she's alpha female, and a valued member of the pack. But she doesn't understand any of that. It's too soon. A month ago, she'd never met me. A month ago, I had no idea I'd — I'd —"

"Fall in love?" Derik asked quietly.

Michael groaned. "How could everything turn to shit so *quickly*? She hates me, Derik, and I can't blame her for that. I've been a disaster for her since I stepped on that elevator. The worst thing is, even if she saw me Change, if she knew we weren't crazy, she'd be terrified."

"But what's the alternative?"

The pack leader had no answer.

"Please, ma'am, please … Jeannie … try some of the bread. Dara saw how much of it you ate yesterday, she made a whole loaf just for you, won't you please try just a piece?"

Moira's entreaty became a soft drone as Jeannie looked out her window, out to sea. The ocean looked exactly like she felt: grey and stormy. The weather matched her mood; it was a perfect day to stay inside and brood. Even the sand looked cold and forbidding, like dirty snow. She'd give anything to be a weredolphin, a weregrouper, a wereminnow, anything that could swim the sea and never never come back to this crazy place. Her stomach, which had been gnawing and rumbling most of the morning, had finally quit and was now a still stone in her abdomen. Vanquished. Defeated.

The way she'd like to defeat Michael Wyndham.

They'd tried to get her dressed. Moira and another woman, one she didn't know, had come in and gently pulled her from her window seat, and dressed her in clothes that weren't hers, clothes Michael had bought for her when he was dreaming about stealing her. She tore them off her, not as spectacularly as Michael had torn hers, but enough to get her point across and then, naked, she had gone back to the window seat, resting her forehead against the panes and wishing she were a wereguppy.

Moira whispered that she understood, she could smell Michael all over her and understood completely, but why punish the baby for the sins of the father, and wouldn't she please try some of this soup?

Somehow, the day passed. Jeannie was thinking harder than she had in her life (ha) but couldn't see a way out of the trap (except to quit letting your pride call the shots).

Night came, and she dozed off in the window seat, ignoring the cramping in her legs. And there came a point in the dark when she was gently lifted, carried, and placed in bed. She roused herself enough to catch Michael's scent and tried to fight all the way back to wakefulness, to get back to the window and look out at the sea and freedom, to get his hands off her, his wonderfully comforting hands …

"Go back to sleep, Jeannie. The window will be there tomorrow."

Reasonable advice, she thought muzzily, and sank back to sleep.

※◌(ĊƆ)◌※

Michael, keeping uneasy watch out Jeannie's window, turned when she sat up. He saw at once she wasn't really awake; her dreaming, wide-open eyes looked right past him.

She got out of bed. Having a good idea of her destination, he followed her out the door, steadying her on the stairs when her sleeping feet stumbled. Jon, back from a late-night hunt, passed them in the dark, his eyes widening appreciatively at Jeannie's nudity. Then he saw she was asleep, saw Michael behind her, and passed on after a polite nod to his pack leader.

She wandered aimlessly on the lower level, until he gently steered her toward the kitchen. Once there, he opened the fridge for her and saw the small plastic container with her name on it. He popped the lid and caught the rich, savory scent of raw ground beef mixed with raw eggs, onion, and lots of salt and pepper.

He handed the container to Jeannie, who did not hesitate to grab a fistful and eat it. She ate until the container was empty, and while he shut the fridge and put the container in the sink, she delicately licked the raw meat from her fingers. He watched her without words.

Then she woke up.

He saw it at once; her dreaming gaze became clouded, then utterly astonished. She looked down at herself, then looked around, saw him, saw where they were.

"I — thought I was dreaming."

"You were hungry," he said simply. "So you sleep-walked down here to feed the baby."

"I ate — I ate all that raw hamburger?" She touched her mouth, revolted. "I can still taste it."

"You were hungry," he said again. "And I think the taste in your mouth is good to you. It's just the idea of it that tastes bad. Jeannie ... can you see me? Do you know where we are?"

"We're in a kitchen. Yes, I can see you." She added, with a snap of her old fire that heartened him, "Ask another stupid question."

"It's pitch dark, Jeannie. A month ago, in equal darkness, you couldn't see anything."

A long, strained silence, broken by her whisper. "What's happening to me?"

"You're pregnant with a shapeshifter," he said simply. "You share a blood stream with the baby. You'll eat raw meat and see in the dark and probably get stronger before you birth the baby. It's natural."

"It is *not* natural. None of this is." She rubbed her face. "Oh, Jesus, I'm catching your delusion, you've all got me turning as crazy as you are ..."

"That's not true," he said, reaching up and stroking her shoulder, lightly, a butterfly's touch. "And I think you're coming to know it."

"It has to be true," she said, almost moaned. "What's the alternative? That everything you said was right? That everything you — everything you did to me was understandable? Okay, even? That's not acceptable, I won't tolerate it!"

"Jeannie ..."

She broke away from him and ran out of the kitchen, navigating her way past boxes and stools without hesitation, though most people would have been effectively blind in such utter darkness.

He came to her room the next morning to find her huddled in the window seat, looking out at the near-full moon with a dazed, almost hypnotized expression.

"Jeannie," he began, and then trailed off helplessly. His fingers itched to touch the smooth skin of her back; luckily, his hands were full. His lack of physical control had gotten her into this mess. Christ, he was like a pup around her, only thinking about physical pleasure, about the sounds she made when she … "I'm glad you ate your breakfast."

"Starving myself doesn't work," she said hopelessly, not turning around. "It just makes me sleepwalk and search out raw meatloaf, for God's sake. Better to have my scrambled eggs, please go away."

He decided it would not be prudent to mention her cravings would get worse, not better, before she gave birth.

"I brought you something."

She didn't answer.

He set the suitcases down, bent, unsnapped all four catches. At the sounds, she snuck a glance over her shoulder, then came off the window seat in astonishment. "My clothes!"

"Some of them," he confirmed, while she elbowed him out of the way and took a closer look. "I went to get them last night. I can't have you running around naked for the next eight months, can I?"

She grinned at him, so wide and natural he actually felt his heart catch: ka-THUD! "Thanks!" She made an aborted movement with her arms; for a moment of pure astonished happiness, he thought she was going to hug him. Then the moment passed and she was wriggling into panties, shorts, and a sweatshirt.

Well, what did you expect, fool? he asked himself bitterly. That she'd kiss you and say, 'Hey, PsychoBoy, I forgive you for the whole raping thing — twice — and love you and want to stay with you forever, thanks for the clothes.'

He turned to leave.

"Michael," she said tentatively.

He turned around, hope jumping in his chest like a rabbit. A continuously lusty rabbit hopelessly infatuated with someone who hated him. "Yes, my — my dear?" He'd almost called her 'my own mate', a common werewolf endearment he was positive she would not appreciate.

"Michael … can I ask a favor?"

He waited. She looked out the window at the moon, nearly full, the moon which would ripen tonight and call to his blood. Her eyes were wide with distress, dilated with fear. "Can I please stay somewhere else tonight? I promise I won't try to get away. I'll — I'll do whatever you want, if you don't make me stay in the house with — with all of you tonight."

"It's not safe for you anywhere else," he said, as gently as he could. "And I'm still planning to leave. You don't have to worry about a repeat of what happened last month." She didn't have to worry no matter where he was, he thought but did not say, because she certainly wasn't ovulating this time. What he would likely want to do in wolf-form is hunt food for her, then stay close. Following her from room to room, drinking in her scent, worshipping her with his eyes. She'd be terrified … or hate it — him … or both.

He closed his eyes against the pain that thought brought, then opened them as she did something he never thought she would do … never thought she was capable of.

"Please!" she begged. "I don't feel safe *here*! It's beautiful here, but I don't feel safe in your home." Every word was a knife in his heart, but she didn't notice, just rushed on in her agitation. "Every minute that goes by, I feel like something terrible will happen, something I'm in the middle of! Please, *please* let me stay somewhere else. I'll do anything, Michael, anything you want."

"Don't beg," he said thickly, "I can't bear it," but she wasn't hearing him. She crossed the room in an instant and flung herself into his arms; he hugged her to him automatically, stepping backward with the force of her assault. "Jeannie, listen. It's not —"

He quit talking because her frantic mouth was on his, her hands were pounding on his chest and then scratching the fabric of his shirt, her scent — orchard ripe, succulent peaches — overwhelmed him. The force of his return kiss bent her backward. "Anything," she hissed into his mouth. "Anything."

The man in him managed, 'Wait! She's giving herself to you for a favor, she thinks if you take her, she can leave tonight. Stop, idiot!' before the wolf took over, yanked her sweatshirt over her head, divested her of her shorts, tore her panties in his haste, tossed her on the bed. He was on her, her limbs were entwined with his and everywhere was her scent and he couldn't get enough, could never get enough of her. He buried his face in the sweet slope of her throat, cupped her breasts with their impudent velvet nipples, kissed her so hard they were both panting when he pulled his mouth from her.

Part of him thought, even as he put his hands on her, his mouth on her, that she must be frightened indeed to give herself to him, a woman who had starved herself and gone without clothes to show her contempt for him. He made a last, heroic effort. "You can't leave," he growled, then bit her earlobe, and wondered how he could make himself leave her with his cock on fire and her musk in his nostrils. "It's not safe."

She bowed her head, resting her forehead against his shoulder. "I know. I knew you wouldn't let me, but I was desperate. I've been watching that damned moon and getting upset and now I'm … oh, God, I'm so ashamed."

He kissed the slope of her breast. "Don't say that."

"I am, though." She seemed content to let him nuzzle her breast; one hand was in his hair, almost absently. He gloried in her touch, in her temporary acquiescence, even as he craved more.

"Because you used your body to try and get what you want?"

She didn't answer, but he felt her swallow hard.

"It doesn't make you bad. It makes you formidable." He chuckled. "The remorse, now, *that* makes you human." He licked the underside of her breast, then nipped the sensitive skin. She jumped and he heard her swallow a gasp.

"I think," she said carefully, trying to ease herself from beneath him, and, because he wasn't cooperating, having no luck at all, "that since you won't let me leave, there's no reason for us to finish this."

"You're not going to send me away, are you?" He probably looked as horrified as he felt, because she got a downright devilish look in her eyes.

"Yes," she said, "I am. You promised you wouldn't force me unless it was to punish me. I haven't done anything wrong —"

"Today," he interrupted dryly.

"— so you have to go," she finished triumphantly. He could tell she was loving it, loving the power she had over him, and was curious to see if he really would leave her, when they could both feel the throbbing below his belt.

"Jeannie, I am *begging* you."

"No," she said, pouting, but she was watching him, watching, and he caught the sharp scent of her wariness. He groaned theatrically and stumbled from the bed, adjusting his jeans to ease the stiffness between his legs.

"About that promise …"

"Out!"

The last thing he saw before leaving was the delighted, surprised look on her face.

Chapter Nine

Jeannie spoke around a mouthful of chocolate. "What do you mean you're all leaving?"

Moira had made the bed, over Jeannie's protests that she 'didn't need a maid, dammit'. Now she was clearing her mistress's lunch plates, and looked up. "Only the females, my lady."

"Why?"

"Because you want us to," she said simply.

"But I never said — besides, Michael's the boss of you guys, not me."

"The alpha female has expressed distress to her mate at the thought of being around us this evening. Thus, we depart." Moira shrugged. "Simple."

"But *I'm* not the —" At Moira's look, Jeannie reversed herself. "Okay, say I am. I never told you guys to go. I only told Michael."

"Werewolf hearing," Moira said with a smile, "is very acute. Besides, we can smell your torment. We don't want to add to it."

"You're really leaving your home tonight? For me? Even though I didn't ask?"

Moira just gave her a look, something along the lines of, 'yes, dummy'.

"Of course," Jeannie said slowly, "you could just be leaving so I don't see you're not werewolves."

"After everything you've seen? Felt? Eaten?"

"Ugh, don't remind me."

"You still think we're crazy? Half the town? And everyone in this house? *And* the father of your child?"

Jeannie harumphed. "Well, I'm not saying you're not convincing …" But she squirmed under Moira's stern regard.

"Well." Moira picked up the tray. "As it is, we're leaving. I'll see you tomorrow."

"Wait!" She bounded to her feet and fought the urge to pluck at Moira's sleeve like a child. "You said the females are leaving. What about the guys?"

"The 'guys'," she said dryly, "think you should get over it. But we won't go there."

"No," Jeannie shouted at Moira's retreating back, "we certainly won't!" She kicked a pillow across the room.

There was a tap on the adjoining door, and Michael poked his head in. "We certainly won't what? And stop kicking that pillow, it's a hundred years old."

Jeannie, bending to retrieve the pillow, dropped it like it was hot. "The girls are all leaving," she said in an accusing tone.

He frowned. "Yes. They told me they were. They've gotten quite loyal to you in ..." He checked his watch. "Seventy-two hours."

"But the men *aren't* leaving."

"No." Seeing the confusion on her face, he added, "The females will do what the alpha female wants, period. The males will do what is best for her. Not always the same thing."

"Fascinating. Really, and I mean that." She yawned theatrically, and rubbed her eyes, feeling sudden, surprising weariness she didn't have to feign. Then she looked at him and said, no screwing around, no wise cracks, "I'm afraid."

"I know."

"Why do you have to sound like that?" she asked crossly, rubbing her eyes again. "All loving and nice."

"Because I have great admiration for you. Not just, as you think, your physical charms." He paused, then said, as baldly as she had stated her fear, "I love you."

She choked in mid-yawn, and stared at him with wide eyes. "No, you don't."

"No?" He smiled, that slow, sexy smile that always charmed her.

"You just love the way I smell. Michael, be reasonable," she said, trying to sound reasonable herself, "you don't know me well enough to love me." Thinking with surprised, giddy joy: He loves me! He loves me!

"Yes, I do," he said casually.

"Michael," she said slowly, wanting to cross the room and touch him, but unable to make herself take that step, "if you really love me, why'd you — why'd you shame me like that?"

"Are you going to run away and find Gerald?"

"No!" She shouted the word before she thought, then blushed furiously. "I mean, yeah, maybe, what's it to ya?"

"*That's* why," he said simply. "I didn't want to punish you. I wanted to take you, but I wanted you to enjoy it. I hated having to scare you." To her astonishment, she saw his hands were shaking. "I hated every second of it," he added with savage emphasis, "but I would do it a thousand times if it meant you would keep away from Gerald."

There was a short silence while they looked at each other. "Um ... thank you? I guess," she muttered.

He smiled a little. "Are you tired, sweet?"

"No," she said defiantly, but her eyelids felt ridiculously heavy. "I want to keep talking about this so-called love."

"Talk while lying down," he said, taking her arm and pushing her gently onto the bed. Before she could turn around or sit up, he had slipped into bed behind her, snuggling against her, spoon-style.

"I don't want to nap with you," she said, wriggling against him.

"If you don't stop moving," he warned, his breath tickling her neck, "you won't be napping."

She went rock-still, and yawned again. "Seriously, though. Why should I reward you for —" He loves me, she reminded herself. "Oh fine, stay then," she grumbled. "See if I care."

His rumbling laugh was the last thing she heard.

꧁⟨♡⟩꧂

It was dark when she woke, but she could see everything in the room quite clearly. She refused to think about what that meant (you've been doing lots of refusing to think this week, huh, babe?) and instead focused on Michael, who was pacing at the foot of the bed. His face was sheened with sweat and he kept running his fingers through his hair. In the gloom, his eyes were a tortured gold. He must have fallen asleep, too, she realized, and now there isn't time for him to leave before ... before ...

"Michael?" The word practically stuck in her throat. He didn't turn, didn't even glance at her. "Are you all right?"

"Fine," he muttered.

Abruptly, she decided: no more fear. She couldn't fear rape if she was the aggressor. And, to be completely honest, the bastard had a touch like nothing she'd ever felt. She wanted it. At night, in her lonely bed, she *craved* it.

"No more fear," she announced, and stood up in the bed. Then she leapt at him.

He caught her, as she had known he would, and staggered back so hard his back slammed into the wall.

"My thinking is," she said into his astonished face, as she looped her legs around his waist, "I've been terrified of a repeat of the elevator scene, right? All week, I've been worrying about it. Hell, I even tried to seduce you so you would send me away. Well, if *I* rape *you*, there's nothing to be scared of. Then I can go back to sleep."

"Are you out of your —"

She kissed him. Then she bit his lower lip. He groaned and staggered with her.

"Jeannie —"

She snaked her tongue inside his mouth. His own met hers in a frantic duel before he wrenched his face from hers. "No! It's not like earlier, it's not — this close to my Change, if you change your mind I won't be able to stop." He set her down and shook her. "I won't be able to stop! And I can't bear to force you again, even for punishment. If I find out in the morning that you were frightened, hurt — no."

She ripped open his shirt.

He spun away from her, panting. "*No*."

"For God's sake," she muttered, and jumped on his back. Looping her arms around his neck, she ignored his hoarse demand that she stop this at once, took his ear in her teeth, and bit. He howled and grabbed for her head, trying to pull her away ... then changed his mind and pressed her face into the side of his head, hard. She bit him again and he groaned, "I will never understand you."

"Tough luck," she said sympathetically, then bit the side of his neck, and licked the spot.

He staggered to the bed and dropped, pinning her beneath him. She released her legs and he rolled over, shoving her sweatshirt to her neck and burying his face between her breasts. "Last chance," he moaned.

"My thought exactly," she grunted, pulling the shirt over her head, wriggling to get free of her shorts. He helped her with hands that shook and in moments they were both nude.

She started having second thoughts when he turned her over and eased her on her knees. "Michael," she managed as he kissed the base of her spine. "Anything else — any other way — but I'm not sure I'm ready for this yet."

He didn't answer, and she was about to try again when she felt his tongue flick past the opening of her vagina ... then delve deeply. She bit back a moan and thought, What the hell am I hiding from? I love it, and he knows I love it.

When his thumbs spread her wide and his tongue lapped at her exposed flesh, she groaned so loudly she was fairly certain Moira, wherever she was, could hear her. He laughed at the sound, a rumble of unbridled delight, and then his tongue was inside her again, darting and wriggling.

In less than a minute she was rocking back against his sweetly busy mouth, keening softly, feeling the familiar delicious warmth start in her stomach, feeling the all-over tightening that meant her orgasm was approaching ...

... then she felt the tip of him, engorged with blood, the head so like a delicious plum, ease into her … and then he shoved forward, the quick, hard thrust instantly jolting her into orgasm.

She shrieked his name and rocked back, meeting him thrust for thrust, on a roller coaster of pleasure, one swooping orgasm instantly merging into another. His low groans, so like growls, fired her blood and made her want to bite something.

She felt his teeth on her shoulder, gently, and then felt him pulsing within her. She thrust back once more, greedily, then felt him slide from her.

"Oh," she said, almost sighed.

"Christ," he groaned, and flopped face down on a pillow. She giggled, and he reached out, snagged her waist, and nestled her against his side. "Tell the truth," he rasped, and when he looked at her, she saw his pupils were huge, his irises only faint rings of gold. "You're trying to kill me, right? Wearing me out before I Change?"

She laughed again. "Does that mean you're not up for seconds?"

He didn't smile at her jibe. Instead he reached out a finger and touched her mouth. Then his rough palm was cupping her cheek. "Don't be afraid," he said, his voice so deep it was difficult to understand him. "I couldn't bear it if you were afraid."

"The funny thing is," she said seriously, "I'm not. The thing I worried about most … I *made* it happen. I had to throw myself at you — literally. But I didn't mind, because it's easier to be scared if you're the passenger, not the driver."

"Don't be afraid," he said again, panting. "I can't hold it off anymore."

He began to Change. And it happened so quickly, if she had blinked she would have missed it. His features and limbs and body seemed to shift, to melt, shrinking into a furred, four-legged wolf with a lush black coat the exact color of Michael's hair, and deep gold eyes. There wasn't a smell. There wasn't even a mess. She had just witnessed a physical impossibility.

"Guh," she said, blinking, staring, before the wolf gave her a sloppy lick on her cheek. The large, furry head bent and licked her stomach, where their child nestled. "Michael, oh Michael," she whispered, reaching out a shaking hand and touching the luxurious pelt. When the wolf — Michael — didn't move away from her touch, merely sat calmly, she gave her delight and curiosity free reign, running her hands over his strong limbs, his tail, stroking the noble head, even burying her face in his rich, black coat. She realized dimly her face was wet as the pent-up emotions — fear, anger, despair — departed as easily as Michael had shed his human form.

It was all true. They weren't crazy fools. She was the fool, for blinding herself to the truth. He was pack leader, she was his mate, she carried the next pack leader. She was in danger as long as Gerald wanted power. Michael had been right to track her and bring her to his home. She had been wrong to escape.

"Michael," she whispered into his fur, "I love you."

She didn't know if he could understand her in his lupine form, but all the same, he made a deep, rumbling noise in his chest, quite like a purr. She hoped he understood. On the other hand, she had a lifetime to repeat the phrase.

The rumbling abruptly shifted in pitch, from purr to growl. She pulled back from him, instinctively knowing Michael was incapable of hurting her in whatever form he took, but still wary. He sprang from her side and arrowed at the balcony doors, slamming into one of them hard enough to crack the heavy glass.

"Whoa!" she said, scrambling to her feet and running for the door. "You want out? No problem, just a second." After a moment she had the door open and Michael dashed past, scrambling up the railing and then fearlessly leaping into the dark.

Behind him, Jeannie watched him drop two stories, landing in a crouch on all fours. "Well, hell," she breathed, "no wonder the elevator fall didn't kill you."

She was still staring, mouth open like a rube idiot, when another wolf darted out of the cover and went for her lover's throat. This wolf had mud-colored fur the exact color of Gerald's hair, and she knew at once who the wolf had to be … and who he had come for. Michael avoided the attack, and the two powerful males squared off and charged.

He's nuts! was her first thought. Taking Michael on in his own territory? Maybe Gerald had heard all the females were gone, and assumed Jeannie would be easy for the taking … maybe he'd also heard Michael had planned to be gone this evening. And probably figured, tonight, or not at all …

Her thoughts were interrupted by a noise; she turned in time to see a buttercotch-colored wolf with Derik's green eyes rocket past her, straight over the balcony railing. Four other wolves had by now surrounded the snarling, fighting males, and Derik unhesitatingly went for the throat of the closest traitor.

Jeannie turned and went at once to the endtable drawer where she had so carelessly dropped Gerald's gun — was it only yesterday? She popped the clip, noted with grim pleasure that it was full, then slapped the clip back in, pulled back the slide, and ratcheted a load into the chamber. So Michael was right, she thought distractedly, walking back out on the balcony. Gerald's gun wouldn't have fired, and he could have killed me then. Well, well. Note to self: apologize to lover, after saving lover's ass.

A distant part of her reminded her that the room was pitch dark and there was not enough starlight for her to see by. Still, she could make out everything as clearly as if it was noon: the wolves' coloring, the lush green of the grass, even some of their eye colors. *Thank you, baby werewolf*, she thought, and then sighted in on Gerald, who had, she noticed with detached rage, just taken a chunk out of her lover's shoulder. She had no idea how Gerald expected to hustle her off Wyndham property in his wolf form. Maybe he was part human and could control his change. Regardless, she wasn't about to stand by and let him damage others — Michael! — in his quest for power.

The two wolves were locked together in an age-old battle for territory and females, and Jeannie, whose cop mother and Marine father knew a little something about battle, waited for her chance. In the meantime, Derik had chased off his opponent and, though one leg was bloodied and one ear gone, was turning hungrily on another.

Gerald reared back and went for Michael's throat. Instead, Jeannie got his — two shots, right where she guessed the adam's apple was on a werewolf.

"How about *that*, Gerald?" she shouted down. She picked off Derik's newest opponent with a clean head shot, and Derik jumped back from the newly-dead werewolf with a yip that sounded suspiciously like a laugh. "In case you didn't realize, trespassers will be shot!" Thinking: thank goodness, the stories about silver bullets aren't true.

The other traitors froze, and looked up at her, except for Gerald, who was coughing out his life on the lawn.

"This is the alpha female speaking," she said, and as the fatally wounded Gerald made one last try for Michael, she put four into his head. "Playtime's over."

The other traitors — only two, now — took off, Derik hot on their heels. Michael looked up at her, coiled, and made a clumsy jump for the balcony. She gasped when she saw his wounds.

"Lucky for us you're a fast healer," she said, and popped the live round out of the chamber. She put the gun away, then went to tend to her mate.

Chapter Ten

In bed, she could hear them chatting at breakfast, even though they were a floor below her.

"And then Michael's trying to keep Gerald off his throat, right?" Derik said. She could picture him holding the group spellbound, talking with his hands, eyes gleaming with suppressed excitement. "And I've got my hands full with those other two assholes. And Michael and I are both thinking, Cripes, are there more on the grounds? Can we take them even though the girls aren't here to help? And we're assuming Jeannie is just about out of her mind, right? I mean, *I* would have been scared at the sight. Then — ka-blammo! Close enough to singe Michael's fur, Gerald's got a couple holes in his throat, and we all look up and there's our pack leader's mate — naked, no less — holding a smoking gun and yelling at Gerald, who's been causing trouble since he was whelped."

"Then what?" Moira asked excitedly.

"Then she drills my guy, puts a few more in Gerald, binds Michael's wounds, and ate a big supper at 2:00 A.M."

"I knew it! I knew Michael had chosen wisely! And *you* said she'd never fit in, Dara."

"I did not. I said after a few months, she'd never fit in her clothes. That's all."

Hearing her staff speak of her with such admiration brought a warm flush to her cheeks. And really, she hadn't done all that much. Just saved the day.

The thought made her laugh out loud. Beside her, Michael was sleeping deeply, and stirred at the sound. She hushed at once and examined his shoulder. The wound looked months old, and she again thanked God for werewolf metabolism.

She touched her stomach lightly, with love. There was a werewolf growing inside her, which should have scared her — should have creeped her out at the very least — but instead, she was filled with a joyful acceptance of her future. She didn't know much about werewolves, but she was going to learn, oh yes. Michael would help her. Her pack would help her.

A large brown hand covered hers, and she looked into Michael's golden eyes. "My own mate," he said slowly, savoring the words, "and so brave. Even when we were in the elevator, you were brave."

"Well, of course. You weren't going to let anything happen to me."

"As you, apparently, won't let anything happen to me," he said wryly. "Remind me to instruct you on the finer points of werewolf etiquette. Number one: never interfere with a Challenge." But he was smiling as he said it, and she knew that, though his male pride might be a bit ruffled, he was pleased with her.

"And number two?"

"Always take a human to mate," he said, and pulled her to him for a long kiss. When he pulled back, she was breathless, and his eyes glinted with satisfaction. "Before we were so rudely interrupted last night, you told me something. I very much want to hear the words again."

"So you *can* understand me when you're a —"

"The words, Jeannie."

"I love you. Dork. What, you think I'd shoot a man for just anybody?"

"For a while," he said seriously, "I wondered if you might shoot me."

"I was an idiot," she admitted. "A blind fool. It was all right in front of me, and I wouldn't accept it."

"You were perfect," he assured her, "considering the circumstances. The words again, Jeannie, please."

"I love you."

"Let me show you how *I* feel," he whispered, and kissed her.

Their lovemaking was slow and almost dreamlike, and for Jeannie, who had only known fierce, fast, couplings with this man, it was like discovering a whole different side to her mate. He took his time, touching her with skilled reverence, gaining pleasure from her own. Even when she was begging him to enter her, tugging on his shoulders and whimpering pleas that made his eyes narrow with lust, he held back. "No," he said, almost moaned, "this time, I want it to last."

Shuddering with pleasure beneath his hands, she had the sense that he was finally touching her as he had always longed to, and she gloried in it. When he slid into her she shivered in his arms and gasped her love, and he closed his eyes in gratitude, deeply moved. He opened his eyes and she stared into his curious gold gaze. "Oh, Jeannie," he breathed, "I love you, too, my dearest, my own mate."

They rocked together, both of them creatures of savagery and passion, and cried out until they were hoarse. And when they were done, and drowsing in each other's arms, Jeannie had time for one thought before she spiraled down into sleep: *Thank God I didn't take the stairs.*

About the author:

MaryJanice Davidson is the author of several romance novels. She's been writing since she was thirteen; **Love's Prisoner** is her first erotic romance. She lives in Minnesota with her husband and two children, loves reading, and has a soft spot for werewolves. You can email her at alongi@usinternet.com or visit her website at www.usinternet.com/users/alongi/index.html.

The Education of Miss Felicity Wells

by Alice Gaines

To my reader:
At a time when all is forbidden, all will be desired …

Chapter One

Marcus Slade had seldom seen a young woman quite as frightened as the one who stood in his study at this moment, alternately biting her lip and toying with her reticule.

"Miss … ," he said, greeting her as best he could without knowing so much as her name.

"Wells. Miss Felicity Wells," she supplied. "It was on my card. But then, you didn't get my card, did you? That is, there wasn't anyone to take it, not a butler nor a servant anywhere." She stopped mid-babble and gave him an uncertain smile. "Oh, dear."

"Won't you sit down, Miss Wells?" he said and indicated an upholstered armchair.

She sat very delicately in it — or perched, rather like a bird ready to take flight. He sat on the matching love seat, crossed one leg over the other, and studied her. She wasn't a particularly handsome woman, but neither was she unattractive. Her wide-set brown eyes and other regular features — straight nose, forehead neither too sloped nor too lofty — made her someone who could easily disappear into a group of women of a similar age and station in life. The healthy glow to her skin and the absence of suspicion in her aspect marked her station in life as one of wealth and privilege. One that cosseted its females and kept them safe from any harsh wind.

In short, she was exactly the sort of young woman who would have been warned away from men like him with scowls and clucking tongues and warnings of debauchery. No doubt that explained her fear, but why had she come here at all? And unaccompanied.

"May I be of service to you somehow?" he asked.

Her gaze darted around the room and then lit on his face. She leaned toward him. "Are we completely alone, Dr. Slade?"

"Completely," he answered. "As you observed, I don't have servants. I treasure my solitude."

"Good." She took a breath. "I need your help with a delicate matter."

"You intrigue me, Miss Wells."

She appeared taken aback at that, as her mouth formed a little O. She had an appealing mouth, actually, almost out of keeping with the rest of her ordinary features. A generous mouth with lush, moist lips that curved up at the corners. Yes, a very appealing mouth.

"I intrigue you?" she said on an intake of breath.

"It isn't often I get a visit from a proper young lady of Boston's Brahmin class. I'm a notorious libertine. Or maybe you didn't know that."

"And a researcher of some note in … how shall I put this … the intimate arts." She bit her lip again and gazed at him as if she couldn't be sure whether he was her salvation or a danger. "That's exactly why I've come to you."

"That intrigues me." He steepled his fingers together and looked at her over the tips. "Innocent young women don't come to my house, especially not unescorted. You are innocent, aren't you?"

Her back stiffened at that. "Of course, I am."

"Mama didn't warn you off men like me?" he asked. "Your chaperon didn't refuse you permission to come here?"

"No one knows I'm here."

"Slip your tether, did you?"

"All right, you find this amusing, Dr. Slade. I understand that. But I really do need your help."

He did find her amusing, but he hadn't lied about finding her intriguing, either. Unfortunately, whatever she wanted, he'd have to send her away without it. Too many young girls sought him out when they experienced the first flush of their own sexuality. Society didn't prepare a girl for the animal side of her nature, and her mother usually made matters worse if the child even dared to ask about the flutterings in the pit of her belly.

No, he'd vowed to keep all virgins safely at arm's length. He'd succumbed to the first innocent who'd turned to him, and he'd lived to regret it. If he hadn't let the girl's father wing his arm in a duel, thereby saving face all around, things would have turned very ugly, indeed. He wasn't about to make that mistake again.

"I'm afraid I can't help you," he said.

"But you don't even know what I want," she objected.

"You come unescorted to the house of Boston's most celebrated hedonist to ask for help with a delicate matter. What else could you want but a good frigging? I'm sorry, Miss Wells, but I'm not in the business of deflowering virgins."

Her cheeks turned bright pink, and her full lips parted as she took in a sharp breath. "But I don't want to be deflowered," she said. "Oh dear, this is very complicated."

He crossed his arms over his chest and watched her as she rose from her chair and walked to the fireplace. She rested her hand against the marble mantelpiece and gazed into the flames of the small fire he'd built to keep away the chill of an early Spring afternoon.

"I'm to be married soon," she said.

"Congratulations," he answered. "Then the sex will take care of itself, won't it?"

"That's just the problem. It won't take care of itself. I have to take care of it, and I don't know how."

"But surely, if you love the man …"

She turned toward him. "Love?" she said. "What does love have to do with marriage?"

"Isn't that what modern young women insist on now? Marrying for love."

"That may well be, but I have no plans to marry for love. Why in heaven's name would I want to give a man that kind of power over me?"

"Power?"

She looked at him as if he were a perfect idiot. "Loving him. Love makes a woman weak. It makes her vulnerable. I don't intend to fall in love with my husband until he's proven himself worthy."

"Oh, really?" He couldn't quite manage to stifle a chuckle at the thought of some poor male having to make himself worthy of the unremarkable Miss Felicity Wells. "And what will you offer your husband as a reward while he's struggling to win your love?"

"Lust," she answered. "I intend to satisfy his lust."

Marc laughed outright at that. What did this woman, with her whalebone stays and the proper set of her posture know about a man's lust? What did she know of desiring and needing and holding back until the woman's cries begged him to take her? Of sweating and groaning and straining for release, only to need more almost immediately? Of a steel hard cock, throbbing to the point of pain, aching to drive itself home in a woman's flesh?

She couldn't know about those things, but he did. And damn him if he wasn't responding to her right now, Priapus growing thick in his pants as he watched the prim Miss Felicity Wells stand at his hearth and talk of a man's lust. His reaction to her was laughable. Preposterous. Out of the question. He wouldn't give in to it. But he could amuse himself with her for a few more moments without harm.

"Men are lustful creatures," she said. "Completely at the mercy of their baser natures."

"You know that from experience, do you?"

She glowered at him, the expression turning her lips into a tempting pout. "Never mind how I know it. I just do."

"And you want to learn how to use a man's baser nature against him."

"No, no, no. You're deliberately misunderstanding me."

"Then, please explain to this lustful beast what it is you *do* want."

Her cheeks flamed again, but she stood her ground and faced him. "I want to be very, very good at … at …"

"At sex," he supplied.

"At the marriage act."

"At sex," he repeated.

"All right, if you insist, at sex. I want to satisfy my husband's every whim. I want him to desire no one but me. That isn't so bad, is it?"

"It's quite admirable," he answered.

"Well, there you are, then."

"And quite impossible," he added. "Monogamy is unnatural, especially for men."

She walked back to the chair she'd vacated and rested her hands on the back, her fingers digging into the crimson velvet of the upholstery. "I don't believe that. I won't believe it."

"Study nature as I have, and you won't find exclusive mating relationships anywhere. Males compete with each other to rut with as many females as possible."

"I don't see how crude language helps this discussion."

"You wouldn't," he replied. "The female is every bit as profligate as her male, although somewhat more subtle in her tactics. No, my dear Miss Wells, monogamy doesn't exist in nature. It's a human invention conceived to make us all miserable."

"What a cynical view of things."

"I? Cynical? You're the one who's come to me to learn how to please another man. A man who'll trust you to be innocent. How cynical is that?"

"I only want to please him," she cried. "Really, that's all I want."

"And what do you get in return?"

She didn't answer but turned her face away. A slight tremble of her chin told him she was trying to contain herself. She badly wanted to cry but wouldn't let him see her tears. What in hell had he said that would make her cry? Oh, damn it all.

He rose and walked to her side. "Miss Wells, I don't mean to be unkind, but you have no idea what you're asking."

"I would if you'd tell me, Dr. Slade," she answered in a small voice. "I'm a quick study. All my teachers have said so."

"This is different." He reached out and turned her face to him. His fingers looked perfectly huge against her delicate chin, and unshed tears added a luster to the warm brown of her eyes. "The physical side of love isn't something that can be taught like history or literature. It has to be experienced."

"I understand."

"We'd have to engage in behavior that society frowns on outside of marriage. Even some things society frowns on within marriage."

"I'm willing to do all that," she said, looking up at him with a clear entreaty in her eyes.

"I'm not. As I told you, I won't take your virginity."

"And as I told you, I don't want you to take my virginity. I only want you to teach me how to satisfy a man."

He ran a thumb over her lower lip and watched as a tiny tremor ran through her. Fear, perhaps. Excitement, definitely. He moved his hand to skim the tips of his fingers along her jaw and then down the soft length of her throat to where her jacket closed very chastely over her collar bone.

"I'll give you one lesson in love right now," he said.

"Please," she breathed.

"Nothing excites a man more than passion in his partner. If I'm to turn you into an irresistible temptress, I'll have to urge your own lustful nature into full blossom."

"Oh," she whispered, and her skin became hot beneath his touch.

"It wouldn't be entirely unpleasant for you." He bent and put his lips next to her ear. "Would you like for me to do that?"

"Yes," she whispered. "Yes, I think I would."

He nuzzled the space behind her ear with his nose, breathing in her fragrance. Something innocent. Rose water and soap. "We'll both become very agitated. We'll both want full consummation. We'll want that very badly."

"Yes," she repeated.

He nipped at her earlobe with his teeth, and she gave out a little cry. "Do you think you can resist?" he asked.

She rested a hand against his chest and pushed herself away from him. "I'll have to."

He looked down into her face. "Are you sure?"

"I'm sure," she answered. "And what about you? Are you sure you can resist?"

He laughed. "Oh yes, Miss Wells, I'm sure."

"Then that's settled," she said. "You will take me as a pupil? I can pay you well."

"I don't want your money. I have plenty of my own."

A look of alarm crossed her face, as though she feared he wouldn't give in. He shouldn't, really.

She'd still be a virgin when he was through with her, though. Still quite marriageable, with no need for her father to come gunning after him. She'd go off and marry her fiancee, and everyone would be happy. But what would he gain in exchange? Nothing. Unless …

"Very well," he said. "I'll serve as your guide to the sensual if you'll do something for me."

She raised an eyebrow. "What would that be?"

"As you mentioned, I've made a study of the human sexual drives. I'd like to use our encounters to observe your sexual responses systematically."

Her eyes widened. "How would you do that?"

"I'd ask you to report — in great detail — everything you're thinking and feeling when I touch you. When you touch me."

She gave a sigh of relief. "Of course, I could do that."

"Think a moment what I'm asking of you," he said. "No dissembling. No hiding anything from me. Your thoughts, your dreams, your fantasies — I could demand them at any time, and you'd be obliged to supply them."

She took a breath and looked him straight in the eye. "I could do that."

"Good." He extended his hand toward her. "Then, you have a teacher, Miss Wells."

She took his hand and gave it a firm shake. "I take my constitutional on Monday, Wednesday, and Friday afternoons. Except when it rains. I'll visit you then until I'm satisfied that I can be a good lover to my husband. Agreed?"

"Agreed."

"Until Wednesday, then."

He gestured toward the study door. "I'll see you out."

"No need," she answered. "I can find my own way."

"As you wish."

Since she hadn't removed so much as her hat or reticule, there was nothing for her to gather up. She simply turned and walked briskly from the room, leaving the scent of rose water in her wake. Marc watched her go and only then realized that he had an enormous, aching erection.

❧✦⟡✦❧

Although comfortably soft and smooth against Felicity's bare skin, Dr. Slade's shirt nevertheless rubbed her bosom in a frankly disturbing way, the friction irritating the peaks of her breasts. Although if asked, she'd have to admit that the feeling wasn't entirely unpleasant. In fact, the sensation stirred something deep inside her — a hodge-podge of feelings and urges that reached all the way to the pit of her stomach. The very idea of that made no sense at all, of course, and the whole of the experience left her rather breathless and confused. But then, she'd never before sat in a man's study wearing nothing but his shirt, so maybe her reaction was entirely normal and to be expected.

The man himself sat across the desk, making notes in a book as though he entertained nearly-naked women every day. He scratched out a few more lines, and the sounds of his pen somehow resonated through the fabric of his shirt to chafe her breasts even further. Oh dear heaven, that last was truly ridiculous. She shifted in her seat, but the movement only made matters worse.

He looked up and studied her face for a moment, a light of intense curiosity in his blue eyes. "First I want to know about your sexual history," he said.

"I don't have one, I'm afraid."

"Nonsense, everyone has had some lustful adventure or other by your age."

"I've lived a very sheltered life."

He set his pen aside and cleared his throat in a stern manner that a minister or headmistress might have admired. "We agreed that you'd reveal everything to me, Miss Wells. It was the one condition I made to tutoring you."

She clutched his shirt around her, even though she'd taken great care to button all the buttons. The action only increased the friction against her nipples, and she shifted again, trying in vain to make herself comfortable. "I'm not holding back, Dr. Slade. I just have nothing to report."

"All right then, let's approach this more methodically." He lifted his pen again. "You've never had full knowledge of a man?"

"I beg your pardon."

He huffed again. "You've never been screwed. You've never taken a man's staff between your legs."

"Of course not," she answered. But oddly enough, just the thought made her tingle in the place where her thighs touched the leather upholstery of her chair.

"Has a man ever touched you there?" he went on. "Has any young fellow ever slipped his hand inside your drawers and fondled your nest?"

"No," she exclaimed.

"You needn't sound offended. This is exactly the sort of discussion we're to have during our sessions," he said. A light flush of anger appeared over his high cheek bones, coloring the pale skin that made such a contrast against his near-black hair. "You'll never learn to accept your lascivious nature if you become shocked at any mention of your pussy."

"My pussy?" she repeated.

"Your pussy. Your cunt. The seat of your husband's delight. Do you understand?"

She looked down into her lap but only found her own naked legs and the hems of his shirt. "I understand."

"Coyness won't serve us here, Miss Wells."

"I know that."

"In fact, you should realize what so few young girls do. Coyness isn't appealing. It's irritating."

"I'm sorry," she said.

"All right, then." He wrote a few more lines in his book, and she studied his face. The flush was still there, although less pronounced, as his gaze stayed fixed on the paper in front of him. His long, black eyelashes cast shadows over his cheeks, softening what were otherwise rather harsh, angular features.

"Has a man ever touched your breasts?" he asked without looking up.

"No."

"Has a man ever kissed you?"

"No."

He glanced up at her, disbelief written in his expression.

"I'm sorry, but that's the truth," she said. "You don't want me to invent stories, do you?"

"No," he answered, his expression gentling. Slightly. "Has anyone else ever kissed you?"

"Anyone else?"

"A boy, another girl … anyone."

"No," she said. "Oh, wait … that's not true. My cousin Henry did once. It was Christmas, and our families were visiting. He came upon me all alone and forced me to kiss him."

"Go on," he answered, bending to his writing again. "How old were you?"

"I was twelve, I think. Yes." She closed her eyes briefly, trying to capture the details in her mind — the cold wind of that December day, the sounds of the horses in their stalls, the feel of the planking against her back as Henry had pressed her back against the wall. "Henry had been looking at me oddly all through dinner, and his foot reached out under the table to touch mine a few times. I'd never liked him, with his fat cheeks and squinty eyes. I escaped as soon as I could and ran out of the house, but he followed me."

"How old was he?" Dr. Slade asked.

"Sixteen and very much enamored with himself. He told me that he'd become a man and that I'd soon be a woman and that he could show me what went on between men and women."

"And what did you say?"

"I told him that if I couldn't do any better than him when I *did* become a woman, I'd stay an old maid. I ordered him to let me go back into the house, but he didn't. He grabbed my hair, pulled me into the carriage house, and kissed me."

"What do you remember of the kiss?" he asked.

She looked at him. His expression held neither approval nor censure, just curiosity as he studied her evenly. "It was wet and unpleasant," she answered. "He pressed his mouth against mine, crushing my lips against my teeth. Then he parted my lips and tried to put his tongue into my mouth."

"What did you do?"

"I bit it."

He smiled at her. "Good girl."

"Good?" she repeated. "I was hardly an obedient female."

"We're not her to teach you to obey, Miss Wells. We're here to encourage the passionate side of your nature."

She reached down and toyed with the hem of his shirt. "And we're going to touch each other in order to do that?"

"Certainly."

She took a breath, a none-too-steady breath. "Do you plan to kiss me?"

"Yes, I think so," he answered. "This very afternoon. I won't put my tongue into your mouth unless you want me to."

She did her best to calmly digest this bit of information, despite the furious beating of her heart. Dr. Slade wasn't her cousin Henry. He wouldn't force himself on her, wouldn't handle her roughly or awkwardly. He was a fully-grown man with a great deal of experience in the boudoir, if any of the stories were true. Kissing him really ought to prove far more interesting than kissing cousin Henry.

"What are you thinking?" he asked. "Right now."

She gazed at him, her attention rivetted on his mouth. His lips appeared gentler than the angles of his face and jaw. But neither were they particularly soft. Would she find them hard? Would the kiss be wet and unpleasant as Henry's had been? Or would it be as exciting as she'd heard kisses can be?

"What are you thinking?" he repeated, putting more force into the demand.

She felt heat rise over her cheeks. "I was thinking that I'm looking forward to you kissing me."

His eyes widened almost imperceptibly for just a moment, and then he looked down to write some more in his book. She could easily learn to dislike the sound of his pen as it scratched over the paper. Here she'd confessed to some desire for him, and instead of saying anything in reply, he'd simply written her wishes down. Still, she'd agreed to this. She sighed.

"In good time," he said. "I'll kiss you after you've answered a few more questions."

Oh, dear heaven. He'd mistaken her sigh for impatience. No matter how great her curiosity about the texture of his lips, no matter how persistent the ache in her bosom, she had no urgent need for his caress. He was only a man, and not even the one she intended to share the marriage bed with. She only needed him for her purpose. Surely, he realized that.

"Dr. Slade," she began.

"In good time," he repeated.

What a ridiculous, impossible situation. She crossed her arms, but that only pushed her breasts upward, showing that the peaks had hardened into stiff, little nubs. When had that happened?

He noticed them, obviously, because his gaze came to rest there and lingered. Then he wrote something else down, damn him. The whole encounter had grown ridiculous and only promised to get worse. She really ought to tell him she'd had enough for one day, get up, dress herself, and leave. If only she could rely on her legs not to tremble.

"Has anyone ever touched you between your thighs?" he asked abruptly.

"I told you no one had."

"You told me no man had. I'm asking if anyone else had."

"Cousin Henry didn't, I can tell you that much."

"There's no need to get waspish, Miss Wells," he said. "You wanted to be tutored, if you'll remember."

"No one has ever touched me between my thighs, Dr. Slade," she said and felt her cheeks positively burn with mortification.

"No little girl school chum sharing your bed?" he said. "No groping under the coverlet?"

"No. The very idea. Another girl."

"It happens all the time, and there's nothing wrong with it," he said, glaring at her.

"It never happened to me."

"Have you ever touched yourself?" he demanded.

"No." Oh dear, except for that one time. "I'm sorry. That isn't quite true. I'd almost forgotten."

"Tell me about it."

Vague memories came back to her. Lying in her bed in the middle of a rainy night. She'd been half-awake, warm and dry. No, hot. So hot there. Surely, he didn't need to know about that. "I'd rather not discuss it."

His ice blue gaze focussed on her face. "I'd rather you did. As part of our agreement."

"Oh, very well." She took a breath and allowed the images to fill her mind. "I'd been asleep, having a very strange dream. In my dream, I'd been riding a horse." She hesitated. "Astride. Without a saddle."

"Go on."

"It was a very singular horse. Warm, chestnut brown. And large. Very, very large."

He didn't comment on that, but made a few more scratches with his pen. After a moment, he looked up at her. Expecting her to continue, no doubt.

She cleared her throat. "The beast was so impossibly huge — his back so broad — that I had to spread my legs as far apart as I could to stay seated. And he kept running and running, and the muscles of his back kept bunching and rolling under me. Faster and harder. Until something happened inside me — some kind of aching. It woke me up."

God help her, it was all happening again. That throbbing between her legs. Right now as she shifted in the chair, the leather rubbing against that part of her body.

"And you touched yourself then?" he asked.

"When I awoke I discovered that my hand was pressed against myself there. So, I moved my fingers, squeezing."

"And … ?" he said.

Sweet Lord, she didn't have to tell him all this, did she? It had all taken place so long ago. What could it have to do with her current problem?

"And … ?" he repeated, insistent now.

"It sent such a shock through me. It frightened me. I could scarcely breathe."

"Was this shock painful, unpleasant?"

"No, it was very pleasant. But too strong. Frightening. Overpowering."

"What did you do?" he asked.

"I moved my hand to pull the covers under my chin. Then I lay very, very still until I could fall back asleep again. It seemed to take hours."

"Thank you," he said. He set his pen aside and reached toward her. His fingers touched the top button of the shirt she wore, and she jumped nearly out of her skin. "I'm not going to hurt you," he said softly. "I only want to look at your throat."

She took a steadying breath and tried to relax as he unfastened the button and moved the fabric aside. He peered intently at her skin, at the violent flush that covered her neck and shoulders. Then he moved his hands to where the pulse beat at the base of her throat. He must have liked what he discovered there, because a tiny smile crossed his lips. He closed the shirt and studied her. "You're embarrassed."

"Yes."

"Is it only that? Or is there more reason for you to color like this?"

She could lie. Anyone would be embarrassed to tell a story like that. He'd believe her if she lied. "There's more," she answered. "Much more."

He made no comment but merely rose from his chair and walked to a book shelf, leaving her to sit where she was. Miserable and ashamed and excited beyond any reason. She hugged the shirt around her and moved once again, trying to find some release. But everything she did made matters worse.

After a moment, he returned with a large volume bound in leather. "I want you to look at some pictures and tell me how they make you feel."

He resumed his seat and set the book in front of her. "What do you know about the male anatomy?"

If it was possible for her skin to grow even hotter, it did. She could feel the blush to the roots of her hair. "I've seen my cat groom himself. I know there's something that grows stiff on a man the same way it does on my cat."

"But you've never seen a man in that state."

"No. Cousin Henry did push his hips against me that time, and I felt a hardness there. I assume that's what that was."

"Charming fellow, your cousin Henry," he said. "You're not marrying him, I hope."

"Certainly not. No one in my family can abide him."

"Good." He opened the book, looking at the pages upside-down. "Look at this picture and tell me what you see."

She glanced down and found a picture of a naked man and woman sitting on a blanket in a sunlit grove. A very distinct protuberance stuck straight out from the man's body. "It looks like a shaft, I imagine," she said. "And there's a rather large, reddened tip on the end."

"Does it frighten you?" he said.

"No," she answered. "That is, yes, a little. But it's not unattractive, either. It's compelling in an odd way."

"Look at some more pictures," he said.

She turned a page and found a brown-skinned couple, both partially clad. The man was fondling the woman's breast while she stroked his shaft. Both appeared to be enjoying themselves immensely. She turned another page, and a little cry of alarm escaped her lips before she could stop it.

"What's wrong?" he said.

"This man," she managed to gasp, looking down at the picture. It showed a man and woman in Asian dress. Preparing to couple, no doubt. But oh dear heaven, no one could be proportioned like this man. His thing was as thick as a woman's forearm and almost as long. "It isn't possible. No man could be built like this."

Dr. Slade looked at the page and laughed. "That's *shenga*," he said. "A Japanese form where the size of the man's cock is exaggerated for stylistic purposes."

"So, it isn't real?"

"No." He turned the page and glanced at another picture. "This is more realistic for the average man."

She studied another depiction of a male nude, his thick cock standing proudly erect. The proportions of this man seemed much more possible, but he was still very imposing, indeed. A woman was supposed to take something this large inside her body?

"May I ask you a question?" she said, looking up and meeting Dr. Slade's gaze straight on. "You're made the same as these men, aren't you?"

"Yes."

"Are you as big as this man?"

He looked again at the picture briefly. "Rather larger, actually."

Oh dear heaven.

"You'll see for yourself soon," he added. "All I'd need to do is stand before you now, and you'd get a very good idea of the size of my rod from the bulge in the front of my pants."

She raised her hands to her lips. "You're in that, um, state now? Even as we sit here?"

"I've been fully erect since you told me about your dream." He smiled at her, more than a hint of challenge in his eyes. "Would you like to see for yourself?"

"Oh, dear," she gasped, too terrified and too fascinated to say yes or no.

He rose and walked around the desk until he stood right in front of her. He parted the sides of his jacket, and true to his word, an enormous bulge distended his trousers. She stared at it and swallowed hard. Heaven help her, her fingers ached to touch the thing. To stroke him and see what he'd do. But she didn't. She just sat and gaped at him.

After what seemed like several minutes, he reached out a hand toward her. "Come."

Chapter Two

Felicity had no idea where Dr. Slade would lead her, but given the fact that she'd put herself in a position where she could refuse him nothing, she could hardly start making demands now. So, like a good, little marionette, she put her hand in his much larger one and rose from her seat. He didn't take her far. Only to a settee at one end of the room, where he sat, spread his legs apart, and patted one knee. "Sit," he said.

"On your lap?"

"You wanted me to kiss you, didn't you?"

"Yes."

"We can do that in a different position," he said. "But this is the easiest."

She stepped between his legs, into the sphere of the warmth of his body and the smell of his shaving soap. He reached up and put his hands around her waist, finally guiding her down onto his knee. She kept her bare toes firmly anchored in the carpet and looked downward, away from his face.

Unfortunately, her gaze settled on the front of his pants. His jacket had fallen open when he sat, giving her a clear view of the bulge she'd seen before. She really ought to look away, but the thing held her gaze. It wasn't shapeless, really, but rather a ridge — long and thick — starting at the base of his torso and straining up toward his waist. Exactly like the shafts she'd seen in those paintings. She could almost make out the contour of the head.

Her heart beat faster just looking at him that way. But no matter how engrossing she found his body, she would have to remember always that she had refused him one thing. He would not put that impressive instrument into her, no matter how much they both wanted it.

"Do you like what you see?" he asked.

She looked into his face and found amusement in his eyes. " 'Like' is a silly word, don't you think?" she replied.

"A good answer, Miss Wells. What word would you use?"

"Compelling. A little frightening. Quite removed from my experience so far in life." She looked straight into his face. No matter what, she would not allow him to catch her staring like a startled doe at that part of his body again. "Am I to touch you there?"

"Not today. Today we concentrate on your body."

"Oh." The sound rushed out of her before she could compose herself. He might have interpreted that one syllable as disappointment, when in fact, it was more surprise. The mere thought of him concentrating on her body had made her even more aware of the pressure of his shirt against her breasts and the heat between her legs where her bare flesh met the wool of his trousers.

He didn't react to her utterance but merely studied her face intently. "What are you feeling, right now?"

Her cheeks grew hot with embarrassment, but she'd made this bargain with him, and she planned to keep her part. "Breathless," she answered. "I feel as if the air is fluid somehow and I can't get enough into my lungs."

"Kiss me," he commanded softly.

"How?"

"However it pleases you. Just touch your lips to mine for a start."

Sitting on his lap, her face was at the same level as his, and she only needed to lean toward him to bring his mouth within reach. He did the most amazing thing as she approached. He closed his eyes, almost the way a cat does when it's being petted. She brought up her fingers to stroke the angular line of his jaw before she covered the last distance and kissed him.

His lips were warm and dry as she tasted them, and although they yielded to hers, they made no movement of their own. He was leaving all the choices to her, it appeared. Letting her decide where to take the kiss. That knowledge warmed her heart, banishing any fear. She took a breath, savoring the scent of him and then closed her own eyes and gave herself over to kissing him in earnest.

Sweet, so impossibly sweet, this touching of mouths. That made no sense, and yet it couldn't be denied. She sampled his upper lip and then his bottom one, nipping at it gently. Tasting his nectar. A sigh escaped her, and she slipped her arms around his neck to pull herself to him.

Finally, he responded. His lips parted and he moved them against hers. At first gently, tentatively, and then with more authority — joining hers in a dance of sorts. Urging and teasing and cajoling. All the while, his hands roamed over her back, warming her and bringing her breasts against the solid muscle of his chest. Reality dissolved, leaving her with nothing but his kiss and his warmth. And the ache that radiated out from her bosom to places below.

He made a soft groaning sound in the back of his throat and ran his tongue over her lower lip. The light rasping sent a tremor through her, and she let her own tongue venture out to find his. When they met, the contact created such a jolt of pleasure, she cried out.

He pulled back immediately. "I'm sorry. I promised I wouldn't do that."

"If I didn't want you to," she answered in a voice that had grown oddly strained. "I was only surprised that it felt so good."

He smiled, and the expression gentled his features, as did the softness of the lips she'd so thoroughly kissed and the drowsy look in his eyes. "You were right, Miss Wells. You are a very quick study."

She blushed at the compliment and also at the rush of unfamiliar sensations. How could simple contact with a man she hardly knew set her heart to racing? And why had her skin grown hotter than any amount of embarrassment could have caused? And why was she throbbing between her thighs when he hadn't even touched her there? Yet.

"Yes," he whispered. "You're an apt student. A perfect delight to instruct."

He pressed his mouth to the base of her throat, where he'd earlier tested her pulse. She let her head fall back in pleasure while he nipped and kissed a path up her throat to her ear. He nibbled on the lobe, and his breath slipped into her ear, making her own breath catch loudly.

"What are you feeling?" he whispered. "Tell me."

"I feel as if my flesh is on fire. As if flames were licking at me instead of your tongue."

"And now?" he murmured, as his lips skimmed the line of her jaw.

"Oh," she cried. "I can't say. That is … it's all so … oh … overpowering."

He pulled his face back and gazed into her eyes, his own eyes heavy-lidded and hungry looking. "But you're not afraid."

She took a shaky breath. "No, I'm not afraid."

"Good. We'll explore further." He reached for the second button of the shirt she wore — the top one still undone from before. She watched in fascination as his fingers worked at that button. And then the next. And the next. Any modest girl ought to stop him. Any decent girl would swoon from mortification. And although she did feel faint, it was only from pleasure and delicious anticipation of what would come next.

Finally, he had them all opened, and he gently pushed the shirt open to expose her body to his view. He appeared as fascinated with her as she had been earlier with the swelling in his pants. She looked down at herself and tried to picture what he saw.

Her skin had turned a bright pink, but then, she'd guessed as much by the way it felt. Her breasts rose and fell with her rapid breathing, and the nipples had turned into hard, little peaks surrounded by rosy flesh. Below lay the curves of her belly and hips. Would he think them too fat?

And there between her legs sat the thatch of brown curls that hid her sex.

"What will my husband see when he looks at me?" she asked. "Will he find me acceptable?"

"Acceptable?" he answered. "My dear Miss Wells, any man who finds you anything less than exemplary is a fool."

"You like what you see?" she asked.

" 'Like' is a silly word." He moved a hand under one of her breasts and tested its weight. "These are small and perfect. Firm like ripe fruit. My mouth waters at the prospect of tasting them."

"Please do," she breathed. Heaven help her, but she ached to have him do exactly that.

"In good time." He moved his hand lower, over her belly to her hip and the outside of her thigh. "Your legs are long and graceful. Your thighs delightfully plump."

"Not too plump?"

"Just right to warm a man's ears during gamahucherie."

"Gama ..."

He smiled — an endearing expression she could learn to love if she weren't careful. "Later," he said. "Much later."

"Are we to put everything off until later?" she demanded, sounding petulant even to her own ears.

"Lust shouldn't be rushed, my eager student. It's most delicious if savored. Besides, I haven't even described your most charming attribute — your cunt. You'll want my opinion of your cunt, won't you?"

Her cunt. That place between her legs that craved him, his touch. "Please," she said.

"Your little cunny is delightful," he said. "Its nest warm and inviting and the lips puckered and begging to be frigged."

"You won't," she said. "You can't. You promised."

"Not with my cock, although he's more than ready and up to the job. My poor ramrod will have to be disappointed today."

"Not today," she said. "Not ever."

"I'm a man of my word, Miss Wells. But there are things I can do that will leave you a virgin. And right now your sweet pussy is weeping against my trousers. I must touch it."

Dear heaven, what such language did to her. She ought to cover her ears and run from the room, but the mere thought of his hard cock — eager and straining to be inside her — made her want to stroke him there. And he had spoken about her pussy weeping. Somehow she'd grown quite wet between her legs, hot liquid burning her flesh. Whatever was building inside her, he could cure it with his touch. She knew that even though she had no idea how she knew.

"May I touch your cunt, Miss Wells?" he whispered. "May I press against the nubbin there and bring you relief?"

"Yes," she gasped. "Please."

He did, and she nearly shrieked with delight, it felt so good. He stroked her fur and then separated the lips and stroked at her core. She clung to his neck as he rubbed and rubbed. "Dear Lord, I'm going to swoon," she cried. "I don't swoon. I never swoon, but oh heaven …"

"You're going to spend," he answered. "Give yourself up to it."

As though she had any choice. The pressure of his fingers, the insistent friction against the seat of her pleasure. The stroking, the fire, the lightening building there. She couldn't endure it. Surely, it would kill her.

If that weren't enough, he bent and covered her breast with his mouth. A whole new set of sensations rushed through her, connecting with the heat at her core. She gasped in her delight as he sucked there. Without knowing what she did, she squeezed her legs together around his hand, sending her ever closer to the something. Something she couldn't name and couldn't avoid.

"Yes, my sweet," he muttered against her bosom. "Yes, that's it. Come now, give me your cream."

He rubbed her even harder, faster. She responded deep inside, the pressure coiling and building. She rested her head against his shoulder and shut her eyes as her hips moved against his hand, seeking out his rhythm and finding it.

Finally, it was on her. A wave of fire, starting where his fingers played with her and radiating out to her breasts, her heart, her very being. She contracted and then convulsed — spasm chasing spasm — as she cried out in delirium. Over and over and over. Oh, heaven, so sweet. So powerful.

And then she felt spent, weak and helpless. She hung on his neck, her head still on his shoulder, and sobbed out her joy. He removed his hand from her nest and brought it to her face as he tucked her head under his chin. Her own scent clung to his fingers — musky and warm. He stroked her hair and made comforting noises in his throat while she felt the life slowly return to her limbs.

"Still not frightened?" he said.

"No," she whispered, her throat quite dry. She licked her lips. "That was … that was … oh dear."

"That was what?"

"That was wonderful," she sighed.

He chuckled and slid his arms around her, pulling her close to his chest. She surrendered to him, to the comfort and peace of his embrace. The feelings were every bit as delicious as the passion he'd just aroused but far more dangerous. In fact, as her brain started to understand what had just happened to her, she realized one more thing. No matter what, she could not give her heart to him. For her very survival, she must not come to love this man.

꼭◦◦(⌒)◦◦꼭

Marc sat and watched Miss Wells pace around his study like a caged cat. She wore his shirts easily now — always buttoned, but never all the way up to her throat. Sometimes she even kept on her boots, stockings, and garters so that he had to make some effort for a glimpse of smooth, white thigh. Today she was barefoot and quite put out with him, if he correctly read the over-the-shoulder scowls she sent him as she padded across the carpet this way and that. Good. He'd planned for her to want a great deal more than she was getting from him, and it appeared his plan had worked.

"The soles of your feet must be burned from so much friction against my carpet," he said. "Why don't you come over here and sit down?"

"Whatever for?" she replied.

"We can talk more easily without so much distance between us."

She snorted, for not the first time that afternoon. "Talk. Is that all you want to do? Talk?"

"Hardly," he answered. "We do a great deal more than just talk."

She huffed and crossed her arms beneath her breasts. The action bunched up those two delectable mounds of flesh and stretched the linen of his shirt over their rigid peaks. By now she had to know that the sight of her that way inflamed him. And sure enough, she glanced at him out of the corner of her eye, her gaze resting pointedly on where his fully engorged member pressed hard against the front of his pants.

She'd turned into quite a coquette in the four weeks he'd been instructing her. But she hadn't learned to win her way in everything yet, and she wasn't going to on this particular afternoon, either.

" 'Talk' hardly describes our afternoons together," he continued. "I've worked hard to bring you to completion on your every visit. Sometimes more than once."

She didn't answer but stared intently at the wall opposite her.

"I've been a very diligent paramour, haven't I?" he said.

Still stony silence from the very obstinate Miss Wells.

"Haven't I?" he demanded.

"Yes," she answered finally.

"But you want more, don't you?"

"Yes."

"You want my cock where my fingers have been, don't you?"

This time chagrin held her tongue, as her cheeks and throat turned a furious red. Dear God, her blushes of embarrassment were almost as appealing as the flush of passion on her skin just before she spent. If she managed to keep that innocence while also indulging her lascivious nature, she'd make the most glorious wanton the world had ever seen. If he were ever to shackle himself to one woman for a lifetime, it would have to be such a woman.

"You promised to hide nothing from me," he said. "You want my cock where my fingers have been, don't you?"

"Yes," she answered in a small voice. "And it's impossible."

He patted the settee beside him. "Come and sit and talk to me."

This time, she obeyed. She crossed the carpet and dropped down beside him. He reached out to stroke her cheek with the backs of his fingers. She sighed in pleasure, the way she always did when he caressed her. The simple trust inherent in her response always touched something inside him, and more and more he found himself stroking her whenever he had the chance.

"Tell me of your impending marriage," he said. "When is it to be?"

"Four months from now."

"You'll have all you could want of a man's cock after that," he said. "Surely you can wait that long."

"I suppose so," she said, but she didn't sound at all convinced.

Poor thing. He really would feel sorry for her if he didn't know beyond any uncertainty that he'd planned the very best introduction to the male appendage that she could hope for. Few men realized how intimidating a stiff rod could be to the uninitiated female. Especially one as large as his own. They simply reached into their pants and pulled out long tom, expecting the girl to swoon with delight.

Miss Felicity Wells wouldn't get a view of him naked, much less a touch of his stiff sex, until she wanted nothing more in the world than to fondle him. Unfortunately, that meant that every Monday, Wednesday, and Friday afternoon he had to allow his cock to swell to almost painful stiffness — a state it had no difficulty achieving at all — so that she could look but not touch.

All would work out for the best for both of them. If the waiting didn't kill him first.

"Tell me about your fiancé," he said. "I don't even know his name."

"George Wilmont," she answered. "Of the textile Wilmonts."

"Very wealthy," he said. He moved his hand to beneath her chin and began to stroke her throat. "Do you love him?"

"I told you I didn't."

"And does he love you?"

She grasped his hand and lowered it from her neck, toying with his fingers. "Why does that matter?"

He settled their entwined hands in her lap where he could burrow his fingers under the tails of his shirt and fondle her thigh. "It seems sad to marry someone you don't care for at all."

"We both know what sort of partnership we're entering. We've been very specific about what we expect."

He slid his fingers down toward her knee and back in the direction of her sex. "And what is that?"

"I'll be a model wife for him. The sort of wife a man in his station deserves. And he'll be a devoted husband."

"You mean, he won't let his affections stray."

She looked at him, a light of defiance in her eyes. "You've told me your opinion of marital fidelity."

"It's impossible. We're all designed to seek gratification where we find it. From as many willing partners as possible."

"I won't," she answered, her expression positively radiating anger. "I wouldn't do that to someone I cared for or even liked."

"Women stray as often as men. Or at least they would if the penalty for being caught weren't so much greater than it is for men."

"No," she insisted.

"It's human nature," he said. "You may try to pretend you're different, but after a while, you'd find yourself noticing other men, wanting them. No matter how happy your husband makes you."

"No!" She started to rise, but he held her with firm but gentle pressure against her thigh.

"Why does this upset you so?"

"Because I've seen what happens. I've seen the damage, the misery."

"Tell me what it is you've seen."

She stared down in her lap and bit her lip, looking for all the world as she had on that day of their first visit. When she'd been near tears. He took her chin in his hand and turned her face to him. "Tell me, Felicity."

"My mother ... that is, my father. He's been such a beast over the years. Everyone knows how he is. I couldn't even have a friend home from school without him trying to molest her in our own house."

She stopped speaking and searched his face for something. He held very still, letting her decide whether to trust him with her story.

"He's always had other women — high born and low. He takes them out in public sometimes. As though he wants us to know what he's doing. As though he intends to hurt us. I hate him. I'll never forgive him for what he's done. Never."

"He's acting out of selfishness, not lust," Marc said. "That's domination, imposing one's will on everyone weaker."

"You can call it what you want, but it's nearly killed my mother. Sometimes I've been afraid she'd harm herself — anything to escape the humiliation." She took a shuddering breath. "That won't happen to me. I won't let it happen."

"And so that's why you came to me — in hopes that I could make you so desirable to your husband he'd always be faithful."

She looked back into her lap again. "Don't laugh."

"I'm not laughing." The poor child had set herself an impossible task. She'd even brought herself to a complete stranger and offered the most embarrassing intimacies in hopes of winning what no man would ever give — perfect fidelity. If anyone deserved what she wanted, it was Felicity Wells. If ever he were to devote himself to one woman, it would have to be someone like her. But that wasn't the nature of men.

Oh, well. The only thing he could do was teach her what he could. And perhaps their amorous sessions would make pleasant memories that would help her through the unhappiness when the inevitable happened.

"Kiss me," he said.

She studied him intently but didn't move toward him. "Will you let me touch you?"

"You touch me all the time."

"Not your face or your chest," she said. "I want to touch you … there."

Great progress. She'd come out and asked point blank for what she wanted. Next she'd have to name it. "Where?"

She looked down at the front of his pants. "There."

"My rod?"

"Yes."

"Say it."

She took a breath. "Your rod."

"My cock?"

"Yes."

He sat in silence, waiting for her to repeat the word.

"Your cock. Your yard. Your sex. I want to touch your prick. I want to fondle your erection. Is that good enough?"

"Very well done, indeed," he replied.

"So, may I finally touch it?"

"No," he said. "You're not ready."

"Damn." She pushed aside his hand and rose from the settee. "Damn you," she cried as she paced toward the desk.

"Such language, Miss Wells." He watched her begin her pacing again and did his best to stifle his amusement. Where before he'd seen a flush of embarrassment, now he found one of pure fury. The woman was magnificent in all her moods. If only she knew how Priapus strained against his trousers aching for just what she wanted to give him.

"You hold back from me exactly what I need to know to accomplish my goal," she said. "You expect me to sit obediently next to you and expose all of myself so that you can toy with me."

"I've never toyed with you."

"I have to tell you everything — my dreams, the unholy fantasies I have about you, every sensation while you take me apart with your fingers. And what do you give back? Nothing."

"I give you those sensations."

"It's not enough," she declared. "I've opened myself up to you completely. I must have some part of you in exchange."

"You're right," he said. She stopped dead and stared at him as if he'd started speaking some foreign language. "You have made yourself open to me, while I've remained hidden," he went on. "It's time for me to reciprocate."

That seemed to take some of the starch out of her anger. "Thank you."

He patted the settee again. "Come and sit down, and I'll tell you one of my favorite fantasies."

She quickly joined him again. "Should I sit on your lap while you tell it?"

"No," he said. "I think it safest that you sit there."

She settled her hands in her lap and waited. How in hell was he going to get through this telling without begging her to give him some relief? Bad enough to tell her his favorite lascivious daydream, but lately she'd played the major part in it. And there was nothing he could do but tell her.

"I imagine I'm at the opera," he said. "With a lady whose body I crave desperately but with whom I'm alone for the very first time. From the looks she gives me throughout the performance and the way she moves against her chair, I can tell that the feelings are mutual. After some time, I become bold and start to caress her throat and bare shoulders with my fingers. When she doesn't object, I lower my hand to her bodice and press it between her breasts."

"And no one else sees you?" she asked.

"It's a private box."

"But they don't have walls all around. Someone could see you."

"It's a fantasy, Miss Wells. I don't plan to actually try this."

"I'm sorry," she said. "Please continue."

He closed his eyes for a moment, letting his mind wander to the images that inflamed his lust more and more often now. Felicity Wells sitting next to him in a brocade chair as he fondled her breasts below the bodice of her gown. As he felt her nipples harden and listened to her breathing grow uneven.

"Eventually, she becomes adventurous, too," he said, opening his eyes again. "She reaches over to the front of my pants and strokes my member. At first slowly and then faster, until I'm quite beside myself and ready to explode."

"I'd like to do that," she said, her voice husky. God in heaven, he'd like her to do it. Right now. It wouldn't take much to make him come. Oh hell, how was he ever to survive this exquisite torture?

"What happens then?" she asked.

"I somehow manage to get my hand under her skirts and up into her pussy. When I realize she isn't wearing drawers and had planned a seduction ahead of time, I almost spend on the spot. But I hold on to my control until I can feel her growing wetter and wetter and I know that she's as desperate to couple as I am."

"Oh, my," she gasped.

"Somehow by mutual understanding, we both know that we can wait no longer. She rises from her chair and lifts her skirts while I unbutton my pants and let my engorged cock spring free. Then, I put my hands around her waist and lower her slowly onto me. Both of us nearly scream with the pleasure, but just then the music is reaching a crescendo, covering our cries. I plow into her as fast and as hard as I can manage, and she rides the length of me until we both spend, the music washing over us in our bliss."

She licked her lips and stared wide-eyed at him. "That's … oh, my … very … um … very …"

"Yes, it is."

Without warning, she reached her hand to him and covered the thick ridge of his flesh with her palm. A jolt of pleasure raced through him, and he groaned. Another moment, and he'd have no control left. He could deny her nothing. But somehow, he managed to grasp her fingers and stop her. "It's time," he managed between his clenched teeth.

"I know," she answered.

"No," he tried again. "It's time for you to go home."

"But I don't want to."

He stared into her face. "If you don't go right now, I'll detain you. And you'll be late, and your mother will miss you."

"I don't want to go home," she said. "I want to stay here with you."

He didn't answer but just glared at her. Didn't she know he didn't want her to go home, either? But what choice did they have?

"Oh very well," she said finally, staring right back at him. "But I'm coming back in two days, and I will look at you and touch you then. I will know you. Do you understand?"

"Go home, Miss Wells."

Chapter Three

Marc knew instantly that it was a dream, but the knowledge in no way decreased the intensity of the images. Felicity Wells lay on a bed of cushions, surrounded by wild flowers, in a sun-drenched meadow. She was wholly and completely naked, her arms outstretched toward him in invitation. God knew he'd seen her unclothed before. He'd often held her in his arms and opened one of his own shirts to expose her perfection to his view. He'd watched her flush with excitement and then surrender to the force of one orgasm after another. And yet, he'd never seen her quite as wanton as she looked right now as she lay there, stretching and turning, her lips parted in a silent plea.

Please, Marc, her mind called to his. *Please, Marc. Take me. The need, the hunger. I can't bear it all. Take me.*

"But, I can't take your virginity. You told me that," he answered.

This is a dream. You can have me in a dream, she said. *Hurry, please.*

She held her arms up toward him, showing him her breasts. How many times he'd kissed them. How many times he'd taken the rosy nipples into his mouth and teased them to hardness. He could do that now. He could devour every inch of her body. He could drive into her, bring himself the completion he'd craved for so long. He could do all that now. But for some reason, his feet wouldn't move.

She reached down and stroked the insides of her thighs, parting her legs. *Please, my darling. Please, my Marc. I need you here. Please.*

He watched her and wanted her and couldn't move. God help him, something always stood between him and the satisfaction she could give him. Even in his dreams.

Come to me, she begged. *I want you as much as you want me. I know you want me.*

"I can't," he said.

You're so beautiful, so magnificent. I want to touch you. I want to stroke you, pet you, make you come.

"I can't," he cried.

Your cock says you can. He wants me, I know he does. He's so big, so hard for me.

Marc looked down at himself and realized that his clothes had disappeared. He was as naked as she was and hopelessly aroused for her inspection. His member had grown to mammoth proportions, as if in *shenga*. He touched himself and nearly came apart. He was going to spurt into his own hand in a moment because he couldn't have her. No matter what, he couldn't have her, and the loss was going to kill him. "I can't," he gritted. "I promised you, and now I can't move."

I release you, my darling. I release you. Come to me.

Finally, his feet moved, and he went to her and dropped down onto the cushions beside her. She immediately grasped his throbbing cock. She stroked him, her slender fingers pale against his reddened sex. He grew even harder and bigger. Impossible, but true.

My pretty man, she crooned to his rod. *So large, so stiff, so hot. You'll find peace soon enough.* She lay back against the cushions and looked up into his face. Her expression made his breath catch. Innocence and lust. Vulnerability and hunger. Her eyes widened, until he felt he could fall into them and lose himself inside her soul. Instead, he'd lose himself inside her body. He positioned himself between her welcoming thighs and drove his sex into hers.

She let her head fall back as a cry of pure, animal pleasure escaped her throat. He pulled almost out of her and thrust back in until his cock was buried in her flesh up to the hilt. She arched her back, meeting his thrust, and her breasts pressed into his chest. So beautiful, she cried. *So beautiful. Oh, my darling.*

He'd made love so many times, and it had never been like this — blood pounding in his ears and fire burning in his groin. Impossible and inevitable. He would have her, over and over. He would make her writhe beneath him. He'd make her spend and spend all over his member until he joined her in bliss.

Only, he couldn't. He'd promised.

In an instant, Marc was awake and lying in his bedroom. He had quite a cockstand pressed into the bed, and in a moment he was going to shoot his sperm onto the sheet. Nothing could keep him from coming, and he might as well make it as good as he could.

So, for the first time since his youth, he took his erection into his hand and began to stroke himself, closing his eyes in hopes of re-joining Felicity in that field. Instead he imagined her in his study. He and Felicity together on the Oriental carpet in front of a fire, and he took his furious member out of his pants and drove it into her pussy. She spent immediately, throbbing all around him, milking his sex with her spasms.

Oh, God, just that image. He bit the pillowcase and kept stroking with his fingers until he could stand no more. Pressure built at the base of his spine, then rushed through his groin to his cock as he spent. Wave after wave of his sperm spilled out of him as he came into the sheets. Finally relieved, he collapsed, gasping for breath.

God, what she did to him, even in his imagination. He'd never wanted a woman so badly in his life. That made no sense, of course. As modest and quiet as she'd been on her first visit, he'd never have noticed her if she'd passed him on the street. Quiet, little things with unremarkable brown eyes and hair had never excited him before. So, why did she have him so at his wits' end?

She wasn't modest anymore. He'd seen to that. She pouted and flirted. She demanded more and more from him, just as he had hoped she would. She'd learned how to take pleasure with great enthusiasm — a trait that would make her husband a lucky man, indeed. The fact that Marc wouldn't take personal gratification from her education didn't make him happy, but it couldn't be avoided. Felicity Wells required nothing less than marriage and total fidelity — things he couldn't possibly give her. So, he'd give her pleasure and take her impressions and feelings for his own pursuit of knowledge. They'd both agreed to that. Why didn't it seem enough now?

Oh, hell. He didn't have to be a martyr in all this. He'd promised to teach her how to satisfy a man, and he could best do that by showing her how to please him. She'd been insisting on access to his body for some time, and he'd only held back to make her want him enough to overcome her shyness. She had fewer and fewer reservations now, and he might as well let her get over the last of them. She was ready to see a fully-grown and fully-aroused man and learn how to please him.

At their very next meeting — two days hence — she'd get her wish finally. He'd bare himself and let her see exactly what happened when a man reached fulfillment. He could think of several ways that didn't involve harming her virginity.

He might have her press her breasts around his cock while he thrust himself between them. He'd spend that way, sure enough. Or he might undress them both and then position himself behind her so that he could press his rod between her thighs. She could reach down and stroke the head while he pumped until he came into her hand. Perhaps he'd have her wear a glove while he did that. Perhaps a black glove so that he could watch over her shoulder as his sperm went onto the fabric.

Damn, what an image. He'd become hard again, just thinking of it. His hand was still closed around his member, and he could feel it growing thick all over again. If she were here now, he'd be ready to take her, to roll her onto her back and bury himself in her and go again. How could that be possible?

Of course, he could stroke himself again and give his body ease. But he already had quite a mess to clean up before he went back to sleep.

He'd save this erection for Miss Wells and her education. Yes, indeed, she wanted to see him aroused. She'd have her wish and more. She'd learn about the male body on her very next visit.

✻✲✐(⌒)✑✲✻

Dr. Slade greeted Felicity in his robe de chambre the next time she visited him. His lack of clothing startled her so badly that she almost went back down the steps and up the street before she remembered that for the past several weeks she'd been insisting he disrobe for her. Now she had what she wanted, and she hardly knew what to do with it. He was so tall, so broad-shouldered, so imposing.

Well, she wasn't about to let him see her hesitation, not after all the effort she'd put into getting him to expose any part of himself — physical or emotional. So she squared her shoulders and gave him what she hoped was a confident smile.

"You were expecting me, I trust, and not some other fortunate female," she said.

"This is our appointed time," he answered.

She studied his face but, as usual, could read little there. His ice-blue eyes looked back at her intently, one might even say hungrily, but he gave no hint of pleasure or displeasure at seeing her. Would she ever fathom the man?

"Shall I have my lessons on your front stoop today?" she asked. "Or would you prefer your study?"

That at least brought an embarrassed smile to his face. He stepped back, pulling the door open. "Please come in."

She walked in front of him and along the foyer she'd crossed so many times now. But today it seemed like a very long walk, indeed. Almost as if she were headed toward her own execution. Dear heaven, what a preposterous idea. She'd nearly begged for this encounter, and now her knees felt like water.

He didn't say anything as he followed her into the study. She turned and gave him another smile. "Shall I undress as usual?"

He gestured toward the screen. "Please."

She noticed the fire in the grate then. A pleasant blaze, although totally unnecessary for the weather. Maybe he'd meant it to comfort her. He'd set some cushions in front of the fire, too. Their trysting site for the day. It looked very inviting.

She glanced at him and found the same even gaze trained on her. As his robe fell more loosely around his person than his trousers, she couldn't even tell if he was aroused. That would come later.

She stepped behind the screen and proceeded to undress as quickly as her trembling fingers allowed. She was already working on her small clothes when he finally spoke. "How long have you been coming here?"

"Six weeks, I think. The weather's been good, so I haven't missed many of our afternoons."

"Have you enjoyed them?" he asked.

Enjoyed? She'd hadn't begun this for her own enjoyment. She'd come to him to learn, and learn she had. She continued removing her clothes. "Have you enjoyed them?"

He laughed, although the sound came out strained. "They've tried me sorely, but I think I'll enjoy today's session."

"Then, I will, too." She took off her drawers and found his shirt where it hung on the regular hook. She slipped into it and stepped around the screen.

He stood in the middle of the room, tall and handsome and as inscrutable as usual. His robe still gave no clue as to the state of his sex, but one way or another she'd find out soon.

He stared at her for a moment and then took a deep breath. "Have I told you how beautiful you are?"

Her heart stumbled in its rhythm. What an amazing thing for him to say. "You've complimented various parts of my body," she answered. "I don't suppose that's the same thing."

"I don't suppose it is."

"Then, no, you haven't told me I'm beautiful."

"Men can be asses. You needed to learn that lesson, too." He stretched out his arms toward her. "Come to me."

She walked into his embrace without hesitation and wrapped her arms around his neck, reaching upward and bringing her body against his chest. He bent and took her lips for a kiss, and she surrendered to the heat of his mouth. Before his clothing had always separated them, and although he still wore a robe and she still wore his shirt, they were nevertheless closer than they'd ever been before. His warmth and his scent surrounded her — an intoxicating combination. As his lips and tongue worked their magic on her mouth, she reached to his chest and parted the robe so that she could slip her fingers inside against his skin.

He was solid and hot under her palms. She smoothed her hands against the curling hairs and moved the robe upward toward his shoulders and then down his arms, baring his chest and watching her palms stroke him. He held perfectly still, but when she rubbed his male nipples with her thumbs, he trembled ever so slightly.

"Dear heaven, you're stunning," she sighed. "I never imagined."

"Not even in your dreams?"

"Not even in my dreams." She reached up and nuzzled the underside of his chin then planted a path of kisses along his throat, downward until she could run her tongue over his collarbone. "I want ... oh dear heaven ... I want so much."

"What?" he demanded. "What do you want?"

She smoothed her hands over the muscles of his upper arms and marveled at the steel-under-satin feel. "I want to devour you, Dr. Slade. One inch at a time."

He groaned — a deep, animal sound in the back of his throat. "I do believe you'll be the death of me, Miss Wells."

She looked up at him. "You won't deny me today, will you? I may have my way with you, mayn't I?"

"Oh, God," he moaned.

"I'll assume that means 'yes.' " She unfastened the belt of his robe and pushed it off him completely. Underneath, he was totally and magnificently naked. And aroused. She could only stare at him in awe.

"What are you thinking?" he said. "Right now."

She looked down at him, at his erect cock where it stood rigidly out from his body. She licked her lips. "I'm thinking that you didn't exaggerate. Not one little bit."

"You're not frightened?"

"No. But if I thought you were planning to use that to take my virginity, I'd be terrified."

"I'd be as gentle as I could," he said. "If I were going to do that."

"But you're not going to do that."

"I've given you my promise more than once," he said.

True, he had. And he'd never done anything to suggest he'd changed his mind. So, why did she fear that so constantly? Because it was something she wanted? One of the many things she'd learned during these sessions was to be honest with herself, and now she had to face the fact that she wanted him to know her fully. She wanted him to take her virginity and make her his. She wanted that desperately. But she couldn't have him in that way. She could, however, have everything else.

No, not everything else. She couldn't have his love. She couldn't even have his exclusive amorous attentions. If she wanted Dr. Marcus Slade, she'd have to share him, and she would not share the man she loved with anyone.

The pressure of his fingers against her skin brought her back to reality. He had reached to her throat and was now pushing his shirt over her shoulders. It slid down her arms and fell to the floor at her feet, leaving her just as naked as he was.

He stared down at her body, his expression heated and his breath coming fast and shallow. She pressed herself against him again, and he closed his arms around her. Of all the things she'd experienced since coming to him, this was the most remarkable. Standing in his embrace with nothing whatsoever between them — the peaks of her breasts pressed against his flesh, the heat of his body encircling her, the evidence of his arousal pressed into her body. If heaven could truly exist on Earth, this must be it. She ran her hands up his back and then down again, stroking his buttocks and pulling herself against his distended cock.

He shuddered in response. "Go slowly, Miss Wells, please."

"I don't want to go slowly."

"But you must, or this will all be over before it gets started."

She looked up at him. "I don't understand."

He gritted his teeth together in an expression that might have been pain or a tremendous inner struggle. "You will soon. Only now, don't rush things."

"Instruct me, then."

He bent and picked her up in his arms as if she weighed nothing at all. A few strides brought them to the hearth, where he lowered her onto the cushions and joined her.

In an instant, he was kissing her, setting fire to her being. His hands moved over her, pulling her against him, shaping her to his body. She let her own hands answer, measuring the width of his shoulders and testing the muscles along his arms. He was so much larger than she and so much more expert in his movements. She could only answer his caresses and pray that she could give him half the pleasure he gave her.

He slid along her body until his mouth found a nipple and closed over it. She arched her back and ran her fingers into his hair, stroking him while he sucked and teased until she could scarcely catch a breath. He moved to the other breast and took that as well. She'd grown so hot being with him like this — his body covering hers, flesh whispering against flesh. The throbbing started between her legs, and helpless to fight it, she squeezed her thighs together. Once, twice, such heavenly friction.

He put his hand there, separating her legs. "Impatient, little thing, aren't you?"

"Hurry, please," she gasped. "I'm burning."

"You have one more surprise coming," he said, and he slid his body lower. He nuzzled her navel with his nose and rained little kisses over her belly. Then his mouth moved lower and lower. Toward her sex.

"You can't," she cried. "You can't mean to kiss me there."

"That's exactly what I mean to do," he answered. "I'm going to devour your pretty cunny until you spend against my mouth."

"Oh, dear God."

"That's right, Miss Wells. Call out to your maker while I show you Paradise."

He lifted her hips, bringing her to his face, and her traitorous thighs parted for him. She reached out her hands for anything to anchor her to reality as he closed his mouth over her sex and licked the bud that was already throbbing for his touch.

He couldn't be doing this, but he was. She couldn't be responding to his caress, but she was. She turned her head and stared into the flames, trying to fight the fire in her belly. Useless. She couldn't fight something this powerful, and she'd die rather than have him stop. He nibbled and sucked and drove her mad with his tongue. She was going to spend. She was going to scream out his name and spasm against his mouth. No power on Earth could prevent it.

She closed her eyes and yielded. Beside her, the fire crackled and sent heat onto her body. She cupped her breasts with her palms and squeezed as he continued his assault. She couldn't stand much more. Another moment and she'd shatter. He nipped and then sucked and then nipped again and she was lost.

The spasms started deep in her belly, and she tossed back her head and screamed with the pleasure. She pulsated inside as the world went crimson with lust. She came and came and came, sobbing and crying, until he finally released her and she fell back against the cushions.

He joined her and pulled her into his arms. Such heaven to be with him this way — sleepy and sated and comforted by the softness of his skin. Without opening her eyes, she reached out and grazed his lips with her fingers. He caught her hand in his and kissed her fingertips. "What did you think of that?"

"Oh, my," she answered. "Will my husband do that?"

He tensed. Just the slightest stiffness to his bearing. She would have missed it entirely if he'd been wearing clothing. "He'll do it if he's a considerate lover," he answered. "Many men don't like to gamahuche their wives."

"Gamahuche?" she repeated. "That's what it's called?"

"The vulgar term. It's also called cunnilingus."

"Can women do that for men?"

His only answer was a groan. She opened her eyes to find that same expression she'd seen before. Pain or struggle, she couldn't tell which. Or maybe pleasure. "Can I do that for you?" she asked.

"Oh, God, you really will kill me."

"I can make you come that way, can't I? Is that what you're afraid of?"

"I'm not afraid of coming with you," he answered.

"Then, why do you resist it so?"

"I'm not. It's only …"

"Only nothing," she said. She reached down and grasped his sex. He shut his eyes and trembled violently. She stroked him, rubbing her fingers along the velvet of his shaft until she reached the head and ran her thumb over the very tip.

He lay back, his eyes still shut, his teeth clenched together. "You don't know what you're doing to me."

"Then, tell me. Show me. I want to make you spend."

He took several gasping breaths and opened his eyes. She almost lost herself in their blue depths as he gazed at her. "All right," he said finally. "Do what you want to me."

"May I kiss your cock?"

He groaned again. "If you want. Only remember, if I tell you to stop, do so immediately or you'll get a surprise I don't think you're ready for."

"What surprise?"

"Never mind. You'll see soon enough."

She took a breath. "What should I do?"

"Kiss my poor Johnnie," he said. "Lick it. Suck on the tip while you stroke the shaft."

She reached to his member and began to stroke. "Like this?"

"Yes. Oh, God help me. Like that." He placed his hand against her cheek. "When I tell you to stop, move your mouth and finish me with your hand."

"Very well."

"I mean it. I won't be able to tell you twice, and I want you to watch what happens."

He rested back against the cushions, and she lowered herself until she was face-to-face with his glorious member. It was long and thick — so thick at the base that she couldn't get her hand all the way around it. It felt smooth and hot in her hand. She squeezed gently and heard a breath catch in his throat. Slowly, she lowered her head and kissed the very tip. Then, bolder, she took the entire head into her mouth and sucked.

His hips bucked upwards, and she had to grasp his shaft to guide it toward her mouth. The sensation was pleasant, really, as she was taking only as much of him as she could. And his surrender, his total vulnerability, the trust it showed — they all warmed her to her core. For once, she held him in her power and she could pleasure him the way he'd done for her so many times. How she loved the feeling.

She stopped sucking and licked around the head, dipping her tongue behind and beneath it. His breath grew loud and labored, and he moaned over and over. His hips continued to move, and she had to work to keep up with him. She sucked him again and stroked and stroked until she felt him tense.

"Now!" he screamed. "Stop now!"

She obeyed immediately, releasing him from her mouth while still pumping with her hand. His body thrust upwards, once and twice, and then a hot liquid spurted out of his cock in waves. He spilled his essence into her hand while he cried her name.

Finally, he collapsed and she moved to him and took him into her arms as he had just done for her. "Was that good?" she whispered into his ear.

He half-moaned, half-laughed. "My dear Miss Wells, you have no idea."

"To the contrary, I have a very good idea."

"Your future husband is a very lucky man."

George. Odd, she hadn't imagined doing that to George. Of course, that was the whole point of this exercise — learning how to please George. But somehow she couldn't picture George surrendering himself to her in the same way as Dr. Slade had. George Wilmont would never allow himself to be that vulnerable.

Dr. Slade pulled her against him and burrowed his nose into her hair. "You've progressed remarkably, Miss Wells," he sighed. "In fact, there isn't much more I have to teach you."

She stared into his face, at the softness of his features with his eyes closed and an angelic smile on his mouth. "You're not sending me away, are you?" she asked. "I may come again, mayn't I?"

"Yes, please." He rested his head against her shoulder. "Please do come again."

Chapter Four

An entire week, and she hadn't returned. Marc stood at the window and stared up the rain-slicked street in the direction from which Miss Wells usually came. She was twenty minutes late already and no doubt wasn't coming at all. Damn this storm.

The weather had to be keeping her away. He wouldn't even consider the other explanation — that she simply didn't plan to return at all. True, he'd told her he couldn't teach her much more, but she'd asked to come back, and he'd agreed. She couldn't have decided to quit their relationship. God only knew what went on in women's minds sometimes, but Felicity Wells had a great deal more common sense than most females her age. She wouldn't take it into her head to leave him without even a good-bye, would she?

He stared out the window at the pelting rain and the leaves whipping around on the trees. The scene was bleak, desolate — just like the void inside him. At least today he hadn't undressed fully but had only removed his suit coat. The previous afternoons he'd stripped and put on his dressing gown, only to wait and wait for her, pacing his empty study. Waiting and wanting like a school boy in the throes of his first love.

For God's sake, two days ago, he'd almost gone looking for her. Imagine her parents' horror if the notorious Dr. Marcus Slade had appeared on their oh-so-proper doorstep looking for their oh-so-virginal daughter. At least that might have amused him for a while. But it wouldn't likely win him a place in Felicity's heart.

In her heart? Damn, he'd better stop thinking in that direction immediately. This had everything to do with her body and nothing to do with her heart. Still, where in hell was she?

He was just about to give up when he spotted her walking quickly up the street. She held an umbrella into the wind, obscuring her face and head, but he knew her body well enough to know it was she. Even with her skirts flapping around her legs in the storm, he recognized her quick tread. It was Felicity. It had to be.

He waited until she reached the base of his front steps and then ran into the hallway to greet her. He had the door open before she could lift the knocker. In fact, she hadn't even raised her hand to knock. She stared up at him, her eyes wide and her hair matted against her head, despite the umbrella. Her clothes were soaked into her skin. She looked cold and bedraggled and infinitely desirable.

He took her into his arms and pulled her into the foyer. She tossed her umbrella aside, and he managed to close the door without letting go of her. He kissed her — hard — pushing her up against the wall and pressing his body into hers. It had been too long. Too damned long.

She caught his face between her hands and pressed kisses first over his eyelids and then his cheeks. "I couldn't get away before," she said. "It rained and rained and rained."

"I thought you were never coming back," he answered. "I thought I'd never see you again."

She devoured his lips with an urgency that took his breath away. Over and over, she kissed him as if she'd never get enough. "I couldn't leave you forever," she murmured against his mouth. "Not that way."

He pulled her sodden hat from her head, sending hairpins everywhere. Her hair fell over his hands and around her shoulders. He pressed his face into it and drank in the smell of rain and woman.

"I thought I'd go crazy waiting," she said. "It never stopped raining, and I wanted so much to be with you."

He worked at the tiny buttons of her jacket. Thoroughly soaked, they resisted the efforts of his fingers. He tore at them frantically, even ripping one off, before he could remove the jacket and start in on the even tinier buttons of her blouse.

She had more luck with his waistcoat and had it open and over his shoulders in an instant. "I wanted to come to you," she gasped. "I missed you, missed your touch. But it just wouldn't stop raining."

"I wanted you, too," he murmured as he removed her blouse, revealing her breasts above her corset. He bent and kissed the soft flesh of her bosom. "God, how I wanted you."

"I couldn't think of any way to get free of the house," she said. "Oh, don't stop. That feels so good."

He slipped a hand into her corset and freed one breast so that he could take the nipple into his mouth. She gave a little cry and tipped her head back. "Oh, Marc. Marc. Don't stop."

Stop? He could no sooner stop than he could stop breathing. He brought his hands down her back and pulled her against him. His cock was fully engorged, and it wouldn't take much to make him spend, but he had to make her come first. To do that, he needed her naked. He unfastened her belt and then her skirt. They both fell into a heap on the floor as she removed his shirt and stroked his chest.

"I finally couldn't stand it," she said. "I told them I was going to the library."

"Thank God you came," he said as he unlaced her crinolines and finally had her down to her small clothes.

"They tried to forbid me, but in the end, I just left," she said. "Oh, please hurry."

"Why did you have to wear so damned many clothes?"

She gave out a strangled laugh and reached to her corset cover, finally pulling it up and over her head. That left only her corset and drawers, aside from her stockings and shoes. But they presented no obstacle. Just the corset and its infernal ties. She removed his shirt and tossed it to the floor. She had him naked from the waist up, and he still had to deal with her corset.

She reached down to the front of his trousers and curled her fingers around his erection. "You'll make me come," he cried.

"I want you," she answered. "I want you between my legs. Hurry."

He caught her hips and lifted her off the floor, pressing her back into the wall behind her. She slid her legs around his waist and pulled him against her sex. Even through his pants and her drawers, the heat of her pussy burned at his cock. He moved, rubbing his throbbing erection against her cunt, and she cried out her pleasure. Over and over he thrust, bringing himself to the edge of madness.

Oh God, he couldn't take her like this. Not partly dressed and in his front hallway. He mustered every bit of control he had and stilled his movements. "Inside," he gritted. "I want to feel your flesh against mine as you come."

"Then, hurry," she answered. "I can't wait much longer."

With his hands holding onto her buttocks, he carried her across the foyer and into the study. She kissed him as he went and moved her hips, rubbing against his member. Up and down and up and down. He had to set her down somewhere and finish undressing her before it was too late for both of them.

He carried her to the desk. "Push those things aside," he ordered.

She reached out with one arm and swept the contents of his desk top to the floor — papers fluttering and the crystal inkwell spilling its contents onto the Oriental carpet. As hot as she'd made him, he didn't care a damn about the rug. He set her onto her back and pulled her drawers down and over her legs. As he did, she fumbled with the buttons of his trousers. Just that pressure nearly unmanned him, but he clenched his teeth and struggled for control.

Finally, she reached inside and freed his prick. Helpless against his own lust, he pressed himself against her naked cunt. He hadn't managed to get rid of the corset, and now he couldn't wait.

He pressed his cock against her so that the shaft thrust between the lips of her sex and the head pressed against her clitoris with every movement. Heaven, or almost. Heaven lay inside her, but he couldn't have that. He moved his hips over and over, listening to her cries grow as her head thrashed in the delirium leading to her orgasm.

"I want you there," she cried. "Between my thighs."

"I am."

"Oh dear heaven, not like that." She shifted, bringing the entrance to her grotto into contact with the tip of his sex. "Inside me. I want you inside me."

"I can't." Oh, God. He'd never wanted anything so desperately than what she was offering, but he'd promised.

"Please, Marc," she begged. "The throbbing there. It's torment. I can't stand it."

He didn't answer, couldn't answer. His cock ached to bury itself in her, to take possession of her and feel her come all around him. What torment, feeling the fire build in his loins and not daring to take what he craved.

"I've dreamed about you," she gasped. "Hot and hard inside me. Moving. Oh, please don't deny me. Please."

"No," he shouted. "I promised you I wouldn't."

"Never mind that. Take me. Now."

He stood as still as he could, his prick ready to claim its prize. One thrust would put him into her. One thrust would let him fill her, would give him everything he'd ever wanted.

"I release you from the promise," she said. "Damn you. What do I have to say to make you give yourself to me?"

"Felicity," he cried, the sound erupting from his chest in agony.

"Now, Marc. Please. Please!"

God help him. He grasped her hips and pushed into her. Past the barrier and into her wet heat. Her virginal muscles clamped around him. Tight, so tight. He was going to come. Any moment.

"Yes," she cried. "Oh, yes, my darling. This is what I've dreamed of."

He held still, fighting for control. His legs trembled, and his knees almost gave way. He had to make this good for her, had to take her to heaven.

"What a feeling," she said. "I never imagined."

Slowly, cautiously, he pulled back and then thrust forward again. Her hips rose to meet him, burying him completely into her flesh. She'd turned wanton and shameless, and her lust inflamed his own, bringing his arousal to almost intolerable levels. He slipped a hand between their bodies and found the pearl between her thighs. When he touched her, she gasped and bucked so hard he had to hold on tightly with his other hand.

"Yes, that way," she cried. "Oh God, I can't hold back. Now. Oh, now."

She was going to spend at any moment. And he could join her in ecstasy. He thrust more deeply, plunging into her over and over again. She sobbed and gasped. He gave in to every urge he'd denied. Deep and hard and fast, he went until he felt her tense around him.

The climax hit them both at once. Her spasms started just as he felt the hot essence spurt from him. One powerful explosion. Then another. And another.

When they were over, he'd grown so weak he couldn't stand. He rested his body over hers while her cries trailed off into soft sighs. He closed his eyes and heard her heartbeat returning to normal. Never, never had he found such completion, such total fulfillment.

❧⁂⧉⁂❧

It was several minutes before Felicity could do anything but listen to Marc's breathing. His head lay on her breast, his face moist with sweat. Evidence of the violence of their coupling. Even now they were connected, with his sex still buried inside her.

Oh, dear heaven, she'd given herself to him when she'd sworn she wouldn't. He'd owned her heart for several weeks, and now she'd given him her body, too. How would she ever learn to live without him?

She lifted her hand and stroked his face, pushing his hair back out of his eyes. She kissed his forehead and then the tip of his nose. He looked so helpless, even innocent, like a sleeping child. Of all the ways she'd seen him — distant, amused, on fire with lust — this was the way she'd remember him through the years to come.

He opened his eyes and stared into her face, his expression dazed. After a moment, he took a few breaths and then raised himself onto his elbows. "Oh, dear God, what have I done?"

You've loved me, she wanted to shout. But he hadn't. He'd made love to her, and that was different. He regretted his actions already. He'd never really wanted her, but she'd made him take her virginity, and now he regretted it. She bit her lip to keep it from trembling. Crying would make her humiliation complete.

He straightened, and the action parted their bodies. She didn't even have that connection any more. Worse, his expression looked completely bereft, as though he'd made some terrible mistake. As though he hated himself for making love to her.

"I'm so sorry, Felicity," he said.

"It wasn't your fault," she answered, trying to keep the tears out of her voice. "I provoked you."

"No, I'm the more experienced. I should have controlled myself."

"Let's not discuss it," she said. "What's done is done."

"This should never have happened." He reached into the pocket of his trousers and pulled out a handkerchief. Dear heaven, she hadn't even pushed his pants over his hips. She been so eager to have him inside her, she'd just released his sex and begged him to drive it home. He'd made her that shameless.

He shook out the handkerchief and gently wiped her thighs. The linen came away bloodied, evidence that she'd crossed a threshold with him, and she could never retrace her steps. If he were capable of giving himself to her exclusively, she wouldn't care. She'd happily live the decadent life right here in his house, married or not. She'd thumb her nose at the world by day and share his bed by night.

That couldn't happen, though, and the tenderness he showed her now — the utter concentration with which he touched her sex — only underscored what she was about to lose. This very afternoon.

He stopped and stood, looking at the stained handkerchief in his hand. "I'm sorry, Felicity. I'm so damned sorry."

"Stop saying that."

"I hurt you."

"It's only the blood from my maidenhead. You didn't hurt me."

He gazed into her face, and the pain she found there tore at her heart. "I shouldn't have taken your maidenhead. This shouldn't have happened."

"Stop saying that, too."

"It's true."

Damn it, she knew that was true. But she couldn't bear to hear it. Not after the bliss they'd just shared. Why couldn't he just tell her he loved her, tell her he'd make everything right, tell her that she meant more to him than any other woman? Why couldn't he want her and no one else?

Tears welled up behind her eyelids and pressed for release. She was going to cry like a spoiled child, and she couldn't let him see it. She couldn't let him see how much she cared. She cleared her throat. "Do you suppose you might find my clothes?"

"Of course." He touched her cheek — more gentleness that threatened to unravel her heart. She bit her lip and willed her chest not to release the sobs choking her.

After a moment, he turned and left the room. She slid to her feet, but her legs wouldn't really hold her, so she rested against the desk and glanced down at herself.

What a spectacle she made. She was still wearing her stockings and shoes and even her corset — although that had been pushed askew during their lovemaking. Her breasts hung over the top of the corset, the nipples still wet from his kisses. She hurt between her legs, and her chest had grown tight with misery.

One sob escaped her, and she clamped her hand over her mouth to stifle it. He'd be back at any time, and she wouldn't let him find her in tears. She'd hold all the feeling inside until she could get home and into her own bedroom. She had to get out of here. Now.

She adjusted her corset as best she could, found her drawers on the floor, and slipped into them just as he re-entered the room. He walked toward her slowly, holding out her clothing. He'd put his shirt back on but hadn't buttoned it. There was no sign of the ruined handkerchief. Lord only knew what he'd done with that.

She took her clothes from him and held them up against her chest. "Thank you."

"What are you going to do?" he asked.

"I thought I'd get dressed and go home."

"That isn't what I meant, and you know it."

No answer came to mind, so she just stood and stared at him, clutching her clothes to her breasts.

"What are you going to do about what happened here today?" he said.

"Dear heaven, can't you even name it?"

"I took your innocence. We have to decide what to do about that."

She knew what she wanted to do about that. She wanted to throw herself into his arms and beg him to love her — only her. Beg him to keep her with him always. But that wouldn't work, and she'd already lost everything but her pride here today. She'd keep that somehow.

"The decision will be mine to make, I think," she said.

"What are you going to do?" he demanded.

"I don't know," she shouted. "I don't think I can lie. Maybe I'll tell George what happened. Maybe he'll marry me, anyway. If he doesn't, I'll manage somehow. There are worse things than spinsterhood."

"A woman of your passions a spinster?" he replied. "A sinful waste, if you ask me."

He'd made her that way. He'd given her those passions, and she only wanted to share them with him. But she couldn't tell him that, no matter how much she wanted to. "I don't know what I'm going to do. I have to think about it."

"If the man's too stupid to have you because of one indiscretion, I'll marry you."

Indiscretion. Oh, dear Lord. Indiscretion. "What a lovely offer, Dr. Slade. You take my breath away."

"Damn." He ran his fingers through his hair. "I didn't mean it to come out that way."

"I know how you feel about marriage," she said. "About fidelity."

"I'm not your father. I would never disgrace you publicly."

No, he wouldn't. He'd have his affairs discreetly. She probably wouldn't even know who his lovers were. She'd have to suspect every woman she met of sharing intimacies with her husband. "I want to go home."

"You're upset. We'll talk later."

"Fine." Only, there wasn't going to be any later for them, but she didn't want to discuss that now. She'd only end up bawling like a child.

"Get dressed," he said. "I'll bring the buggy around and drive you."

"I can get home on my own," she answered.

"Like hell," he answered. "I'm not going to take my pleasure with you and then send you out into a storm."

She looked into his face and found steely determination there. He wasn't going to let this be simple. He was going to make her ride with him to her house. She sighed. "Fine. Get your buggy."

❧⟨♋⟩❧

Felicity let him drive to within a few blocks of her house and then told him to stop.

"But you don't live here," Dr. Slade — Marc — answered.

"It's not far, and the rain's letting up."

"You don't want to be seen with me?"

"It's better this way."

He didn't look pleased at that answer. In fact, he looked rather as if he'd bitten into something sour as he gazed around them at the puddle-strewn street. But at least the rain was slowing to a trickle.

"All right," he said finally.

She moved to climb out of the buggy, but he caught her arm. "I will see you again," he said.

"Of course," she lied.

"When?"

"I don't know."

"We're not through with this," he said. "We still have to talk."

"About what?" she demanded. "You've apologized. You've told me how much you regret our indiscretion. You've offered to marry me if my fiancee won't have me. You've even promised not to humiliate me — at least not publicly. What's left to discuss?"

"A little matter of pregnancy," he replied. "What to do if you're carrying my child."

Oh God, a child. His child. How could she have been so stupid? She'd wanted him for so long — thought of nothing but having him, even dreamed about having him — that she hadn't thought of the consequences. Now, she loved him, might even be carrying his child, and she couldn't have him without dooming herself to the very fate she'd been hoping to avoid from the beginning.

"Felicity," he said softly, as he reached up to stroke her cheek, "what if you're going to have my baby?"

His tenderness undid her. She could have withstood anything but that. Anger, sarcasm, blame, maybe even indifference, but not tenderness. A sob escaped her, followed by another and another. Her shoulders shook, and tears blurred her vision.

He gathered her into his arms, resting her face against his chest. "Don't cry," he whispered. "I won't abandon you."

"I know," she managed. "I know you wouldn't."

"And I'd never ignore any child we conceived," he said. "We'll be married, of course, if you're pregnant."

"No," she sobbed. "I can't."

"Don't be silly. I will take care of you and the baby, if there is one. You have no choice in the matter."

She pulled away from him and swiped at her eyes. No one was on the street because of the rain, but Lord only knew how many people could see them from the neighboring houses. She must look exactly like what she was — a woman who'd ruined herself and was now suffering the consequences. She had to get away from here, calm herself, and go home. With any luck, no one she knew had seen them.

"Let's not argue, please," she said. "We don't even know if there's anything to argue about."

"I must insist. I won't be put off about this."

She lowered her face into her hand and took a few breaths. "Fine. I believe you. Now, really … I have to go."

"When will you know?" he demanded. "When are your menses due?"

She looked up at him and felt her cheeks turn hot. She never discussed *that* with anyone. But how could she feel shy with a man who'd made love to her less than an hour before? "It should be in about three weeks. I'm usually fairly regular."

"I'll expect to hear from you in three weeks time, then."

"Three weeks," she repeated and moved to leave the buggy.

Once again, he stopped her with a hand on her arm. "Either way, I'll expect you to visit me then."

"All right," she said, glaring at him.

He glared right back. "If you don't come to me, I'll find you. And your parents, if necessary. Do you understand me?"

"I understand," she cried. "Now, let me go."

"Three weeks, Felicity."

Chapter Five

Callie Houseman looked every bit as plump and appealing as ever, but somehow today her charm wasn't working. Marc looked down into the sweet smile she always gave him after their first kiss, and he wanted to want her — desperately. But somehow he just couldn't manage any real passion.

"Why don't we go into my study?" he said.

She looked at him out of her twinkling blue eyes. Despite her "advanced age" of almost ten years Marc's senior, Callie still could turn heads. But she only indulged herself with Marc. He'd find that a bit overwhelming if she didn't have such a wonderful independent streak and sense of humor.

Right now one of her eyebrows went up, making her appear amused and a bit perplexed. "The study, not the bedroom?"

"I haven't seen you for months," he answered. "I want to hear what you've been doing. Where you've been. What — and who — you've seen."

"You want to talk?"

He gestured toward the study door. "Let's."

She shrugged and walked across the foyer into the study. He followed and found her standing by the love seat, pulling off her gloves. Her reticule already lay on the table nearby.

"So," she said. "Who've you been entertaining?"

"I beg your pardon."

"Someone's tired you out," she answered. "Usually we head straight upstairs on my visits."

"Really, Callie, can't we have some intelligent conversation? You're worth more than just a tumble, you know."

She removed her hat and stuck the pin into it then cocked her head and studied him. "Uh-huh."

"Do you find that so hard to believe?"

She set her hat on top of her gloves and reticule. "Not at all. We always have things to tell each other, things to laugh about together. Afterwards."

"Perhaps I feel like showing some restraint today. Perhaps I've matured."

She laughed at that. "Marc, sweetheart, this is Callie. We know each other better than that."

Damn, he should have known not to try to fool Callie. She'd been married for twenty years and had no doubt heard every excuse a man had to offer. But did she have to choose today to become so perceptive? "Alright, then," he snapped, "if you're so hungry for me, let's go to bed."

She laughed ever more loudly at that. "Now, I am curious, love. Some woman has tied you in knots, and I want to hear all about it."

"Don't be ridiculous."

She sat and patted the cushion beside her. He joined her and took her into his arms. If Felicity had him in knots, he didn't have to surrender to the knots. A delightful roll in the hay with a dear friend was exactly what he needed to make him forget the fact that it had been three weeks and two days since he'd seen Felicity.

He pulled Callie against him and bent to kiss her. She responded instantly, as she always did, opening to him and offering her softness. She made such a delightful armful of womanly curves, he usually grew hard and hot instantly. But somehow today she wasn't enough. The sweetness of her breath didn't satisfy, not as it usually did. The scent of her perfume seemed merely pleasant and no more.

She pulled back from the caress and studied him. "There is something wrong, isn't there?"

He dropped his arms to his sides and smiled at her. "No, really. You're making something out of nothing."

"I know nothing when I see it, young man," she said, sounding for all the world like any stern schoolmistress. He'd never heard her sound like that before. "This is far from nothing," she continued. "And I want to know what's bothering you."

He took a breath and searched for an answer. How could he tell anyone — even Callie — that an innocent young woman had come to him for help and he'd taken advantage of her? How could he admit that he'd taken the young woman's virginity, may have gotten her with child, and he didn't even know what had happened to her? He could hardly say the words aloud to himself. How could he tell anyone else?

Three weeks and two days. He should have heard from Felicity by now.

"I've been very stupid, I'm afraid," he confessed finally.

"A woman."

"What else?"

"Who is she?" Callie asked.

"No one you know."

She reached up and stroked his face. "Whatever you've done, you'll fix it."

"I'm not sure that's possible."

"I know you, Marc. You'd never do anything cruel. Anything else can be fixed."

He took her hand in his and lowered it to his lap. "I appreciate your faith in me. I'm not sure it's deserved."

"Come, come. Tell Callie everything. How bad could it be?"

He didn't answer, but just looked into her face.

After a moment her gentle smile turned to a frown. "You didn't get her with child?"

"I may have."

"Darling," she said. "You didn't use a French letter?"

He couldn't bring himself to admit exactly how idiotically he'd behaved, so he merely shook his head.

"But that isn't like you. You'd never lose your head like that," Callie said.

Damn it, he knew that. He'd always protected the woman and himself in the past. Always. But that afternoon with Felicity — three weeks and two days ago — had been different. He couldn't have waited to get a French letter or anything else. He'd played the encounter over and over in his head ever since then, and he kept coming back to the same answer. He'd needed her *then,* not a day from then or a minute from then. As hard as he tried, he still couldn't make sense out of how he'd felt that day.

"Marc?" Callie prompted.

He rose and crossed the room, running his fingers through his hair. When he reached the desk, he turned and faced Callie. "I can't explain it. I lost my control. Completely."

She looked at him for a moment, and then a smile crossed her lips. For God's sake, he'd just told her that he was the world's greatest idiot, and she was smiling at him.

"I can explain it," she said, sphinx-like. The way women acted when they were at their most irritating.

"Then perhaps you'd like to try."

"You've fallen in love."

"Oh, for heaven's sake, Callie."

"You have," she declared. "That accounts for everything. Why you're so morose …"

"I am not morose."

"Morose," she repeated. "Distracted. Why you have no interest in bedding me."

"What makes you think I have no interest in bedding you?"

She laughed again. Normally he loved her laughter, but this particular afternoon it grated on his nerves. To make matters worse, she looked pointedly at the front of his pants. She couldn't help but notice his total lack of an erection. Damn it, she saw entirely too much.

"I do wish you'd stop laughing at me," he said. Oh hell, now he sounded petulant.

"I'm sorry, darling. It isn't funny, is it?"

"No, it isn't." Damn, that sounded even worse.

She rose from the love seat and walked to him, finally reaching out and taking both his hands in hers. "Falling in love isn't funny. It's deadly serious and the most magnificent thing that can happen to anyone."

Could Callie be right? Could he have fallen in love with Felicity Wells? Timid, virginal women like Felicity didn't even appeal to him. But then, she'd gotten over her timidity during her tutelage, and he'd disposed of her virginity well enough.

Still, he didn't believe in love, at least not in the way society had invented it. Love restricted people unnaturally. It blocked the natural expression of the sexual drives. Only fools believed in that idea of love.

"I knew this would happen one day," Callie said, "and I couldn't be happier for you."

"I don't feel very happy."

"You will, darling. You'll make things right with the young woman, and you two will have a lifetime of happiness."

"How can you say that?" he asked. "You and your Robert loved each other, and you didn't have a lifetime of happiness."

"We had over twenty years. Not nearly enough time, but I wouldn't trade a moment of it for all the pearls in the ocean."

"That's fine for you, Callie," he answered. "But I'm a scientist, a researcher. My intellect tells me that love doesn't exist."

"Pig's piddle," she declared. "What does your cock tell you?"

More of her blasted perceptiveness. How could she know that for the last three weeks and two days he'd wanted no one but Felicity Wells? He'd tried imagining himself with other women — had even welcomed Callie's visit to prove to himself that he wasn't hopelessly smitten with his wanton, little Brahmin. Now he had to face the fact that his member was interested in one woman only. But where was she?

"I thought so," Callie said. She squeezed his hands. "I'll miss our afternoons together, Marc."

"Who said anything about ending our afternoons?"

She clucked her tongue at him. First laughter and now tongue clucking. She could be a real nuisance if he didn't like her so damned much.

"Marc, darling," she said. "You need to find the woman you love and be with her. Marry her, for heaven's sake. It wouldn't kill you."

"This whole conversation is ridiculous."

"You know I'm right." She waved a finger in his face. "Now, you go and make things up with her. Today."

He took Callie's hand in his. "All right. I do need to find her, in any case."

"Good, then. I'll expect an invitation to the wedding."

He slipped his arms around Callie and squeezed her. "I'll miss you."

"And I you." She smiled at him — that delightful combination of sweetness and mischief that he'd grown to love. "But I've been thinking it's time for me to open myself to love again."

"Any man would be lucky to have you."

"You've been wonderful for me, Marc. Just what I needed after Robert died, but it's time for both of us to move on, I think."

"Perhaps you're right."

She backed out of his arms and walked to the table where she'd deposited her things. "I'll see myself out, then. You go do whatever you have to do to win your lady back."

"Thanks, Callie, I will." Only how in hell was he going to do that?

Marc's door wasn't locked, not even latched. When Felicity raised her hand to the knocker, the door swung open on its own, so she stepped inside and listened for some sound of life. Except for the ticking of the grandfather clock, the house was silent. Surely, he wouldn't go out and leave his door ajar.

She ought to just close the door behind her and go home, but she'd spent all last night and this morning readying herself for this visit. If she ran away now, she'd might never have the courage to come back. Courage indeed — the news she had to share would end things between them for good. After today, they'd never have any reason to see each other again.

She stood for a moment, doing her best to commit the hallway to memory — the stairway that curved out of view, the mahogany wainscoting of the walls, the plush carpet runner that passed the door to the study and disappeared into the back of the house. The study door itself stood half-open. She could go in and take one last look around. If Marc appeared, she could simply tell him that his front door had been open and she'd let herself in. She could chide him for his carelessness. She could look at him one last time.

Dear heaven, melodrama wasn't going to win her anything. She'd go back outside and knock properly. If he wasn't home, she'd come back tomorrow. She turned to go, but a sound stopped her. A sigh, from the direction of the study door. Someone had sighed. Marc had sighed.

She took a step in that direction and stopped. She'd heard him sigh before — when she'd kissed him. When she'd caressed him so intimately she could hardly bear to remember it. Was someone else in the study with him?

Lord, this was why she'd vowed to protect her heart from him. Why hadn't she kept that promise to herself?

He sighed again, and her cheeks grew hot with humiliation.

"Felicity," he whispered.

Her name. He'd whispered her name.

"Felicity," he said again. "Damn, where are you?"

She walked to the study door and looked inside. Marc sat on the settee, alone. He was bent over, his elbows on his knees, his head in his hands.

"I'm here," she said.

He looked up, his eyes wide, and rose immediately. "Where have you been?"

"I told you I wouldn't come back for three weeks."

"Three weeks were up two days ago."

She shrugged. She ought to tell him that she could have come several days before, but if she told him that, he'd ask for the answer to the unspoken question between them, and then she'd have to leave. For just a few seconds, she wanted to drink in the sight of him.

He'd always looked calmer than he did today. More in control. Today he wore no jacket, and his waistcoat hung open. He'd rolled his sleeves up, exposing dark hairs over his forearms. With no cravat and with his hair all askew, he appeared positively wild, and the angles of his face seemed even more pronounced than usual. He was so different from the Dr. Marcus Slade she'd first confronted in this very room, but he was still every bit as mysterious and beautiful.

"If you hadn't come today, I would have gone looking for you tomorrow," he said.

"I'm sorry."

"For all I knew your parents had packed you off somewhere, and you'd left without a word to me."

"I wouldn't have done that," she answered.

"You might not have had any choice." He ran his fingers through his hair, demonstrating how it had arrived at its present state of disarray. "You can't imagine what's been going through my mind. I might have lost touch with you, with my own child."

That did it. As much as she couldn't even bear to hear the words, she could avoid them no longer. "There isn't any child."

"Oh." He stared at her blankly for a moment and then ran his hand over his chin. "Oh."

"My monthly ran its course. A little early, in fact."

"Oh," he repeated.

Is that all the man knew how to say? She'd come to tell him that he was free, and all he could say was "oh"? Well, she'd planned to keep this light, and his terseness could help in that regard.

"I suppose you're relieved at this news," she said, doing her best to smile.

"I should be," he said.

"Well, I should say so. We can both get on with our lives now. You can do your research, and I can be married." She didn't add that she hadn't yet told George that his fiancée was no longer pure. That was her own personal hurdle to face, if she decided to marry George at all. The idea became less and less appealing the longer she stood and gazed at Marc Slade.

"That's it, then," he said. "The problem is solved, and you'll marry someone else and just forget about our ..."

His voice trailed off, and he looked away. As though he couldn't face her.

"Our what, Marc," she demanded. "Our research? Our indiscretion? Our what?"

"You'll forget about me."

If only she could. If only she could forget the way he'd made her feel, the way his touch had made her come alive. The way his kisses had set her free to soar. She wasn't likely to forget any of that. Nor would she forget the way he looked right now, as if he was lost in a mist of pain and confusion. Damn him, why couldn't he just give her a cheerful good-bye and let her go home to try to recover from loving him?

"I don't understand you," she said. "I thought you'd be happy at my news."

"Happy?" he repeated.

"Relieved. I've released you from any obligation."

"Obligation."

"Would you stop repeating what I say and tell me what's wrong with you?" she shouted.

"I wanted you pregnant," he said. "I wanted you to have my child."

"Why?"

"I thought that way I could talk you into marrying me."

She stood and stared at him. He looked like the Marcus Slade she'd been visiting these past weeks. He had the same broad shoulders, the same high cheekbones and pale skin. But this man made no sense at all.

"You're exactly the man I can't marry," she said. "I won't live my mother's life — worrying who my husband is bedding every time he's out of my sight. And you can't be faithful to one woman. You've told me that over and over."

"I know I told you that," he answered. "But can you believe I've changed?"

She'd love nothing more than to believe he'd changed. She'd give anything for that. But she didn't dare delude herself on this point. It was too important.

"These weeks without you have been hell," he said. "I haven't been able to sleep or eat. All I could do was think of you and how much I wanted you. Only you, Felicity."

"Oh, Marc." The words rushed out of her before she could stop them. "You don't know how much I've wanted to hear you say that."

"It's true. I've been such a fool — trying to deny what was happening inside me. I might as well try to will the sun to orbit the Earth. I love you. I can't live without you."

"I love you, too. Oh God help me, I do. But can I trust you?"

"An old friend visited today," he said. He squared his shoulders and gazed at her straight on. "I'll confess this, and it will be the last confession I'll ever have to make to you, I swear."

"Please."

"She and I have enjoyed each other many times. I thought we would again today, but I had no interest in her whatsoever. She saw instantly what I've been hiding from myself for weeks. You're the only woman I want — the only woman I'll ever want, for the rest of my life."

"Oh, my love." She opened her arms and went to him. He took her in an embrace, clasping her tightly to his chest. How she'd missed the feel of him, his scent, his warmth. She tipped her face up to his, and he kissed her — desperation mixed with tenderness mixed with love. She answered in kind until the world spun around them.

After a moment, he pulled back and stroked her face with the tips of his fingers. "And what about you?" he asked. "Have you changed?"

"I don't think so. I've loved you from the very beginning."

"But you said you'd never marry for love. That you'd never give a man that much power over you."

"Oh, that." She toyed with a button on his shirt. "I don't know what sort of silly fool would say something like that, do you?"

"The sort of silly fool I'd fall in love with, that's what sort."

She gazed up into his face. "I don't suppose I have any choice in the matter, anyway. You own my heart, and that gives you the ultimate power over me. Use it carefully, please."

"I'll only use it one way. As your husband." He looked down at her with such devotion and tenderness in his face that her heart almost stopped beating. "Will you have me?"

"Oh, yes. Oh, yes, my love. Oh, yes."

"Good," he said, smiling at her wickedly. "Because I have the most tremendous cockstand just now, and Priapus will accept no one but you. Can you accommodate him?"

"I think so." She reached down and fondled his erection. Even through the fabric of his trousers and her gloves, she could make out the hardness and the length of it.

He sucked in a harsh breath. "Mercy, woman. It's been over three weeks. For once, I'd like to keep enough control to make love to you properly. In a bed."

"Then, take me to your bedroom."

"Our bedroom," he corrected, as he took her hand and led her into their new life together.

About the author:

Alice Gaines also writes as Alice Chambers for Leisure Romance. Her next full-length book, **Always a Princess,** *will appear in May of 2001. Alice loves to hear from readers. Contact her at algaines@ pac-bell.net or write her at: Alice Gaines (or Alice Chambers); 5111 Telegraph Avenue, PMB #197; Oakland, CA 94609. Or visit her web-site at http://home.pacbell.net/halice.*

A Candidate for the Kiss

by Angela Knight

To my reader:
I was watching James Bond do something impossible in one of his movies when I thought, "This would be a lot more believable if he was a vampire." And just like that, this story was born.

Thanks to Alexandria Kendall for letting me play in her *Secrets* sandbox with my handcuffs and handsome hunks. And thanks to the readers who said, "When are you going to do another vampire story?"

Well, here it is.

Chapter One

If they caught her, they'd kill her.

Dana Ivory looked out the window of the rotting treehouse, peering down at the four men gathered around the bonfire below. She knew that if they discovered her, they'd put a bullet in her brain and dump her body so far out in the woods nobody would ever find anything but bones.

But if Dana could keep the four from catching her, she'd live to blow their plans to hell and make her own reputation. All she needed was guts and luck. Guts she had. Luck … well, she'd see.

Her hand shaking, Dana angled the microphone further out the window to better pick up the conversation going on below.

"Nothin'll put the fear in the mongrel races and traitor whites like killing the President they all elected."

"Shit, they'll piss themselves wonderin' where the next bullet's coming from!"

"And right-thinking whites'll flock to our banner. It'll finally be the start of our holy war."

The voices carried clearly in the warm summer air. Dana just prayed her tape recorder was picking them up half that well.

She swallowed against a queasy blend of terror and excitement. This time tomorrow, her byline wouldn't just be on the front page of *The Adamsburg Weekly Tribune*. Once the national wire services picked up this story, the words "By Dana Ivory" would be on every paper in the country.

And four white supremacists would be in jail for plotting the assassination of the President of the United States.

All thanks to Dana and their ringleader's nephew.

Jimmy Satterfield had sidled up to her just that morning to whisper that the local chapter of the White Aryan Brotherhood was meeting in the woods outside town. That in itself got Dana's attention, because Jimmy was so terrified of his uncle, he'd normally never breathe a word about anything Joe Satterfield or the WAB was up to.

"I ain't no snitch," Jimmy whispered, his voice hoarse and earnest with terror. "But this thing is so fuckin' big, anybody who even knows about it could go to jail. And not in no candy-ass state prison either. Hard time. Leavenworth time. Time I ain't gonna do for no Hitler-lovin' bastard, even if he is my uncle."

"But what are they planning?"

"Hide in the old treehouse just before sunset. You'll find out."

Dana had gone to the sheriff, of course. Steve Hannah should have jumped at the tip; he already suspected Joe and his crew in a string of convenience store robberies and drug deals he'd never been able to prove in court.

But instead of mobilizing his men for a raid — or even sending a deputy with Dana to investigate — Hannah had given her a verbal pat on the head and told her the elementary school was holding a nice pageant she ought to do a story on.

Well, she'd already written that story, dammit. Six times in the six years she'd been at *The Adamsburg Weekly Tribune*. What Dana hadn't done was an exposé that would send the WAB straight to jail, leaving the crime rate of Adamsburg, S.C. to plummet for at least a decade.

So she'd headed for the treehouse a couple of hours before the boys were due, picked her way over the rotting pine boards to a relatively solid spot, and started setting up her microphone, tape recorder and camera.

The treehouse wasn't the most comfortable perch in the world. Neighborhood kids had built it in the limbs of the old oak more than ten years ago, cobbling together pine plank walls and a sloping roof now pocked with several fist-sized holes. The whole thing smelled damp and unpleasant from the rot, mildew and wildlife that had moved in over the years.

But if the ambiance wasn't exactly Martha Stewart, it also wasn't enough to keep Dana away from a good story. She'd pushed a desiccated mouse carcass aside with the toe of her running shoe, swept off a relatively clean patch next to the opening that served as a window, and sat down to wait.

The four WAB boys had showed up just before sunset, jouncing through the woods in a rusted white pickup, one man holding on for dear life in the back. As they got out of the truck, Dana recognized them as a fairly sinister quartet she knew from covering various bond hearings over the years.

There was round, snake-mean Bill Mason, who put his wife in the hospital once a month; Skeeter Jones, a tall man who reminded Dana of a ferret with his long body and narrow head; and buck-toothed Tony Brown, who grew marijuana out in the woods and guarded his crop with a sawed-off shotgun. But the worst of the bunch was Donnie Anders, hulking, bearded and fresh out of prison for beating a buddy to death over a bar tab. Oddly, there was no sign of Joe Satterfield, the leader of the Brotherhood chapter. Dana wondered where he was.

They'd built a fire, rolled a couple of joints, and started working their way through a couple of twelve-packs as they told lies about women and who'd told whose boss to go to hell. Dana began to suspect she was courting the attentions of the area's chigger population for nothing.

Then the conversation wandered to President Daniel Grayson's up-coming speech at the University of South Carolina. Dana was just wondering what possible interest the boys could have in that surprisingly intellectual topic when Skeeter Jones drawled, "This'll be bigger than the time we bombed that church."

She almost dropped her mike. The Mount Zion Baptist Church in nearby Newberry had blown up on Christmas day last year, killing the African-American pastor who'd come in to open up for services.

"No kidding, asshole," Anders said, spitting a spray of tobacco juice into the fire. "Putting a bullet in the President is definitely bigger than blowing up a preacher."

"Too bad the damn bomb went off early," Mason grumbled. "We coulda got us a whole church full."

Being a pastor's daughter, Dana was so horrified they'd bombed the church that the assassination plot took a moment to register. By the time she'd recovered from the shock, the four were already discussing the expert they were bringing in to murder Grayson.

Oh, God, Dana thought, as her heart began to lunge in her chest. *These bozos are actually planning to murder the President of the United States.*

She spent the next half-hour listening in appalled fascination and planning the biggest story of her career.

Now Anders popped the top on his beer with a violent gesture of one grimy hand. "It's a helluvalot of money to give some bastard from out-of-state. I still say we should do it ourselves and keep the cash."

Mason hooted. "Yeah, right. We'd have the Secret Service so far up our ass we'd be pulling badges out of our teeth. This guy is good. Hell, Joe said he's the one that did that judge in Alabama …"

"Maybe he's good. Maybe he ain't." Anders' little black eyes gleamed in the firelight, feral and mean over his scraggly beard. "And if he ain't, maybe he gets caught and sings to the Feds about what we hired him to …"

Something growled.

A rush of blackness detached itself from the night and snatched Anders off the ground, then swung him around like a rag and slammed him against the nearest tree.

Dana jumped.

Anders must have tipped the scales at well over two hundred pounds, but now a man held him pinned so far up the trunk his cowboy-booted feet swung six inches from the dirt.

"Let's get something straight, asshole." The man's voice was cold, calm and so deep it seemed to rumble in the bones. "I do not sing for the Feds, I do not tap dance for the Feds, I do not provide the Feds with entertainment of any kind. And I sure as hell don't tell the Feds who hired me to do a job!"

That was the assassin?

Anders' square face twisted with rage. But as he met the stranger's narrow gaze, his expression slowly changed, eyes widening until the whites showed. Wheezing from the pressure of the big hand pinning him to the tree, he gasped out, "I didn't mean nuthin'."

Dana blinked. Anders had just done five years in prison for voluntary manslaughter. What had he seen in the other man's face that was nasty enough to make him back down?

True, the stranger was big, with a good four inches on Anders' six feet. Thick biceps shifted and bulged in his extended arm as he held the ex-con pinned, and the black T-shirt he wore molded to the curves of a powerful chest. But Anders was pretty beefy himself, despite the layer of fat covering his muscle, so it wasn't just the other's brawn that had him sweating.

Gazing at the stranger, Dana silently admitted he could make her sweat a little too. His profile looked as if it should be stamped on a Roman coin: handsome and arrogant, with an aquiline nose, high forehead, starkly masculine cheekbones and a square chin. The only soft thing about him was the wavy dark hair that brushed the tops of his broad shoulders.

But handsome or not, he stared at Anders with such menacing intensity Dana felt the hair rise on the back of her own neck. She was relieved when Joe Satterfield stepped out of the woods, his smile placating. "Uh, Jackson, you can turn him loose now. Donnie's harmless."

Like hell, Dana thought, but the assassin stepped back and let Anders drop. As the ex-con stumbled and tried to regain his balance, Jackson turned his back and walked away. An act of either courage or ignorance, considering Anders had hit the last man he'd killed from behind.

"So let's talk business." Accepting a beer from Skeeter, Jackson popped the top and took a long swallow. "Jonah said you want me to kill somebody big, but he didn't say who."

"How do we know you ain't wearing a wire?" Anders demanded, sullen hostility growling in his voice as he stumped toward the fire. Dana tensed, suspecting he'd feel compelled to do something nasty after the way he'd been humiliated.

Jackson shrugged, handed his beer back to Skeeter, and reached for the hem of his black T-shirt. In one easy gesture, he pulled it over his head.

Oh, my.

Why the hell was the man making his living with a gun when women everywhere would have paid just to look at his body?

Broad expanses of fluid muscle formed Jackson's pecs, and his abdomen and ribs were sculpted in tight ridges that could have been chiseled by Michelangelo. Dark chest hair grew in a silky ruff across his chest, narrowing to flow downward toward the snap of his jeans. When he turned his back, the firelight gleamed across smooth, rippling contours that formed a beautiful V from broad shoulders to narrow waist, drawing attention to a pair of buns clad in black denim that were as tight and round as cantaloupes.

The man could have played the lead in one of Dana's guilty fantasies.

God, she thought, *it's a shame he's a racist pig.*

When Jackson faced around again, he lifted a thick brow. "Is that enough, or do I have to drop my pants?"

Satterfield gave an uncomfortable laugh. "Hell, boy, I think you've made your point."

A small voice in the back of Dana's mind whispered, *Damn!* She winced in guilt. Here she was, ogling a killer. No matter how sexy he was, his job description included sniper scopes and grassy knolls. Her parents were probably spinning in their graves.

Jackson shrugged back into his shirt with a lithe twist of his torso, reclaimed his beer, and sat on the ground next to Skeeter, stretching his long legs out in front of him. "Now that we got that settled — who am I killing?"

Satterfield wandered over and eased his considerable bulk onto a fallen log, his checkered shirt straining over his belly. He splayed his jeans-clad legs far apart to balance his gut and scratched the two-day growth of grey stubble on his chin. "Like I told you on the phone, what we got for you ain't gonna be easy. But Mr. Howard says you're the man to do it, and that's good enough for me."

Dana frowned. Was he talking about Jonah Howard, the Idaho racist who'd founded the White Aryan Brotherhood?

Jackson sipped his beer. "Yeah, I've done a lot of work for Jonah."

Which answers that question, Dana thought.

And what kind of "work" had Jackson been doing? A magazine article she'd read a few months back had called Howard "the suspected mastermind behind the WAB's domestic terrorism." Had Jackson been involved too?

"Well, now you can do something for us." Satterfield leaned forward and looked Jackson in the eye. "We want you to execute Daniel Grayson as a traitor to the white race."

Jackson's beer hesitated in mid-tip. "That is big." The assassin resumed his sip. "And you're right — it's not going to be easy. Not gonna be cheap, either. What do you have in mind?"

Satterfield told him about the President's planned trip to South Carolina. Dana listened, barely breathing, her hand sweating on the barrel of the boom microphone, her mind buzzing with questions and half-formed plans.

Should she call the FBI or the Secret Service? Did the Secret Service even have a South Carolina office? Could she get an agent to meet her so she could turn over the tape? She'd have to make some phone calls and find out.

Then, while the Feds were rounding up the WAB and their handsome assassin, Dana would write the exclusive of a lifetime. No more living on chicken salad sandwiches and driving a ten-year-old Mazda. No more working for a small town weekly for slave wages. This was her ticket to *The New York Times.*

"… really think you can do this?" Bill Mason asked. Dana snapped back to attention.

Jackson propped his beer can on his flat belly. "It's gonna take some planning." He slanted Satterfield a look. "And money. Figuring out the best time and place to hit him …"

"We thought you could do it in the Carolina Coliseum as he gives the speech."

Jackson snorted. "I'd never get out of there alive. It'll have to be before that, while he's on the way. Or after."

"Could bomb the Coliseum," Tony Brown suggested as he picked his buck teeth with a match.

The assassin shot him a scornful look. "What, you think the Feds are going to let me park a tractor trailer full of fertilizer on the lawn? Get serious. I'm gonna have to work on this awhile, use my contacts in the Service." He turned to meet Satterfield's hopeful stare. "And you're going to have to make it worth my time."

"A real patriot would do it for free." Anders spat into a pile of dead leaves.

Jackson smiled, his teeth flashing white in the firelight. "Even a patriot's gotta eat."

"We got money." Satterfield nodded at Mason, who pulled a suitcase into the light and flipped it open with a flourish.

Jackson leaned forward to peer at the bundles of green inside. "Quite a stash."

"We been raising cash for months," Satterfield told him. "Robbed a couple banks, a few convenience stores, sold a lot of dope. We was planning to buy a truckload of fertilizer and fuel oil, maybe blow something up. But then I heard Grayson was comin', and I thought — here's a chance to make a real difference."

"We'll be famous!" Skeeter said happily.

Satterfield shot him a look. "I hope to hell not. That would mean we got caught, and I ain't getting caught. Some other fool can be Lee Harvey Oswald."

Jackson got to his feet and stretched, putting one hand to the small of his back as he arched his spine. "No, he's right. Y'all are gonna be famous." In one smooth gesture, he pulled out a flat black case and flipped it open on something that glittered in the firelight. Something that looked a lot like a badge.

His white teeth flashed in a malicious grin. "I'm a federal agent, and you assholes are busted."

Dana's jaw dropped.

Safe, she thought, dizzy with relief. *I'm safe. And so is the President.*

"I knew it!" Anders howled, exploding off the ground where he'd crouched in a sullen knot.

"Freeze!" a strange voice barked. "Federal agents! Throw down your weapons and raise your hands."

There was a concerted rustle, the crunch of feet stepping on leaves. A ring of men stepped out of the darkness, bulky and menacing in black body armor, their assault rifles leveled.

Donnie froze, staring wild-eyed at the muzzles ringing them.

"You heard the man, y'all." Jackson grinned mockingly. "Dump the guns and raise your hands."

As an assortment of hardware began thudding to the ground, it occurred to Dana that she'd better reveal herself to the Feds as quickly as possible. Especially if she wanted an interview with J. Edgar Gorgeous down there. Which she did.

God, what a story this was going to be. And it looked like she'd even live to tell it.

Trying to decide when to draw attention to herself, Dana watched as the agents handcuffed their prisoners. Anders was being his usual charming self — cursing, demanding a lawyer, refusing to lie on the ground so he could be searched. Frustrated, the agent guarding him stepped closer, gesturing with the muzzle of his gun.

Then all hell broke loose.

An agent moving to help Anders' captor tripped on a root and fell against his comrade. The first agent automatically braced him with one hand … and Anders struck like a snake, grabbing the man's gun and ripping it out of his grip. The guard snatched for it, but Anders jumped back, bringing the weapon to bear on both men. Even as everyone else swung to cover him, he opened fire in a thunderous explosion of sound. The two agents went down in a heap.

Before Anders could fire again, Jackson was on him with a roar of rage, smashing the gun out of his hands as he grabbed the ex-con by the hair.

Dana was still wondering how anybody could move that fast when the agent opened his mouth — *were those fangs?* — and dove, growling, straight for Anders' throat.

What the hell is he doing? Dana thought, incredulous.

Anders grabbed Jackson's head to try to force him back, but his jaws were locked tight. Blood poured down the ex-con's throat, black and wet in the firelight.

"Let go, you bastard! Somebody get him off me …" He clawed at Jackson, who ignored him, jaws working. Anders' voice spiraled into a shriek. "Shit! *He's drinking my blood!*"

Jackson growled like a rabid wolf.

Around them, the other agents watched while their prisoners stared in horror. One of the Feds made an abortive movement toward the two, but none of the agents seemed surprised by Jackson's bizarre behavior.

Dana fumbled for her camera. She didn't know whether the photo would even come out in such poor light, since she didn't dare use a flash. But she damn well wanted a shot of a Federal agent trying to rip out a prisoner's throat with his teeth. Bringing up her Canon, she started clicking off shot after shot.

"Archer, they're all right!" an agent yelled at Jackson as he knelt beside the two men who'd gone down. "He caught 'em in the body armor. Looks like broken ribs. Somebody call EMS!"

Jackson — Archer? — stiffened, then jerked up his head and shoved the ex-con away. An agent began yelling into a radio, calling for medical assistance.

Anders stumbled back, clamping a hand to his bleeding throat as he stared at Jackson. "You were drinkin' my blood! What kind of sick motherf …"

"Go to sleep!" Jackson roared.

Anders dropped as if somebody had put a bullet in his brain.

Dana blinked at the ex-con, sprawled flat on his back in a bramble bush. She hadn't even seen Jackson hit him.

There was a long, long silence, broken finally by Anders' gentle snore.

"Jesus." Satterfield lifted his head off the ground to stare at Jackson with an expression of wild-eyed horror. "You're some kinda fuckin' vampire!" He rolled his eyes at the agent crouching next to him, naked terror on his face. "We knew there was Jews running the government, but nobody said nuthin' about no vampires …"

Vampires in the FBI, Dana thought. *Yeah, right. That hood you like to wear must cut off the circulation to your brain.*

As for the fangs she'd thought she'd seen when Jackson had grabbed Anders — well, that had obviously been a trick of the light.

"You ain't gonna get away with this," Satterfield babbled. "I'm gonna tell my lawyer. There's laws against drinkin' people's blood ..."

Jackson looked at the white supremacist coldly. A smear of red glistened on his mouth, and he wiped it away with the back of his hand. "You too, mastermind. Sleep."

Satterfield's eyes rolled back, and his head hit the ground.

Dana gaped. This time she knew Jackson hadn't touched the white supremacist; he'd been all the way on the other side of the clearing. The agent had just ... commanded Satterfield to sleep, and he'd slept. Like magic. As if Jackson really did have a vampire's psychic powers.

But that was impossible.

The man who crouched beside the fallen agents got to his feet and walked over to Archer. "You always go out of your fuckin' mind when one of the men gets hurt." He shook his helmeted head. "It's a good thing you're magic, or we'd never be able to explain this kind of shit."

"Yeah, well, the smell of blood makes me cranky." Archer shouldered past him to kneel beside the two injured agents, who'd just begun to stir. "How you doing, guys?"

"Ribs feel ... like I got stomped ... by the Dallas Cowboys," one of them gasped. "What the hell happened?"

"You got lucky. It could have been your head." Archer rocked back on his heels. "You want me to do something about those ribs, Roberts?"

The man winced and took a deep breath. "Yeah. I'm not ... feeling particularly macho at the moment."

"Okay, look me in the eye." He bent close to the injured man and gentled his tone. "Feel the pain drain away, George." His voice was a low, hypnotic croon. "Going. Going. And gone."

Roberts let out a sigh of relief and relaxed, the white lines around his mouth smoothing. "Thanks, Archer. You're better than Demerol any day."

Hypnotism, Dana thought desperately. *He's not a vampire, he's some kind of hypnotist.*

Yeah. That made sense. The vampire thing ... well, that was just plain ridiculous.

"You're welcome." Archer straightened. "But I still don't want you jumping up and running around until you get the ribs taken care of. You could hurt yourself without knowing it." He glanced over at the other man. "How about you, Stevenson?"

The second agent licked his lips and looked uncomfortable. "I'll pass, boss. I'm not that bad."

"Don't be a dumbass." Roberts sounded annoyed. "Archer's not gonna hurt you. I know you haven't been with us long, but ..."

"It's his choice, George." Archer shoved to his feet. "Stevenson, if you decide you want help after all, don't be too proud to let me know."

"It's not that I don't trust you," the agent said hastily. "It's just the idea of somebody else being in my head ..."

Jesus, Dana thought, stunned. Maybe this guy actually does have some kind of psychic powers.

Uneasily, she flashed on the image of Archer's teeth buried in Anders' throat. Could it be true? Could he be a vampire — the kind of soulless demon her fundamentalist father had always said was abroad on the earth?

No. No way. This was getting too much like an episode of *The X-Files*. She didn't know what was going on here, but it couldn't possibly be what it looked like. There had to be some kind of perfectly logical explanation for all this that didn't involve capes and coffins.

There'd better be. Otherwise the only paper that would touch this story would be *The National Enquirer.*

Licking her lips, Dana aimed the camera at Archer and prepared to take another photo — just as he lifted his head, looked straight up at her and called, "Get any good shots, Ms. Ivory?"

Dana froze.

"Who the hell are you talking to, Archer?" The agent who'd checked on Roberts and Stevenson moved to join him, looking up at the tree-house over their heads.

"Remember the newspaper reporter the sheriff warned us about? She's up there taking pictures." Propping his fists on his lean hips, Archer stared upward. Dana knew the treehouse window was shrouded in utter blackness, yet he looked as if he could see her clearly. But that was impossible. Unless ...

Jesus, she thought, unable to deny the weight of the evidence any longer. *He really is a vampire.*

"She's been up there with a microphone since before we arrived. I can hear her breathing and the tape recorder running." Archer shook his head. "Then she started snapping photos, though God knows why — she's not using a flash, and there's no way in hell they'll come out."

"Oh. Well, you can handle it." The agent looked around at his com-rades. "Come on, let's load these morons up. Where the hell is EMS?"

"Dispatcher said they're on the way," somebody called back.

As Dana watched, frozen, the men hauled their prisoners to their feet. It took some sharp calls and shakes to rouse Anders and Satterfield, both of whom staggered and blinked once they were finally upright, disoriented as drunks.

"Look, Ms. Ivory, nobody's going to hurt you," Archer called, his tone patient. "You can come on down now. I just want to talk to you."

And then he'll look me in the eyes and make me forget the whole thing ever happened, Dana thought.

Like hell. She wasn't losing the story of a lifetime to some vampire's mental magic, badge or no badge.

Dana looped the camera strap over her head, then grabbed her tape recorder and mike and jumped to her feet. Wheeling for the door, she took a single lunging step forward.

Her left foot smashed through a rotten floorboard.

Dana fell, equipment tumbling. She caught herself on her hands and one knee, only to feel her ankle twist with an agonizing wrench of pain.

Biting back a frantic curse, she tried to jerk free. All she got for her trouble was a jagged board digging more deeply into her trapped leg. Dana gritted her teeth, grabbed her thigh in both hands and pulled. The board dug deeper, bringing tears to her eyes. Something hot rolled down her ankle.

Great. Here she was, trapped and bleeding with Tall, Dark and Toothy waiting to pounce.

"Calm down. You're just making it worse."

Dana looked up to see the vampire standing silhouetted in the door of the treehouse.

Chapter Two

He could see the reporter plainly with his vampire night vision, though Gabriel Archer knew the room must be pitch black to her.

"So," she demanded as she glared up at him through her platinum blonde bangs, grey eyes narrowed with a mixture of fright and defiance. "Are you going to bite me next?"

Archer killed the impulse to purr, "Oh, could I?" Instead he gave her an easy smile. "I wasn't planning on it."

"Well, that's a relief." But she didn't look relieved as she crouched there on the floor, one long, slim leg caught in a jagged hole in the rotten wood, her full breasts quivering with every agitated breath.

She was young, Archer judged. In her mid-twenties at most. And lovely, with a narrow, delicately angular face and a thin nose that tilted just slightly at the end. Under that shaggy mop of moonlight-pale hair, her eyes were the misty grey of clouds after a storm, wary and wide. It was the kind of face you'd expect to see peering out from beneath a mushroom — except there was nothing fairy-like about those centerfold breasts.

Or that courtesan's mouth, Archer thought with a stir of hunger. Her lips were full, pouting and exotic, parted slightly to reveal straight, white teeth. There was a wealth of erotic potential in that mouth.

Her feminine scent only added to the temptation: gently musky, blending with the sharp copper of blood to set Archer's appetite burning. She must have cut herself in that fall.

God, he'd love to kiss it and make it well.

Looking at her, scenting her, Archer felt a ravenous heat. He might consider himself a professional, but his body was a creature of sex, blood and seduction. A woman like her could feed all his favorite hungers.

Unfortunately, the middle of a mission was not the time to indulge.

While Archer worked for self-control, Dana's features smoothed as though she were reaching for calm herself. She sat back, bracing her hands behind her. The position arched her spine, and Archer took shameless advantage of the darkness to eye her breasts. She was wearing a bra under that cotton shirt, but he was willing to bet it was little more than a veil of lace over her tempting flesh.

"Just how many vampires does the FBI have on the payroll?" Dana asked, sounding as cool as Sam Donaldson grilling the President. A real feat considering the rapid heartbeat he could hear slamming out her terror.

The question startled an admiring laugh out of him. "Damn, you've got guts. No brains to speak of, but guts to spare."

"Just doing my job, Agent. And you didn't answer the question."

"I'm not with the FBI. It's another federal agency altogether."

"Called?"

"I could tell you." Archer smiled slowly as he put his own spin on the old spook joke. "But then I'd have to bite you."

"I could guess, and you could nod," Dana suggested boldly. "The Bureau of Vampire Intelligence? The Central Vampire Agency?" Her full mouth twitched in an impish smile. "Fangs 'R' Us?"

"The Federal Office of Inquiry and Analysis." She wouldn't remember it in ten minutes anyway.

"Never heard of it."

"I'd be worried if you had."

"Sounds more like accountants than vampires."

"That's the idea."

"How long have you been a vampire, anyway?"

Archer shook his head. "I can't believe you're trying to interview me. Not thirty minutes ago, you watched me come close to tearing out a man's throat. Most people would be babbling right about now."

"I'm babbling on the inside. How long have you been a vampire?"

"Two hundred and twenty-six years." He just wanted to see her reaction.

She didn't give him one. "How long have you been working for the government?"

"Two hundred and twenty-three."

That stopped her, but she rallied. "So what were the Founding Fathers like?"

"That thing about the cherry tree is a myth, Washington's teeth were ivory rather than wood, and Congress was just as big a pain in the ass as it is now."

"That doesn't surprise me."

"Nothing much does, does it?"

She smiled slowly, ambition and confidence in her eyes. "I mean to play in the big leagues, Mr. Archer. I can't afford to be taken by surprise."

I'd like to take you. Slowly. "Why don't you come down to the fire where we can see each other better, and we'll continue this conversation," he said, his voice far more husky than he'd intended.

"Where we can see each other better. Right," she said, sounding surprisingly tough for somebody with that face. "Translated: where I can look deep into your eyes and you can put the vampire whammy on me. And suddenly all my questions will disappear."

Archer grinned. "Smart girl."

Her tempting lips peeled back from her pretty white teeth. "You're not messing with my head."

"Don't you think it's best all around? It's not like anybody will believe you."

"They won't have to." Dana snorted and gingerly pulled at her trapped leg. "What kind of moron do you think I am? I'm not blowing my chance at a national story because of your overbite."

He walked lightly across the rotting flooring to kneel beside her. She shrank back, but Archer ignored the movement and reached down to twist the broken length of board away from her calf. "It won't hurt you to forget a detail or two. You'll still get your exclusive."

"Forget it. I'm not thrilled about having somebody else edit my copy. I sure as hell don't want you editing my head." Dana pulled her leg free with a tiny gasp of pain, then cautiously felt for the wound in the darkness. He could see it wasn't serious, though she could probably use a tetanus shot.

Archer sighed and stood, reaching down to pull her to her feet. "Ms. Ivory, I'm afraid you've missed the point. I'm not giving you a choice."

Dana narrowed her cloud-grey eyes in anger. He could almost see her busy little brain working out her chances of escape. The results evidently didn't please her; her shoulders slumped. Then she mustered a glower. "You've got no right to rape people's minds just so you won't be inconvenienced."

"Inconvenienced?" He snorted. "Ms. Ivory, if people knew what I am, they'd hunt me down like a rabid dog."

"So what about government officials? They've got to know about you." Dana bent and started to feel around in the dark for her camera.

"Only the few who need to. To others, I'm just another operative. The rest have never heard of me at all. And I keep it that way." Archer scooped up the camera, microphone and tape recorder, then handed the whole armload to her.

"Thanks," Dana grumbled. He took her elbow to guide her toward the door, where she ended up giving the pile back to him so she could climb down the treehouse ladder.

She moved stiffly as she crouched to feel for the first rung with her foot. Archer suspected her injured leg was hurting, but when he offered to help, Dana aimed such a cold look up at him that he shrugged.

Delicate jaw set, she began to descend, her long, slim hands white-knuckled as they gripped the rungs. He climbed after her, holding her gear in one arm.

When Dana reached the ground, she immediately turned her back on him. Archer smiled in reluctant admiration, recognizing her stubborn determination to make his job as difficult as possible.

The clearing was empty except for the dying fire. His men had gone, headed for the sheriff's office and the nearest jail to book their prisoners. His unruly body immediately began to see the possibilities, but Archer reined in its eager leap with his habitual self-control. Business first. He wanted to change her memories and be done with it; he'd had enough of her pricks to his conscience.

But he'd make it up to her, Archer told himself. As soon as he checked on his men, he'd give Dana an exclusive about the arrest and finish up the paperwork.

Then, once duty was served, he'd turn his attention to seducing her.

Archer loved a good seduction. The sweet, hot quest to discover what aroused a woman most, the erotic dance of temptation once he found the key to her heat. Especially when the woman had this one's fire and will — not to mention edible little body. She'd be both a challenge and a pleasure.

He dumped her equipment on the ground and moved up behind her. "Look at me, Dana." Softly, he added, "I promise I won't hurt you."

Dana whirled on him, grey eyes snapping in the firelight. "The hell you won't."

"Then I'll be quick." Archer locked his gaze on hers, the way the Countess had taught him two centuries ago, and reached for her mind with his own. He expected the usual easy tumble into alien memories, feelings, hopes and fears.

Instead he felt … Nothing.

Her grey eyes didn't widen, didn't glaze, didn't falter from his in their cool, defiant stare. It was as though she looked at him through a glass shield.

Archer felt a quick spurt of delight at the unexpected resistance. He forced it down. He'd gotten his hopes up before when he'd encountered this kind of mental barrier, only to be disappointed again and again. If he pushed a little harder, her mind would yield to his control the way all the others had.

He gathered his considerable psychic power and stabbed it like a rapier straight between those wide grey eyes.

There. He waited for her to open to him …

"Are you going to do whatever it is, or not?"

God. Archer stared at her, staggered. His mental thrust should have punched right through her resistance, opening her mind to his. But it hadn't.

She was a candidate for the Kiss.

Finally, after two hundred and twenty-six years, he'd found a woman who could survive rebirth as a vampire.

Maybe, Archer cautioned himself. She had the psychic strength, but there was more to it than that. Much more. He needed time, time to examine and probe. Time to decide what to do.

Suspended between hope and wariness, Archer stared at her. She met his gaze stubbornly, her features set in rebellion.

Candidate or not, he realized Dana Ivory was going to be a problem.

For one thing, what was Archer going to do about her knowledge of his vampirism until he decided whether to change her? He had no idea if she could be trusted. He'd survived in his country's service all these years through ruthless secrecy, but Dana could force him into the glare of a national spotlight even if she never used the word "vampire." Once her story hit the Associated Press wire service, he was screwed. There was no way he could influence all the thousands of editors who used the AP into killing the story.

He had to get her under control.

Fortunately, Gabriel Archer had two centuries' practice in controlling women.

At first it was all Dana could do not to shake when she met his gaze. Archer's eyes looked so blue and cold and merciless as he stared into hers. And so knowing, as if he were immensely old. Looking into that immortal stare, she finally *believed* he was a vampire.

Her father's religious teachings stirred uneasily in her mind. If he was a vampire, didn't that make him some kind of demon?

Yet a demon would have helped the kind of men who bombed churches. Archer had jailed them. So he couldn't be a demon.

But what was he?

As she stared up at Archer, Dana suddenly realized his expression had softened, becoming less ruthless, almost seductive. His lids lowered, pupils expanding into dark pools set in his crystalline blue irises. The tight line of his mouth relaxed, taking on a sensual curve, and his nostrils flared as if scenting her. He took one step closer, then another, until he was so close his big body seemed to surround hers.

Her mouth went dry as she remembered the way he'd looked with his shirt off, the intensely male contours gleaming in the firelight. She took a step back.

"Are you afraid of me, Dana?" Archer murmured, closing the distance between them again.

God, his chest was broad. It seemed to fill her vision. And the T-shirt fabric clung, so she could see all that fascinating masculine topography.

Like the way the black material tented over the tiny nub of his left nipple. She wet her lips and resisted the impulse to look down, see if something else might be protruding beneath his jeans.

"You shouldn't be afraid," he said, his velvet and whiskey voice curling around her senses. Archer lowered his head toward hers, his hair falling forward. Dana watched, hypnotized, as strand slipped over dark, gleaming strand, tumbling in slow motion against the stern rise of his cheek. She wanted to touch his hair, feel its silken length slip through her fingers.

"I have no desire to hurt you," he said softly. "There are so many better things to do." His breath gusted over her lips, warm and smelling faintly yeasty.

"Beer," Dana blurted, groping for a way to resist the lush spell he was spinning around her. "I didn't think vampires drank anything but blood."

"Don't believe everything you hear." Gently, Archer reached up and smoothed her own tumbled hair back from her forehead. His fingers felt warm, almost feverish. Wasn't a vampire's skin supposed to be cold? *Another myth shot to hell,* she thought, fighting dizziness.

"Don't be afraid of me, Dana," he said, his voice a deep, seductive rumble. "I'm one of the good guys." His eyelashes cast long shadows against his elegant cheekbones as he lowered his head. "Very, very good."

And then his lips touched hers, hot silk, brushing once, then clinging, slowly drawing her lower lip into his mouth to gently suckle. His tongue slipped across it, wet and clever, tempting her to open her own mouth, let him inside.

Her head went into a long, slow spin. What was happening to her?

He was touching her now, gentle little strokes, here on her shoulder, there on her cheek, a fingertip dance on her waist, slipping into a caress of her hip. How could a man who could throw Donnie Anders around with brutal strength touch her with such delicacy?

Dana dragged her mouth away from his and gasped. "I thought you were supposed to hypnotize me, make me forget."

"Oh, I want to make you forget." His mouth moved to her ear, nibbled, breathed. "I want you to forget how to say no."

Dana tried to brace her hands against his chest to hold him back, but she couldn't seem to summon the strength. And that alarming weakness spread quickly, rolling from her arms to her knees. She tried to stiffen her legs and stand erect, only to find herself leaning into his chest, surrendering to those hot, seductive hands.

One of them had discovered her bottom. He traced the curve of a jeans-clad cheek with long fingers, then slipped into the cleft to exert a suggestive, wicked pressure. Dana tightened reflexively, unintentionally thrusting forward against his groin. Where she felt the thick, hard length of his erection jutting against the zipper of his jeans. He rolled his hips, letting her feel the massive ridge. She gasped, and he purred a laugh in her ear.

He's got me acting like a skittish virgin, she thought, appalled. "Stop that. Aren't you on duty?"

"I'm taking a dinner break," he whispered, and bit her earlobe. One of those quick hands found its way under her shirt and slid upward toward her breasts. "How about it, Dana. Wouldn't you like to be dinner?"

The hand captured her, slipping over her breast to encircle it with long, possessive fingers. She caught her breath as the sensation unfurled along her nerves. He squeezed gently, his heat searing her skin through the lace of her bra. "No," Dana protested. It came out as a tiny, helpless whimper, sounding arousing even to her ears.

"But you'd make such a lovely feast. And I'm so hungry." He delicately pinched her nipple, which drew into a tight, tingling peak at his touch. "I could spend hours devouring these beautiful breasts. Let me see them, Dana."

"You've done something to me," she moaned.

"Not yet." He grabbed her shirt and ruthlessly pulled it off over her head, then dragged the bra down. "But I'm going to."

Dazed, Dana looked down to see her own bare breasts glowing pale in the firelight, the nipples hard, rosy points. Then Archer's head covered one breast while his hand claimed the other. His mouth sucked and bit as his fingers tormented until need jerked tight in her belly.

Dana's feet went out from under her. She yelped, grabbing at Archer for support, only to realize he'd swept her up in his arms. Still suckling greedily at her helpless nipple, he lowered her to the ground. Dry leaves crunched under her bared back.

For a moment Archer loomed above her, his massive shoulders edged in moonlight before he descended on her to continue his leisurely feast.

Dana twisted helplessly at the sensation created by his swirling, lapping tongue, then groaned as a hand slid between her legs, pressing into her cleft through her jeans until she thought she'd burst into flames. She panted, past protest now, her body yowling for him, for his mouth and his fingers and his erection.

Distantly, she heard the erotic whisper of her zipper sliding down. Then his hand touched her silk-clad belly, slipping past the waistband to search out wet curls and tight, soft lips. One long finger dipped inside, gliding through the thick cream of her arousal to slowly pump. Then another joined it, and another, filling her full. She moaned.

It had been so long.

This was just like her fantasies, Dana thought, in helpless, shamed excitement — the ones she never told anyone about because they were so sinful. Being taken by a stranger in the woods, letting him touch and taste and bite.

Bite.

The word stabbed her with a sudden realization that sliced through the heat in her mind like a dagger of ice.

He wasn't just any stranger. He was a vampire.

And this wasn't about love or even sex. He intended to feed on her.

"Stop it." Her voice was low and determined. "Now."

Archer froze, his mouth filled with hard nipple, his fingers buried in tight, lush sex. He was triply erect, fangs and cock, lust searing his veins until he ached.

But he didn't ignore that tone. Ever.

"I said get off me!" Her hands pushed at his shoulders.

"All right, dammit!" He jerked away and shot to his feet, retreating several paces as Dana jumped up and began to jerk and zip at her clothes. Aching, frustrated, Archer watched her pale breasts bounce as she scooped her shirt off the ground and shrugged into it.

"I thought you were supposed to be one of the good guys," she said bitterly.

"You weren't complaining a minute ago." Archer barely managed not to snarl. Showing fang at a time like this would be too much like a threat.

Dana jerked her head up. Her grey eyes swam with betrayed tears. "You said you would make me forget you're a vampire. You didn't say anything about making me sleep with you."

He gaped at her. "You think I did this with psi?"

"Didn't you?"

"I'm a seducer, not a rapist," Archer snapped. "I'd never use psychic influence to get a woman into bed."

Dana fisted her hands on her hips. "Oh, right. One minute you're going to hypnotize me, the next, I'm on the ground letting you suck my nipples. But you didn't use 'psychic influence.' "

"I'm *good*," he snarled.

"You're a vampire," she hurled at him. "You couldn't be good if you tried. You're damned by God."

For a moment Archer couldn't believe she'd said the words. This was the twenty-first century, and she was giving him the same line he'd heard in the eighteenth. "God and Satan have nothing to do with vampirism. It's a virus. You catch it."

That stopped her. Her pale brows drew down over those cloud-grey eyes. "How?"

"I'm not in the mood for another fucking interview," he ground out.

"I've just been rolling on the ground with you. I think I'm entitled to know."

She had a damn good point. "You have nothing to worry about." *At the moment, anyway.* "You can't catch the vampire virus from a kiss. Or a toilet seat, or a sneeze. You'd only have to worry if you drank my blood."

She wrinkled her pert nose at him. "Ugh. Well, I'm certainly not going to be doing that any time soon." There was a long, tense pause. Finally Dana drew herself upright, evidently deciding to defuse the moment. "When are you going to do your psychic amnesia thing?"

"Already tried." He shrugged. "It doesn't work on you."

She blinked. "Why not?"

"I don't know." A lie, but she wasn't ready for the truth.

A relieved smile spread across Dana's face, winsome and sweet. "Well, in that case, I'll just be getting back to the paper. I've got a story to write." She turned on her heel and started out of the clearing.

"No." He couldn't let her leave. Not now.

She whirled back to him, eyes widening. "But I told you, I'm not going to use any of the vampire stuff. Nobody would believe me anyway."

"I'm not even talking about the 'vampire stuff.' I just don't want this story out right now."

"Too bad. It's out."

"Dana, I flushed Satterfield's plot by using psi on the WAB's founder and ordering him to recommend me to anybody planning something big. If you report this, Jonah Howard will get suspicious, and he won't let me get close enough to influence him again. And I have reason to believe the WAB is planning other terrorist actions."

Well, it sounded plausible, anyway. In reality, Howard would have a hell of a time keeping Archer away no matter how suspicious he was. All Archer had to do was walk up to him in the grocery store, look him in the eye and give him an order, and Howard would do whatever the hell he wanted. But Dana didn't know that.

She shook her shaggy blonde head. "Archer, those men were going to assassinate the President. You can't keep something that big a secret."

He laughed. "Oh, I've kept much bigger secrets than this."

"But …"

"I am not letting you go, Dana."

She bared her teeth at him. "You can't keep me."

Archer reached into his back pocket and pulled out a pair of handcuffs. "Can't I?" He started toward her. "You have the right to remain silent …"

Dana backed up. "But I haven't done anything!"

"How about interfering with a federal investigation?"

"Interfering, hell, I'm just reporting it. Or did they repeal the First Amendment when nobody was looking?"

"Sorry." Archer grabbed her shoulder and spun her around. Catching her slim wrists, he pulled them behind her, trapped them in one hand, and snapped on the 'cuffs.

"I want a lawyer, you toothy jerk!" She turned her head to glare over her shoulder at him, her grey eyes snapping. Those moonlight pale curls framed her face, and her full mouth looked mutinous, kissable. "Now."

"You'll get a lawyer when I say you get a lawyer. In the meantime, you'll stay in my custody." Temper simmering, Archer leaned close to her delicate little ear and whispered mockingly, "How *do* you feel about bondage, Dana?"

Her heartbeat leaped.

"Ahh." A smile of delight spread across his face. "Does innocent Dana have a guilty secret?"

As he watched, a tide of red flooded from her cleavage right up to her hairline.

And he knew he had her.

Chapter Three

Dana picked nervously at a hole in the vinyl seat of her chair, then realized what she was doing and forced herself to stop. She was in enough trouble without destroying the property of the Adams County Sheriff's Department. Guiltily, she looked around the office, but none of the detectives were watching her.

And Archer and his handcuffs were nowhere to be seen.

Thank God. An hour had passed since he'd hit her with his wicked suggestion, but her skin still felt hot from that blush. Damn her misspent adolescence anyway. And damn big brother Mark and his stash of Victorian erotica.

She slumped. At least Archer'd had the courtesy to take the handcuffs off before he'd escorted her into the building. It would have been mortifying to be cuffed in front of the deputies she'd been working with for the past six years.

Unfortunately, he'd killed the spurt of gratitude she'd felt by leaning over and whispering in her ear, "They go back on … later."

That last "later" was spoken in such a tone of velvet suggestion that she'd felt the blush roll right back up to her hairline again.

Dana glowered, remembering the curious looks her red face had gotten from the deputies as they'd walked in. She'd promptly blushed even hotter. She just wasn't equipped to keep her cool in the face of Archer's sophisticated games, not with her upbringing.

From the day Dana had turned thirteen, her evangelist mother had exercised her considerable talent for fire and brimstone preaching on the subject of sex. "Intercourse," as Helen Ivory called it, was powerful and innately corrupting, and should only be risked under the protection of marriage for the purpose of begetting children. Anything else was sinful.

Helen also laced her lectures with well-meant misinformation: the AIDS virus would go right through latex condoms, and abortions would leave you sterile and suicidal.

Dana's outrage when she'd discovered she'd been lied to was one of the reasons she'd gone into journalism, the business of spreading truth whether anybody liked it or not.

But that strict upbringing also left her hungry for any knowledge whatsoever about sex. So the day she discovered her brother's hidden porn cache in the attic when she was sixteen, she'd pounced on it.

At first Dana had been horrified at the stories, with their blatant misogyny and streak of cruelty. But she'd been equally excited by their eroticism. Even though guilt had quickly driven her out of the attic, fascination had repeatedly lured her back. She'd spent hours up there on a discarded couch, reading in the light from a tiny attic window as she caressed herself in guilty excitement.

From then on, her fantasies revolved around wickedly handsome rakes and bound virgin prisoners. Hell, she still had those fantasies, and she still felt guilty, not so much out of a fear of brimstone as the knowledge she shouldn't be aroused by the idea of submitting to anybody's domination.

Unfortunately, her libido didn't seem to have a social conscience. And it loved Archer, archetype of wickedly seductive dominance that he was. The man was the sum total of every fantasy she'd ever had: handsome, built like a Roman gladiator, and gifted with enough erotic skill to make a woman get down and beg. Dana would bet her last notebook Archer had actually *been* a Victorian rake. He certainly seemed to sense her darkest fantasies, knowing just how to drive her right into a frenzy.

Yet he'd stopped when she'd said no and meant it.

Unfortunately, he was also planning to book her on some pretty serious federal charges.

Dana slumped, discouraged, and braced an elbow on the battered desk beside her. Brooding, she turned her attention to the federal agent who was typing with two fingers on a small black laptop. He must have brought the computer with him; God knew the Adams County Sheriff's Department couldn't afford any tech that high.

"Did Archer really fight in the Revolutionary War?"

The agent looked up and gaped at her, then glanced around hastily for eavesdroppers. Seeing none, he whispered, "He told you that? And let you remember it?"

"His psychic thing doesn't work on me. Did he?"

He frowned. "His psychic thing always works." Hazel eyes focused on her, sharp in the agent's middle-aged face. He was in his fifties, Dana estimated, with tired, lived-in features and thinning sandy hair, but his body was as hard and lean as a teenager's in its black fatigues. "No comment."

"But ..."

"I'm not telling you a damn thing, lady," he interrupted, his voice cold. "Especially not if Archer's psi doesn't work on you."

"Fitzroy," Archer said from the doorway.

"Yes sir?"

"I need to talk to you a minute. And you." He shot Dana a hard look. "Quit trying to interview everything that moves."

She slumped down in her chair with a sigh of disgust.

Michael Fitzroy followed Archer into the interview room and shut the door. "How'd it go?"

He closed his eyes and rubbed his temples. Repeated psychic sessions always gave him a murderous headache. "They'll cooperate fully for the next forty-eight hours or so. You'll need to gather all the evidence they'll give you before my influence wears off."

Fitzroy lifted a greying eyebrow. "You sound like you don't plan to be there."

Archer shrugged. "You can handle them. Besides, I've got another project." *Which should be a lot more fun.* "By the way, I want you to do a full security check on Dana Ivory — the works. I want to know her bank balance, her work history, her parents, her shoe size, what her third grade teacher thought of her and who gave her that first kiss. Everything, right down to the ground. The same check we give prospective agents. Then e-mail the data to me. I'll be at the house in Charleston."

Fitzroy stared at him, gaze sharpening. "Why? What the hell's going on, Archer?"

"She's a candidate, Fitz."

"For the *team*?" He looked horrified.

"More than that — for the Kiss."

"*You want to make her a vampire?*"

Archer gave him an annoyed look. "Would you hold it down?"

Fitzroy moved closer and dropped his voice to a hiss. "Shit, Arch, are you getting Alzheimer's? She's a kid. She can't be more'n twenty-five. You can't seriously mean to give her your kind of power. Besides, she's a *reporter*."

He said the word in a tone of such deep loathing Archer had to grin. "It's not a dirty word, Fitz."

"The hell it's not. Look, Arch, this little bimbo makes a living telling morons things they've got no business knowing. And you want to hand her the biggest secret in U.S. history? Why not make a fuckin' sixty-second commercial and run it during the Superbowl!"

"Once she joins the team, she won't tell anybody anything." Archer scrubbed both hands through his hair, trying to make his second-in-command understand. "Look, I believe Dana has the strength to become a vampire without going insane. And I have never met anyone else I could say that about in my entire life, including you. That makes her a potential intelligence asset we can't ignore." He looked up and caught his friend in a determined stare. "I have to check her out."

Agitated, Fitzroy turned and began to pace. "What if you change her, and she misuses the power?"

"Then I'll kill her."

The agent snorted. "Oh, you are so full of shit. You hate hurting women, up to and including psychopathic terrorists. This kid would just look at you with those big grey eyes and you wouldn't be able to lay a finger on her. And we'd all be fucked."

"I said I'd handle her," Archer snapped. "Look, I'm not going to change her unless I'm sure she'll work, all right? Besides, she may not even agree."

Fitzroy threw up both hands. "Fine. You do whatever the hell you think best. You always do. But you'd better damn well be right."

Archer set his jaw. "Don't worry. I know exactly what to do."

≈⚔❦ᗺ❦⚔≈

Dana looked up as Archer stalked back into the detective's office and gave her a smoldering look. "Come with me."

She rose to her feet, eyeing him warily as he strode over to grab her by the elbow. "Where are we going?"

"You'll find out." Archer pulled her around and propelled her out of the office and down the hall toward the front door.

"Am I under arrest or what?" Dana tried to set her feet, but his relentless strength kept her moving. "Look, you haven't booked me, which means I haven't been charged, which means you have no right to hold me. I could report you for this. Who's your supervisor?"

He angled her an amused look. "Don't try to bluff me, Dana. Even if you did file a report, do you really think I'd let anybody take action against me?"

Damn. She hadn't thought of that. She could scream bloody murder clear to the President, and all Archer would have to do is whisper in the right ear to make it all go away. True, she could go to the press — he couldn't use his psi on everybody – but he could have the right people declare her a nut, and she'd be written off. Maybe even hospitalized.

A sudden chill skated Dana's spine. *He could do anything he wanted to her, and nobody would ever say a word.*

Feeling helpless, she stumbled after Archer as he pushed open the department door and pulled her out into the dark.

"What are you going to do to me?" Dana licked her dry lips.

He laughed, a low, seductive rumble. "I don't know yet. I'm still trying to make a list." With a flex of his arm, Archer swung her around the corner of the building. Her foot slipped as a piece of gravel rolled under it, but before she could smash into the brick, his big hands caught and steadied her. Then he planted a palm between her shoulder blades and gently pressed her face-first against the rough surface of the wall.

"Let's start with a frisk, shall we?" Before Dana could jerk back, Archer kicked her feet wide, then moved up behind her. She gasped as he slid his muscular thigh up between her legs until it pressed against her sex, forcing her to ride him. She was just gathering the breath to protest when his big hands began to explore her body as if he owned it.

"Archer, what the hell are you doing?" she gasped. "One of the deputies could drive up!"

"It's so dark back here the only one who can see a damn thing is me." His breath gusted warmly against her ear as he dragged her back against his powerful body, then cupped his hands around her breasts. His thumbs strummed her nipples through her shirt. She felt them harden. "Hell, you can't even see what I'm doing, can you? But I can. You've got beautiful breasts, Dana." His tongue flicked out, tested one of the straining cords of her neck.

"Archer ..."

"Ever been strip-searched?" Archer's voice was so darkly suggestive, she shivered. "How about a body cavity probe? We could play pretty little hooker and bad, bad cop. I'll bet you'd like that."

Dammit, how did he do this to her? How did he know just the right notes to hit? Thirty seconds, and he had her creaming. It was humiliating. "I'm not interested in playing anything with you," Dana gritted.

"It's against the law to lie to an agent of the Federal government, Dana." He brought his leg up higher, lifting her off the ground and forcing her sex hard against his thigh. Heat scalded her. "Do it again and I'll have to pull down your pants and spank you."

It was all she could do not to writhe as she rode his leg. "This isn't right," Dana gasped. "It's just a game to you, isn't it? It's a role. Dominant male."

"It's what I am," Archer purred in her ear, fingers plucking her nipples through the thin fabric of her shirt. "There are too damn many of you and only one of me. I've got to dominate you or I'm dead."

He pressed closer until Dana could feel the entire length of his body against her back. She licked her lips as his rigid erection ground against her bottom. "I've got to find out what you need and give it to you, so you won't notice when I steal what *I* need. And what I need is you spread wide and wet under me, ready for my fangs and cock." He pressed her against the wall until she could feel every thick, powerful inch of him. "And Dana, you're going to give me just what I need."

"No," she moaned.

"Oh, yes. Over and over, every way I can think of." Slowly, Archer rolled his hips against her bottom, forcing her to imagine what it would be like to be at the mercy of his power. "On your belly with your ass in the air and your hands cuffed behind you. Tied spread-eagle to my big tester bed while I lick and taste all that creamy white skin. On your knees, sucking my cock until I shoot into your mouth."

"I won't!" Dana gasped, hot cream flooding her sex.

"You will," he retorted, his voice rich with velvet menace, his strong hands kneading her breasts. "Again and again. And you'll love every minute of it while I show you just what a vampire can do to a bound and naked woman."

"You'll have to use force," she said, trying for toughness.

"Oh, I will." He twisted her nipples. "Just the way you've always dreamed."

Shame and excitement stung her. "You don't know a damn thing about my dreams."

"I know how your heartbeat speeds when I talk about what I want to do to you. And I can smell how wet you are right now. I'd like to take your jeans down and lap you all up while you writhe and beg." He took her earlobe between his teeth and gently bit. "But you'd love it even better if I handcuffed you first. Admit it."

"No." She swallowed.

"At night in your lonely bed, you dream of being at the mercy of a man like me. Bound and spread and helpless. Ready to be fucked."

Humiliation shafted through the languid desire he'd roused. It was as if he'd eavesdropped on her darkest fantasies, the ones she hated to admit even to herself. "I'm not a toy, damn you!" Dana cried, her voice ragged with shame. "Don't treat me like one!"

Archer froze. She felt the hot wind of his breath gusting hard against her ear, heard him swallow. "No," he said, his voice hoarse. "You're not a toy."

Then he was gone, releasing her so quickly she would have fallen if he hadn't caught her again. He spun her around, gathering her wrists in one hand. She felt the touch of something cool around one of them, heard a snap, a musical rattle.

He was handcuffing her again. He was going to take her right here in the parking lot.

"No!" Dana fought to pull away, but he was too strong. "Not like this. Please, Archer!"

"Calm down," he said roughly. "I'm not going to do it here."

Panting, she subsided. He led her to the passenger side of one of the big, government cars parked in the lot and bundled her inside. Dana sat there, dazed, while he leaned in to buckle the seatbelt around her. His hair brushed her face as he snapped the belt together. She remembered what he'd said about smelling her wetness. She shivered in arousal and shame.

Archer pulled away from her and closed the door with a solid thunk. A moment later the driver's door opened, and he got in. The car started with a well-mannered growl.

"Where are we going?"

"Charleston. I have a house there." He threw the car into reverse and began to back up.

"Charleston. That's a two hour drive." Two hours in the car with him. Alone. And then they'd be at his house.

Alone.

She just wished the idea didn't make her feel so hot.

There was something about Dana that made him lose control.

Archer had planned to take it slow, play the dark master of seduction until he had her begging. It was a part he'd acted for countless partners until he knew every leisurely step, every stylized gesture.

So when he'd pushed Dana against the wall, he'd intended nothing more than the opening act. Then he'd touched her, tasted her skin, scented her growing arousal, seen her blend of trembling desire and shame. He'd taken those full breasts in his hands, and hunger had roared over him in a wave so strong he'd come within a hair's-breadth of ripping her jeans down and taking her. Right there against the wall.

But the game was not supposed to affect Archer this way. He was supposed to be in control — of her and himself. An actor, playing a role. That was, after all, what he did best: act, whether the part was white supremacist assassin, Nazi S.S. officer, or demon lover. Whatever it was, Archer wrapped himself in the role, but he never lost sight of his goal and never forgot he was acting.

Yet somehow, Dana Ivory made him forget. This game was about gaining control of a potential vampire agent, yet he was the one who was being seduced. She kicked his hunger so high and so hot that all he wanted was to sweep her up and take her. Take her body, take her blood, take her heart. Take her and own her, until she was his without question, without possibility of escape.

And Dana responded deliciously, but she also fought that response, refusing to simply go along with the game. Archer wasn't sure he understood why. Usually women were more than happy to let him play the demon lover, never questioning what his real feelings were. He suspected they thought of him as nothing more than a fantasy given delicious life. And nobody cared about the feelings of a fantasy.

Yet Dana seemed to want something more. He had no idea what, or how to give it to her. Or even if he should.

Still, she responded to his demon lover. And that would have to be enough — for both of them.

She should be afraid of him, Dana thought.

For God's sake, the man was a vampire. He'd handcuffed and abducted her for sex and bondage. He could even kill her and make sure no one ever caught him. Yet she felt no physical fear of him at all.

Paranoia stirred. Maybe she was under some kind of spell after all.

But … She stole a look at Archer's Roman coin profile as he drove. There was, despite every wicked thing he'd threatened her with, a basic core of decency under that dominant male mask of his. There wasn't even any real cruelty. He wouldn't hurt her. Not physically.

Emotionally, she wasn't so sure about. Dana didn't like the way he was getting to her, the way he'd figured out her darkest fantasies and turned them against her.

"How do you do it?" She asked the question before she realized she was going to. "How do you always know how to make me respond?"

Archer looked at her. His eyes reflected a glow of red in the light of a passing car, making her heart leap at the eerie shimmer they gave off. Dana expected him to give her another one of those suggestive lines of his, but his tone was serious when he answered. "I've been at this two centuries and more, Dana. I serve my country out of duty, but I seduce to survive."

"Why?" she demanded, not sounding nearly as cool as she wished. "Why does it matter to you what my fantasies are?"

Archer turned his head again to watch the road. "A vampire feeds on strong emotion as much as blood. The higher, the hotter, I can get my partner, the stronger the psychic charge she gives me in her climax. I learned a long time ago how to read the needs a woman can't speak, that she can't even allow a lover to guess. When I feed that hidden need, the response is explosive."

She stirred uneasily against the leather seat. "Then what? You just walk away? You've been fed, and that's it? What about how she feels?"

"You imagine a trail of broken hearts in my wake?" Archer snorted. "Women don't fall in love with a guilty fantasy. Generally they can't forget me fast enough."

Dana frowned, studying his profile in the dim, soft light of the dashboard. Was that a flash of vulnerability? "Are you the one with the broken heart, Archer?"

He laughed, a short, bitter bark. "Demon lovers have no hearts, Dana. We fuck, we feed and we walk, and everybody's happy."

"Are you?"

"Ecstatic." A flash of red. "You can't imagine what it's like, seeing a beautiful woman stretched out in chains, helpless and writhing and hot. Knowing that in a moment I'm going to possess her, sink my cock and my fangs into her delicate flesh …"

Archer tormented Dana like that for the next half-hour, until she finally blurted out, "So how do you become a vampire?"

It was such a transparent attempt to change the subject that he had to smile. Still, talking dirty to Dana was just a little too stimulating, so Archer decided to play along. "Are you asking about me in particular, or vampires in general?"

She licked her lips. "In general, I guess."

Archer eyed her. She looked flushed and flustered, he noted with satisfaction. Not exactly the cool reporter who'd started grilling him the moment they'd met.

"You'd need a weakened immune system, then you'd have to ingest a large amount of infected blood." Nothing like talking about infected blood to wilt an erection. "All of which would probably kill you anyway, but if it didn't, the virus would move in and change the DNA in your cells. That in turn would change your muscles, your bones, your nerves. You'd become enormously strong, and your immune system would be able to heal almost any injury."

Dana frowned. "I thought viruses weakened their hosts, not made them stronger."

"This is more of a symbiotic relationship," Archer said, repeating the explanation a CIA researcher had once given him. "It has to be. The vampire virus is so weak it only survives by making the few who do catch it practically immortal."

"Huh. I'm surprised the government's not infecting people in droves."

Archer winced, remembering one of the CIA's more boneheaded stunts. "They tried. Once. They had this program going in the Sixties, during the Vietnam War. It was so secret even I didn't know about it. They took samples of my blood when I went in for surgery to remove a few bullets. Then …"

"Infected somebody."

He nodded. "I found out about the project when I had to kill the vampire they made, and I made sure they never tried it again."

"You killed him? Why?" Archer could almost see her taking notes in her head. "How'd you stop them?"

"You never quit hunting a story, do you?"

"Nope. Why'd you kill him?"

"He ripped out the throats of the research team." Archer grimaced, remembering the battlefield gore he'd seen in that lab. "One by one. Then he killed the strike force the CIA sent in after him. Twenty-three people died before they finally called me to take care of the problem." He shook his head. "The crazy son of a bitch almost got me, too. God, I was pissed. You can't just pick somebody at random and infect them."

"Why not?"

He glanced at her and told her a crucial truth, knowing she wouldn't recognize it until later. "Because very few people can handle the change. You become aware of the thoughts of others, the beat of their hearts, the blood in their veins — blood you're desperately hungry for. If you're not one of the very few who can generate a psychic shield, you go mad. And it takes another vampire to recognize a potential survivor."

"So they dropped the experiment?" Dana looked uneasy, as if she didn't quite buy it.

"I told them that if I ever found a candidate, I'd let them know. Don't worry, nobody's got a lab somewhere turning out vampires. Not in this country, anyway."

"I can't tell you how relieved that makes me feel," Dana said, rolling her eyes. She was silent a moment, mulling over everything he'd told her. "There must not be very many of you."

"I've met only two, other than the one the CIA spawned. About thirty years ago, there was a Soviet agent named Pavel Andronovich …"

"The Russians have vampires too?"

"Not anymore."

"Oh." Whatever Dana read on his face kept her from asking for the details, thank God.

"Then," he continued, remembering a fall of silken dark hair and hungry eyes, "there was the Countess Isabeau de Vitry, who gave me the Dark Kiss in 1774." Catching her puzzled expression, he explained, "That's what she always called making a vampire, the Dark Kiss. I don't know if that's a universal phrase with vampires, or just another example of Isabeau's French hyperbole."

She eyed him, frowning. "Why not just ask her?"

"The Countess has been dead two centuries." Archer paused, remembering the day of guilt and grief when he'd gotten that last letter from Isabeau's steward. "A French mob took her head during the Terror."

A long, dark pause went by as he fought off black memories, until Dana said, her voice gentle, "It must be lonely."

"I have my work. I have my co-workers." He smiled slightly. "I have women, though usually not for long." Glimpsing Dana's appalled expression, Archer grimaced. "Quit believing everything you see in bad movies. There's something like two gallons of blood in the human body;

I couldn't drink it all in one sitting if I tried. On the other hand, I can give someone a good case of anemia over time, so I tend to go for one night stands."

"No girlfriends? Couldn't you …" She gestured. "… Not bite? At least not every time?"

"Yeah, I could. And I do. Or rather, don't." Archer shook his head. "But it's best not to form close relationships with my partners. It's not fair, it's not practical, and after awhile, it becomes painful." His eyes caught on the delicate curve of her face. "I outlive people, Dana. I'm tired of grieving."

She glanced away. "Yes, I can see how you would be."

"Besides," Archer added wickedly. "There are so many more interesting things to do …"

Dana groaned as he started describing them.

❧❦❧

By the time they pulled into the long, winding driveway, Dana had her legs tightly crossed against the wet ache between them.

Archer had spent the rest of the trip into Charleston describing the things he'd done to eager female victims, recounting acts of sensual decadence in that deep, drawling velvet voice of his until she was squirming and dry-mouthed.

Still feeling dazed, she looked across the darkened expanse of lawn to see a sprawling brick mansion with thick square columns and wide wings stretching out to either side.

"My father built it," Archer told her as he parked the car in a spacious garage. "Of course, I've made some additions." As he opened the driver's door, he flashed her a wicked smile that showed his fangs. "Manacles in the bedroom."

"Daddy would have been shocked," Dana said as he came around to open her door and unbuckle her seatbelt.

"Not really," Archer said, pulling her out of the seat and into his arms with easy strength. Another flash of those teeth. "We owned slaves."

Dana stared at him, so caught between fascination and revulsion that she forgot to protest as he picked her up. "You're kidding."

"Nope." He straightened, cradling her. "Don't look so self-righteous. I freed them all after the war ended." He shrugged. "It didn't feel right, keeping slaves after we'd just fought the British over natural rights. But God, it pissed the neighbors off."

Archer turned and started across the garage, still carrying her like a child. For a moment the novel sensation stunned her, and she froze in his arms, feeling the warm power of his body, breathing his exotic scent.

He smelled faintly of sandalwood and spice, male and tempting. Too tempting.

Sudden panic rose, and she kicked out, trying to squirm her way from his powerful grip. "I can walk!"

"Only if I put you down." He ducked his shoulders so he could open the door without turning her loose, then swept her inside.

She subsided reluctantly. "You are such a high-handed bastard."

He shrugged. "Comes with the territory."

Curiosity overcoming her desire to struggle, Dana peered around the darkened house as he carried her through it. The kitchen was spacious and modern, likely a recent addition, with gleaming white appliances and a surprising array of copper pots hanging over a central island.

As they walked into a hallway, Dana glimpsed a painting of a sailing ship rolling against the sunset in the aftermath of a storm. Archer's booted feet clicked against slate-tile flooring, then they headed up a broad, curving stairway. Toward a bedroom, no doubt. She clasped her hands in the handcuffs, feeling intensely vulnerable.

Just as Dana expected, Archer ducked into a huge bedroom at the top of the stairs, where he put her down at the foot of a gleaming mahogany bed, canopied in what looked like navy brocade and spread with a matching comforter.

Nervously she looked around as he stepped away from her and began to rummage in a drawer. The room was flooded with a golden glow from countless white candles that sat on the mahogany dresser and bureau. The floor was polished hardwood, set here and there with thick woven rugs.

"Who lit the candles?"

"Called the caretaker before we left." Returning, Archer reached for her wrists. There was a coil of gleaming rope in his hand that looked like silk. He smiled into her eyes. "I commit my best sins in candlelight."

"Archer!" Dana pulled away, but he was already backing her against the side of the bed and pulling her arms over her head. "What the hell are you doing?"

"What do you think?" Quickly, efficiently, he tied the rope around the handcuff chain and the overhead canopy support, reaching underneath the canopy to lash them together with a few smooth turns.

She watched him, dizzy with a combination of outrage and desire. "I can't believe I'm letting you get away with this."

"Could you stop me?" Feral eyes locking on hers, he grabbed the front of her shirt between his big hands and gave it an easy tug. Buttons popped, bouncing on the polished wooden floor with a salvo of tiny clicks. Dana looked down to see the white flesh of her breasts swelling in the pretty lace cups of her bra.

Archer made a pleased purring sound in his throat and took hold of the fabric that held the cups together between her breasts. He tore it like paper, then snapped the shoulder straps one by one and threw the ripped bra aside.

Dana tried to swallow the moan. Her knees shook.

Archer stepped close, looking into her eyes. She felt his big hands at her waist, heard a snap, the hiss of her zipper. "Actually," he said, pushing the jeans off her hips, "you could stop me. All you have to do …" The fabric slid down her thighs. She could feel his warm hands brushing her legs. "… is say no."

He went to one knee to slip off her running shoes and socks, then tossed them and the jeans aside. His hair brushed her belly in a stroke of cool silk that made her shiver. Then his mouth was there, pressing a soft kiss to her stomach just before his hands came up to grip the thin silk of her panties. He looked up at her, his eyes pale and hypnotic in the candlelight. "Do you want to say no, Dana?"

She licked her lips, swallowed. "Would you really stop?"

"Yes."

She should say it. She knew she should say it. Her parents would have been appalled that she even hesitated.

She didn't say it.

He smiled. Silk ripped.

Chapter Four

Wrists bound over her head, her heart pounding, Dana looked down at Archer as he tossed aside the remnants of her panties. Then, slowly, he leaned forward until his face was barely an inch from her wet, aching sex. His broad chest lifted and fell as he inhaled, scenting her. She quivered.

He brought a hand up, stroked one long finger over the delicate flesh of her outer lips and the blonde fluff that covered them. "Such pale, pretty curls."

Archer leaned forward, extending his tongue. She could see it, pointed and pink in the instant before it slipped between her lips in a single hot, searing stroke.

"Oh, God!" Unable to help herself, she rose on her toes and rolled her hips forward to give him better access.

"You're so wet," he said, his voice a dreamy drawl. "So ready to be fucked."

Slowly, skillfully, Archer licked at her wet folds, stopping occasionally to suckle her clit and set off a detonation of pleasure. Dana writhed in her bonds, tormented by delight, on the verge of climax. But each time she almost went over, he stopped, waiting for her to subside.

Only to begin again, licking and feasting, driving her higher.

"Archer!" she screamed at last, unable to take any more. "God, now! Please!"

He surged to his feet, one hand at the snap of his jeans, the other catching her under the thigh to pull her legs apart as he stepped between them. The expression on his handsome face was feral, blue eyes narrow and hot, his lips pulled back from white fangs. Dana gasped in a combination of fear and arousal.

"Shit!" Archer let her go and spun away, jerking his black T-shirt over his head as he strode across the room.

"Don't stop!" She stared at his magnificent back and pressed her thighs together, burning to feel him between them. "Why are you stopping?"

"I don't want it over this quick," he growled, without turning around. "I want more."

Bewildered, aching in frustration, Dana watched as he stopped at the bureau, where a crystal decanter sat beside a pair of wine glasses on a silver tray. His hands shook with a fine tremor as he picked up the decanter and poured a stream of something dark into one of the glasses.

Archer took a sip as he turned to face her again, then shook his head. "Almost lost control. I never do that." He took another, deeper sip, then grabbed a wingback chair sitting in a corner and carried it across the room, where he put it down directly in front of her. Dropping into it, Archer eyed her broodingly. "How do you make me break all my rules?"

"The same way you make me break mine." She licked her lips. His chest was a tight, curving sculpture of brawn that shifted in the candlelight as he lifted his hand to drink from the cut crystal glass. The snap of his black jeans was undone, and his cock formed a long, thick ridge under the denim. As she watched, the zipper began inching downward on its own, yielding to the strain of that powerful erection. Dana squirmed, imagining how it would feel driving into her.

Any minute now, she was going to start begging.

Archer had played this scene so many times it should have lost its ability to move him. Hell, just yesterday he'd thought he was getting bored with it all — with the women and the dominance games they so often wanted, with the act he'd always thought was light years from his true personality.

But that was before he'd tied Dana Ivory to his bed in nothing but an open shirt that framed her pert centerfold breasts and the tempting moonlit curls of her sex. Below the shirt, her legs looked as long as his life. The way she kept pressing those sweetly muscled thighs together was slowly driving him insane.

Her grey eyes looked huge in her small face, staring at him with a kind of erotic panic as her tongue slipped out to wet her carnal mouth.

Archer drew in a deep breath, trying for control, but the scent of blood and wet woman mingling in the air almost snapped his grip. He burned to jam himself inside her, sink his aching fangs into the delicate column of her throat and ride her without mercy.

But he couldn't give into that lust, no matter how it tormented him. He had to make her so hungry for what he could do to her that she'd agree to anything if he'd only give her more.

Even if it meant becoming a vampire.

A quick, driving fuck wouldn't force her to that level of desperation. He had to keep building her hunger until she was enslaved by it. And him.

If only he could avoid losing control of his own demanding appetite for her …

Dana pulled at the rope that held her handcuffs, less to get free than to express some of the tension she felt under Archer's devouring stare.

Those crystalline eyes kept flicking from her hard nipples to her sex, then up to her face, then back to her nipples again, around and around while he sprawled there in that chair, his cock thick as a truncheon.

"Are you going to do something?" she blurted. "Or just look?"

He took a sip of his wine, lids shuttering over his glowing eyes. "I like to look."

Dana's gaze slid helplessly to his erection. "I can tell."

"Are you feeling … neglected?" Archer bent over and put the wine glass down with a click on the hardwood flood. He stood up in an entrancing display of bare chest and long legs. One corner of his pirate's mouth curled. "Can't have that. A good host keeps his guests satisfied."

She bit her lip, watching in helpless need as he stalked toward her until his broad shoulders were blocking the candlelight. He loomed there, wolf-pale eyes locked on her face, his features sharp with hunger.

Slowly, Archer knelt, first on one knee, then the other. And slowly, so slowly, he lifted his hands to her breasts and put his face to her sex again.

Dana felt the long stroke of his tongue just as his fingers took her tight nipples and began to gently pinch.

She almost screamed. *Not again.*

Oh, yes. *Again.*

Her head fell back, too heavy for her neck, and her eyes slid closed as his skilled tongue savored her, explored her lips, slipped inside, circled delicately over her clit. The sensation was heart-stopping, hot, maddening, like the feeling of his hands squeezing her flesh, rolling and thumbing her nipples until they sent waves of pleasure to her helpless brain.

"God, Archer!" She instinctively ground her hips, pushing against his face as he licked and bit.

One hand abandoned her throbbing breasts, lowered to slip between her legs. A long finger slid into her. "You're tight as a virgin," he whispered, his voice rough velvet. His eyes glinted red as he tilted back his head to look up at her. "It's been a long time for you, hasn't it?"

"College." She shuddered, eyes closing, refusing to think about the callow, greedy young men who hadn't had a tenth of Archer's sorcery. "Once, twice. Too much guilt, not enough pleasure. It was never, never like this … Archer, please … "

A second finger, and she writhed. He was focused on her clit now, circling his tongue until she strained against his mouth.

A third finger, stretching her. Dana imagined what it would feel like when he drove that big, satin-slick cock into her. Her hands fisted in the handcuffs. "Archer!"

He twisted his wrist, pressing his fingers hard up inside her, stuffing her, almost lifting her off the floor as his tongue fluttered over her clit.

Pleasure roared over her in a great, burning wave, about to surge into climax …

Archer drew back. The wave began to die.

"No! Please, Archer, how do you want me?" Her voice spiraled into a scream. She had no idea what she was saying, and didn't care. "Whatever you want! *Anything*!"

He stood in a hard rush, his hands jerking down his zipper, then dragging at his jeans just enough to free his cock. She whimpered with need when she saw it jut out at her, an inch longer and twice as thick as anything she'd ever had.

Then Archer's strong hands were under her ass, lifting her, spreading her as he speared forward in one long, relentless thrust.

"God, you're so wet, so tight," he growled in her ear, forcing deeper. "It's like fucking my way into a peach."

Dana clenched her teeth, shuddering, her back arching, as he tightened his grip on her hips and dragged her down on his cock until she was utterly impaled. She felt stuffed with him, surrounded by his hard body, wrapped in his massive arms. Overwhelmed and helpless.

And God, she loved it.

She'd never felt like this — the strength and the heat and the power, the thick, greedy cock driven into her like a spike. She thought she could come just like this, just from having him inside her.

Then Archer began to move. His slow, slick glide out of her body sent curling spirals of heat up her spine. Then in, and in, and in, his muscled belly flexing against her softer one, his organ forcing her walls to spread around him. Dana twisted helplessly in his arms, wishing he'd grind, needing him to show her no mercy. Instinctively, she wrapped her legs around his waist and locked her feet together, squeezing him between her thighs.

"Oh, yeah," he purred. "Like that."

Archer picked up the pace, shortening his strokes, digging into her. Pleasure coiled tighter and tighter in Dana's belly. His powerful torso rolled against hers as he hunched, fucking her faster. His breath gusted hot in her ear. Spasms of delight rippled through her body.

"Look at me," he demanded in a harsh whisper.

Dazed, she opened her eyes. Archer's face was inches from hers, eyes glowing red in the candlelight. His teeth were bared, fangs fully extended.

"Offer me your throat," he growled. "I want to drink from you as you come."

The image seared her — the thought of his teeth piercing her as his cock tunneled deep. "Oh, God. Yes." Dana let her head fall back.

"Yeah, that's right." Archer gathered her closer, pumping even harder between her thighs, his glowing vampire eyes narrow as they focused on the arch of her throat. "Let me have it all!"

His head lowered. The silk of his hair brushed the underside of her jaw. His teeth pierced her skin, then slowly pressed deep, the sensation building to a deep, hot burn. His lips moved against her throat, warm and smooth, suckling in time to the long, driving thrusts of his cock. His torso stretched and rolled as she held him tight between her legs.

Her climax built, hot and cold at once, the contractions in her sex growing into a brutal pounding. Screaming, Dana convulsed as pleasure exploded through her in a long, fiery cascade down her nerves.

Archer's growl rumbled in her ears as he stiffened in climax, his cock jerking deep inside her, his mouth greedy on her throat.

Until finally she lay limp in his arms, exhausted from the power of her orgasm, unable to move, the vampire still buried deep.

Still feasting.

~⌒(♥)⌒~

Finally Archer carefully released her throat and lowered her feet to the ground. Dana staggered and almost fell, but he caught her close. She could feel the muscles in his arms quivering and jumping. He was still breathing hard.

"Are you all right?" Archer asked, his voice a little hoarse. "I didn't hurt you, did I? I was … rough."

Dana shook her head. It spun, and she stopped. "No. You were …" She couldn't think of a word incredible enough. "I've never felt like that. Though I realize you've probably …" *Driven thousands of women out of their minds.* She let the sentence trail off, realizing it sounded like a plea for empty reassurance.

Archer lifted her chin with a gentle forefinger. "I've never felt like that either, Dana. You are *not* just the latest in a long line."

She gave him a quavering smile, knowing he had to be lying. A kind lie, but still, a lie. She'd never been the sort of woman that drove a man to that kind of passion. She had no intention of spoiling this lovely moment by saying so, though.

Archer reached up into his back pocket and pulled out the handcuff key, then freed her wrists. Leaving the metal bracelets still lashed to the canopy, Dana lowered her stiffened arms with a groan.

"You okay?" He lifted her hands in both of his to examine her wrists anxiously. "They're bruised. I'm sorry, I didn't think I had them that tight."

"You didn't." She felt herself blush. "I seem to remember pulling on them pretty hard, there at the end."

Archer ducked down to bring one arm up under her thighs, sweeping her into his arms.

Dana giggled as he stepped around the bed with her. "What is this thing you've got with carrying me?"

"It's all part of the service." He bent down, caught the navy coverlet with the hand under her knees, and flipped it back out of the way before laying her down on the cool cream sheets. "Masterful Vampires 'R' Us."

Sitting down beside her, he went to work massaging her aching arms. Dana sighed under his strong fingers. "God, I'm tired. You wore me out."

"You've had a busy night — spying on white supremacists, getting busted by a vampire federal agent, then driving him right up the wall with lust. Anybody'd be tired."

She grinned and let her eyes slip closed. Just for a minute.

It was the last thing she knew for hours.

Archer woke curled possessively around Dana's lush little body. He lay there for a moment, allowing himself to savor the sensation of her warm curves nestled against him. From the sound of her breathing and heartbeat, she was still asleep. He lifted his head to look into her profile, at the long fan of her lashes against her cheek, that silly nose, the full, rosy lips slightly parted.

He had a sudden mental image of sliding his cock into that carnal mouth, maybe while she was on her knees with her hands bound between her legs, her fingers stroking her hard little clit …

Jesus, Archer thought as his erection stiffened into a spike, where had *that* come from? He didn't even have bondage fantasies anymore, not after all the times he'd played those scenes in reality.

But only one of them had been with Dana. And he wanted more of her. Much more. Every way he could think of.

Right now.

Archer started to reach for Dana, then hesitated. He'd taken her pretty hard last night. She'd probably be sore. Despite his rapacious hunger, he didn't want to hurt her.

He wondered how long they'd been asleep, and threw a calculating look at the window. The curtains were heavy navy velvet, but there was enough light creeping around the edges to tell him the sun was up. Well up, judging from the clock on the bureau and the "3:45 p.m." glowing on its face.

Archer glanced back at Dana. His gaze caught on her long, slim back as she lay on her side, and followed the curve of her spine down to the tempting mounds of her ass. He thought of another way to take her —

draped belly down over a mound of pillows, her wrists tied together at the small of her back …

Breakfast. It was time to fix her breakfast, or she'd be breakfast.

Archer flipped the covers aside and rolled to his feet before stalking, naked, in search of a clean pair of jeans. No shirt, she liked him without a shirt. Almost as much as he liked her wearing nothing at all.

Archer had started work on a batch of crepes when the phone rang. He let go of the whisk to scoop the handset to his ear. "Hello."

"What's this about some new vampire?" Richard Fleming had never been one for pleasantries.

Sandwiching the phone between his head and shoulder, Archer went back to whipping the batter. "Her name is Dana Ivory, Fleming, and she's not a vampire. She's a candidate for the Kiss, that's all. I've put Fitz to doing a background check on her."

Fleming snorted. "Who gives a damn about a fucking background check? I want to know what *you* think. A background check can be fooled, but nobody lies successfully to Gabriel Archer — and God knows, I've tried."

He had, too. Fleming was a dyed in the wool ex-Cold War spook who firmly believed in not telling anybody a damn thing they didn't have good reason to know. It had taken Archer years to break his superior of the habit of automatically lying to him about anything and everything. But the effort had been worth it. Fleming was damn good at covert ops, and after his years in the intelligence community, he was an invaluable resource. Which was why Archer had recruited him away from the CIA to begin with.

"So what do you think of this girl?" Fleming demanded.

I think she's hot as hell and I want to keep her tied to the bed for at least a decade. Instead Archer said, "She's intelligent, and she's got nerve …"

"Huh. Yeah, setting up in that treehouse to spy on those assholes took either nerve or no sense of self-preservation. Which ain't necessarily a bad thing in an agent."

"It's practically a requirement," Archer, agreed, grinning. "But other than that, I don't know enough about her yet to make a decision. I need to find out more."

Fleming cracked out a nasty laugh. "And judging from the photos on my desk, I'll bet research is a ball. God, what tits."

"And which photos are these?" Archer inquired in his best tone of silky menace.

"Jesus, Arch, you're paranoid. No, we didn't put a guy outside your house with a telephoto lens — not that I'm not tempted. It's just a couple of Polaroids Fitz got from one of her old boyfriends. Ivory at the beach in a bikini." He whistled. "Speaking professionally, that's some package of intelligence assets. If you do make her a vampire, tell her she can bite me anywhere, anytime."

Archer was surprised at the flare of jealousy he felt. Fleming was a good-looking bastard, Marlboro-man handsome. It was far too easy to imagine that Dana might find him a tempting meal. "She has better taste."

"And if anybody'd know how she tastes, I'm sure it'd be you," Fleming said, with another annoying laugh. "Whatever you decide, keep me posted."

"It's not just my decision," Archer told him, still frowning at the strength of his own jealousy. "She gets a say in this, too."

"No, she doesn't." His voice went completely flat, with that cold, deadly tone Archer knew well. "If Ivory's a good prospect, recruit her. She can get used to it later."

"Fleming …"

"I mean it, Archer. I've never liked the fact that we have only one of you. Your abilities are too goddamned invaluable to this country. Hell, if not for you, Manhattan would be glowing in the dark and half the eastern seaboard would still be coughing up blood. We need another vampire agent in case somebody puts a stake in your heart."

He snorted. "Nobody's killed me yet. And believe me, it's not for lack of trying."

"We've been lucky," Fleming snapped. "I'll make it a direct order — if you decide she's trustworthy, bite her."

"Betrayal's a hell of a reward for being worthy of trust."

"You're a fucking secret agent, Archer. It's what we do."

⁂

Dana awoke to the feeling of soft lips brushing hers, a tongue slipping sweetly between her teeth. "Rise and shine, sleepyhead. There's a nice, hearty breakfast downstairs with your name on it."

She blinked up at Archer's handsome face as he leaned over her. He'd opened the curtains, and sunlight poured into the room, painting his delectable torso with light.

"I gather the whole bursting-into-flames-at-dawn thing is a myth, huh?" Rubbing her eyes, she sat up.

"Mostly, though you won't catch me sunbathing in the nude anytime soon. Second degree burns in half an hour. I'm okay with overcast days, though."

"Hmmm." Dana yawned and stretched, then stopped in mid-gesture, remembering her would-be exclusive. "Have you seen the news? Has the story broken yet?"

Archer raised an arrogant eyebrow. "That story won't break until I'm good and ready for it to break. And I've made sure everybody who knows anything will keep their mouths shut."

"Somebody could check the jail logs, find out that way." It would kill her if another reporter beat her to the punch.

"Isn't the *Trib* the only paper in town?" Archer moved to the mahogany armoire, pulled open the door, and contemplated the contents. "Who checks police records for you?"

Dana gave him a sheepish smile. "Me."

"And right now, the only thing you'll be reporting on is how mouthwatering my crepes are." She was about to launch an indignant protest when he pulled out something long, black and gleaming and brought it to her. It turned out to be a silk robe.

"Here, put this on," Archer said. "All that naked Dana makes my blood supply head south. Hard to have an intelligent conversation when my cock keeps interrupting."

The mention of his cock — and the thought of what he could do with it — deflated her interest in argument. "You do say the nicest things."

He watched with lecherous interest as she rolled out of bed and shrugged into the robe. "The things I do are even nicer. Like letting you eat instead of ravishing you right now."

Dana licked suddenly dry lips. "You could serve me breakfast in bed."

"True, but I thought we could do something really radical — try to hold an actual conversation like people who aren't compelled to couple like crazed mink." Archer caught up her hand and folded it into the crook of his muscular arm. "Come on. I don't know how long this burst of self-control will last."

"But I like coupling like crazed mink," Dana said, trying to make it sound like a joke as he towed her out of the bedroom and down the sweeping staircase.

"Couple later. Talk now."

"I thought it was the woman who always wants conversation instead of sex. Men are supposed to be the insatiable ones."

Archer raised a brow, a humorously dangerous gleam flaring in his eyes. "Are you suggesting I have a weak sex drive?"

"Who me?" Dana squeaked. "Never. I would never do that."

"Good," he purred. "Because my fragile male ego would be compelled to prove you wrong."

"That's not necessary," she assured him. "I like being able to walk."

He laughed. "Beauty and brains. What more could a vampire ask?"

Five minutes later Dana was watching from the breakfast nook as

Archer poured crepe batter into an electric skillet with the same graceful skill he'd used in combat.

"How can you cook when you don't eat?" She plucked a ripe strawberry from the bowl of sliced fruit at her elbow.

"I can taste." Archer popped a forefinger into his mouth to suck off the batter. "Besides, I've always thought if a woman feeds me, it's only polite to feed her. Would you like some eggs? Bacon?"

"No, crepes and fruit are fine."

For a moment they were silent as he flipped the crepes, then transferred the finished product to a plate. "I actually enjoy cooking. It's relaxing. Nobody dies, nobody gets screwed. If you mess up, you throw it in the trash." He carried the plate to her, then sat down to watch her eat.

Dana cut off a forkful and popped it in her mouth. Her eyes widened at the burst of delicate flavor as the crepe simply dissolved on her tongue. "God, that's good!" She took another bite and closed her eyes to savor the sensation. "You're an incredible cook."

"Thanks. It's a useful skill," Archer said, smiling slightly as he watched her devour her breakfast. "Chef is one of my favorite covers. You can find out all sorts of interesting things about a household in its kitchen."

"How did you become a spy, anyway?" Dana took a sip of her orange juice. Fresh squeezed, judging from the juicer and pile of orange halves on the cabinet.

"Ah, well. That's a long story."

"I'm not going anywhere." She lifted a brow at him. "Give."

"I'd rather talk about you."

"I'm not nearly as interesting as you are."

"But I know my story, and I don't know yours." Archer's lips curved into the charming smile that had probably been the downfall of many a female spy. "Tell you what, we'll trade. All my evil secrets for yours. How about it?"

It was a tempting proposition. "Okay. But I want to hear about all the spy stuff."

"I'll even show you my secret collection of espionage toys."

She grinned. "I'll just bet you will."

So as they cleaned up the kitchen, Dana told him about herself and her work. She related the challenges of putting out a weekly newspaper: the stories she'd done, the people she'd interviewed, the Byzantine machinations of small town politics — who was sleeping with whom, who was cheating whom, and why.

"You're good at this, aren't you?" Archer asked thoughtfully, as he led the way to the library when they were done with the cleanup. "Sounds like you found out where all the bodies were buried pretty fast."

Dana shrugged. "It's just a matter of listening, getting people to open up to you. You can pick up a lot chatting at the neighborhood diner. Then you hit town hall and start researching the records, and you find out whether there's any truth to the gossip."

"Why bother? Why go to all that effort?" He flung himself into a massive leather wing chair as she settled onto the matching couch. "You work for a weekly. You could be doing stories about the county fair and school kids winning essay contests."

"I have done those stories." She shrugged. "But I have a responsibility to the community. If somebody's using public money to advance his own agenda, people should know it."

He eyed her thoughtfully. "I imagine that goes over real well with the powers that be."

Dana smiled in reluctant amusement at his cynical tone. "Oh, I'm considered a huge pain in the butt. And the public isn't always pleased when I drag things out in the open. At one time or another, the whole town's been furious at me." She tucked her legs beneath her and settled back in a corner of the couch. "But once they calm down, they always wind up doing something about whatever set me off, so I figure I did my job."

"What do your parents think about what you do?"

Dana looked away. "They died just after I got out of college. Car accident."

His eyes darkened in sympathy. "I'm sorry."

"They were strict, but they loved me," she said, staring out the window over the rolling lawn. "They were evangelists. Had a syndicated radio show that was aired around the country in a hundred and twenty markets."

Archer lifted a brow. "Somehow you don't strike me as the daughter of a minister."

Dana laughed. "Oh, I'm the stereotypical P.K." Catching his questioning look, she explained, "Preacher's kid. Rebelling against my upbringing, fighting authority, the whole bit."

"I thought you liked authority." He smiled slowly. "At least the handcuffs."

She glowered at him. "Cheap shot."

"Sorry." He sobered. "Seriously, what was it like for you growing up?"

Dana found herself telling him everything: the frustration, the guilt of never being good enough to meet her parents' high standards, the sense of suffocation under their strictures. And the love she'd felt for the mother and father who always acted out of love and a desire to do what was right.

It was only later that Dana realized how skillfully Archer interrogated her. Before long he had her telling him things she'd never told anyone, seduced by his interest and humor.

She even told him about Mark's collection of erotica.

"I don't know what it is about all that stuff that gets to me," Dana told him, studying her bare toes as a blush heated her face. "I don't believe in women being submissive. God knows I'm don't submit to anybody or anything in my daily life. I'm a dedicated feminist."

"Oh, I know exactly why you like bondage." Archer gave her such a teasing, masculine grin that she lost her discomfort and grinned back.

"Oh? And why is that?"

"You don't have to do any of the work. You can just lie back while the guy licks and nibbles and thrusts in a desperate attempt to please you."

Glad to have the conversation back on a comfortable footing, Dana sat back in her chair and eyed him. "Are you saying I'm lazy?"

He smirked. "If the handcuffs fit."

"For your information, there's a lot a woman can do with both hands tied behind her back."

Archer reached into his back pocket and pulled out his handcuffs, let them dangle by a thumb. "Prove it."

"You're on." Dana stood up and shrugged off the black robe. It landed in a silken pool around her ankles, leaving her wearing nothing but a smile. "Take off those pants, Double-O-Fang, and we'll see who's lazy."

Grinning, he skimmed his jeans and briefs down his hips in one, smooth motion, then stepped out of them. It was the first time she'd seen him totally naked, and for a moment Dana just stopped and stared. His legs were long, roped with muscle, and his cock was a thick, aggressive thrust over the tight, furry pouch of his testicles. He lifted a brow at her. "Well?"

Dana marched over to him and held up both wrists.

"Nope." He gestured for her to turn. "Both hands behind your back, remember?"

She spun around and crossed her wrists at her spine. A moment later she felt the cool caress of metal, heard a double click. Dana turned back around to find him grinning down at her.

"So what are you going to do now, Gloria Steinem?"

Chapter Five

"The possibilities are endless," Dana shot back, grinning. But as she let her eyes play over his face, across his bare, powerful shoulders and down his brawny torso, she felt her amusement fade, replaced by something more urgent. She wanted to touch him, to see how all that male strength felt under her fingers. But her hands were bound behind her.

Inhaling sharply, she caught his scent — dark, spicy. She leaned forward, wanting to draw that tempting Archer smell more deeply into her lungs. The froth of hair covering his chest tickled her nose.

Impulsively, Dana leaned even closer, put out her tongue, licked at a ridge of muscle. He rumbled in approval. She eyed his chest, the swell of a pectoral muscle, the tiny dark bead of his nipple. Testing, she bent her head and flicked her tongue over it. He stiffened, catching his breath.

Encouraged, Dana edged closer until the tips of her breasts brushed his chest, the sensation sending a flare of pleasure through her. She sighed and licked him again, a long pass of her tongue over the hard bulge of his pecs. Intrigued by the sensation, she caught his nipple between her teeth, gave it a slow, gentle bite. His breathing roughened, his chest rising and falling more quickly against her face.

Suddenly there was the breath-stealing sensation of fingers stroking her nipple in a light, velvet flutter. Archer's other hand brushed down her spine to linger on the upper curve of her ass.

Dana shivered at the sensation and lifted her head. Archer looked down at her, his eyes intensely blue, the lids heavy. She stood on her toes and stretched her neck up until she could taste his firm mouth. A quick brush of the lips, once, then again, then a slow foray with her tongue into the warm cavern of his mouth. He opened for her, letting her explore his lips and trace the edges of his teeth. She touched the point of a fang and drew back, startled. Archer looked down at her, eyes shuttered, subtly challenging.

Quick as an impulse, she leaned forward again and slipped her head up under his jaw to the strong cords of his throat. Taking the smooth skin there between her teeth, she gently bit down. He tasted salty, tempting, male. He moaned.

"I see why you like to bite," she whispered against his skin, and began to nibble.

"It does have its ... pleasures," Archer agreed, his voice rasping.

Slowly, Dana worked her way lower, using her tongue and teeth, lapping and raking in turn, exploring his chest, the ridges of his abdominals, the ripples of his ribs. As she moved, the tips of her breasts brushed against him, the pressure sending curls of rosy pleasure through her.

Until she was on her knees, the rigid length of his cock thrusting out beside her face, the hair of his thighs caressing her nipples. She felt languorous, hungry, as bewitched by her own gentle teasing as he was.

And he was bewitched. When Dana tilted a look up at him, she found his azure eyes locked on her, watching her every move with a kind of tortured anticipation. She could almost see him wondering when she was going to take his cock into her mouth, see him aching for the firestorm of sensation her tongue and teeth and lips would bring.

Watching him wait, Dana felt a burst of feminine power. She was doing this to him, just as he'd made her writhe and ache last night.

She turned her eyes to his cock again, studying it, admiring the thick stalk, the big, heart-shaped head that blushed dark with the force of his passion. It quivered and lengthened, taking on a pronounced upward jut.

Dana put out her tongue and licked away a drop of pre-come. He jolted against her mouth. "God, Dana ..."

She licked the head again, watching it bob under the stroke, then leaned closer and caught it in her mouth. And began to suck. Gently at first, then harder. She felt him dip, as if his knees had gone weak for an instant. Smiling around his width, Dana pressed her head forward until the thick shaft moved deeper between her lips. Then pulled back, tightening her lips at the same time to create a demanding suction. She closed her eyes as smooth length slid from her mouth, remembering how it had felt when he'd stroked it into her sex.

A strong hand came to rest on top of her head, fingers lacing through her curls. She felt him shudder and reversed her stroke, taking him deeper and deeper, until the big head brushed the back of her throat.

Archer gasped as her mouth drew at him with such power it made his head swim. It felt so good, so hot.

And the sight of her, slim and naked, kneeling between his feet with her wrists bound behind her back and her lips wrapped around his cock. God, he could come just looking at her.

She slid forward again, pleasuring him until he wanted to explode down her throat. Yet it wasn't enough. He needed her sex clamped where her mouth was, hot and tight and wet. He wanted her body pressed to his, flexing against his strength. Surrendering.

And he wanted her blood. He wanted it flooding his mouth in a wave of liquid copper.

Now.

Half-maddened, Archer pulled out of the unbearably seductive suction of her mouth, almost groaning at the loss of her wet heat even as he bent and scooped Dana off the floor.

He turned to the couch and dropped her lush body belly-down over its padded leather arm. The position thrust out her rounded, heart-shaped ass, inviting his possession.

Dana moaned.

Archer grabbed his cock in one hand, aimed for the glistening red folds of her sex. And thrust.

God, she was wet. Sucking him must have aroused her as much as it had him. And she was just as tight, clutching him like a slick fist, her grip so strong he had to bear down to force his way deeper. The sensation seared its way up his spine to his skull with brutal intensity.

Shivering, Archer settled against her until the full curve of her bottom nestled into his groin. And slowly, he began to thrust.

God, he felt so big in this position. Thick, forcing her to spread. And strong. She couldn't have kept him out even if she'd wanted to.

And she didn't.

Dana hung there over the couch arm, head down, feeling his powerful hands clamping her hips as he tunneled in and out. It felt as if each thrust impaled her to the heart, sending sparks of pleasure spiraling along her nerves. She whimpered in raw delight.

Archer leaned over her, slipping his arms under her torso to gather her close. His fingers found her nipples, plucked and strummed as he fucked her. His thrusts grew even faster, harder, winding the pleasure like a spring. He felt huge inside her, too much, far too much, yet she could only hang there in his hands, bound and helpless. The thought made her close her eyes in wicked delight.

Suddenly Archer crowded hard against her, his thighs trapping hers against the side of the couch as he reamed her in short, hard strokes. One hand gripped her breast as the other dragged her head back by the hair. She stiffened, realizing what he intended.

Just as he sank his fangs into her throat.

Dana convulsed helplessly, the combination of pleasure and pain kicking her over into a long, rolling orgasm that continued to shake her while he drank, still pistoning into her, ruthless, hungry and possessive.

Until he lifted his head from her and roared out his own climax.

It took Archer thirty minutes to recover enough to carry her back to bed. Dana protested sleepily that she was perfectly capable of walking under her own steam, but he suspected she was lying. He shouldn't have drunk from her so soon after the last time; he never did that. He had a firm rule against taking from the same partner twice in a six-week period.

But then, he'd never made anyone a vampire before.

Holding her as she sank into a doze, Archer realized that was exactly what he was going to do.

She was everything he'd spent two centuries searching for. A vampire had fantastic power, and he'd always feared giving the Dark Kiss to someone undeserving. But Dana would never misuse those superhuman abilities; she had too keen a sense of idealism and morality. She would be the perfect agent.

More than that, she'd be the perfect wife.

Archer loved her humor and intelligence — not to mention all that shy sensuality. He could easily imagine spending the next three hundred years being fascinated by her, working with her, making love to her.

He almost woke her up right then to blurt out his proposal. But there was no rush.

They had forever.

So he let her sleep, savoring her warm, smooth curves as she nestled into him. Until finally she stirred against him and woke.

Then, heart in his throat, he began telling her everything.

"I met the Countess when I went to her estate in France to negotiate the purchase of a wine shipment," Archer said, his chest vibrating under her chin.

Dana had been staring dreamily into his handsome face. Now she sat up, attention instantly caught. The Countess had been the one who'd made him a vampire. "Shipment?"

"We were merchants," he explained. "My family owned a number of ships, and I'd heard she bottled the best wine in France. We traded letters for a year before she finally invited me to her chateau to finish the negotiations." Archer smiled faintly. "God, that house. I'd never seen anything like it. The furnishings, the art. We were wealthy, but not like her." The amusement drained away. "She realized I could survive the change the moment she met me."

"And seduced you." Dana felt a sting of jealousy, then was instantly ashamed when she remembered he'd said the Countess had been killed by a French mob.

Archer nodded, the look in his eyes distant with memory. "She was lovely — all dark beauty and wicked fascination. It didn't take me long to fall in love. I was willing to do anything for her. Even become a vampire."

She propped her chin on her fist and studied him. "Was she in love with you?"

Archer shrugged. "She said she was. And I know she was lonely. It gets very lonely, after a hundred years or so. You become willing to do damn near anything for company." He hesitated. "But we were very happy in the three years we had together.

"Then my brother wrote to tell me my parents had been murdered."

As Dana listened in horror, he described how his father, James, had thrown his support behind the American fight for independence. During a trip to Boston to meet with leaders of the rebellion, a rival British merchant and a gang of Tories attacked James and Archer's mother at the docks. The men dragged them into a warehouse, where they used clubs to beat James Archer until he was broken and dying. Then they turned their attention to his wife.

The couple was dead by the time they were found two days later.

"Their deaths haunted me," Archer said, his voice distant and terrible. "The thought of my parents dying in that filthy warehouse, each knowing the other was suffering, neither able to help. All because some greedy bastard wanted to get rid of a rival, and some Tories wanted to make a point."

He'd booked passage back on the same ship that had brought his brother's letter. The Countess had cried and begged him to stay, but Archer had turned a deaf ear. She finally told him she'd get her affairs in order and join him.

Archer arrived in Boston like an avenging demon. He used his powers to hunt down the men who'd murdered his mother and father, then systematically killed them all.

"I had no mercy," he said. "They deserved none. My parents weren't the only innocents they'd killed trying to terrorize supporters of the rebellion." Archer paused, his eyes chilling. "And they weren't acting alone. Before he died, one of the Tories told me they'd been carrying out British orders. A particularly brutal Redcoat major out to build a name for himself." His voice flattened. "He told them to make my parents an example."

"What did you do?" Dana swallowed, caught between fascination and horror.

Archer looked away, refusing to meet her gaze. "I slipped into British headquarters when he was working late one night. And I made him an example."

But that wasn't the end of Archer's war. He left the major's bloody body and headed straight for the nearest Continental commander to offer his services. Archer couldn't join the army because he couldn't fight daylight battles, but he could become a spy. It was no job for a gentleman, but in his hate and grief, he didn't care.

Archer spent the rest of the war among the British, assuming various guises to observe their fortifications and troop strength, sometimes even gaining access to commanders and using his psychic influence to discover their plans.

"You could have influenced them into deliberately losing," Dana observed.

He frowned, stroking her slim fingers absently. "There were times I was tempted, but I always drew the line. It didn't seem honorable. Like beating a bound prisoner, there are some things you just don't do."

As Archer went on telling her about his experiences, Dana realized he'd become addicted to the idealism and the danger of his cause. Even after the war was over, he continued using his talents to gather information and undermine the country's enemies.

Yet even in his zeal, he hadn't forgotten his Countess. Archer continued to exchange letters with her, even traveling to France for frequent visits, but he never stayed long. Conditions in the fledgling United States were too uncertain, and he couldn't stand to be away. The Countess swore she'd join him, but busy with her estate and the worsening conditions in France as the country spiraled into revolution, she never did.

Until the day came when Archer got word she had been murdered.

"A mob is the greatest danger to a vampire," he said, his voice soft, bitter. "Once it gets going, you can't stop it. Influence doesn't work on that many people in the grip of bloodlust." He stared broodingly at nothing. "They hacked off her head with a scythe."

Guilt-stricken, Archer returned to France to try to find her killers. This time he had no luck, and he finally returned home to the cause that was now all he had left.

"As the years went on, America became everything to me," Archer said. "Friends and enemies age and die, but she remains. I've watched her grow from a sickly newborn to the queen of the world. I've watched her act from greed and gallantry. I've seen her whore to rich men, then turn and sacrifice her own children for the freedom of others. There is no other nation like her. She's worth every lie I've told, every life I've taken, every morning I've faced with dread."

As Dana listened in spellbound fascination, Archer described the wars he'd fought and the missions he'd carried out. He was brutally frank, describing not only the triumphs but the failures that still made guilt flare in his eyes decades later. His stories were an enthralling glimpse of the past, of the people and events that had molded the country.

And as he spoke, he unwittingly revealed himself — a powerful man moving invisibly among powerful men, using his abilities to play a prominent role in history that he allowed few people to even know about. A ruthless man, yet quietly, intensely honorable.

"Why are you telling me this?" she asked at last, uneasy. It didn't seem in character for a man who'd made secrecy a way of life for two centuries. "You can't make me forget it."

Archer rolled over on his side and braced himself on one elbow. He met her eyes, his expression so serious her unease increased.

"Dana, the Countess knew I could become a vampire because she tried to influence me into giving her a better price on the wine. And it didn't work."

Understanding hit Dana like a punch so brutal she lost her breath. When her heart began beating again, she whispered, "Like me."

"Like you."

Dana licked her lips. "All this ... These things you've told me ..." She stopped and almost lost her courage, then forced herself to continue. The words came out in a rush. "Archer, are you saying you want to make me a vampire?"

His blue eyes were steady, staring into hers with a quiet intensity. "If you agree."

A crazy joy bloomed in Dana's chest. He wanted her to stay with him. Forever.

"We could do so much," Archer said, and reached out to cover one of her hands with his own. "Dana, you have no idea how I need you — how the country needs you."

She froze.

"Even with all my abilities, I'm only one man. But working together, we ..."

A wave of shock washed over her skin, so cold that for a blessed moment she went completely numb. Humiliated understanding roared in behind it.

Archer had been planning this from the first. He had guessed her secret fantasies, and he'd used them to bring her to heel. He'd played the demon lover, tied her and taken her and made her hotter than she'd ever been in her life. But to him it had been just another mission. It had never touched him at all.

She had never touched him at all. While he had made himself everything to her.

"... Have to undergo training, of course. Weapons and tactics. Languages. You'll need to ..."

"No."

Archer blinked. "What?"

Biting off the words, Dana said, "I'm not going to spend the next two hundred years whoring for this country." *I'm not going to spend the next two hundred years in love with you, watching you seduce an endless succession of willing women.*

It was only after she'd thought the word "love" that she realized she meant it.

Jesus, it had only been twenty-four hours. You didn't fall in love in a day. Not with a normal man.

But Archer was not a normal man. He was so damn good, so damn seductive — not just his body, but his intelligence and idealism and that damn honor. He'd slipped into her heart like the spy he was, and he'd taken it.

"You're not just a spy," she said brutally, wanting to hurt him. "You're a whore."

"No." The word came out as a whisper, sounding somehow wounded. Another of his actor's tricks. "I've … done some things I'm not proud of, but I've also saved a lot of lives." For once his eloquence failed him. Dana could almost see him groping for a way to defend himself. "Just last year there was this terrorist with a nuclear …"

"I need to get dressed." She couldn't take any more of this, or she was going to humiliate herself and start sobbing.

Dana lurched off the bed, then realized she was nude. She couldn't stand to be naked in front of him — he'd stripped her enough as it was. She grabbed the hem of the sheet and tried to drag it off the bed, but it wouldn't come, caught under one of Archer's trim male hips. Dana gave it another ruthless jerk.

Immersing her in a glare that was beginning to sizzle with growing rage, Archer freed it.

"Thank you." Back rigid, Dana wrapped the length of cloth around her body, then turned and made for the bureau where she'd stashed her folded jeans. "Look, do you have a T-shirt? You ripped mine."

"I don't understand you." His voice rumbled with anger, threatening as the thunder before a storm. "I could make you immortal."

In one fluid movement, Archer rolled off the bed and strode naked toward her. She refused to look at that magnificent, deceptive body as he stopped inches away. "You would never grow old. You could take a shotgun blast to the chest and survive. Hell, you could bench press a Toyota, see in the dark …"

"Leap tall buildings in a single bound and turn into a bat. I know." Dana jerked on the jeans with trembling hands.

The corners of his mouth twitched in a bitter fragment of a smile. "The bat thing is a myth."

"Well, if I can't turn into a bat, why bother?" She zipped the jeans.

"Hell, I don't know. Maybe for the men who died at Bunker Hill and Gettysburg and Normandy." Fury emanated from him like his potent body heat. "That old cliché is dead-on, Dana — freedom ain't free. Sometimes people have to step up and pay the bill."

"Oh, that's right — 'The tree of Liberty is watered by the blood of Patriots.' Or however the hell that goes." She dragged open a drawer and searched for a shirt. "Well, that tree has all of my blood it's getting." Dana lifted her head to glare back at him. "You drank it already."

For a moment, such rage blazed in his eyes that she instinctively hunched her shoulders.

Seeing her flinch, Archer snarled and spun away. He strode to the door and flung it open, then slammed it shut again behind him.

Dana still couldn't find that damn shirt.

Staggering back to the bed, she collapsed as the tears began.

Damn her! He took the stairs in a rush, pounding down them, still naked and not giving a damn. She was everything he'd always wanted, always needed, and she'd blown him off, left him to the mission that never ended and the women he could never have for more than a single night.

Archer stormed into the kitchen for lack of any other destination. The phone rang just as he passed the counter, and he snatched it up.

"How's the girl working out?" Fleming's rough voice asked.

"Oh, she's just fucking perfect," Archer snarled. "She'd be a great agent. Unfortunately, she just told me she has no interest whatsoever in having anything at all to do with us."

"And that stopped you?" The acid sarcasm in his tone made Archer's lips pull back from his teeth.

"If I did turn her, how the hell would we get her to cooperate? You can't force a vampire to do a damn thing. Believe me, it's been tried on me, and it never worked."

"I know of at least one cell even you couldn't get out of."

"I will not let you lock her up and starve her, Fleming."

"Fine. So convince her. Even after she's a vampire, you'll still be proportionally bigger, stronger and more experienced. Right?"

He frowned. "Yeah. So?"

"So we need this girl, Archer. Quit fucking around and bite her."

Fleming's right.

The words whispered through his skull, chill and tempting. He fought them, knowing it wasn't right to force her.

Until a demonic voice asked, *But what about the lives that could be saved?*

And he couldn't think of an answer.

A wave of burning cold washed over Archer — the same deadly psychic frost he felt when he knew he had to kill.

When he spoke, his voice sounded flat and emotionless in his own ears. "I'll call you when it's done."

ᔕᕈᕉᔕ

Dana wiped her eyes. He'd be back any moment, and by then she had to have a shirt on and some fragment of self-control.

God, she felt wrecked.

Get hold of yourself, Dana. Concentrate on the practicalities. How was she going to even get home? He'd driven. She'd have to call a car rental company and arrange to have them send over a …

The door opened. Dana whipped around, her arms automatically covering her bare breasts.

Archer filled the doorway like a Roman god brought to life, all beautiful naked strength. But the expression on his handsome face was cold, closed. Flat. She felt a shiver of unease.

Summoning her courage, Dana stood up. "I won't reconsider, Archer, so don't waste your breath."

He didn't even acknowledge her attempt at a preemptive strike, just started toward her in a long, silent stride. Something about the way he moved made her feel stalked, and she took an instinctive step back.

Archer's pale eyes watched her retreat like a cat focused on a canary. "I just got a call from my boss with my next mission." His tone was soft with velvet menace. "You."

One instant he was halfway across the room. The next, she was on her back on the bed, his powerful, naked body pinning her down, a superhuman hand gripping both her wrists. His wolf-pale eyes were merciless. "Dana," he told her, his voice emotionless, "you've been drafted."

Archer fisted his free hand in her hair and pulled her head back to arch her throat. He opened his mouth, revealing the sharp white length of his fangs as he bent to bite.

And she screamed.

Archer hesitated an inch from her flesh and looked up as she bucked under him, terror and rage contorting her face, her hands jerking helplessly in his. Pity stirred beneath his mental chill. "I'm sorry," he said softly. "This won't be pleasant. I can't even make it quick."

He would have to drink from her several times over the coming days, partially draining her before forcing her to drink his blood. What followed would be worse. Archer could still remember the raw agony he'd suffered two centuries ago as his body was reshaped by the vampire virus. And he, at least, had been willing.

"You have no right to force this on me!" Dana spat, struggling to drag her hands out of his grip.

"No." He contained her desperate jerks carefully. "But I do have a duty. There've been so many times when I have accomplished things no ordinary man could have. Foiled plots, saved lives. If I die, I want to know there's someone to carry on the work. And there's no one else but you."

Realizing she was helpless, Dana subsided to glare up at him bitterly. "I thought you were supposed to be invulnerable."

Archer shrugged. "Not to being crushed, burned, staked or decapitated. Given my lifestyle, the odds that I'll encounter something I can't walk away from are pretty good."

"I don't give a damn. I will not work for you!" She gritted out the words, her gaze as defiant as a martyr's.

"Yes, you will." Archer smiled sadly. "You're an idealist. No matter how pissed you are at me, when a crisis comes along, you'll have to help."

Recognition and despair flickered in Dana's eyes until she squeezed them closed. She took an angry, hitching breath, half sob, half curse. "Do it then, damn you," she spat, "And get it over with."

Archer started to lower his head — just as something glittered on the side of her face. A lone tear, sliding slowly down the fragile curve of her cheek as she sank her small white teeth into her lower lip.

Something twisted in his chest.

He had done worse things than this, dammit. Betrayed men who believed him a friend, killed gallant enemies and innocents who knew too much. He'd done whatever his country had demanded. Besides, he was giving her a precious gift — immortality. Freedom from the twin mortal curses of old age and disease.

In the end, she would forgive him. He'd see to it, spinning a spell of sex and pleasure around her until she forgot her anger. He already knew he was her weakness.

Another tear beaded on her lashes.

"God *damn* it!"

Suddenly Archer was sitting on the side of the bed, and she was free. Dana blinked at him in bewilderment. His broad shoulders were hunched and knotted as he scrubbed a big hand over his face.

"Goddamn it," he growled again. "I can't do it. I should, and I can't."

Cautiously, Dana sat up, confused. "What's happening? What are you talking about?"

He rose from the bed and strode away from her to brace both arms on the bureau. "I mean you're safe. Now get out before I change my mind."

She stared at the strong muscled V of his back, blinking at a sudden wave of disappointment. *Oh, God,* Dana thought, stunned. *I actually wanted him to do it. Force me to stay with him, even if it meant watching him make love to other women. Never loving me.* "What about all that stuff about duty and country and …"

He whirled on her, fangs bared as he growled, "I said get out!"

She should. She should run like hell, and she knew it. But some perverse demon drove Dana to find out why he'd stopped. "Is this another game? The stories you told me … You never walk away from a job, even when it turns your stomach."

"Which is why you should get the fuck out while you can."

"Not until you tell me why."

He stared at her, bewildered and furious. "You little idiot. Don't you understand what kind of danger you're in? I want to throw you down on that bed, feed from that white throat of yours and *keep* you. And to hell with what you want. So if you don't want to stay with me for the next three hundred years, you'd better get your tight little ass right out that door. Now!"

Hope began to expand through Dana's chest like a slow motion explosion. "Why?"

"Why what?" he roared.

"Why do you want to keep me?" She rolled to her feet and moved toward him, feeling the cool air against her beaded nipples. Deliberately, Dana arched her back and watched his gaze slide hungrily to her breasts. "For duty? For truth, justice and the American way? For sex? What?"

"If that was all it was, I'd already have my fangs in your throat. Get out."

"No." She put a deliberate roll in her hips. "Not until you give me the truth."

He peeled his lips back from his fangs and growled, "Keep it up, Dana, and I'll definitely give you something. But since you've already said you don't *want* it, I strongly advise …"

"Why do you care what I want?" Daringly, she stroked a forefinger over one of her own hard nipples and watched his eyes blaze. "Why aren't we on that bed right now, Archer? I couldn't stop you." His cock was lengthening between his muscled thighs, thickening, tilting slowly upward. "You could tie me down and feast on me, indulge every hunger your keen sense of morality has never allowed you to feed. And you're so good, it wouldn't take you long to make me want it."

He lifted burning eyes to hers and asked in a seductive purr, "Do you want me to rape you, Dana?"

"No." She licked her lips.

Archer watched the movement of her tongue hungrily. "I'm not convinced." He took a long, gliding stride toward her, his cock swaying, fully erect.

Dana stepped back quickly. "I want to know why you didn't take me."

The sensuous mask dropped, and he drew himself up. "Luscious games notwithstanding, I'm not actually a rapist."

"You're whatever your country needs you to be, Archer." She dared to step close enough to look up into his eyes. "Including a rapist. Yet you let me go. For once in your immortal life, you ignored your duty. And I want to know why."

His expression closed, chilled. But his cock was still hard. "Because I've fallen in love with you. And I couldn't stand to doom you to a life you don't want."

Her heart leaped. "We've only known each other twenty-four hours."

"It doesn't seem to matter."

Dana met his gaze with a long, steady stare. "No. It doesn't."

Archer's eyes widened and blazed with incredulous joy, only to cool into caution an instant later. "What we're feeling could be just a product of truly amazing sex."

She grinned. "Got a pretty high opinion of your skills, don't you?"

"I've had a lot of practice."

"I love you."

He moved with that astonishing vampire speed again, and she was in his arms, every inch of his muscled body pressed to hers. She cried out in utter joy, both arms going around his broad back as his mouth met hers greedily.

Dana matched Archer kiss for searing kiss, tongue dancing with his as their demanding hands explored one another, dizzy with love and lust. Until finally she pulled back enough to pant, "Make me a vampire."

Archer stilled. "But you said …"

"I thought you didn't really want me, I thought you were just doing a job," she said in a breathless rush. "And why the hell didn't you know that? You're the bloody telepath."

He gave her a look. "But I can't read *you*. Where you're concerned, I'm just like every other poor bastard, wondering what the hell's going on in his woman's head."

Dana grinned. "If it's any consolation, it sounds like you'll have plenty of time to figure it out."

He smiled slowly, sensually. "Why don't we get started?"

Her grin widened. "Oh, yeah. Let's."

Archer bent down, swept her into his arms, and started toward the bed. "Now where," he purred, "did I put the rope?"

Dana froze in the act of caressing his shoulders. "Rope?"

"What was it you said a minute ago? Oh, yeah. 'You could tie me down and feast on me.' I liked that idea, Dana. I really did."

"I was speaking rhetorically!"

"But I'd love to try it."

She tossed her head, enjoying the game immensely. "Not a chance."

He sighed in mock sympathy. "That's the trouble with being a feast. You don't get much choice."

Archer tossed her on the bed. Dana immediately rolled off it.

And the chase was on.

Just to be polite, he allowed her to elude him for two quick circuits of the bed, slowing down his lunges just enough to let her dart free. Round breasts bouncing as she danced on the balls of her feet on the opposite side of the lake-sized mattress, Dana giggled. "Slowing down in your old age, Archer?"

He grinned and vaulted the width of the bed, enjoying the way her grey eyes widened when he hit the floor beside her and caught her into his arms. "What do you think?"

"Archer!" she squealed, as he swooped in for a hungry kiss of her laughing mouth. He kept her distracted with his tongue while he waltzed her backward to the bedside table, pulled open a drawer with one hand and reached inside. When his fingers found the silken coil of rope, Archer grinned against her lips.

Dana shrieked out a laugh as she felt herself flying through the air to land on the soft surface of the mattress. Before she could even think about rolling off again, Archer was on top of her, jerking her left hand over her head. He tied it to one of the bedposts with a few twists of rope while she playfully pounded at his chest with her free hand.

He ignored her until she sank her teeth into the muscled ribs that were so temptingly close to her face. "Cut that out, you little devil," Archer ordered, stretching out to snap the remaining length of the thick rope so he could tie her other wrist with it.

"Brute!" Dana accused, trying to sound outraged. "Rapist! Pervert!"

"You bet your sweet ass."

As he went about binding her to the bedposts, Dana squirmed, trying to look as tempting as possible as she slowly twisted her half-naked body. The ploy worked; she saw his blue eyes heat as he eyed her struggles. But his hands never hesitated in the task of tying her down. At last she was completely immobilized, arms and legs stretched wide.

Archer straightened to stand over her, scanning her bound body with an expression of lecherous triumph, his cock at full, magnificent erection.

"I hate to mention this, but there's a fatal flaw with your plans," Dana observed, swallowing as she stared at his cock. It looked as thick as her wrist.

"I don't think so." Archer grinned, showing the long points of his fangs. "You're tied up and helpless, ready to serve my every evil appetite."

"Not in these jeans."

"Oh, that." He scanned the tough blue fabric, then focused his attention right between her legs. "That's not going to be a problem."

And it wasn't. Archer reached down, grabbed her waistband in both hands and yanked. The thick fabric tore with a loud rip, splitting right down to her left thigh.

Stunned by the display of raw vampire strength, Dana blinked, then mustered a grumble. "Great. Now I don't have anything to wear at all."

"You don't need anything to wear," he told her, and licked his fangs as he reached for the fabric again. "At all."

Archer shredded the jeans off her body like a greedy boy tearing into a birthday present. In seconds, she was completely nude.

Wide-eyed, Dana watched him toss aside the shreds of her clothing and rock back on his bare heels to give her a long, hungry stare. The air felt cool on her pebbled nipples and spread, wet sex. She tugged at her bound wrists with a blend of excitement and unease.

Archer watched the nervous movement like a starving wolf. "Feeling helpless?" His stare flicked back to her full breasts, then down between her thighs. "You look helpless. And you are. I can do anything I like to you." He looked up into her eyes. "Does that worry you?"

She licked her dry lips. "Should it?"

"Oh, yeah." Slowly he began to stroll around the bed. "I'm remembering all the wickedly creative things I've done to pretty victims over the past two centuries." His eyes glinted. "Sometimes they were a little reluctant to try this or that at first, but I soon had them begging for more." His voice deepened, drawled. "I'd like to make you beg, Dana."

She remembered his tongue, spinning spells of pleasure and frustration around her clit. "You *have* made me beg."

"True." Archer's grin was white and wicked. "But somehow I never get tired of hearing 'Please, Archer!' and 'I'll do anything, Archer!' Gives me a feeling of power." He stopped by the bedside table and pulled open a drawer.

"A feeling of power," Dana repeated, watching him dig around. "Yeah, I can see how that's something alien to you. What are you looking for?"

He pulled out a length of bright red silk. "Ever been blindfolded?"

"Hey, now, wait …" She tried to jerk her head aside as he sat down next to her and covered her eyes with the scarf. "But I like looking at you!" she wailed as he tied it off.

"But I want to keep you in suspense," Archer said, laughter in his voice. "And since I'm not the one who's tied up, guess who gets his wish?"

"Rat," she grumbled, staring into the blackness over her eyes.

Despite the moment's frustration, she felt her anticipation began to rise as she waited for his hands, his mouth, his first, heady touch.

Nothing.

"What are you doing?"

The bedroom door closed with a soft click.

"Archer! Did you just leave? What the hell are you up to?"

Damn. Frowning, Dana blinked against the blindfold. He'd damn well better not be planning to just leave her here like this. She'd kick his vampire butt clear to Washington.

Great, she thought. *Here I am, naked, bound and blindfolded. And my demon lover leaves.*

Hadn't he?

What if he was still in the room? He moved so quietly, he could be standing right beside her and she wouldn't know it. He could be standing over her right now, looking at her hard nipples, thinking about where to touch her first.

Then again, he might be downstairs watching *60 Minutes*. She was definitely going to kick his ass.

Dana stewed behind her blindfold for what seemed an hour but was probably only fifteen minutes before she heard the door open and close again.

"Sorry to leave you hanging, but I had to get a few supplies," Archer said with disgusting cheer.

"When I get loose, I'm going to hurt you," she told him. "How'd you like to have a clove of garlic shoved up your …"

"Oooh, you are pissed." Something rattled. "I hate to disappoint you, but the garlic thing's a myth." A wicked purr entered his voice. "But if you'd like to experiment, I could get some and see how *you* like it."

"That's not what I had in mind at all."

"May I remind you, you're the one who's tied up. It doesn't much matter what you've got in mind."

Dana felt her irritation drain at the note of velvet threat in his tone.

The bed shifted under her, the mattress dipping as though he'd sat down beside her.

Now, she thought. Now he'd touch her.

Something brushed her skin, then retreated. His fingertips?

There it was again, dancing over the tip of her right nipple, faint and delicious. Not a finger. Something thin. Several somethings. Filaments gliding over the sensitive skin of her breasts, swirling circles, tracing the full lower curves. Dana couldn't help squirming as she stared into the darkness of the blindfold and wondered what he was using to inflict those delicately erotic sensations.

"I love to watch a woman writhe," Archer said, his voice silken and deep. "Especially when she's bound."

Now the thing was dancing between her legs, tickling the sensitive skin of her thighs, drawing ghostly patterns of delight. "What is that?" she gasped. "What are you ..."

Warm, strong fingers touched her most sensitive flesh, parting the delicate lips of her sex and spreading them, then holding them that way for the filaments' tender dance. Dana gasped at the fairy-like sensations playing over her wet lips, only to zero in on her erect clit, circling and brushing it. Unable to stop herself, she began to roll her hips, not even knowing whether she was trying to elude the sensation or get more.

"No, darlin'," Archer murmured. She felt his warm weight settle across her hips, pinning her down. He must be draped over her on his side, Dana thought, a little dazed.

The filaments continued their play, but now she felt a hot puff of air as well, gusting over her clit. He was blowing on her sex, she realized. The idea of his head so close to her hungry core made her grow even wetter.

His tongue slipped down, flicked over her button. Dana moaned, waiting for more of his delicious mouth.

Instead he rolled off her.

"No!" she whimpered. "Archer, don't stop!"

"Patience, darlin'." There was a rumble of laughter in his voice.

"One of these days I'm going to tie you down and torture you," Dana growled. "We'll see how patient *you* are."

"Promises, promises." Something rattled. She thought she heard his bare feet padding on the floor. Then the mattress shifted, moved. Something rattled again.

He was crawling up between her legs, she thought in growing excitement. Something warm pressed against the inside of both thighs that she recognized as his shoulders.

Rattle.

For a long moment he didn't move as she waited breathlessly for him to begin feasting on her sex. Dana could feel the cream flooding her core in heady anticipation.

Then his mouth was there at last, sucking her clit, hot and wet and setting off a firestorm of burning pleasure. Dana cried out as he drew strongly on the tiny bud, the feelings so intense she could hardly bear them.

Maddened, she rolled her hips. One of his arms clamped across them to pin her down. Another rattle, just before he took his skillful mouth away from her sex. As she was about to groan a protest, she felt the brush of his fingers at her opening.

Cold!

Dana yelled and convulsed as she felt him slide the ice cube up her heated, creamy core, but he held her pinned. Then her clit was in his mouth again, and his free hand was rolling and pinching one nipple. She squirmed and writhed, cursing breathlessly as the ice melted inside her hot sex, the chill warring with the sensation of his wet, clever mouth on her bud, the skilled fingers tormenting her breast.

The orgasm hit her out of nowhere, rolling over her like a train as he suckled her ruthlessly. Dana screamed, unable to bear the raw, brutal pleasure.

Suddenly he was on top of her, his gloriously naked body pressing into hers, touching her everywhere. A hand snatched the blindfold away.

She blinked as Archer reared over her, his fangs bared, taking his big cock in one hand and aiming it for her core. Archer shoved it deep, sucking in a breath as he felt the chill.

"That's what you get for putting ice up my ..." she gasped.

"I'll melt it," he growled, and began to drive, fucking her hard and ruthlessly, his thick organ shuttling in and out with such strength she could only twist and moan in her bonds.

The sterling silver ice bucket tilted against her hip, but before it could fall and dump ice on them both, he stopped long enough to grab it up and put it down on the floor. Dana spotted a long ostrich feather curling among the sheets and realized what he'd first used to pleasure her with.

Then he was shafting her again, and she didn't care about anything else except that massive satin cock and the ecstasy it drove into her with each merciless stroke.

Another orgasm swamped her, and she threw her head back in pleasure. She saw his eyes lock on the column of her throat. Deliberately, Dana held the arch, offering herself as he lowered his handsome head. The sting of his fangs pressing deep kicked her climax even higher. He drove to the hilt and stiffened, his cry muffled against her throat.

As the last aftershocks of her climax shuddered through her, she collapsed into the mattress. His big hands stroked her, gentling and soothing as he fed.

Finally Archer drew away.

Dana blinked up at him, a little dizzy, a lot satisfied. "That was ... amazing," she sighed.

He stroked tender knuckles over her cheek. "You're pretty amazing yourself. Which must be why I love you."

She felt a goofy smile spread over her face. "I love you too. You want to untie me now?"

Archer's smile took on a wicked cant as his long fingers found her nipple. "I don't think so. I'm nowhere near done yet."

And he started again.

Epilogue

Dana stumbled into the hotel room, staggered to the bed, and fell across it. Archer sauntered in after her, looking, she thought resentfully, disgustingly fresh for a man who'd just spent the last month posing as a terrorist.

"You did good today, darlin'," he told her, pulling his gun out of his shoulder holster. "I was proud of you. Even Fitz thought you handled yourself well."

"It's about time. That man has made my life hell for a solid year." Dana gave him a narrow look. "Come to think of it, so did you."

Archer shrugged as he unloaded the nine millimeter Smith and Wesson. "We had to make sure you were well-trained. And you are. You took down those three mob guys like a pro."

"The look on Galleni's face when I bent that gun barrel ..." She laughed, savoring the memory. "I wish I had a picture."

"We probably do. I'll ask." He unbuckled his shoulder holster and shrugged out of it.

Watching the flex of his powerful chest, Dana felt a familiar wash of heat. She rolled to her feet and began to stalk him.

He looked up as she slid nearer and smiled. "Why, Mrs. Archer — whatever do you have in mind?"

Dana grinned, exposing the fangs she'd finally gotten used to. "Just thought we could celebrate the successful closing of my first case." Reaching to the belt of her black combat fatigues, she whipped out a pair of silver bracelets and dangled them from a thumb. "In fact, let's break in my new handcuffs."

With a wicked laugh, Archer reached for them. "I do like the way your mind works, wife."

"Then try this." She grabbed his shoulder and spun him back around. "Up against the wall and spread 'em! I need to practice my strip search."

His rich laughter rolled as he obeyed.

About the author:

Angela Knight is a newspaper reporter who lives in South Carolina with her cop husband and her teenage son. She's written three novellas for Secrets, and loved doing every one of them, since, she says, "Nobody else lets me get away with this stuff."

She welcomes e-mail and letters from readers, and may be contacted through her publisher, Red Sage.